WINTER OF ICE AND IRON

ALSO BY RACHEL NEUMEIER

The Mountain of Kept Memory

WINTER
OF
ICE
AND
IRON

RACHEL
NEUMEIER

SAGA PRESS

LONDON SYDNEY **NEW YORK** TORONTO NEW DELHI

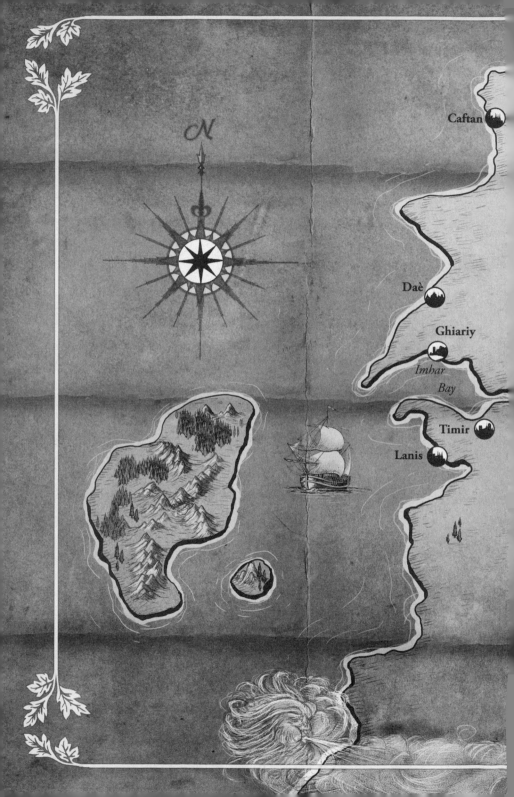

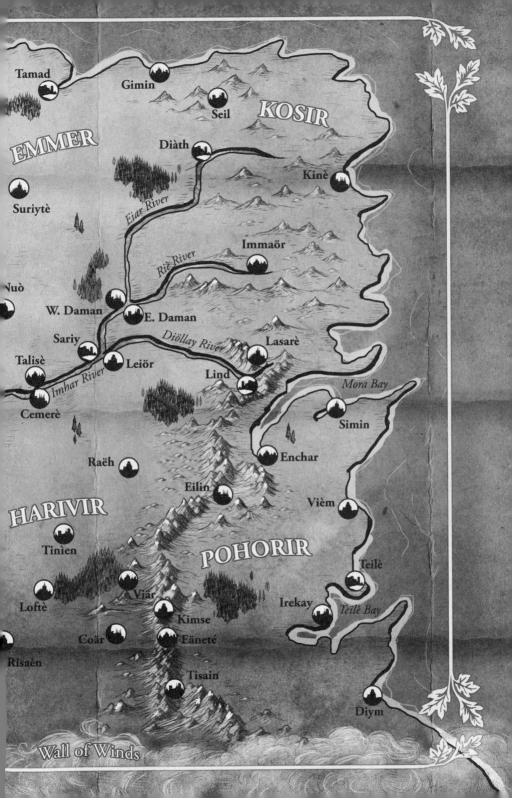

SAGA PRESS

AN IMPRINT OF SIMON & SCHUSTER, INC.

1230 AVENUE OF THE AMERICAS, NEW YORK, NEW YORK 10020

FOR CAROLINE EVARTS, *who read an early draft many years ago, fell in love with the Wolf Duke, and never quite stopped nagging me to knock this story into shape. Here you go! I hope you love this incarnation even more than the first.*

ACKNOWLEDGMENTS

With thanks to my agent, Caitlin Blasdell, who was, as always, instrumental in knocking a rough manuscript into shape; and my awesome editor, Navah Wolfe, whose advice was indispensable for those final tweaks that make all the difference.

There are twelve months of thirty days, except the hinge months each end on day twenty-nine. Following the twenty-ninth day, there are four uncounted hinge days before the year turns and the next month commences. The Golden Hinge marks the turning of spring into summer. The Iron Hinge marks the turning of autumn into winter.

THE MONTH OF DEEP COLD

WOLF MONTH

THE MONTH OF BRIGHT RAINS

APPLE BLOSSOM MONTH

THE BURGEONING MONTH

THE GOLDEN HINGE MONTH. THE HEIGHT OF THE YEAR.

THE FATTENING MONTH

THE MONTH OF HONEY

THE HARVEST MONTH

FIRE MAPLE MONTH

THE MONTH OF FROST

THE IRON HINGE MONTH. THE END OF THE YEAR.

PROLOGUE

Jeneil inè Suon was a beautiful girl. Her beauty did not serve her well: not as a child in her father's house and not in her youth and certainly not when, as a woman grown, she caught the eye of Iheraïn terè Iönei Eänetaì. The Iron Duke, the Wolf Duke, the Black Duke: Iheraïn Eänetaì, possibly the cruelest of all the lords of Pohorir. The very first lord of Eäneté had possessed a difficult temperament that had unhappily found an echo in the emerging Eänetén Power. The Immanent Power that formed from those mountains, from their thin soils and their broken stones, from their forests and creatures and the folk dwelling within their small, scattered villages, had even from those earliest days exhibited a savage disposition. That savagery had echoed back and forth between the lords of Eäneté and their strengthening Immanent, until cruelty no less than molten fire burned beneath the stone of its mountains.

Jeneil loved music and painting and small pretty songbirds: nothing that flourished in the house of Iheraïn Eänetaì. Her lord permitted her paints and canvas because these could be used silently and alone, and because sometimes it amused him to take them away. Jeneil's mother had taught her to love music, but her lord forbade instruments in his house. When she sang, she had a voice pure as the voice of a lark—or so said the servants of the house, pitying her. But she seldom sang after she entered the Black Duke's keeping, and never when her lord was anywhere in his house, because in that house she became as fragile and timid as a little bird.

Jeneil had always known fear. Her own father had taught her that lesson well. But in the Black Duke's house, she found that lesson refined. She grew more delicate every day she lived there. Even so, at first she stole moments of happiness; moments when, just for a little while, she forgot to be afraid. Small things might give Jeneil a moment of happiness: a spring crocus blooming through the snow, a bird coming to her hand for bread, a line flowing from her brush to the canvas in just the way she had imagined it.

She found love in that house too. She loved one of the duke's stewards, a young man named Gereth Murrel, for Jeneil had a generous and loving heart and she needed to love someone. He loved her in return. But for Jeneil this was a wistful and distant love, and for the young man a cruel one, for neither dared break her marriage vows. Iheraïn Eänetaì would have known, as he knew all things that occurred in his house and his city and his province.

Even so, Jeneil turned to the young steward for companionship in her misery, though she feared for him lest her lord destroy him as he sometimes destroyed her paintings. She turned to Gereth for comfort anyway, just as she turned to painting to create the illusion of freedom; just as she sang, when she dared, to distract herself from her unhappiness. But in the face of her fear, neither the love of the steward nor her own wistful thoughts of what her life might have been gave Jeneil reason enough to hold to life. A year after her marriage to the duke, she turned to her child-bed with relief, knowing she might die of the birth. She wished to die, because she no longer hoped for any other escape from her life.

There was nothing especially difficult about the birth. Jeneil Suon delivered the child, a son. When the midwife cut the cord and laid the child in her arms, Jeneil gazed for some time upon his small, wrinkled form. If she had borne a daughter, perhaps it would have been different. But even so young, this boy-infant had his father's black hair and, rather than the cloudy blue eyes of any common newborn, his father's yellow wolf eyes. So after gazing upon him for a little while, Jeneil set the child aside in his crib and turned her face to the wall. She died on her next breath.

1

When he was fourteen, Innisth terè Maèr Eänetaì tried for the first time to kill his father. He did not succeed. He found out instead something that he should have realized beforehand: that the Immanent Power of Eäneté protected the Duke of Eäneté from any ordinary attack.

No Immanent Power was concerned with action or achievement or triumph, not when it was young and new and first stretched itself out in the earth and stone and forests and creatures of its land. Such matters were human concerns. But Immanents took something of the character of those to whom they were tied. Ambition and domination and triumph had been the driving concern even for the first of the Maèr line. So Innisth should have realized that the Immanent Power would move to shield his father from any attack. Even an unexpected attack. Even an attack by the heir.

He also learned that it is a great deal easier and less painful to discover such things through logic than it is to learn them through trial and error. Both lessons proved useful, in time.

Innisth survived his father's punishment and the subsequent years of his youth. When he was twenty, he tried again to murder his father. This time he succeeded. This time he thought out his plan with cold deliberation, and when the opportunity presented itself, on the twenty-eighth day of the Month of Wolves, he seized his chance.

Wolf Month was the starving month, the bitter month, the month when winter stores grew lean and the new growth had not yet come, the month when the long haunting cries of the wolves drifted almost nightly from the high mountains. It was a hard month. The cold lingered. But one could look forward from the Month of Wolves to the approaching spring. It was a good month for sharp change, for renewal, for the rekindling of life out of grim silence. Perhaps that, too, drove Innisth to make and seize his chance.

This time, he knew that the Eänetén Immanent would block any attempt to stab or bludgeon or poison its master. But there was nothing it could do to preserve a man flung down a sheer thousand-foot cliff.

The Immanent Power of Eäneté came down upon Innisth after his father's death. By that time it was immensely strong, for the dukes of Eäneté had always, despite their cruelty, been intelligent enough to steward their province with an eye toward the prosperity of both land and people. It was not a Great Power such as ruled and bound lesser Immanences into a unified nation. It was not quite that. But it had learned ambition and pride—not in any mortal or human way, but in the way the soul of the land could learn such things from those most closely bound to it. Now only stark will could rule it.

Generally, a duke's heir mastered his Power while surrounded by supporters and allies, men and women bound to allied lesser Immanences, who knew best how to help a new heir survive the often brutal transference of the deep tie. Innisth Eänetaì mastered the Immanent of Eäneté alone, in the cold heights, lying in the trampled snow at the top of the ice-edged granite cliff. It was a cruel and ferocious Immanent, long shaped by the sharp-edged mountains and the high cutting winds of Eäneté and by the savagery of a long, long line of Eänetén dukes, none of whom had taught it much of gentleness.

But Innisth was his father's true son. He encompassed the Eänetén Power, and mastered it, and bound it, and he did not freeze to death there in the heights because Eänetaìsarè would not allow its master to die such a death.

By the time he got to his feet and brushed the snow off his face and out of his hair, it was nearly dusk. Innisth did not look toward the cliff edge where his father had fallen. He found his horse and his father's horse not far away, in the shelter of the firs in the lee of the mountain's high ridge. Though he was stiff with cold, he mounted and rode down the long steep way to the gate at the mouth of the pass.

The men stationed there knew immediately what had happened. At least, they knew the important part of what had happened. They knew because Innisth Eänetaì came out of the pass alone, leading his father's horse by its reins. And they knew because of the look on Innisth's face, or by some subtle difference in his manner, or perhaps because they could feel the dense, invisible presence of the Eänetén Power spreading out above and around him. They knelt there in the snow and made their vows.

Innisth did not accept an escort back to the house that was now his: the massive house that loomed, gray and thick-walled and forbidding, dominating the town below. He told the men where to look for his father's body. They took his orders with white-faced impassivity. He left his father's horse with them and rode his own black mare down from the gate of the pass toward that great grim house. He did not look back.

There were more men-at-arms at the courtyard gate, of course. They were not so quick to understand, until Innisth said, "I am now Eäneté." Then he said, "Send for my seneschal, and for your captain, and bid all the household staff assemble here in the courtyard."

It was cold, with the frigid stillness that sometimes lay across the mountains during the winter dusk. But the courtyard was the only place large enough for all the staff to assemble. And there were other advantages to the courtyard besides its sheer size. Even at night. "Light all the lanterns, and light torches," Innisth commanded the men-at-arms. They ran to obey.

If one included all the men-at-arms, the household staff comprised well over a hundred men and women. There were the stablemen and grooms, the huntsmen and kennel girls, the kitchen staff and scullery maids, the old women who stayed in the attics of the servants' quarters and spun wool and wove cloth, and the seamstresses who made the cloth into finished clothing. In the back of the assembly hovered the girls who endlessly polished the wooden floors and the brass doorknobs and the boys who clambered dangerously about on the outside walls to wash the house's many fine glass windows. To one side stood the house physickers and the grim old librarian with his assistant scribe. To the other side stood the men-at-arms, drawn up in their neat ranks, with their captain at their head. Before them all, with the torchlight casting his heavy features into unreadable shadow, stood Innisth's father's seneschal and his father's personal servants—including the special servants, with their rusty-black clothing that did not show blood.

They all knew the old duke was dead. Innisth did not have to tell them so. Word must have run through the house, even in the few moments they had required to assemble, but he believed they would have known anyway. He thought the empty space where his father should have stood echoed with the old duke's absence. To him it seemed that absence echoed through the entire house, louder than a shout. The assembled staff were utterly silent. They did not know yet how the shift of power from the old duke to the younger would affect them.

Innisth looked along the silent lines of the gathered staff. He said flatly, "Captain Tregeris," and beckoned with the crook of one finger.

The captain of the men-at-arms stepped out, approached Innisth, and saluted. He was not a young man, but not old; his shoulders were broad and his mouth narrow and he thought much of himself and little of others—except for Innisth's father, whom he had always feared and admired and sought to emulate. His eyes ran up and down Innisth's frame, curious and scornful, for he had, following the old duke's lead in this as in all else, never much regarded his son.

Innisth took one step forward, flicking his smallest knife out of his sleeve and into his hand. He stabbed the captain in the stomach and then stepped back while the man's mouth fell open and he sank down, quivering, his hands clutching at the hilt of the knife. The knife was small, but it was a vicious quilled blade, and when the captain steeled himself and jerked it out, a great dark gush of blood followed, and his breath followed it in a voiceless moan, and he died.

It had all been very quick, though at the same time the moment seemed to Innisth to stretch out and out, until he was half surprised that, when he looked up again, the whole assembly was still frozen in shocked quiet.

Innisth said, "Sergeant Etar."

There was a pause. Then the man he had named stepped out of the ranks and came forward to face him. Etar was nearly of an age with the dead man, perhaps twenty years Innisth's senior. In other ways he was not much like his former captain, for he was a plain man who did not seek to come near power. That was why he was still merely a sergeant, despite his age and competence. He met Innisth's eyes now, expressionless save for the tightness of his mouth.

Innisth said, "Captain Etar. The men-at-arms are yours. Over the coming days, you may set them in what order you think best. Dismiss men you do not think suited to your command; recruit other men as you see fit. I will expect you to inform me of what you do, but I do not expect I shall countermand your decisions. Is that clear?"

Small muscles around Etar's mouth twitched; that was the only sign of surprise. He gave a measured nod. "Your Grace."

Innisth sent him back to his men with a small gesture and said, not raising his voice, "Now, where is Gimil Sohoras? Where is my father's seneschal?" His voice, though not loud, fell into the echoing silence of the courtyard as clearly as a shout.

His father's seneschal was, of course, right there at the front of the assembly. He was a big man with heavy bones and heavy hands and a heavy voice. He glowered at Innisth and started to speak. Innisth lifted an eyebrow, and the man closed his mouth without a word.

"Gimil Sohoras," said Innisth, in that same quiet, carrying tone. "Though I appreciate your years of service to my father, I find I have no need of your service myself. You may have until dawn to gather all your possessions and leave Eäneté. You are not to count the girl Ranè among your possessions, however. She will remain here. Nor are you to damage her before you depart." There was a murmur from the gathering. Innisth pretended not to notice the young woman he had named, who turned and embraced an older woman. The woman eased Ranè away out of sight through the crowd. Innisth pretended not to notice that, either.

The big man stared at Innisth, plainly stunned. "But—"

"Or, of course, you may refuse to go," said Innisth. "That is certainly an option, if you prefer." He glanced thoughtfully down at the dead man who had been his father's captain and then once more regarded his father's seneschal.

The man closed his mouth.

"Dawn," Innisth reminded him. "Captain Etar will provide you with the assistance of two of his men. You would not wish to risk mistaking the hour as the sunrise approaches."

"No," said the man, his voice husky with suppressed rage. "No." He backed away awkwardly, nearly bumping into one of the men-at-arms Etar had sent to oversee his departure. He wheeled on the man, but then shot a wary glance at Innisth and smothered his anger.

"Gereth Murrel," said Innisth, naming a man who had been a factor and steward in the great house all Innisth's life. When the man made his way forward, Innisth met his eyes and smiled for the first time in all this long day.

Returning his smile, Gereth came forward to take the new duke's hand and kneel at his feet. "Innisth," he said, but very quietly. Then he said more loudly, "Your Grace. Command me."

Gereth was not young, being already in his fifties, but he was the man to whom everyone turned when they were in need. Quiet and methodical, Gereth was seldom noticed: a manner he had learned bitterly in this house and taught, as well as he could, to Innisth, when he had still been young enough to sometimes escape his father's notice. Innisth was confident that Gereth Murrel knew everything about running the house. And he knew the older man was kind.

Resting a hand briefly on the older man's shoulder, Innisth told him, "You are my seneschal," and another murmur, louder than the rest, whispered through the assembly.

Gereth said clearly, "Yes, Your Grace." His eyes searched his new duke's face. "Mastering Eänetaìsarè cannot have been easy. No one will challenge your right or your tie. There's no need for you to reorder the entire province tonight."

Innisth gave him another thin smile. "I have one or two more tasks before I rest. But you may certainly assign factors and stewards as you please. You will need an adequate staff, and I do not suppose you will find many of my father's factors suitable." He turned his hand palm-up: permission to rise.

Then he turned to his father's . . . special servants. He looked them over, one and then the next and then the third, and then raised his hand to signal to Captain Etar and said briefly, "Hang them all."

"But—!" protested one of the men, taking an involuntary step backward before stopping himself. Men-at-arms were already moving swiftly to seize them; Etar had plainly anticipated this order or one like it, and there would be no escape. The man flung himself to his knees instead, pleading. "But, Your Grace! We served your father well—we would gladly serve you—we only obeyed your father's commands, Your Grace—we had no personal animosity—I'm sure none of us ever wished—"

Innisth cut the man off with a lift of his hand. He said softly, "Yet I seem to remember a quite personal relationship between us. I advise you, do not protest overmuch. There are far more unpleasant fates than mere hanging. As you of all men are certainly aware."

The man closed his mouth.

"Be quick," Innisth said to his new captain, careful that his tone was merely impatient and held no trace of unease—though to himself he acknowledged that he would not truly be able to believe himself secure until these three servants, among all others, were dead. On that thought, he added to Etar, "And assemble a punishment detail. I do not care what failings the men have shown, but there should be at least half a dozen of them. I will see them, and you, downstairs. In half an hour."

There was the slightest stiffening of Etar's expression. But the captain only asked, "Tonight, Your Grace?" But he added immediately, "Of course it will be as Your Grace commands. Six men in half an hour."

Innisth had actually forgotten the time. If he had thought, he might have ordered Etar to bring his men downstairs in the morning, but he did not wish to seem indecisive, so he only gave a curt nod and turned to watch as the third of his father's torturers joined the other two in strangling death. It was not the death the man deserved, but it would do. It would do. He glanced across the courtyard toward the assembled staff. They were very quiet now. If anything, the silence had deepened. He met Gereth Murrel's wide gaze and said to him in a low voice, "I will speak to you further on matters of law and custom. Both will change now. You may advise me. Tomorrow. Late tomorrow."

Gereth bowed acknowledgment. "Your Grace."

"You are dismissed. You are all dismissed," added Innisth to the gathering, raising his voice. "Save for male servants of my household between the ages of twenty and thirty. The rest of you may all go." He paused, and then added flatly, "Go."

There was a general movement, not precisely a retreat, but nearly everyone was clearly glad to be permitted to escape without being singled out in any way. A few of the staff lingered, however, braver or more curious than the rest, or perhaps having friends among the young men whom Innisth had commanded to stay. Innisth pretended not to notice this minor disobedience. He said to the young men—there were fourteen of them, from a young groom to a senior huntsman—"I require a personal body servant. If any of you are not content with your current position, you may inform my seneschal of your interest. Your duties as my personal servant would be light, but various."

Only the stupidest of men could fail to understand, and even those would assuredly be enlightened by their fellows. Even now, a few of the sharper or more daring of them were exchanging significant glances. Innisth said, "This position will remain open until it is filled," and gestured dismissal.

The young men all edged away toward the staff entrance or toward the stable—none of them daring to speak, not yet, not while Innisth might overhear. But when Innisth turned to go into the house, he found the librarian's scribe in his way. He stopped, startled and prepared to be offended.

The youth clasped his hands in front of his belt, glanced down nervously, but then raised his gaze to meet Innisth's eyes. "Your Grace. I'm—I—if it pleases you, Your Grace, I would be glad to—to ask for the transfer of which you spoke."

Innisth looked the scribe up and down. He had the bony look of a boy who has not yet grown into himself. His clothing was plain but of good quality, as befit a young man who earned his bread with a quill rather than with the labor of his hands or a hunting bow. But he did not look delicate. His wrists were too big for his hands; his shoulders promised eventual strength. He was plain, with a rather ordinary face and untidy brown hair, but his gaze was sharp enough—though nervous, at the moment.

"Caèr Reiöft," Innisth said, pulling the name from his memory after a moment. "How old are you? Am I to understand that you have been dissatisfied with your place as a scribe?"

"Nineteen, Your Grace," the young man answered immediately. "But near enough twenty, if it pleases you. I don't mind the scribing, Your Grace, and if you wished me to—to write letters for you, or anything you wish, I would be glad to do that. But I would be glad— that is, I believe I understand the duties you will expect of a personal servant, and I would be very glad to serve Your Grace in any capacity that pleases you."

Innisth's eyes narrowed. "You mean: instead of the librarian. Is that what you mean?"

Reiöft took a quick breath. "I've no complaint of him, Your Grace. But I would—I've lived all my life in this house, Your Grace, and I would be glad to serve you, if you will have me. I know I'm not—I don't want to be presumptuous, Your Grace—"

Innisth lifted one hand a fraction, and Reiöft stopped. "We may at least try the arrangement," he said. "Inform Gereth of the matter. I am going downstairs for a little while. Then I will come up to my rooms. I will wish to bathe and rest. I will expect you to have everything ready for me."

Reiöft nodded swiftly. "Your Grace." He looked slightly stunned now that it was settled. His eyes were wide and vulnerable. Innisth liked that. He had never much noticed the young man before, but now he thought he might like him well enough. He gave him a brief nod of dismissal and walked away, for the black door and the narrow steps that led downstairs.

A long table, scarred by iron and knife, dominated the large antechamber of the old duke's dungeons. Beyond it stood an ornate chair with a high, carved back and carved arms and a cushion of black leather. The chair was a handsome piece, out of place in this room. Save for the space directly around the chair, the floor was matted with straw and sweet rushes, originally laid down to absorb blood and other matter, but left far too long. The stench of moldy straw and rotted blood and filth hung in the room; even the torches seemed to burn low and flicker unevenly in the close air. A vast fireplace took up most of the wall to the left, though at the moment no wood was arranged there. Tools of all sorts occupied racks and shelves along the wall to the right. In the far wall, an iron door stood open, leading to the small cells where the old duke's less fortunate prisoners might linger for . . . some time. There was no sound from beyond the iron door. Innisth could not remember whether his father currently held any prisoners in those cells, but if any were there, they were too cowed to make a sound when they heard men come into this antechamber.

Drawn up in an uneasy row waited the men-at-arms Innisth had ordered be brought to this place, and their new captain. The men were afraid, Innisth saw, but not terrified. That was Etar's influence. He met the new duke's gaze with level fortitude before inclining his head. "Your Grace."

Innisth gave him a small nod. He glanced around, his gaze catching on the chair. He nodded toward it. "Burn that."

"Your Grace?"

"Burn it." Innisth scuffed the toe of one boot through the filthy straw. "Clean away this mess. Clear the air. Burn cedar—burn incense, if necessary." He didn't actually care for incense, but better that than this current stench. "Scrub the floor. Clean and polish the table. Replace those torches with clean-burning lanterns and clean the soot off the walls."

The men were exchanging glances in which dismay and relief mingled. Even Captain Etar let his breath out. He gave Innisth a crisp nod. "Those?" He nodded toward the racks of whips and knives, irons and needles and clamps. "Shall we dispose of all of that as well?"

Innisth hesitated, wanting to say, *Yes, burn it all.* But Eänetaìsarè pressed him, drawn by this place with a force he had not entirely expected. The Immanent wanted blood and screaming; already he could tell he would eventually need to give it something of that kind. Already he could tell he would eventually want to.

"No," he said at last. "Clean away the old blood and rust. Sharpen the blades; replace anything worn or damaged and leave everything in good order."

Some of the relief faded. But Etar met his eyes and said quietly, "Of course it will be as Your Grace commands. But as your captain, I must ask that Your Grace leave the discipline of your men-at-arms in my hands."

That was brave. Of course, Innisth had known Etar was brave. It took a moment of effort to appreciate that courage, to set down offense. There was a tiny stir among the men as they waited for his response, a general catch of breath. Their fear was . . . seductive, in a way Innisth had only half expected.

Nevertheless, at last he managed a thin smile. "So long as they respect my law and my commands, my own people will have nothing to fear from me, my captain. Neither your men nor my staff nor any of my folk." He made this a promise, flat and uncompromising, and swore to himself that he would keep that vow.

Captain Etar bowed his head briefly, accepting this assurance. If he let out a covert breath, Innisth couldn't tell it.

Setting aside the pressure of the Immanent as well as he could, Innisth made himself look around with careful consideration. "The cells," he told the captain. "Clean them all. If there are prisoners, inform me. If any could benefit from the attentions of a physicker, summon one. If any would best be granted a swift knife, then supply that need and, again, inform me." The men were once more looking faintly dismayed. He ignored them. He had, after all, told Etar to assemble a punishment detail.

"Your Grace," Etar acknowledged. "I think this will take more than one night's work, if I may say so."

"In this, I prefer thoroughness to speed."

Etar gave a nod. "I shall inform you when the task is completed, Your Grace."

Innisth returned the nod and left the men to their labor, turning back toward the narrow stairway. The stench of this place clung to him even after so brief a time, following at his heels as he mounted the steps and returned to the clean air above. He did want a bath now. Though . . . that was not all he wanted. But the bath, certainly, first. And then he would discover whether Caèr Reiöft did indeed understand the duties Innisth expected of his personal body servant. And then . . . and then, Innisth thought, he might at last be able to rest.

✻ ✻ ✻

The old duke's body was returned to the house, where it lay in state for a day and a night. The Immanent Power of Eäneté did not take it up, and thus the body was finally interred in the duke's garden of remembrance. Innisth did not attend the ceremony.

There were quiet celebrations all through Eäneté as the season eased from the Month of Wolves into the new spring. Nothing obtrusive. No one wanted to risk offending their new young duke. But on the twenty-eighth day of the Month of Bright Rains and then again on the twenty-eighth day of Apple Blossom Month, townspeople made cakes with brandy and berry preserves, then broke the cakes to share with strangers on the street. The wealthy bought lambs and young calves, took them up to the pine forests, slaughtered them there, and left them for the wolves. This might have been the old custom of propitiation, to turn wolf and misfortune aside, save that the month was wrong and the day was wrong. Innisth knew, though no one would say so, that it was a gesture of homage to the new Wolf Duke. Those who could not afford lambs bought larks and other songbirds in the market and set them free in a new custom that had, Innisth gathered, already become quite widespread.

"I believe some of the larks have been caught and released a dozen times by now," Gereth told Innisth, who lifted one shoulder in a deliberately disinterested shrug. But he was pleased. So he also rode down to the town on the twenty-eighth day of the next month, which was the Golden Hinge Month.

As the month ended, the world would enter the uncounted four days of the Golden Hinge, the days of good fortune and celebration during which spring turned to summer. Already the town was fragrant with baking and decorated with streamers of flowers. Delicate strands of blown robins' eggs had been draped over the lintels of doorways where marriages would take place during those golden days. Innisth strolled through the Open Market. No one had the temerity to offer him a bit of cake. But folk caught his eye and smiled as they bowed, tentative and hopeful, and though Innisth did not smile in return, he offered no rebuke to this familiarity. And he bought a lark from the first woman he encountered offering them for sale.

Innisth took the little bird out of its cage and held it in his hands for a moment, feeling its heartbeat rapid and delicate against his fingers. And then, in the middle of the market square, in full view of all his people, he opened his hands and let it fly.

2

The sixteenth day of Fire Maple Month offered a bright and pleasant autumn morning, here at the edge of the kingdom of Harivir, in the province of Cemerè, in the town of Cemerè from which the province took its name. The season gave a particularly pleasant aspect to the garden wrapped around the house of Liyè Cemeraiän, Lord of Cemerè.

Kehera irinè Elin Raëhema, daughter and heir of the King of Harivir, found both the morning and the garden disconcertingly pleasant. It seemed to her a starker season and a bitter wind would have been more in accordance with the exigencies of the day.

Kehera was keeping company with Liyè's wife, Soë Cemeraiän, while they both pretended confidence and waited for day's end. The breeze was soft and warm, wisps of cloud chased one another through the brilliant sky, and from the garden, the fighting along the river was only barely audible.

Kehera sat gracefully poised across from Soë by the courtyard's central fountain. They were surrounded by their women, who were supposed to be a comfort. They even were, in a way. At least, the need to present a serene face to the women was useful. Kehera slipped a needle back and forth through a panel of fine cloth and hoped that her pretense of unworried calm was a little more difficult to penetrate than Soë's tense smile.

The women spoke of everyday things, of cheerful things. But Soë, a comfortably rounded woman of fifty or so, in Kehera's experience placid to the point of stolidity, was this morning as silent as Kehera, and for much the same reason, though Soë feared for her husband and her sons rather than her father or brother. And for Cemerè, of course. They both, they all, had reason to fear for the town and province of Cemerè. And for Harivir itself, if Cemerè fell today to the Mad King of Emmer.

It might. Mad Hallieth Suriytaiän might be, but Emmer had long been the wealthiest and strongest of the Four Kingdoms and not even the maddest of kings could ruin Emmer's prosperity or break its strength in a day. Not in a year, nor even in five years, nor eight. As Hallieth Suriytaiän seemed determined to prove, judging from his efforts over that entire span to seize first the nearest provinces of Kosir, which bordered Emmer to the east, and now those of Harivir, to Emmer's south.

Starting, in Harivir's case, with Cemerè.

Dark blue cloth and dull gold embroidery thread fell in disorderly waves across Kehera's lap, along with a fine strand of pale hair that had escaped the careful nine-stranded coil Eilisè had put it in that morning. Nurses and ladies-in-waiting had instructed Kehera in needlecraft since almost before she could talk. Now, after years of practice, her fingers knew the skill. Embroidery gave Kehera a way to seem occupied and busy while in fact lost in her private thoughts. This was a valuable talent for any lady, especially for her father's heir: heir to Raëh and its Immanent Power of Raëhemaiëth and the throne of all Harivir. Especially in times like these.

Kehera's eyes might have followed the needle, but only the smallest part of her mind needed to be concerned with the abstract pattern of stars and waves that her hands were creating with blue and silver thread. She might have heard the murmuring voices of the women, but she did not listen to them. Her bodily ear was tuned to the distant battle and her inner ear to the angry tension humming through the

Immanent Power of Cemerè. She felt guiltily relieved that she perceived the Cemeran Power only through her tie to Raëhemaiëth. That swelling anger was frightening enough, even though she was only the heir. For her father it must be worse. She could hardly imagine how Liyè Cemeraiän endured it.

No one had actually expected this war. The threat of war, yes. There was always that threat. Even before he had gone mad, Hallieth Theraön Suriytaiän, King of Emmer, had pressed now and again to expand his borders. Sometimes he threatened Kosir and sometimes Harivir—sometimes both at once. Particularly when withering spring frosts or long summer droughts or any such misfortune drew the strength and attention of Immanent Powers from the affairs of men and into the long, slow dreams of field and river, forest and mountain. That was the time for an ambitious king to see whether his strength might be enough to overwhelm some border lord's territory, to force a lesser Immanence to accept a bond to his own.

Thus had kings been made since the beginning of the world: through the deep, slow strength of the Immanent Powers that arose naturally from their lands and were then channeled by the focused will of ambitious men—or occasionally women; one of Kosir's earliest rulers had been a queen, though at the time Kosir had lain more to the west and had not extended as far south. That had been before the apotheosis of first Emmeran Great Power, an Immanent that had once dwelt in the far north of Emmer. It had risen during one particularly ill-omened midwinter, when the Unfortunate Gods were closest to the world. It had become an Unfortunate God itself, as Immanent Powers did when they rose at midwinter, thus creating the northern desert.

It was nearly two months yet before the Iron Hinge of midwinter, and Kehera doubted that even Hallieth Suriytaiän was mad enough to let the Great Power of Suriytè seek apotheosis. But the Mad King was certainly ambitious enough. Thus Gimin in the far north had recently become an Emmeran town, when until five years ago it had belonged

to Kosir; and similarly, last year, another Kosiran town, Diàth, a prosperous town surrounded by good farmlands, which mountainous Kosir
could ill afford to lose.

This year, the summer had been hot and dry in Harivir—yet
another hot, dry summer, the fifth in a row. The drought had lain
heavy on the land from the Month of Flowers right through the Harvest
Month, with little rain falling anywhere north of Coär. So now Hallieth
Suriytaiän looked to press Emmer's borders south of the broad Imhar
River and take Cemerè for his own. And then, no doubt, he would look
east toward Leiör or west toward Timir, smaller towns that also lay
along the Harivin border with Emmer.

All this summer, every day, it seemed to Kehera Raëhema, her
father had become a little quieter, a little older. She worried about
him—she had worried about him even before this trouble with Emmer.
Raëhemaiëth, the Immanent Power of Raëh, drew on her father's own
strength so that its lands flourished. The ruling Immanent of all Harivir,
it drew on his human strength so that it could support all the lesser
Immanences of the drought-stricken provinces of Harivir. Raëhemaiëth
was important. It prevented each Immanent from encroaching on the
lands of its neighbors; it encouraged generosity and liberality from land
and human folk alike. During the lingering summer months it supported
the peace and calm and burgeoning life brought by the Fortunate Gods.
Thus even in a difficult year, when little rain fell and day after day the
cloudless skies stretched out above the lands, the grain ripened in the
fields, and the acorns ripened on the trees, and the deer and foxes and
saplings flourished. And thus the harvests did not falter. But the golden
grain ripening in the fields and the swelling apples in the orchards and
the fattening of the land all wore at Kehera's father. It was the price of
being king; or at least, it was the price of being a good king, a king who
loved his Immanent and his people and set the well-being of his lands
above his own span of years.

And so now, of course, Hallieth Suriytaiän had decided that
Harivir's misfortune presented a fine chance to press the border. And

so there was this war. This little war. This attempt to take Cemerè away from Harivir, to carve its Immanent Power away from Raëhemaiëth, the Great Power of Raëh. To bring all the southern bank of the river into Emmer, binding those provinces into Suriytè instead, forcing Harivir farther south and expanding Emmer's grasp.

Of course Hallieth Theraön Suriytaiän would not succeed. Kehera was certain he couldn't succeed. She'd told herself so firmly every day for the past month. But throwing back the Emmeran offensive cost her father too—in the lives of men and in his own strength. It cost him a little more with every passing day, and would, until the Mad King of Emmer turned his attention to some weaker target. No doubt another Kosiran border city would prove an easier—

Kehera lifted her head and held up her hand for quiet. Only after the startled women had fallen silent did she realize what had changed. It was the distant sound of battle. The clamor had stilled, or at least quieted so far as to become inaudible from Liyè Cemeraiän's house. The stillness should have been welcome, and yet dread ran through her, though she did not know why. Turning her head, she met Soë Cemeraiän's wide, stunned gaze.

That was when she realized that another kind of silence had fallen as well.

She rose to her feet, blue cloth and golden thread falling unheeded to the fine gravel. She looked around the garden, not quite seeing the yellows and oranges of the maples, nor the russets and golds of the chrysanthemums, nor the mute horror of the ladies. What she saw instead, with her inner eye, was a great blank emptiness that a moment before had been filled with the vast living Immanent of Cemerè.

Then Raëhemaiëth swelled up beneath the emptiness, and Kehera let out a slow breath of profound relief and looked around the garden once more, meeting each woman's eyes. Even, at last, though it was difficult, Soë Cemeraiän's.

"We have lost Cemerè," she said quietly, because someone had to say it. "I am so sorry, Soë. Liyè was a strong lord and Cemerè prospered in his hands. But Raëhemaiëth holds. I promise you, Raëhemaiëth holds and will not fall. I am sure my father will withdraw toward Raëh. You and your family must come with us. You must all come."

"We've lost Cemerè . . . ?" faltered Soë. "You are certain . . . ?"

"I am sorry," Kehera said gently. "I must ask now for haste. I am sure we must withdraw at once to the south. If you will all—"

The sound of a man's heavy, hurried tread on gravel interrupted her, and Kehera turned—they all turned—steeling themselves as women must for the news of the disaster they already knew had fallen upon them.

Liyè Cemeraiän burst into the garden, swung around the gatepost, cast down the helm he had been carrying as though only at that moment realizing he held it, came forward with long strides, and folded his lady in a fierce embrace. Though many of the women cried out and exclaimed, Soë herself did not make a sound, but gripped her husband's surcoat with both her small hands and pressed her face against his chest.

But after the first moment, the Lord of Cemerè raised his head and met Kehera's gaze over his wife's head. He said, his voice cracking a little, "Your father—your father must speak with you, Your Highness. If you will . . . if you will go to him at once. He is—he—my men will show you—"

Kehera saw that half a dozen men had come with Liyè. They waited now by the gate. She wanted to demand Liyè tell her what had happened by the river; she wanted to cry, *But what happened? How could my father let the Mad King of Emmer take Cemerè? How is this possible?* But she smothered all this and said only, "Of course. I'm grateful—I'm glad to see you well, Lord Liyè. I'm grateful it was not worse."

"It could not have been worse," Liyè said bitterly, and bent his head over his lady's.

"We could hardly have seen a worse outcome," Torrolay Elin Raëhema told Kehera when she found him.

Her father had proved to still be in the encampment by the river, in his pavilion, which occupied a slight rise toward the rear of the Harivin force. The king's pavilion was set a little apart from the soldiers' tents and the larger physickers' tent. It was made of bleached canvas put up on gilded rods, with sheer curtains at front and back to let in the breeze, and Kehera had always thought it rather pleasant. But at the moment the pavilion was also surrounded by the aftermath of battle: men weary and wounded, physickers and women hurrying to attend them. Too many wounded; Kehera had seen that already. Too many young men laid out in the rows of the dead. That contributed to her anxiety, because she could see that the Hallieth Suriytaiän must have done more to Cemerè's Immanent Power than just take the deep tie from Liyè. That would have been bad enough, but he must also have disrupted all the thin, barely perceptible ties that bound ordinary people to the Power of their land. Otherwise the Power would have healed many of the wounded and taken up more of the dead.

So she was not surprised by her father's grim manner, though clearly he did not expect another attack—not, at least, a physical attack with blade and bow and weight of arms. If he had, he would hardly have sent for her to come here. Indeed, from what little she had glimpsed as she hurried through the encampment, the Emmeran force had already retreated through the drought-shallow river back to their own camp on the opposite bank. Kehera was surprised by that; she knew she did not have any great grasp of battlefield tactics, but she would have expected whatever general was in command of that force to claim the town of Cemerè now that Hallieth Suriytaiän had forced the Power of Cemerè to yield to his own. But the Emmeran soldiers had withdrawn to their neat rows of canvas tents. Even from this distance, if she glanced out the door of her father's pavilion, she could see their long standards whipping in the rising breeze, the White Stallion of Suriytè before the others. Kehera could not keep from giving that banner a mistrustful glance even as she nodded attentively to her father.

He had been seeing to whatever details attended the loss of an important Power—she was sure there must be a thousand grim minutiae that needed arranging. Her younger brother, Tirovay, was with him, which relieved Kehera's mind and heart of at least one great worry. Another man Kehera did not know was also present. The stranger was a mystery. She'd thought she knew all her father's captains and advisers. But she didn't ask. She assumed her father would tell her who this man was if it were important for her to know.

"It's not this day, though that's gone badly enough," her father told her now. He ran a hand through his sweat-dampened hair. He repeated, grim and weary, "It's not this day. It's the threat of tomorrow."

Kehera nodded again earnestly, and continued to wait, with a patience she was far from truly feeling, for him to explain.

Though Torrolay Elin Raëhema was not old, he had been King of Harivir for years and years, since long before Kehera was born. His own mother had died young, and so he had mastered the Harivin Power and ascended the throne when he was only a little older than she was now. Ever since, he had dealt with the Fortunate and Unfortunate Gods, with generous and recalcitrant Immanent Powers, with aggressive Emmer to the north of Harivir and untrustworthy Pohorir to the east, with quarrelsome nobles at home and with every possible crisis with the imperturbable composure and patience that every Raëhema stamped more firmly into the character of the Harivin Power and received back redoubled.

But he did not look entirely calm now. He said, "You felt it, of course—the death of Cemerè's Immanent." This wasn't a question, and he went on before she could do more than blink in surprise at the word "death." "Hallieth Suriytaiän didn't rip Cemerè away from Raëh and force an Unfortunate bond between Cemerè and his own Great Power. That would have been bad enough, but hardly unprecedented. I thought I could stop him doing that—and I thought that was as bad as it could get."

Of course they had all believed the Mad King's intention was just as her father described. That was why her father had come here to Cemerè himself, bringing several companies of his men, but more importantly bringing his deep tie to Raëhemaiëth. That was why he had brought her and Tiro; because Kehera was his heir and had to be ready to take the tie if the worst should happen and the king fall to mischance on the field or to the foreign Emmeran Power. And, of course, if that should happen, Tiro had to be ready to step into the heir's place in his turn. He was old enough, at least. If there was no direct descendant old enough to establish the necessary resonance with the Immanent, no heir's tie would be possible. That was never safe. If any lord or duke or king—or queen—died without a proper heir, the tie might go anywhere, to an unknown distant cousin, wherever it could find that resonance. In the case of a Great Power like Raëhemaiëth, that sort of succession could ruin the good order of a kingdom for generations—disaster in time of war.

Tirovay was seventeen; he was rather a young seventeen, Kehera thought, with his baby-fine brown hair cut a little long and his wide mouth that smiled readily. Ordinarily he was quick and cheerful and ready to believe the best of everything and everyone. He had always had a child's confidence that nothing so very terrible could happen. Kehera believed it wasn't the few years between them that made the difference, but her memory of their mother's death. Tiro did not remember their mother at all. Kehera, on the other hand, though she had been only three, had learned then that terrible things could indeed happen, and that nothing you did could make the world go back to the way it was supposed to be.

Today she thought her brother had learned that too, and she was sorry for it, but she still did not know what exactly had happened. She asked plainly, "But what *did* the Mad King do, if not take Cemerè's Immanent away from Raëhemaiëth and force it to submit to his own Power? What do you mean, its death? Immanents can only deepen in the earth or become Gods. They can't *die*."

Tiro cleared his throat, and Kehera looked at him, appalled. "You mean they can?" Her brother, always fascinated by the oldest stories, knew more than she did about the creation of the Four Kingdoms. Diffident in the presence of their father and the stranger, Tiro nevertheless ducked his head and said, "It kind of happened in Sierè, people think."

Kehera didn't like that idea much at all. The greatest calamity the world had ever faced was thought to have been caused by the Great Immanent of Sierè, a land that had once lain far to the south.

Tiro glanced at their father, who gestured briefly that he should go on. So he explained. "The southern king used the Immanent of Sierè to force the lesser Immanences of neighboring provinces out of their lands. It's thought . . . Scholars think he meant to make those lands his own, creating new Immanences in them so he could rule them utterly. But midwinter overtook him, and the Unfortunate Gods tilted all his ambitions to serve their own ends. All those dispossessed Immanences entered apotheosis all at once. Or maybe one after another; no one knows."

Kehera shook her head, doubting it had mattered. The apotheosis of some gentle Immanent into a Fortunate God was destructive enough to the lands from which it tore itself free. Far worse was the apotheosis of a cruel, ambitious Great Power into an Unfortunate God. That was the part of the tale she knew: the part where the Immanent of Sierè had ascended to Godhead in a storm of shattering chaos. By tempting it into their company, the Unfortunate Gods had nearly succeeded in destroying the world they hated and despised.

Nothing was left of the southlands now, as far as anyone could tell. Actually, no one knew, since directly after the disaster, a servant of the Fortunate Gods had somehow raised the impassable Wall of Storms between the northlands and the southlands, to stop the spread of ruin.

Servants of the Gods were something like extremely powerful sorcerers, but they drew their strange capabilities not from a forced tie to an Immanent, but directly from the Gods. Tiro could probably list all the differences and advantages and disadvantages attendant on being such a servant compared to an ordinary sorcerer, but Kehera knew only a little about such things. Potent, unpredictable, no longer precisely human, a servant of the Fortunate Gods appeared when circumstances were most dire, but such sorcerers solved problems—if they solved them—in ways that weren't always kind to the world. The Wall of Storms was the most dreadful thing Kehera knew of; the dragons it spawned at midwinter were the most terrible sign of the enmity the Unfortunate Gods held for the world.

Tiro, plainly thinking along the same lines as Kehera, said in a hopeful tone, "If the King of Emmer is trying anything too much like what the King of Sierè tried, maybe a servant of the Fortunate Gods will move to stop him."

"It's never wise to depend on the intervention of the Fortunate Gods," the stranger commented, his tone absent, as though he weren't very interested in the topic. "Generally, even if such a servant is made at an opportune moment, his ability to intervene—or hers—depends primarily on dedicated human action."

Tiro turned to the man in surprised interest, plainly wanting to go on with this topic, but their father waved the whole abstract matter aside. "Whatever the Mad King has in mind isn't quite as dangerous as whatever happened in Sierè, probably. Hallieth Suriytaiän tore the Immanent away from Cemerè and away from the earth. But it's definitely not going to ascend, because it's *gone*." He gestured sharply, frustrated with the limitations of words. "He gave it entirely to his Power. The Immanent of Suriytè . . . devoured it. We are nearly certain. Poor Liyè," he added. "I hardly knew what to say to him. He thought at worst he might be forced to kneel to Hallieth Suriytaiän, and now . . . this."

"The Mad King . . . left Cemerè empty?" Kehera tried to imagine the unmooring of an Immanent Power from the land and people from which it had arisen. She hardly knew what to think. Except it was horrifying.

But if Cemerè's Power had actually been *destroyed* . . . no wonder . . . no wonder there were so many dead left lying on the now-soulless earth; no wonder the wounded had no help but ordinary physickers. She said, hearing the blankness in her own voice, "But . . ." Her voice trailed off.

"Yes," said the stranger, his tone dry. "Hallieth Suriytaiän *is* mad."

Torrolay Raëhema let out his breath and shook his head, but obviously not in disagreement. He said to Kehera, "I was warned the Mad King would destroy Cemerè if he couldn't take it. I was warned he'd leave Cemerè hollow. I didn't quite understand that warning. Or believe it." From her father's glance, Kehera surmised that this stranger must have been the source of the warning.

This was a dark man, not tall, with an ambiguous cast of feature and a cool manner. He was clearly not a soldier. So far as she knew, she had never seen him before.

"This is a man of mine who has been in Emmer for some time," her father told her. "Quòn is his name; or at least, it is what he is called. He had been keeping an eye on . . . things, for me. You understand."

Kehera understood perfectly. He meant the man was an agent of his who had been spying on the Mad King. "Yes?" she said, wishing that one or the other of them would start at the beginning and just *explain* everything. If the Mad King had destroyed the Immanent Power of Cemerè, that was terrible, but though that seemed more than enough, there was something else to all this. She knew there was.

"I used to believe Hallieth Suriytaiän's entire hobby was petty provocation," Quòn said in a soft, wry voice. "But of late it has become clear that whatever his ambition, it is not *petty*." He slanted a sidelong look toward Kehera.

Torrolay Elin Raëhema took a breath.

Outside, somewhere beyond the encampment, Kehera heard a bird sing, a liquid trill of notes. A breeze wandered in, stirring the sheer draperies, bringing in the scent of sun-warmed earth and horses, of blood and physickers' salves. Out there, wounded men still cried out and the women who tended them murmured reassurance and sympathy. But here, within this gilded pavilion, the whole world seemed somehow to have paused.

Her father said, his tone level and quiet, "Quòn came to me . . . not quite in time, with warning that Hallieth Suriytaiän had taken the Immanent Power of Talisè and fed it to his Great Power. Alas, I did not understand in time what he meant, or that Suriytaiän might do the same to Cemerè. Or what he might do next, or threaten to do."

Kehera didn't understand. Talisè was the Emmeran sister-city of Cemerè; it lay directly to the north, right across the Imhar River. Kinder days saw a good deal of trade move back and forth between the two towns. She said, "But Talisè is an *Emmeran* city. Surely even the Mad King wouldn't have . . ." She faltered.

"I came from there," Quòn told her. His tone was perfectly matter-of-fact. "I can tell you: Talisè is indeed hollow. It's unmistakable even to me, though I haven't a drop of Talisaiän blood. Its Immanent is gone. As is Cemerè's now. One must hope the Fortunate Gods will protect the folk of Talisè and Cemerè from the dragons that ride the midwinter storms and from the Unfortunate Gods. It will surely take many long years for another Immanent Power to grow in either province."

Kehera couldn't help giving the man an incredulous look. Without an Immanent Power actually inhabiting the land, it would be almost impossible for Raëhemaiëth alone to turn aside the terrible storms of midwinter. Everyone knew that the Fortunate Gods were weakest during the uncounted Iron Hinge days between the death of the old year and the birth of the new. Those were the days on which the Unfortunate Gods sent their dragons riding the obsidian winds, destroying what they could. Even a child knew how perilous those days would be for every creature living in a land with no Immanent Power to turn the storms and the ill luck.

She could not understand how anyone could say things like that and sound as Quòn did. Unmoved. Unaffected. As though none of it were anything to do with him.

Her father did not seem surprised nor offended at the man's tone. He didn't even glance at him. All his attention was on Kehera. He said quietly, "Hallieth Suriytaiän sent word to me just before he . . . did what he did to Cemerè. Unless we prove able to stop him, he intends to take one Harivin town after another and give their Immanences to his Great Power of Suriytè, until all Harivir lies empty, vulnerable to storms and winter dragons and all Gods Fortunate and Unfortunate. Or"—and her father took a breath and then finished, his voice steady—"or else, he declares he is willing to take Harivir peacefully, through you. Through your children, heirs to both kingdoms and both the Great Power of Raëh and the Great Power of Suriytè."

For a long moment Kehera could not quite parse her father's meaning. Her brother was staring at her, plainly as stunned as she felt. His eyes were wide, dark with horror. It dawned on her at last that this horror was on her account. Only then did she begin to feel horrified herself. Then she wished she were still numb. She said, "No."

Her father came to her and touched her cheek, but he said nothing.

Quòn said, "I believe Hallieth Suriytaiän has been feeding the least among Emmer's Immanences to his own Great Power for some time. I fear Caftan's Immanent has disappeared. Possibly Tamad's as well. Some reports suggest so. I'm bound for Suriytè myself, next, in fact, to see if I can find out precisely how all this has been affecting its Great Power and whether some method for countering its . . . startling innovation may suggest itself."

Kehera shook her head in dismay, but Tiro said angrily, "Well, maybe it's not true! It's all *you believe, you fear, reports suggest,* but maybe you're wrong! Maybe—"

Torrolay Raëhema began, "Tiro—"

The boy spun back around. "Devouring Immanences? That's not a Great Power; that's a monster! Let the Mad King meet us outside Raëh, let his Immanent Power meet Raëhemaiëth, and *then* let him make such threats and demands!" He took a step toward their father and said fiercely, "You can't *possibly* send—"

"Tiro," the king said again, gently. "I may not have a choice. Raëhemaiëth could not protect Cemerè's Power. Obviously. How many other Immanences shall we spend, how many towns leave open to the malice of any Unfortunate God that has a whim to meddle with the lives of men and beasts? We—*I*—have little time to consider. By dawn. That is the ultimatum. At dawn, if Kehera Raëhema has not set foot on the north bank of the Imhar, Hallieth Suriytaiän will ride upriver and do to Leiör what he has done to Cemerè. Do you know how to stop him? Because I do not." He turned quietly to Quòn, who had waited, to all appearances unmoved by the exchange between prince and king. He asked the same question again. "Do you know how to stop him?"

Quòn inclined his head. "I fear not yet. No one has stopped him so far."

Her father nodded. He had expected just that answer, obviously. He said, "Kehera?"

Kehera shook her head. It seemed a terrible idea, but of course she would feel that way, and she had never studied tactics. Her father must think this was the wisest course, the best course for Harivir, or he would never have frightened her with the merest suggestion of this plan.

She tried to think what it would be like, to leave Harivir—to leave Raëhemaiëth—to go into Emmer, to the court of the Mad King. The whole idea seemed worse and worse the more she tried to imagine it. "Dawn? Tomorrow's dawn?" she asked. She tried not to let her voice falter, but she sounded weak and uncertain even to herself. "If the Mad King presses for so swift a surrender, perhaps that means—mightn't it suggest he is constrained somehow, that time is running through his hands faster than through ours? Perhaps it would be better to play for time—to put him off, to try to find a way to stop him, stop the Suriytè Power. Perhaps he will prove weaker later than he does now—"

Tiro nodded emphatically, but her father only asked her, "And if we don't find a way? If he in fact does to Leiör what he has already done to Cemerè? There are many towns north of Raëh. If we can't stop him until he reaches the very boundaries of Raëhemaiëth's own lands, how many of those towns will be left hollow and empty?"

"But—" said Tiro. "No, listen, what's to stop the Mad King from taking Kehera and then destroying Harivir's Immanences anyway? This is a *terrible* idea."

This seemed all too possible. Kehera looked at their father.

"It might be," their father said quietly. "It might be ill will and treachery from front to back, but what it will *not* be is the surrender Hallieth Suriytaiän demands. I need you to do this, Kehera, not because I intend for you to wed the Suriytaiän and bear him an heir with a double tie. I need you to do this so that I have time to prepare an adequate defense. And an adequate offense."

Kehera stared at him. "You mean—" she began in a small voice. "You mean you—oh. You think you can get Kosir to help us?" Kosir, to the northeast of Harivir, was the smallest and poorest of the Four Kingdoms, and generally it tried to avoid the affairs of its neighbors, but if the Mad King of Emmer was truly feeding lesser Immanences to his own Great Power, well, she could see how that might very well be enough to force the King of Kosir to ally with Harivir.

"I believe I already have a useful understanding with Corrièl Immariön of Kosir," said her father, with the ghost of a smile. "But this will compel a practical alliance. If Harivir cannot withstand Emmer, then certainly Kosir will not be able to do so. Corrièl cannot help but understand this. However . . ." The smile disappeared again. "I will move as swiftly as I can, Kehy, but it may all take some time. I'm sorry, but I can't promise to move against the Suriytaiän quickly . . . quickly enough to prevent this . . ." His voice tightened. "This utter *obscenity* of a marriage. If that is indeed the Suriytaiän's intention. But I promise you, Kehera, I *promise* you, I will never abandon you. I *will* bring you home, as soon as may be. Yet I see no alternative but to ask you to take this risk. And, utterly unfair as it is, to pay this price."

She could see that. She understood that. She did. It seemed terrible, and terribly risky—dangerous for her and not offering enough hope for Harivir. But her father seemed to think it was necessary, and she knew he would never ask it of her unless he were sure.

Tiro took her hands in his. She could feel the pressure of her brother's grip, but it was as though she felt that pressure from a long way away. He met her eyes and shook his head, just a little. "You can't," he whispered. "Don't you know—you *know* what it would mean."

Kehera pressed her brother's hands in return. She did know. She wanted to say to Tiro, *Of course you're right. Of course I can't. This is impossible.* She wanted to cry to her father, *I'm your* heir. *I'm heir to Raëh and Raëhemaiëth. I can't leave the lands bound to Raëh!* Because of course that part was true. Her father's *heir* could not possibly leave Harivir, or enter a foreign land bound to a foreign Great Power. Of course his *heir* couldn't do anything of the sort.

It took her a long moment. It took time enough to almost fool herself that if she only tried, she would be able to think of something else. For that lingering moment, she thought she would turn to her father—she could almost *see* herself turning to him—and say, *Of course I can't leave Harivir and Raëhemaiëth, but listen, here's what we can do instead.*

But she couldn't think of anything. Not though the seconds trickled by like grains of sand down a glass.

When she was silent, her father, bound more deeply to Raëhemaiëth than any of them, said gently to them both, "We can't let the Mad King destroy Harivir's Immanent Powers. Can you imagine what might happen to us, if more and more of our people were left helpless before Hallieth Suriytaiän in the north, aggressive Pohorin lords coming across the mountains to the east, and winter dragons riding the winds down upon us at the dark turn of the year? Never mind the Unfortunate Gods."

Tiro began to answer, but Kehera shook her head because she knew her father was right. She could see everything he said coming true: all the northern and eastern provinces and the smaller towns being torn away from Raëh and from Harivir. And then the winter dragons coming down upon lands with no Immanent Powers to protect them. She said unsteadily, "Tiro, if it's true . . . if it's true, then you must see that I have to do this." Turning to her father, she said to him stiffly, forcing out each word, "I'll do it. If you think I must, then I will." It was harder to say so than she'd expected, even with her father's promise that he didn't mean to abandon her to the Emmeran king. Because whatever happened to her later, what must happen to her first was terrible enough. Nevertheless, she managed to tell him, to tell everyone, "I'll do it. I'll go to Emmer and—and marry Hallieth Suriytaiän. If that's what he demands, I'll do it."

Her father gave her a quiet nod. "I know you will. Be brave, Kehy. We have a few hours yet—we will need every one of them, I fear."

She nodded. It all still felt oddly distant, as though her father were discussing an academic situation that had everything to do with tedious political maneuvering and nothing to do with her. That was fine. She didn't want to feel that any of this really had anything to do with her. Not now. Not yet. It was only going to be worse. Because . . . She said, feeling each word fall off her tongue as though a stranger was speaking, "I can't take a deep tie to Raëhemaiëth into Emmer—to the Mad King." They all knew this, but saying it aloud made it feel more true and more real. Every word seemed to cut her like a knife: as though in a moment it would hurt quite a lot. "I'm sure Hallieth Suriytaiän couldn't actually *do* anything to Raëhemaiëth, but it's not worth any risk. If I have to do this, then I *have* to give up the heir's tie, let Tiro take it—" She flinched and stopped at the look in her brother's eyes.

"Yes," her father said. "That is necessary, whatever else we may contrive. You have always had a fine grasp of a ruler's necessities." He sounded unlike himself on those last few words; his voice went flat and steady and hard.

Tiro shook his head in unvoiced protest.

"My son," their father said in that same flat voice, "I fear that you, too, must develop that clear sense of necessity. I know you will. You are my son, a Raëhema born, and you must recognize your sister's necessity, and your country's, and your own."

Tiro swallowed. He didn't protest, *But I don't want it*, though Kehera knew this was true. He didn't say, *But you can't send Kehera off like this. What if it doesn't even work? You can't sacrifice her just to buy time.* He didn't say any of that. Because he *was* Raëhema, and he knew as well as Kehera did what kings and queens were for: to stand between their country and the Gods Fortunate and Unfortunate, to channel the Great and lesser Powers of the land, and to bear whatever burdens fate or chance laid down for them in order to protect their kingdom and their people.

"Very well," said Kehera, distantly surprised at the steadiness of her own voice. "Very well. How do we do it? Shall I . . . ?" And now she faltered and had to start again. "Shall I repudiate Raëhemaiëth once I am across the river?"

She could do that. She knew how. It wasn't even difficult. One gathered up a handful of the earth that had given rise to the Immanent and stepped outside of its precincts. One cast the soil away and repudiated the Immanent and its tie upon one's heart and blood and bone. She knew how it was *done*, but she could not actually imagine *doing* it. Even if she had wanted the Immanent Power of Suriytè to lay claim to her, which she passionately did not, she could not imagine rejecting Raëhemaiëth so entirely.

Her father took her shoulders and drew her close. "Kehy, no. I would never ask that of you, and I hope it will not happen. You must give up the heir's tie. That is unavoidable. But we shall ask Raëhemaiëth to keep a claim to your heart. A thin tie. A thread of a tie. But enough you shall not be utterly bereft. Enough that at need you may yet hope that Raëhemaiëth may hear you."

Kehera nodded, her face against his chest, hoping it would prove so, terribly afraid that she would lose everything. Everything except the knowledge of her duty. Which would have to be enough, even if she lost everything else.

It was surprisingly easy to do this, in the end. Also far more difficult than Kehera had believed possible, but . . . also easy. Kehera only had to tell Raëhemaiëth what she wanted in her heart and mind and soul. The words were just for herself, so she could know her own intention clearly, because that would help Raëhemaiëth understand. Immanent Powers weren't like people; they didn't understand the same things. But they understood some things. Kehera said out loud, holding Tiro's hand, "I, Kehera irinè Elin, renounce the Raëhema name and the throne of Harivir. I renounce Raëh and Raëhemaiëth. I relinquish forever all rights and privileges, all duties and responsibilities of the throne and the tie to my brother, Tirovay arrin Elin Raëhema."

And her father murmured, "A thin tie, a whisper of a tie, do not let go entirely of our daughter, Raëhemaiëth! Wherever she goes, let her be drawn back to us!"

And the Great Immanent let her go. The air became warm and heavy for a long, lingering moment. That was all. It didn't hurt, except that Kehera felt the weight in the air was both somehow a part of her and something outside herself. It rose fast and then it dwindled . . . and dwindled . . . and was gone, as the Power withdrew from her mind and heart.

It had happened so fast. So easily. She hadn't understood how easily the Power of Raëh, where she had been born and had lived all her days, might let her go. As though Raëhemaiëth didn't even care. That was . . . Actually, that was one more grief in a day filled with sorrow and anger and fear. She gave the heir's tie to her brother, and Raëhemaiëth let him take it and let her go, even though the heir's deep tie had been part of her for her whole life, since the moment she was born. If any thin tie was left, she could not feel it. Maybe there was a thread, but she felt . . . so alone.

It was like giving away her own body. It was like her own body was glad to turn away from her.

Kehera had meant to give up the tie. But she had not known how much it would hurt, to have the Raëh Power give her up as well. She thought it must be as though a lover turned his back on her. No. Worse: as though her own mother turned her back and walked away. She felt as though she could not quite draw breath. It felt as though she had been pithed like a reed and left hollow. It did not actually hurt her. It was the worst thing she had ever experienced.

She blinked, and blinked again, feeling her vision had failed, and found her father holding her. Her face was against his chest. What they had done had hurt him too. She knew that, and she was almost glad of it, and ashamed she should feel that way. Tiro was kneeling beside her, but his head was bowed and his attention turned inward: He was discovering what the heir's tie would be. For just a moment, Kehera almost hated her brother, and that was worst of all. She shut her eyes and pressed her face harder into her father's shirt, trembling.

"Kehy," he said, very gently.

"I know," she whispered. "I know. It's all right. I'm all right." Actually, it felt worse and worse. She felt as though she had forgotten how to breathe, as though she might never be able to breathe again.

"Brave heart," her father murmured, and stroked her hair again as though she were a much younger child, until she was finally able to still her shaking—mostly—and push away from him. She rubbed her hands across her eyes and face and straightened her shoulders.

He said gently, "You still hold a thin tie, Kehy. You don't feel it? I thought not. But I see it in you. You may not feel it now, slender as it must be, but nothing can take that from you. I hope it will be enough if you must call upon it."

Kehera nodded, though she felt nothing now of Raëhemaiëth, nothing at all. She prayed to all the Fortunate Gods that he was right, that he was not just lying to her to be kind.

Her father nodded. Then he said, "Tiro." It was not quite a question.

"Yes," answered Tiro, a little shakily. He looked up, blinking, and then looked quickly and helplessly at Kehera. He opened his mouth, but closed it again without saying anything, because what was there to say, except this wasn't his wish? And she already knew that.

Poor Tiro, who had never wanted the heir's deep tie or to be king, and would now have to learn everything about being heir right now, at once.

Feeling sorry for her brother almost distracted Kehera from feeling sorry for herself. But not quite.

❋ ❋ ❋

They returned to Liyè Cemeraiän's house to make what other preparations could be made—few enough, so far as Kehera could tell. What possible preparations could there be for unexpected exile, with who knew what to follow once she set foot in Emmer? All the preparations that mattered were her father's. Maybe he would share his plans with Tiro, but certainly not with her. Not anymore.

For her, there was only the long afternoon and then the night to get through, pent up in her room in the apartment set aside for her father and his household.

Kehera had loved her room in this house as a child: All the wood was carved and gilded and all the rugs and curtains and seat cushions dyed indigo and vermillion and deep purple. Now this extravagance somehow seemed to contribute to a haunting feeling of unreality. Eilisè moved quietly about, taking dresses and jewels out of the wardrobes and laying them out, deciding what Kehera should take with her. Kehera couldn't bring herself to care about such small matters and did not watch. As the sun slid down lower in the west, she moved to the window and looked out over the garden instead. And farther than that. From this window, she could see over the garden wall and right down to the Imhar River, the wide expanse of water stretching out black in the gathering dusk. It was going to be long and dark, this night. It was going to feel endless.

She wished it would never end. Because in the morning, in the dark hour before dawn, she must cross the Imhar and let Hallieth Theraön Suriytaiän claim her like a prize, like the spoils of the war that her father would not now fight, not openly, because if he fought it openly now he could not win.

And she would have no one to help her in Emmer. Not even the firm sense of herself that had always, she knew now, actually been due to the presence of Raëhemaiëth.

Kehera hardly knew how she could bear it. Except that if she carried this through, Harivir might have a chance to win, later. So she had to trust her father to arrange everything, and bear the part appointed for her.

"I'll go with you, of course," Eilisè told her. She had been Kehera's companion since they'd both been little girls; now she was closer to Kehera than anyone save Tiro. She had come to keep the night from being so lonely, and also to help Kehera choose what she would take with her.

But Kehera had never thought until that moment she might be saved from having to go alone. "Oh," she said, and began to cry. Eilisè stopped, horrified, and hugged her. Kehera cried not with the vigorous sobs of unselfconscious childhood, but with a nearly silent gathering of tears. She fought the convulsive breaths that shook her.

"It'll be all right," said Eilisè urgently. "I'm sure it will, Kehy."

"It's just," whispered Kehera, "it's just I hadn't thought till now that I won't have you, either, in Emmer. No, I won't," she added fiercely. "How could I let you come? It's too dangerous. Who knows what Hallieth Theraön intends? I can't possibly take you with me."

"Of course you can. How can you not?" Eilisè regarded her with exasperation. "Why make it harder for yourself than it has to be? If he's to marry you, he can't simply lock you in a dungeon or anything, and it would look very odd if he denied you ladies of your own. It's my choice, isn't it, if I want to risk it?"

"I can't ask you to leave your family—"

"You haven't asked, and I wrote my mother already. She'll say I was right, not that I needed telling. You Raëhema! You always want to bear the weight of the world. It's that Power of yours, I suppose, the memory of all those responsible, kind, patient kings in your blood, but you ought to have more sense, Kehy!"

Kehera looked at her uncertainly. "Well—"

"Now that's settled, perhaps you could hold still for a second and let me finish laying out these gowns, and then you can tell me which ones you want to take." Eilisè studied the pile on the bed with a critical eye.

"I'd be very glad if you did come," Kehera admitted in a small voice.

"There!" said Eilisè briskly. "As if I'd stay behind! Now, I think this plain dress is what you need for traveling, but don't you want to take this blue for later? It's your most beautiful gown, Kehy, and all those tiny little opals at the hem make it plain you're a princess and no mere lord's daughter."

"Whatever you think," Kehera said meekly.

There was a quiet tap on the bedroom door, from someone who had come quietly right through Kehera's reception hall and sitting room and breakfast room. Kehera was not surprised—indeed, she would have been surprised if that tap had not come. She glanced at Eilisè, who, nodding, moved to answer the summons.

It was Tiro, of course. He came to Kehera without a word, Eilisè slipping quietly out to leave them alone. His eyes looked bruised. His face was drawn with unhappiness. Kehera held out her hands to her brother and drew him down to sit on the edge of the couch beside her. She put her arm around him and leaned her head against his shoulder. He was taller than she was. He had got his growth more than a year ago, but it still surprised her, that she could lean against him and find him so tall. Her little brother. He had grown up.

She said gently, "You'll be a good king, you know, Tiro."

He shook his head, not answering. After a while he said, "There've been four times I know of where a king or queen or duke renounced his—or her—recognized heir and set the heir's tie in somebody else. Twice the original heir tried to get the deep tie back later."

"I don't expect it worked."

"No," Tiro said, his voice muffled. "Or, it might have worked for Tamareìs' Immariön. No one knows, because she died in the attempt and the next king of Kosir came from a cousin's line. Tamareìs's brother fought her for the tie, though. Or that's what Kesenorel wrote, but there weren't any witnesses. At least not that survived."

"Ah."

"They're lucky it didn't shatter all its bonds to its land and people and become a God, though at least the Immaör Power ought to make a Fortunate God if it ever does break its ties to men and its bonds with the land. Kosir's lucky the Immariön line has always been responsible."

Kehera nodded solemnly, although she was not able to worry just at the moment about such distant possibilities. Whatever the Immanent Power of Immaör might do at some possible day in the future, she knew Raëhemaiëth would never try to break its own ties to its people nor to Raëh nor to the Raëhema line. She didn't care right now about anything that might have almost happened a long time ago in the heart of Kosir.

"Anyway, listen," Tiro said earnestly. "A hundred thirty years ago, Secheier Maran Lerè, of the province that was then Ceroran, gave his tie to his cousin Luka Nouriy because he was so angry about the way his family treated Luka. But then later, after his mother finally died, Secheier tried to reclaim his tie, but he couldn't just take it back, even though his cousin tried to give it back to him. The tie has followed Luka's bloodline ever since, and Secheier's children lived and died plain Marans."

"How do you ever remember these things?" But Kehera wasn't surprised. Tiro remembered practically everything he read, as long as he was interested. Though not much about subjects he disliked. She told him, "I won't try to take back the heir's tie, not if it might hurt you or Raëhemaiëth." That was too solemn, so she tried to smile. "You'll have to study law, you know. And etiquette."

"No. Because even if you can't take back the tie, you'll be here. Father will get you away from Hallieth Suriytaiän. Or you'll get away on your own. You're stubborn, Kehy. You always get your own way in the end if you really want to. You'll be fine. I know you will. So when I need to know about law or whatever, you'll be here to tell me."

Kehera let out her breath and nodded.

"Be stubborn," her brother whispered. "Get your own way. Promise me."

"I will. I promise."

"Good," Tiro said. "Good."

"Help Father, Tiro. Don't let him worry too much. Make sure he gets enough rest."

"I'll try."

"And you. Don't you worry too much either."

Her brother laughed, not with much humor.

"Well, maybe you can worry a *little*," Kehera conceded. "Stay with me tonight, Tiro, will you? I won't sleep. We can play tiahel, if you like." Her brother had made her the set when he was only twelve, carving the rods himself out of blackwood and pale maple and finding dice he knew she would like, of agate and jasper, no two alike. He had burned the symbols onto the pale rods and inlaid them in mother-of-pearl on the black ones—he had always been good at such fine work, though he had given it up when he turned fifteen and got interested in horses instead. But Kehera had never let anybody give her any other tiahel set, not even very fancy sets of griffin bone and wind-sparked obsidian.

"Yes," Tiro said. And, with forced cheer, "Best two games out of three means I get your cream cake. Eilisè will get us cakes and sweet rolls, won't she?"

"She will, but I'll win your share," Kehera told him, and looked around for the tiahel box.

Two hours before dawn was time enough for Kehera to choose what traveling dress to wear and for Eilisè to help her with the buttons and then put her hair up in an elaborate nine-stranded knot. Her father had ordered a repast to be served in the apartment. There was an abundance of sweet rolls. Neither Kehera nor Tiro ate any. Nor did their father. Kehera ate an egg and half a slice of plain bread so that her father wouldn't worry so much. The food sat uneasily in her stomach. She pretended so hard that she was fine that she almost made herself believe it, though she doubted anyone else did.

She wondered what Hallieth Suriytaiän was actually like. She supposed he would be waiting for her on the other side of the Imhar. He would take her to Suriytè. She dreaded every step of the journey that would take her ever farther from Harivir and Raëh. She knew her father knew she was afraid. He could hardly fail to know it. But she didn't admit it, and neither did he. Tiro was pale and quiet and said almost nothing.

After breakfasting by lantern light, everyone came out into the courtyard of the house to witness her departure—Liyè Cemeraiän and Soë and all their household. Everyone knew now that she was being surrendered to the mad Emmeran king. Everyone with any sense probably guessed that this was only an opening move in an unstated slow-motion struggle that did not—at the moment—involve armies or clashing swords. Armies and swords, Harivir could have faced. The silence in Cemerè was different.

The silence in the courtyard was deafening as Kehera mounted her gray mare. It was a silence that was somehow not broken by the sound of hooves on the paving stones and the jingle of the horses' bits, though those ordinary sounds rang through the morning stillness. It was a silence of waiting. It was the silence before war, because no one thought that Kehera's departure would end anything. Everyone knew it was one move among many still to come.

So they rode slowly through quiet Cemerè, Kehera with her father on one side and her brother and Eilisè on the other and a whole company behind. It was dark, but the road was lined with lanterns. Despite the clatter of the horses' hooves on the cobbles, despite the many people who had come out to line the streets and witness her departure, the town echoed with silence. Even without the heir's deep tie, Kehera could hear that emptiness. It stole her heart and at the same time strengthened her determination. She could never have let this happen to another Harivin province. Not if she could prevent it.

Then they left hollow Cemerè and rode down the slope toward the river, through the quiet encampment, and halted at last on the cracked clay flats where, but for the lingering drought, the river should have run. The ferry had been brought up, its ramp extended across the flats, so that she would not need to trail her skirts in the muddy water.

Kehera drew rein and sat still, gazing north. She could hear the river, washing against the ferry's hull out where the water was deeper. The sky in the east was just beginning to lighten with the coming dawn, but from this distance she could see nothing but darkness on the other side of the river.

Kehera's father dismounted. Coming to her side, he took her hands and looked earnestly up at her. She could make out nothing of his face but a pale blur in this predawn gray. She felt rather numb and distant and hoped he would not say anything kind or sorrowful, because she was afraid if he did she might cry, and she couldn't bear to weep. She tried to tell her father this without words, with just the pressure of her urgent gaze, and he might have understood, because he didn't say anything of the kind.

Instead, he said, "You won't spot him, and it's best if you don't look for him. But I'm sending Quòn after you, just in case . . . well, in case."

This was not what Kehera had expected. "Quòn?"

"If you need him, Kehy, he'll be there." Her father's voice tautened. "I'm not sacrificing you, Kehy. I'm moving you onto the board, but I'll not watch you fall to the Mad King. If—when—you need to get out of Suriytè, Quòn will get you out. He'll do whatever is necessary to protect you, whatever we've arranged or haven't arranged with Kosir. And we'll go on from there, however the rods fall out afterward."

Kehera nodded. She thought of the man she'd met in her father's study and did not know quite what to make of him. But she was glad a man of her father's would be there, in Suriytè, keeping an eye on her. She said, "Thank you."

Her father lifted her hands in his, to touch his forehead. Then, releasing her, he gave her the gesture that wished for good fortune, hand to his heart. "May the Fortunate Gods watch over your road, my daughter, and may the Unfortunate Gods never notice you at all, and may your thin tie to Raëhemaiëth comfort you, even in foreign lands." He stepped back.

Kehera swallowed. But the urge to cry seemed to have left her, thankfully. Her eyes felt dry and gritty, but no tears threatened. She was able to incline her head to her father with proper dignity, rein the mare around, and ride straight up the ramp onto the deck of the ferry. Her mare's hooves thudded on the wood, sounding like the hollow drumbeat of a dirge. Elisè, impossible to dissuade, followed, and Kehera was grateful. She did not dismount, but kept her hands low, pressed against her gray mare's neck, to hide their trembling. When the ferry pushed away from the shore and began its slow progress across the river, she did not look back.

3

On the sixteenth day of Fire Maple Month, Innisth terè Maèr Eänetai, these seven years the Duke of Eäneté, absolute ruler of the largest and most powerful of all the western Pohorin provinces, stood with his hands resting on the railing of the upper gallery of the tallest tower of his great house, his eyes closed, and reminded himself that he was far too mature and sensible to murder the Irekaïn lord with whom the King of Pohorir had seen fit to burden him. Satisfying as that murder might be, it would not be practical. The king would certainly take exception.

In a sense, the province of Eäneté prospered despite its distance from the sophistication and wealth of Irekay, capital of Pohorir. Irekay lay far away, a white city carved of the white stone of those rugged cliffs where the sea flung itself in constant assault against the far eastern coast of Pohorir. It was the *western* border of Pohorir that Eäneté guarded. The eastern and central provinces always benefited from the nearby wealth of Irekay, while more remote provinces received little in return for the taxes and tribute they sent to the capital.

In another sense, Eäneté prospered because of its remote location, far from the political maneuvering of the court. Not only were all the western provinces relatively untroubled by the king's unpredictable whims, but also Eäneté controlled the Pohorin side of Roh Pass. Even in high summer, more than half of all trade goods to or from Harivir came through Roh Pass. When winter closed its icy teeth on the mountains, almost all traffic must come through Roh.

Of course Methmeir Heriduïn Irekaì, master of the Great Power of Irekay and King of Pohorir, knew this full well. The Heriduïn Irekaì kings were accustomed to both enrich themselves and keep Eäneté close at heel through the imposition of high taxes upon that trade. The Kings of Pohorir might not be able to rule the far-flung border provinces with as tight-drawn a rein as those that lay closer to Irekay, but they well knew how to curb any province that showed signs of becoming too wealthy or powerful. But first Methmeir Irekaì's father and then Methmeir Irekaì himself had been a friend of Innisth's father, and so for a generation no Pohorin king had showed any great inclination to check Eäneté's prosperity. So Eäneté had done well in those years.

Now, however, here was Lord Laören of Irekay, newly arrived in Eäneté, sent by the king's own hand. Innisth knew exactly what judgment Laören was expected to render: a judgment on the docility of the new Duke of Eäneté and on the strength of the Eänetén Power. Five years, six years, seven years since Innisth had become duke, and the king had not sent any man of his to Eäneté. Innisth had begun to believe that Methmeir Irekaì was too much taken up with his own affairs to be much interested in the provinces distant from his capital. He had been glad of it. He remembered the king from his one compulsory journey to Irekay, when his father had presented his heir to the king and the court. Innisth had been twelve, Methmeir Irekaì eighteen and very much a son of his father. The experience had left its scars, and while Innisth did not precisely fear the Pohorin king, he was far from willing to repeat that visit.

And now, seven years after Innisth's assumption of the deep tie and the title, the king's attention was far more dangerous than it might have been earlier. Because Eäneté had indeed prospered and grown strong.

If Lord Laören suspected that Eänetaìsarè was on the verge of becoming a Great Power and told the king so . . . or if he, on some random whim, compelled Innisth to accompany him when he returned to Irekay . . . if Innisth was forced to come before Irekaì and look into the king's eyes . . . Methmeir Irekaì was not precisely clever. But he had a cleverness for identifying men who might someday become rivals, and a delight in cutting such men down before they could challenge him. And he could not fail to realize how strong Innisth terè Maèr Eänetaì had grown in these seven years; he and the Immanent Power whose tie he bore.

Yet Innisth dared not openly defy any command to appear before the king.

Either to come before the king in Irekay or to refuse to come would lead to disaster, for the King of Pohorir desired vassals, not rivals. Methmeir Irekaì might break Eäneté's prosperity for a generation, if he believed the province had grown too strong or its duke had become too arrogant.

The king would not likely put Innisth Eänetaì to death. Certainly not before midwinter. Innisth had no recognized heir of appropriate age and trained strength of will. Killing him would cast Eänetaìsarè's tie to some unknown by-blow of the Maèr line, or to some distant cousin of some other line whose connection to Maèr and Eänetaì everyone had forgotten. If that cousin failed to hold the tie and master Eänetaìsarè, then so violent and strong a Power might even tear free of the bonds that held it to the mortal earth. It might become a God. From that disaster, even if Eäneté's Immanent Power became the most Fortunate of Gods, Eäneté would be a long, long time recovering.

Or if the Power became an Unfortunate God—which seemed likely enough from the apotheosis of so harsh and grim a Power—then the province and surrounding lands might *never* recover. The desert in the north of Emmer was a warning to even the most reckless and brutal king. Innisth hardly fancied himself a scholar and would not have hazarded a guess as to the intentions or desires of either the Fortunate or the Unfortunate Gods, but he knew that was one belief: that the

Unfortunate Gods hated themselves and hated the world. Perhaps they did. Certainly the notion accorded well enough with the violence and calamity brought by the apotheosis of a Great Power to an Unfortunate God. Though even kinder Immanences that eventually ascended to join the Fortunate Gods wreaked some degree of destruction upon the lands of their birth when they rose.

Either way, it seemed unlikely a desert would form here in mountainous Eäneté. Probably this land would become a rugged, barren landscape of broken stone and ice, cut with streamers of molten rock where the violent heat below broke through into the chilly world above. Innisth could imagine just what that blasted land might be like. Then Pohorir would lose not merely its strong westernmost province, but also the goods that came and went from Harivir through Roh Pass. No, the king would not wish to go quite so far.

But imprison the Duke of Eäneté away from the lands of Eäneté, hold him in some grim captivity far away in the east past the dark turning of the year, force him to name some unfortunate minor cousin his heir, then kill Innisth in the spring . . . that would break Eäneté's strength far more safely. And Methmeir Heriduïn Irekaì would no doubt enjoy the cruelty of it.

Innisth could not prevent the king from ruining Eäneté if that was his pleasure. For all Eänetaìsarè's strength, the Immanent Power of Irekay was older and deeper, bound to wider lands and strengthened by its bonds to all the provinces of Pohorir. And the Heriduïn Irekaì kings had ruled in an unbroken line for many generations. Irekaìmaiäd must still be far stronger than Eänetaìsarè. There was no hope in defiance.

Thus Innisth must placate or cajole or bribe or threaten Lord Laören, so that at length the court lord returned to Irekay with a good report of Eäneté and its duke. A safe report, of a lesser Power and a tame duke.

The situation called not for violence, but for flattery and bribes, and perhaps a carefully designed distraction or two. Nothing broad, nothing overt. Subtlety was the key. Murdering the king's pet, however satisfying, probably would not prove sufficiently subtle.

Innisth opened his eyes and turned to look again upon the face of Methmeir Irekaì's pet. He knew what Lord Laören saw: a provincial duke, feigning aristocratic tastes but woefully out of fashion, his spare face further removed from the current standard of beauty by yellow eyes: the eyes of a wolf, set in the face of a man with the wolf as his seal and his standard. Laören must not be allowed to guess what Innisth saw: a careless little dog too stupid to understand that he had trotted into the wolf's den.

The Irekaïn lord gazed back at Innisth with the smug complacency that only the king's lapdogs could afford. It would have been very easy to strip that complacency away from him. But that would not be wise. No.

Mastering the impulse, Innisth said gently, "Of course I am delighted at the notice of His Majesty. How generous of him, to deprive himself of your company, my lord; and how dedicated of you to endure the discomforts of such a journey. I trust that you will not find Eäneté too bleak, after the"—*decadence*—"luxuries of the capital. Alas, here on the border, we must make do without the amenities of Irekay."

"Of course," said Lord Laören. "I assure you, Your Grace, I have come prepared to withstand privation. I have brought my own servants with me, that I need not impose upon your hospitality."

The insult was intentional, no doubt of it. And the servants would spy on Innisth's staff, almost as dangerous and annoying as their master. "I shall order the upper level of the west wing dedicated to your use, my lord," Innisth murmured with strict courtesy. "Two connected suites— rustic, no doubt, but I hope you will find them adequate. Perhaps you would be so gracious as to permit my seneschal to show you the way." He glanced at Gereth Murrel, who immediately came forward and, murmuring polite nothingnesses, extracted the court lord, like a thorn, from the duke's presence.

Innisth looked down again into the inner yard, gazing at the activity below without seeing it. Brilliant sunshine just saved the afternoon from an unpleasant chill. There was a wind, as always, from off the mountains, but today it was merely a breeze. A pleasant autumn day, if not for the king's little whims.

Behind him, his seneschal, Gereth Murrel, coming back out onto the gallery, said with distaste, "A typical court lordling, that one. He thinks he holds the wolf on a short chain."

"He does, unfortunately," Innisth answered, allowing a trace of humor to enter his voice.

"I know you. You'll send the king's pet yipping back to his kennel, never knowing how close you've come to ripping out his throat."

"One must hope you are correct." Innisth himself did not feel quite so assured, but Gereth's confidence pleased him. He turned slowly to look at the older man, lifting a hand to shield his eyes from the lowering sun. "Laören holds a stronger tie than most to the Irekaïn Power, I believe. All that family are of Irekaïn birth, are they not? And his grandfather married a Heriduïn cousin, is that not so? Yes, I thought I recalled that. No doubt that is why the king selected him for this . . . tour of the west." Innisth paused. Then he went on. "I would not be surprised if Laören sees more than we might wish. I fear he will end by commanding me to accompany him to court."

Gereth nodded. "I know you cannot outright refuse any command he gives you, Your Grace. Far less any command His Majesty sees fit to give. But I trust you will find some means to evade anything that might harm Eäneté."

Innisth inclined his head. "I imagine Laören is clever, in a small and petty way. But such men can be distracted by their own cleverness. Perhaps he might discover some shameful plot to evade Irekaïn taxes. Not here, of course. I shall have to decide which of our neighbors might have engaged in so despicable a practice."

"I shall trust Your Grace's capability to devise something suitable."

"Indeed." Innisth paused. "In the meantime, Laören's servants will make themselves a nuisance, I am sure. They will be spies as well. This will take careful handling, I fear."

"Indeed, Your Grace. I will instruct the staff most carefully."

"See to it that some pleasure girls and boys are brought up from the city. They can pretend to be nervous young servants of the house. That will both distract Laören and protect our own people. Have our younger staff warned to keep out of their way. If some serving boy or girl is careless and must be rescued, I will not be amused."

"I will be very clear on that point, Your Grace."

Innisth nodded slightly and drew a long breath of the cold air. "I do not . . . The air within the house seems close today. I will take a small force and ride the bounds, I think. Laören may inquire after me. You may inform him I request the honor of his company at a late supper. He may be annoyed I am not here, waiting at his word. That will be as well. It may be useful to see that he is annoyed and impatient. Not, however, truly angry. Be sure he is entertained."

Gereth made a slight face. "Yes, Your Grace."

"My old friend," Innisth said, and laid a hand on his seneschal's shoulder, lightly, in passing.

So Innisth spent the day in the saddle, riding around to many of the garrisons guarding the roads that led through his province and around his city and the outlying villages. He spent little time at each, taking only a few moments to speak to the commanding officers. Most of his attention remained on the problem Lord Laören posed and on various stratagems that might suffice to send the man away prepared to make a useful report of the province's docility.

Eventually, however, Innisth noticed how little traffic they passed on the roads. Rather less than usual. What there was moved mostly toward the city of Eäneté. That was interesting. If it was part of a trend, it might indicate trouble in the neighboring provinces, the lesser folk, as always, feeling it first.

Innisth kept an eye on his escorting guards, marking which seemed particularly nervous to be riding under the eye of their duke and which were calm, which took the long day in stride and which wearied and dragged. The officer, one Verè Deconniy, was young and not well known to the duke. Deconniy had only recently come to Eäneté from the neighboring province of Tisain, having gotten into some manner of difficulty there; Gereth had explained something about it, but Innisth had paid little attention. He knew Deconniy had been an officer of Lord Geif's house guard. Beyond that, he knew only that he must have impressed Etar, for he had quickly been promoted to one of the lesser captaincies. Thus Innisth had requested Deconniy's escort specifically.

The officer knew he was being evaluated, of course. He was tense, but had the sense to keep his mouth mostly shut. His occasional comments were brief, to the point, and quiet. And, though this was not strictly required in an officer, he was a good-looking young man. Strong featured, not precisely attractive in any typical sense, yet he was the sort of man who drew a second look. Innisth thought he might approve of him.

They had left the city riding south and made a quarter circle to return, at sunset, riding almost due west. The setting sun blazed behind the duke's hall, poised to slide below the Takel Mountains. The late sunlight ran like honey across the walls and flagstones of the wide courtyard. Innisth tilted his face up to the lowering sun and fancied he could feel the subliminal purr of the Eänetén Power, like a low voice murmuring just outside the range of hearing.

The duke rode through the eastern gate without glancing at the guards. In the yard, Innisth dismounted, tossed his reins to a waiting hostler, and dismissed the escort with a brief nod. He kept Deconniy back with a gesture, then crooked a finger for the young officer to walk aside with him into the relative privacy provided by the turn of the outer courtyard wall. Deconniy obeyed this silent command without a word, as sparing of speech now as he had been during the ride, but Innisth could see the tension in his back and shoulders.

"You find yourself comfortable in Eäneté?" the duke asked him. "You do not find a lingering Tisain tie draws upon your heart? I know it can take some time for the tie to the land of one's birth to lighten, for the new tie to set itself in one's blood and bone."

"No, Your Grace," Deconniy answered firmly, meeting his eyes. "I repudiated the tie to Tisain the moment I set foot on Eänetén soil. I repudiated Lord Geif Tisainiär, cast Tisain earth away, and gladly took the tie to Eänetaìsarè, as I swore to Senior Captain Etar and as I swear to you now, Your Grace."

A low purring of possessive satisfaction came from Eänetaìsarè at this declaration. Innisth smiled. "Bravely spoken. Very good. Etar thinks highly of you."

The young man answered steadily, "I am glad to think so, Your Grace."

Innisth reached out to touch the younger man's cheek. Deconniy stood very still. Innisth slid his hand down the man's jaw and rested his hand on his throat. The pulse under his fingers was light and rapid. He said, keeping his tone impersonal, "You are afraid of me, Verè Deconniy." It was not a question.

"Yes, Your Grace," the man said, his voice now not quite so steady.

"What did Captain Etar tell you of me?" Innisth slid his hand up again, cupping the man's jaw, thumb resting still on the pulse.

The tiniest pause. Then Deconniy answered, "Senior Captain Etar told me you will not compel your own people. That Eäneté is not Tisain and you are not Lord Geif. That in matters of this kind, I can refuse without fear of punishment." He met Innisth's eyes across the little distance that separated them and added, "Whatever order you give, I will obey. But Senior Captain Etar told me this is an order you will not give."

Innisth almost smiled. "What else did he tell you?"

Another very small pause. Then the answer came, in a low, even voice, "That you would press me and try to make me afraid, but that you like a man who will not back away even if he fears you."

"Yes. He would have said that. Do you believe him?"

"I thought I believed him, Your Grace. I wish to believe him." The beat of the young man's pulse was still fast against Innisth's thumb.

"You should believe him. Etar knows me very well." Innisth lifted his hand and took one step back. "You should fear me," he added. "But not for this. I will not command this." He looked the younger man up and down. "Unless you wish to be commanded?"

Deconniy flushed, slowly but comprehensively. "No," he said stiffly. "Your Grace."

"Pity," said the duke, careful to keep his tone impersonal. He turned away, but added over his shoulder, "You did well today." But he did not stay to observe the young officer's response.

4

As the seventeenth day of Fire Maple Month dawned slowly silver, Kehera irinè Elin, no longer Raëhema—though she certainly didn't intend to say so unless she had to—rode her gray mare down the ferry's ramp and onto the northern bank of the wide Imhar River. Just as her mare's hooves touched the beaten earth of Emmeran soil, the sun edged at last above the horizon and the river turned to gold behind her.

It felt . . . very strange, to have set foot on land that was not connected through even the slightest bond to Raëhemaiëth. It felt . . . disturbing. Disturbingly *wrong*, as though she had made a terrible mistake to come here. More than anything, she wanted to turn and flee—not back onto the ferry; that would be too slow—straight into the river and back to Harivir. Hating her own cowardice, Kehera refused to even turn and look. She stared only ahead, at the Emmeran soldiers drawn up to meet her.

She had feared that the Mad King might seize her the moment she descended from the ferry, gloat about his victory, parade her like a trophy before his soldiers. Or that he might meet her coldly, produce the twice-braided cords and candles necessary for even the most abbreviated wedding ceremony, and marry her right there on the riverbank. She had not been able to guess what he might do.

But the man who stood at the forefront of the assembled Emmeran soldiers was not the king. She knew it right away. This man, whoever he was, was dressed too plainly, obviously a soldier; and he was not old enough; and he was not mad—or at least she could find no madness in his face or eyes or manner. She glanced beyond him, expecting the king to be waiting in the encampment, perhaps, if he was not here at the river's edge. But she could see that nearly all the tents had already been rolled up and packed away. There was only the trampled ground, and away to the left, not far, the Emmeran town of Talisè. Perhaps that was where Hallieth Suriytaiän had gone to wait for her. She stared searchingly at Talisè. It was a handsome town, all its yellow sandstone gilded by the rising sun. But even from the riverbank, a disturbing silence echoed here, too: the absence of the Emmeran Power that should have inhabited every street and home, every alley and shop and all the surrounding lands where farmers lived. Even without the deep tie to Raëhemaiëth, she could feel the flatness here almost as vividly as she had felt it in Cemerè.

The Immanent Power that had grown up out of Talisè should have inhabited all the land for miles in every direction. It should have within every man and woman and newborn child, every dog and goat, every tree and blade of grass. But there was nothing there. Quòn had been right. Talisè was empty, exactly as Cemerè was empty. The mare's hooves thudded on the packed earth of the riverbank. The mare tossed her head uneasily as though she, too, felt the terrible emptiness of the land. Kehera bit her lip and turned her gaze from the hollow town to the face of the man who had come to the foot of the ramp to meet her.

This was a big man; not young, but powerful. His hair was mostly dark, but his short-cropped beard was grizzled, and the lines around his eyes and on either side of his mouth attested to long years of patience and discipline. He met her eyes with a direct confidence that she did not trust in an Emmeran officer, then bowed his head in a deference she trusted less than that. He wore the uniform of an Emmeran officer, but she was not certain what rank was indicated by the badge at his shoulder.

Taking her mare's rein, he said to her, his manner respectful, "Princess Kehera Raëhema. I am Enmon Corvallis. Allow me to welcome Your Highness to Emmer and assure you of my goodwill. My king is not here, but he will come to Suriytè before you."

Much about this little speech seemed odd to Kehera. *His* goodwill, was it, and *his* welcome? And no mention of the goodwill of his king. Who was not here. Kehera wanted to ask where Hallieth Suriytaiän had gone and why, but she did not think the question wise. Even if she had the goodwill of General Enmon Corvallis.

She knew who he was now that he had offered her his name. She perhaps knew a little more of General Corvallis than he might expect, for her father had mentioned this man's name on more than one occasion. She knew her father thought him the ablest of the Emmeran generals. Her father had said once that General Corvallis was the sort of man who would choose his own means of carrying out operations, who would sometimes even choose his own objectives over his king's. That afterward he would look anyone who challenged him straight in the eye and declare that he had kept strictly to his exact orders, even when it was perfectly obvious he hadn't. Her father had not been speaking to Kehera at the time, but the description had struck her and she had remembered it.

Now, looking at him searchingly, she found she could believe it. He certainly looked confident enough, even in these peculiar circumstances. Indeed, Corvallis's sheer arrogance seemed to have carried him through the Mad King's reign very well. Where more timid men incurred the king's displeasure and were cast down, here General Corvallis was, in command of this important Emmeran force and now trusted to escort her to Suriytè. She thought—she hoped—that the goodwill of this man might be a true asset to her in the days to come.

"I thank you for your welcome, General," she said quietly. And asked no questions at all, not about his king, nor about his king's intentions, nor about what his own goodwill might be worth. Not yet. Though she hoped perhaps she might find a chance to ask such questions sometime before they reached the walls of Suriytè.

It was eight or nine days' ride from the Imhar River to Suriytè in the heart of Emmer, if one went at a dignified pace. Eight or nine days was going to be a long time for Kehera to keep up a brave pretense in front of her Emmeran escort, a long time to watch Eilisè worry about her, a long, boring time to fill with fears of the future. She did not quite wish that the Mad King had seized her forcibly as soon as she'd set foot in Emmer, but no matter what waited for her in Suriytè, Kehera almost longed to arrive there just to put an end to this terrible uncertainty.

Whatever happened in Suriytè, this was certainly not a future or a marriage she had ever imagined for herself. She still flinched from imagining it now. Of course she trusted her father to bring her back to Harivir; of course she did. Quòn would help her, or she would get away on her own. She would get out of Suriytè somehow and back to Harivir and Raëh.

But even then, she didn't know what her future might hold. Tiro might try to return the heir's tie to her, but Raëhemaiëth had accepted him already, and from the story he'd told her, no such effort was likely to work.

She had known all her life that she would someday take the ruling tie and become Queen of Harivir. Raëhemaiëth would strengthen her in good years and draw on her own strength in harder years, and she would listen carefully to the concerns of her people and do her best to make good and just decisions about the problems they brought her. She would marry some important duke or lord and bear children to come after her, children with solid ties to her lord's province as well as to Raëh, thus strengthening the bonds between Immanents that held Harivir together and kept the whole country secure.

Of course, love was not something she had ever counted on when considering whom she might wed. Of course not. A princess or a queen married to strengthen Harivir. Raëhemaiëth was a generous Power, and all the bonds it made with lesser Powers were Fortunate bonds, bonds through which they could draw upon its strength and surety. Thus, every marriage of a Raëhema to a lesser lord reinforced those bonds, and thus the lesser Powers of Harivir grew stronger. Thus all of Harivir became more secure. Or that was how it was supposed to work.

Even as recently as last winter, Kehera had not quite been able to decide whom she should marry, though she had puzzled over the question for several years—ever since she'd become a woman. She had thought first of Duke Riheir Coärin of Coär, who was always kind. He was only ten years older than she was, which wasn't so bad, though he was dedicated to his land and so looked a little older than he was. She liked Riheir's voice, which was cheerful and warm. She liked the way he looked: not precisely handsome, but athletic, broad in the shoulder and narrow in the hip. On one visit to Raëh, he'd taught Tiro and her how to make wonderful things out of paper—swans and fish—and he'd taught them how to make and fly kites; he'd made her a beautiful one, all the colors of fire. She had thought then that perhaps someday she might like to marry Riheir Coärin. Other considerations also made this a reasonable idea. Coär was an important province, set as it was far to the east and south of Raëh, at the foot of the Takel Mountains, directly west of the Pohorin province of Eäneté. The pass there was the only pass through those mountains that never closed, and the trade that moved through it was important. But Pohorir was always slyly aggressive, the dukes of Eäneté always strong and cruel. In order to safeguard all of Harivir, it was important for Coär to be as strong as possible.

But then Riheir married a woman from his own province. The woman had a daughter right away and then a son. Then she died, but Duke Riheir wore black and lavender afterward and showed no sign of putting off his mourning even years later, so Kehera had known he was not planning to marry again.

Gheres Risaniòn, Duke of Risaèn, was nearly forty. Risaèn was not as strategically important as Coär, but centered the important farmlands that stretched out in south-central Harivir. Those lands were more important than ever when, as now, drought weakened the northern provinces of Harivir.

Kehera could have borne marrying a man as old as Gheres Risaniòn, but he was also far too grim. A forbidding sternness had echoed back and forth between the dukes of Risaèn and their Immanent Power for generations, intensifying with every new Risaèn heir, and as the family had taken no pains to bring in bonds to gentler, more joyous Powers, that sternness was now set deep. The dukes of Risaèn were strong and loyal and mindful of their duty to their people and to Raëh, but Kehera had never liked either Gheres Risaniòn or his Immanent Power.

The Duke of Lanis was younger and recently widowed, but he was also impossibly annoying. He couldn't tell minor irritations from major disasters and complained about everything equally, a constant whine of disapproval and disappointment, and though that was just him and not his whole family or his Power, Kehera had never seriously considered him.

There were two boys she had thought might do. One of them, the heir to Viär, was bright and funny, and she thought she might like him, but he was also only nine years old. The other, the heir to the important town of Timir that sprawled along the southern edge of Imhar Bay, was tall and handsome and only a year younger than Kehera, but he was not very clever. Kehera had supposed the little boy in Viär would get older, whereas the dull boy in Timir probably wouldn't get smarter, but she was not eager to wait another ten long years and finally marry a boy ten years younger than herself. Besides, Viär, north of Coär and hard against the mountains, was so small a province, its namesake town hardly more than a large village. She could not see how she could justify marrying its heir.

So it had been difficult to decide what would be best for Raëh and for herself. One day soon she would have gathered her nerve to speak to her father about such matters, if he hadn't spoken first.

Then late this spring, in the Golden Hinge Month, the month when spring turned to summer and all change was counted fortunate, Riheir Coärin had finally put off mourning and sent her a courting poem. Kehera remembered every word of it. He had written:

> *In Risaèn the roses bloom red,*
> *red as the heart of the burning fire.*
> *In Eilin the roses bloom gold,*
> *gold as the sun on summer wheat.*
> *In Coär the roses bloom white,*
> *white as the snow on the mountains.*
> *But in Raëh the roses open blue,*
> *blue as the sky that stands above,*
> *blue as a fountain under the sky,*
> *blue as the ribbons in your hair.*

And he had sent with the poem a tiny rose carved of lapis, strung on a silver chain. Kehera had considered the needs of Harivir and the choices available to her. And she still liked Riheir Coärin well enough. So she had put on the pendant to let her father know that she approved of Riheir Coärin's suit and would accept him when he asked for her.

But the summer had passed into autumn, and he had not yet asked. And now there was this. Everything had changed. Nothing was as it was supposed to be, least of all her. She was so out of place and nothing that had been turned wrong could ever be made right again. Not even if she wheeled her horse this moment and rode back to the Imhar River and crossed it back into Harivir.

Kehera tried to forget where she should be and what future she should be facing and think about this moment and this day and this future now stretching out before her, whatever it might hold. It was hard, though. She would have liked to question General Corvallis about his king, about what Hallieth Suriytaiän was like, what he might intend. But she understood that he would not be able to answer such questions, so she didn't ask. But sometimes, as the day wore on, the general commented on some bird that flew up from the fields or some flower blooming by the roadside, and eventually Kehera concluded, with some surprise, that he was trying to be kind. He had brought Kehera up to ride beside him at the forefront of the company, and he always addressed her carefully as "Your Highness." He did not, she concluded, much like orders that involved forcibly taking girls from their homes and compelling them to marry mad kings. He might be an ally, if not a friend. She made careful note of that.

To the north of Talisè the land changed from the rolling hills to flat plains. Off to the northwest, the land stretched unbroken as far as Kehera could see, except for scattered farmhouses and fences. It gave her an odd, exposed feeling, as though the sky had grown too large. Grain swayed in the fields, golden with the turning of the year. She tried to remember whether there had been drought here as in Harivir, but doubted that Hallieth Theraön Suriytaiän would have spent his own strength and the days of his life to protect his lands from want and suspected Emmer had simply been more fortunate with rain.

She saw none of the sheep that would have been scattered along the hills at home, only occasional herds of short-horned cattle. Sometimes they passed farmers in the fields, or other groups of travelers on the road. All these people gave wide berth to the Emmeran soldiers.

Twice as the afternoon drew on, the general asked her if she would like to rest. Each time, Kehera refused. With every step her mare took north, she wanted more desperately to turn and flee south. Every moment that passed was another in which she had to resist that stupid, useless desire. She treasured the numbness that weariness brought.

At sunset on that first day, she waited wordlessly for her tent to be set up and water brought for a bath. She let Eilisè help her bathe, requested that she be served the evening meal privately, and retired as soon as she decently could. But she could not sleep. Not right away.

The quiet camp sounds did not disturb her, but somewhere close at hand someone was singing.

> *"In Tinìen, the winter roses come up pale through the snow,*
> *hope of spring in the months of deep cold,*
> *and the black winds blow less sharply for their blooming.*
> *But this year, no pale flowers open in my heart.*
> *This year, no girl comes out to meet me,*
> *with flowers in her hands, walking with a light step.*
> *The silence of midwinter has crept into my heart,*
> *and I pass by the gentle fields of Tinìen."*

The singer was a man with a clear tenor and the accent of the north, but the song was from Harivir. Kehera half wanted to go out and ask the man to stop, but it seemed right that her first night outside Harivir should be marked with a lament, and a lament from the home that she had ridden away from and might, if her father's plans went wrong, never see again. The song's plaintive words mingled with her own exhaustion and fear, and Kehera rolled over, hugged her pillow hard, and cried herself to sleep.

She was rewarded for this escape by a too-early waking. She lay on her pallet for some time, hoping that she would either go back to sleep or that the rest of the camp would begin to stir. Neither happened. Finally, unable to lie still any longer, she sat up. Eilisè did not wake. Kehera dressed herself. Traveling dresses at least had the advantage of simplicity. She pinned her braided hair up in a simple coil and slipped out of her tent quietly.

The camp was quite still. Stars glittered in the cloudless sky. The air was cool and still, but without the briskness that, at home, suggested the coming winter. Probably it was her imagination that suggested she could already taste the northern desert in the air.

The constant wind that blew during the daylight hours had stilled sometime during the night. Kehera walked a few steps away from her tent and stood still, looking up into the sky. Silence and stillness and the shimmer of distant stars: the hour before dawn was an hour for oath taking, for the Gods would hear any promise made under the silent stars.

The Gods were mysterious and nameless, uncountable and unknowable. Folk prayed to the Fortunate Gods and hoped for their favor, but in ordinary days, no one expected them to take much notice of one person or another. But these did not seem like ordinary days to Kehera.

At least the Fortunate Gods wanted the world from which they had risen to prosper. They wanted the land to produce Immanent Powers that would someday rise to join them. The Unfortunate Gods wanted to shatter every land and force the apotheosis of every Immanent into their own company. Or something like that.

Tiro had explained all that to her, but it had been ages ago and Kehera hadn't entirely understood it, or cared. People prayed to the Fortunate Gods, and part of what they prayed for was protection against the Unfortunate. But usually Immanent Powers were more important. Immanences protected their lands against the influence of any Gods that might do them harm. Fortunate Gods quickened the warming earth in the spring and the seed in the fields and the baby in the womb; Unfortunate Gods brought the killing winds and the winter dragons. That was all an ordinary person needed to know; it was certainly all Kehera needed to know.

Even so, she made a silent oath, to the Fortunate Gods and to Raëhemaiëth and to her people: that she would do what she had to do to protect Harivir, and that if she came back to her home, she would strive to accept whatever small and minor tie she might yet hold to Raëh. That she would try to find a way to be useful to Raëh and Harivir and her father, and that she would do her best to make sure that she gave nothing of bitterness or resentment to Raëhemaiëth, so that in its time, far in the future, when it rose, it would become a Fortunate God.

In the predawn stillness, the unvoiced oath had the feel of truth. A light wind from the west ruffled the grass stems and picked up dust from the road to swirl into tiny whirlwinds. A vast sweep of cloud stretched across the line of the road and off to the east, dark slate against the pearl of the sky. It was going to be a beautiful morning, and almost against her will, Kehera felt her spirits lift.

Suriytè was an amazing city, Kehera was forced to admit. It spread out in the wide and level lands of north-central Emmer, even reaching some way into the northern desert. Its walls rose against the sky as they approached, rooftops showing beyond, ornate as though the whole city was filled with palaces: rose-pink and white and gold. The city of Suriytè commanded the plains as though it had been set down deliberately in this flat country by the Fortunate Gods and shaped into glory for the awe of travelers.

But the tales of Suriytè were not all about its beauty. Everyone knew that Suriytè had survived the northern cataclysm when the apotheosis of a Great Power engulfed hundreds of square miles in calamity and made all that country into the great northern desert. By this time, the dust of the road included a lot of red sand, and the breeze had grown warm and dry. The air tasted of dust and copper, a northern wind carrying the breath of the desert to the travelers.

There was a great deal of traffic on the road this close to Suriytè, no matter how unsettled the times. Fruit and linen and lumber from Kosir came in from the east, while goods from Pohorir traveled a longer road, first through Anha Pass and then by barge down the Diöllay River to the great Imhar before being carried north by ox-drawn wagons. Those goods mingled with the fish and salt that came from Caftan and Daè and Ghiariy on the western coast of Emmer.

But above and beyond the trade caravans were military encampments and columns of soldiers. Kehera had counted these through the days of travel, her heart chilling with every one she numbered. It was uncomfortably clear that Emmer was indeed well prepared for conquest, and there were few signs that military preparations had lightened with her forced betrothal.

The escort had formed up in a compact column, with men riding ahead to clear the way. Folk stared as she went past. Some probably recognized General Corvallis and by that perhaps knew who Kehera had to be; the pressure of their curiosity pressed on her like the dusty wind. She set her face straight forward and tried to look regal. The towers of Suriytè rose before them, spreading out until they seemed to stretch along the entire horizon. Unlike Raëh, there was not the long sprawl of low walls and estates and little villages outside the walls. Only the city, rose-pink and white, glowing beneath the endless sky.

Kehera's traveling dress was dark-brown linen with a little green embroidery. Kehera had thought it suitable. Now, as the city rose, she felt small and plain. She was glad she'd had Eilisè put her hair in a figure-eight braid, threaded with green and silver ribbons and a single strand of lustrous gray pearls. The style made her look older, she hoped, and the pearls, at least, should make her look like someone to respect.

And then they were there, at the gates.

The gate guards had clearly been alerted to their approach. They stood to either side, stiff and formal. Traffic had been cleared off the road and the gates stood open, a vivid blaze of sunlight in the shadows cast by the walls. A delegation of some sort waited by the gates.

"The king . . . ?" she asked Corvallis, leaning forward in her saddle and searching that company with an anxious glance. She half hoped the Mad King would be there so she could get the initial meeting over with, and half hoped he was not there, that he was even out of the city, finding another small Immanent to feed to the Suriytè Power.

"He will be in the King's Hall," General Corvallis told her. "These are courtiers and officials. That man in the fore of the gathering, do you see? That is Lord Geiranè. He will welcome you on behalf of the king." The general hesitated, as though he might add some other comment to this, but then did not.

Kehera nodded and did not ask any more questions. When they

came to the gates, she inclined her head a tiny fraction to Lord Geiranè and then straightened her shoulders and tried to look regal and unimpressed, maybe even a little bored. Her brother, Tiro, could have managed it; playing roles was one of the many things he was better at than she was. Kehera was afraid she mostly just looked stiff and nervous.

Lord Geiranè was a narrow-faced man with a flat mouth and opaque eyes. Kehera instantly disliked him. She disliked his voice as well: It was too polite, a voice that hid everything he felt. And she was, now that she sat on her mare beneath the very shadow of the walls, uneasy for a different reason. Something about Suriytè felt . . . wrong, somehow.

The breeze still smelled of the desert, but it seemed that a chill ran through the city, almost as though the desert air carried within it a hint of ice. . . . That was ridiculous, and Kehera didn't even know exactly what she meant. But she didn't like it. When Lord Geiranè murmured flowery phrases, she barely heard him. When he fell silent, she blinked and drew a breath and said, grateful she had thought this out beforehand, "I thank you for your gracious welcome, my lord. I shall think of my coming, not as the loss of my home, but as the gaining of another home, of incomparable beauty and splendor. I must add my voice to those which, through the centuries, have proclaimed with delight the peerless elegance and glory of Suriytè." *There, criticize that,* she thought, satisfied despite her distraction and nervousness. Whatever Lord Geiranè thought of her, he could hardly fault that little speech.

Lord Geiranè looked slightly surprised. Had he thought she would be too frightened to speak? "Your Highness will be the greatest ornament possible," he returned politely. "Suriytè is the most fortunate of cities to boast of your presence."

Kehera inclined her head politely and nudged her gray mare forward, and the company formed up behind them as they rode through the gates and into the Queen of Cities. And Suriytè deserved the title, reluctant though Kehera was to admit it. She had never imagined a city as . . . as *polished* as Suriytè. Perhaps the blowing sand scoured walls and cobbles clean, but even so there was a surprising lack of sewage in the channels that lined the roads and no trash at the edges of the streets. Men rode astride or walked, and women rode in carriages or in veiled litters, but the veils were usually pulled back so that those who occupied them could see the streets. All the people they passed were well dressed, in red and brown and tawny gold and rich blue, and she saw no poor folk or beggars—though probably such unfortunates dwelt in a lesser area of the city.

The streets were wide, too: wide enough for four carriages to travel abreast, fronted by buildings of dressed stone—white or pink or pale gold—and everywhere she looked, she saw ornate columns and porticos. And then the streets opened up to a wider view and she saw the King's Hall, and knew that nothing else in Suriytè could possibly compare to that grace and strength.

The King's Hall was all smooth pink stone; not sandstone, but something smoother, something that took a finer polish. The windows were high and arched, screened against the sun with latticework shutters; the doors were made of wrought iron. Between the Hall and the city stood a high fence of wrought iron, its elaborate gates guarded by men in Emmeran colors, men with cold eyes and tight mouths, who looked at her as though they knew who she was and didn't approve of her at all. Kehera felt her heart sink as she studied that fence and the guardsmen and the forbiddingly ornate hall. It looked to her like the kind of palace that was probably easier to enter with a proper escort than slip away from on one's own.

General Corvallis did not enter the King's Hall with her, though he met her eyes as if he meant to convey an important message. But all he said was, "It has been my honor to escort you, Your Highness. I know you will do well and bravely in everything." He saluted her gravely, turned aside, and rode away with his men along the curve of the wall. Kehera stared after him, wondering if she were foolish to think there might be some hidden message for her in those words, not feeling brave at all.

The rooms to which Lord Geiranè at last escorted her, following a long, involved route through the King's Hall, were very elegant indeed. The rugs and couches and walls of the sitting room were peach and pink and powder blue, with ruffled lace everywhere; the bedchamber had been done in rose and gray. The bed itself was more than twice as broad as the one she had slept in at home, and the wardrobe larger as well. A massive bathtub, pewter and enamel, stood behind a screen against one wall; a beautifully carved rosewood table followed the angles of another wall. Several vases of flowers had been placed on the table. Kehera's chests had been brought here already and sat on the hardwood floor by that long table, waiting attention. Once Lord Geiranè had taken his leave, she looked around at the elegant room and wished desperately for her simpler apartment at home in Raëh. It had been a terrible mistake to come here. . . . Of course her father must have been right to send her, but she couldn't *feel* that he had been right. She wished she dared flee at once; that she had an open road before her that led straight back south.

There were several windows through which slanted the sunlight of the late-autumn afternoon, rather stronger and warmer than it would have been at home. All the windows were high and narrow. Standing on tiptoe, she managed to peer out one of the long slits. It gave a view of a nice little courtyard; across the way were more of the narrow windows, and a glimpse of color and movement within.

Eilisè slipped past her, went to the largest chest, and began unfastening the buckles. "I'll unpack," she said. "Why don't you rest a little? I'll send for water; I'm sure you'll want to bathe. What gown do you suppose is suitable for meeting a mad king who's going to make you marry him? Do you suppose he will formally present you to his court? Though perhaps even a mad king wouldn't do that tonight, before you have a chance to rest properly."

Kehera wished she could guess what Hallieth Suriytaiän might do. She went over to the bed and tested it with one hand. "Too soft," she judged. "And I'm filthy with road dust, anyway. I do want another bath.

I suppose you might lay out my best gown, though you'd think Lord Geiranè would have said something, if the king were going to present me tonight."

Eilisè glanced up from the gown she was shaking out. "If no servants show up soon, I'll go find someone to carry water." She opened the wardrobe and put the gown away. "There're quite a few gowns in here already, Kehy. That's a good sign, isn't it? We'll have to see how they fit after you have your bath." She shut the wardrobe door again. "Beautiful material, at least. They'd be worth the trouble of altering."

Kehera was unable to work up interest in this prospect. She sat down on one of the couches and leaned back, shutting her eyes. Briefly, she allowed herself to entertain the fantasy that when she opened them, she would be back at home in her own rooms, but the feel of the couch and the smells in the air were too different.

"Oh," Eilisè said suddenly, in an odd tone. She held up a small, flat box, carved of blackwood, perhaps a handspan wide and just a little more than that long, with scrolling inlaid across the lid in abalone shell in the shape of the Harivir Falcon. Kehera knew exactly what was in it: thirteen four-sided rods, each with its own name and symbol, and four dice of agate and jasper. The tiahel set Tiro had made her. Her brother must have slipped it, at the last, into her luggage: a final, private gift.

Kehera took the box. She unlatched the lid and slowly lifted out the first rod of the set. This was the King Rod, engraved with the suits— Emmer's White Stallion, Harivir's Red Falcon, Kosir's Azure Griffin, and finally Pohorir's rather horrible double-headed Winter Dragon—it said a lot about a kingdom, in Kehera's opinion, that it chose the winter dragon as its sign and symbol.

The King Rod ruled the hand—or lost it, if too many other rods came up in opposition. Kehera turned it gently to the Falcon, then gathered up all the rods and cast them across the bed.

The King Rod came up with the Dragon on top, one narrow head arching forward on its snakelike neck, the other turned to glare back over its shoulder. Tiro had painted in tiny red dots for its eyes, giving the Dragon what had always seemed to Kehera a particularly savage expression.

Winter dragons weren't actually so terrible, at least not for Raëh. People who lived in the south, in Viär and Coär and such towns tucked in against the roots of the mountains, had more reason to fear the midwinter storms that carried dragons north from the Wall of Endless Storms.

The Wall of Endless Storms, the Wall of Winds, the Hurricane Wall... It had many names, that vast cyclone of black, churning winds that the Fortunate Gods had long ago created between the northern lands of the Four Kingdoms and the disastrously ruined south. Kehera knew everyone should be grateful for the Wall of Storms, but during the Iron Hinge days, the uncounted days during which the year pivoted around the long midwinter night, winter storms spun away from the Wall and came down upon the lands of men. Dragons rode those storms, ice falling like knives from the shadow of their wings; the obsidian winds streaked the sky with dark translucence. The dragons that rode those winds cried with the voices of the doomed southland, the voices of men and women and Immanences and all the creatures that had been destroyed in that cataclysm.

Or so tales claimed; Kehera had never glimpsed a winter dragon nor heard one cry. But she had always thought it said a lot about Pohorir that one of that country's distant kings had chosen a double-headed winter dragon to represent his country on the King Rod.

Some people thought a tiahel cast divined the future; they thought the Fortunate Gods nudged the rods to fall in an order one might read. But certainly Kehera could not imagine what the Dragon of Pohorir might have to do with anything. She glanced over the pattern the rest of the rods had made, but saw nothing she could interpret. She told herself she hadn't expected to. She didn't believe in divination, anyway. But the tiahel set was like a breath of familiar air in this strange desert-scented place.

She said in a small voice, "Eilisè? Do you really think there's a chance we'll see home again?"

Her friend put the gown she'd been holding back in the wardrobe and came quickly to take Kehera's hands. "Kehy. Of course. A chance always comes, if one holds to hope. The trick is to recognize it when the Fortunate Gods put it in your way and catch it before it's gone. But we'll be watching, and we'll catch it, and we'll get out of this and fly straight home to Raëh and everything will be fine. You'll have bought your father the time he needs, and he'll do something clever and crush the Mad King, and everything will go back to how it's supposed to be."

Kehera nodded and said, "Yes, of course," and tried to believe her.

No one came for her that night, nor the next day, nor the day after that. Kehera could not imagine why Hallieth Suriytaiän was waiting, but he did not send for her. For three full days after her arrival in Suriytè, Kehera saw no one but Eilisè and a scattering of servants who would not speak to her, nor even to her companion. The Mad King sent her neither messages nor commands nor courting poems. Of course he had no need to court her, but still, his utter silence frightened her. In this unfamiliar palace in the heart of this foreign land, she would have found such a gesture reassuring, even without blue roses carved of lapis.

Servants brought water for washing, simple meals that were always cold by the time they were carried from the kitchens, and, when asked, sewing materials. Kehera and Eilisè spent their hours altering some of the gowns that had been provided, and without quite commenting to each other about the matter, stitching some of Kehera's pearls into the hems of a selection of the plainest dresses. Just in case.

Kehera wished her father's agent, Quòn, would make himself known. That would have made her feel safer even than the hidden pearls. She thought perhaps he might disguise himself as a servant and slip into the King's Hall that way. She couldn't think of any other way for a stranger to approach her. She looked closely at the male servants who came, but no matter how Quòn might have disguised himself, all the servants seemed too old and too stupid, and none of them whispered her father's name to her. Kehera told herself she must be patient. She did not feel patient at all. She felt anxious and helpless and very much alone, and she was glad Eilisè was with her even though she was sorry she had let the other girl come into this strange and frightening place.

On the morning of the twenty-eighth day of Fire Maple Month, the king sent for her at last. By that time, Kehera welcomed the summons, only so she would find out something of his intentions. He would tell her the date they would be wed, or perhaps inform her they were wed now even though there had been no ceremony. Perhaps she was only frightening herself, but three days of silence had given her a lot of time to frighten herself.

At least now Hallieth Suriytaiän must surely give her some idea of what her life was to become here in his Hall. She did not know; she could not guess. It was better to find out, and so she was glad of the summons and willingly followed the man-at-arms.

The man guided her by convoluted ways, along ornate corridors, past doors of carved, polished wood, and up long, curving stairways. All the corridors were deserted and all the doors closed, though sometimes Kehera thought she heard voices within the hidden rooms. Then, when she was already lost, the man led her up more stairways and along more corridors, which grew plainer as they ascended, and finally up a long spiral stairway illuminated only by the daylight let in by the narrow windows that pierced its thick walls. Even the undressed stone of this stairway was handsome: pink and cream and gold. But Kehera felt her stomach knot with dread at the silence and loneliness. She wanted to ask the man where he was taking her, whether the king in fact waited for her somewhere ahead, but she was afraid he would not respond, and more afraid that he would and that she would not want to hear his answer.

But Hallieth Theraön Suriytaiän was there at last, in the small round chamber to which the man finally led her.

Kehera knew the Mad King was in his sixties, but he did not look so old; clearly he had not spent himself over the years to support his Immanent Power, but had chosen instead to take strength and vigor from his land and his people. His hair was white, his lips thin and pale, but otherwise he looked like a man in his midforties. The deep lines engraved at the corners of his mouth spoke not of age, but of anger and malice. She tried not to stare at him, but he stared at her. He did not look at her as a man looks at a woman. His look was odd, almost of triumph, but not of honest triumph for a political victory gained, which Kehera could have understood. It was more the satisfaction of one who has gotten away with something wicked. She could not bring herself to meet his eyes, but looked around at the room instead.

The chamber stood above the world, at the top of a slender tower. The walls were pierced all around by those slitted windows, and where there were no windows, there were long, narrow mirrors, so that all the light that came into the chamber was cast back and forth in a confusing dazzle. The air smelled close and dusty, except once again there was that strange bite of ice behind the heat and dust. She thought the cold was coming from the Emmeran king, though that made no sense.

He said to the man, "Good. Bring her here."

The man gave Kehera a little shove forward, like she was too stupid to understand, like she was only an object to be pushed where real people wanted her to go. An object that had climbed all those stairs with her own feet and strength. Maybe she should have struggled and made the man carry her. But it was too late now. She thought she ought to say something, protest or ask a question or even plead, but she had no idea what to say or what she might plead for, and her mouth was so dry from the long climb and from fear that she could not speak anyway.

Hallieth Suriytaiän reached out with one bony hand and took Kehera by the throat. When she would have backed away, his man shoved her forward and held her. The king's fingers were cold. He stared into her face. His eyes were a strange color between brown and green, flecked with gold. His white hair was tangled; his breath was stale. He said, "Raëhemaiëth." Then he stopped and frowned, the lines of his face deepening. "Where is Raëhemaiëth? Where is your tie, girl?"

"*It is not here. It has not come. It does not dwell in her,*" hissed a long, cold voice that was not the voice of the Emmeran king, that was not the voice of any human man and never could have been, that was not a real voice at all. But though it was not a real voice and made no real sound in the world, Kehera heard it clearly, more clearly than she had ever heard the voice of her own Power even when she had held the deep tie. She heard it in the place within her heart where she had once heard Raëhemaiëth. It spoke almost in words, almost as a man might speak, but it was *horrible.* Immanents did not think or speak as people did; it was all wrong that she should hear this one so clearly. This terrible thing must be the Suriytè Power, and no wonder, no *wonder* the king who held its deep tie was mad: It had taken enough of his mind and his soul that it spoke now in his voice. Although it was strangely unlike *his* voice. But that couldn't be right; of course his Immanent must speak with his voice if it spoke at all; she must be mistaken.

The bitter, biting voice whispered into her heart, "*No, I see. The Immanent remains in her, but it has hidden. Its tie is buried so deep and is so slender that I cannot use it to draw Raëhemaiëth. Not from so far. Fool! You allowed this girl to break her deep tie before bringing her to me.*"

With a gasp of rage, Hallieth Suriytaiän let Kehera go and hit her across the face, hard, so that she stumbled and fell. She let herself fall; anything to get away from him. Forgetting pride in her terror, she scrambled away on her hands and knees, but the servant caught her. He held her by one wrist and by her hair, and though she tried to wrench herself free, she couldn't break his grip. The king paced away, turned sharply, and came back to glare at her.

"*How am I to take Raëhemaiëth now?*" whispered the voice, thin and bodiless. "*I must have Raëhemaiëth.*" There was a slight pause. Then it said, "*You must send her to me. My agent will take her and bring her and deliver her to me. Once she is within my precincts, I will draw Raëhemaiëth no matter how thin its tie to the girl.*"

Kehera didn't understand this. Here she was, in the heart of Suriytè, so she certainly was within the precincts of the Great Power of Suriytè. Probably she was too stupid with fear to understand—or maybe she mistook what the terrible Power whispered; it wasn't *actually* speaking in words, not words the way men would speak them. Yet she could understand it, or thought she could, through her tenuous link to Raëhemaiëth. The Immanent she seemed to hear must be very deeply tied to Hallieth Theraön; generally the awareness and concerns of Immanences were too removed from mortal awareness and concerns for any such understanding. That was why a human lord or duke or king or queen could draw so freely on an Immanence's strength—at least if they remained open to its drawing on their own. Their levels of awareness and interest were too different for either to interfere with the other.

Yet *this* Immanent Power could be understood almost as clearly as a man. It seemed to Kehera that Tiro might have explained something about that once, but she couldn't remember, and she was too frightened now to remember. She tried to listen and flinch away from listening, both at the same time, and found herself frozen and shivering with confusion and terror.

"I will send her to you," agreed the king.

"*Yes,*" hissed the voice, even more clearly than before. "*But the way is long and the days run past. I must have sustenance. What will you give to me, little king, if I cannot yet take Raëhemaiëth for my own?*"

"We don't need it. I will take every city in Harivir and make each one a gift and sacrifice to you—"

"*I must have sustenance now,*" hissed the voice. "*What will you give to me?*" The Immanence that was speaking was deathly cold, Kehera realized. It was the source of all the cold in the chamber, all the cold in the Emmeran king. Frost spread across the red tiles, delicate and implacable.

"No!" cried the Mad King. He flung up his hands and stepped back, and back again. But Kehera felt it at almost the same time the king must have: a sudden savage struggle beyond the merely physical, and then a great hollow echoing emptiness. But the emptiness was impossible, because the cold voice of the Power was still there, hissing with malice and satisfaction. Kehera pressed her hands to her mouth, cowering as Hallieth Suriytaiän cried out, a thin, desperate sound, and clutched at his face, staggering. He tottered in a circle and tore at his own face, and she knew, she *knew* that Suriytè was empty, hollow, devastated as Cemerè had been devastated, yet at the same time, despite the hollow booming emptiness that flooded the city around them, the terrible Suriytè Power was *still there*. It was impossible. She didn't understand, but it was screaming, too; she couldn't hear it with her ears, but she could hear it with her mind, and it was screaming and screaming—or maybe laughing, but its laughter was like screaming.

Kehera tore herself free from the slack grip of the servant and fled. She slammed the tower door behind her and wished there were a bar, but there wasn't, so she fled down and down the spiral stair, clutching at the rough stones of the wall to keep from falling and slamming every door through which she passed. There was no way to bar any of those doors, but if anyone followed, she didn't hear them. Even so, she feared she might still hear the Suriytè Power in her heart, and wasn't sure she would be able to hear any ordinary human voice over that terrible soundless voice.

She found her own rooms by simply running down and down and then asking the first servant she met. She didn't know what the girl made of her. She knew she must look wild and terrified, but the girl at least pointed the way, which was all Kehera cared about. So she found the right door at last and flung it open and darted in, already calling for Eilisè. She barely recognized her own voice, thin with fear and shock.

"Kehy! What did he *do*?" Eilisè cried, leaping up and coming to catch Kehera by the arms, and at least she sounded normal, if frightened.

The door slammed open again before Kehera could get out more than the briefest stumbling explanation. Both girls whirled around, but it was General Corvallis, his lieutenant, Alen, at his back. The general looked grimly furious, but what he said was, "Here you are, thank the Fortunate Gods! Done it at last, hasn't he, lost control of the dark Power he's been playing with and put the knife in his own heart—you, you brought him a mouthful he couldn't chew, didn't you, girl? I mean, Your Highness. At last! Thank the Fortunate Gods, it's over at last!"

The general sounded both glad and deeply horrified at one and the same time, as though he'd hoped for exactly this, but dreaded it in equal measure. Kehera had hardly any idea what he meant, and no idea at all how to answer him. Everything in that tower room had been horrible, but she was sure *nothing* was over. "Do you know—do you understand what—?" She did not know how even to ask.

But General Corvallis said with grim satisfaction, "He's let that foreign Immanent he's been toying with consume his own Power, which is no more than he deserved, making that alliance with Irekaì. Both mad, the pair of 'em, as though the world needed more than one mad king."

"Irekaì?" Kehera said, faltering. She didn't understand at all. Methmeir Irekaì was King of Pohorir. A cruel king for a cruel country, which everyone knew, but even if Methmeir Irekaì were as mad and ambitious as Hallieth Suriytaiän, she didn't understand how the Great Power of Irekay could have allied to the Great Power of Suriytè. Nor did she understand how any sort of alliance could have led to . . . whatever she'd felt in that tower.

General Corvallis said impatiently, "Suriytè has been made hollow; surely you feel that, Harivin as you are? I'm not of Suriytè myself, and I assuredly felt it go! But we may be glad of it; nothing else could have broken the Theraön line. Hallieth Theraön won't last a week now—not an hour, if I have my way! But this is the tricky part, of course; everyone's going to move at once. I believe I've countered Geiranè, but the man's no fool; likely he's moved against me already as well. Assuredly he'll want *you* in his hand, Your Highness."

Kehera shook her head, still too bewildered and frightened to think, but understanding that the cold frost-ridden voice must not have

belonged to the Irekaïn Power, the Great Power that bound all the lesser
Immanences of Pohorir—or through the Irekaïn Power, it might have
been the voice of Methmeir Heriduïn Irekaì himself. *That* made more
sense. That would explain why it had come so clearly and understand-
ably to her, but there was no time to think about it now. She declared,
"We have to get out. Can you get us out?"

"There's no hope of settling matters here while your presence stirs
everything up, so I certainly mean to try," Corvallis answered grimly.
"When you get the chance, Your Highness, you tell your father he's
in my debt and I mean to collect! I'll take Emmer if I can; Fortunate
Gods know, someone must! But you're absolutely right, Your Highness.
We've got to get you back to your father; that's essential." He beckoned
to his lieutenant. "Alen will take care of you—I must go—I'll give you
the best start I can. Be careful, be safe, be brave, go! Alen, see to it!" He
turned on his heel and strode out before Kehera could even thank him.

Lieutenant Alen stepped forward with a quick nod. "We've prepared for this. We have men waiting all along the way, but we must go
immediately. If we can only get to the edge of the city, we can get you all
the way south and safe across the river. The trick will be getting away
from the King's Hall—for this we need stealth and speed, not force of
arms. You and your woman must change at once to something plain, as
plain as you have. I must ask you to be quick."

"That brown for you," Eilisè said quietly, and met Kehera's eyes.
The brown dress was not only one of the least likely to draw attention,
but it had a handful of large pearls stitched into its hem.

Lieutenant Alen stepped out, and Kehera let Eilisè unhook her rose
silk and changed quickly to the plain dress, then made herself sit still
while Eilisè took down her hair and rebraided it quickly, then knotted
it up carelessly at the nape of her neck. "Not much we can do about the
color," Eilisè said, stepping back to view the effect with a critical eye.
"But you look almost not like a princess at all now."

Kehera nodded. "At least fair hair is more common this far north.
Shall I do yours?"

"I can probably do it faster," Eilisè said apologetically. Fingers flying, she rapidly redid the mass of her own light brown hair, putting it up in a knot similar to the one she had done for Kehera.

Kehera tucked a few more jewels in various pockets of her skirts and called to Lieutenant Alen, waiting in the outer rooms, that they were ready.

He came in at once, handing Kehera a small bag and tossing a second to Eilisè. "A few coins, a few jewels, enough to last, I hope! Here, girl, take my dagger. Have you a place to hide it in that dress?"

Eilisè pulled the dagger out of its sheath for a moment, turning the unfamiliar length of it over in her hand with matter-of-fact interest. "I'll find a way. Kehy, we'd better also have those pouches that go under the skirts. I've got one, but let me see if I can find one for you as well." She rummaged in the bottom of one of the chests, pulled out a pouch and tossed it to Kehera. Kehera put a lapis and pearl confection in it, and some more coins that Lieutenant Alen gave her. There was a lot of room left. She glanced around, hesitated, and suddenly picked up the tiahel box. It would just fit, if she forced it. She slipped the bag under her skirts, cinching tight the straps around her thigh, Alen politely turning his back.

And that was all. It had been only moments, and they were ready to escape. Yet it felt like too much time had slipped through her fingers. It felt like it was already too late.

There was only heavy silence in the King's Hall when the lieutenant opened the door. Except Kehera could not help but read that silence as ominous. Suriytè had lost its Immanent Power; it had been hollowed out.

"We've cleared the way, but that won't last, so fast is more important than sneaky," Lieutenant Alen declared. "Though we'll do sneaky soon enough." He led the girls boldly down the hallway and through one of the doors, which proved to lead to another hallway and then a stair. After that, the hallways Alen chose rapidly became narrower and less inviting. Here at last they began to run across people, but only servants. Most of them seemed to have been shocked silent by what had happened, by the death of the Suriytè Power. None of them seemed to care if a hundred Harivin girls hurried past.

Then Alen led them down a narrow flight of stairs and pushed open a plain, unguarded door, and suddenly they were out in the daylight, in what was plainly a tradesman's yard. Surrounding this yard was a high wall, probably separating it from the finer areas of the King's Hall, and across from their door, a gate. The gate was standing open, but it was guarded by five soldiers who stood together, arguing in low voices.

Lieutenant Alen cursed in a low voice. "This gate was to be clear," he explained. "Someone is countermanding the general's orders. Still, I know those men; we'll see if we can just pass through. Please don't speak, either of you."

Kehera nodded. Fear had tightened her stomach into a small, hard knot.

"If it comes to a fight, forget about me and just go. I'll have the surprise, so I should be able to get clear of them, and I'll catch you up. If I don't, you must go to the house of Norrey Behalla, on the Street of Drapers, on the east side of the Open Market. You have that? You'll remember?"

Kehera nodded again. At her side, Eilisè took a deep breath and nodded too. They all walked forward briskly and openly, as though it were the most ordinary thing in the world. Nothing in the world to hide here, Kehera thought, suppressing a devastating impulse to laugh. Just fleeing the King's Hall in the wake of destroying the Suriytè Power, and Gods know what's become of your king or what will become of any of you now. She tried not to believe her guilt for all this was emblazoned on her forehead for everyone to see.

"Sir!" said one of the men as they came up, sounding surprised. He lifted one hand in the beginning of a salute, and then, since Alen was not in uniform, changed the gesture at the last moment to a respectful nod. "Do you know what's been happening, sir? His Majesty—the

Power—what *happened*? What's it *mean*?" He barely seemed to notice Kehera or Eilisè at all, too much caught up in the disaster that had fallen upon his city.

"I don't think anyone knows yet, Voll," answered Alen. "Corvallis has some people he wants to talk to, the sort of people who might be able to answer for all this, but I don't know—if you ask me, we'll never know. Somebody will figure it out, but they won't tell *us*."

"You're right, yeah," the other man said miserably. "Don't ask us what it's worth, tearing up half the Immanents of Pohorir or starting fights with Kosir and Harivir both at once. Don't tell *us* what it costs—"

"We can win it all, take it all back, if we just don't back up when it gets tough!" declared one of the other men.

"When it gets tough? When it gets *tough*?" cried Voll, his voice rising. The other man sneered at him.

"No time to debate," Alen said easily, and waved the girls forward, through the gate and into a much wider outer courtyard. Before them stood the high iron fence, here draped with flowering vines, and beyond that the city itself and relative safety. She didn't know about Eilisè, but she felt horribly conspicuous. She could hardly believe that no one stopped them, but the soldiers were arguing again and not paying attention to anything else.

Then, from the door behind them, a voice shouted. Lieutenant Alen didn't turn, but he quickened his stride.

The *second* shout had words in it that were all too distinguishable. Kehera risked a glance back. Several new guardsmen were running toward the gate. The men stationed there still looked more confused and angry than alarmed. That would last all of thirty seconds, Kehera was sure.

Alen thought so too, and broke into a run, sweeping Kehera and Eilisè before him. Kehera ran with a will, the hidden pouch thumping heavily against her leg.

Even after the alarm had been raised, for a few minutes it looked to Kehera as though she and Eilisè and even Lieutenant Alen, who had fallen back to protect them, might after all gain the outer fence and the maze of streets beyond without having to fight.

"Can you manage a bit of a climb?" Alen asked them.

"Easily," Kehera panted, observing the wrought-iron curlicues of the fence and the tough-looking vines.

"Head left once you're across. That's the way the Open Market lies, and a hundred fugitives could get lost in that."

Kehera skidded on the damp cobbles. Eilisè steadied her, and both young women threw themselves at the fence. Kehera's skirts snagged on a sharp bit, and she used a word that she wasn't supposed to know and ripped it loose. Behind them, Alen had turned to cover their retreat.

"We're going to need you!" Kehera reminded him urgently.

"I know!" the lieutenant called back. "Move!"

She moved. She was more than halfway up the fence already, a good twelve feet, somewhat ahead of Eilisè. It occurred to her suddenly that the other woman was holding back, a second line of defense in case Alen couldn't hold the guardsmen. She used another unsuitable word and climbed faster.

The first guardsman arrived, well ahead of the others. "Hold it right—*Raft*?" he said. "Raft Alen? What are you—?"

"King's business," Alen lied instantly. "Can you hold this line of retreat for me, Pennon?"

"I—" said the guard, hesitating.

"Come on, man!" Alen snapped urgently. "You know me!"

"Yes, but—"

It was hard to know what Pennon might have decided, because at that moment two of the other guardsmen arrived. Kehera, looking over her shoulder in dread, saw how they threw themselves forward without hesitation, and how when Alen ducked aside and killed the first man, Pennon quite reflexively took out the second with a fast sideways cut across the stomach. The man went down, in shock so deep he could not even try to gather up his own spilled intestines. Alen didn't wait to look; he jammed his bloody sword into its scabbard, whirled and took the fence at speed, with a reckless disregard for his own safety that carried him halfway up in an instant.

Kehera dragged herself up the last bit of the fence and crouched on top. She lingered just long enough to watch Pennon, lifting his sword against the mass of arriving guardsmen, be cut down and fall.

Lieutenant Alen gained the top only a second after Eilisè. He threw an arm around each woman's waist and simply jumped, which wasn't quite suicidal because the street level on this side of the fence was rather higher than on the inner side. It was not a particularly enjoyable exercise, even so, and Kehera picked up a brand-new set of bruises on her knees. Alen dragged her up with a ruthless yank and half shoved her forward, heading left into a tangle of narrow streets.

Behind them, they could all hear the shouts of their pursuers. The leaders were too close for comfort, and gaining. Alen had his bloody sword out again, running with it in his hand. At least the sight did clear the street in front of them handily.

The steps of their pursuers seemed so close behind them that Kehera found herself bracing against the expectation of a sudden grab. Lieutenant Alen turned so suddenly she did not at once miss him, and took out the first pursuing guardsman with a vicious slash across the chest. It slowed the other five. Eilisè fumbled out the knife Alen had given her and threw it. It hit one of the men in the chest hilt first and bounced off, but it made him hesitate just a second, and Alen, taking advantage of his distraction, killed him, too. He ran forward and struck a third through the chest in almost the same movement.

Three left. One of those put up a pacifying hand. "Look, Raft," he began, "I don't know what this is all about, but—"

"Sorry, Voll," Alen said, and over his shoulder added, "Fortunate Gods look on, girl, run!"

Eilisè grabbed Kehera's hand and hauled her down the street. Kehera yielded and they ran together. Not having Alen to clear the way made it harder, but at least none of the surprised people they passed tried to stop them.

Then a guardsman stepped out in front of them, and then another, and now they didn't even have a knife. Both Kehera and Eilisè backed up as the men advanced with drawn swords.

"Aren't you supposed to take us alive?" Kehera asked, bumping into a stand stacked high with hot meat pies and piles of fritters. The owner of the stand had sensibly disappeared.

"Who cares?" said one of the men. "Harivin bitch, look what you've done to Suriytè." He stalked forward.

Kehera backed up, wishing she could protest that she hadn't done anything, knowing it didn't matter. Of course everyone would blame her—they weren't even wrong, exactly.

Eilisè caught up the deep pot of oil used for frying the fritters and, stepping forward, flung the boiling contents in the man's face. He screamed, one hand going to his face. With the other he slashed wildly. By pure chance the blow connected with Eilisè as the young woman tried to scramble back. For a long, stretched moment Kehera thought he had missed. Then, turning, Eilisè fixed a wide, surprised stare on her and crumpled; not all at once, but slowly, clutching at the fritter stand with hands suddenly too weak to support her weight.

Kehera leaped forward to catch her, too shocked to cry out. She cradled the other woman's head in her lap. "Eilisè?" she said shakily. "Eilisè?" Her companion's eyes were open, but quite blank.

The burned man was blundering around, blind. Kehera had completely forgotten about his partner, until the man, outraged at the injury dealt his companion, lifted his sword and started forward. And then she couldn't even move.

Lieutenant Alen ran him through from behind, planted a foot on the body, and wrenched his sword free, all in the same fast movement. Dropping to one knee, he made a quick, cursory examination and straightened to meet Kehera's eyes. "She's dead. Unless you want to join her, you've got to get up."

"Yes," Kehera said, not moving.

The lieutenant grabbed her wrist with bruising force and hauled her to her feet. "She won't thank you for sitting still like an idiot and letting yourself be killed or captured, and the general won't thank me for letting it happen! I can't carry you and fight at the same time. Be in shock *later*."

He was right. Kehera pulled free of his grip, rubbed her hands hard across her face, and made herself say, "What now?" Her voice was unsteady, but firm.

Alen looked profoundly relieved. He led her away from the bodies at a fast walk, down one street after another, rapidly tracing a path through the narrow, confusing alleys. He seemed to know exactly where he was going, which was just as well, as Kehera not only did not know but could not bring herself to care.

"Try to look normal," said Alen.

Kehera blinked at him.

"Can you?"

She took a deep breath and shook her head, not in denial, but trying to wake up. She felt . . . very strange. "Yes," she promised numbly.

"Good." Alen took her hand and guided her quickly between two buildings, down a short alley, and into a tavern. Kehera had never entered a public tavern in her life. The low crowded benches, the heavy smells of smoke and grease and ale, and the low roar of talk were all rather overwhelming. She tried hard to look *normal* and allowed Alen to lead them quickly through the crowded room. For some inexplicable reason, no one seemed to take special notice of them. She had never felt so conspicuous in her life, but maybe everyone was too wrapped up in the loss of their Power to notice anything as trivial as a man dragging a woman through their tavern.

The lieutenant seemed to know his way through this tavern very well, and led them straight to the kitchens at the back. The heat was like a blow in the face after the brisk outdoor air, and the smell of grease and cheap ale nauseatingly strong.

"Hey, Raft," said a fat man, heaving himself to his feet from his place at a broad table. "Got trouble?"

Alen rolled his eyes expressively. "He turned out to be the jealous type," he said, his tone indescribable. "*And* clever enough to use what's happened as cover for murder. He's got more buddies with him than I think I want to deal with. May I use your back door?"

"O' course," rumbled the fat man. "Come on through here, then. Mind the steps, girl. Steep, they are."

The stairs he had led them to were in fact extremely steep. And dark. Kehera gripped the handrail and descended cautiously. In front of her, Alen was moving ahead with the confidence of familiarity. He stopped at the base of the stairs to collect a torch from a stack against the wall and light it, the snap of his candlelighter sharp against the heavy silence that had enwrapped them. From a hall to the left came muffled voices, accenting the quiet rather than troubling it.

"That's where the real gambling goes on," Alen murmured in her ear. "Fortunes, bodies, and souls won and lost, sold and bartered. I doubt they've even noticed anything's amiss. We'll go this way." He lifted his torch and led her to the right-hand door, which let into a short hall and then another steep stairway.

"What's down here?" Kehera whispered. These stairs were not only steep and dark, but slimy. And a disagreeable smell was starting to make itself far too apparent.

The lieutenant slanted a quick sideways look at her. "You aren't going to like it."

Refusing to give way to rage or tears, she said, "I'll cope. What?"

He steadied her with a hand at her elbow. "The sewers."

"Oh, Lieutenant, Fortunate *Gods!*"

"Yes, I know. But the general's plan has turned belly-up, that's clear, and with any luck this will get us right away. As long as we meet nothing worse than rats, I shan't complain."

"There are . . . other things we might meet, down there?"

"Only the other kind of rat," Alen said grimly. "Thieves and beggars and other low folk; they sometimes come and go through the sewers. But it's worth the risk; too many guardsmen up in the streets, too many of them too close behind us. We've no choice, and this should get us right away. Can you bear it?"

Kehera took a deep breath, and then wished she hadn't as the smell, thick enough now almost to taste, seemed to crawl down her throat. She coughed, then started to say that of course she could *bear* it—that wasn't the question—but what if their pursuers figured out where they'd gone. Wouldn't having gone to earth in the sewers limit their options terribly? They would be like a fox that had gone to ground, only one way to run and enemies waiting at the places they might come up. Could they count on no one knowing where they might come up? Wouldn't it be better to say aboveground, where streets went off in all direction and every door offered potential escape?

But Alen had not actually waited for her answer. He was ahead of her, pushing a door open with his foot with wary caution. Feeling overwhelmed, Kehera followed, trying not to breathe.

The sewer was not quite as bad as she'd imagined. It was actually a broad channel, perhaps eight feet across, with a ledge on either side of it wide enough for easy walking. The water, thick with its unspeakable flotsam, flowed sluggishly a good foot below the level of these ledges. The torch Alen carried cast its light forward and received it back, glinting red, from numerous little pairs of eyes.

Kehera said tautly, "I hate rats." She was appalled to feel the tight prickle of tears behind her eyes. It wasn't the rats, of course. It was Eilisè. Eilisè had hated rats worse than Kehera ever had, and now she wasn't even here to worry about these rats. Because she'd been so brave, because she'd insisted on coming to Emmer. Worse, because Kehera had let her insist, and then let her get killed. Kehera struggled to pull herself together, knowing grief could be more crippling than any physical injury.

Alen gave her a quick weighing look. "You must bear it."

Not being stupid, she realized perfectly well that his brusque tone was meant to straighten her spine, where kindness would—indeed—have let her go to pieces. She was still angry. That was fine. Anger was much better than sick disgust or wrenching grief for walking through sewers. She met his eyes and bit out, "I'm fine."

He nodded just slightly. "Carry this." He handed her his torch. "If I have to fight, get back against a wall and hold off any attacker with that. Don't try to run unless you truly must; it's an absolute maze down here."

"I—I thought you said we'd left the guardsmen behind?" A glance around showed clearly that there were only two ways to go from this place: ahead or back. She more and more feared they should not have come down here.

He nodded. "I'm sure we have. Merely a precaution. This way."

The ledge seemed rather less wide when one actually walked along it. The disgusting water lapped the stone far too close on one hand, and on the other the arching curve of the wall dripped and stank. Both ledge and wall were unpleasantly slimy. A green scum coated the stones, and the wall was dotted here and there with round, pale lumps, like the unhealthy growths of some obscure and particularly disagreeable disease.

The next little time was a nightmare. The ledge, which had been wide enough at first so they might almost have walked side by side, narrowed to half that distance, and then narrowed again. It became increasingly difficult for Kehera to maintain her balance, especially when she was distracted by the fervent desire not to touch the filth of the wall. Worse, in places the ledge actually lowered, or the water level rose, so that the liquid lay over the stones in horrible puddles. Lieutenant Alen lifted her over these wordlessly, his boots far more suited to the necessary wading than her light shoes. Kehera thought she should perhaps not allow the man to put his sword arm out of action this way, but in the end she could not endure the thought of wading in the ordure, and she said nothing.

They turned into a side tunnel, and then turned again. And again. Kehera was hopelessly lost very soon. The touch burned lower. She watched uneasily as the flame crept closer and closer to her hands. She mentioned it finally, and Alen cast a quick look back. He judged the length left on the torch and said reassuringly, "It'll last till we get above. Another half hour, a little more. Are you going to last? We could rest here for a few minutes."

The thought of remaining in these horrible tunnels one second longer than necessary was intolerable. "I'm fine."

Alen nodded without speaking, as if he understood her thought, and turned again to lead the way. Then he stopped, after only one step. Kehera only just barely stopped herself from letting the torch strike him in the back. She bit back an exclamation of angry surprise and stood still, watching his taut stance, trying to decide what had caught his attention.

The scrape of metal across stone, at their backs and not at all like the scuttlings of rats, answered this question unpleasantly. Kehera discovered that the phrase "a chill down the spine" was founded in literal fact. She shuddered helplessly. The shadows from the torch she carried betrayed her shivers with ruthless clarity.

Alen pressed himself against the wall of the tunnel and beckoned urgently for her to pass him. The ledge right at this point was at its narrowest, not at all wide enough to change places comfortably. Kehera gritted her teeth, took the hand so urgently offered her, and let the man swing her dizzily wide over the offal-thick water and back with a thump against the suddenly welcome support of the tunnel wall, slime and all. They walked on, not too fast on the uncertain footing.

"Turnings," Alen murmured in her ear, so close behind her he was all but treading on her heels. "We need to take the next tunnel left, and then skip the next side turn, and then the next left again. It slopes up all that way. Then there are several little side tunnels both ways. Keep to the main passage. Got that?"

Kehera went over it in her mind. Left, skip one, left, don't get distracted by smaller tunnels. "Yes," she whispered over her shoulder.

"You'll find stairs, up and down. You'll want to go up, but go down. Two doors at the bottom. Knock on the one to the left and tell the man you're sent by Jagharis. He'll let you in and ask what the water level is.

Say it's full five and likely to come up. Walk past him and then up the stairs. Got that part?"

"Yes," Kehera hissed back over her shoulder, repeating under her breath, *Full five . . .*

"A door at the top. Don't knock, just go through. You'll be in a wineshop hard by the Open Market. You remember where to go from there?"

She indicated that she did.

"The house is around to the east from the wineshop. About half a mile. Use my name and they'll help you there. Don't mention the general. *Don't* use your own name."

"Are we going to be attacked down here?"

"Probably," Alen murmured. "Yes."

"By whom? Guardsmen, or—"

"Hush." The lieutenant obeyed his own injunction, walking with catfooted care, his boots nearly silent on the slimy stone of the sewer ledge.

Kehera bit her lip and watched the ledge before them carefully, holding the torch low to illuminate their path. Even so, it was Alen who was the first to see the new threat in front of them. His touch on her shoulder stopped her in her tracks, and peering forward, she followed the direction of his stare to the gleam that was metal and not damp stone, the darkness that was black cloth rather than simply lightless air.

"I'll go in front again," he said quietly. "You come close behind—a good span back so I don't need to worry about taking your head off with a backstroke."

She started to acknowledge.

Another voice cut hers off, grim and oddly flat in the echoing tunnel: "And then what will you do when one of my men comes and takes her away from you from behind?" Before them on the walkway, a man watched them steadily. Kehera couldn't tell whether he was a guardsman or one of the thieves Alen had mentioned. For a second she had hoped he might be Quòn, but this was a stranger, and the disappointment of that was crushing.

Alen said swiftly, "I'll put her in the water and take both sides at once. How many of your men are you willing to lose trying to take us, and for how little profit? Back your people off and I've some coin I can spare."

Kehera screwed up her nerves and her stomach for the suggested jump into the filthy sewer water. She promised herself that, whatever happened, she would not throw up.

The unseen man answered heavily, "I am not a patient man. Nor have I a need for patience. Put up your sword, or I will have my bowmen shoot. Up lanterns, there."

Flame bloomed ahead of them, and behind, several lanterns in each direction, each held by a man with a sword. The men who weren't holding swords held small wicked crossbows. Kehera looked at Lieutenant Alen in dismay; she could think of nothing they could do against crossbows. Jumping in the water probably wouldn't help; she doubted it was that deep. The men in front were close, not more than thirty steps ahead; even indifferent bowmen could hardly miss their targets from that distance.

"If you're guardsmen, you're out of uniform," Alen said sharply. "And you're not plain thieves or I'm a granny with wooden teeth. Who are you?"

The leader took one step forward, lifting a lantern. Kehera's skin prickled all over as she stared at him. She didn't understand. He looked . . . like anyone. Big. Heavyset. There was nothing out of the ordinary about him. Except there was something . . . there was something *wrong* about him. Something almost familiar, though she knew she had never seen this man before in her life.

The man shook his head. "The question is, who are you? No one, I think. No one of use to me." He made a slight, impatient twitch of one hand, and two crossbow bolts were suddenly standing in Lieutenant Alen's chest.

Alen staggered. His sword sagged in his grip, its tip gritting across the slimy stones. Kehera tried to catch him, to break his fall, but he was too heavy. He sank down to his knees, his eyes glazing as his blood ran out. Kehera knelt beside him, clinging to his hands. She felt stunned. Too much had happened in the past few days. She felt her comprehension would never catch up. The death of earnest Lieutenant Alen, whom she had only just begun to know, seemed in that moment more unbearable than any other thing that had ever happened to her.

"You are the Raëhema heir," stated the man. It didn't have at all the tone of a question. His heavy voice was flat and unexpressive. "Yes. You have the tie still. It's drawn out thin and buried far underneath. But you have it. I know you."

Kehera shook her head, but not exactly in denial because denial was too plainly hopeless. "Who *are* you?" But she was more and more certain she knew him, too, though she was equally certain she'd never seen him before in her life. She thought she could see a tie in him—or not exactly *see*, but she thought he carried a tie. It felt to her like a thing of cold and frost. It felt to her like the voice had sounded, in the Mad King's tower. She could almost hear its hissing voice in her mind: *"My agent will take her and bring her and deliver her to me. Once she is within my precincts, I will draw Raëhemaiëth . . ."* Kehera wanted to scream. If this was that agent—if this man belonged somehow to the King of Pohorir, to Methmeir Irekaì . . . he must have found her by her tie, somehow. She thought she might have been able to find him by his. She thought she would recognize that cold Immanent anywhere.

The man might have seen something of her horror in her face, but if so, her terror didn't interest him. He answered her indifferently, "My name is Gheroïn Nomoris. And you are the Raëhema heir. You are the daughter of Torrolay Raëhema and the heir direct to Raëhemaiëth. I see your tie. You will not be able to escape me."

Habit straightened her back and lifted her chin. Kehera said, "I think you will someday come to regret what you have done here." She was amazed at the coolness of her own voice, so at odds with the trembling of her stomach.

Gheroïn Nomoris shrugged indifferently, already turning away. "Bring her," he ordered curtly, swept up one of the lanterns, and walked away.

Kehera let the man who held her shove her forward. She knew she couldn't get away. Not now. Not yet. She thought again, with the flat clarity of shock, *A chance always comes*. Very well, then. She would hold to hope, and wait.

And when the Fortunate Gods put the chance in her way, she would catch it with both hands and never let go.

5

Over the next two weeks, the king's little pet proved just as much trouble as Innisth had feared. By the end of Fire Maple Month, Innisth was heartily sick of the sight of him and the sound of his voice. Lord Laören was arrogant with the Eänetén folk and dangerous to the duke's servants. Innisth had been forced to pay more than double the normal rate for the pleasure boys and girls, whose masters had continually to replace damaged goods. And Laören's servants were almost as arrogant and annoying as their lord, a constant strain on his own staff.

Laören wanted a bribe, of course: a bribe to go away, a bribe to persuade Methmeir Irekaì to turn his attention elsewhere. Innisth was perfectly willing to pay it. Let the King of Pohorir play his games with the lickspittle provinces of the east and leave be the western provinces, among which none could measure its strength against Eäneté's.

The only questions were the amount Innisth would have to offer and how the bribe would be paid. Infuriating as it was to yield to such extortion, Innisth could see no way around it. Unless, to be sure, he could supply a *truly masterful* distraction. He had ideas for that, but could not yet see quite how to manage it.

Worst of all, if Innisth could not finesse the current . . . situation, then he might offend Laören to such an extent that the man would refuse any bribe and ignore any distraction, but rather become a true enemy, focused on Innisth's destruction and perhaps the ruin of all Eäneté. Innisth wanted very badly to feed the king's lapdog to the wolves of the mountains. Instead, he must use *finesse.*

Because Gereth had reported most urgently that one of the young women of the household had, despite all precautions, caught Lord Laören's eye and Gereth did not know how to get her away.

Gereth, being the sort of man he was, was very much distressed. The girl was not originally from Eäneté, Innisth gathered, but from Lord Geif's province of Tisain. In recent years, as Innisth's reputation for restraint had spread, not a few folk of Tisain and Kimsè and other nearby provinces had come to Eäneté seeking refuge from their petty lords. This pleased Innisth; both the knowledge that his own people trusted him and the gradual weakening of the neighboring provinces. In time . . . neither this year nor next, but eventually, he had some hope he might make something useful of Eäneté's increasing strength and the comparative weakness of Tisain and Kimsè.

Though not unless he could be rid of the close attention of the king. Which meant, now, the close attention of Lord Laören.

Though this present situation with the girl was exasperating. She had suffered in Tisain and suffered further on the road before at last the Fortunate Gods had cast her up at Gereth's feet. Now the seneschal was frantic for Innisth to protect his foundling. Innisth would have been willing to intervene simply for Gereth's sake. But the girl was, after all, now one of his folk and a member of his household. Innisth's pride could hardly permit him to allow her to be abused by some posturing court lord.

Innisth strode straight up the stairs toward the upper level of the west wing and entered the interconnected suites he had ceded to Irekaï's pet. Laören's servants scattered, squawking, from his path, and Innisth flung open one more door and stepped forward, putting on his most arrogant manner.

"Lord Laören," he said, taking care to sound cool and remote and not at all as though he had just run up two flights of stairs. "I fear there has been an inexcusable error on the part of my staff."

The court lord turned, astonished and angry at this interruption. Two of his servants held between them a fine-boned girl with delicate features, porcelain skin, and rose-brown hair, falling now around her tear-streaked face. Her eyes were huge, like the eyes of an arrow-struck doe. Though she was making tiny whimpering noises, she was not struggling. Evidently her life had taught her not to fight back.

The girl was naked. Several vivid welts crossed her back and buttocks. Laören held the riding crop. Whether he and his servants had yet had their use of the girl was difficult to say; Innisth had never seen reason to question the pleasure girls regarding Laören's habits. He supposed it made little difference; either way, he had clearly failed to protect her.

"What error?" Lord Laören demanded. "The girl's not really spirited enough, but even if she's a trifle limp, she's a pretty little thing. I certainly see no reason for Your Grace to burst in unannounced—"

"Indeed, I am ashamed to disturb you and outraged that the girl—" Innisth recovered her name after an instant of thought; of course, Eöté; yes. Gereth had told him. He had no idea what position she held on his staff. She looked too fragile to work at anything demanding. He said almost without a pause, "That Eöté did not inform you that she is possibly carrying. You will understand, Lord Laören, that one hardly wishes to confuse any issue that may possibly bear upon the succession. I have no recognized heir, you know."

There was a brief, frozen silence. Lord Laören stared at Innisth, who added blandly, "I must certainly commend your taste, my lord. She is indeed a pretty creature."

After another moment, Laören signaled for his servants to release the girl. Sinking down, she huddled on the floor, making faint efforts to gather up the torn rags of her dress. She was not weeping or screaming, for which small favor Innisth was grateful. Laören looked down at her, grimaced in disgusted embarrassment, and offered Innisth a short, reluctant bow. "I intended no trespass," he muttered. "She did not tell me she was carrying your babe."

"We are not quite certain just at present. The girl believes she is, however, and I consider it prudent to hold her aside until the issue becomes clear. I think you quite overpowered her with your attention," Innisth added smoothly. "And then, she is not very intelligent. But biddable, ordinarily." He collected a tumbled blanket from the nearest couch and dropped it over the girl, adding in his coolest tone, "Eöté, go up to my rooms and wait for me."

The girl, fortunately, was not actually stupid. Or perhaps she was in fact biddable. Either way, she nodded shakily, clutched the blanket around her shoulders, and slipped away. No one tried to stop her.

"I do not mean to be inhospitable," said Innisth, making his tone apologetic. "I would be pleased to send you other girls. I rather thought the bath attendants I provided would do. I apologize if they did not please you. You should have spoken sooner."

Lord Laören shrugged. "You have been more than generous, Your Grace," he said, though not with very good humor. "You have made my stay most comfortable and pleasing in all ways." He bowed.

The duke returned the bow as gravely. "I hope I may expect the honor of your company for a late supper, my lord? I shall hope that the girls who serve at table will please you." He would make sure of it, though it might require hiring staff from every pleasure house in the city.

Eöté waited in his rooms, as commanded. Innisth found his body servant with her; good. Caèr Reiöft was both imperturbable and thoroughly competent. Caèr had found the girl a robe and, when Innisth entered, appeared to be making some progress in persuading her to let him tend her hurts. But he set basin and cloth aside when the duke came in, gathering himself neatly to his feet and proffering a slight bow.

The girl had perched nervously on the edge of a wooden chair before the fire, a damp cloth gripped in both hands, but she leaped to her feet when she glimpsed Innisth and stood wringing the cloth and trembling.

"You'll spend the evening here," the duke told her. "Indeed, you will spend the better part of your time here, until my Irekaïn guest departs. You understand what tale I told him?"

The girl opened her mouth, closed it, and shook her head. He could hear her teeth chattering from where he stood, a careful distance away. He said patiently, "You are carrying my child. At least, the possibility exists. In the fullness of time, we will discover whether it is so." He paused. "You are not married? You have no young child?"

Another wordless shake of the head. Innisth was beginning to wonder whether she *could* speak. He said merely, "Good. Best to avoid such complications. Yes. Your ordinary duties may be set aside for the next little while. I believe I can guarantee that neither Laören nor any of his people will venture to disturb you here." He looked her up and down. She *was* pretty. Quite startlingly lovely. She looked very young and exquisitely vulnerable. So fragile. Like a little bird, a lark or timid finch, that, captured, might simply die of terror. The Eänetén Power trembled through him, seduced by her fear.

Caèr Reiöft cleared his throat. Innisth met his eyes and shook his head slightly. He asked the girl, with what gentleness he could muster, "What have your ordinary duties been? If you can speak, answer me."

"I—I sew." Her faltering voice was exactly as he might have imagined: tiny and timid. But she managed to add, "I sew, Your Grace. Embroidery . . . I do embroidery. . . ." Her voice trailed off. Perhaps she was in fact not very intelligent. Or perhaps she was merely frightened. It could be hard to distinguish between the two conditions, in Innisth's experience. He said, carefully moderating his tone, "I will see that appropriate tasks are provided. As this suite is large, you should have no difficulty keeping out of my way."

From her trembling nod, keeping out of his way was the girl's whole ambition. Innisth dismissed her with a gesture, nodded for Caèr to go after her, and waited, his teeth set, for the edge of desire to subside. He wanted to go after her himself, send Caèr away. . . . He did not yield to the impulse by even a single step, but the Eänetén Power was reluctant to settle and he was grateful when Gereth arrived, anxious on the girl's behalf and worried about Lord Laören.

"Your Grace—"

"The girl will do well enough," Innisth told him. "She will stay here. Put it about that she might be bearing, and that if so the child is mine. That should be explanation enough for any inquiry, whether from our own folk or from the Irekaïn lord."

"Ah!" said Gereth. "Yes, that will do. Ah . . ." He gave the duke a different kind of look.

"I have no such intention," Innisth told him, a touch impatiently. "You should know better, Gereth. Indeed, you must say something reassuring to her. Remind her that when the king's pet departs, she will no longer be required to remain near me."

"Yes," murmured Gereth. "Poor little thing. What a pity Laören's eye should fall upon her! She was a highborn lady's maid in Tisain, you know, and I gather the lady used to hand her around to her guests—and now Lord Laören—"

The duke flicked an impatient hand. "Her fragility drew him, no doubt, as blood scent draws wolves. She is safe now. Caèr will make her believe so. However, you must be sure she understands she must say and do nothing that contradicts her supposed position with me."

"Indeed, I will, Your Grace."

"My reliable Gereth. Of course you will. Find me a girl to gift to Lord Laören. Someone willing to play at being new and innocent, and with enough skill to bring it off. The man is a brute, but the girl may be able to advance in his household if she is clever. The chance may appeal to an ambitious whore. It would be best if you found such a girl before supper."

"I'll see to it without fail, Your Grace."

The duke moved toward his study. "I'm going to prepare some

papers, invoices and such, to indicate that I have been skimming illegal profits off the trade from Harivir. Not much. Just enough to assure Laören that I will not jibe at a considerable bribe, not enough to compel official notice. It's a delicate balance. I'll want you to give me your opinion."

"Certainly, Your Grace."

"I believe I will also prepare something to indicate Lord Geif's involvement in something more noticeable than skimming, in order to draw Laören's attention away from Eäneté. I have not quite thought what this might be. Eventually, however, I'll want your opinion on that as well."

"Yes, Your Grace."

The duke took another step toward his study, then paused. The girl was moving around somewhere in the depths of his suite. He could hear her. She had a light, quick step, nothing like Reiöft's. A pretty, feminine step. The sound of it was . . . much like blood scent in the air. He said slowly, "Gereth . . ."

"Your Grace?"

"It is fair outside this morning, is it not?"

"Indeed, Your Grace. A beautiful morning."

"Then I believe I shall go for a ride. It will give me time to think." He caught up a cloak and, leaving his startled seneschal behind, strode out of the room.

On an impulse he did not quite permit himself to question, Innisth summoned the captain with whom he had ridden the bounds so recently. Verè Deconniy, the man who had come so recently, like Eöté, from Lord Geif's domain of Tisain. Innisth considered Geif of Tisain, whose people fled him so frequently. What sort of evidence might best be set to bait Laören toward Tisain? An idea seemed to hover at the edge of his mind, but nothing came clear to him. He waited impatiently while his favorite mare was saddled and another animal tacked up for Deconniy. The officer arrived just as the grooms finished with the horses. He came into the stable yard collectedly enough, but his breathing, deep and even, showed that he had been running.

Innisth swung up onto his tall black mare. "Join me," he ordered, and turning his mare, signaled her at once into a neat canter. Behind him, he heard the clatter of hooves across the cobbles as the captain hastily vaulted into the saddle and hurried to catch him up. Innisth did not look back, tracking the other man's movement by ear, putting his mare to a faster gait as Deconniy came up with him. He took his mare out of his castle's gates and past the guards without slowing.

The captain stayed at his side, his bay gelding pounding alongside the duke's mare. Innisth turned off the causeway immediately outside the gates, jumped his mare over the retaining wall, let her have her head to slither down the shallow hill, and reined her in to a sedate walk at the base of the hill. The mare, beautifully responsive, put her ears hard forward and extended her gait, showing that she would like to run if he would let her. Her breath plumed in the cool air.

Deconniy had stayed by the duke almost perfectly, only reining in a fraction after Innisth had done so. He turned his gelding back, face still, and came in neatly at the duke's shoulder. Innisth might have believed him relaxed, had the gelding not dropped his head and mouthed the bit uncomfortably and so betrayed the rigid hands of his rider.

"Well done," Innisth said, and watched sardonically as the gelding relaxed and came back on the bit. Deconniy, eyes firmly on his horse's neck, said nothing. "We," Innisth informed him, "are going to go riding. A pleasure ride, nothing more. You are my escort."

Deconniy nodded. But he also met the duke's eyes and said, briefly, voice stripped of expression, "One man is not a sufficient escort, Your Grace. I beg Your Grace will reconsider."

Innisth smiled and let his mare pick up her pace to an extended trot and then a collected canter. Deconniy fell in behind him. The duke led him into the clean trails that curved through the forested foothills of this western province. He rode lightly, alternating an easy canter with a trot, heading nowhere in particular, but tending steadily westward. The peculiar all's-well purr of the Eäneté Power was a low murmur at the back of his mind. The Power was much calmer in the open mountains—though Innisth was always aware of Verè Deconniy. So near. So vulnerable. One of his own people now, however. No longer Geif's man. No longer fit prey for man or beast in these mountains.

The foothills steepened and the trails grew rougher as they rode farther away from the city. Innisth ducked a low branch and turned up into a secondary trail, hardly more than a deer path, that angled up a steep slope. A little stream, barely a handsbreadth across, dropped as a miniature waterfall across their way. Light prismed in its spray. The mare jumped the little waterfall without fuss, the gelding after a second's urging, and Innisth turned around the corner of a massive granite boulder up to the crest of the hill.

Deconniy came up beside him. Through a cleft in the hills, the province spread out below them. The city looked clean and tidy in miniature. The greater part of it nestled back into the hills like a spring fawn cuddling back against its mother. A long scattering of farms and outlying villages stretched off to the east. The forest, of course, ranged to either side: oaks russet and tawny in this season and the lingering green of pines, which in turn gave way, far above, to the stripped rock of the peaks.

"I used to come here as a child," Innisth said, and paused. He was not ordinarily given to impulsive confidences. Deconniy, wisely, said nothing at all. The duke dismounted, tossed him the reins, and walked away. He stood for a moment, regarding the view, and then stepped lightly up onto an outreaching spur of granite that struck boldly out over the gulf. A branch, ready to grip, just here, a foothold, just there, and he was up. His father had stood here beside him once. Briefly. Setting the memory aside, Innisth glanced back at Deconniy.

The captain had dismounted and was holding the reins of both horses in one hand. He stood facing slightly away from the duke, looking at nothing in particular. Innisth was suddenly unable to bear the sight of him intruding on this spot. The young captain, as if guessing this, stood perfectly still.

Innisth turned away, stepping around a spur of granite, and lowered himself down to a seat on the bare stone. The cold of it struck even through his heavy cloak. He rested one hand, lightly gloved, in the place that had always seemed made for an armrest. The cold was there too, clean and knife-sharp through the glove.

He used to come here, indeed. After some brutal punishment from his father. Or worse, one of the exquisitely savage, derisive, unbearable tongue-lashings that flayed more than skin, of which his father had been so perfectly a master. Innisth caught his breath with the force of memory and sat still, still as the granite of these mountains and cold as the wind that sang so piercingly at their peaks. After a time, he found himself able to think of other things.

He had used to look down at Eäneté and think, *This will be mine. When he dies, this will be mine, and it will have been worth everything.* And so it had been, when the old duke had fallen from this very cliff to his death far below. Seven years on, and the memory of the old man was still so strong that at times it stopped his breath. He had made a vow once, sitting here, red blood on the cold stone, long before his father's death, that he would rule the Eänetén Power and never be ruled by it. That under his rule, the town and province of Eäneté would prosper. That his passions would be his own, and never corrupted by those of the Power.

He had kept the first two parts of this vow. He'd had no idea then, of the impossibility of keeping the other. What could a child know of the deep tie? He'd had no idea how his own passions and those of the Power would blur until there was no way to say, *This, out of everything, this is mine.*

Even so, he had kept the more important vow. The years of his rule had seen his city and his province and his Power prosper and grow strong. Too strong, perhaps, if Methmeir Irekaì guessed that the Immanent Power of Eäneté might come to rival even the Great Power of his own Irekay. He must not permit the king to realize this was so.

He got to his feet, hand on the shallow ledge to take his weight, and walked back along the granite spur of the mountain. Deconniy was still—or again—assiduously studying the air. No doubt he did not realize how the light picked out the strong line of his jaw, the vulnerable length of his throat. . . . Innisth took his mare's reins without a word and mounted. He turned her back down the narrow path and headed for the lower trails without glancing over his shoulder. Deconniy stayed at his back, wordless as before.

They came out of the narrow trails into a private little clearing. A tiny stream came down alongside the path and spilled across a granite face at one end of the glen, where boulders had been tumbled together in the past by the careless hand of some great flood. The stream deepened and broadened into a quick brook as it came into the meadow, curved through the clearing, and vanished again at the far side. The babble of the water and the wind through the barren branches of the trees were the only sounds that disturbed the quiet of the hills.

Innisth dismounted again in the little clearing, walking slowly, leading his mare on a long rein. She dropped her head to nibble half-heartedly at the yellowed grasses. He was aware of Deconniy, who stayed mounted, eyes warily on the trees, mindful of the possibility of brigands in these woods.

"Dismount," he called, not quite on impulse. "Leave the horse and come here."

Deconniy opened his mouth, shut it again, and swung down from his gelding. He twisted the horse's reins about a low branch and walked over, slowly, to stand before the duke.

Innisth regarded him, his gaze carefully ironic. The captain was commendably steady. He had the dark hair of the south, the wide brow more common in men from eastern Pohorir. He said nothing, as seemed his habit when uncertain. Innisth approved. He preferred men who did not open their mouths only to fill an uncomfortable silence with foolish babble.

"It was right and proper for you to ask for a larger escort," said the duke, "but unnecessary. You are thinking of threats a man such as Geif, with a tie to only a very minor Immanent Power, might face. Draw your sword."

After a second, Deconniy did so. He held it awkwardly, blade pointed down and across his body, trying to pretend that he was not holding it. It was clear he had noticed that Innisth himself was unarmed.

"Now," said the duke softly, "raise your sword and strike at me."

Deconniy looked at him helplessly. He shifted his grip on the sword hilt. Innisth could see him trying to figure out what he should do.

"Go on," commanded the duke. "I *order* you—raise up your sword and strike at me. Strike hard." He stood still, empty hands at his sides, smiling a little as he stared at the other man.

The captain met his eyes, took a smooth, long breath, lifted his sword, and struck at the duke. Innisth had just time to see that he struck with the flat: a hard blow, one to cause a bruise, but not one that might kill.

The sword did not touch Innisth. It rebounded in Deconniy's hand, twisted out of his grip, and fell to the ground. It cut a long furrow in the damp earth, laying bare the rocky soil beneath the dying winter grasses. Deconniy looked at it for a long moment, rubbing his sword hand slowly with the fingers of his other hand. After a moment he lifted his eyes again to meet the duke's gaze.

"Well done," Innisth commended him sardonically. "Pick it up, my captain, and put it away."

The officer stepped away, bent, and picked up his sword delicately, as though he were not quite sure whether it might twist around of itself and cut at him. He cleaned the earth off the blade against his cloak and sheathed it, gaze studiously on the task as though it required all his attention.

"That will work throughout a large part of the province," the duke told him. Once, that had been all that had prevented him from killing his father. That protection had not, of course, saved the old duke in the end. He said blandly, setting all those memories firmly behind him, "I prefer not to advertise the fact unduly, lest the knowledge inspire an enemy toward . . . creativity."

Deconniy cleared his throat. "Indeed, Your Grace."

"I notice you did not strike with the edge of the blade."

Deconniy met his eyes uneasily. "You didn't order me to strike a killing blow, Your Grace."

Innisth laughed briefly, but with real, unexpected pleasure and amusement. He did like this young man. He thought he did. Above and beyond the urging of the Eänetén Power. He liked the unease—but he liked still more that the man met his eyes. "What would you have done, my captain, had I ordered you to strike to kill?"

The man did not answer at once. He said finally, "Faked it, Your Grace."

The duke laughed again. Then, sobering, he examined the captain with care. Deconniy waited, stoic. "You'll do," Innisth told him. "I think you will do." Yes. The man did not lack courage, plainly. Nor good sense. A stroke of good fortune that this man of Tisain had come to Eäneté at this moment. He might prove very useful. Innisth did think he might.

Unless he was a spy, of course. Though Geif would have had to be uncharacteristically subtle, to send this man.

"We shall see," the duke said aloud, and watched with amusement as the young captain's brow creased just a little in worry.

"Get your horse," Innisth ordered. He tossed the reins back over his mare's neck and mounted, waiting impatiently while the other man strode across the clearing to fetch his gelding. But he made himself take a plain, easy path down toward the city.

He sent for Captain Etar the moment they passed back through the gate into the courtyard of the house, and for Gereth, and as the boys ran to take those messages, he indicated with a curt gesture that Deconniy should come with him as well. He had to stop himself from taking the stairs two at a time, but still Gereth met them at the outer door of his suite.

"A profitable ride, Your Grace?" the older man said, smooth and a little bit amused—only Gereth would have the temerity to be amused at anything the duke did—and only very slightly worried.

"I trust so," Innisth told him. Then Etar arrived, and Innisth signaled Deconniy to wait in the outer chamber while he swept the other men through two interior doors and into the main room of his suite. Windowless and spare, with one narrow couch and two angular chairs drawn up by the fireplace, and beyond that only paintings of the winter forest on all four walls, the room offered no chance for any lingering servant to overhear anything said. Innisth said without preamble, "You are certain the young man is not a spy for Lord Geif."

Etar's blinked. He was grizzled now, in his fifties, but still powerful; he wore experience and confidence like armor and was seldom surprised. He said, "I would have said not. I did say not. Have you reason to suspect him, Your Grace?"

"I do not. I wish to use him against Geif. It would prove awkward if you were mistaken." He turned to Gereth, who was shaking his head. "Well?"

"Your Grace, Geif took his sister, his only close family. He got her with child. As he has legitimate sons and did not want the child born, he accused the girl of theft and sentenced her to be publicly flayed. Deconniy spent every coin he had and called in every favor he was owed, but he couldn't get her away. The best he could do was get someone to slip her poison. Geif was furious. Deconniy got out of Tisain only because his friends in the guard didn't put much effort into capturing him. I believe he would welcome any plan of yours that would strike against Lord Geif, but he would be recognized in Tisain—though, of course, he must still have friends there."

"You are confident of this story?"

"I always investigate those who enter your household, Your Grace."

"Gereth," the duke said, with real affection. "Of course you do."

"The tale was all over Tisain. Dealing so with a girl would be characteristic for Lord Geif, but the tale does not flatter him, so it seemed true on its face. More, Deconniy proved to have many friends. So did the girl. No, Your Grace, I'm certain the story is true. That's why I recommended him to Captain Etar."

"He's a straightforward young man," added Captain Etar. "I imagine you have found him so as well."

"Indeed," said Innisth. "Straightforward. Yes. Bring him in, my old friend, and we shall put it to him."

Verè Deconniy was plainly nervous. He could hardly be otherwise, told to wait while all his seniors held close consultation about some undisclosed topic. But he came into the room with a firm step and stood straight, his eyes on the duke's face. He said nothing.

"I hear nothing but good reports of you," Innisth told him. "You did well today. You showed good sense, rarer than obedience—and you are, of course, lately of Tisain. I understand you bear no love for Lord Geif. I have a small task for you. I wish to implicate Geif in some criminal dealing, something large and expensive that will draw the attention of Lord Laören, whom we shall hope finds coin even more riveting than malice—" The idea that had been niggling at the back of his mind all day leaped clear.

Innisth had been thinking of paper evidence, of planting records suggesting tax evasion. But now he said, "I wish to make it seem that Geif has been striking his own coins. That he has been weighting the gold with pewter or lead. Yes. Base coin bearing the king's own image." Now he had to work to tamp out a real smile. That would do very well indeed. Making base coin was certainly a significantly greater crime than merely skimming illegally from the top of legitimate trade.

And striking base coins with Methmeir Irekaì's own image and sign . . . yes. Lord Laören would by no means pass over *that* insult. Merely extracting a girl or two from his grasping hands was nothing in comparison. Yes.

"Yes," Innisth said aloud, and focused his gaze once more on this new young captain of his. "You have no fondness for Lord Geif, I think.

You would be willing to do this? You would be capable of the task?"

Captain Deconniy's face had gone blank and still. He said slowly, "Indeed, no, Your Grace. I mean, yes, Your Grace, if you . . . I have friends in Tisain. I could . . . yes." He looked suddenly at the duke. "I could put anything you wish in that man's house—but if he found it before Laören—he has a hunting lodge, you know, Your Grace. He loves the hunt, does Geif. He loves the kill. Everyone knows that. It would be—I could—if I may suggest—"

"The hunting lodge sounds ideal," said Innisth. "An excellent suggestion, my captain."

Captain Etar said, "You'd be willing to take Laören hunting, make sure he finds the right lodge, the papers, the coins?"

"Yes," said Deconniy, and turned urgently to the duke. "Let me do this. I would be glad to do this. That will be enough, won't it? The king will kill Geif. For passing bad coins. Coins stamped with his image. He will *flay him alive*."

"This pleases you, my captain?" Innisth was amused.

"Yes," said Deconniy, and smiled at last, a small, tight smile.

"Very good," Innisth said, satisfied. "Yes, very good. Base coins cannot be created instantly. But I believe—Gereth?"

"Yes, Your Grace. I believe some are already available in your own treasury. Carefully set aside, of course."

"Of course," Innisth said. "Now. Coins. And appropriate papers . . . accounts and so forth."

"A coin stamp?"

"That, we don't have," said Gereth regretfully.

"Well, it is not necessary. Geif has his stamp hidden elsewhere. Naturally it is well hidden. No doubt Lord Laören will ask many close questions regarding that stamp, but Geif will prove surprisingly recalcitrant in providing accurate information. Or perhaps one of his own people betrayed him and took it. There are many possible reasons it might not be found."

"Yes," Gereth agreed. "That should work, particularly as Lord

Laören will want very much to cast his find at Irekaì's feet. He'll want Geif to be guilty; he'll probably think of his own reasons why that stamp can't be found. Yes, this should work."

"Yours is the dangerous part," Innisth said to his young captain.

"I will do it," Deconniy declared fiercely. "I won't fail you."

"Very good," Innisth murmured, and rose, smiling.

6

On the fifth day of the Month of Frost, Tirovay arrin Elin Raëhema stood on the river wall of Leiör, watching one of the giant ferries as it prepared to undock from the Leiör side of the river. Despite the bite in the air, he found this a spectacle well worth watching, though he could see that the folk of Leiör were too accustomed to the sight to even glance toward the river. There were at least fifty people on the deck of the ferry, lining the rails or settled under awnings. Fawn-colored Emmeran cattle crowded together in pens along one side of the ferry, lowing unhappily. Spotted goats occupied a pen along the other side. Two horses had been led to the rear of the ferry, while more delicate poultry were crated and carried below. The massive cables that were strung across the whole width of the river sang with tension as the signal flags signed for the casting off and the long line of coupled heavy draft horses leaned into their harness. Tiro watched the powerful gray horses stride slowly past, their drover calling encouragement and gesturing with his long whip, and the ferry moved slowly out into the river.

Leiör was a prosperous town, sited as it was at the confluence of the great Imhar that here came down from the north and the smaller

Diöllay that curved its way from the east. It wasn't only a confluence of rivers; here at Leiör three of the four kingdoms met as well. The Imhar, of course, marked the border between southern Harivir and northern Emmer; but just there where the river turned north, the boundary it demarcated was between Emmer to the west and Kosir to the east. And the Diöllay, of course, showed the boundary between Harivir and Kosir. The ferry that was now crossing the Diöllay would draw up to the quay of Leiör's sister-town of Sariy in Kosir. There it would take on iron and copper and whatever passengers wished to make the return crossing to Harivir. The larger Emmeran town of Sariy was also visible to the north across the wide confluence, and in gentler days perhaps some of those cattle would be destined to cross the Imhar at the narrower width above the confluence. During these unsettled days, though, Tiro knew that very little traffic would be making that crossing. But a scattering of small river craft slid down the rivers to the west, or made their more laborious way up one river or the other.

The source of the Diöllay lay in the high mountains of Kosir; if one followed the river upstream, one would find the town of Lind, and from there the long, winding Anha Pass, which led along the edge of Mora Bay on the eastern coast. Anha Pass came out above Enchar, which had belonged to Kosir until Meriön temè Heriduïn Irekaì, King of Pohorir in Tiro's great-grandmother's day, had taken all the land around Mora Bay for his own and forced the Immanent Power of Enchar to yield to the Great Power of Irekay. Even today, Enchar's Immanent and its people and the very stone of its land remained restive in Pohorir's grip; tremors were still felt now and then as far away as Eilin, on Harivir's side of the mountains. Tiro honestly didn't understand why Meriön Irekaì had wanted to subdue a land so opposed to his rule. . . . Well, he understood it in *theory*. No doubt Meriön had been glad enough to bind another lesser Immanent to the Great Power of Irekay; no doubt he had been glad to steal Enchar's virtue and strength for Pohorir and for Irekay, glad to use that virtue and strength to extend his own life. Tiro supposed Meriön's descendants had been just the same, right down to the current King of Pohorir, Methmeir Irekaì himself.

It was an ugly business, a king annexing foreign provinces not just for ordinary human ambition, but to fatten his own land at the expense of the conquered province. Entirely the reverse of a king spending his own strength so that his Immanent Power could support the outlying provinces . . . But that was Pohorir, and had been for many generations.

Tiro's grandmother, ruler of Harivir before his father, had moved swiftly to fortify the Anha Narrows, the summer pass just south of Anha Pass itself. The Narrows led from Enchar to Harivir's town of Eilin. But so far Methmeir Heriduïn Irekaì seemed content to leave the borders as they stood.

Tiro could see one boat that was making its way up the river, carrying goods or passengers from somewhere in Emmer into Kosir. The boat was moving a little more quickly than some; its owner had not hired one of the ox teams that generally did such work, but a relatively fast team of heavy horses, a big hitch that was hauling the boat upstream at an impressive pace.

Perhaps the urgency implied by that pace caught Tiro's eye; he found himself lingering on the river wall, watching that boat glide past. Small, as such boats were always small; sharp-bowed and broad in the stern, with a shallow draft and a cabin taking up a good part of the deck . . . not meant for cargo, he guessed, but for passengers who wished an easier or quieter or more private passage upriver than afforded by riding along the road. For a moment Tiro let himself imagine that Kehera might be on that boat herself, having made her way somehow from Suriytè to the river and bribed or bought her passage. It was not impossible. The timing would be just about right, from everything they knew about when some mysterious crisis had struck Suriytè. If Kehera had somehow precipitated that crisis and then gotten away . . . Tiro was almost sure about the former—nothing else made sense—but he could only pray for the latter. But he counted days in his head and watched that boat and wished that it would put in at the Harivin landing, that he would be standing here watching and actually see his sister step off that boat's deck and set her foot back on Harivin soil. . . .

It didn't happen, of course. The boat went on up the river, and a quiet sound behind him made him straighten and turn. Then long training made him smile and nod. "Lady Taraä."

Lady Taraä inan Seine Leiörian, Lady of Leiör, nodded back, but she did not smile. These recent days had been difficult for her, as everyone waited to see what the Mad King of Emmer might do. Specifically, whether he might try to do to Leiör what he had done to Cemerè.

The Lady of Leiör was young, though older than Tiro—practically everyone was older than Tiro. She was a solidly built woman, pleasant rather than pretty, with the steady temper and good sense of all the Seine line. Tiro knew his father had been thoroughly satisfied when Leiör's tie had come to Seine from a line of flightier cousins. He knew as well that his father, wishing to encourage the Leiör tie to follow the Seine line, had considered Lady Taraä a possible match for Tiro. Tiro would not have objected. He liked Taraä. She was not very pretty—she was too big-boned and sturdy to be pretty—but her steadiness reminded him of Kehera. Anybody could guess that her Seine line would cross well with his Elin. But the awareness made him awkward around her. Whenever he had to talk to her, he felt young and not very clever.

Lady Taraä was in her midtwenties, but she looked years older, as happened to those who took a ruling tie in hard days. Taraä's grandmother had died several years ago, her death no doubt hastened by the long drought, and unfortunately her mother had died many years ago, and so the ruling tie had come to Taraä early. Now the Mad King became less and less predictable, and so she had Emmer's ambition to worry about as well as the continuing drought.

That was why Tiro had come to Leiör: His father had to stay

in Cemerè, to anchor Raëhemaiëth into that newly hollow town and province because now the Immanent of Raëh was all the protection that whole central part of the border possessed. But when the Mad King's standard had moved east, *someone* had needed to bring Raëhemaiëth's attention here so it could better support Leiör. So Tiro's father had sent him, hastily.

It should have been Kehera. Tiro knew it should have been Kehera. His sister should have held the heir's tie; *she* should have been the one here in Leiör, ready to raise up Raëhemaiëth and support the town's Immanent against any attack or incursion. No matter what happened, she would have known what to do, because she always did; and she wouldn't have given up even if Hallieth Suriytaiän had struck against Leiör, because she never did give up. Tiro had lost enough tiahel games to his sister to know she would give the Mad King a harder game than Tiro himself could.

But Kehera had gone north eighteen days ago, and Tiro had had no choice but to take the heir's part. Then, just six days ago, word had made its way south to the Harivin border; news of some sort of trouble in northern Emmer. Tiro couldn't be *sure* Kehera had caused that trouble. But he *was* sure of it. He only waited for word from his father, about what was going on in Emmer and whether Tiro himself should stay in Leiör or return to Cemerè, or go back to Raëh, or . . . he didn't know. He had to just trust that his father would know what would be best to do now, while they all waited for . . . whatever would come next.

Now, seeing Lady Taraä's unsmiling face and tense-set lips, he thought perhaps the waiting had ended. Or at least changed shape.

She nodded toward the river, still unsmiling, and said, "The river's wide there, but not wide enough."

Tiro had to agree. What had happened at Cemerè had made it quite clear that the river ought to be much wider—a real barrier to armies and, more importantly, to Immanent Powers anchored by mad kings. He wished the whole river were as wide as Imhar Bay on the western coast, with miles of water between Harivir and Emmer. He wished Emmer were an island kingdom, with a wide and wild ocean between its ambitious Great Power and all the rest of the world.

But the world was as it was, and no use wishing. "Someone's crossed it," he said, not quite a question. "A Suriytaiän messenger?"

"Probably," said Lady Taraä. "But he's not raised up the White Horse standard, nor any other. A senior Emmeran officer, but come in a small boat with a small escort, asking for Torrolay Elin Raëhema— expecting to find your father here, evidently. I suppose he's had word that a Raëhema is here in Leiör and expects His Majesty would have come here to support me."

Tiro nodded. "I'll see him," he said at once. Maybe the man brought news about what had happened in Suriytè. Or maybe he could be made to yield such news, even if he'd come with some sort of demands from his king.

Tiro glanced around. The ferry was well out across the Diöllay now, the other ferry nearing the landing; the riverboat was nearly out of sight upstream. Everything looked so . . . ordinary. To a first glance. "Not here," he said, though he had no idea what other place might be better.

A senior Emmeran officer. The man would probably try to overawe a seventeen-year-old prince. Whatever further concessions Hallieth Suriytaiän wanted, this officer would surely be pleased to try to get them from Tiro rather than his father. Tiro had no doubt of that at all. He made sure his expression was untroubled. He was not going to give any concessions; he fixed his mind on that. He would put this man off, whatever he demanded, and send word to his father, and hope that nothing too dire happened before his father could decide what to do. . . .

"Under Leiör's banner," Taraä said, her intelligent glance suggesting she knew just what Tiro had been thinking. "That's where my grandmother used to see people when she wanted to keep them off-balance. I'll show you."

The place Lady Taraä showed him was perfect. Leiör's standard was the graceful willow, such as stood close by the banks of the rivers—not an intimidating standard, except the tree in the rear courtyard of the lady's house was vast, with a girth four men couldn't have compassed and branches that swayed so far overhead they seemed to catch at the passing winds. The leaves were yellow now, the draperies of twigs half naked with the approaching winter, but it was still an impressive tree. More importantly, there was a heavy table of willow-wood under that tree, and embedded too deeply in that table for any man to withdraw, a great ax that looked old enough to have been slammed down into the wood of the table at the very dawn of the world. The streaks of rust that ran down the blade were unsettlingly close to the color of blood.

"Ah," said Tiro, studying this tableau. "I remember the story."

"Not many do," murmured Lady Taraä. "But you would, wouldn't you? It was your . . . what, great-great-grandfather who put it there." She gave him a smile at last.

"One more great," said Tiro. "And if a Seine had been Lady of Leiör at the time, I doubt he would have found it necessary." Then he blushed, realizing how this might sound. Lady Taraä probably knew his father had been considering a possible match between Seine and Elin. He felt younger and clumsier than ever. "It's a memorable story," he muttered.

"Yes." Lady Taraä ran a hand across the oiled wood of the table. "My grandmother told me it didn't matter whether a petitioner knew the tale or not. That blade's unsettling either way."

Tiro nodded. "Yes, it's perfect."

"Then I'll send for the Emmeran officer. With your permission, Your Highness."

Tiro gave it with another nod and added impulsively, "You'll stay by me to receive this man, of course, Lady Taraä. As he's seen fit to seek out a Raëhema here at Leiör."

His invitation pleased her, he saw, though she'd no doubt meant to be present in any case.

The Emmeran, when he was escorted into the courtyard, proved to be a big man: tall and broad, with powerful shoulders. Not a young man, but not yet old, with a dark-grizzled beard and deep-set eyes in a hard face. He came into the courtyard alone except for his Harivin escort, moving with quick, impatient strides, but he checked—rather satisfyingly—at his first sight of the table and the ax. It took him a second to look past the ax to Tiro, seated behind the table, and Lady Taraä standing behind Tiro. Though his expression didn't change, his eyes widened just perceptibly.

Tiro rose politely—*Always be polite to your enemies,* his father had told him. *Courtesy leaves you with more options, and besides, it disconcerts them.* This Emmeran officer didn't look very easy to disconcert. Tiro nodded to him and waited.

The Emmeran walked forward, more slowly now, and made his bow. "Prince Tirovay," he said. He didn't say *I expected your father,* though that was obvious. He glanced at Lady Taraä and offered her a slighter bow. "I'm Enmon Corvallis," he told them both, obviously expecting them to recognize his name, as of course Tiro did, and he was sure Lady Taraä as well. "Eighteen days ago, I met Her Highness Kehera Elin Raëhema on the other side of the river and escorted her to Suriytè."

Tiro tried to hide his sudden eagerness behind a polite court smile, but wasn't entirely sure he succeeded. "Go on," he said, trying to brace himself against whatever news, good or otherwise, this man might have brought.

"On the twenty-eighth, Hallieth Suriytaiän tried to use Her Highness to take the Power of Raëh," General Corvallis said bluntly, and went on at once. "He overstepped his ambition at last; he failed and lost his own Power, and I got Her Highness away—my man was to get her away. I had hoped to find her here, or news of her." He stopped, tilting his head interrogatively.

"Go on," said Tiro. He sat down again, closing his hands into loose fists to stop them from shaking. He couldn't stop himself from listening for a messenger's rapid footfalls—someone bringing word that Kehera had come back across the river—but he knew she hadn't. He would have felt it. He would have known it. Raëhemaiëth would have felt it. She was not in Harivir, or he would have known.

The twenty-eighth. And it was now the fifth of the Month of Frost. Seven days. The weather had been mostly good. She *could* have made it this far by now. At least, a man on a fast horse, a man with no need to evade enemies or fear pursuit, could very well ride from Suriytè to the Imhar River in less time than that. For Kehera, even with help, it might have been different. He shouldn't count her overdue. Not yet. But his heart clenched in fear even so.

"She's not come here, then," Corvallis surmised, though Tiro hadn't said as much. "I'd hoped she had. I won't hide from Your Highness that I should have had word long since, from my man and from others posted along their route. Her Highness was to be brought to a certain place in Suriytè and go on from there, but she never came there. Getting off the route's one thing, but whatever's happened, my man should have found a way to send me word, and I've heard nothing. I've people searching, of course, in Suriytè and along the roads south."

"So you rode at a hard pace all the way from Suriytè to inform His Highness that you'd gotten Her Highness away from the Mad King and then immediately lost her somewhere in Suriytè, and despite all your efforts haven't found her again," observed Lady Taraä while Tiro was still trying to catch his breath. "This seems an uncommon enthusiasm for delivering bad news, General Corvallis."

"I confess I'd hoped to find her here," the general repeated without heat. "Or news of her. Seven days' hard pace, as the lady says, and I pray to the Fortunate Gods you'll see her safe in another day or two. Without that, I'm in a bad position. I don't deny it. Worse than you know. I'd meant my men to deliver her safely back to your doorstep long before I had any need to speak to Torrolay Raëhema on my own account. But matters in Suriytè are a good deal more complicated than I'd expected, and I couldn't delay. Hallieth Suriytaiän's lost his rightful Power, which you'll say is all well and good. I certainly said so. But he's got a tie yet, and that, I will confess, I didn't expect at all. It's a deep tie and no mistake. Someone more ambitious and less mad than he has forced a tie on him—that's what I think."

"How very unusual," said Tiro, startled into attentiveness despite his fear for his sister. "How very strange. What Power is it?"

"I don't *know*," said the general, impatient and angry. Then, collecting himself, he went on more calmly. "Irekay, I think. He made a fool's alliance there, or so I believe. I felt the king would overreach when he set himself against the Immanent of Raëh, yes. I wanted that. I was waiting for that. Then I felt the Suriytaiän Immanent disappear from the city and the land—I'd felt that before, at Cemerè and Talisè. So I thought I'd been right. I'd meant to take Suriytè myself the moment it became hollow, you understand."

Tiro actually did. He guessed now that General Corvallis had actively maneuvered his king to take Kehera, betting that Raëhemaiëth had the strength to pull down the Immanent Power of Suriytè and not much troubled at the danger this plan posed to Raëhemaiëth. Corvallis could not have expected much interference from so far away as Irekay in Pohorir. He had meant to take Suriytè, hold the city and the province until a new Immanent Power grew up from the land and the city and the people. Then he would be in position to take the ruling tie to that new-forming Immanent. He—or his heir, if it took so long—would master the new Immanent of Suriytè, bind it to their line, and become a true king. No one would be in a position to interfere, given how many of the lesser Emmeran Powers Hallieth Suriytaiän had destroyed.

It was ambitious. But it was exactly such ambition that let a man—or a woman—take a new tie and shape a developing Immanent Power. If Corvallis could have done that, he could have guided the new Immanent in almost any direction he wished; it was human intention and determination that set human priorities and achieved human ends. The Immanent itself was a thing of being and becoming, not a thing of doing or deciding—unless a man were foolish enough to reach through the deep tie and, striving for greater and greater influence over his Immanent, force into it too much of himself. Then, taking on human ambition, the Immanent might in turn master whoever had tried to rule it. There were certainly stories about that—vivid, exciting stories about terrible events that no one would want to actually live through.

Corvallis would not have let anything of the kind happen, and anyway, there was almost no chance of it from a newly formed Immanent. He would have been king of a weaker and probably smaller Emmer, but his kingdom would still have had the wealth of her wide, fertile lands. No doubt General Corvallis had intended for his eventual heirs to rule a kingdom that would become stronger and stronger, until its borders were back where they had been—or pressed out even farther than that.

Except now, whatever had happened, Suriytè had proved not to be empty after all. Someone else, someone holding a deep tie to the Great Power of Irekay, perhaps, had reached across those miles . . . somehow. Tiro couldn't quite imagine Raëhemaiëth managing anything of the kind. That was more terrifying still, a Power that ambitious and that strong and that much more aggressive than Raëhemaiëth.

He said, "This is certainly all very disturbing, General Corvallis. And you believe it was the Irekaïn Power that reached across the miles to anchor itself into Suriytè?" The Pohorin king was, in fact, the most ambitious man Tiro could think of who also held a ruling tie to a Great Power. Tiro glanced at Lady Taraä, whose province was a good deal closer to Pohorir and Irekay than Suriytè. "If Methmeir Irekaì can reach so far, that's . . . not good."

"Makes me particularly glad you're here, Your Highness, I'll say that," Lady Taraä agreed forthrightly. "I'm not such a fool as to let a foreign Immanent anchor itself into Leiör whatever it promises us, but invite Raëhemaiëth into a closer bond with Leiöriansé? That I'd do in a heartbeat to keep out this ambitious enemy. Raëhemaiëth, we trust."

Tiro nodded, not knowing how to answer this. He was fairly sure he was flushing, though she hadn't meant anything personal by that, he knew. He tried to steady his mind, think about what Corvallis had said.

He could think of just one time where a king had forced his Great Power to anchor itself into foreign lands to which it had no proper bond, promising to support the lesser Immanences while instead— this part was surmise—intending to forge his own ruling tie to each Immanent Power, superseding the lords who already bore those ties.

Actually, every part of that story was surmise. That had been in the south. Not much was known about the calamity that had consumed the entire south. Something had gone wrong, and the Great Power had become an Unfortunate God, a thing of chaos and terror. Such disasters were not common; that was the best known of such apotheoses, and almost nothing was known even of it. But every child knew at least that the lands of the north, too, might have been destroyed except the Fortunate Gods had raised up the Wall of Storms to utterly and forever divide south from north. And even the Fortunate Gods had not been able to prevent the Wall from spawning black storms at midwinter, nor dragons from riding the obsidian winds across the northlands.

Or had not cared to prevent such things. Even the Fortunate Gods were mysterious and chancy; one prayed to them for favor and luck, but their wishes and intentions were only a matter for speculation. Tiro himself agreed with the school of thought that argued that the Fortunate Gods mostly wanted Immanent Powers approaching their apotheosis to become Fortunate rather than Unfortunate Gods, and that it was only happenstance that this goal also led to happier outcomes for mortal creatures. But even that was only speculation.

"What I think," General Corvallis said in his blunt, straightforward way, "is that Methmeir Irekaì wanted to anchor his Power to a land far in the north, where black storms and dragons never come. If he ever needed any reason other than ambition to do . . . whatever he thought he was doing. And if this *was* his work, which we don't actually know."

Tiro nodded, but he was almost grateful to think of the King of Pohorir merely destroying the Immanent Power of Suriytè in order to anchor his own Immanent to that land. That was peculiar and frightening and probably boded ill for what Methmeir Irekaì might do next, but destroying an Immanent was surely a great deal safer than forcing one out of its land and into apotheosis. Methmeir Irekaì might be leaving lands hollow, which was bad, but Tiro couldn't see how anything the Pohorin king was doing could lead to the apotheosis of his own Great Power into an Unfortunate God. Rather the reverse; it should force the Irekaïn Power to stretch itself out thin. It might even force it to fracture into smaller Immanences, though . . . Tiro wasn't sure that was actually possible. He knew just the books he wanted to consult, but they were all back in Raëh, unfortunately.

And of course if the Great Power of Suriytè had been destroyed, *it* was no longer a threat at all. Surely whatever Methmeir Irekaì was doing, bad as it might get, couldn't lead to anything like the calamity that had fallen on the southlands.

"Your news is alarming, certainly," Tiro said. "We're pleased you brought us this word. Yet I'm not sure just what you meant to ask my father to do." Obviously General Corvallis must have ridden south almost at once to be here in Leiör so soon after these events he described. Which meant the general had been driven by some urgent necessity. Tiro went on, careful not to imply agreement to anything. "May I ask what it is you want from Harivir, precisely?"

The general gave him a short, acknowledging nod. "Your Highness, I would very much like to see Emmer and Harivir come to a useful understanding. That will obviously not be possible while Hallieth Theraön Suriytaiän remains King of Emmer. I ask you—I ask His Majesty Torrolay Elin Raëhema—to help me bring down the

Mad King. I'd hoped force of arms alone would be sufficient. Force of arms *should* have been sufficient if he'd lost the Suriytè Power and stopped there. But clearly that's not the case. This new Power that's reached across the miles to anchor itself in him and in Suriytè . . . This complicates matters, whether it's Methmeir Irekaì's doing or another's. I ask—I ask humbly—for the assistance of Torrolay Raëhema and Harivir in this cause. But I must point out that if Hallieth Theraön Suriytaiän is not brought down without delay, he may well reach some accommodation with this lord who has bound a foreign Power into Suriytè, and then Harivir may very well find itself at odds with both the Mad King *and* his new overlord—surely not a situation any of us can wish to see develop."

Yes, that was very humble. Tiro kept his face smooth. This moment was the kind that would be remembered forever by every historian in the Four Kingdoms; he knew that as surely as though he were opening a dusty tome right now and reading an account of the general's words. He only wished the next words didn't have to be his own, because he didn't know how to answer this. He wished he were watching this scene from behind his father's chair. Lady Taraä wasn't leaping into this moment, either. Which would be very wrong of her, of course, but Tiro would not necessarily have minded.

Except . . . if he'd been standing behind his father's chair, he would have known what he would *suggest*. It's just that he wouldn't have had the responsibility for things going horribly, irretrievably wrong if his advice proved terribly mistaken.

He took a deep breath, let it out, and said, he hoped calmly, "Harivir would want some form of surety, I expect, General Corvallis. A demonstration of your sincerity. For example . . . Sariy."

Lady Taraä smiled. "Oh, now, *there's* an excellent notion."

Tiro nodded to her. Obviously she had understood at once that if he could bring Sariy into Harivir, bind it to Raëhemaiëth when it had been bound to Suriytè, then that would be the beginning of a buffer between the Mad King and the southern bank of the Imhar. It would most particularly serve as a buffer between the Mad King and her own Leiör.

Corvallis looked like a man who'd bitten into a summer-ripe plum and found it unexpectedly sour. But he didn't reject this counter-offer out of hand, either, though Tiro was proposing to cut down the size of his potential kingdom right from the beginning. Corvallis probably had not expected to hold all the lands once claimed by the Kings of Emmer who had held the close bond to Suriytè. The general only said, "Sariy has belonged to Emmer for a long time. You know that, of course."

"Certainly. And as Suriytè has become hollow, then Sariy has no true overlord at all. While the lord of Sariy may find that an excellent state of affairs at the moment, it will put him in a dangerous position if a stronger Power moves to force a bond on Sariy's Immanent. For example, this Power that has, you say, anchored itself in Suriytè. Aran Sariäna must be aware of the danger. I can promise—I do promise—that any bond Raëhemaiëth establishes will be Fortunate. That's all I have in mind: an ordinary Fortunate bond. He knows Raëhemaiëth will do no harm to Sariy. Do you think he'll hope as much for the Irekaïn Power? Do you hope for as much from Irekay?"

The sour-plum look deepened, but Corvallis said reluctantly, "I don't think anyone sensible expects anything good from Methmeir Irekaì."

Tiro nodded. "Later, I do expect to find out whether Raëhemaiëth can extend itself all along the river. But Sariy will do, for a start." He paused and then asked with real curiosity, "What else did you have in mind when you crossed the river, if not this?"

General Corvallis shook his head, by which Tiro understood that he had hoped to get a lot more for a lot less. Probably he'd hoped to somehow finesse the situation to make sure the Mad King faced Torrolay Elin Raëhema on *this* side of the river, on Harivin soil. That might not even be a bad idea, if it came to true battle: Raëhemaiëth was strongest in the land to which it had been bound the longest. But

Tiro was very sure his father would be even better pleased if the whole grim situation could be worked out in some way that kept any battle right out of Harivir entirely.

He said, "If you want Harivir's help in this, then you'll have to persuade Lord Aran of Sariy. Such a bond between Sariy and Raëh would benefit us all. Once Raëh has established a bond to Sariy . . ." Tiro opened his hands. "Perhaps we make the same arrangement with other towns along our common border. Daman, perhaps, and even Luòriy. I only wish there were still an Immanent in Talisè to which Raëhemaiëth might be bound."

This was true, but a regret unexpectedly nudged at the back of Tiro's mind. He frowned, but it would not come clear.

Corvallis said shortly, interrupting his thoughts, "Your Highness, we can discuss Sariy. And Talisè. But anything farther north is out of the question."

Tiro focused again on the present moment. He said carefully, picking his words, "General Corvallis, Harivir's interest isn't in helping you establish a ruling line of Corvallis Suriytaiän kings. I'm sure that's clear to you. It's in protecting our own people and countering the continuing threat posed by Hallieth Theraön, whatever tie he carries now. And that means expanding our own reach and reducing his, by whatever means are necessary."

The general gave him a level look. "I'm in no position to lay down terms. I know that. But, Your Highness, *neither are you.* Harivir must help me, and quickly, or it'll be the Mad King you have on your border again, and I don't mean some new border that stretches east to west on the other side of the Imhar River. Nor can you expect to face Hallieth Suriytaiän alone, but also whoever's forced this new tie on him. Methmeir Irekaì, as you say; I wouldn't be surprised. Tell your father that, Your Highness. I'm a reasonable man, but no one besides me is in position to pick up the land the Mad King's left in broken pieces. If I fail, who knows what enemy Harivir will find itself facing by midwinter?"

"Sariy," said Tiro, clenching his hands together under the table and forcing himself not to look away. "And then we'll talk about the next step."

This got a long pause, as General Corvallis plainly hadn't expected such a lack of give. At last he nodded, grudgingly. "I'll speak to Aran Sariäna. I agree in principle. But, no offense, Your Highness, I'd expect Lord Aran would be happier if it were Torrolay Raëhema himself who established that bond."

So would Tiro. He started to say so, stopped himself, and said instead, "How many days' grace will Hallieth Theraön give us? Can you say? Can Aran Sariäna? This doesn't just benefit Leiör. Sariy would also be far safer bound to Raëh." And he got to his feet, leaned forward, grasped the heavy haft of the massive ax, closed his eyes, and called inwardly, *Raëhemaiëth!* Beside him, he was aware of Lady Taraä drawing a shocked breath, but he was *mostly* aware of Raëhemaiëth's rising around and within him. The bond between the two Immanences was normally Fortunate, with strength flowing from Greater to lesser; but now Raëhemaiëth rose hard, and Leiöriansé gave way, and Tirovay Elin Raëhema lifted the ax smoothly from its long rest. The deep, deep gash in the wood was stained with rust that looked red as blood in the afternoon light.

Then Tiro let out his breath and the glittering strength of the Power faded, and suddenly the ax was so heavy in his hands he could barely hold it. Stiffening his back, he offered it across the table to General Corvallis. "Take this to Aran Sariäna," he commanded. "And tell him that I will reclaim it in friendship or otherwise, as he chooses."

It was almost exactly what Tiro's own great-great-great-grandfather had said to that remote, slantwise relative of Lady Taraä's, when he'd slammed this very ax into this very table. Very soon after that, Leiör had become a part of Harivir without any other weapon being lifted.

Whether or not General Corvallis knew the story, he took the ax with a respectful nod that was close to a bow. "I'll tell him . . . I'll tell him, if he desires to forge a bond between his Immanent and yours, he need have no concern regarding the strength of your tie."

"Yes," Tiro said, a shade too quickly, and made himself pause and then go on in more measured tones. "I shall pass this word to my father, I promise you, General Corvallis, but I think we won't wait for his answer. Speak to Aran Sariäna, and send me word . . . tonight?" He couldn't quite bring himself to make that an order, but he knew his tone had definitely become too uncertain on that last word. "Or by dawn tomorrow," he said, as firmly as he could. "I'm sure His Majesty my father *will* agree that Sariy would do better bound to Raëh than to whatever Great Power has taken Suriytè." He couldn't stop himself from adding, "And I'm sure my father would be even more disposed toward assisting in a change of line and authority in Emmer if someone were to find my sister and return her to us safely."

Whatever the general thought of this—he looked grim enough— he nodded. "I'll find Her Highness," he promised in his turn. "If she's still anywhere in Emmer, I'll find her and send her back safe to you."

7

Kehera Raëhema entered Pohorir sometime during the early part of the Month of Frost. She did not know the exact day. In the pass that led from Kosir into Pohorir, all the days blurred together in one endless sweep of cold and apprehension and exhaustion.

She knew she and her captors had approached most closely to Harivir on the fifth day of the month; they had been *so close*. The riverboat Nomoris had hired had passed *right by* Leiör before beating its way upriver and into Kosir. Kehera had stood at the tiny window of her private cabin and stared out at the town as they passed it. She couldn't help but wonder whether her brother or father might be in Leiör at that exact moment, watching her boat pass by the town and never knowing she was a prisoner upon it.

She had tried so hard to think of a way to escape. But she had failed, and lost her chance. And then she'd lost track of the days as well, which made her feel strangely disconnected from the world and from herself.

Or maybe that was lingering grief and guilt for Eilisè. And increasing terror for herself. She felt so alone. She *was* so alone. At least that meant no other friend would die to save her, but she felt so helpless, and so afraid. No wonder she clung to the numb distance born of loneliness and cold and silence.

At home they would still be waiting for the first frost to whiten the stubble in the fields. It would not snow near Raëh, not this month, not until midwinter. But here on the border between Emmer and Pohorir, traveling into the teeth of the mountains, her captors had carried her into what already seemed the depths of winter.

If someone had asked her a month ago, Kehera would have said that traveling through the Takel Mountains was impossible even early in winter. No one dared Anha Pass once the snow began to fall. She knew it must be worse later, but to her the bone-grinding cold of the heights seemed terrible enough already. It drained strength, killed thought, and paralyzed the will.

Kehera rode with her head bowed and her hood pulled across her face. She had learned to pry shards of ice out of the hooves of her shaggy horse, handling her borrowed hoof-pick with fingers she could scarcely feel. She had not realized that chunks of ice and frozen pebbles could be so dangerous until she had allowed her first horse to go lame. Gheroïn Nomoris had put her on a different animal and left one of his own men behind with the lame horse, abandoning man and beast without regard for the man's pleas. The man who was left behind had been one of her captors, and Kehera had told herself firmly that she didn't care about his fate, but riding away from him had been horrible. After that she checked her new horse's hooves every time she felt any worrisome change in his gait.

No one stopped her from pausing to care for her horse or for her own needs, or seemed concerned that she kept the hoof-pick in a pocket of her skirt. It was the cold that held Kehera prisoner now.

Nomoris had driven them all mercilessly, hoping to get clear of Anha Pass before the deepening snow could close it off. When they did not quite succeed, he rode out before them and spread out a hand into the teeth of the wind, and the winds rose and threw the snow back.

Kehera had been horrified to discover that Nomoris was a

sorcerer—a man without a natural deep tie, a man on whom a deep tie had been forced, a man who now held something of the power of a king at the cost of allowing Methmeir Irekaì's will, even the king's identity, to subsume his own. Even worse, the Irekaïn Power itself would draw out Nomoris's life and strength through that unnatural bond, feeding both gradually and steadily to Methmeir Irekaì, preserving the king's youth and health and strength as Nomoris withered into age and infirmity before his time.

There were stories about sorcerers and sorcery. None of them had happy endings.

The King of Pohorir must have set that unnatural deep tie into Nomoris, and Nomoris must have allowed it to happen. Maybe Gheroïn Nomoris was the sort of man who thought all of that was a fair trade for the power that came with the deep tie. That was horrifying in a different way.

Once she knew of the tie he carried, Kehera was also terrified of the hissing cold in his voice and behind the winds he called up. She flinched from Nomoris, avoiding his eye as best she could. She didn't understand how he could call on any Pohorin Power when he was so far from its precincts.

It had said it wanted her. It had said that once it got her to its own precincts, it could take Raëhemaiëth. She didn't understand how the Irekaïn Power could do that. It was no older than Raëhemaiëth— more aggressive, yes, but no deeper. On the other hand, she truly didn't want to find out how it would carry out such threats.

She had to get away. But she saw no possibility of escape.

They met no other travelers. Only an occasional owl, floating by on silent wings, reminded her of life outside the endless days of snow and silence. Kehera rode with her eyes fixed on the mane of her horse, cold sunken so deeply into her bones that she could no longer believe it was possible to be warm. At first there was only the blank gray rock of the mountains and the occasional iron-black leafless tree, stunted by the savage winds and the lack of good soil. When they passed the

Anha Narrows, where the pass divided and they might have turned west, toward Harivir, there was a gap in the ranks of the mountains. But of course there was no way to break away from her captors, and the Narrows would be impassable already anyway.

After that, only other mountains could be seen, and sometimes a stand of the twisted black trees. As they went on, the pass become lower and wider and the trees stood more thickly along the road. Occasionally there was an evergreen among the leafless black, green needles vivid against the gray stone and white snow and black trees, a reminder of color in the world.

There were wolves in the forest. Kehera had seen them first in the middle of the pass, shadowy gray flickers of movement across the snow. One great wolf, passing quite close, had stopped and looked at Kehera, amber eyes the only color in a world of white snow and black branches. Her captors did not seem to have noticed it, and Kehera did not speak of it, feeling the wolf less a threat than Nomoris.

They passed finally into Pohorir itself on a day as cold and clear as any day from the first winter of the world. The trade town of Enchar lay just to the east, at the base of the mountains. They were still high in the mountains here, and ice had rimed the logs and stone of Enchar's walls and towers so that the city glittered in the clear air like a jeweled child's toy placed there by a giant hand.

From Enchar a wide road ran south through the foothills toward the southern provinces of Pohorir, the little towns with their lords and the larger ruled by dukes. Another road ran east to the edge of the world where the King of Pohorir ruled from Irekay, the white city carved into the chalk cliffs above the sea. That was the way Gheroïn Nomoris would take her, she knew.

At least once they left the mountains, it would not be so cold. Behind them a wolf called again into the clear sky, and she lifted her head to listen. She felt odd, as though she were waking out of a long night's dream into a bright day. The cold here was not much less, but the icy wind seemed somehow less oppressive than it had been.

Behind them, the wolf howled again, the long singing cry lingering in the still air.

Nomoris turned his horse's head toward Enchar. The animal started forward wearily. The continual cold of the pass had been hard on man and beast alike. Well fleshed and energetic in Lind, all the horses now seemed like different beasts entirely, with staring ribs and rough coats.

Kehera followed Nomoris. She let her horse pick his own path down the slick road, sitting passively in the saddle with her hands tucked inside her sleeves, hardly gripping the reins at all. She could not imagine the tired animal plunging off the road voluntarily, even if the wolves did come unexpectedly out of the mountains to leap at its throat.

The rest of the party strung back up the road, single file. None of them spoke. The pace was slow. Enchar hardly seemed to grow at all with their movement. Kehera could easily have imagined that the town was moving away from them as they approached, retreating to leave them forever in the mouth of the pass. When the road turned around the lowering curve of a mountain, Enchar slid from sight as though it were departing from the world entirely, never to return.

The black trees crowded closer to the road here, as the bare rock gave way more and more to earth, dormant but living. Leafless branches interlaced overhead, supporting a solid roof of snow, here where the trees were protected from the wind by the bulk of the mountains. It was like riding through a tunnel fashioned of ice, ribbed with trees of wrought iron and spangled with diamonds. In this closed place, sound flattened and echoed oddly, and the thud of the horses' hooves sounded dull and heavy as if they trod on a thick layer of muffling cloth.

It was hard to judge the passage of time in this place, with the sun hidden and even the daylight, filtered through the snow, taking on a strangely artificial feel, like light glowing through opaque porcelain. It made the breath come short and the heart thump with the creaking of the ice-laden branches. It felt like anything could happen . . . no, like anything was *about* to happen, any minute now, unstoppable, and the frozen world was waiting for it with its own tense expectation. Every muffled hoof-fall seemed a drumbeat carrying the party forward to some climactic moment of a play. Even Nomoris seemed to hunch his shoulders forward against some anticipated blow. Kehera fixed her gaze on her horse's mane, coarse black hairs sliding over his bay neck with every step, and took a firmer grip on the reins.

The road turned again, widening, the trees spreading out from it to give a clear view, and Enchar emerged to glitter again before them in the daylight. Kehera took a slow breath of relief without consciously realizing just how oppressive the close press of the winter forest had been.

A man stepped out of the forest to stand before them in the center of the road.

Nomoris drew up his horse sharply, lifting a hand to halt his people. He said in his flat, deep voice, "King's business, man. You would be wise to get out of my way."

The man did not appear to be impressed. He was dressed plainly, a heavy gray cloak close-drawn about his body. Lifting one hand, he put back his hood. Dark hair and dark eyes, a level stare and no sign of fear; Kehera thought he looked somehow familiar but couldn't remember where she might have seen him before. He said calmly, "I think this is as near Irekay as the princess needs to go."

Kehera, watching in amazement, felt her heart begin to pound. *A chance always comes.* And so, at last, one had come, though she couldn't tell yet just what this chance comprised.

But Nomoris tilted his head with what seemed recognition. "Ah. The lesser Gods think to take a hand. They think to balk me and so they have made a servant. But they have left it too late, and I am beyond their reach. Certainly far beyond *your* reach. The greater Gods favor my design. Your masters, too, would be wise to get out of my way."

Kehera stared from one of them to the other. The *Gods* thought to take a hand? The *lesser* Gods, and the *greater*? She was sure Nomoris meant the Fortunate Gods and the Unfortunate. She had never heard the other terms. Tiro would have. He'd have known just what Nomoris meant, and all the implications. He'd know all the stories about "servants of the Gods"; he'd know just what it meant when the Gods reached into the mortal world to twist luck and coincidence and providence. She longed for her brother beside her, though at the same time she was so glad Tiro was safe in Raëh.

The dark man did not answer Nomoris, but he lifted an eyebrow in what seemed dry skepticism. She recognized him at last. This was her father's man. Quòn. Or not exactly her father's man after all. Nomoris seemed to think Quòn was in the direct service of the Gods, somehow. Surely he had to be. How else could he have gotten ahead of them?

Nomoris started to say something else, but Quòn didn't wait to hear it. He raised a small crossbow smoothly from within his cloak and shot the Irekaïn agent in the chest. The quarrel made a little *whick* sound through the air and a muffled *thunk* as it struck home, and Nomoris sat very still for a long, long moment, looking utterly shocked, and then slowly toppled sideways from his saddle. His horse shied sideways as he fell but was too weary to go more than a few steps.

The men behind Kehera began to surge forward, but Quòn, seeming completely unconcerned, put out his other hand and was holding another small crossbow, and shot the first among them in the face. And he dropped that crossbow and suddenly had yet a third in his hand, the bolt already in place, and the rest of the men reined up hastily, lowering their own weapons. Kehera though it was Quòn's complete lack of emotion that brought everything and everyone to a halt. Such utter lack of fear was frightening—though the crossbow didn't hurt either.

"A hard journey through the pass?" Quòn said to her. "I've been waiting for days. I'm glad to see you at last. It would have been seriously inconvenient if you'd been snowbound on the way." He didn't sound annoyed, though. He sounded, if anything, slightly bored.

"You . . . serve the Fortunate Gods?" Kehera asked him. "Not my father?"

"The two services run parallel at this present," Quòn assured her, seeming unconcerned.

"But how—"

"One becomes disengaged from mortal concerns," Quòn told her. "Indeed, such detachment is a necessary prerequisite, though not sufficient. However, this is not perhaps the most appropriate moment to discuss such abstruse matters, Your Highness." He added, in a conversational tone, "I'll shoot the next man who moves, and the next after that, but I won't be able to hold them all forever. That wretched animal of yours had better have a gallop left in it."

"Yes," Kehera said. "I mean, yes, I'll do whatever you say, but we—you—we'll go back through the pass? Because I'm not sure—"

"No," Quòn told her. "The pass is impossible now. The snows have buried that road too deeply. Enchar. It's the only way open, so it will have to do. Take this." He held up a stiff roll of paper in his free hand. "I've made arrangements. Follow these directions. I'll find you there. You'd better go."

She took the paper, but then hesitated. "What about—" She glanced uneasily over her shoulder at the glowering men.

"I don't anticipate any difficulty," Quòn told her. "If these men wanted to die, they would have rushed me already. I expect we shall come to an arrangement once you are out of their reach and not so compelling a temptation toward stupidity. Go on. Don't look back. Don't look for me. I will find you in Enchar."

Kehera believed him. He was a servant of the Fortunate Gods; she could hardly imagine what that might mean, but of course he would find her in Enchar. Anyway, she knew she was done hesitating. *A chance always comes.* A chance always comes, and if you miss it, it's gone forever.

She guided her horse past Quòn and kicked the tired animal to a canter. The wind blew icy past her face, and her horse's hooves rang on the hard, frozen earth of the road.

Enchar grew ahead of her. No odd turns to the road this time; it was a straight run to the city walls. . . . How to get past them? She knew, without doubt, that she would find a way. No more tame acquiescence to the will of her father's enemies. No more captivity. There on the winter road, riding out of the mountains, Kehera made that a vow. She would never again let herself be made into a pawn, to be moved across the world at the whim of others.

Enchar was a wooden city, built of timber from the endless Pohorin forests. As she came closer, Kehera examined the walls of the city. They grew taller as she approached, the towers withdrawing modestly out of sight behind their protection. How to get in? Perhaps Quòn's directions had something about that. She let her horse slow to a walk and unrolled the paper—brittle and stiff with cold, the wax of its outer weatherproofed layer cracking as she unrolled it—and found there only terse directions: *Third street west of the square, perfumer's shop. Follow your nose. Kereis is the proprietor, he'll hide you. He's already been paid half. Destroy this.*

Kehera tore the paper into tiny bits as she rode and worried about getting into the town and finding the perfumer's shop. And once she found the shop, what if Kereis didn't think he'd been paid enough? What would she do then? She bit her lip and tried to stop thinking so far ahead. Get into Enchar, find the perfumer's shop, just that, and *then* worry about everything else.

She need not have worried, in fact, about getting into Enchar. The walls were indeed formidable, but the gates were thrown fully open and unguarded. After her first startlement, she was less surprised by this seeming carelessness. It wasn't as though an army was likely to come charging through Anha Pass in *the middle of winter,* no matter how mad the Emmeran king might be. It had been hard enough for

Nomoris to get their small party through, and as Quòn had said, every day that trickled by buried the mountains under more layers of snow. And the open gates let the people of the surrounding villages move freely in and out, which was probably good for keeping up market activity in the winter. It certainly made Kehera's life very much easier. She rode through the gates unquestioned, picking up no more than a few quick glances from the sprinkling of other passersby, and so entered the city.

Enchar was the first Pohorin city Kehera had ever seen, and there was something about it. She tried to decide where the difference lay. The streets were narrow, but that was only to be expected in a provincial city. Perhaps the difference was in the buildings on either side of the streets: tall and blank and oddly faceless, as though deliberately concealing their identities from strangers. She recognized an apothecary only by the sharp smell of pounded heart's-blood and fireflower that hung in the air in front of the shop, and a restaurant or tavern by the scent of hard cider and ale before it. There were no signs marking out these things; presumably if you didn't know what the shop was, the proprietors didn't want your business. It seemed a strange attitude, but it made her understand Quòn's directions a little better. If there were no signs, you might very well follow your nose. Once she found the square, the perfumer's shop should be possible.

Or perhaps it was the people in the streets who lent Enchar its distinct character. There were plenty of them, and they seemed normal enough, but it was odd how few of them took a second to look directly at the stranger in their midst. They peeked instead, quick covert glances as though they did not want to be seen looking.

Perhaps, Kehera thought, it was the horse that was drawing the glances, and not her. There were very few other horses on the streets. Probably she should get rid of it; if Nomoris's men were going to be looking for her, and she could hardly see how Quòn could stop them all, she certainly didn't want to help them out. Without a horse, though . . . Well, perhaps Quòn intended to hire passage with a merchant's train or something. That would make sense if they needed to get south to Roh Pass.

She told herself firmly to concentrate on the immediate necessities. Get rid of the horse. Find the square—no doubt it was in the center of town. Then the perfumer's shop.

The market square. With a mental shrug, Kehera looked about, trying to judge where the center of town might lie.

A man in a dark red cloak turned as she passed and stared up at her, his eyes narrowing. Then he put a hand on the bridle and swept back his cloak to lay his other hand on the hilt of a sword. "Who might you be?" he demanded coldly. "Get down off that animal at once."

Kehera stared at him for a second, shocked. Then she lifted her leg as though she meant to dismount, braced herself on the pommel, and kicked the man in the face as hard as she could. He fell back with a cry of outrage and pain, and she lashed the horse with the reins to make him jump forward. Behind her there were shouts. People were certainly staring now, although the street was emptying with amazing speed. The horse skidded on a patch of ice, and she threw her weight to the other side to balance him, terrified he would take her down with him. Break her leg now and she'd be in real trouble. *As if I'm not in real trouble now.* She felt an appalling desire to laugh, or perhaps weep with terror.

After the next corner, she dragged the animal to a stop and swung down from the saddle. She jumped at him, waving her arms, and he shied violently and lunged away, back around the corner. Kehera glanced around hastily. The horse was too tired to go very far. She had to get away from here. She started walking quickly, first picking a direction at random, then turning and walking toward what she guessed might be the center of town and the market square.

Her pale hair would mark her. She put her hood up. Just how badly did she stand out, in her ragged travel-worn clothing and Emmeran cloak? *Just walk.*

She tried to think. If she couldn't find the square, she still had to get off the streets. An inn? They would search the inns first, wouldn't they? A restaurant? But how long could she sit in a restaurant without attracting attention?

There was a shout behind her, not yet very close, but maybe the red-cloaked man had seen her. Without thought, Kehera turned a corner sharply and strode through the door of the first shop she came to. It was not, unfortunately, any kind of perfumer's shop—that would have been a lot to ask even if all the Fortunate Gods had been looking after her. It was a sausage shop. Strings of sausages hung in the windows, the fat kind in casings and the long, slim spicy ones that were air-dried to keep.

A bell on the door rang as it swung closed behind her. A young man brushed a curtain aside from a doorway to another room and came in. "May I assist you, mistress?" he asked politely, as if he found nothing odd in her worn dress and wide-eyed stare.

Kehera leaned back a little and peeked out the door. There were several men in red cloaks just coming around the corner, walking fast and looking as though they meant business. Straightening, she smiled nervously at the young man. "Um, do you have any pork sausage with sage and thyme?"

The young man glanced from Kehera to the door and back. "We have very fine pork sausages of all kinds," he assured her. "We offer a sampler tray to new customers, mistress, if you'd care to step into the back room?"

The thud of boots on frozen earth was close enough to hear. Or was that her heart pounding? "That sounds wonderful," Kehera assured the young man fervently, and almost stepped on his heel as he led her out of the main shop through a curtained doorway and into a little room. It was comfortably if shabbily furnished. There was a small table with several chairs drawn up to it along one wall, and a little couch at an angle to a roaring fireplace set into the opposite wall. The table was plain and scratched, but there was a large, deep bowl of water with several floating candles set on it as a decoration. The couch, too, was slightly shabby, but redeemed by a pretty throw tossed over it. There was no other door out of the room.

The bell on the door rang.

"I'll just fetch that tray," said the young man, and ducked hastily back into the shop. To alert the hunters? Kehera stood by the curtained doorway. The urge to pull the curtain aside enough to let her see into the shop was nearly overwhelming, but she knew it would be stupid to risk letting the curtain be seen moving. She stood still, listening.

"May I assist you, sirs?" said the brisk, polite voice of the young man.

"It might be to your benefit if you could," a heavy, deep voice answered, with a significant emphasis on the word "benefit." "Have you seen a young woman in the last few minutes, tall, with light-colored hair? Dressed ragged, like she'd been on the road?"

Kehera held her breath. She undid her cloak and slipped it off, laid it gently on the floor and started unbraiding her hair with flying fingers.

"I only wish I had, sir," said the young man regretfully. "Business has been slow of late. But I'm afraid I can't help you. No one like that has come in here."

"What's through there?" said the heavy voice. Kehera had a feeling she knew where the owner of that voice was pointing. She hurried on the stays of her dress, fingers stiff with fear.

"Only a sitting room we use when business is slow, sir. As it has been lately, as I said. May I interest you in some sausages? Nothing better to keep up your energy in this cold weather. Or we have some very nice smoked cheeses—"

"Check that room," said the heavy voice. Kehera shoved her boots out of sight under a chair and dove for the couch, ripping her dress in her haste to get out of it. Thank the Fortunate Gods for the floating candles! She dunked her head quickly in the water and threw it back over her shoulders, dripping heavily.

"Really, sir," protested the young man, "this is hardly necessary, I assure you—" There was the sound of a minor scuffle.

Someone ripped the curtain aside. Kehera sat up on the couch, rubbing her hair briskly with her skirt. "Oh, darling—" she began, saw the men in the doorway, emitted a small shriek, and whipped the blanket from the couch up around her shift. The discarded skirt dropped to the floor, where she hoped that any casual glance would take it for a towel. Her hair, sodden and dark with water, dripped icily down her back.

"I'm so terribly sorry, my dear!" said the young man, and turned helplessly to the other men. "Sirs, please! *My mother doesn't know!*"

One of the men smothered a laugh behind his hand. Another, owner of the heavy voice, said curtly, "Our apologies." He grabbed the sniggering one by the arm and dragged him back, letting the curtain fall. Kehera knelt on the couch, clutching the blanket and trembling slightly.

The bell on the door chimed. There was a pause.

"Are you decent?" said the young man, from the other side of the curtain.

Kehera started. "Just a minute," she said, and looked at her filthy and now damp dress with loathing. Even the pearls sewn into the hem couldn't make it look attractive. She stood up and experimented with the blanket. Yes. Not wonderful, but acceptable. "Come in," she called.

The young man brushed the curtain back and stepped in. He looked at Kehera and hastily averted his gaze. "I meant to tell you where the hide is, but there wasn't time," he said apologetically. "You were very clever, but—that is, you were very clever." Was he blushing? He was. He must be younger than he looked.

"I was desperate," Kehera said. "I was praying you weren't going to give me away—I'm so grateful you didn't. I hope I didn't get you in any trouble with those men?"

"No, no, not at all."

"Or with your mother?"

Their eyes met. A smile tugged at the corner of the young man's mouth. Kehera smiled back, and then lost control and started giggling.

The young man laughed with her, in a half-hysterical release of tension. "I can't believe you *did* that! Did you see their faces?"

"Did you, when you said that about your mother?"

The young man shook his head, still laughing. He walked across the room to perch on a corner of the table. "You must have been inspired."

"More like desperate." Kehera sat down gingerly on the couch, trying not to lose control of the blanket.

"I'm a fool," said the young man, striking himself in the forehead with the heel of one hand. He sprang back to his feet. "You need different clothes, of course. Here, I hope these'll fit well enough for now." He shoved the table aside and knelt to pry up some of the floorboards. Kehera watched with fascination as a whole section of the floor lifted up in his hands. He reached down and pulled up folded clothing, brown and tan.

"I don't mean to be ungracious," Kehera said tentatively, "but why are you helping me? Does this sort of thing happen often? I mean, forgive me for prying, but you do seem to be extremely well prepared, if you don't mind my saying so."

The young man grinned at her over his shoulder. "Anyone running from the redcloaks gets a place in the back parlor, that's one of the rules. People help out. They don't have us quite as sewn up here as they'd like to think. Someday we'll see our province go back to Kosir—or so we hope." He picked up his armful of cloth and stood up. He looked at her doubtfully, reddening slightly. "Uh, excuse me, but would you like a bath before you change?"

Kehera closed her eyes at the vision this offer summoned up after so many days on the road. "I would *love* a bath," she said fervently.

"I'll bring some water, then. More water, I mean. You already seem to have started on your hair. . . ." He grinned at her appreciatively and went on. "You'll have to be quick, you know. I don't think you'd better stay here very long, in case those redcloaks get suspicious and decide to come back for another look. As soon as you're ready, we can decide what you should do next." He hooked the curtain up and went into the outer shop. Kehera leaned against the doorframe and watched as he found a large basin and started to fill it from a spigot in the wall.

"Do you mind if I ask your name?" she asked suddenly. She couldn't keep thinking of him as That Nice Young Man in the Sausage Shop.

"Teier Lamis. Everyone knows me," he said cheerfully, and hefted the full basin with a grunt to carry it into the back room. He put it down without slopping much of the water out, which was pretty impressive, as big as the thing was. "The water's not very warm, I'm afraid. Let me get you some towels. And soap. There you go. Need anything else?" Was it significant, that he didn't ask her name in return?

Kehera accepted both towels and soap, shook her head at his question, and let him retreat beyond the curtain. The basin wasn't big enough to sit in, of course, and the water wasn't warm enough to be very inviting anyway. Kehera did the best she could standing up, trying to confine her dripping to the towels. It was much better than nothing, anyway. Amazing the things one could learn to appreciate.

The new clothing smelled strongly of camphor, but at least it was a *clean* smell, she told herself. There was a brown skirt and a matching brown outer tunic to go over a light tan blouse with long puffed sleeves. The skirt was a little too short, but not so much as to draw the eye. She got her hold-out pouch from the pile of damp cloth that she had been wearing and strapped it back to her leg, taking an odd sort of comfort from the now-familiar weight.

"I'm ready," she called, and Teier Lamis came in quickly. He carried yet another bowl of water, which he set on the table. The look he gave her was approving. "You look much better," he said. "I think you'd better dye your hair, though. Not many people have hair like that."

"Don't tell me you have dye?"

"I live to serve." Teier extracted a twist of paper from his pocket with a flourish. "It's for coloring some of the sausages, but it'll also turn your hair dark brown. My mother used it when she started going gray. Lasts pretty well too. I'll give you another packet."

"Thank you." Kehera took the packet. "How am I supposed to do this without getting it all over my new clothes?"

Teier turned diffident again. "Well, uh, I think it would be fastest if you were to, you know, sit at the table and let me do it. . . ."

"Good idea." She sat down with her back to the table, sweeping her wet hair behind her shoulders with both hands.

Teier stirred the powder into the water, gathered up her hair, and started to work in the dye. It was a lot like having Eilisè wash her hair with the delicate scented soaps used for special occasions. Except completely different. Kehera winced away from the thought, expecting a surge of grief, but the emotion she felt was only a shadow of what there had been. Had grief, too, been lost somewhere in the silent cold of the pass? *Too high a price,* she thought, and then wasn't quite sure what she meant by that. But maybe she was just tired. If the lingering numbness made it easier to think through the exhaustion, that would be helpful. She had better try to figure everything out now, then, before unbearable grief and fear crashed over her again like the black storms of winter.

Teier finished and wrapped her hair in a towel, helping her sit up. "Better rub it dry. Do you want to keep those?" He gestured toward the heap of discarded clothing.

Kehera thought of the pearls in the hem of the skirt. "Yes, please."

"Amazing," said the young man. "No offense. Now, let me get that sampler platter and you can tell me what else you need."

The young man, relieved that Kehera actually knew what to do next, was perfectly willing to show her the way to Kereis's shop. It apparently wasn't even very far. He handed her a basket of sausages to complete her disguise and then led her out of his shop, pausing to lock the door behind them with a little brass key. Kehera stood beside him nervously, trying not to look like a fugitive.

"Walk like you can't imagine why anyone should be interested in you," the young man advised her. "Nothing makes a person look so ordinary as a basket full of sausages, you know." He offered her his arm, smiling.

It was a ten-minute walk through lightly peopled streets. No one showed the slightest interest in them, although once, spotting a couple of redcloaks, Teier whisked them quickly into a shop. They spent several uneasy moments examining scented candles and fancy perfumed soaps while the redcloaks passed by. Teier insisted on buying Kehera a bit of hard soap in the shape of a swan, scented like sweet lemon.

"It surpasses even camphor," she murmured gravely, and put it away carefully in a pocket while he chortled.

But when they reached Kereis's shop, it was closed and locked, the shutters shut over the windows and two redcloaks stationed at the door.

Teier and Kehera walked past on the other side of the street, pretending not to see the redcloaks, and turned a corner, strolling on in a random direction. "So, new plan," he said to her, his voice just a little strained. "Any ideas?"

Kehera shook her head mutely. She blinked hard and rubbed her eyes, feeling like she should cry, but too tired even for that. It was so hard. Everything was *so hard*. She wanted to just stop and magically find herself at home and everything back the way it had been, the way it should be, Eilisè humming in the next room and Tiro barging in to tell her some old tale about the servants of the Gods that he'd read in some dusty book that made sense of everything that had happened. . . . Tiro at least might someday tell her old stories. Eilisè would never again sing any songs at all. Kehera might never even have a chance to tell Eilisè's mother how Eilisè had saved her life.

She had no idea at all how to get home now. She felt like she would never have another idea as long as she lived.

"All right," the young man said gently, and they walked for a while in silence. Then he said, "I'm not asking who's after you. Someone powerful, someone who can set the redcloaks hunting, obviously, and that's enough for me. You need to hide for a while, right? We can find a place. You could stay with my mother, maybe. Or do you need to get clear away from Enchar, hide in the country?"

Kehera nodded helplessly. That was what she needed. To get away. To hide. If she couldn't go back through Anha Pass . . . she had no choice, obviously, but to go south. The only pass that was open all winter was Roh, in Eäneté. She had no idea how she could possibly get all the way to Eäneté without being caught. But the thought of traveling south *felt* right somehow, and no other possibilities came to mind.

She didn't see how she could possibly wait for Quòn. She guessed something had gone terribly wrong, because how else had her enemies learned about Kereis's shop? She couldn't imagine what could have stopped Quòn, but Nomoris had *said* he was too late. And now those soldiers were right there in her way. She greatly feared she was on her own—and if not, then she had to trust Quòn would find her no matter that she left the path he'd meant her to take. She looked anxiously at Teier, wondering how far he was willing—or able—to help her. "I need to get through Roh Pass," she told him in a low voice.

"Roh!" he exclaimed, but quietly. Then he was silent for a time while they walked on. But at last he drew her to a stop, looking at her seriously. "It's a long way. You'll have to leave Enchar, travel right through Kimsè and far into Eäneté. They say no one comes or goes through Roh Pass save under the eye of the Wolf Duke, and they say the yellow eyes of the Wolf notice everything that moves."

Kehera nodded, but she wasn't actually listening. She felt overwhelmed enough without counting off the obstacles. Or listening to someone else count them off. "If Roh is the only pass open all winter, then it has to be Roh. If I can get to Eäneté, I'll find a way."

"Well . . ." The young man hesitated. "Well, if you have to travel quietly, the journey will probably take you some weeks. I doubt you'll reach Eäneté until after the Month of Frost turns to the Iron Hinge Month, and then you'll be looking to cross through the pass at the worst time of year." When she did not seem deterred by this idea, he went on, a trifle reluctantly. "But . . . if you're sure, then I know a way that might work. I know . . . a man. He smuggles people sometimes. For a fee, of course." He gave her a doubtful look, clearly wondering if she could pay.

"Can he be trusted?" Kehera asked, avoiding the other question for the moment.

"I think so. He's honest. Everyone says so. If you pay him, he'll do what you hire him for and won't try to gouge you again halfway to Eäneté. But I don't think you'll like his method."

As it turned out, Teier was right. Kehera hated everything about the proposed method.

8

On the twenty-eighth day of the Month of Frost, in the high country of Eäneté, snow fell from a pewter sky.

The town and the mountains beyond were lost to the snow, which constricted the world to a narrow view of blowing white. The snow worried Innisth. A storm such as this might drive a hunting party to shelter. Cold, clear winter weather: that was best for hunting. Scent lingered in the cold, and the voices of the hounds carried well in the crystalline air. But this . . . No one hunted in such weather.

This storm had descended days ago, and since then broken only twice, each time briefly, before closing in again. That would not matter if Deconniy's party had reached Geif's lodge, but if they had been forced into shelter too early, then he did not see how his young captain could recover the plan. He turned over ideas in his mind, looking for another that might work as well. Unfortunately, killing Laören and giving his body to the wolves still seemed impractical.

Gereth rapped quietly on the doorframe and came in. He was not smiling, Innisth saw at once, and consciously forced himself to relax his shoulders because he would not allow himself to appear concerned before his household.

"Captain Deconniy has returned, Your Grace," Gereth told him. "Lord Laören and his servants chose not to return with him, as Lord Laören decided suddenly that it would be best if he went on to the town of Tisain to speak to Lord Geif about urgent business."

"This seems promising," Innisth observed, his tone neutral. "I look forward to hearing the full report. You may admit Deconniy at once."

"Ah. As perhaps Your Grace has ascertained, it's possible that not everything in the tale will please you."

"I see." The duke considered what might have happened to put that note of constraint into his seneschal's voice, and Gereth was right: The possibilities that seemed most likely did not please him. He said, his tone remote, "Nevertheless, you may admit him."

"Your Grace." Gereth went out, and Innisth heard muffled voices. Then the seneschal returned, this time accompanied by the young captain.

Deconniy stood straight and looked Innisth directly in the face, but the duke could not miss his pallor, which was more than weariness and cold.

"All went well," Deconniy said immediately, his tone crisply professional. "I spoke to your huntsman and made sure we rode toward Tisain; we put up a stag at nearly the ideal place and rode hard after it, and your huntsman made sure when it circled back north that we lost it and went on south and east. The huntsman did a good job all through, Your Grace; he made it look just right, and I want to commend him."

Innisth inclined his head in acknowledgment.

"So we were well placed when the snow began. I told your huntsman to declare it looked like a blizzard—so it proved, of course—and then I said I knew of a hunting lodge where we could pass the days comfortably; not in Eäneté, but as Lord Laören was of our number, that would not signify. So we came to the lodge after a hard ride. Geif's staff made us welcome, of course, because of Laören, and the next day one of his people turned up the first of your papers, Your Grace, carelessly left out in Geif's bedroom, which of course Laören had taken for his own. Once Laören became suspicious, he quickly found the base coins and the accounts. Thus, when the storm lifted, he took his people and went on to find Lord Geif at his own house."

"Ideal," said Innisth without emphasis. "Well done, my captain."

"Yes," said Deconniy, and then added, his tone flattening, "Lord Laören . . . Unlike Your Grace, Lord Laören does not permit refusal."

"Of course not." Anger built in Innisth, anger on Deconniy's behalf, yes, but also a surge of outraged possessiveness at Laören's trespass, to touch what belonged to *him*; and beyond even that, outrage that Irekaì's pet had dared take a pleasure Innisth had denied himself. Tamping down his rising temper, he said flatly, "I regret to hear so."

"Yes," said the young officer. Color rose in his face and subsided again, leaving him paler than before. "I assure Your Grace, I would have refused. But Laören—" He cut that off. After a moment, he said instead, "I would not have told you, except he said he will return to Eäneté before he turns again toward Irekay. And that he will ask you to give me to him when he goes. And that you will not be able to refuse. He will take me, because if you balk, he will order you to accompany him yourself. He knows I will tell you that, and he knows you would yield me up to him to avoid that command—"

"Enough," said Innisth. "Get out." A moment before, he had thought himself angry. *Now* he was angry. It was as though the very stone of the mountains had cracked to let forth fire, a dark and heavy fire that rose against the lowering sky. He wanted violence and blood and death; he wanted to tear down wounded prey. Deconniy hesitated, perhaps began to speak, but Gereth gripped the younger man's arm and drew him away.

His own anger, the anger of the Eänetén Power, Innisth could hardly tell where one ended and the other began. But it did not matter. At the heart, they were the same. He moved from room to room in his apartment, but found solace in none of them, and went at last up to the high gallery. He paced there, back and forth through the white wind, until his anger at last burned out its first violence. Then he stood for some time, his hands gripping the icy railing, refusing to flinch from the bitter violence of the wind, gazing out at the snow and the glimpses of the mountains beyond until the muted light began to fail and the early darkness of the storm closed itself down around the tower.

At last, having mastered himself, he turned back into the house. He believed he had mastered himself. Until he walked through his outermost reception room and through the audience chamber beyond and turned without thinking into his private sitting room, and found Eöté there, tucked into his favorite chair. The chair had been drawn close by the fire, the heavy table shifted to one side to make room for it, though the girl still looked cold. She was all but lost behind its high arms. A bundle of dark blue cloth and silver thread lay across her knees, but she was not setting stitches into the cloth. She was still as a mouse, gazing up at Captain Deconniy, who stood with his hands tucked into his belt, his head bent a little, his own gaze not on the girl but on the leaping fire. The air in the room was fragrant with burning cedar.

The anger he had put aside rose again in a violent rush. Innisth clenched his teeth, took tight hold of his temper, and asked, his tone measured, "Well, Captain? You thought of some other detail I must know?"

The girl seemed to shrink into the chair, but Deconniy, visibly bracing himself, faced the duke. "I'll go with him. I'll go with him, and once we're well away, out of Eäneté, I'll get clear and cut around north. I won't double back; there'll be no reason for him to think you've set me to it. I'll head for Enchar; let his people track me that way. It'll be none of your doing. Then he'll have no reason to blame you—especially not if he's got Geif to content his malice—"

"Did you share this clever plan with Etar?" Innisth asked. "What advice did he give you? That you would not escape, that Laören is well versed in malice and would not be so careless?"

Captain Deconniy began to speak, but hesitated.

"You would go bound and under guard and you would not escape," said the duke. "No. Bravely offered, but no."

"There's no other way!" Deconniy said. There was expression in his voice now. He sounded desperate.

"There is always a way," Innisth told him. The beginnings of an idea touched the back of his mind, but the remnants of anger were too much in the way and he could not make it out. He shook his head, but . . . no. It would take time. He said curtly, "Attend me tomorrow. For tonight, you may retire."

"But—" Deconniy protested.

"You may retire," repeated the duke. He stepped to the side and lifted a hand to indicate the door.

Deconniy said stubbornly, "I would rather—"

Innisth, his patience at last fraying beyond bearing, took the one step necessary, closed a hand on the young captain's arm, and shoved him back. Deconniy, caught by surprise, stumbled and caught at the tall chair. The girl made a tiny, terrified noise, cowering. Ignoring her with an effort, Innisth threw Deconniy back against the heavy table, using his thigh to block the man's instinctive twist away and his own weight to pin him. One hand went to control Deconniy's right wrist; the other closed on his hair, dragging his head back.

Deconniy's eyes were wide with shock and fear, but he had not made a sound. After his first reflexive struggle, he drew a swift breath, shut his eyes, and gave up all resistance, yielding to the duke's grip, letting himself be pinned.

Innisth closed his own eyes, battling briefly and savagely with himself and with the Eänetén Power, and somehow managed to find the will to loosen his hold. He stepped away, shaking with the effort of restraint, and turned his back to conceal his expression. His hands were shaking. He closed them into fists to hide the fact. Behind him, he heard Deconniy get unsteadily to his feet. The room was so quiet, he could hear even Eöté's quick, frightened breaths. He wanted her, suddenly and ferociously—her very terror was seductive; he knew exactly how she would tremble and whimper. In her fear, she would yield to anything. He cut the compelling images off sharply and locked them away, refusing to think of it. Better to take his young captain than the fragile girl—but he was not Laören. He was not Geif. He would not do that, either.

When he thought he would be able speak without his voice shaking, he turned. "Do not defy me," he said. "Especially not when I am already angry." Despite all he could do, his voice cracked and broke. He bit off the last word savagely.

Deconniy had also used that brief moment of time to collect himself. He stood very still. His gray uniform shirt was torn where it had been raked along the edge of the table. He drew breath. "Your Grace—I—"

"Don't speak," Innisth said curtly. He had disciplined his voice, savagely, to something approximating its customary impassivity. If he moved, he was afraid of what he might do. "Go," he said briefly. And when the man still hesitated, repeated harshly, "Go!"

Deconniy backed away, eyes still wide with shock, reached the door, and fled. The duke strode away as well, the other way, toward the privacy of his own bedchamber, where no one would dare intrude without a very explicit command.

Caèr Reiöft, who had once received that exact command and had never viewed that order as ceasing, came in only a very few moments later, carrying a decanter of dark wine and two crystal goblets.

"Deconniy?" Innisth asked him.

"I sent him away. Don't concern yourself," Reiöft said softly. "You did not harm him, and another time, he will know better." He set the goblets down on the sideboard with the tiniest click of glass against wood and poured, expertly.

"And the girl?"

"Far too fragile to bear your presence. She has been broken too often, I believe, and never given sufficient peace to heal. Eäneté is better for her than Tisain, but I doubt she will ever feel confident of any Pohorin Immanent. Or any Pohorin lord." He paused, then shrugged.

"It's a pity Lord Laören ever set eyes on her, but there, it can't be undone. I told her to make up a pallet in your other sitting room and called another woman to tend her. Ranè. You don't mind Ranè, my lord, and she's good with the damaged ones. She'll keep the girl entirely out of your way."

"You think I want her *out of my way*? Perhaps tonight I want her very much *in* my way."

Reiöft lifted one eyebrow. "Well, I don't think so, my lord. You're in a rare temper just now, every inch the Wolf Duke, and if you're going to be in a temper, better you take it out on me." Leaving the goblets, he moved softly across the room and poured a basin of water for the duke to wash his face and hands.

Innisth had known exactly what the other man would say. The moment was all but scripted. Even so, he gave him a hard look. "Is that yours to decide?"

Reiöft set the basin down and bowed his head. "No, lord. I beg forgiveness, lord." He glanced up through his eyelashes. "Will you want me to stay with you tonight, lord?"

Innisth reached out, almost involuntarily, to touch the other man's face. The willing submission satisfied the ferocious possessiveness that drove him, and at last the Eänetén Power began to subside. He murmured, "I should have called for you earlier."

"Of course," agreed Reiöft. "You should always call for me. Though it's a little cold on the gallery. But exciting, when the winds are high and wolf-fierce." He was smiling, a tender expression with only a trace of fear in it—just enough to be seductive.

But Innisth dropped his hand. "No," he said. "I would be cruel tonight, Caèr. No"—as Reiöft made to speak—"I know you are willing, but I should not like the memory tomorrow." He stepped back decisively, mastering himself, the anger settling to the back of his heart. "You may retire," he said. "Tomorrow—" He paused.

"Yes, Your Grace?" Reiöft asked respectfully.

The idea had leaped clear at last. Innisth turned it over in his mind. A steady hand, and a steady will, and courage. And loyalty. He did not doubt three of the four. The fourth, he seldom trusted. Now, after the past hour, less still. But fear of Laören and hatred of Geif . . . yes. Leaving aside any questions of trustworthiness and loyalty, Verè Deconniy of all men would have reason to want this plan to work. More, to work *perfectly.* "Well, we shall see," said the duke aloud. "We shall see. I think perhaps I shall not retire just yet. I think perhaps I must call for Captain Deconniy after all."

"Lord?" Reiöft asked, his tone faintly reproving.

Innisth almost laughed. "Not for that reason! No. However, do not reassure him. Let him assume—let all the household assume—that is exactly why I want him. Inform him I have sent for him, Caèr. And collect two practice swords and bring them here. But quietly. Quietly."

"Your Grace is always wise and clever," Reiöft murmured, which was his way of asking if the duke was quite sure. But when Innisth only gave him a brief nod in return, he smiled and bowed and went quietly away to do as he had been ordered.

It took some time for Deconniy to present himself. Innisth was not surprised. He would not have been entirely surprised if the man, driven beyond endurance by the lords of Pohorir one and all, had simply fled. North toward Enchar, if he were wise, rather than risk the pass. It would not have been an unreasonable choice.

But the young captain did come, in the end. He came very quietly. He had put aside his sword and carried not so much as a knife at his belt—that was a statement, of sorts, along with his very presence.

Innisth was now clad in a light short-sleeved shirt and hose, and over this only a long robe. Deconniy's eyes went to his face, dropped lower, and flicked away at once. Color rose in his face.

"Sit down," Innisth said, gesturing to a chair close by the fire. He took a facing chair and waited.

Deconniy sank down as ordered. His hands shifted restlessly across the arms of the chair until he finally folded them in his lap like a polite child. Innisth saw his throat move as he swallowed.

"Regardless of any other impression you might have gathered, I actually sent for you," said Innisth, somewhat regretfully, "in your professional capacity. Please compose yourself."

Color came and went in the captain's face. "I thought—but you said—I—" He stopped and took a breath, then said more firmly, "I did not mean to defy you. Forgive my insolence."

Innisth nodded slightly. "You were afraid. I understood that. But I was angry, and the Eänetén Power was pressing me. You must learn to recognize such moments. But that danger is past, and the other you need not fear. Now. Your professional opinion, if you please. Rate your skill with the sword for me, my captain, in comparison with all other soldiers in my service."

Deconniy closed his eyes, visibly disciplined his mind to the task, opened them, and said, "Captain Etar can beat me four times out of five. Mattin Periyr is better, at least with sword alone. Hetgaiy Simil is better . . . in some ways."

"Vaì Tejef?"

"I would rate myself . . . about equal to Lieutenant Tejef, Your Grace, or a little better."

"But it would be safe to say that you rate your skill quite highly."

The captain flushed a little again. He said simply, "I'm very good, Your Grace, yes."

Innisth stood up and walked across the room. He poured a goblet of water from a carafe on the sideboard and raised an interrogative eyebrow at Deconniy. The captain started to shake his head, reconsidered, and said, "Thank you, Your Grace."

The duke poured a second goblet and brought it to him. Deconniy took it gingerly, sipped, and cleared his throat.

"There will be a sparring accident," the duke told him. He leaned his hip against the arm of his chair. "A misjudged blow during a practice bout, a failure to block adequately. Such misfortunes are common, I believe. I will be wounded in the leg. The injury will be sufficiently severe as to render me unable to travel for some considerable time, but not, of course, so severe as to permanently deprive me of the use of the leg. Because you dealt such a blow, you will be arrested and held for execution, but naturally the execution will have to be delayed until I have recovered sufficiently to attend. That recovery will take some time. Certainly long enough that Lord Laören will not be able to linger to witness the event." He paused, lifting one shoulder slightly. "It is possibly a trifle obvious, but we shall be certain the injury is severe enough to put off suspicion."

The captain said nothing, even though the duke paused to give him a chance to do so.

"You may speak," Innisth said patiently. "In this matter, I depend upon your judgment, and you may speak freely. Say what you wish to say."

Meeting his eyes, Deconniy said, "Your Grace, forgive me, but this seems very dangerous to me. Sparring accidents with sharp weapons can be serious. A wound in the leg—I understand your intention, but a slip, a misjudgment, you could be crippled. You could even die, Your Grace."

"That would indeed be unfortunate. I give you leave to suggest a different plan. One that would protect not only me from Laören's malice, but also yourself."

"It's not plausible. You never spar with us."

"Does Lord Laören know that? Still, you are correct. There must be a reason I would spar with you in particular. One obvious reason suggests itself. You are not unattractive. Sparring is . . . another form of exercise, perhaps. As an added benefit, Lord Laören should be both offended and jealous, and this should distract him further. You will not, of course, be able to deny that I have taken you to my bed."

Color had risen in Deconniy's face. "I see. That's why—all right. I do see. That will provide time for us to practice, then. Because this will take practice, if it is to look real." He looked at the duke, waiting for an acknowledging nod, then added, "You intend Laören to witness the accident?"

"Indeed. Which carries dangers of its own. I am, in fact, not a master with the sword. Making it look real will be your task. I will be fighting quite in earnest. Your part will be threefold: to avoid injury to yourself; to avoid injuring me, aside from the necessary blow; and, I fear, to avoid winning so quickly that the match appears obviously thrown."

"I . . . see."

"If you know yourself to be incapable of the described procedure, tell me now."

"I . . . believe I can do it, Your Grace."

"Practice will, of course, be necessary. As you observed. We will begin tonight. I have two swords here. Practice weapons, of course. No one will hear. These rooms are quite well muffled against sound."

Deconniy flushed again, but stood hastily and went to examine the swords Reiöft had brought. They were good, plain practice weapons, lead drilled into the wood to mimic the heft of real weapons. Deconniy handed one to the duke, hilt first, laying the blade across his forearm as courteously as though he surrendered an actual sword. Innisth accepted the practice weapon gravely. He set it across the arms of his chair long enough to remove his robe.

Deconniy shifted the chairs and the table out of the way, then turned to collect the other sword. Turning back, the captain started to lift his sword in salute and then paused. He said, "What of your tie to the Eänetén Power? Or . . . as this is not a real weapon . . . but even a wooden sword . . ." He hesitated.

Innisth gave him a cool, ironic stare. "Yes," he acknowledged. "I will persuade Eänetaìsarè to set its close guard aside for this purpose. Any blow you strike will not be blocked. It will be quite possible for you to kill me . . . even with a wooden sword . . . if you do not take care."

There was a pause. The quiet room suddenly seemed much quieter. The red light of the fire gilded Deconniy's cheek and arm and made the sword he held look almost real.

Deconniy took a deep breath. "How can you trust me so much?"

"Are you not trustworthy?" Innisth picked up his sword and lifted it in a slow, careful salute, moving out into the center of the room.

The first exchange was rapid and brief and left the duke with a bruised hip and a worse bruise across his thigh, where Deconniy had pulled a blow not quite in time.

Flinching back, the captain grounded the tip of his sword and lifted his other hand to signal a break. "Your Grace—" he began, and shook his head. "Forgive me. I thought you would block that blow."

"Did you not believe me when I told you that I was not skilled? It is generally assumed, of course, that a duke *should* be skilled. It is, however, a rare soldier of mine who could not defeat me in an even contest."

Deconniy stood still, bemused.

"I'm better with knives," Innisth added, and advanced.

Deconniy jerked up his sword. The second exchange was much more careful, as the captain delicately probed his duke's skill. Several minutes into it, Innisth found himself suddenly advancing, pushing back the younger man, who retreated, and retreated again, circling the room, face taut with concentration. The thud and clatter of the swords, the harsh breathing of exertion, the muffled thud of footsteps on the floor filled the room. The exertion was not unpleasant. Desire rose, fierce and aggressive, and Innisth drove his young captain back in truth.

Until, with a sudden step and twist, Deconniy evaded a slashing blow and caught Innisth's sword hand in a tight hold. Simultaneously he brought his own blade across and down in a sharp arc that ended, lightly, against the duke's thigh. For a moment both men stood motionless, body to body, as close as lovers.

Deconniy broke the hold and stepped back.

"Very good," Innisth commended him, catching his breath. He put his sword down and opened and closed his sword hand carefully, investigating the bruises where his fingers had been crushed against the wire-bound hilt of his sword. His whole arm and shoulder ached from the unaccustomed weight, in fact, and he thought he could feel every bruise.

"I'm sorry, Your Grace," said Deconniy, watching. "I'll be more careful next time."

Innisth glanced at him sharply. "You will be as careful as is consonant with the exigency of the moment. I am hardly likely to fret over a bruise or two, my captain."

Deconniy bowed his head in acknowledgment.

"I gather you will indeed be able to perform as will be required."

"Yes, Your Grace." The captain nodded with conviction. "It needs practice, to make it look real, but it can be done. The most difficult part will be judging the strength of the blow." He hesitated. "You understand, Your Grace, I am quite serious when I tell you this is dangerous. There is a chance of crippling—a cut to the muscles of the leg can be very serious—"

"I shall, of course, have my physicker standing ready," Innisth told him shortly. "And Eänetaìsarè should assist me in that regard. Still, I understand that practice will be important. It will probably be some days before Laören returns. We shall practice every night. You may sleep here. On the couch, of course."

Deconniy hesitated, began to speak, then changed his mind and nodded.

Innisth set his teeth against a sudden, powerful urge to order him to strip. Why not the reality, if there must be the appearance? It would not take from the young captain anything Laören had not already taken. Deconniy would still cooperate in this little play—he could not possibly risk doing anything else—

Except, of course, it would be an unconscionable abuse of whatever trust Deconniy might have given his duke.

Innisth said, his tone remote, "Go to bed. Reiöft will be in quite early to wake me, and you may then depart about your other duties." He walked away, into the inner bedchamber, and shut the connecting door. It closed with a quiet *click*, leaving him alone. Dimly from the other room came the sounds of his officer making ready to retire. Innisth set his teeth. However hard the Eänetén Power pressed him, he could not send for Caèr if he was supposed to be lying with Deconniy. It was going, he feared, to be a long night.

❋ ❋ ❋

Over the next days, practice shifted from wooden swords to edged steel. Innisth learned to keep an even tempo of steps and blows, to take the opportunities Deconniy let him have, to block the blows he knew were coming. The young captain was a good teacher, far better than the armsmaster Innisth's father had once set to the task of instructing his son. . . . Innisth turned his mind deliberately from those memories.

With Verè Deconniy, it was like a pattern dance. One learned the steps more easily with a partner whose lead could be trusted. Deconniy would not let him learn the exact time the true blow would come, however. That, he varied, lest the duke learn to flinch and so give the whole gambit away.

With the duke's leave, Deconniy also spent one whole afternoon at the slaughterhouse outside of the town, and came back quiet and pale. "It's harder than I thought, to make the blow only so hard and no harder, to deliver a cut only so deep and no deeper," he told Innisth. "And I spoke to your physicker—only in general terms, of course, Your Grace. This is more dangerous than I thought. And I already thought it was dangerous."

"Your alternate plan?" Innisth asked him, impatient with this timidity.

Deconniy shook his head. "I will go back to the slaughterhouse tomorrow, Your Grace. I've told them it's a study of mine, which method of putting an edge on a sword is better."

"There's more than one method?"

Deconniy, easier with the duke now, laughed. Innisth almost smiled.

But it was a difficult week. He had to keep Verè Deconniy close; nor could he send Eöté away, lest she be endangered when Laören returned. The Eänetén Power pressed him, wanting them both.

At least Eöté did not seem so very frightened of Deconniy. They were both originally of Tisain, had both fled to Eäneté; they had that in common. Both had been abused by Laören; perhaps that produced a kind of bond. Or perhaps the girl reminded Deconniy of his sister. Or perhaps he favored her on her own account. Innisth could hardly deny the appeal of extreme vulnerability.

However, it seemed to him that with every day that passed, the girl became even more subdued. Innisth had no patience to spare to reassure her, though this mattered little, as he was aware she would not find any word or gesture from him reassuring. He made sure she was provided with small tasks: the embroidery she liked and intricate lacework she clearly enjoyed. But he also made sure she kept out of his way. The restraint wore at him.

"You might spare yourself a little of the generosity you offer your servants," Gereth told him, the third time he brought the duke a supper tray and found it untouched on his return. He cut a sliver of ham, folded it into a bit of bread and held it out.

Innisth gave him an austere look.

"Eat it," Gereth said sharply. "You worry us all. You will need your strength when Laören returns. Do you want to bleed to death because you've weakened yourself through all this unnecessary abstemiousness?"

"Gereth," the duke said, his tone warning.

"You are frightening Reiöft. You are frightening Deconniy. You are frightening Etar. And you are frankly terrifying me. Is that what you want?"

Innisth sighed, and took the food.

"Good. Thank you. I hope you will do us all the favor of finishing this entire tray. Now, I've worked out one or two things we might do if you are incapacitated and Laören becomes difficult. I have discussed these plans with Etar, who requests the opportunity to put them to you, Your Grace. I am going to be otherwise occupied for this next little while, because I am going to go into town and find someone suitable for your . . . other needs." He held up a hand as Innisth started to speak. "Lord Laören will return very soon. The word from Tisain is that he had been much involved there. But we know he left the lord's hall early yesterday, Geif in tow—"

"I am aware of this," snapped the duke.

"Of course, Your Grace. And so naturally we are all on edge. How not? But better for us all if *you* are . . . not so much on edge as the rest of us. I will find someone suitable. And when you meet Laören, he will recognize at last that he should be afraid of you."

"Will he?"

"You do have that effect on people, Your Grace. Particularly at moments when you have allowed your Power to sate its . . . other desires. That will be half the contest right there."

"Gereth, I will go myself. You do not gladly take on the role of procurer."

"You don't have time. You must work with our earnest Captain Deconniy. Which will further strain your hold on your Power. I know," the seneschal added in a gentler voice, "that this is not something you like to hear spoken aloud. But I know you, and I know how the Eänetén Power presses you. This is something I can do. I will do it."

Innisth was not often compelled to yield an argument. Not even to Gereth. But he could not argue any point his seneschal had raised. He said after a moment, "Someone who will not be missed. Someone whose death will benefit Eäneté."

Gereth lifted his eyebrows. "Yes," he said. "Of course. I will find precisely the right sort, Innisth. I am hardly likely to make a mistake in this."

"True," Innisth conceded. "You, least of all. Very well." His stomach clinched hard with anticipation. He smiled, knowing his face now was the face of the Wolf Duke. He said, "Yes. Go, then. Tonight—no, I know, very well. Tomorrow, then."

"Assuredly," Gereth murmured. And withdrew, leaving Innisth still edgy, but with a different and more welcome kind of tension.

9

Kehera hated Teier's suggestion. But it seemed the only way.

Slavery was illegal in every country but Pohorir. Kehera had never even met a slave, much less considered what it would be like to pretend to *be* one. To travel as a slave in a slave trader's wagon train, at the mercy of the slave trader. It seemed a dreadful idea.

But Teier said this man regularly smuggled people from one town to another. Mostly from other parts of Pohorir to Enchar, mostly in the summer when the folk he smuggled might make it through Anha Pass and then go anywhere they liked. They paid, of course. But Kehera thought a couple of her pearls would probably meet the slaver's price, and who would look among a slaver's merchandise for a free girl?

"It's the only way I know," Teier told her, and in the end Kehera agreed to at least meet the slave trader.

His name was Parren. Once she met him, she had to admit that he seemed surprisingly normal. Even . . . nice.

He was a big man with a deep, rumbly voice, tall enough that the top of Kehera's head would not quite reach his collarbone, wide enough that he probably outweighed her three times over. He had long red hair pulled back and bound at his neck in the mountain style, and a thick curly beard of the same color framing his broad mouth. His arms, and the vee of his chest visible through the open throat of his shirt, had the same curly red hair. Combined with his direct look and warm smile, it made him look like a particularly friendly bear. Kehera returned his smile involuntarily.

"Oh, aye, I can do it right enough," he promised her. "No doubt about it, and the redcloaks none the wiser for it." He looked Kehera up and down, smiling, his blue eyes shrewd and kind. "It's the Eänetén pass you're heading for? Then it's not the redcloaks will be your problem. It's the Wolf Duke."

"You know how to stay out of his way," Teier observed. "Or so you've told me any number of times, Parren."

A rumbling laugh. "Very true. Very true. You get good, plump girls in Eäneté, even in winter, fetch a top price in Irekay. Mind, you don't want to catch the Wolf's eye while you're in his lands. But I'll get you there, right enough, and what you do after that is no concern of mine."

"I will manage," Kehera told him quietly. Just that quickly, she was committed. It was . . . terrifying. But she was intensely relieved, too, to have found a way out of Enchar, to be moving again, this time on her own terms and toward home. She turned to Teier. "I'll remember all the help you gave me. I'm so grateful for your kindness."

The young man gave her a last shy smile, and that was the memory she knew she would carry away from Enchar: the young man from the sausage shop, with his shy manner and quick kindness, who in a moment of danger had bought her a piece of soap in the shape of a swan.

Parren guided her across a wide, muddy yard bordered on every side by warehouses and cluttered at the moment with waiting wagons and a few men on horseback. More men stood in a loose cluster near a smaller group of girls. Kehera realized with a slight shock that these must be Parren's slaves. She did not know exactly what she had expected, but not such quiet, normal-looking people. There was no evidence of chains and no guards with whips standing over them. A few even held bundles that she guessed must contain their own possessions. Yet they were slaves. She could see the brands when she looked more closely: a little hourglass shape on the right cheek of each man, the mark old and white on a couple, vividly fresh on others. The girls were branded on the shoulder where it wouldn't show. Buyers preferred that. She'd heard so, at least, and thought it barbaric, as everything about Pohorin slavery was barbaric, but mostly she was just relieved that girls weren't ordinarily branded where the mark would show.

Brand or not, she would have to be a slave too, until they arrived in Eäneté. Then she would pay Parren and escape through Roh Pass and go home. And all these other people would be left behind. They would be taken away to be sold to anyone who wanted to buy them. It seemed impossibly awful. But none of these people looked especially frightened. They mostly looked cold and bored.

"You'll be traveling in the wagon with the other girls," Parren told her. "Only a few others. They don't often sell their girls here in Enchar. I mostly get men here and girls in Eäneté, but this trip I've got a few, including a real little one. Tell her you're her new big sister, you hear? Little ones, they like to play that kind of pretend—anybody pokes his head in, get her babbling. She'll do it perfectly. People believe babies' chatter, see?"

This was actually a very clever idea. Kehera's estimation of the slave trader rose. She asked, "How long do you expect it will take us to get to Eäneté?"

An expansive shrug. "Who can say? If the weather is good, not so long. Maybe eighteen, maybe twenty days, maybe a little more. Me, I plan for bad weather, but not too *much* bad weather! I hope not much more than twenty days. Once we're past Kimsè and into Eäneté Province, the roads will be good. The Wolf Duke keeps his roads in good repair, whatever else you might say about him. Here, that's the wagon, with the other girls. It's lucky you caught me! We will finish loading very soon."

Two of the girls looked like they were probably about ten, possibly twins. Both were pretty, one actually lovely. Then there was the little girl, a child of perhaps five or six years. An older girl, maybe fourteen or fifteen, held her by the hand. Kehera thought at first that they must be sisters, but they did not look at all alike, so perhaps they weren't.

The men stood a little distance away from the girls. There were more of them than of the girls—nine, she counted. One, young and sullen, his brand new and painful, looked about her own age. He stood slouched, his hands tucked under his arms to keep them warm. Kehera found herself in sympathy with his sullen expression. Another man, bigger and older, with a plain face and a crooked nose, watched without expression as Parren's employees loaded the wagons. His brand was new as well, she could see. He stood straight, like a soldier, his arms crossed over his chest, but after a moment Kehera saw that unlike the rest of the slaves, he was chained—an iron manacle around each wrist, the chain just long enough to let him cross his arms. Maybe he had been a thug, a brawler, a thief, something of the sort, and so arrested and condemned to slavery. She didn't know how people became slaves here, but that made sense. But the oldest of the men was about fifty, with ink stains on his hands. She couldn't believe *he* was a thief or a brawler. Kehera wondered how he had come to be standing in the muddy court-yard with the rest of them.

The biggest difference between these slaves and ordinary people, Kehera decided, was that the slaves were quieter. They hardly spoke among themselves at all, and none of them spoke to her. Taking that cue, she said nothing herself. They watched the wagons being readied with no sign of either pleasure or displeasure, as if their imminent departure from Enchar was a matter of indifference to them. The exception was the little girl, who swung impatiently on the hand of the girl minding her and asked questions.

"Are we going in the wagons, Reilliy?"

"Yes, of course we are. You know that," said the girl impatiently. "Please don't fidget so, Geris. Aren't you a big enough girl to stand still?"

"Yes!" the child asserted. She stood still for a minute and then tugged on Reilliy's hand again. "*When* are we going in the wagons, Reilliy?"

"Soon. Hush!" Reilliy answered.

"Let me take her for a minute," said the man with ink stains, stepping over. He swung the little girl up into his arms. He murmured to her in a low voice, and she giggled and whispered back. Reilliy looked relieved.

"Load!" Parren bellowed from the side. He pointed to one of the wagons. "Girls there! Men and boys in that one over there." He scowled suddenly at the man holding Geris. "What are you doing there?"

The man lowered his eyes. "Nothing, sir." He put the child down and gave her a little push toward Reilliy. "Go to Reilliy now. Go let Reilliy hold your hand now, Geris."

The little girl stuck her lower lip out rebelliously, but she let Reilliy take her hand again.

"Load up," Parren commanded them all indiscriminately. He swung away on his horse.

Kehera followed Reilliy and Geris and the other girls toward the girls' wagon. It was a much bigger wagon than was necessary to accommodate the five of them. Presumably it would become more crowded when Parren picked up more slaves in Eäneté. Kehera took a deep breath and climbed in.

The wagon was dark after the daylight, close and warm even with the flaps tied open. Sacks and bales and crates took up the rearmost part of the wagon, but there were blankets in the front part for the girls to sit on. And at least it was out of the wind. After riding through Anha Pass, it didn't seem so bad to sit in a wagon for a while, and Kehera couldn't deny that she felt safer out of sight. She found a place near the front opening and sat down, cross-legged, back braced against the wood of the side. Reilliy sat across from her, wordlessly, and Geris knelt where she could see out and peered out excitedly. The other two girls curled up together at the back and were quiet; they seemed completely uninterested in anything that was happening.

A man leaped up to the driver's seat and took up the reins, the horses leaned into the harness, and the wagon lurched and started forward.

They came up on the city gates very quickly. Kehera got a look at the walls with their wide-open gates and thought suddenly, *What if they're searching outgoing traffic?* On the very heels of that thought, she saw men in red cloaks at the gates, stopping and searching wagons as they exited. She told herself that Parren must have known about the inspection, but her heart sped anyway.

"I'll take Geris, if you like," she said to Reilliy casually. "She's almost the age of my youngest sister."

Reilliy nodded. "Good, yes, you take her! Geris, would you like to go to—?"

"My name's Eilisè," Kehera told her. "Geris, sweet, want to come sit with me? You're just the age of my sister, did you know that?"

The little girl came over willingly and plumped down in Kehera's lap. "What's her name?" she demanded.

"Um, Taviy," Kehera invented hastily. "Did you have any big sisters, Geris?"

"No, never!"

"Well, you should," Kehera told her. "Every little girl needs a big sister to take care of her. Would you like me to be your sister for a little while?"

Geris laughed, pleased. "Yes! You be my sister. Can Reilliy be my sister too?"

Kehera glanced at Reilliy for permission. "Sure, why not? We'll all be sisters." They were almost at the gates. The first wagon had already stopped. Parren was speaking to one of the redcloaks. Kehera thought she saw something change hands. A bribe? She hoped the redcloak would stay bought. The wagon rolled to a halt.

A redcloak walked over and jumped up on the running board to peer into the wagon. He said to the driver, "What all have you got here, then?"

The driver shrugged laconically. Kehera sent a quick prayer to the

Fortunate Gods and whispered to Geris, "You want to tell him?"

Geris said loudly to the redcloak, in her piping child's voice, "He's got us! I'm Geris. This is my big sister, and that's Reilliy; she's my other big sister! Big sisters take care of little girls!"

The redcloak grunted, looked them over disinterestedly, and jumped back off the running board. Kehera hugged Geris. Perfect! She promised herself that she would indeed take care of the little girl as well as she could, and hoped that the child wasn't heading for any future too terrible.

The wagons started up again, rolling through the gates and out of Enchar. Nothing ahead of them now but the open road, all the way to Eäneté! Her heart lifted at the mere thought that she was finally moving. It felt *right* to be heading south toward Eäneté, as though at last she was moving in exactly the right direction.

It was hard to believe she had come so far so fast, from being a prisoner on her way to Irekay to being a fugitive on her way home. For a moment she let herself think of her father's face when she rode safely through the gates of the palace in Raëh. The picture was so vivid it was almost like she was actually there, and she prayed to the Fortunate Gods it might happen that way.

Then, trying to be sensible, she settled down in the wagon with her arm around Geris and set herself to endure the miles and days that inescapably rolled out before that hope could become real. Eighteen days or more until they might reach Eäneté. It wasn't so very long. With the favor of the Fortunate Gods, she might be home before the beginning of the Iron Hinge and midwinter. She wished for that, fervently.

It took eight days to reach the limit of Enchar's precincts and the beginning of Kimsè Province. At first the days were so clear and cold it seemed that a sharp cry should shatter the air into frozen crystalline fragments. But, as often happened during the Month of Frost, the weather warmed and chilled and warmed again. That was unlucky, as the roads were much harder on the animals when the ruts thawed to ice-edged mud. But Parren seemed pleased enough with the pace by what Kehera could see.

They traveled mostly south and a little east, the road curving its serpentine way along the foothills of the Takel Mountains. Kehera watched the mountains roll slowly by on the right, all black leafless forest and sharp gray reaches of stone, and thought about home. Raëh lay just on the other side of those mountains. Somewhere on the road through Kimsè they would pass opposite Raëh, but then they would keep on south a hundred miles or more too far. She longed for the wings of a bird, so that she might fly straight west over the mountains. But the wagons only rolled south, one slow mile after another, and that was good enough. She cherished every mile.

Kehera was grateful for Geris. Looking after the lively little girl gave her full-time occupation and settled her nerves. And Reilliy was openly glad to have the child taken out of her hands. The other girls provided little enough company. Reilliy was spiteful and angry. Her parents had sold her, she said, so they would have enough to feed her brothers through the winter. A common enough story, it seemed, for Geris had become a slave in exactly the same way; but where the younger girl had a sunny disposition undimmed by her circumstances, the older seemed to have taken the transaction as a personal insult. While being sold as a slave was not a very nice thing to have happen, Kehera privately thought that Reilliy would do better to take her manners from Geris. Eight days in her company, and it was all Kehera could do to restrain herself from taking her by the shoulders and shaking the meanness out of her.

The male slaves were kept strictly segregated from the girls except at mealtimes, and even then the girls kept to one side of the common pot and the men to the other. This was a pity, Kehera thought, because though some of the men looked like the kind a girl would want to be protected from, others looked like they would probably be pleasant company. The older man with ink-stained fingers, Hallay, had an easy manner and a good voice when he sang around the fire at night, as the men sometimes did. Even the man with the chains and the crooked nose showed evidence of dry wit. The snatches of talk she overheard at suppertime suggested he had an inexhaustible supply of quite unbelievable stories.

Then they entered the province of Kimsè and the journey became truly unpleasant. All through Kimsè the road was horrible, both icy and muddy at once, churned up and then frozen and then half thawed. Everyone had to walk, the mud freezing their feet even through their boots. The male slaves were pressed into service over and over to get the wagons through muddy holes.

The guards had all along been businesslike and impersonal when they had anything to do with the girls, but now Kehera saw how ready they were to use a riding whip on the male slaves if the men failed to get a wagon out of a hole as fast as the guards thought they should. Then she guessed that only Parren's orders made them leave the girls alone. After that, she was afraid of them—though they continued to leave the girls alone.

Kimsè itself proved to be not so much a town as a string of miserable villages, ruled over by a brooding castle and, she gathered from overheard comments made by the guards and the other slaves, an equally brooding lord. Kehera stared up at the castle when they passed it, squatting gray and heavy on its hill, and loathed the lord who would let his people live like this.

Whenever they passed through a village, gaunt dogs ran out to bark from a safe distance. The guards threatened them away with shouts and raised whips when they came too close. They warned off men, too, who now and then came out to the muddy road to hold up a coughing child or push forward a thin, frightened girl. Kehera was horrified when she realized the people of Kimsè wanted to sell their children, but guiltily grateful Parren did not seem to want to buy them. She understood now why he had spoken approvingly of the plump girls of Eäneté, if he had meant to contrast them to the poor children in these villages.

Then at last, on the twenty-eighth day of the Month of Frost, they crossed out of the precincts of Kimsè into the province of Eäneté.

They were still a week or so from the city itself, Kehera knew, because the province was a big one. But just as Parren had said, the road was suddenly much, much better. It ran smooth and level, frozen hard but without so much as a snowflake to slow the wagons. Kehera almost thought she would have recognized the border without that evidence of the change from one Immanent Power's precincts to another: she thought she could feel a faint shock of recognition in her bones, almost as though Eäneté belonged to Harivir rather than Pohorir. But perhaps it was just the way the land opened out and began to resemble more the lands of southern Harivir. They began to pass through pasturelands much like those near Coär, and here the cattle were fat and the boys who herded them far less skinny.

Parren stopped to bargain for fresh meat and good potatoes and apples from the folk of the first village they came to, as he had not done in Kimsè, and the villagers had all this to sell. Neither the animals nor the people were as starveling and poor as the Kimsèn villagers. No one tried to sell their children, and Parren made no attempt to buy any girls. Kehera supposed he meant to purchase his much-admired plump Eänetén girls in the city itself. She could imagine that perhaps girls sometimes disappeared, in a crowded city. Stealing girls would certainly keep costs down. Would Parren steal girls? Would the young man in Enchar have recommended someone like that?

Would he have known?

When they reached the town of Eäneté, Parren was supposed to help her find a money changer and supplies, and then he was supposed to let her go. Kehera was uneasily aware that she could not make him do any of this. And even more uneasily aware that it was too late to change her mind about this plan.

It would work. It had to work. All she had to do was get through the town and away into the pass, and she'd be safe. She'd come through so much already. Surely she could manage to slip into and out of Eäneté without coming to the notice of the duke.

"The Duke of Eäneté can't be so bad. Everything here seems so much better," Kehera said aloud that evening, when the slaves had gathered together for their soup and bread. Even the cold seemed less bitter in Eäneté, and the fire seemed to burn with more heat and less smoke.

Reilliy's lip curled. "Better think again. The Wolf Duke is worse than the lord of Kimsè." Her tone was almost cordial—she liked to sneer at the ignorance of the other girls, and she liked to tell them bad news.

Kehera understood that Reilliy wanted to feel superior to someone and there wasn't anyone else she could sneer at, but knowing this didn't make her like the other girl any better. She didn't want to seem ignorant of things she should know, but she did want to know more about the Eänetén duke, so she raised her eyebrows skeptically.

"He is!" insisted Reilliy. "They say if you offend the duke, you'll die screaming. That's what my father says. He says it's better to deal only with people in Enchar and leave Eäneté out of it."

"It's not quite that bad," murmured the older man, Hallay. He looked drawn and tired. He was not the kind of man who was used to hauling wagons through frozen mud, and he had taken the brunt of the guards' ire over the days it had taken to get through Kimsè. "The Eänetén duke likes good work. He'll pay fair measure for it, and a contract from him is like iron. That's what we—they—know of him, in the guilds in Enchar. You needn't fear him unless you try to break a contract from your end, or pass off shoddy work."

"He's dangerous," Reilliy insisted. "He's horrible and cruel and it would be better to *die* than have *him* buy you—"

The big man, the one who was some kind of criminal, laughed outright at that. "A lord of Pohorir? Of course he's dangerous and cruel and vindictive. That's not the question. The question is whether he can be trusted. Hallay's right. Deal honestly with the Wolf Duke and you've nothing to fear."

The man's name was Tageiny. He was the only slave the guards treated warily. As they'd passed through Kimsè, she'd twice seen him fix one of the guards with a thoughtful stare when the man raised a whip to hit Hallay, and both times the guard had contented himself with a curt order or a shove. Kehera had no idea who would want to buy a big, dangerous slave like Tageiny, who had to be kept chained up like an untrustworthy dog. But she'd noticed that the other male slaves didn't seem to fear him as the guards did. Hallay plainly trusted his good nature far more than that of the guards, staying close to Tageiny when he had a chance. Not only that, but the young rough-looking Luad, though obviously a street tough, kept a constant eye on Tageiny, helping without comment when the chain got in Tageiny's way— assistance that the older man accepted with a matter-of-fact patience that she liked.

And now Tageiny spoke of the Eänetén duke as though he knew him, or at least knew of him. Though she feared to reveal too much of herself, she couldn't resist asking, "Are you from Eäneté?"

"I lived in the city for a couple years not so long ago," Tageiny said mildly. He said almost everything mildly, as though he never saw any reason to raise his voice. He added, "You wouldn't have wanted to catch the old duke's eye, but the current duke is all right. You don't see that very often, an heir that comes out better than his father and grandfather—guess he reached some sort of accommodation with the Immanent. I actually saw him once. Yellow eyes; you can see right away why they call him the Wolf Duke. He didn't notice me. But I wouldn't have worried if he had—unless I was stupid enough to try selling him brittle steel or spoiled grain or short measure."

Hallay smiled briefly, something in this comment amusing him. Tageiny slid a glance his way and a corner of his mouth quirked upward. "Yeah, like you ever sold short measure in your life."

"Ah, well," said Hallay. "It's an easy accusation to make and a hard one to answer—especially if the accusation's made by Conanè Sochar, and especially for a man with a family."

"Ah," said Tageiny, as though this answered a question he hadn't quite asked.

"You were working for Sochar yourself, weren't you?" Hallay's tone wasn't quite casual.

Tageiny gave him a lazy look and a little shrug. "Yeah, well, that turned out to be an easy job to take and a hard one to quit. I admit, when I decided to walk away, this wasn't quite what I had in mind."

Luad laughed, not sounding very amused. Tageiny's mouth tugged upward again in that not-quite smile. "Yeah. Life's full of the Gods' little jests, and sometimes it's a trick to figure out whether it's the Fortunate or Unfortunate have you in their eye." He shied a pebble off into the dark—it got dark very early now, as the year turned toward the Iron Hinge—and said meditatively, "I can tell you, I'd rather the Wolf Duke bought me than, well—" His eye fell tolerantly on Reilliy. "Let's just say there are several possible buyers I do not want to see bidding."

Kehera suspected she herself had the best chance of meeting the Eänetén duke, if he caught her trying to slip through his pass.

But it would be fine. She would be careful, and quiet, and the Wolf Duke would never know she had so briefly visited his city. And the moment her foot touched Harivin soil, she would be home, and everything would be *fine*.

But though she told herself this as firmly as she could, it all sounded far less likely than when, back in Enchar, she had so firmly declared her intention to head for Roh Pass.

That was why she waited for Tageiny to head around the wagons toward one of the shallow trenches he and the other male slaves had earlier dug in the snow at the side of the road. Then she left the fire as though she were going back toward the girl's wagon to get out of the cold, but instead followed Tageiny. In the winter dark, no one noticed—she hoped no one would, if she was quick. Behind her, Hallay was beginning to sing, which would probably help, too.

> *"I left you in the morning,*
> *in the pearl light of morning.*
> *I left you calling for me,*

in the silver morning glow.
I came back to you in evening,
in the ashen light of evening.
I heard you calling for me,
that you would have to go. . . ."

She knew that song. Everyone knew it. Probably everyone would listen straight through to the tragedy at the end, but if one of the guards did come after her, Kehera supposed she could say she had forgotten which trench was supposed to be which. The guard might be angry, but she was almost sure she could make any guard check with Parren before he dared hit her.

She was afraid she might not catch Tageiny alone, and she was afraid she might be caught herself, but she hadn't expected him to be actually waiting for her. He was standing balanced and wary, his chained hands not making him look at all helpless. But he straightened when he saw her, his eyebrows rising. "Well," he said. "Didn't expect you. Thought you were that pig's turd of a guard." He looked her up and down, his expression neutral. "I could say this isn't a good idea. But you already know that. So be quick."

Kehera nodded. This was a risk. She knew it was a risk, but she'd had days to watch this man. Days in which she had come to trust him more, and Parren less. And she knew she had to offer enough to make Tageiny truly commit to helping her. She said rapidly, not letting herself hesitate now that the decision had been made to speak at all, "You were going to leave Pohorir, weren't you? That's what you meant when you said you'd intended to quit that job in Enchar. If I bought you from Parren myself, if I hired you to help me get through Roh Pass and into Harivir—you know you'd be free in Harivir—"

Tageiny's eyebrows went up again. "Fortunate Gods, yes, count me in," he said without even a second's hesitation. "I'll hire on for a promise and a poem—I'll swear any oath you want and never betray you, Fortunate Gods witness! Listen, girl, if you've got enough, if you can get Luad away, too, I could use another man if we're to try the pass. You think you can get that bastard Parren to let you have me and him?" He hesitated just perceptibly. "You haven't paid him up front, have you? He's a bastard, right enough, a bastard and a liar and not one to trust unless you've plenty of coin in your hand, or better still a friend with a knife standing behind him."

Kehera nodded, all her past doubts about Parren rearing up, ugly in the dark. "He was recommended to me—he's done this before, I was told—half up front, yes. He's to get the other half when he brings me to the walls of the town."

Tageiny's skepticism was clear in the tilt of his head. "If you're Harivin, and I'm sure there's a tale in that, then who's to miss you on this side of the mountains? There's more than one way to get a reputation, and t'other is to make sure the wrong sort of story doesn't get around—" He cut the last word off sharp, jerking his head at her, and Kehera slipped away into the dark, as quick and careful as she'd ever been in her life, but feeling cold to her bones.

She still didn't know for certain whether she could trust Tageiny. But there was no way to tell except to put him to the test, and she'd surely seen at least a glimpse of the hearts of all her traveling companions through those wretched days in Kimsè. And she thought she trusted him more than any man who bought and sold slaves, even if Parren did seem friendly. She could see at once that Tageiny was the kind of man who'd know about such things. And *he* had no reason to lie to her.

She couldn't help but understand that Parren had every reason to lie to her. So she took the chance, while the slaves gathered around the next morning's common fire for porridge and tea, to give Tageiny a significant look. That was all she could manage: a straight look into the big man's eyes. That was all it took, because two hours later one of the horses drawing the second wagon came up lame, and just as the driver got it out of harness and began to put in one of the riding animals in its place, the rest of the team suddenly spooked so hard—at nothing

Kehera could see—that the two nearer the verge were shoved right off the road, dragging the two left wheels after them into the ditch. One wheel cracked its rim, and the new horse, not accustomed to being part of the wagon team, took that excuse to shy and rear like a green yearling, drawing yet more of the men into the unexpected fray.

Kehera hadn't seen Tageiny anywhere near either the horses or the wagon, but somehow she wasn't surprised when he turned up next to her among the group of watching slaves. She moved a few steps apart from the group to watch the cursing men argue about how to get the wagon back on the road without cracking another wheel, and of course Tageiny drifted after her, and there they were, as private as they needed to be for at least a moment or two.

"You're thinking maybe you don't trust Parren after all and maybe you want to shake free on your own," he murmured without preamble. This wasn't quite a question, though she nodded, barely. He went on in the same low voice. "You want to wait till we're closer to the city, I won't say you're wrong. On the other hand, you want to clear out before Parren expects it, that might offer the best chance right up front, but it'd have to be today or tomorrow, and it'd mean covering some rough country off the road—I'll tell you straight, this time of year, I wouldn't be eager to take a girl any distance through the mountains."

"But you do think you can get us away?" Kehera asked, trying not to sound too doubtful. "And your friend, too?"

"You branded? Right, I figured not. On our own, just me and Luad, I don't mind saying it'd've been tricky. With an unbranded woman as can say she owns us, well, that gives the rods a nudge toward a fortunate throw, as they say. Not that canny folk aren't suspicious of that little trick, only there's ways to make 'em believe it's all right and proper—or ways to make 'em pretend to believe it, which is good enough, mostly." He added, "Likely we'll get only one try, so my advice is, closer to town opens up more options."

"Whatever you think," Kehera murmured.

Tageiny barely nodded. "A day or so out from town, then. Now, what do we have to work with? I don't mind saying money is a big help. You paid that bastard Parren half up front, you said." He rubbed the side of his face, looking at her out of the corner of his eye while the men unharnessed the horses and led them aside so they could replace the cracked wheel.

Kehera hesitated only a second before saying in a low voice, "I've a handful of jewels hidden away."

"Best if we can count on nobody looking where they shouldn't for an hour or more. If you'll pass me something, I'm pretty sure I know which guard to bribe." At her sideways glance, he added, "I know. But, listen, girl"—he ran a thumb across the brand on his cheek—"*this* means Harivir sounds damn good to me; that's damn sure something you can trust. It's the Fortunate Gods put you in my path. Or me in yours, whatever. I believe that, either way around."

Kehera thought she might believe that too. "I'll give you something," she murmured. And then they had to go in opposite directions as the men finally got the wagons back in order and started to shout at the slaves to get back on the road.

That evening, at supper, when she handed around the hard bread everyone ate with their soup, she made sure Tageiny's portion had a pearl tucked into it. If he swallowed it and choked, she would feel pretty stupid. But she was sure he wouldn't.

Then Geris ran over, wanting bread of her own, and Kehera found herself blinking back unexpected tears as she pretended to have to search for a last piece for the little girl. She hadn't thought of having to leave Geris behind. . . . It made no difference, she told herself sternly. She would never have been able to take a child with her through Roh Pass in any case. She would have had to leave her anyway. And Hallay, and the rest. She had never had any way to rescue every slave in Pohorir.

So the next morning, when Tageiny caught her eye and one of his eyelids shivering in a suggestion of a wink, she made herself nod. She knew he must have put that pearl to good use. She wondered which guard he'd bribed.

She wondered if she trusted him to have bribed a guard on her behalf and not just on his own. She thought she did. But it was hard to be sure, and the uncertainty wore at her nerves through the next day's slow travel toward Eäneté. This was heavily settled land, here so near the town. Every hill had a farmhouse or a barn nestled against its lee side, where the land would offer shelter from the black midwinter winds that spilled from the wings of dragons. . . . Eäneté was as far south as Coär, which meant the Wall of Storms lay only another hundred miles or so to the south. Kehera guessed, from the feel of the air and the early dusk, that the Month of Frost had probably turned to the Iron Hinge Month. No doubt the Wall of Storms was already boiling with the obsidian winds, terrible and beautiful and capable of flaying a man to the bone in seconds.

She wished that everything were over and past and no one needed to try anything difficult and chancy during the month of ill fortune.

If Tageiny shared her impatience, it didn't show. If Luad knew anything was going on, Kehera couldn't tell it, though he might have looked a shade less sullen. But maybe that was just because they were getting close to the town of Eäneté at last, which promised a few days' rest for everyone and better shelter than a couple of wagons could provide. Except that Kehera could hardly bear to imagine spending days in Eäneté. . . . Even if Tageiny couldn't manage to get her away, or if he betrayed her, maybe Parren had brought her here in good faith anyway. He offered her a warm smile when she caught his eye. But he always had, right from the beginning. He *looked* trustworthy . . . and Tageiny looked like a thug.

But that evening, the last before they were supposed to reach the town, when Kehera started back toward the girls' wagon after supper, Tageiny caught her eye and glanced away, toward the bushes where the girls were supposed to go for their needs. She didn't nod, but she looked just once more toward Parren, sitting and laughing expansively with a couple of his men. He clapped one of them on the shoulder . . . a brute of a man. All the guards were brutes: What other kind would work for a man who bought and sold slaves? Parren's manner with those men was just as bluff and friendly as it was with her, unless he was angry. Then it was something else. She'd seen that, too, during the long days of travel.

Kehera let her breath out. Then she got up and wandered off toward the bushes.

Luad met her, with a low *"Hst!"* and a tip of his head, and she hesitated—after this it *would* be too late to change her mind—but then followed him down the road the way they'd come. It was bitterly cold. The young man seemed to know where he was going, though Kehera couldn't imagine how. He glanced back now and then to make sure she was still with him, but didn't offer her a hand when she stumbled over frozen ruts at the side of the road. . . . She wasn't sure she wanted him to offer her a hand; she wasn't sure she trusted him. She'd decided to trust Tageiny, but that decision was seeming possibly ill-advised now too.

She couldn't help but think about a night out in this cold, and think again of the relative warmth of the girls' wagon. . . . At least the moon shone on the snow, so there was enough light to see. Though she wondered if that was so much an advantage to those who might soon be hunted. Maybe Parren had always meant to do exactly as he'd promised and she'd been a fool to be persuaded away from the wagons by men she didn't actually know. . . .

Ahead of them, snow crunched. Tageiny shifted away from the shadows of a stand of trees, so close that Kehera jerked back with a startled gasp. Even Luad cursed under his breath, which was a slight comfort.

"You blind, boy?" Tageiny said, sounding amused. "Never mind. It's a different kind of dark out here."

"Yeah, I'll take a town," muttered Luad. "Probably got wolves out here."

Tageiny chuckled. "In Eäneté? You bet. Never you mind, boy; it's too early in the winter to worry about wolves. This way; let's go."

"*I'm* not worried about *wolves*," Kehera said tautly, following him up the slope, among the trees that came down almost to the road. They were mostly firs and cedars here, which at least broke the wind. She was trying not to believe she heard steps behind them, or distant shouts. Surely that was just the wind across the branches. . . .

"Good girl! That's the way," Tageiny told her approvingly, apparently taking her rejoinder for bravery, when it was quite otherwise. He went on with good-natured calm. "We should have a little time. Enough. *If* the man stays bought. Though I'll tell you, I wouldn't put a man like that at my back if I had a choice, so best we move along briskly. There's a farmhouse I have in mind, just the kind of place to pick up a couple horses, not too far back this way. How're your hands? Tuck 'em in your sleeves. We'll get you a proper coat if we can."

"I'm perfectly fine—I'm not cold," Kehera told him firmly, trying to sound like she meant it. It helped that they were walking fast. "What did you tell the guard—what will he tell everybody else? The other girls—they'll know I'm missing—" She couldn't imagine now how she'd thought this could work.

Tageiny laughed under his breath. "Well, now, I'm almost sure you don't want to know the story he'll pass along. Nice girl like you. In a way it's too bad the guards have kept themselves to themselves this trip—well, no, probably just as well, only it's a bit hard to see one of 'em breaking discipline at this point. On the other hand, this close to town, might as well drink the rest of the beer, right? And that'll give some boys ideas. By the time the rest figure he's not coming back, we'll be well away."

Kehera was pretty sure he was right: She didn't want to know any more than that. She said hastily, "But Parren will know where to look for us, surely? At least, won't he check all the nearby farmhouses?"

"Sure, and he'll figure out who's lost a couple horses, if he bothers asking around, but that'll take time, and meanwhile there'll be little trails all through these woods, all kinds of tracks on 'em, and what's a man to do? Even if he knows you're heading for Roh Pass, lots of ways to get there from here, and is he going to leave the rest of his merchandise sitting by the roadside so's he can chase down one girl who already paid him up front? I don't see a man like him being real *committed* to getting you back. Plus, a couple of brawlers like Luad and me, those men of his won't necessarily want to catch up to us all that damn fast, if you get what I mean."

This made sense. Kehera began to feel cautiously optimistic again. This was going to work. Tageiny obviously knew what he was doing—and if she'd been wrong to trust him, surely that would already be clear. "How did you get rid of that chain?" she asked.

Luad surprised her with a quite friendly sounding chuckle. "Yeah, I took care of that," he said confidently. "*That*, I can do."

"He can," Tageiny confirmed comfortably. "Boy's scared of wolves, but he's a natural with a bit of wire. It's a real handy skill."

"I'm not *scared* of *wolves*, Tag—"

"Good thing, in Eäneté, boy—"

Kehera let herself be comforted by their easy argument, by the welcome effort of the uphill pace—*away, away,* every step seemed to say; after so many days of slow and uneasy travel, she felt that she was finally *moving*.

The farmhouse was a bit ramshackle for an Eänetén farmhouse; its combined byre and stable was a mere lean-to, closed to the mountains from which the midwinter winds would come, but open to the east. And as far as Kehera could tell, there were no dogs, which was surely a favor from the Fortunate Gods. She could see why the place had caught Tageiny's eye when they'd passed it. *She* hadn't noticed it at all, or not to think of it as a place to steal horses. She didn't like to think of stealing the animals, though. Not from folk who probably needed them and might not have the coin to buy others. Maybe she could leave another pearl somewhere those people would be sure to find it. . . .

"Right," said Tageiny. "Right, girl, listen, I'd just as soon have you wait here, but it's too cold. So we'll all go down, but quietly, hear? Don't talk and be careful how you set your feet. It'll be warmer in with the beasts, though we won't dawdle about. Likely we can pick up a bit of blanket for you, if nothing better. Then we're off. We'll pick up the rest of what we need in Eäneté—I know people, so that's no problem—and find out who to bribe to get through Roh Pass. But first, gotta have a couple horses. So let's go. Quietly."

They were quiet. But it didn't matter. There were no horses in the shelter, nor cattle. Parren was waiting there instead, with several of his men, all of them armed with the small crossbows men carried for hunting and for protection against wolves.

They couldn't even run, not with the crossbows and the moonlight. Tageiny caught Luad's arm when the younger man might have tried to break away. Luad was cursing under his breath, steadily and uninventively. Tageiny didn't say a word. Kehera, whose first incredulous thought had been that he'd led her deliberately into this trap, changed her mind at his expression. Or non-expression.

"I thought *you* might try something as we got close to Eäneté," Parren said to Tageiny. "You and your buddy. Figured this was the kind of place that might catch the eye of a clever man who wanted to run."

"Not so clever. Not clever enough to figure *you* were clever." Tageiny sounded disgusted, but not afraid. But in the lantern light, Kehera could see the tension in his body, as though he might be right on the edge of attacking Parren despite all the crossbows. They would just shoot him, she knew, and maybe that's what he wanted, but she couldn't stand the thought and laid a hand on his arm to stop him. He did ease back, though he wouldn't look at her.

"People don't figure that, somehow. I don't know why that is." Parren shook his head in mock wonder. "The one who surprised me is the girl." He looked Kehera up and down. "Yeah, *you,* I didn't expect. Didn't trust me after all, hey?" He didn't look friendly at all anymore, despite his smile.

"I did," Kehera whispered. "*Teier* trusted you."

"It's my face," Parren said, smiling even more broadly. "Everybody trusts me. It's very, very good for business—two payments for the same goods! Your young friend in Enchar isn't the only one to keep me supplied. I didn't figure you'd guessed, and now look at you! Not many come so close to getting away. That wouldn't have been good. I've got *just* the buyer for you. A special buyer with special needs." And he laughed, not friendly or warm at all.

Kehera asked, because she couldn't understand how this had happened and she thought Parren might answer, "How did you even *know?*"

"Ah, that was your fault, girl," Parren told her cheerfully. "Reilliy told me. *Worried* about you, she was. Malicious little snip, but I guess she likes you—or she wanted to get my man in trouble. He'll get *trouble,* all right, if I get my hands on him. Not the cleverest boy in the Four Kingdoms, that boy, if he let you bribe him. I'm betting I know just where he'll go to drink up whatever you paid him. Either way, I'll get enough for *you* to make up for all this bother, not just in coin, but in the prettiest bills of sale you ever saw in your life, just the thing when you happen across the chance to pick up a pretty girl who might not technically be a slave."

Kehera said nothing. There seemed nothing to say. She felt physically ill. How many other men and women over those years had stood, as she was standing, on the threshold of freedom, only to find it giving way beneath them, crumbling into a pit of slavery and despair?

10

Gereth was only just entering the outskirts of the merchants' district on the north side of town when the wheel of His Grace's carriage broke. Despite the fine cushions and the carefully woven suspension of leather straps, the jolt flung him forward and then back harder than was comfortable for a man of his years. He caught the edge of the window to brace himself, bruising his hand on the closed shutters. The driver cursed, and the carriage settled at a distinct slant.

Gereth shut his eyes and sighed. This sort of errand was difficult enough without adding trivial annoyances.

A moment later, the lieutenant in charge of his escort cautiously opened the door on what had become the lower side of the carriage and peered in. "Sir," he muttered. "The driver hit a hole, sir, begging your pardon. These damn cobbles get worse every winter. The whole street needs to be reset and sanded, but the wheel, it must've been cracked already, I guess. You all right?"

"Merely a little startled," Gereth assured him. "Better now than a moment when His Grace was within." He began moving, slowly, to extricate himself from the interior of the carriage.

"Fortunate Gods forfend!" said the lieutenant—Nikas, a

responsible man, not one to be flustered by minor disasters. He offered Gereth a hand, but added, "The wind's wicked, sir, and I don't see anyplace comfortable to wait. You might want to just stay inside there till the driver brings down another wheel. Or maybe another carriage; that might be faster. Or do you want I should get somebody along here to loan you a carriage?"

"No. The driver had better go fetch another of His Grace's carriages," Gereth told him, a little distractedly. "I don't want to hear what His Grace would say to me if I went about his business in a borrowed conveyance."

"Sir," said Nikas, which was as close as he could come to agreeing without skirting dangerously near impudence.

Gereth nearly smiled, but then his amusement ebbed. He feared Innisth had pressed himself far too near the razor edge he rode with the brutal Eänetén Power. That was too often the young duke's way: to refuse to notice his own limitations until he was perilously close to going beyond them. He thought he should be able to endure anything, and while he had indeed been trained in endurance, *anything* was a bit beyond mortal reach.

With the lieutenant's assistance, Gereth clambered down from the tilted carriage, standing with one hand braced against the ornamented door as he considered the street. It was deserted at the moment, save for the half dozen men of his escort, all of them looking at the moment thoroughly disgusted with this turn of events. This wasn't a much-trafficked area at the best of times: all guild offices and such, with just a scattering of townhouses. Earlier in the morning the servants would have been out; later in the afternoon men of rank would pay calls on one another to deal with matters of business, but at this particular hour, few folk of any degree would find reason to brave the weather. Though there was one other carriage: the heavy, plain sort hired by the moderately well-to-do, pulled up before an establishment a little way down the street. The sign above the door showed a black rose, a single drop of blood clinging to one petal. Gereth made a slight face and looked away.

Then he thought again. "It might be good fortune that caused the accident to happen just here," he told Nikas. "I intended to visit the magistrates, but . . . this may do. Perhaps I shall be able to complete His Grace's errand even before the other carriage arrives."

"That'd be good, sir," Nikas answered distractedly, keeping an eye on the driver, who had moved to the horses' heads, murmuring to them as he fussed with their harness.

The horses were both gray geldings, His Grace favoring black and gray animals for his personal use. One was younger and darker and more heavily dappled than the other, but otherwise they were well-matched beasts, with handsome heads and sloping shoulders and powerful quarters. The driver rearranged the harness of the darker and clambered from the driver's seat of the carriage to its back, gathered up its reins and the trailing reins of the other horse, and started off with a clatter.

The low sky began to spit a nasty mix of freezing rain and sleet. Gereth squinted up at the clouds and sighed.

"It's not a pleasant day and that's a fact," Nikas agreed.

Gereth nodded, gathering his nerve against anticipated unpleasantness. "I believe I know just the door to knock on, Lieutenant, and we'll get in out of the weather for at least a few minutes." Beckoning to his escort, he headed down the street toward the Black Rose Guildhouse.

This particular guildhouse was one of the older buildings in the town of Eäneté, and one of the grander on this street. The brick steps were wide, the porch generous, the door polished and inlaid with brass to form another rose image. The servant who answered the knock was a silent old man with a narrow-lipped mouth and unfriendly eyes. He looked first at Lieutenant Nikas and the other soldiers. Then his gaze flickered to Gereth's face, and he stepped back and swung the door wide without a word.

The hall Gereth entered was warm and welcoming, richly carpeted and well lit. A little way down the entry hall, a door stood half open, revealing light and voices. One of the voices was familiar: the light, smooth voice of Baraka Ris, one of the guildmasters who sometimes represented the Black Rose establishment to His Grace. The other, deeper and warmer, Gereth did not recognize. Nor did he care, but gestured to his escort to wait and headed that way, Lieutenant Nikas at his back, without waiting for the servant to announce him.

Gereth had never actually set foot in this guildhouse before, nor wished to. The room he surveyed from the doorway was smaller and plainer than he had expected, looking much like his own office in the duke's house, desk and straight-backed chairs and scrolls filed in a rack on one wall. But here the rose symbol of the house was picked out in black iron on the fireplace screen and inlaid in some dark wood on the surface of the desk.

Baraka Ris had turned swiftly as Gereth came in, his hand falling to the knife sheathed at his hip. Then, recognizing the duke's seneschal, his mouth tightened and he whipped his hand away from his knife. Though he gave the servant a sharp look, he said only, "Sir! What an unexpected honor! Pray explain how we may serve His Grace."

Gereth studied the guildmaster in silence for a moment. Then he considered the other two occupants of the room. One was a big man he didn't know. Not Eänetén, or Gereth thought not. He had the feel of someone carrying a thin tie to some other Immanent Power. He had a bluff, friendly look that Gereth did not trust at all, considering the company he was keeping.

The other, not at all to Gereth's surprise, was a young woman. Hardly more than a girl to Gereth's eyes. Pretty enough, though nothing out of the way. She was clearly frightened, which also was not a surprise; but she stood with her back straight and her chin up, and though her eyes were wide, she was not trembling. It was perfectly plain what had been going on here, at least in broad strokes. Gereth asked in a level tone, "Is this a private viewing, or is anyone allowed to bid?"

The guildmaster hesitated for an instant. Then he said smoothly, "Of course there is no need for His Grace to bid. He need only make his wishes known, and of course the Black Rose House will be honored to serve. However, this girl has already been purchased by a . . . special client. I must ask His Grace to permit us to honor our prior contracts. We have no shortage of superior stock, as you know, sir, though of course not here at these offices. I would be delighted to arrange a viewing at any establishment you wish—or at His Grace's house, if you prefer."

Gereth ignored all this, studying the girl. He could see that, like the man, she wasn't Eänetén. But he thought she carried a quite different tie. Not Kimsè or Tisain . . . somewhere farther away and unfamiliar. Though he had no idea who she was, he was curious. And sorry for her, of course. And if the guildmaster didn't want Gereth to take her, one had to wonder just why that might be.

Also . . . all that aside, even though the duke might be annoyed, Gereth knew he couldn't walk out of this room and this house and leave this girl to her fate. He said absently, "His Grace will naturally pay for any service done him by the Black Rose House."

The girl said, quickly and unexpectedly, before the guildmaster could answer, "Lord, I appeal to you! This man"—she gestured at the stranger—"contracted to guide me to this city, and now he is unlawfully attempting to sell me into slavery. I appeal to you for aid and protection."

"This girl is my lawful property," the man protested, glaring at her. "I'm a licensed merchant, sir, and I've a proper bill of sale." He picked up one scroll from among others on the cluttered desk, proffering it to Gereth. Guildmaster Ris twitched and half reached after the scroll, then caught Gereth's eye and stopped dead.

Gereth took the scroll, fastidiously avoiding brushing the man's fingers. Unrolling it, he scanned the few lines and considered the stamp. The document did *seem* official. And yet the woman spoke so vehemently. He asked her, "*Are* you this man's slave? I advise you to answer me truthfully."

"No, lord," she declared at once. "I swear it. I am without friends here, and this man seeks to take advantage of my helplessness. Please, I appeal to you for protection."

"I am no lord," Gereth told her, but gently. "And you appeal not to me, but to the Eänetén duke. You insist this document is forged?"

"She'd say anything—" the slave dealer began. Gereth raised his eyebrows, and the guildmaster gripped the stranger's arm with urgent force. The other man closed his mouth.

The young woman glared at both of them and said quickly to Gereth, "Sir, it's not just me. That bill of sale is one among many! He was arranging to buy free Eänetén girls from this man. It's not right, sir, and I appeal to you and to His Grace."

Guildmaster Ris drew himself up in deep offense. "That accusation is entirely false—"

Gereth lifted a hand to halt them both. "It is a very serious accusation, guildmaster. But of course His Grace will not act without determining the truth." He added to Nikas, "His Grace will wish to question both these men, I'm sure."

"Sir," Lieutenant Nikas said grimly, and leaned out the door to beckon to his men.

Guildmaster Ris said reluctantly, "Sir, of course it will be just as you command. But I assure you, the Black Rose House has never participated in any such traffic! We are most strictly mindful of His Grace's law, I promise you. If this man has forged bills of sale or trafficked in Eänetén folk, it is entirely without our knowledge." He completely ignored the slave dealer's sputtered protests.

Gereth said, "Of course I'm sure that's true," without making any effort to disguise his skepticism. "And that being the case, I am sure you need not fear His Grace's judgment, Guildmaster Ris." Nodding to the young woman to follow, Gereth led her out of the room.

"I am Gereth Murrel, the duke's seneschal," he told the woman, taking her elbow to steady her down the steps to the cobbled street. "I shall take you to the duke's house, but you needn't worry. There should not be any need for you to meet him at all, unless you've lied to me about your legal status."

The woman showed no sign of terror at the idea of venturing into the Wolf Duke's house. She said, "I don't know how to thank you. I told you the truth, sir. That man has no legal claim on me, and he *told* me he would get forged bills of sale from that man." She added more slowly, sounding hesitant for the first time, "I hope . . . I wished to go through Roh Pass. Parren said he could bring me this far. If you are the duke's seneschal, sir, then may I ask you for leave through the pass? I would be very grateful."

Gereth regarded her with some astonishment. Harivin? He might believe it; he truly thought he might; she did have that foreign feel to her, not unlike the feeling one occasionally experienced when dealing with Harivin merchants. But . . . He said aloud, "But what possibly brings you to Pohorir, then? How did you become stranded here without your lord or father or anyone to protect you?"

The woman looked at him in some confusion. "It's . . . complicated," she said weakly.

"Well, I shall look forward to hearing your complicated tale." He expected she would probably lie, and didn't mind that. For a Harivin girl on her way home, what could it matter who she was or how she'd gotten into such trouble? "Here's my carriage," he said, but looked it over doubtfully. He had not wanted to spend another moment in the Black Rose Guildhouse, and surely this young woman agreed, but the carriage *was* tilted at a most uncomfortable angle. Still, the cushions were good ones, and the leaping wolf picked out in silver on the door would certainly guarantee that no one importuned or annoyed a girl waiting within.

He explained, although it was obvious, "The wheel's broken— that's the only reason I happened to stop just here. I meant to go on to, well, that can hardly matter now. When the wheel broke, I thought I might complete my errand here instead." He smiled at her. "The Fortunate Gods must be personally watching over your steps, young woman."

The young woman nodded earnestly. "I think that might be so."

She sounded as though she thought this might be literally true.

Well, perhaps it was. Gereth said kindly, "You can wait out of the wind, at least. Another carriage should be arriving very shortly. Can you manage the step? Good. Mind the tilt."

The carriage seat was luxuriously upholstered in blue and cream, and must surely be inviting to a young woman in need of protection. She allowed him to assist her, seated herself with care, and let out her breath in a long sigh. If she were afraid of Gereth, it didn't show.

"I hope I haven't interrupted your errand, sir, or imposed on your work with this ridiculous situation," she said politely once Gereth had joined her. Yes, polite, and also startlingly assured. Gereth did not permit himself to stare at her, but he knew this was not the manner of a common woman, nor of a slave woman, nor of any young woman who had been badly treated or who had learned to expect hard treatment. He was more and more certain that this was indeed a Harivin woman, and a woman of good family as well.

"Not at all," he assured her, keeping all these thoughts out of his voice. "Besides, it was the carriage wheel breaking that was the true interruption; your company for the wait fortunately makes it a pleasant interlude rather than an irritation."

"Allow me to thank you again, and ask, if I may—" But the young woman's tentative request or question was interrupted by the clatter of hooves and the rattle of wheels as the new carriage arrived.

Not an hour later, as they turned up the high road toward the duke's house, Gereth watched his foundling's eyes widen. The duke's house was big. It lifted arrogantly above the city, snow whirling around its heavy towers. The mountains might as well have been set deliberately behind the house to serve as a backdrop, for they certainly showed it to best advantage. The house commanded the western approach to the province and the town, powerful and aloof.

It proclaimed the duke's wealth and taste as well. Pale oak formed the massive guarding walls of the Wolf Duke's house, but fine-grained black wood had been set between the pale timbers in an abstract design like an embroidery pattern. The tall gates were forbidding, but also ornate, the iron worked into patterns suggesting fir trees and running wolves. As they approached, a cold wind rushed by them and flung out the long banner above the gates: argent, a gray wolf leaping, with eyes the color of beaten gold. The banner snapped in the wind, so that the wolf seemed to move and breathe, as though in the next moment it might leap out of the cloth and land before them in the snow.

The gates swung open in good time, so that the carriage need not pause. The span of those gates was great enough to let more than one carriage pass through abreast, and the courtyard they entered was broad enough to hold thirty such carriages without crowding. The house itself was of pale stone and pale wood, oak and pine and ash. It towered, many-storied, so that the young woman peered up at it in astonishment.

The driver drew up the carriage by the stables. A boy sprang forward at once to take the horses, and another hurried to open the door of the carriage and place steps on the damp stones to aid the passengers in alighting. The young woman stepped gravely down to the flagstones, moving with what Gereth was certain was trained grace, and turned to wait for him to join her.

Descending, he gestured his guest toward the house. She walked at his side toward the broad door and entered without hesitation, then paused to look around the entrance hall with obvious curiosity. Though Gereth wanted to tuck her away somewhere unobtrusive before he reported to His Grace, he paused too.

In the old duke's time, the entry had been dark and forbidding. Now it was far more welcoming. The hangings that had once covered the high, narrow windows had been removed and the rugs taken up from the parquet floor, so that one might admire the many shades of wood worked into an intricate, repeated pattern. The walls were paneled now with pale wood, and the windows set with both clear and colored glass. The glass sent rainbows of refracted light slanting across the floor. The grim hunting scenes and scenes of battle had been replaced with large paintings, mostly landscapes of the city and the forested mountains in all their seasons.

The young woman stopped by one such painting, and Gereth couldn't help but catch his breath. No doubt it was meaningless chance she had chosen that particular painting, but he couldn't help but wait to see her reaction. This one was taller than she was, framed on either side by a wide fall of midnight-blue draperies so long the cloth puddled on the floor. Set off by that dark frame, the painting stood out as vividly as though it were a window rather than paint and canvas. It showed the city as a bird, winging high above, might see it. The sky had been shown as a broken scape of leaden clouds, with brilliant beams of sunlight lancing through; in the painting, the play of light caught out the duke's house while leaving the city below in shadow. The arrogant power of the house had been caught exactly. To one side of the painting, slanting in swift flight, went a lark. The little bird had been rendered in beautiful detail, darting across the heavy sky on a course that would, in the next instant, carry it out of view entirely.

"What do you think of it?" Gereth asked at last.

The young woman answered quietly, "I think the artist was more in sympathy with the bird than the walls. . . . I don't think he loved this city. Or was it this house he did not love?"

Gereth, struck to silence, could only stare at her. She looked up to meet his gaze, and he managed after a moment, "The artist was the current duke's mother. She was brought here at nineteen to marry the old duke, and she died at twenty bearing his heir. I think it was the only way she could find to escape him."

"I'm twenty," the woman said quietly. "She was just my age." She looked again at the painting, her expression grave and a little sad, as though she imagined herself in the Jeneil's place.

Twenty-seven years since Jeneil inè Suon had died, and Gereth had hardly thought of her in years. Now, all in an instant, she seemed again a presence in this house. He almost believed he might hear her light, tentative step, that in a moment she might come out into the entryway and speak to him. She would probably look at him reproachfully. *Gereth, why did you bring her here? This is no house for a gently bred Harivin girl.*

And, for all Gereth had loved and served Innisth terè Maèr Eänetaì every day of the young duke's life, he knew Jeneil would have been right.

He said in a low voice, "It may take a day or so to arrange matters, but I shall see you through the pass."

She lifted grave eyes to his face but did not fall into effusions of gratitude. She merely murmured, "May the Fortunate Gods bless you and the Unfortunate pass you by. I and my father will both be so grateful."

Gereth did not ask her for her father's name, or her own. He didn't want to know, in case the knowledge might compel him to inform Innisth of this young woman's presence in Pohorir and Eäneté and in this house.

11

Kehera looked back at the painting to disguise her relief at the sene-
schal's promise. She suspected from his tone that the seneschal had
cared about that other young woman. Studying the flying lark, she felt
a strong kinship with that other girl, just her own age and even more
bitterly trapped by circumstance.

Before she could ask anything about Roh Pass or her own circumstances, however, a tall man strode into the hall, the heels of his boots
sounding crisp beats on the polished wood of the floor. Kehera knew
instantly, even without the seneschal's slight flinch, that this must the
Wolf Duke himself. She saw at a glance that he bore a ruling tie to
a Great Power—of course he held a tie, but she had not realized the
Eänetén Power was among the Great. But the tie blazed in him like fire,
brilliant and dangerous. Even so, it wasn't only the tie that told her who
this must be. There was also something in the tilt of the duke's head,
something in the set of his shoulders or the way he moved, a confidence
of his own mastery so absolute that she could never have mistaken him.

His hair was dark, his face lean and spare, his hands narrow and
elegant. His eyes were the eyes of the wolf on his banner: amber-gold;
topaz-gold; a color startling and disturbing in the face of a man. It was

impossible to judge his age: he might have been twenty-five or thirty or thirty-five, but he would probably look little older at fifty. He brought into the hall a tremendous, tightly leashed vitality. It was immediately hard to remember that anyone else was present.

"Ah," murmured the seneschal, making a tiny, abortive movement, as though to draw Kehera away and out of the duke's sight. But it was clearly too late.

The Wolf Duke paused, took in Kehera's presence, and said, his tone cutting and yet not without humor, "Gereth, a girl? She hardly seems suitable. Am I to gather you found yourself distracted from your other errand by a mission of mercy?"

The seneschal cleared his throat. "I admit I was distracted, Your Grace, but I may have fulfilled my other errand as well. Lieutenant Nikas should be arriving shortly with a slave dealer who requires close questioning—he may have been taking free people, our people, to sell as slaves in Irekay. A bad business, if so. Also, he will bring a Black Rose guildmaster who might have been involved in forging bills of sale for this purpose. Though we do not know with certainty that either of these men is guilty," he added hastily, as the humor disappeared from the Wolf Duke's face. "I can go back, visit the magistrates as I intended, find someone more certainly guilty of serious wrongdoing—"

"Unnecessary. I shall determine the truth," said the duke. "I assure you, I am not in such straits I cannot take appropriate care. Well done. Well done, indeed, if you have discovered such traffic. But this is not one of our folk, I perceive." He studied Kehera narrowly.

"Your Grace?" The seneschal glanced, with a trace of reluctance, at Kehera, who tried to look unimportant.

"Harivin," murmured the Wolf Duke, his gaze still fixed on Kehera. "Yes, I think she is Harivin. Not Pohorin, certainly." He looked at Kehera more closely, golden wolf's eyes flicking with impersonal curiosity down her body and returning to examine her face.

The seneschal sighed, almost imperceptibly. He said in a faintly apologetic tone, "She has appealed to me for leave to go through the pass, Your Grace. I thought she might very well join a merchant's company."

Kehera continued to concentrate on looking like any random girl who might somehow have gotten herself trapped in Pohorir through . . . she could not quite imagine what set of circumstances. She hoped the duke would simply shrug and agree with his seneschal, but she could not believe he would. She felt as though all the layers of deception were being peeled ruthlessly away from her by that fierce topaz stare. It struck her silent, bereft of words, almost of thought, like a rabbit crouching before the wolf of his banner.

A clatter from outside interrupted this moment before anything had been resolved. A man came in hastily and said, half announcement and half warning, "Your Grace, Lord Laören."

"A bit beforehand, it seems," muttered Gereth, sounding grim, and took Kehera's arm to lead her aside.

The Wolf Duke straightened his shoulders, tilted his head at an even more arrogant angle, and turned toward the door. The new lord was already coming through the doorway. He was nothing like the Wolf Duke. He was shorter and softer, and though he also carried an air of arrogance, in him it had a thin, sharp edge of contempt. Kehera didn't know him, but she was afraid of him immediately. Without thinking, she stepped back, tucking herself softly behind the midnight drapery on one side of the painting. Then she thought how stupid that was, because of course the seneschal would exclaim in surprise and make her come out—or the Wolf Duke would say something sardonic and drag her out himself. Then, his interest firmly captured, this other Pohorin lord, Laören, would surely want to know all about her.

The Eänetén duke had recognized her as Harivin; so had his seneschal. Lord Laören, as any lord, must hold some stronger tie to an Immanent Power than a common man; he would see that in her as well. Kehera found herself certain of this. He would know she was Harivin, and who knew what else he might find out?

But rather than revealing her, Gereth actually stepped away from her hiding place, and the Wolf Duke only said, in measured, chilly tones, "Lord Laören. I have heard your hunting party turned up unexpected quarry. Allow me to congratulate you. I am certain His Majesty will be pleased."

"Your young Captain Deconniy was instrumental in my success," answered the other man. "Such a modest young man, but I trust his modesty did not prevent him from informing you of that as well." Kehera couldn't see his face, but something in his voice made her shiver. It was something beyond mere satisfaction. Something colder and more malicious.

"Indeed," said the duke, his own voice flat.

"Yes, yes. I must say, I so much appreciated your loaning him to me. I'm sure he feels the same appreciation. Irekay offers so many more opportunities for advancement than the provinces, though I mean no insult in the world. It is merely a fact. Of course any ambitious young man must be glad of the chance to acquire patronage within the court. I so much appreciate Your Grace permitting your young captain to seek his fortune in Irekay. Not every provincial lord is so understanding of a young man's desire to seek greater opportunity elsewhere. But I'm sure you agree that Irekay will broaden anyone's experience of the world."

"Indeed, I have often said as much," answered the duke, his tone even flatter.

"I have so looked forward, all through the long ride from Tisain, to renewing my acquaintance with the young man," said the other, and Kehera could hear the smile in his voice. It was the smile not of a wolf, but of a viper. She tried not to shiver, afraid the draperies that concealed her might tremble.

"I am gratified Captain Deconniy gave such complete satisfaction, my lord," said the duke, his tone colorless. "I shall instruct him to present himself to you when he is at liberty. You will be weary after your journey. Allow my servants to conduct you to your suite. They will see to your every comfort. I am told you have taken Lord Geif into your custody. I assure you, this house possesses secure cells for miscreants."

"Oh, I think I will keep him with me," answered Lord Laören. "My staff knows very well how to keep miscreants secure."

"Of course," murmured the duke. "Just as you wish, my lord."

Then Kehera listened to the small sounds of people sorting themselves out, murmured politenesses, the sound of echoing but muffled footfalls, and the kind of quiet that told her nearly everyone had gone. She felt profoundly relieved, though that was foolish. She knew perfectly well the Eänetén duke must be just as dangerous to her as any other Pohorin lord. But somehow she didn't *feel* that. She felt . . . she felt as though something in herself recognized him and as though she had come to the place she should be. She didn't understand that. She no longer carried a deep tie to Raëhemaiëth, and even if she had, Eäneté was not bound to Raëh.

The Wolf Duke himself folded the draperies aside and offered her a steadying hand. Kehera met his eyes, took his hand, and stepped forward.

She knew at once that touching him had been a mistake, for she felt the mountains of Eäneté in him, with their ungiving stone layered over buried fire. And though he shouldn't have been able to, she knew he also perceived something of Raëh in her. She could see the certainty in the slight narrowing of his eyes. She gazed at him helplessly.

"You know whom you have brought into this house, of course," the Wolf Duke said to his seneschal. "No? Not even yet? But of course you cannot perceive her tie as clearly as I do. It is greatly attenuated, yet quite unmistakable." Reaching out, he pulled a pin out of Kehera's hair. The gesture was at once so quick and so smooth that he had completed it before she thought to flinch. Her disordered hair fell past her shoulders, its damning pale-blond roots grown out past the dye.

"This is Kehera irinè Elin Raëhema," said the duke. He was speaking to Gereth, but his eyes were again on hers. "This is the Raëhema heir, for whom all men in the world have been searching these past weeks. Hallieth Suriytaiän took her and lost her, and Methmeir Irekaì has reached out from Irekay to the four quarters of this kingdom to gather her in. Yet here she is. The Fortunate Gods have cast her at my feet like the key to a riddle I did not know to ask."

The seneschal drew his breath in slowly. He said, "I didn't know. I thought . . . When I found myself outside a Black Rose house, I thought I might find someone for you among their more perverted clients. But when I saw her there, I could not bear to let them have her. Even before she insisted to me that she is not a slave."

"Well, after all, that is true. She is certainly not a slave." The Eänetén duke did not smile, but an indefinable lightness had come into his face like the shadow of humor or affection.

Kehera finally managed to find her voice despite the duke's wolf-eyed regard. "My father would be grateful to have me returned to Harivir. I would be grateful too."

"Kings have a short memory for gratitude."

"In Pohorir, perhaps. Not in Harivir."

The Wolf Duke smiled, more an expression of his eyes than a movement of his lips. "Perhaps. We shall see. How clever of you to avoid Laören's notice. I do think it better if no lord of Irekay sets eye on you. Particularly no lord in direct service to Methmeir Irekaì."

Kehera certainly agreed with this.

"Indeed," the duke added to his seneschal, "the more quickly we can be rid of Laören, the better pleased I will be. How very convenient that we have already fed him our bait and designed our little play." He gave Kehera an unreadable look. "I believe I may even see a way to contrive a more permanent solution by which Eäneté might be made safe from Irekaïn attention. Indeed, I believe it must have been the Fortunate Gods who brought Your Highness to me. But while Laören lingers here, we must certainly keep you well out of his way. That is very clear."

Kehera nodded uncertainly. That last bit sounded like a good plan to her, although she wondered what the Wolf Duke meant by "a more permanent solution" and why he spoke of her safety in the same breath. An alliance with her father—could he hope for that, could he hope to break away from Pohorir and bind his province to Harivir instead? She would be willing to urge her father to such an alliance, but she feared Harivir was already facing too great a threat from Emmer for Raëh to easily support Eäneté . . . though she didn't know what might have happened in Emmer during these past weeks. She looked speculatively at the duke, wondering what news he might know from Harivir and whether he would tell it to her if she asked.

Gereth was saying, "Yes, Your Grace, but Laören *is* a problem—his servants snoop everywhere, and Laören himself is so unpredictable—"

"She must stay close; she must stay hidden; she must not be made the object of gossip. Or at least, not of such gossip as might be dangerous if it makes its way to Laören's ears." The duke gave a slight nod. "I see no alternative. She must lodge in my own rooms."

Kehera stared at him, recalled abruptly to the moment. She did not have to struggle to find words, however, because the seneschal protested, "Your Grace, that is hardly proper!"

"But safe," said the duke. He sounded amused and annoyed and resigned all at once. "My suite is becoming quite crowded of late, I admit. I can hardly imagine the gossip that will run through the house. First Eöté and then Verè and now I snatch up this girl the very moment I lay eyes on her. But gossip will not matter so long as no one suspects her name." He added to Kehera, "There is nowhere else in this house I can be certain you will be safe from Laören's prying. Do not fear. I will offer you no insult." He held out a hand in invitation for Kehera to accompany him.

It definitely wasn't proper. But Kehera thought of the Pohorin lord's silken malice and followed the duke's gesture without hesitation.

The duke's private suite proved to be enormous, all its large rooms warmly and richly furnished: two different reception chambers, each leading away to a different sitting room, a bedroom—he did not show her that, for which she was grateful—a study, a sort of conservatory with red-flowering plants hanging in front of wide windows, a private dining room, and a luxurious bathing room. Kehera looked wistfully at the wide tub, but the Wolf Duke did not seem to notice. He guided her to one of the sitting rooms. It was a wonderful room, with fires roaring in each of two massive fireplaces and tall, arching windows that let in the pale light of the winter noon. Stands of cedar and spicewood supported clean-burning oil lamps. The fragrance of the oils made her think of summer afternoons and new-cut hay and flowers, and the fear that had constricted her heart for so long began, despite everything, to loosen its grip.

Shelves reaching higher above Kehera's head lined two of the walls, holding not only books but also lithe wooden carvings that suggested the forms of running deer and leaping wolves. One wall was occupied mainly by a single tall painting, trees and tangled branches and golden leaves and a single bird, a lark, flashing away, half hidden behind leaves. Kehera was sure this painting, too, had been painted by the duke's mother. Kehera moved to study it and only then realized that the room was already occupied. A girl knelt by one of the hearths, but when she saw Kehera looking her, she shrank back. The other, a man perhaps a little older than Kehera, rose with alacrity from his chair.

"Your Grace," he said, and stood straight, his hands at his sides and his expression professionally blank. Kehera decided he must certainly be a soldier.

"My captain," said the Wolf Duke. "I gather you are aware of Lord Laören's return."

"Yes, Your Grace. I came straight here, as you ordered."

"As well for you that you did. He expresses a desire to renew your acquaintance. I have assured him you will attend him when you are next at liberty." The duke paused. The young man said nothing, but his mouth tightened.

"I am certain you have much to occupy yourself with here for the rest of today," the duke told him. "I expect your duties will keep you busy until late into the night. Tomorrow, you might have time to accommodate Laören, save that I believe events may intervene. You are ready for our little play?"

A nod. "Yes, Your Grace, if you are."

The duke inclined his head. "The choreography will take some care. I am determined Laören shall witness the incident. Otherwise his suspicion would be twice as sharp. He will be acutely suspicious in any case, so we must be convincing in every detail. I shall see to it he has word that you will be sparring against others of the young men. That should draw him to watch. Then we may perform the rest of the play."

"Yes," the captain said again, not sounding very happy about any of this.

"Indeed. This lady is my guest. My valued guest. She, too, must be at some pains to avoid Lord Laören. Thus she will stay here—I trust for only a short time. Laören will not dare intrude here in my private rooms, but if he does, my captain, from this moment, your first duty is to protect this lady by any means you might find necessary."

The young captain gave Kehera a curious, assessing look. "I understand, Your Grace."

"Eöté," said the duke, and waited until the girl rose timidly and came forward, clutching her hands together and not looking at any of them. The captain moved as though to lay a reassuring hand on her arm, but she flinched and after a second he let his hand fall.

Ignoring this, the duke said to the girl, "As the lady had no attendants of her own, you may attend her. I give you my word she is a kind and gentle lady. I do not believe you will find the duty onerous."

Eöté gave a tiny bob of her head and whispered assent. Kehera wondered at the girl's obvious terror. She had not thought the duke's people feared him so much. Or, if it were herself the girl feared, that was even more disturbing because she had no notion why.

Before she had quite decided whether to speak or what to say, a man put back the great door that the duke had left ajar and came in. By his dress and his manner, he was a ranking member of the duke's staff, a quiet-seeming man perhaps in his late twenties, with dark blond hair and calm eyes. The man bowed slightly to the duke. "Gereth said you wanted me, Your Grace?"

"Gereth anticipated me," agreed the duke, nodding. "Yes. This lady will need proper clothing and"—he gestured, a minimal flick of the fingers—"whatever else she requests. She will not leave this apartment until Laören has departed. Do not speak of her to the staff, save as a woman who has caught my eye."

"Another one?" the man said. He was not actually laughing, but his sideways glance at the duke was alight with silent humor.

The duke cast his gaze upward.

"I'm jealous," said the man cheerfully. "I'm sure Laören will hear all about your . . . vigor. But never fear, Your Grace. I will defeat all my rivals in the end."

The duke ignored this. Kehera found her eyebrows rising and hastily turned her gaze out the window, making sure her expression reflected polite inattention rather than incredulity.

"I will leave you in Reiöft's capable hands," the duke told her. "Do not leave these rooms." He swept a narrow glance at the others, including them both in this command as well. Then he added, only to her, "You will join me for a late supper. Caèr, get the lady something from the kitchens if she wishes. Bring it yourself." He did not wait for a response, but turned sharply and went out.

The man—Caèr Reiöft—gave Kehera a small bow. He was not very good-looking. His mouth was too wide, his eyes set too close together. But Kehera liked him. His good humor was enormously reassuring. "I will draw a bath for you, lady," he told her. "And I will endeavor to find satisfactory clothing that will do until better can be properly made up for you."

"Thank you," Kehera said fervently. "You are very kind." All else aside, she wanted a bath above anything. At least, anything that didn't involve a fast horse and a straight path through Roh Pass. But at least she could have the bath. Immediately, she hoped. "Eöté?" She turned to the girl.

"Of course my lady will wish to bathe," Eöté whispered. "There are bowls of special soap for your hair." She backed away toward the bathing room.

Eöté found soaps and scented oils. She still seemed very much afraid, even once they were alone in the duke's enormous bathing room. Her fear made it impossible for Kehera to relax. She wanted to say, *Please, Eöté, don't be frightened of me. I think I'm going to need a friend here.* It wouldn't help—and this girl was not Eilisè, and was far too terrified to be a friend. Kehera missed Eilisè intensely now that she had found herself in relative safety. If Eilisè had been here, Kehera would not have felt so alone or so lost. If she had only known her friend was alive and well in Raëh, she would have felt less alone. If she hadn't been responsible for her friend's death, she knew she would feel braver and more able to try again to get away, get home.

But now she had abandoned that poor little girl Geris as well, and Tageiny and Luad . . . even spiteful Reilliy and the other girls, poor Hallay who'd obviously never deserved to be made a slave. Everyone she would have wanted to protect was lost somewhere behind her, and she could help none of them.

"Did the duke—has he hurt you?" she asked Eöté directly. "Is he that sort?" If he had, Kehera was determined to do something to help this girl, at least. Somehow.

Eöté knelt frozen by the tub, a warm towel in her hands, her eyes enormous in her delicate face.

"I'm sorry to ask," Kehera said sincerely. "But I do think I had better know the worst. You—I mean—I can't help but see you're afraid of him. So—"

"*He* hasn't," the girl answered suddenly, with bitter emphasis. "But he *could. Anyone* could. A woman is never really safe. No one is safe. Not even here." Then she paled again and dropped her eyes, clearly wishing she hadn't spoken.

Kehera wished she could promise that she would keep Eöté safe. But she knew she could promise nothing.

Despite her doubts, being clean, really clean, was a tremendous luxury. Kehera let Eöté wrap her in a soft blue robe and then sat in a low-backed chair for the girl to work the tangles out of her hair with a broad-toothed comb. The dye still colored most of it dark, startling Kehera whenever she caught sight of herself in one of the bathing room's mirrors.

Eöté braided Kehera's hair, a complicated braid with the ends turned under and hidden, but left the heavy braid swinging loose down Kehera's back. Kehera looked in the mirror Eöté held for her, and she nodded in approval, then frowned. The pale roots of the hair were quite noticeable now that her hair was clean, and all the dye was wearing off in streaks.

"I could get you some more dye, my lady. . . ." Eöté offered hesitantly.

"Thank you." It was probably a good idea, and she was glad the girl had been brave enough to offer.

"Would you like to see the gowns Caèr Reiöft found for you, my lady?"

"If I am to join His Grace for supper . . . is there one suitable for a private but formal supper?"

"I think so. If my lady pleases, I will show you. . . ."

The dress Eöté found was like the room, all pale cream and soft blue. Delicate beadwork spread in a smoke-colored fan from the bodice down the long skirts. Kehera stood still to let Eöté do up the lacings. The fine, heavy cloth seemed doubly luxurious after the coarse material of her recent garb. The thought reminded her of other things she had carried all this way, and she asked, suddenly, "Eöté, the pouch I had with my traveling clothing. Would you bring it here, please?"

The other girl retrieved the pouch wordlessly. Kehera weighted it in hand for a moment. It had come so far with her . . . incredible that she still held it safe. A memory of home, a thing Tiro had made just for her. She dared not hope that she might ever play another game of tiahel with her brother with these carefully carven pieces. Still . . . "I'd like to put this somewhere where it won't be lost, Eöté. It's only a tiahel set—you can look, if you like. But my brother made it for me, and I would like to keep it safe."

The girl looked at the pouch doubtfully. "I think my lady will be sleeping on a pallet in the smaller sitting room. I can put it there for you, if you wish. . . ."

Kehera handed her the pouch and watched as the Eöté took it away, perhaps to examine its contents, or report them, or something. But after all, it honestly was a tiahel set, ordinary to anyone but Kehera. Probably the pouch would wind up on her bed, just as it was supposed to.

While Eöté was gone, she also quickly retrieved her few remaining pearls. There were only five left, but they were the biggest and the best. Kehera tucked them away in a pocket of her new dress.

She wanted nothing quite so much after that as a chance to lie down somewhere private and close her eyes for a little while. But there was no privacy she could trust in these rooms that were not hers, and if she lay down, she would crush her skirts. She went back to the larger sitting room instead, perched upright on the least comfortable chair, gazed out the window, and tried to think. Her thoughts only went in circles, but the view from the wide window was stunning, the lowering sun gilding the tops of the Takel Mountains. In the shadowed curves of the mountains, she thought she could make out the way Roh Pass must run.

Captain Deconniy had taken a seat by the fire, and Eöté had tucked herself down on the hearth near him, half out of sight behind his chair. Kehera wanted to ask them whether they thought the Eänetén duke might give her leave to go through the pass. But probably they would not know. She said instead, as though idly, "It was so kind of Gereth Murrel to help me. But he does seem kind."

This proved the right thing to say. Eöté actually brightened a tiny bit. "Oh, yes! He's so kind to all of us. Without Gereth, His Grace might—he might do *anything*, but he listens to Gereth."

Kehera was glad to hear this. After Parren, she wasn't very certain of her ability to judge people. Although she could see now that hints of the slave trader's true nature had been there all along. . . . She supposed Parren was probably here in this house now. The duke's seneschal had said he was to be brought here. Whatever the duke did to Parren, he deserved it. But she said, "Yes, it seems to me His Grace might do anything. I have heard that he's cruel."

This time it was Captain Deconniy who answered. "His Grace isn't cruel, my lady. I mean . . . it's the wolf tie. But he . . . controls it. He's not really *cruel*, not like Lord Geif of Tisain. Or Lord Laören." He and Eöté exchanged a glance of what seemed complete accord.

"Him," Kehera said, and shivered.

The captain gave her a little nod. "I see you've met him. Not—" The man hesitated. "Not closely, I hope." He and the girl exchanged another glance. Then Deconniy moved to touch Eöté's hand, just resting the tips of his fingers on the back of her hand, and though the girl dropped her gaze, she didn't flinch away.

"No," said Kehera, and definitely didn't ask just what either of them had suffered at Laören's hands. But she turned back to the more important topic, obliquely. "I understand how it is, to have a deep tie. But it shouldn't be like that for your duke. I mean, something you have to fight to control. It's more like . . . something that shapes the person you are. But not something that makes you into someone you never could be."

The captain's eyebrows went up. "With respect, my lady, in Pohorir, you don't want a deep tie to shape your lord. You're Harivin, are you not?"

"Everyone seems able to tell," Kehera said, discouraged. She had thought herself so well disguised.

"I don't know about that, my lady. It's just, it's what you seem to expect from a lord with the deep tie. Mind, His Grace *is* a hard man. But—I've seen this, since I came here. He's hardest on himself. You can trust his self-control." He gave Eöté a tiny nod that Kehera couldn't read, but the girl only looked away. Deconniy turned back to Kehera and went on. "But you have to understand, managing his tie takes a lot of . . ."

"Strength of mind?" Kehera suggested. "I understand. You're new to Eäneté yourself, Captain Deconniy? Why did you choose to serve the Eänetén duke, then? Him, especially? If I may ask?"

Captain Deconniy gave her a long look. "There aren't any other lords in Pohorir who would choose a man like Gereth Murrel as their seneschal, or regard his opinion if they did. I knew just from that. And from Senior Captain Etar. And there's not another lord in Pohorir who would trust a man from another lord's service. Or go to . . . enormous trouble, to protect such a man from an influential Irekaïn lord who wanted him. His Grace . . . he's a great man, lady. I believe that."

Eöté shivered.

Kehera made a mental note not to try to suborn the young captain. But perhaps she wouldn't need to try to suborn anyone, if she could only persuade the Eänetén duke to simply let her go. If he wanted an alliance with her father, perhaps he would. She hoped for that.

The duke's private dining room was beautifully appointed; it was not large, but the wide windows made it seem more expansive. This room, too, had the inevitable fireplace, the light of the fire flickering across the slate of the hearth and the polished brass of the spoons, but the room smelled more of cooking than burning cedar. The table was oak, carved with leaves and acorns around the edge. The chairs, too, were carved, but with stylized deer and wolves with eyes of yellow topaz.

The Wolf Duke stood up with that same strict courtesy as Gereth Murrel escorted Kehera into the room. "Lady," he said—not "Your Highness," a caution she appreciated, though there seemed little chance of anyone outside the duke's intimate servants overhearing. "Please join me. I hope you have found yourself comfortable despite the rather close accommodations."

"Yes, quite comfortable," Kehera answered, automatically coming forward to take the chair he indicated. She studied him, at once wary and fascinated. She could see the tie in him. It seemed . . . less obtrusive now than it had earlier. She could not tell whether the Eänetén duke had bound his Immanent Power more firmly through sheer self-control or whether he had done something else to content his Power and make it settle. The duke was, in fact, very hard to read.

But the food was good. Caèr Reiöft served, unobtrusive but quietly good-humored, so that Kehera found herself almost at ease. There was a winter soup of leeks and potatoes, rich with butter; and bread; and apples with honey; and little skewers of meat served with some spicy sauce that took Kehera by surprise so that she had to reach quickly for bread to cool her tongue.

The duke smiled slightly. It altered the angles of his face and made him seem less forbidding. But he said only, "Lord Laören may depart as early as tomorrow. Then we should enjoy a peaceful interval in this house, during which we may consider the course of the future."

Kehera inclined her head. "I must thank Your Grace again for protecting me from . . . our common enemy." She meant Methmeir Irekaì as well as Lord Laören. And if the King of Pohorir was the Eänetén duke's enemy . . . surely that was all to her advantage. She added, "I pray Your Grace will have nothing but good fortune before you for the years to come."

"In your coming to my house and my hand, I hope we may indeed perceive the intentions of the Fortunate Gods." Strict patience glinted in the duke's yellow eyes, ruthless as winter.

"There is surely no reason why the Gods should not favor us both. Especially if Your Grace is kind enough to allow me passage to Harivir. Such kindness would surely find favor with the Fortunate Gods." *And my father*, she meant, though she did not say this out loud.

"Perhaps. We shall see. In fact, you might do better to claim refuge here. I think you may not know that Harivir has of late found itself much engaged against its enemies to the north." The duke paused.

Kehera suddenly found her mouth dry. She took a sip of wine and asked, calmly, she hoped, "Perhaps Your Grace would be so kind as to tell me the news from Harivir?"

"Rumor has crossed the mountains in some confusion," murmured the duke. "For example, some weeks ago, toward the end of Fire Maple Month, word came to Eäneté that Hallieth Suriytaiän had compelled Torrolay Raëhema to deliver up his heir in tribute, but that the Mad King had quickly found reason to regret his demand, for Torrolay Raëhema had sent a trap of some sort as well as his daughter." He regarded her with thoughtful interest. "Shortly thereafter, I heard that Hallieth Suriytaiän was dead. Then that he did not die, but rather lost the Power of Suriytè, and with the tie, the kingship. Then that he had lost the Suriytè Power but gained a different tie; that a foreign Immanent Power reached out of the wild desert and set its tie in his heart and in Suriytè. You will understand my bewilderment."

Kehera considered this assortment of tales. "He was not dead when I . . . left Suriytè," she said after a moment. "But I think it's true that the Great Power of Suriytè had been destroyed."

"Do go on. I am most interested."

Kehera was sure he was. She said, "An Immanent Power out of the empty desert? Is that the tale? That seems strange to me. The foreign Power I saw there seemed no small wild Immanent newly risen out of those abandoned lands. Nor do I see why an Immanent rooted in the desert would reach out to a great city such as Suriytè; nor do I understand how such an Immanent could have challenged the Great Power of Suriytè even were it so inclined." She hesitated, but she couldn't see how reticence could help her now, so she added, "The foreign Power I saw in Suriytè was . . . cold." She shivered. All her memories of those horrible moments in the tower of the King's Hall of Suriytè seemed blurred and strange. But she could say with confidence, "The man who brought me through Anha Pass was an agent of your king, I am certain. He was a sorcerer. He bore a deep tie, and I would swear that the Power he carried within him was that same cold Power and not some other."

The Eänetén duke's interested regard sharpened. "Indeed. How very intriguing. You were there, of course, when Hallieth Suriytaiän lost his namesake Power. And Methmeir Irekaì is uncommonly ambitious, even for a King of Pohorir. Of course, his father was ambitious, and his grandmother before that; one expects the Irekaïn Power to be acquisitive and aggressive. Still, to strike so ruthlessly and so far from Irekay is certainly unexpected."

Kehera nodded. Everyone knew that an ambitious king might use his Immanent Power to overwhelm a rival, force another Immanent into an Unfortunate bond, bind the land to his own. An unfriendly king might then strip the vigor and strength of the subjugated Immanent to enhance his own land and extend his own life.

But a king using his Immanent Power to actually *destroy* another was something she had never heard of, and a king reaching so far from the precincts of his own Power to do it was something she had never imagined. She guessed now that this had been Gheroïn Nomoris's role: to carry a deep tie from Irekay into Emmer so that his king might reach through him. She had never heard of anyone doing that, but she had never studied history assiduously. Probably her brother, Tiro, could list half a dozen times it had happened.

But she hardly cared about any of that at the moment. "But Harivir?" she asked, unable to disguise her need to hear whatever the Wolf Duke might know. "Your Grace, what has happened in Harivir? You say my father is hard-pressed?"

"Indeed. Well, the rumors that have come to my ear suggest that Hallieth Suriytaiän in fact continues to hold Suriytè and all the land north and the east; that no one within his demesne dare raise sword or hand or voice against him. But Emmer has fragmented, with the south and the coast breaking free of Suriytaiän authority. An Emmeran general, an ambitious man called Corvallis, has taken the south of Emmer and seeks to claim the kingship there, I gather." The Wolf Duke sounded faintly approving. He added, "Rumor suggests that Torrolay Elin Raëhema has allied with General Corvallis and they work together to resist Hallieth Theraön Suriytaiän. But yes, one hears they are indeed hard-pressed despite their alliance. From which one gathers Methmeir Irekaì must indeed be supporting the Mad King of Emmer."

This made sense. Kehera wished now she had pushed Hallieth

Suriytaiän out a tower window when she'd had the chance. She said, "Your king must wish to rule the whole world." But she added with what she hoped was quiet dignity, "Yet whatever rumors make their way to Eäneté, it is unwise to discount Harivin strength or determination."

The duke inclined his head, faintly ironic. "You will find that I do not discount the possibilities Harivir may yet hold for the future. However, if you would now be so kind as to describe for me what you witnessed in Suriytè?" He gave her an inviting flick of a hand. "In a little more detail, if you will."

"It was . . . very strange." She did not remember exactly what Hallieth Suriytaiän had said to her, nor exactly what the cold Power had said, but she described the scene as well as she could: the high tower, the Mad King, the hissing frost that had spread across the room. Then the rest of it, stumbling a little, leaving out Eilisè because she couldn't bear to see the Wolf Duke not care about her friend's death. But she carefully described Gheroïn Nomoris.

"Gheroïn Nomoris," murmured the duke's seneschal, speaking for almost the first time since the conversation had become fraught. "We know that name. A hound of the king's. A hunting hound; one is not astonished the king should set him to an important task. But carrying a tie such as you describe?" He glanced at the duke, frowning. "The Nomoris family is not known to be above common."

The duke himself made a slight, dismissive gesture. "Gheroïn is a cousin of the family. A by-blow with a tangled inheritance. I am not surprised to learn the Heriduïn Irekaì line has crossed the Nomoris line once or twice."

"Your Grace has met Gheroïn Nomoris?" Kehera asked, catching a note of familiarity in the duke's tone.

"When I was presented at court as a boy," the duke answered distantly. "I became closely acquainted with the man, unfortunately." He was not, evidently, inclined to speak more of that, moved a hand to encourage Kehera to go on with her story.

"There's not much more," she said, and edited her father's man out of the tale because she did not feel equal to explaining Quòn. She only said she had gotten away and found help in Enchar. And His Grace knew how that had come out.

"Yes," said the duke, his yellow eyes glinting. "Perhaps it will please you to know that the slave dealer who betrayed you did not survive questioning. I regret that you cannot be offered the chance to attend a proper hanging."

"Oh," Kehera said again. "No. I mean, that's all right." She couldn't quite decide what she thought about Parren's death. But she was glad not to actually have to watch him hang.

"He should have known better than to kidnap Eänetén folk," Gereth told her, perhaps guessing at her discomfort. "The Black Rose House does appear to have been complicit, for which the entire house will likely be . . . dismantled."

Kehera was surprised at the grim satisfaction in his tone when he said this. But then she thought again. "I had the impression that perhaps the . . . Black Rose . . . sells girls to men who will murder them. Perhaps I didn't understand."

"Oh, you understood," the seneschal told her. He gave his duke a sideways look. "Not quite legal, but very hard to stamp out."

"I am perfectly aware of your opinion," the Wolf Duke said dryly. "Indeed, I could hardly fail to be aware of it." He added to Kehera, "The Black Rose House tithes directly to Irekay, so I have been constrained in dealing with its excesses. Your Parren, however, set the house into my hand. And chance or the Fortunate Gods seems to have arranged . . . various other tactical elements. I believe I will now be able to destroy the house, root and branch."

"Not before time," muttered Gereth.

"Precisely at the right time," the duke corrected him. "And not before Laören has departed. Be patient, my old friend."

The seneschal nodded.

Kehera said cautiously, seeing a chance to make good a promise she had thought beyond hope, "The other slaves that the slave trader Parren brought with me to your city—"

"Lady?"

"Your Grace. I should be pleased if those slaves were to find good places. If they might even be freed, if they could find honest work. I would be . . . I would be grateful."

"Slaves are not customarily freed. The brand marks them as unfit for ordinary employment."

Kehera had not realized this, and was quietly appalled.

Perhaps the Wolf Duke saw this, for he added, "However, I am not necessarily concerned for this custom. But what are those people to you, that you should care for them?"

"People," Kehera said, not quite sharply. "What else would they have to be?"

A trace of amusement informed the curious fire-ridden eyes. The duke inclined his head slightly. "My household can no doubt absorb a handful of freed slaves. I shall be pleased to issue the appropriate orders." He glanced at his seneschal, who nodded with obvious satisfaction.

"Thank you, Your Grace." Kehera hesitated. "I had . . . before everything . . . one of those men—two of them, in fact—were going to help me get through the pass. But it went wrong."

"Indeed. You might have found this challenging, even with two men to help you."

"Well, I knew it might be difficult, but Tageiny seemed like the kind of man I would be glad to hire for something dangerous and difficult. I thought I might trust him, that much at least, especially since he would have been free as soon as we entered Harivir. I cannot now redeem my word, I know. . . ."

"Indeed," repeated the duke. "Tageiny."

Kehera nodded. "And a younger man, Luad."

"I see."

"I would be truly grateful if they were freed, Your Grace. And there was a little girl, Geris . . . and an older man. I believe he had done nothing wrong. . . ."

"You wish *all* of these people freed, I gather." The duke was plainly amused, but he added, "They shall be. Gereth will see to it, and he will be able to find suitable employment for them, I am sure."

Kehera bowed her head. "You are generous, Your Grace."

A dismissive shrug answered this. "I can afford to be generous, can I not? I would prefer that you view me as . . . potentially, your ally. Certainly not any simple enemy."

"Your Grace, I would be glad to think of you as a friend, but I don't think I would ever think of you as a *simple* enemy."

For a moment those wolf's eyes lingered on her face, and she wondered whether she had offended him. She had not meant offense. But he only said softly, "You may retire, if you wish. I hope our circumstances will all be greatly improved by this hour tomorrow."

Sometimes a retreat in good order is as much of a victory as is possible. Kehera stood up thankfully. "Of course, Your Grace. Good night."

12

The sun gleamed dimly, low in the flat winter sky, veiled by cloud the exact color of beaten silver. Later those clouds would probably yield to the sun and the day would become almost pleasant. But at dawn, it was cold.

Innisth called for bread and fruit preserves because that was his invariable habit. But he did not eat. It seemed unwise to break his fast, given the coming charade. It would be a small play, for an audience of one, but the injury would be real.

He felt very little fear. The blow would not be crippling, or else it would; he expected the former but did not doubt his ability to cope with the latter if it became necessary. If his physicker was incapable of repairing the damage, he would still be the Duke of Eäneté. He did not rule his province with his leg. Nor did he need to fear the pain. There was nothing unfamiliar about pain. It would not touch his dignity.

Verè Deconniy did not seem to share his sanguine outlook. The young captain also refused breakfast, but neither could he settle. He moved restlessly from table to window and back again, waiting for Innisth's signal that they might go down to the practice yard. It was too early. The men would not begin training for another half hour.

But Deconniy plainly wanted to go down at once.

Eöté also did not touch the food. She sat very still in the chair nearest the fire, her hands folded in her lap and her eyes on the table. "You may both eat, if you like," Innisth told them. "You will need your strength, my captain. There is no reason you should go without, Eöté."

Two pairs of eyes lifted to his face and immediately fell again.

Annoyed, Innisth pushed back his chair and rose. Let them be dismal alone, if they were so inclined. He himself felt, so close to the departure of the despised Irekaïn lord, that a weight was lifting from his shoulders. Or perhaps that was due to the Raëhema girl's appearance on his doorstep. He felt that the world was wider this morning. As though every possibility waited to fall into his hand.

He said to Deconniy, "Do not come down to the yard until the usual time." Then he said to Eöté, "Do not come down at all. Laören will be there, and we shall not put easy temptation in his way." He did not wait for acknowledgment, but strode out to find Captain Etar.

The senior captain was on his feet, pacing from one side of his small room to the other. He, too, plainly wanted to go down to the practice yard and was having to exert himself to resist. He turned sharply when Innisth rapped on his open door and grimaced. "Your Grace. It will go well. No reason it should not go well."

"Of course," said Innisth.

"I think it unlikely you will be badly injured," said Etar. "Still, your physicker will be . . . where?"

"In the barracks, attending some recent minor injury. That cannot cause suspicion. There is always some minor injury among the men. That will place him as near as seems practicable."

Etar paced again, then nodded at last. "I want to warn him. But that's not wise. So I will also be ready to tend you immediately after the wound is dealt, that no time may be lost. Deconniy?"

"He is ready to play his role, I think. You must be sure he suffers no undo harm after he is arrested. If Lord Laören attempts to bribe his guards, this must be handled with delicacy."

"I'll see to it."

"Indeed." Innisth paused, then added evenly, "If I should happen through some mischance to be killed, the Eänetén Power must go to someone."

"Yes. Have you any idea where the tie would go?"

"A difficult question, unfortunately. To the best of my knowledge, I have no child of my body. The Power's choice will thus be unpredictable. A distant cousin, an unknown by-blow of my father, who can say? Nor can I say how much of an imprint I have myself set on Eänetaìsarè. My father held the deep tie for much longer than I."

"And your grandfather was worse," said Etar. "I know."

"Just so. In the event you must take what steps you see fit, but it would please me to think that you would strike down any man who took the tie unless he were such a man as should do well by Eäneté. In all such matters, I would trust your judgment. As you no doubt remember, a fall from a high place will kill any man, deep tie or no." The duke paused.

Etar bowed his head. "Your Grace may depend on me. I give Your Grace my word that should this tragedy occur, I will without fail see the tie goes to a man you would approve."

"You reassure me, my old soldier." Innisth gave this first and oldest of his captains a spare nod of approval. "Shall we go down?"

The younger men were already at their practice when Etar and the duke came into the yard. It was sheltered from the wind by the barracks and the house, but cold. Still, some of the men stripped to the waist to spar, particularly the unattached young men, as was the custom. Girls gathered at the windows of the house to watch; that too was traditional. Innisth did not look to see whether Lord Laören also watched. Making certain the Irekaïn lord witnessed at least the end of the morning's practice was Gereth's task. Innisth trusted he would see to it.

The practice weapons, made of weighted wood, were edged with chalk to leave clear marks as well as bruises. But as they warmed up, some of the men, more expert than the others, switched to real swords.

Verè Deconniy came into the yard at last to the ring of steel against steel.

Deconniy saluted the duke, but casually. He acknowledged Captain Etar with a more formal salute and an apology for his tardiness, then strode across the yard to claim a sword. He was already undoing the laces of his shirt. Innisth could not quite restrain a glance up toward the windows, but light slid across the glass and he could not tell whether Laören was there or not. Looking away again, he strolled closer and leaned against a post to watch Deconniy spar with Lieutenant Tejef. Steel rang. The light ran down their swords—the sun had come out; Innisth had not noticed until that moment. Their boot heels rang on the flagstones. Sweat gleamed on Deconniy's shoulders and chest. He was not over-large, but, shirtless, one could appreciate the muscular definition of his body. Innisth allowed himself to watch the young captain with open attention.

Etar called the match and waved Tejef away toward one of the younger men. "Tem extends too far when he lunges; work on that," he told him, and turned toward Deconniy. But Deconniy had already taken a deliberate step toward the duke. He was smiling, flushed with exertion, and when he beckoned to the duke, anyone watching would certainly see more than one kind of invitation in the gesture.

"Practice weapons," Etar ordered, and jerked his head toward one of the other men.

"No need," Deconniy said, light and amused, meeting the duke's eyes with a lover's boldness. "I won't slip—and His Grace won't get even a single touch."

"Indeed?" said Innisth, allowing the corner of his mouth to crook upward. He had designed this little play and set it in motion; but even he had not expected Verè Deconniy to be quite so convincing. His own part was easier. He only looked Deconniy up and down, allowing the Eänetén Power to rise and look out of his eyes. Heat flushed through him, sensual and savage. He made no effort to hide that heat. He knew that Laören, lord as he was and holding some minor tie of his own, must see it. Feel it.

"Your Grace, this is not wise," Etar protested.

"Practice weapons aren't the same," Deconniy said with careless confidence. "Dancing on the sharp edge of danger adds savor to life." He was still smiling, though his expression had become a little strained. Only a close look would see that strain. But anyone would see the smile. And if Laören was not watching, Innisth was going to be very angry with Gereth. He did not let himself glance around, but only beckoned for one of the other men to bring him a sword.

Astonishingly enough, the match went exactly as it had been planned. There was the same tentative, slow beginning as in their practice sessions, the same smooth acceleration of the pace. Deconniy retreated briefly, then seemed to gather himself and press the attack. Innisth, as always, found himself forced to narrow his attention, concentrating on the choreographed swordplay. It prevented him from anticipating the coming blow, which was perhaps the point.

Deconniy struck, too quickly for Innisth to evade.

Innisth was aware first simply that a heavy blow had been struck; it felt like the kick of a horse. He stumbled, but did not fall. Deconniy took a step forward and caught his arm, supporting him. Etar was there as well suddenly, taking the sword from his hand. A wave of dizziness swept through Innisth, and he staggered again, catching his weight on the injured leg.

That was when the pain finally hit. Innisth had been right; he did not lose his dignity. He lost consciousness. His last memory was of Deconniy, who, white and stricken, caught him as he fell.

Innisth Eänetaì dreamed he walked along a path that ran through a forest. The path was covered with a blanket of snow. Fine dry snow drifted in the air and blew stingingly against his face and hands. The black trunks of trees crowded close on each side of the path, reaching tangled and leafless branches overhead. A pale light, like and yet unlike that of the moon, glowed against the white snow. It was bitterly cold. He felt distantly that he should turn back, but he did not. A cold wind rattled the naked branches against one another and hissed through the light snow. His boots crunched on the snow. There was no other sound.

Then there was. A lighter, quicker step: a wolf wove through the trees, paralleling his path, a lean gray wolf with yellow eyes. It slanted back its ears and dropped its jaw in a silent wolf laugh, savage, but not without humor. Its shadow stretched out long behind it: the shadow of a man and not of a wolf. Innisth stopped and turned. The shadow lying on the snow behind him was the shadow of a wolf.

A cutting wind rose, whipping through the black wood, sending the snow stinging into the air. Somewhere not far distant came the long humming cry of a winter dragon, like the resonant voice of the wind itself. Innisth turned toward that threat, but a small falcon, a buff and slate kestrel, darted through the air before him, quick-winged, visible for only a second and then instantly gone again into the snow. He paused, not knowing quite why. Turning again, he found the wolf pacing gravely toward him out of the blowing snow, no more than a few feet distant.

"Eänetaìsarè, it is, walking in your shadow," a quiet voice told him. A woman's voice, oddly familiar. He stopped, listening, his heart leaping up and beating fast as though this was the one voice he had longed to hear.

The falcon flashed once more through the air before him, its flight as sharp and sudden as a lightning strike: there and then gone again. It called as it flew, sharp and fierce. Somewhere the dragon cried again, but this time it seemed more distant. The wind died and the snow fell quietly, large silent flakes drifting downward around him. The wolf took a step closer and looked into his eyes.

The woman's voice said, "It is Eänetaìsarè, but you have mastered it. You know your own name. What is your name?"

Innisth opened his mouth to answer, but the sound that came out of his throat was the long, eerie song of a wolf.

"Innisth," the woman named him. "Innisth terè Maèr Eänetaì."

The wolf came close. "Eänetaì," it said, and its voice was his own.

"Eänetaìsarè," cried the falcon, speaking with the voice of a woman. Then the falcon said, "Innisth," and darted away on narrow wings through the interwoven black branches and the silvery light.

He turned and took one step to follow the bird, but stopped, looked back at the wolf. Its yellow stare seemed as measureless as the deep forest. He said, "Eänetaìsarè," and woke.

Innisth blinked up at the ceiling, trying to focus his eyes. For a moment he thought he looked at black branches laced across a field of snow, but he saw then that it was the dark spicewood trim over the white ceiling of his own bedchamber. He was terribly thirsty, and his leg hurt abominably. He tried, weakly, to sit up.

A hand touched his shoulder, pressing him back irresistibly. "Don't try to move," said Gereth, and shifted into his field of vision. His seneschal looked as though he had aged years. His skin was fine-drawn, the lines etched deeply around his eyes and mouth. Such deep lines, to appear in so little time. Innisth said without thought, "I am sorry."

Gereth moved his head in quiet negation. "No. You did well in everything. You have always done well, Innisth. You lost a great deal of blood, that's all. It certainly made for a most convincing performance. That was the day before yesterday. Hush! Do you think me so incapable that I cannot manage for a single day and night?"

Innisth closed his eyes and sank back, accepting the rebuke wordlessly, knowing it was deserved. He asked huskily, "Help me sit up."

The seneschal obeyed, shoving pillows to brace him. "Drink this," he said, and gave the duke a tall wooden cup.

Innisth tried to lift it, but found that even so light a vessel wobbled alarmingly. Gereth caught it and held it steady for him to drink. It was water, plain and cold. Innisth drained the cup.

"More?"

Innisth shook his head slightly and leaned back against the pillows. "The Raëhema girl? She was here?"

Gereth paused. "How did you know?" Then he said, "I knew you wouldn't like it. But she insisted she could help you. That she could help your Power hold you. You almost . . ." He stopped.

"The falcon," said Innisth. He lifted one hand to rub his eyes. Even that small movement tired him. He said, "She did help me." He frowned, trying to remember, but the dream had faded as dreams do, and he could remember nothing but a flash of wings and the sharp quick cry of a falcon.

He shook his head slightly, not so much dismissing the dream images but setting them aside. "Laören is still here." He knew it was true. He thought he could feel the Irekaïn lord's presence, like a canker festering in the roots of an otherwise healthy oak.

"He declares he is waiting to see you recovered before he goes. I allowed him to see you immediately after you were injured, as soon as your physicker said it could be allowed. I'm sorry, I know you would *truly* hate that, but he might have doubted the severity of your injury. No one could doubt it after seeing you as you were then. And Amereir was very convincing." Gereth almost smiled. "I believe he suspects you did this to yourself on purpose, and wishes you would warn him before you do such things."

"But Laören is *still here*," Innisth repeated, though he knew he sounded sulky.

Gereth touched his shoulder, a comforting gesture. "He tells me he will depart as soon as you are strong enough to see him off. I imagine he is waiting to see if you will live. As everyone has been. Captain Deconniy is being held for your judgment; no one has presumed to touch him. Eöté is quite safe; I had her stay in your rooms here to help nurse you. Everything is quite in order."

"Why did the wound . . . bleed so much?"

"Amereir said the sword managed to nick a major artery. A fluke, he said. He stitched the artery and said to tell you that the cut itself was not especially serious. You may expect to regain full function in the leg, though he was very stern about not rushing the recovery. That is for your ear," Gereth added. "Everyone else has been informed that you may never again walk without a cane."

"Good. Very good. I will see Laören gone tomorrow."

"No."

"Yes. I want him away from here."

"The day after tomorrow," Gereth said, and raised his hand as Innisth started to speak. He held his arm out before the duke. "Pull my arm down to the bed," he commanded.

Innisth eyed him with weary anger. Then, without speaking, he reached out and gripped the older man's arm. He tried to pull it down. Gereth resisted the pressure with no evident effort. Innisth tried harder. Pain rose from his leg through his body in sickening waves.

"You're going to faint if you keep that up," Gereth observed with pitiless accuracy.

Innisth stopped, panting, just before he would have fainted, black lines (*branches against white snow*) cutting across his vision, his head swimming.

"Day after tomorrow," Gereth said gently. "The rest of today, and tomorrow, you rest."

Innisth leaned his head back against the pillows, defeated. A novel sensation. Had it been anyone but Gereth, he would have refused to accept it. The older man touched his arm again in affection and reassurance, a familiarity, but one Innisth had no heart to rebuke.

Gereth said, "There is broth and bread. You must eat, and then rest again. Amereir left very stern instructions." He helped Innisth eat, with care so matter-of-fact and impersonal that the duke found it possible to accept his help without shame. And he made him sleep, after eating, with the same tactful authority. "I will be here when you wake—I will be here all the time. I, or Caèr Reiöft, or Etar. So you see, you may rest easy."

"Or the Raëhema girl," Innisth murmured, his eyes already closing. "She too may come and go." But he sank down and did not hear Gereth answer.

The second time Innisth woke, he was clear-headed enough to know that he had not been entirely clear-headed earlier. And stronger.

Strong enough to push himself slowly up until he was sitting nearly upright, leaning back against the pillows.

As promised, Gereth was present, sitting in a heavy chair drawn up close to the bed, his head tilted back, his eyes closed. A ledger was open on his lap, his hand lying across its pages in abandoned effort. Innisth found himself with no desire at all to disturb the older man and remained perfectly still in the bed.

But Gereth, perhaps feeling Innisth's regard, or sensing the new stillness greater than the quiet of sleep, opened his eyes and lifted his head. For a moment he only looked at the duke, a look that held, in that one moment, all he had felt of strain and fear in the past days. Then he smiled, and that strain seemed to fall away. "You're looking much better, Your Grace."

Innisth said dryly, "I see you are using my title again. Does that mean you are now willing to accept my orders?"

"I suppose I must be," agreed Gereth. He stood up, laying the ledger aside. "What orders do you have for me, Your Grace?"

The duke considered this. "Deconniy? The Raëhema heir?"

"Kehera Raëhema is safe and well. Verè Deconniy is also well. The staff is evenly divided between believing this was an accident and believing Deconniy struck you down purposefully, so there is some tension there. But Etar is keeping an eye on him."

Innisth nodded slightly. "Such doubt is perhaps unavoidable. That can be dealt with later. The great thing must be to send Laören on his way. You may inform him that I shall be strong enough to see him on his way no later than the day after tomorrow. Add my apologies for the delay I have occasioned him and my thanks for his courtesy in remaining to take formal leave."

"Your Grace, I will see to everything."

"I know you will, Gereth. I depend on you entirely."

The seneschal smiled. He bowed, more deeply than was strictly required, and went out.

❋ ❋ ❋

Three days after Innisth's little play, on the twenty-seventh day of the Month of Frost, Lord Laören and his staff assembled at last in the courtyard, more than a dozen men and horses, Lord Geif of Tisain close-guarded in their midst and looking already more than a little worse for wear. Innisth had intended to take his leave of Laören from his reception hall or his library—somewhere warm and comfortable. Forcing the duke to have himself carried into the frozen courtyard was a small, spiteful gesture that did not surprise Innisth at all; he very much hoped it was the last such gesture he would be required to suffer.

"I'm so glad to see you recovering, Your Grace." Lord Laören drew on his furred gloves slowly, smiling his little, dangerous smile. "Such a pity about your injury."

The duke sat in the high-backed chair brought out to the courtyard for the purpose. He inclined his head, showing neither pleasure nor displeasure, and murmured that he, too, regretted it very much. It was even true—at least true enough. He certainly regretted the pain and the incapacity. This was important, because he did not dare to lie too blatantly to the Irekaïn lord.

"And a pity that it should have been your young Captain Deconniy who made such a serious error," added Laören. "You were a bit fond of him, I thought. A shame."

Innisth said, his tone remote, "You may certainly enjoy the hospitality of Eäneté long enough to witness his punishment. If you wish it, I will set the day forward as far as possible to accommodate your need for haste, my lord."

"Alas, I dare not linger so long." Lord Laören put out a hand without looking, and one of his men put the rein of his horse into it. "I have certainly enjoyed my visit, Your Grace. A very useful trip." He glanced over his shoulder at Geif and then smiled at the duke. "I do so like to be of service to His Majesty. As do we all, of course. Perhaps the king will send for you when you are well enough to travel. Or perhaps I will ask him if I might visit your province and city and house again. Next year, perhaps."

"I will, as always, be delighted to serve His Majesty in any way possible," Innisth said flatly. This time he did not care if Laören heard the lie. He bowed, a slow, deliberate bow that made it clear he considered the interview at an end. "May you have fair weather and good roads for your ride."

Laören, smiling, returned the bow with one a little less deep, and turned away to mount his horse. And he rode away, across the width of the courtyard and out the gate and away, gone. Innisth gazed after him, watching until he was out of sight and then tracking his progress through his tie. Four days, five days until the court lord would ride through the borderlands between Eäneté and the inner provinces and be truly gone.

But he was gone enough now. At last. Innisth let out a slow breath and unclenched his hands from the arms of his chair. Gereth moved forward, but Innisth signed him to silence. He murmured after a moment, "He may yet turn back. He might enjoy that. I will not be confident he will not play that game until he is at least a day's ride away from the city."

"He will want to drop Geif at the king's feet, like a dog bringing back a stick to its master. Whatever he or Irekaì might suspect of you, the king will surely deal with Geif first. As you intended."

Innisth lifted one shoulder in a tiny shrug. "Yes. Even so. The Raëhema heir—"

"Your Grace?"

"I will see her." Innisth set his hands deliberately on the arms of his chair, preparing to push himself to his feet. His leg twinged alarmingly, and he sank back, thinking better of the movement. "Tonight. A private supper, as before. Arrange for her to be given proper accommodations at once. The suite adjoining mine will do. However, we will not announce her name to the household." He paused to consider. "Eöté can continue in her service. That will do, as we have few enough women in the household. But the men Kehera Raëhema particularly wished to bring into her service, I will see them. After supper, I think. Yes. She may attend while I interview them. Yes, I think that would be best. And send Etar to me. That, first of all." He added last, pretending grimly that he did not find this dependence humiliating, "And have someone assist me inside."

Captain Etar strode into the duke's reception room with a firm step and straight shoulders, neither of which quite hid the tightness of his mouth or the hard-held weariness of his eyes. He looked the duke up and down, a swift, summing glance, and some of the tightness eased. But some of it did not. He gave the duke a curt nod and drew himself into a pose of relaxed attention.

Innisth considered him for a moment. Then he said, "My old soldier."

Etar relaxed, though Innisth could not have precisely pinpointed the difference in his stance. "Your Grace. I am very glad to see you well. Or nearly well. I hear from Amereir you are expected to recover fully."

"So he insists," said Innisth, just a little wry. "At the moment it is tedious enough. You have Verè Deconniy safe in your keeping, I understand."

"Yes, Your Grace. Your Grace will understand that the young man is much distressed."

"Is he? So, tell me, my old soldier. Was the fault in the man who dealt the blow, or the man who received it? Or was there no fault at all, but only mischance?"

Etar answered straightforwardly, "You moved in exactly the wrong direction at exactly the wrong instant. I thought Deconniy had managed to compensate until I saw the blood. Allow me to say that your recovery is a great relief to all of us, Your Grace."

"Indeed." Innisth considered. "Bring Deconniy to me here," he ordered eventually.

"Immediately, Your Grace."

Deconniy still wore his uniform, but he had been stripped of his weapons and of the signs of his rank. There was a bruise along the line of his jaw, and even in so few days, he seemed to have lost weight. Other than this, however, he showed no sign of rough usage. But he was pale. His expression was closed, the line of his mouth ungiving. Captain Etar escorted him, but the senior captain stepped aside as soon as they entered the room and stood by the door, expression professionally blank. Deconniy, after one swift, urgent glance at the senior captain, came forward alone and stood at attention.

The duke regarded him for a long moment. Then he said plainly, "I do not suspect your motives in the blow. I accept that the bleeding was an accident."

A weight seemed to lift from the young captain's shoulders. He bent his head. "Yes, Your Grace. I swear by every Fortunate God, it *was* an accident—"

Innisth waved a dismissive hand. "Yes. Do not concern yourself. You played your role skillfully and acquitted yourself well. I am pleased with you and with the success of the stratagem. Of course I am not pleased to have been injured, but that was always the price I intended to pay to rid myself of Laören while keeping you here. You are not to think of the price as one set on your life, but rather as one I set on my own honor and my pride, which to me are beyond value. Do you understand?"

Deconniy closed his eyes for an instant. A little color came back into his face. "Yes," he said, and after a second, "Your Grace."

"I count your loyalty, as I do my pride, beyond price. Do you understand me, my captain?"

"I . . . Yes. I understand, Your Grace."

"Then we need not speak of this again," said the duke. "You know that Laören has indeed gone, with all his people and with Geif? Yes, good. In a day, perhaps two, when we are confident he will not turn back, you may reclaim your insignia and your weapons and return to your ordinary quarters. However, I believe caution is warranted. You will have to remain here for the immediate present. You may retire to the outer rooms, however. I am going to rest."

"Understood, Your Grace. If . . . if Lord Laören does return . . ."

"In that case, it would be as well if the staff did not realize you had been released. Stay close and stay quiet."

"Yes, Your Grace. I—" But Deconniy only shook his head and withdrew, still subdued, but no longer with quite so closed an expression.

Innisth found himself exhausted, which was ridiculous, as he had done nothing but sit in a chair this whole morning.

The afternoon found the duke much recovered. He slept and waked and dozed again, and ate the food Reiöft brought him, and found himself impatient and restless, yet still bone-weary when he attempted to rise. Still, as the evening approached, he insisted on putting aside the ledgers and reports with which he had been passing the time. He had Reiöft help him to his chair in his private dining chamber, so that the Raëhema girl would not see how he struggled to manage the least task. Reiöft arranged cushions and brought a low stool on which the duke could rest his foot and generally fussed, but so quietly Innisth found it possible to tolerate his hovering. And he placed a blackwood walking stick where the duke could reach it. The walking stick was topped with a carved wooden wolf with topaz eyes. Innisth raised his eyebrows.

Reiöft cleared his throat. "I know, it was your grandfather's," he said apologetically. "But the wolf is yours now. Perhaps you will not object to taking possession of the stick as well."

"Very thoughtful," said Innisth after a moment. "Thank you, Caèr."

There was a sound from the doorway, and he glanced up. The Raëhema girl stood there. He could see the tie in her more clearly now, thread-thin but vivid as the first green shoots of spring. Warm, quiet, lending her a calm strength, which she gave back to it, a circular gift that could not have been more different from his own constant struggle with his Eänetén Power. Yet he felt Eänetaìsarè stir in response, not rousing in jealous anger, but as a wolf might stretch and yawn and settle in front of a fire if it were a dog. His breath seemed to come more easily. Even the ache of his leg eased.

He said with careful restraint, "Welcome, Your Highness. Forgive me for not rising."

There was a concerned line between her brows, but she met his eyes and smiled. "Your Grace, I am relieved to see you so much improved."

"I believe I have you to thank for that. My memory . . ." He thought of the dream, black trees and winter dragon, the wolf and the swift-winged bird, and frowned. "My memory seems uncertain. But I thank you."

"I'm grateful your people let me help you," the girl said gravely, and came forward to take the chair Reiöft held for her.

"I trust your new suite pleases you. Eöté may continue to serve you, if you wish."

A slight nod, but the girl was frowning. "That is kind of you, Your Grace, but there is no need. You may simply give me leave through Roh Pass. I assure you that I am willing to risk whatever danger may threaten Harivir and Raëh and my family."

Reiöft served the soup, a clear consommé with slender mushrooms and a few thin bright-green leaves floating in the broth, very elegant. The Raëhema girl did not touch her spoon, waiting instead for the duke's answer.

Innisth inclined his head. But then, because he felt obscurely that he owed the girl at least something of the truth, he added, "I fear that I intend to wait for the situation between Harivir and Emmer to become clear. And the situation between both of those countries and Pohorir. I am unable therefore to give you leave at once. I will try to be generous in other matters, as I gather you were generous enough to assist me when I was . . . incapacitated."

A faint line appeared between the girl's brows, but she didn't argue. At least, not yet. He was confident she would seize some other moment. But for now she merely answered, "I . . . It seemed to me you were sliding away from the world, away from . . . Eänetaìsarè, is that its name? I feared you might . . ." She hesitated, not saying, *I feared you might be dying.*

And she had stepped forward with inborn kindness and generosity to help him, though he was her captor and her tie so thin. She had even risked Eänetaìsarè overwhelming her own tie in order to help him. It was the generosity born into the heirs of the Raëhema line. Innisth should have found this weakness contemptible. Instead, he found it . . . charming.

He said merely, "Yes. I am in your debt. Especially as I have no proper and acknowledged heir and cannot say to whom the tie might have gone. Some distant cousin, perhaps, and who can say whether such a one could have mastered Eänetaìsarè? It is not an easy or generous Power."

Kehera Raëhema had picked up her spoon. Now she put it down again, her gaze troubled. "Eänetaìsarè is nearly a Great Power, is it not? It seems so to me."

The Wolf Duke inclined his head. "Indeed. So a weaker duke with an uncertain tie might suit Methmeir Irekaì well enough. The King of Pohorir does not desire rivals, and such a succession would weaken Eäneté for a generation. Perhaps two." He added kindly, "But all is well. Laören will take Geif of Tisain to Irekay, and the king will be much occupied by that and less concerned with Eäneté. At least for a time." He found he did not wish to explain to the girl the use to which he was considering putting this interval of relative safety. Not tonight. Later would do. He turned firmly back to his supper.

Then, wishing to please the Raëhema heir in at least some small matter, Innisth glanced up again and added, "I believe Gereth has located the . . . people with whom you traveled south. As it is always best to keep one's word, I have asked him to bring before me the men you intended to hire. I shall interview them after supper. You may attend. If they satisfy me, and if you wish, you may hire them as you promised. You should have your own bodyguards in this household, as you should have your own servants."

A faint line had appeared again between those wide-set eyes, but she only said, "You are generous, Your Grace."

He wished to be. Yet the only thing she truly wanted from him was freedom through Roh Pass, and that he already knew he would refuse her. He said merely, "Try the soup. Or if it does not please you, we shall have the next course." He signaled for Caèr to bring the leeks and roasted duck and the other dishes. He wanted the girl to speak again simply to listen to her voice. She had a pleasant voice with an accent that fell kindly on the ear. He thought of asking about her family or her home or her journey—but he was keeping her from her family, and her home was in danger, and her journey had been filled with privation and fear. He hardly wished to discuss the future. Every topic seemed unkind.

She might have thought conversation chancy too, or she might have been lost in her own thoughts, or shy of him, or too bitterly angry to speak to him, for she said nothing, save to Caèr Reiöft now and again. For him, she had a smile and a quiet word. Innisth found himself actually jealous of Caèr.

Ridiculous. He was only tired. The evening stretched out before him, seeming endless. But he had promised the Raëhema girl he would interview those men this evening. It was important to keep one's word. He caught Caèr's eye and flicked his eyes toward the door in command.

The older of the men, Tageiny, had a tough, weathered face, not at all handsome, but with a great deal of character. He looked to Innisth like a brawler; his nose had plainly been broken at some time in the past, and two fingers of his left hand were knotted with old injuries. His wrists were marked with recent manacle scars. But his manner was professional. He stood straight and his eyes met the duke's with commendable directness. The younger man, thin and wary as a kicked cur, was unremarkable. Luad. Yes. Innisth would have taken him for a common street thug and never given him a second look. But the young man kept one eye on Tageiny and tried clumsily to copy his manner. That was interesting.

Gereth and Captain Etar had joined the duke for this interview.

Gereth's air of quiet reserve meant he wanted the duke to be generous but was not sure he would be. Etar's closed expression meant he did not approve of these men and wanted them out of the house. Caèr Reiöft, who had retired to a position to one side, observed curiously but without concern; he would be perfectly content with any decision the duke made.

The Raëhema heir sat with her back straight and her hands folded on the table before her. She gave the two men a small nod but said nothing.

The duke said to Tageiny, "Your name? Your background? How did you come to be a slave in that man's keeping?"

The man bowed his head. "Heris Tageiny, Your Grace." His voice was deep and quiet, his tone calm. He said, "I'm from here and there. I've been a soldier and a merchant's guard and a bodyguard. A laborer now and then, when I couldn't get better work. I've worked in Vièm, Simin, Irekay for a little while. Here, for a few years. I worked for a man named Inmar Corsiön, a jeweler. Your Grace may have known of him; he did good work. He died—old age. His heir and I didn't get along, so I moved on. Went up to Enchar. In Enchar I hired on as bodyguard to a man named Conanè Sochar. He's a big dog there. You probably haven't heard of him."

The duke made a little *go on* movement of one finger.

Tageiny nodded. "Well, Your Grace, I got tired of the job. It didn't seem like a good idea for me to tell Sochar that. I figured never mind my back pay, I'd just slide out of Enchar. I thought maybe I'd go north, get through Anha Pass just before the season shut down the pass and I'd be right out of Pohorir and clear for sure. I thought I was subtle enough getting ready for the trip." He shrugged, a minimal lift of one shoulder. "Guess not."

"My fault," muttered the younger man. "I let it slip."

"Not your fault," Tageiny contradicted him. "Anyway, you'll know better another time, boy." He said to the duke, "Luad here, he was one of mine."

"So you also worked for this Sochar," the duke said to the young man.

"Shit, no," Luad said in obvious surprise. "Conanè Sochar wouldn't of noticed me, m'lord. I worked for Tag, is what."

The duke leaned back in his chair, raising one eyebrow.

"I hired him, I gave him jobs to do, I paid him. He wasn't part of the regular staff," Tageiny said. He didn't give the impression of speaking hastily, but he got all that out before the duke lowered his eyebrow. Then he said, still with no appearance of haste, "Boy, you don't say 'shit' to His Grace or in front of a lady. Haven't I taught you better? And a duke is a good sight higher than just a lord of some petty township. Say 'Your Grace' to him and 'my lady' to her, and be very damn polite, you hear me?"

The young man ducked his head. "Sorry, Tag. Sorry, m'lord—Your Grace."

Innisth almost smiled, but caught himself. Ignoring the young man, he said to Tageiny, "When you say you were Sochar's bodyguard, you mean you were . . . muscle. An enforcer. In short, a thug. You intimidated, beat, or killed men who offended him. Correct me if I am mistaken."

On the other side of the table, Kehera Raëhema tilted her head. She didn't look shocked. She didn't even look surprised. Innisth, watching her covertly, was mildly surprised at the girl's lack of reaction. But perhaps a princess was not as protected from such things as an ordinary well-bred girl. Or perhaps her recent experiences had broadened her understanding of lesser crimes and brutalities. The duke would understand that.

There was a slight pause. Then the big man said slowly, "You're not mistaken, Your Grace."

"It wasn't like that," protested Luad.

"It was exactly like that." Tageiny, Innisth was interested to see, glanced sidelong at the Raëhema girl, though his face was professionally blank. He said, "There was real bodyguarding in the mix, too. But, yeah, mostly it was breaking fingers. Or legs. Didn't usually come to murder. But it got so I didn't much like Conanè Sochar. Then it got so I didn't much like myself. So I thought I'd quit."

"Why did you agree to work for this Sochar in the first place?" Kehera Raëhema asked, her voice quiet.

Tageiny faced her at once, seeming to give her his whole attention. The man was really very good. Innisth was certain he had not for an instant lost track of anyone in the room. A dangerous man. No wonder Etar didn't like him.

But Tageiny only said smoothly, speaking neither too quickly nor too slowly, "My lady, the job paid well—and it was supposed to be bodyguarding. It *was* bodyguarding, mostly, at first. Then the job description got broader. And broader. But when you take a job like that from a man like Conanè Sochar, it's not easy to quit. You've got blood on your own hands, see, and his hands are clean, and he's got friends because he does favors for powerful men, and, well, yeah, it's not a good situation to get yourself into. I must've been stupid, because if I'd been smarter, I wouldn't have gotten myself into it."

"He got Sochar, though," Luad burst out. "When we knew they had us. He cut around and got back in the house and made like no problem and walked right past that fucking bastard Timon and—" He made a sharp, illustrative gesture with one hand and grinned.

Tageiny had closed his eyes. Now he opened them again and said in a pained tone, "Luad, I wasn't exactly going to mention that."

"But, Tag—"

"Because explaining how you knifed your previous employer doesn't generally count as a job recommendation," Tageiny said gently.

"But, *Tag*—"

"It does show both uncommon audacity and commendable resolution," observed the duke. He was thoroughly amused, which he had not expected. He approved of this Tageiny. And he liked the younger man's loyalty. Despite his . . . rough edges. He glanced at the Raëhema girl. He expected her to be horrified, alarmed, certainly disturbed. She was leaning back in her chair, but she certainly did not seem alarmed. A finger was crooked over her mouth, but her eyes were alight.

She said, her tone a little stifled, "Your Grace . . . I am inclined to take that tale as a job recommendation."

"Your Grace, no—" Etar began.

The duke cut off his senior captain's protest with the lift of a hand. He did not need Kehera Raëhema to explain her decision to him. She wanted Tageiny in her service because she was a prisoner in the house of an enemy, and she, too, judged the man possessed of uncommon audacity and commendable resolution.

He said calmly to Tageiny, "It is the lady's choice to offer employment as she sees fit. You may decline, and I will find you other employment. If you accept her offer, you will be her man, not mine. Nevertheless, I swear on my name and on the name of the Immanent Power of Eäneté, if you fail her, I will kill you. If you betray her, I will destroy you. Do you understand?"

The girl had stiffened in offense. "That's hardly necessary!"

"I think it is," the duke said mildly. "You do not know these men, or not well. They do not know you. Let them know me, then." He could not stand, but he leaned forward, set his hands flat on the table, and called up Eänetaìsarè. The Eänetén Power rose through him, roaring heat and passion overlain with the endless strength of the mountains, given voice in the long singing cry of the wolf. He blinked, and blinked again, his vision filled with stone and fire, until gradually he found himself again, on his feet, his hands still braced on the table, but his awareness once more limited to the perspective of a man. He did not remember standing, but Caèr Reiöft was at his side, ready to brace him if he suddenly found himself at the limits of his strength. His leg hurt, not merely a dull ache, but as though the original blow had just slashed down. He set his teeth against a gasp and straightened, though he had to grasp Caèr's arm for balance and support.

"I knew that already," Tageiny said in a level voice. "But, yeah, I know it better now." He had bowed his head and did not look up, not risking meeting the duke's gaze while the Eänetén Power filled him. But he slid a glance sideways at Kehera Elin. The duke could not read that glance, but the man said, "We'll take the lady's offer, if she's willing, me and Luad both."

The girl nodded and rose to her feet. Her own tie seemed a little brighter, a little more vivid—responding to Eänetaìsarè, perhaps. She did not appear to notice. She said, "You may consider that the offer stands, exactly as I first made it."

"I shall see to the notation," murmured Gereth, and made his bow to the duke, then offered the lady his arm and his escort. Tageiny and Luad followed, and then Captain Etar, probably meaning to get Gereth off by himself when he got the chance, so he could vent his feelings properly.

Innisth waited until the room was clear. Then he said to Caèr Reiöft, between his teeth, "I cannot walk. I don't think I can sit. Get me to my bed."

"It would heal faster if you wouldn't *do* things like that," Caèr observed, not quite a rebuke. "But lean on me. I won't let you fall."

"I know you won't," said Innisth, and allowed the other man to take his weight.

13

Kehera wished she understood what the Wolf Duke meant by encouraging her to establish a household of her own within his. That he wished her to be content—so much was plain. He thought she could help him somehow against the King of Pohorir, and if that was true . . . if that was true, wasn't she obligated to try? Someone had to stop Methmeir Irekaì. Maybe a Pohorin duke had the best chance. So maybe the best thing Kehera could do was accept the gilded cage he offered her and pretend she did not see the bars.

Eöté—Eöté was a question. Kehera glanced at the door to her bedchamber. She could hear the girl moving about, no doubt with bed warmers and things. She was actually singing to herself, very quietly, a child's song:

> "One for the silver sunrise,
>   two for the golden noon,
>   three for the iron nightfall,
>   lit by the shining moon.
>
> One for the frozen winter,

two for the budding spring,
three for the fragrant summer
that the turning year will bring. . . ."

Kehera was astonished the girl could be happy enough to sing. But then, she'd guessed Eöté might be friends with Captain Deconniy, who had played a part, if Kehera understood it all correctly, in the duke's ruse to get rid of Lord Laören. Deconniy had been arrested, and released only today. So perhaps she understood after all.

As much as she understood anything just now. She was so tired she could barely think. She knew it was the relief of Lord Laören's departure. She should not feel safe here; she wasn't *safe*. She knew she couldn't trust Eöté, who belonged to the Wolf Duke as certainly as Captain Deconniy or Gereth Murrel. But sometimes it was best to know who in your household owed service somewhere else. Or more than service. Kehera was almost certain the Wolf Duke's relationship with Eöté was not entirely . . . appropriate. Yet something in that suspicion seemed not quite right.

That moment when the duke had called up his Power . . . he had frightened her. Eänetaìsarè was so strong, and for all his pretense, the duke was obviously not recovered from his injury. But she knew he had not come close to losing control of the Immanent. She knew it because Raëhemaiëth had not been disturbed. Her tie, thin as it was now . . . just being near the Wolf Duke seemed to strengthen it. Helping him when he'd been injured seemed to have strengthened it further. That didn't make sense, because Raëhemaiëth was a Harivin Power and the Eänetén Power was Pohorin. The two could not *be* allies. Except it seemed they were.

She remembered how awful she'd felt when she'd first set off north for Suriytè, how much better she'd felt when she'd finally gotten away from Nomoris and decided she had to come here, to Eäneté. Both times, the feeling had been so strong. Understandable, of course, but . . . oddly resonant, the way feelings were sometimes, when they echoed between herself and Raëhemaiëth.

She'd given up the heir's tie to Tiro. Raëhemaïëth had given up its deep tie to her. Or she'd thought so. Now . . . now she wondered. She didn't understand *any* of this. She wished Tiro were here with her—well, of course she didn't, except that her brother could undoubtedly have told her if ever before in history an Immanent Power had hidden itself so deep within a person that neither she nor anyone else could quite perceive the depth of its tie. Or whether one Immanent Power had ever decided on its own to ally with a foreign Power to which it had never been bound and somehow nudged a person who held its tie into the territory of the other Immanent Power. And why. And whether the Gods had been involved somehow, or servants of the Gods. And what the outcomes of those incidents had been.

She had doubted the alliance between Raëhemaïëth and Eänetaìsarè. She couldn't doubt it any longer. She had been unable to feel her tie to Raëhemaïëth until she came to the Wolf Duke's house, and now it ran like a thread of light through her mind and heart. When the duke had been injured, she had found it so *easy* to call on Raëhemaïëth to help calm the Eänetén Power, coax it around to support the duke rather than fight him. She didn't understand that, either.

Nor did she understand what the duke intended, giving her Tageiny and Luad, as though he were handing a gift to a child during the Golden Hinge of the year, when all the world celebrated the turning of spring into summer.

Heris Tageiny had moved right to the middle of Kehera's sitting room and stood now at a kind of relaxed attention, his gaze fixed on nothing in particular. Luad stood at his shoulder, watching Kehera with unconcealed interest.

"You took service with me because you were afraid of what *other employment* the duke would find for you if you refused," Kehera told Tageiny. "If it comes to it, you'll spy for him and take his orders over mine. Right?"

The big man met her eyes without any sign of surprise. "I remember your original offer just fine. That's why I took the job. One reason why.

Though you're not wrong about me being scared of the duke. But spying on you or taking his orders over yours would count as betraying you. You've thought of that, too, I expect."

"You think the Wolf Duke will find that a persuasive argument, the first time he wants something from you and you refuse?"

"We'll see, won't we? Or I suppose we can hope it won't come to that." Tageiny didn't sound like he found this hope very persuasive. "You're a prisoner here."

"Yes."

The man glanced around the room, and by implication the entire suite. "Nice accommodations. Right next to the duke's. You're Harivin, of course. That's why Roh Pass. But you're important to His Grace, who doesn't seem inclined to let you go."

"Yes."

"Right. You're so important he wants you guarded by men who aren't from Eäneté, men whose loyalties won't be divided, no matter who they're scared of."

"Apparently so."

"Mine won't be divided." Tageiny glanced at Luad. "Ours. You want us to swear to it? Or can you just see who's telling the truth?" He gave her a shrewd look. "You've a tie. More so than most. You're someone's heir, maybe a second daughter, but you're in someone's bloodline. I'm guessing. But I think so."

Kehera found herself smiling. "Yes. You are certainly not stupid. How in the world did that Sochar person hook you into his service?"

"I was overconfident. That's worse than stupid sometimes. It's not likely to happen again, under the circumstances."

Kehera suspected this was true. She nodded to Luad. "He's not stupid, either, I assume."

Finding himself suddenly the center of attention, Luad blinked and flushed slightly, and looked quickly at Tageiny. Tageiny only said mildly, "He's not used to dukes and ladies, but no, he's not stupid. Taking down an enemy who's done it to you first *is* a job recommendation, in certain circles. But you guessed that, I think. You were kind to ask for him as well as for me, and I thank you."

"Oh," said Kehera, reminded, and went quickly to retrieve her pearls. "I don't have much money right now. But I have these." She held two of the pearls out, and said when Tageiny hesitated, "I said I would hire you, and I will. You're free men, not slaves. So take these. I doubt His Grace will allow me to leave this house, but I expect you can go into town and get what you need. Swords, whatever you need. Better clothing."

"Well," said Tageiny, sounding for once nonplussed. "This should certainly be enough. Call it a quarter's pay plus a signing bonus." This seemed to amuse him, though Kehera didn't understand why. But he took the pearls and gave one to Luad. She felt better then, as though these indeed were her men and she actually had hired them.

And Tageiny had said he remembered the terms she had first offered, when she had said she needed help to get through Roh Pass. For the first time since the Eänetén duke had recognized her, she felt that might truly be possible. Or, at least, if these men took her pearls and went to town and then actually came back . . . yes. Then maybe the pass would be possible.

Though now she wasn't sure she would be doing the right thing, to run away and make her own way home, abandoning the Eänetén duke when Raëhemaiëth—or the Fortunate Gods, or both—seemed possibly to want her here so she could support him. Against Methmeir Irekaì and the Unfortunate Gods, she presumed. It was all so complicated and peculiar and she didn't know what to do.

She was so tired.

There was a room in the suite that was meant for bodyguards. Gereth had pointed that out to her. It held beds that could fold up into couches, so it could serve either as a bedchamber or a second reception room. That explained why the duke's suite and hers each had two reception chambers. Naturally, the bodyguards' room lay between the outer door and the rest of the suite, and naturally there was no other door that led from the suite to the rest of the house. Actually, the arrangement *did* make her feel safer. She went to look into her own bedchamber.

Eöté had turned down the bed and taken the chill off the linens with a heavy iron bedwarmer filled with coals and wrapped in a towel. Now the girl jumped up, bobbed a hasty little curtsy, and hurried to hold up a robe she had laid out to warm by the fire.

Though she wanted that robe and her bed more than anything, Kehera took a moment to introduce the girl to Tageiny and Luad. Naturally Eöté was terrified of them, though she didn't say so. Tageiny barely glanced at her, assuming a studied air of complete disinterest. Luad set himself to charm her, an attempt Kehera suspected was doomed to failure. She couldn't find the energy to worry about it now. She left Tageiny in charge of everything and retired to her own private room.

She was tired. She was so tired. So much had happened. But she didn't think she would be able to sleep easily. What she wanted most desperately was solitude, time to think about . . . well, things. Everything. She settled on the window seat rather than in the warm bed. The broad glass windows reflected only the room within, as though the outside world had been packed up and put away for the night. Kehera blew out the lamps and pushed aside the heavy curtains, and the winter night leaped into existence: dark mountains against the sky. Curling up on the window ledge, she leaned her cheek against the cold glass and watched the high gibbous moon lighting the streamers of cloud.

At this very moment, her father might be watching this same moon. She thought of him in his study, leaning back in his chair to consider some difficult problem brought to him for solution. Or perhaps he was at the border, directly confronting a problem that might in the end prove too much even for his care. What in the world was going on between her father and General Corvallis? Her father would have to deal with whatever was happening in Emmer. Tiro would be . . . at home, in the heart of Harivir, at Raëhemaiëth's heart. At least Tiro was surely safe.

She missed her brother *so much*. He would know everything about the history of Eäneté and its dukes, about Pohorir and its kings, about the maneuvering of the Immanent Powers that were bound to the earth and the Gods that had torn themselves free of the mortal world and yet sometimes tried to tilt the outcomes of human strife one way or another. . . . She wished he were here to tell her all about it. Or better, that she was there, with Eilisè, and Tiro was explaining it to both of them just because he was interested and they were patient enough to listen, not because the history of this province mattered to any of them.

She wanted her father so badly she could taste it. If these past weeks couldn't be turned back, then she longed to warn him. She wished she could tell him what had happened in Suriytè, and what she suspected now about Methmeir Irekaì and the Immanent Power of Irekay reaching all the way north to unseat the Suriytaiän Power.

Perhaps her father already knew. If he didn't . . . perhaps she could send a letter. The duke would surely permit her to explain everything they knew and had guessed.

The Wolf Duke, whose Power walked through his dreams in the shape of a wolf . . . She pressed her hand against the cold glass.

She didn't want to send a letter. She wanted to *go home*.

A chance always comes. She was so close. And now . . . if she could trust Tageiny. She thought she could. Surely the Fortunate Gods, who must surely have guided her journey so far, would not deny her one more chance.

Kehera let the cold of the night strike through the glass into her palm and whispered a private prayer, but she honestly did not know for what she prayed, or whether she hoped more that Fortunate Gods were listening to her or that They hadn't noticed her at all.

She woke suddenly, much later, confused. She sat up, gasping at the chill in the air, not knowing where she was, or what had happened to wake her. For the first seconds, recognizing nothing in the cold room with its dark wood and white plaster, in the pale light slanting in through the wide windows, she felt herself utterly adrift.

Then she remembered. For another few seconds, she thought she must be remembering fragmentary bits of a dream—it all whipped through her mind: the snow and the wolves in the forest, Gheroïn Nomoris dead at her feet, Parren, the duke, a wolf's yellow eyes set in the face of a man.

It wasn't a dream. Nothing of the past days or weeks or months was a dream. She was still in the house of the Wolf Duke, and he was not going to let her go through the pass because he wanted to . . . use her against the Power of Irekay somehow. She couldn't even blame him. In his place, she would use anything she could lay hand to against that cold Power.

She should get up. She was cold and stiff and still half asleep. She should get up and wash her face, call for Eöté to help her dress, and venture out of this room so she could find out what was going on. But the room was cold, and Eöté was probably not waiting for her call with a robe warmed by the fire the way Eilisè would have been. Kehera felt very much alone. She wanted nothing more than to tuck herself into the bed, pull the blankets up over her head, and pretend she had never woken up at all.

But even so, after a moment, she threw back the blankets and sat up, shivering at the shock of cold.

Eöté slipped in quietly as Kehera was struggling with the highest hooks of the dress she had chosen from those in the wardrobe. It was plain, a soft blue-gray with darker slate gray for the collar and the wide cuffs on the sleeves and the heavy hem. The fabric was heavy and soft and warm, and it fit well enough. But the hooks at the back were hard to reach.

The girl did up the hooks of Kehera's dress silently, seeming distracted, and then brought her several thin silver bangles and earrings of silver and smoky crystal. "Your hair, my lady . . ." she whispered, and Kehera smiled at her reassuringly and sat down to allow the girl to unbraid her hair and then braid it again more neatly and put it up in a figure eight. Kehera checked her reflection in the mirror the girl held and nodded. She looked . . . not as pale and frightened as she felt, at least.

Today, she was determined, she would find out exactly what use the Wolf Duke meant to make of her. She would at the very least to learn enough to let her make a reasonable guess about what he might intend.

And she knew how to start. She would start with Gereth Murrel, the duke's seneschal. She told Eöté she wanted breakfast for four, served in her morning room in half an hour.

She found Tageiny first, however. He was lounging quietly on a couch in the inner sitting room, but he immediately stood and bowed when she came in. "Good morning, my lady," he said crisply.

Kehera looked him up and down, astonished. He wore slate-gray trousers, a dove-gray shirt, and a russet vest. His hand rested on the hilt of a sword, and a thin knife was sheathed at his opposite wrist. He looked completely professional and not like a thug at all, despite the broken nose and crooked fingers. He gave Kehera a sense of confidence, which she knew was not justifiable: She was no less powerless in this house. But she no longer felt so dependent on the whims of strangers. It occurred to her, with a sense of surprise, that Tageiny was the first man she had ever had in her service who looked only to her; all her childhood servants and guards had been her father's men. Tageiny was hers.

She glanced around. "Where's Luad?"

The bodyguard jerked his head toward the outer part of the suite and the main house beyond. "Seeing the armorer about a sword. You have to have a weapon that suits your hand and reach, and I didn't want both of us out last night." He touched the hilt of his sword. "I apologize for not asking your permission before leaving you to Luad's guard alone. You had already retired, and the duke's men are on your door—did you know? Right. I promise you, the boy *is* trustworthy, my lady—and better in a fight than I am, at least at close quarters, especially if all there is to hand is a letter opener."

"I trust your judgment. I'm impressed you found everything you needed so late in the evening."

Tageiny's eyes glinted. "I had to get the armorer out of bed. He was remarkably accommodating, eventually."

Kehera decided not to ask. She said instead, "I'm going to ask the duke's seneschal for permission to go for a ride in the city. I don't expect permission to be granted, but I expect Gereth to come in person to tell me so. One of those men outside my door can carry my request to the seneschal. I wouldn't be surprised if he comes at once. I told Eöté I would need breakfast for four."

"Should have made it five, my lady. The boy eats like two. Do the duke's people always leap to obey you?"

"They have so far. He . . . I . . . It's complicated. His Grace extends to me every possible courtesy." She seated herself on a low couch and regarded him. Tageiny, standing in front of her, looked back very soberly. "I don't yet know what he wants from me. Or, in a way, I think I might know, but not . . . really. It's all very strange. I think . . ." But she hesitated, not certain whether she should try to explain that everything seemed suddenly to involve Powers and Gods and kings. That it was all much bigger than one man using her as a hostage to win concessions from her father. In the end, she only shook her head wordlessly.

Tageiny gave Kehera a look she could not interpret and stepped over to open the door. Kehera had heard nothing, but Luad was there, grinning, bouncing a little on his toes. He was dressed much like Tageiny, but besides a sword he had a knife on each wrist and another at his belt.

"Lady," he said to her, but still smiling. "Lots of good sh—stuff in the armory here. All kinds of knives. Got this sword, too." He tapped its hilt. "I'm a knife man, really, though."

Tageiny sighed. "His heart's in the right place," he told Kehera, and crossed the room to lean out and tell the duke's men that the lady wanted to go riding and could they check with the seneschal, and if someone could tell the kitchens breakfast for five, the lady would appreciate their kindness. Then he came back in, looking satisfied. "They do leap to obey you," he told her. "That's useful to know."

"Any moment, that might change."

"Sure. Still, good to know that's how it is right now."

Kehera privately agreed.

"Want to see my sword?" Luad asked Tageiny.

"*Later*, boy . . ."

Kehera left them to it and went to find the morning room. It wasn't the room opposite her bedroom, though that one also had an eastern window—that one was a maid's bedroom, though clearly Eöté hadn't slept in it. The room after that was a tiny, comfortable library, with handsome volumes of classical poetry and histories and novels—she would like to give those a closer look, later.

The next room was the morning room. Big eastern window, with a view of the city past the stone and forest of the mountain's slopes. A table of cream-colored wood, with narrow legs and a carved edge, and six matching chairs. Against one wall, a sideboard and a cabinet for the porcelain dishes, both of the same pale wood. The dishes were beautiful, glazed an unusual silvery green that Kehera had never seen before. She was still admiring them when Eöté came in to tell her Gereth Murrel requested permission to enter, and then almost at once two other girls, both carrying trays.

Kehera went quickly out to welcome the duke's seneschal. He looked exactly as always—kind and faintly harassed—but with a tiny hint of reserve in his manner, which she guessed meant she was not allowed to leave the house and ride into the city. She was aware of a little kick of dismay even though she had not expected otherwise. Inclining her head, she said gravely, "Good morning, Gereth. I was just preparing to break my fast. Might I persuade you to give me the pleasure of your company, if you have not yet broken yours?"

The duke's seneschal's smile might have been reserved, but he pulled up a chair with alacrity, peering at the serving dishes the girls were placing on the table. "I'd be delighted, my lady. That seems like a lot—oh, of course, your, ah, staff." He discreetly pretended not to notice as Tageiny handed one of the dishes of shelled eggs and a loaf of bread to Luad. Tageiny himself did not sit, nor take any food. He leaned his hip casually against the windowsill and crossed his arms over his chest, keeping an eye on everything.

"I've been entirely too much on the move this morning," Gereth told Kehera. "I did mean to attend you later in the day—I've drawn up a list concerning the disposition of the remaining slaves Parren Dihaft brought south." The seneschal extracted it from his belt and handed it across the breakfast table, adroitly avoiding dipping his sleeve in the currant jelly. "If any of my decisions displease you, or if you wish on reflection to claim any of these people for your own household, don't hesitate to let me know. But I think you'll find most of my placements acceptable. The little one, Geris, can go in with the kennel girls. They're nice girls, that lot, and little Geris took to the puppies right off. I plan to try one man on my own personal staff, an educated man, Ren Hallay. Geran Lhiyré—my senior factor—has been after me to find him someone competent with figures. Lhiyré's always overworked, poor man, and more so now as we've lost two of our younger factors recently. To marriage and businesses in town," Gereth added at Kehera's concerned look.

"Well, I'm glad you've found a place for Hallay. I liked him." Kehera put the paper aside to examine at leisure later. "Thank you, seneschal," she said formally.

"Entirely my pleasure, my lady, I assure you. Now, as for riding out. I fear—" He turned his hands palm-up.

"I'm not surprised," said Kehera, and sighed.

"Yes, I know," the seneschal said sympathetically. "Many things may change once Lord Laören is finally out of the province."

Kehera sighed again, but nodded.

"Unfortunately, it is likely to take at least three more days for Laören to cross the border. Eäneté is a big province."

Kehera nodded politely. "Of course, or it would hardly support such a strong Power. May I ask you an impertinent question, Gereth?"

He gave her a wary glance. "Of course, my lady."

"How long ago did His Grace take the deep tie to Eäneté? It's only," she added apologetically, "that I seem to have heard of the Wolf Duke of Eäneté all my life, and his tie seems very strong and, well, *committed*. I'm almost sure his Eänetaìsarè deliberately sought help from my Raëhemaiëth rather than risk his death. Yet he doesn't seem that old. So I am curious. I told you it was impertinent," she said ruefully as the corners of Gereth's eyes crinkled.

"The first part is easy enough: Innisth's great-great-grandfather, Imhaèr, was the first to be called the Wolf Duke—called that by everyone, I mean, rather than just his own people. The Wolf Duke, the Black Duke, the Iron Duke—I doubt anyone called him by his name. I believe it was during Imhaèr's lifetime that the Immanent Power of Eäneté grew into itself and took its full name. At first it was called Eän, which is 'mountain,' you know. And then for a little while, Eänetaìsa— 'mountain of fire.' The wolf symbol came later."

Kehera made a small interested sound.

"Eäneté was a smaller town for a long time. The Power has strengthened since Imhaèr's day, and I believe the duke's tie has deepened with every generation since. But it is only since Innisth took it that I think it could fairly be said to become nearly Great."

Kehera nodded thoughtfully. "Yet he can't have held the true tie long? When did his father die?"

"Innisth took the tie when he was twenty. He is now twenty-seven."

"Oh." So he had taken the full tie when he was just her age. Kehera tried to imagine that. "Eänetaìsarè can't have been an easy Power to master," she said aloud. "How tragic that His Grace should have been forced to take it so young." Something in the seneschal's silence caught her attention, and she looked at him, frowning in question.

"It was difficult for him, I believe," Gereth murmured. "But hardly tragic. They still celebrate the occasion in town."

"Oh." Kehera thought about this. "So the old duke, His Grace's father was . . . He must have been a . . . difficult lord."

Gereth was not going to be drawn, but Tageiny snorted quietly and put in, "A vicious, sadistic wolf's whelp, Iheraïn Iönei Eänetaì, and no mistake. I was way off in Vièm then, and that wasn't a mistake either. It was a good time to not be anywhere near Eäneté."

Gereth smiled ruefully, caught Kehera's raised eyebrows, and shrugged, not disagreeing.

Kehera said to him, "But *you* were here in Eäneté, of course?" She thought the seneschal must have been. But he didn't answer, and she could see a certain constraint in the set of his shoulders that hadn't been there before. She said, "Tageiny, would you go make sure Luad got enough breakfast, please? And take some of this for yourself, too; I know you must be hungry."

Without a word of objection, the big man collected a plate of sliced sweet cake and another dish of eggs and retired into another room. As soon as he was gone, Kehera asked quietly, "What was he like? The duke's father? I think . . . I think I had better know. If I am to be His Grace's guest. Or . . ." Something about the quality of the seneschal's silence drew her. "What was *she* like? His mother? You said she died when she was twenty, but . . . the old duke didn't *kill* her, surely?"

There was a little silence. Then Gereth gave her a small, stiff smile. "Innisth does that too. Asks the question he shouldn't know how to ask. Your man is quite correct about what Innisth's father was like. A vicious, sadistic wolf's whelp. Yes. That's fair enough. And Jeneil was a lovely girl, who deserved . . . so much better. Iheraïn didn't kill her with his own hand. But he hounded her to her death as surely as though he'd set his wolves on her." He fell silent, eyes focused inward, on a private vision, an echo of memory.

"I'm sorry," Kehera said softly. "That's why you serve Innisth, then."

"I saw only Jeneil in him, at first. I was a fool there again, you may well say. . . . He's far more the old duke's son than hers, for all he has her fine cast to his face and her graceful hands. By the time I saw Iheraïn in him, it was too late. I loved him too much by then ever to turn away from him."

"Not just for her memory," Kehera said with quiet certainty. "I don't find it astonishing that you found something in him to love."

"Well." The seneschal gave her a little nod, half-surprised. "Yes. There's more under that stony facade he's built up than you'd ever think, seeing him as he is now. He's not gentle. The Eänetén Power doesn't lend itself to gentleness. He's possessive, and merciless, and passionate. His temper . . . well. He's not kind. Or, that's not quite fair. Sometimes he *is* kind. He can be generous. And strong. My sweet Gods, you can't imagine the kind of endurance it took even to survive, under his father's attention."

"Even with your protection," Kehera murmured.

Gereth laughed, a laugh edged with bitterness. "How much protection do you think I could be? Oh, I tried, that's true enough. There was little enough I could ever do. I could help against the servants, but it would have taken the Gods themselves to protect Innisth from his father. And the Fortunate Gods, more's the pity, didn't seem overly inclined to take a hand. Not that they ever seem to, in Pohorir."

"It must have been . . . very hard," Kehera ventured.

Gereth laughed again, still bitterly. For a long moment Kehera thought he wasn't going to speak. Then he gave her a direct look and said, "The first time Innisth tried to kill his father, he was only fourteen."

Kehera stared at him.

"He didn't manage it, of course. Not then. That . . . was a hard time for all of us."

In a hushed voice, Kehera asked, "What did his father do to him?"

The question got her a sharp look. "I talk too much," the seneschal said, in quite a different tone. He stood up. "Forgive me, my lady. I have a great many tasks I must see to. Forgive me that I cannot allow you to leave the house. Please do not even visit the stables. It would worry His Grace's men. I hope it will not displease you to know that His Grace will most likely invite you to join him for supper."

Kehera nodded, since that was what he expected. She stood up to see Gereth out, feeling as though her new knowledge were actually weighing her down. She had wanted to understand the Wolf Duke better. Now . . . now she wasn't at all sure she was comfortable with what she had learned. That *Not then* was . . . fraught. She tried to imagine what Innisth terè Maèr Eänetaï's life had been like as a child in this house. It was not a comfortable thing to imagine. But she thought she understood him better now. No wonder he was so determined to have everything his own way, to gather all power into his own hands, to make every decision and force those around him to accede to his will. She suspected that he had learned young to value his own power and strength as the only possible guard against ill will and cruelty.

At least she was convinced he also valued his own power and strength as a means of providing safety and well-being to his people. That was why he was so utterly self-disciplined; because he put his whole sense of self-worth on forcing kindness and generosity from an inherently cruel Immanent.

It all seemed so complicated. And she might still be wrong. Except she was sure she was right. This was her captor. In a way, knowing this little bit about his history made her look forward to supper. She wondered how much of his history she would now see in his face or hidden within his yellow eyes.

14

Innisth woke before dawn, in pain. The wound had been healing. He had been foolish, forgetting himself, reopening the injury, and now he paid for that foolishness. For a time he lay still, teeth set, enduring. The throbbing ache grew worse, spreading to involve his whole side. Finally he thought, *This is ridiculous*, and threw back the blankets. There was an infusion of willow bark in the other room, left by his physicker for just such a need; ridiculous not to use what remedies were available. He gripped the headboard of the bed and pulled himself up, allowing himself a grimace in the privacy of the darkness. There was a lamp on the table, hardly a step away. Caèr had set the wolf-headed walking stick close by the bed. He reached for it and felt in the dark for the candlelighter. The lamp cast a flickering mellow light across the quiet room. A dozen steps to the door, perhaps a dozen more to the remedy the physicker had left. Not an impossible distance. He picked up the lamp and made his way grimly across the room. The stick had certainly been an inspiration of Caèr's.

The door opened quietly. The lamp threw light in a long trail across the outer room. For a moment Innisth thought that the sharply arrested movement to one side was an illusion of that flickering light, and even when he realized it was not, it took him a long moment to determine just what it was that he was seeing.

Deconniy was on a couch there, and Eöté was with him. They were frozen in horror, staring at the duke, faces deathly in the chancy light of the lamp. Eöté had been on top of Deconniy, with the blankets thrown over them both; now the young captain moved convulsively, putting the girl behind him and coming to his feet between her and the duke, his expression stricken. He was quite naked.

Innisth spun away violently, back into the inner room, and closed the connecting door with real force. He nearly fell as his weight came onto his injured leg, and swore savagely. But in one way, the pain was no longer unwelcome: it was a distraction, and Gods knew he needed one now. He hardly required the stick at all on his way back to his abandoned bed. No one, thankfully, tried to come after him: neither the earnest young man, nor the frightened girl, for which slight mercy Innisth was truly grateful.

The sunrise was welcome, when it finally came: as an end to the night if for no other reason. Caèr Reiöft helped the duke dress, as on any morning. It was impossible to guess whether Reiöft knew of the eventful night. He was very quiet, but he understood the duke's moods, so that meant very little.

Deconniy and Eöté both stood up nervously as Innisth came into the breakfast room, their eyes on his face. Leaning on Reiöft's arm, the duke surveyed them with cool detachment. He permitted Reiöft to assist him to a seat at the table. Reiöft gave him a wry look, but withdrew without a word to bring the breakfast tray. Both the young captain and the girl stared after him, as though they had hoped Reiöft might save them from the wolf. Innisth was almost amused.

"Your Grace—" Deconniy said cautiously. His voice shook a little, and he stopped.

"Silence," ordered the duke. He examined Eöté narrowly. The girl twisted her hands together painfully and stood still, eyes on the floor.

Weak. Fragile. He let his breath out slowly. He asked her, "Did he importune you? Force you? Tell me the truth."

Eöté paled, and flushed, and paled again. "No," she whispered. "Your Grace. I—I asked him. Truly."

"Indeed," Innisth said coldly. "Very well." It was, he supposed, the coin a frightened woman might most easily barter for protection, though why she should suddenly feel the need escaped him. He could not quite prevent a sharp stab of offense that she would not consider his own protection adequate. . . . But that was foolish. Of course she would not seek shelter from *him*. He said, still coldly, but not so cuttingly as he might have, "Why are you here? Should you not be in the adjoining suite, assisting the lady?"

Deconniy drew a breath, but said nothing. The girl did not look at him, but flinched and whispered, "Yes, Your Grace." She slipped away carefully, like a mouse under the regard of a wolf.

Deconniy said steadily. "I beg leave to ask—"

"Denied," the duke said curtly. "You may go. Do not leave this suite, however."

Deconniy nodded. But he did not retreat. Instead, he came forward and knelt beside the duke's chair, reaching out to touch the back of the duke's hand with the tips of two fingers, very lightly.

The Eänetén Power rose instantly, its heat edged, as always, with violence. Without thought, Innisth lifted a hand, tracing the line of Deconniy's cheek. Deconniy turned his face deliberately into the duke's touch, brushing Innisth's palm with his lips.

For an instant, Innisth was still. Eänetaìsarè rushed through his blood, so that his heartbeat quickened and his breath came short. Nevertheless, he exerted himself to free his hand from the young man's hold. "You don't want this. You wish to fix my attention on yourself, thus protecting the girl. It speaks well for you. But it is not necessary."

"Your Grace, I am very sorry for my insolence. You have been all that is generous. I'm willing, I swear it. You aren't Laören."

"That, at least, may be said to my credit," the duke agreed with some irony. "No, I am indeed not Laören. So I will not permit you to . . . sacrifice yourself. No. Enough. Get up. Don't argue. Get up. Good. Step back. Farther than that. Enough." The pressure of the Eänetén Power was subsiding, slowly, as he refused to yield to it. He leaned back in his chair, breathing deeply, gradually recovering himself. He said after a moment, "You are fond of the girl, I gather?"

The young man was clearly embarrassed. But he met the duke's eyes with determined effort. "I have become so. She is so . . . delicate. Elegant. Gentle—"

"Oh, stop."

Deconniy flushed. "Forgive me, Your Grace—"

"You were careless. Young love is said to impair judgment, I believe. The remedy is, as I recall, equally well known. I am aware that a girl may suffer when she is set aside by a man of rank. It will be thought that I have set Eöté aside. A suitable marriage may ameliorate any difficulty. It would therefore seem advisable for Eöté to be married as quickly as possible."

Deconniy had drawn his breath in sharply midway through this speech. The captain had already been pale; now he paled further. He said huskily, "I would be glad to marry her, Your Grace, with your permission."

"Indeed. A match with a captain of mine will give the girl adequate rank. If Eöté is agreeable, the match may be announced as soon as I have clearly put you both aside. I expect to do so very soon. I will leave it to you to address the girl with the suggestion."

The man had got his balance back. He said simply, "Yes, Your Grace."

"You may go."

Deconniy bowed. Then he said much more forcefully, "*Nothing* like Laören. Nothing like Geif. I *am* your man, Your Grace. Whatever you ask. I swear it."

Innisth found himself genuinely moved. He said flatly, truthfully, "I value your loyalty, Verè. Nor will I abuse it. You are dismissed."

The young captain hesitated one more moment. Then he bowed, to the precisely correct degree, and withdrew.

Though the incident might be said to have come to a satisfactory conclusion, Innisth was nevertheless in a fine temper. He knew it, and knew it would be seriously unjust to indulge it against his household, but today he could not seem to cast it off. He wanted to pace, but his injury still made that impossible. He wanted to order his black mare brought up from the stables, ride a wild course up into the mountains until the whole world turned into snow and stone and leafless trees and the distant voices of the wolves. That, too, was out of the question for at least another day or two.

The household ledgers were open in front of him, but he could not focus on them. He wanted to kill someone. He wanted to take his time about it. That slave merchant, Parren, had died not so long ago. Even in this bitter season, the desire should not press him so hard for some time. Weeks, at least; perhaps months.

Possibly it was the injury. Or perhaps it was—

He straightened in his chair. Then he laid his hands flat on the table for several moments, steadying himself as he stared into the blank air.

Then he rang the bell to summon whatever servant was waiting.

The servant was Timàs, an elderly man who had served first Innisth's grandfather and then his father, and who as a consequence did not fear Innisth himself. He came in and bowed in silent inquiry.

"The lady, my guest," Innisth told him. "I will see her at once."

Kehera Raëhema arrived quickly, as her rooms were adjoining. Her man Tageiny came with her, at her back, watchful, which even under the circumstances Innisth found faintly amusing. The pressure of his tie eased the moment the girl stepped into his presence. That was not so amusing. It was too important to be amusing.

She gave him an unsmiling look, cautious but in no way fearful. He knew she was aware of Eänetaìsarè. Its presence did not frighten her. It never had. Her own tie to the gentler Immanent of Raëh protected her

. . . or Eänetaìsarè became gentler in her Immanent's presence. He truly thought it might be so. He had not expected such a phenomenon. Yet it seemed it might be so.

Innisth said none of this, but only gave his guest a small nod. She returned it, though she still did not smile.

"We have had a surprise," he told her. "Lord Laören has crossed the border. He is no longer within Eäneté's precincts."

"Already?" she asked, frowning. "I thought Gereth said three days more."

"Indeed. My eastern border lies eighty miles and more from these mountains. A four-day ride in good weather, for a man who wishes to travel comfortably."

She thought about that. Then she asked, "Why would this Laören ride good horses to death just to get out of Eäneté? What would be so important? Do you think—but that doesn't make sense." That small, thoughtful line appeared between her eyebrows.

"He did not ride fast," the duke told her. "A normal pace. He was just passing Padné. That is a village two days' ride from the city of Eäneté, still well within the province. Then he was gone. Toward Irekay, I imagine, though I cannot be certain. But gone from the province entirely. Of that I am certain. He is gone." The duke paused. The girl didn't ask how it was possible for a man to step, between one breath and the next, from Padné to the Eänetén border. She knew it should not be possible. She was waiting for him to explain how it could be true.

"Methmeir Irekaì has reached out and gathered Laören up, him and all his party," Innisth stated. It was surmise, but what other explanation could there be? "He wished to question him about Eäneté, about me. He persuaded the Great Power of Irekay to extend its awareness and its reach and snatch Laören away from Eäneté. I see no other likely explanation. Only a Great Power could do any such thing." He paused, because of course the princess knew that. Then he added, "But the man you knew, this servant of Pohorir's king. Gheroïn Nomoris. He bore a tie to the Irekaïn Power. So much seems clear. Nevertheless, he walked from place to place like a normal man, not covering miles in a step. Methmeir Irekaì did not use his strength so to bring Gheroïn and his men and you yourself to him. I surmise events have begun moving more swiftly or more urgently."

"Or perhaps he couldn't do for Nomoris what he did for Laören," Kehera suggested. "We had barely entered Pohorir when I got away. We were still nearly in the mouth of the pass, just above Enchar. And Enchar is different, isn't it? Because it belonged to Kosir until fairly recently. So I don't know what Nomoris or—or your king might have done as we came nearer Irekay's precincts, if I hadn't escaped."

The duke considered her. She did not appear frightened. Concerned, yes. He could hardly fault her for that. He said, "Sit, if you wish. Tell me again of Gheroïn Nomoris and the tie you saw in him. How *did* you escape once Gheroïn had brought you into Pohorir? I would not think your thin tie could have gotten you clear of a sorcerer who carried the sort of tie that could cast back deep snows and open Anha Pass when it should have been closed." The quality of the silence alerted him, and he studied the Raëhema girl with narrow attention. "Well?"

"I had help getting away from Nomoris," she admitted. "He's dead; I told you that, didn't I? A . . . a friend shot him with a crossbow and killed him. But I won't tell you about my . . . my friend. In case he . . . in case."

She met his eyes with quiet certainty. Normally he took defiance as a challenge. Normally he enjoyed breaking it to cringing submission. This girl . . . Eänetaìsarè stirred behind his heart, but softly. The Immanent did not take her defiance as a challenge. And Innisth . . . The girl would not answer him, and he found her defiance merely . . . appealing.

The Harivin princess was not what he had expected. He did not know what he had expected, but after a scant few days of her unwilling company, he did know that Kehera Raëhema was not it. She feared nothing, not even him. She looked at everything, including him, with the same clear gaze, a line of thought springing into existence between her calm gray eyes, and kept her own counsel about what she saw. Or she said what she thought, with an astounding lack of fear.

Innisth found, remarkably, that he had very little desire to break that calm. He began to say something to her, he did not know what, and instead found himself surging to his feet, gripping the edge of the table, his leg blazing with the pain of the abrupt movement. Eänetaìsarè was abruptly fully roused and furious. Kehera Raëhema stepped back and tucked herself against the wall by the window, shrinking half behind the draperies. Her man, naked sword in his hand, had stepped to one side where he could help conceal her and still have room to move. And all of them were staring at a dead man.

Aside from Kehera's tale, Gheroïn Nomoris seemed both like and unlike the man Innisth remembered from his visit to Irekay in his youth. The Gheroïn he remembered would have been laughing, derisive. *This* man looked exactly like he had died, and remembered his death. But, despite Kehera Raëhema's tale, he certainly did not look dead now.

It was impossible twice over for Gheroïn to have come here like this, of course. When an Immanent Power took up the dead within its precincts, as sometimes happened, it did not *raise them up*. It took them into itself, certainly. That . . . was whatever that was, and it was different for every Immanent, but it was certainly not *this*. But Gheroïn did not know he had revealed so much to Innisth by coming here. He could not suspect that Innisth knew that he, Gheroïn, had been killed in the mouth of the pass above Enchar. He must think he showed the king's strength in stepping through the miles. But he surely could not guess that he showed Innisth the king's impossible ability to raise up dead men and send them walking through the air.

A king who held the deep tie to a Great Power . . . a king could sometimes do amazing things. From the princess's tale, Gheroïn Nomoris had carried a strong tie to the Irekaïn Power, and he had been about the king's business. But none of that explained a man who had died and now lived again, a man who had—what? Snatched Lord Laören across the miles from Eäneté to Irekay and then stepped in the other direction himself?

It *was* impossible. And yet here was this dead man, alive and standing here in the heart of Eäneté.

"Innisth terè Maèr Eänetaì," Nomoris said, paying no apparent heed to Innisth's astonishment. His voice was flat and chill, nothing like the voice Innisth remembered. He said, "We are rising up in our strength. We are ready to move now in every direction. We have taken Immaör in Kosir and thrown down Corrièl Immariön; the King of Kosir is no more, and his heir has fled."

Innisth stared at him in utter astonishment. "Is that the king's ambition? To take *Kosir*? Why Kosir?" That *we* could hardly refer to anyone but the king as well as Gheroïn Nomoris. He asked, hardly believing it, "You say he has taken Immaör in the heart of Kosir; you say he has thrown down the King of Kosir. Does he intend to strike from Kosir against Emmer and Harivir at once?" He hesitated a breath, then went on smoothly, as though it were a reasonable question and he expected a reasonable answer. "Had he not already thrown down Hallieth Suriytaiän and destroyed the Great Immanent of Suriytè?"

"Hallieth Theraön resists us," Gheroïn said, still in that flat voice. "So we took Immaör in order to establish our hold in the north. Corrièl Immariön is dead. The Great Power of Immaör clings now to Cimè Immariön, but she will not long survive. We will find her. We will take her tie and entirely subsume her Great Immanent. All Kosir will fall before us. Then we shall press west from Kosir into Emmer and force Hallieth Theraön's submission. But we shall not wait for that before we move against Harivir. Raëhemaiëth has proven our bitter enemy. Now we will strike west through Roh Pass. If we are swift, we will deal Torrolay Raëhema a mortal blow. We must press forward against Harivir and take Raëh as quickly as we may."

Innisth said, carefully deferential, "And you wish Eäneté to serve this aim."

"We will strike west through the mountains here. Once we have established ourselves in Emmer, we will strike against Raëh from the north. Once you cross through Roh Pass and take Coär, we will also be able to come against Raëh from the south." He must have felt the anger rising in the duke, or in Eänetaìsarè, for he added, "You will not refuse. Your Immanent is not sufficient to withstand Irekaìmaiäd."

Anger rose, and sudden understanding. This had been Laören's report, the only part of it that had interested Gheroïn, or perhaps the part that had interested the king. That the Immanent of Eäneté was not strong enough to withstand the Great Immanent of Irekay.

Innisth had intended Laören to make exactly that report. But he had not expected *this* result.

"Two days," said Gheroïn. "You will be prepared to yield the soldiers of Eäneté to us within two days. We will take Coär. We will take its Immanent. We will take it. Then we will come against Raëhemaiëth from two directions at once. Raëh will fall, and all Harivir will be ours."

Kehera Raëhema made a small noise, not quite a gasp, quickly stifled. But it was enough to catch Gheroïn's attention. He turned, gazed at her for a moment, and then said, not even seeming surprised, "Raëhemaiëth. Here you are." He paused and then added, *now* sounding surprised, "But sheltering with Eänetaìsarè?"

The girl shrank back, cowering from this man as she had never cowered from the Eänetén duke.

Tageiny, his expression calm, stepped smoothly around and made as though to run the man through from behind. But his sword rebounded, twisting in his hand. He had struck hard and not expected the block; he dropped the weapon. His little wrist knife was already in his left hand, but his expression suggested he knew he would do no better with that than with the sword. Gheroïn had not even turned to look at him.

Innisth, with a feeling of inevitability, stepped to the side, reached out, caught Tageiny's left wrist, and held out his own hand, palm-up, in silent command.

"I saw you die! Quòn killed you!" Kehera said, all her attention on Nomoris. Then she said, sounding even more horrified, "There's nothing left in you but the tie, Fortunate *Gods*, you're hollow. You're not Gheroïn Nomoris at all. You're *dead*. There's *nothing there*—" She backed away, but there was nowhere to go. Nomoris was between her and the door.

Tageiny opened his hand and let his knife fall into Innisth's hand.

"Heir of Raëhema. Give me Raëhemaïeth," said Nomoris, or the dead man that had been Nomoris. He stepped forward, coldly expressionless, reaching out to seize her.

Innisth terè Maèr Eänetaì, the Wolf Duke, the Iron Duke, raised up the Immanent Power of Eäneté. Eänetaìsarè roared into him and through him, brilliant and furious and terrified. He laid the strength of the mountains into the blade. Eänetaìsarè sent the brilliant leap of fire and the sharp fury of the high winds slicing along its edge, and they stepped forward and drove the knife into the lower back of the man who had been Gheroïn Nomoris, angled upward, aiming for the kidney. This time, the knife did not rebound.

Nomoris, or the man who had been Nomoris, uttered a short hissing cry, jerked back and away, and was gone, into a swift blur of shadows and light.

Innisth Eänetaì bowed his head, closed his eyes, and raised the borders of Eäneté. All the borders, from the edge of Kimsè to the border that ran hard against southern Tisain, and the other way, away from the mountains, east nearly eighty miles. Eänetaìsarè reached through him like fire exploding through stone and struck along every boundary, marking Eäneté off from the rest of Pohorir, raising a barrier to anyone carrying a foreign tie.

For some time, Innisth was unable to perceive anything besides Eänetaìsarè.

At last that faded, and he discovered himself seated at his table, in his own house, in his own body. He drew a long breath. Another. Eänetaìsarè still simmered beneath his skin, but the great roaring fire had burned itself out. He was aware of the Raëhema heir near at hand.

Of the attenuated presence of her Immanent. Raëhemaiëth had supported him—supported Eänetaìsarè—he was aware of that, now that the pressure had eased.

Another breath, while he tried to judge whether he might have returned to himself enough to think.

"Your Grace?" someone said. A hand touched his—an outrageous familiarity. He guessed it was the Raëhema girl by his very lack of outrage. It might have been Caèr Reiöft. But the voice was not Caèr's. The touch was not Caèr's familiar touch.

His eyes were closed. He had not realized. He opened them and lifted a hand to his face gingerly. He had become strange to himself.

"Your Grace," Kehera Raëhema said again. "Your Grace, are you . . . all right?"

"Send for Gereth," he said. His own voice was unfamiliar to his ears: worn and husky. His throat hurt as though he had been shouting. He did not remember shouting.

"I'm here," Gereth said from the doorway. "I'm here." He sounded shocked. Innisth wondered distantly what he saw. Some length of time must have passed, for others crowded behind Gereth: Captain Etar, of course. A scattering of other staff.

Innisth rubbed his face hard with both hands. He said huskily, trying to order his thoughts. "That was a sorcerer. We already knew that Methmeir Irekaì made him into a sorcerer. But he is something else as well now."

"I've no doubt Your Grace is correct," Gereth said.

"He was hollowed out," Kehera Raëhema said shakily. "Wasn't he? I wasn't wrong about that. He was a sorcerer when he caught me in Suriytè. He already had a tie then. I told you about that. Not a natural tie such as everyone is born with, but a deep tie your king had forced on him. It was in him then. The Irekaïn Power, I mean. That's how you make a sorcerer, I know. But that . . . that's not what I saw in him now."

"I doubt the king had to force the deep tie on him," Innisth said grimly. "Gheroïn was the sort to grasp at power, believing he could sidestep the cost. But you are correct. That is not what is in him now. That was a dead man. There is nothing in him now but the Irekaïn Power itself."

"Is that even—" the princess began, and stopped. Plainly it was possible. They both knew it had happened. They could both sense it through their Immanences. Their own Immanences made sure they knew it.

Innisth said, "The Immanent Power of Tisain is not strong, and it will have been weakened further because Geif has left its precincts, even if he still lives."

"Tisain matters, after all this? How?" Gereth sounded exasperated.

"This is the time. This is the moment," Innisth said to him—to all of them. "This is the only moment we may ever have. We have betrayed ourselves completely, to an enemy more inimical and far more powerful than we had guessed. We must move at once. Forward, as there is no way back. Tisain is vulnerable. It is small, but taking it will strengthen Eänetaìsarè. So we shall take it." He held his hand out to the Raëhema girl. "Your Power steadies mine," he told her plainly. She already knew it, and though her eyebrows rose, she answered the implicit command, taking his hand. Her fingers were slender in his hand, but her grip was firm. She met his eyes, quizzical and fearless. She had never feared anything. Except the Irekaïn Power. That showed good sense.

"Now," said the duke, and raised up Eänetaìsarè a second time. This time it came more easily, with less fury. It was surprisingly easy to fling its power south, a hundred miles and more. Wolf-wild, wolf-fierce, he met the border of Tisain . . . of Tisaniceì. Vicious, but small. Like a little weasel, a stoat. Quick and sharp-toothed and angry, not dangerous to the wolf, but eager to bite. Its anger met his, and both flared, but the thin, silvery presence of Raëhemaïëth drew him back and steadied him. Stone shrugged upward and settled; fire rose upward and settled. The wolf closed its jaws on the little stoat, but gently. Gently.

For some measureless time, Tisaniceì continued to struggle. But then, recognizing that it was not being crushed, it grew still. It was not exactly afraid. Immanent Powers were never exactly afraid. But it was *like* fear. It knew Eänetaìsarè was much stronger. "Yield," Innisth whispered. "Yield."

Tisaniceì stilled. He held it. He did not let it go, and it lay still and did not fight him.

Fiercely satisfied, he released the Raëhema girl's hand. His awareness of that deeper aspect of the world faded, yet he remained aware of Eänetaìsarè. The satisfaction mostly belonged to the Power, though some of it was also his. He was still aware of the Immanent Power of Tisain. It did not fight him—Eänetaìsarè—it did not fight them, even now, when it might have tried again to free itself. Its submission was satisfying. The bond he had forced upon it would feed his own strength. But Eänetaìsarè did not draw on the bond, not yet. It ruled Tisain now, whether to support it or take its strength . . . that was entirely Innisth's choice. And Eänetaìsarè's, of course.

"It needs . . ." he began, and looked at Verè Deconniy. "I will take the tie from Geif, lest he become a weakness through which our enemies can reach the Immanent of Tisain. To whom should it go?"

The young captain blinked and drew a slow breath, visibly turning this question over in his mind. "Innè," he said at last. "Perhaps Innè Gereïné. She is his niece. She is not *kind*. But she likes her people to prosper—to show her own strength, that she has the power to protect them." He stopped, swallowing, and added, "I don't know what she would be like, without the need to resist her uncle."

"She will do," Innisth said. "I will make it plain that she must protect her people from me. And if she displeases me too greatly, I can always kill her and set the tie elsewhere. I will make that plain to her as well." He looked at Gereth. "Send a man to Innè Gereïné with a message informing her of my intention. She must be ready to take the tie. Be sure this is clear to her."

"Yes," said Gereth, sounding a little bit stunned.

"I will take Kimsè as well," the duke added. "That tie may go where it will, and if it discards the line that has held it, that is very well." He added thoughtfully, "Perhaps in time I will be able to take Enchar as well."

Kehera Raëhema said quietly, "You are trying to carve out a fifth kingdom, aren't you? You don't have any choice now. You intend to make yourself into a king. But—" She hesitated. "You can't extend your Immanent's grip far enough to the east. As you reach toward Irekay . . . your Power isn't quite Great, is it? You can't actually tear the Irekaïn Power out of any provinces where it's had a strong hold for a long time."

"I have no hope of that," Innisth agreed quietly. "No. I fear that will be impossible. Yet to acquire sufficient land and strength to block Methmeir Irekaì . . . for that I must take more than a handful of these minor provinces of western Pohorir." It was ironic that he should, for once, wish to ease the pressure of his hand and find himself unable to do so. Ironic, and not pleasant. He found in himself a profound reluctance to break the Raëhema girl's hard-held calm. Yet the opportunity, once it appeared, must be grasped firmly with both hands. In this one moment, all he had ever desired lay within his reach. It could never be so again if he did not take it now.

But he regretted the distress he must inevitably cause his . . . prisoner. Yes, his prisoner. She had never been truly a guest.

He said, "You will recall that I said, from the first day of your—captivity—here, that I would find some use to make of you."

The gray eyes had widened. But she would not ask. That was the measure of her pride.

Innisth paused. Then, unable to think how to soften the blow, he said, "Tomorrow I will send a message to Coär and to your father. I will hold Roh Pass in return for Coär. Your father will recognize the necessity. He will have no choice. The Immanent of Coär is old and deep and strong. I could not take it by force. But it will yield to Eänetaìsarè if the Duke of Coär yields to me. Riheir Coärin *will* yield to me, and when I move to establish a bond between Eäneté and Coär, your father will release the bond between Coär and Raëh. Your Raëhemaiëth will release the Immanent of Coär—we have both seen that Raëhemaiëth supports Eänetaìsarè."

"It does," she said reluctantly. "On this side of the mountains. On the other side, it may be different—"

"Your Raëhemaiëth fears the Immanent Power of Irekay more than it fears Eänetaìsarè. It does not fear Eänetaìsarè at all. How else would you explain anything that we have seen between them?"

Kehera Raëhema said nothing. He knew from her silence that she must know what he said was true. He said gently, "I will claim Coär and establish Eäneté as the ruling province on both sides of the mountains. Thus will I acquire the strength I must have to defy my—the King of Pohorir." He paused and then went on. "One cannot, of course, expect the people of Coär to yield themselves willingly to my rule. I will therefore make you my wife. Thus the folk of Coär will see that you accept me, and so they will accept my hand over them."

There was a small, heavy pause. Then Kehera Raëhema said with careful steadiness, "Your Grace, my father will not surrender Coär to your hand. Nor will he surrender me. Even if he would, you cannot think I will accept any such . . . stratagem."

"Your Highness, neither he nor you will have any choice. Your father cannot hold the south against me, not when he must also face enemies from the north. You heard what Gheroïn said—what the King of Pohorir said through him. The strength of the Irekaïn Power is clearly greater than anyone could have expected. Taking up the dead of Irekay, that's one thing. But setting a deep tie into a dead man, raising him up so that Methmeir Irekaì can speak through him, as we see must be the case . . . that is something quite other, and the King of Pohorir commensurately dangerous. Your father must ally with me or lose everything. As I must extend Eäneté's sway, or inevitably fall. But with this alliance, I will hold. We may both hold. You must see this is true. So you will accept this . . . proposal. You have no practical alternative."

The girl said nothing.

Innisth continued relentlessly. "In every age, a king takes what he can hold. Or gives up what he cannot hold. Yet we *shall* be allies. Coär *will* ally with Eäneté, and the alliance will hold. Our two provinces have long been familiar to each other, sharing Roh Pass as we do. Our Immanences are familiar to each other. Our lands are similar. Both provinces lie in the shadow of the mountains, though Eäneté lies to the east and Coär the west. There are ties of blood: some Harivin folk of Coär dwell here—not many, but some. And a scattering of Eänetén people have made lives in Coär. We are natural allies, as Eäneté has never been with Irekay. And when the Duke of Coär yields a ruling tie to Eäneté, I shall have the strength to defend my borders against Methmeir Irekaì. I give you my word, I shall hold this side of Roh Pass. No enemy shall pass into Harivir through it. But your father must yield Coär to me, and you must accept marriage to me so that he may do so. Once I hold it, I will defend it. Your father cannot defend it himself. Coär—and you—are the price of alliance. Your father will yield both Coär and you to me because he has no choice."

Everything he said was true. He already knew Kehera Raëhema had no talent for denying to herself what was true. He did not expect her to shout or storm, having taken in the past days some measure of her quiet strength. He could see she understood at once that it was all true. He said, almost gently, "I would therefore trouble Your Highness to write a brief note to your father confirming this plan. I will send a man of mine to bear it through the pass to Coär, along with my message. It would be kind, I think, to suggest to your father that you are not entirely overwhelmed with personal revulsion at the match."

He watched her consider refusing. He could trace, in the minute shifts of her face, the exact path of her thoughts. She was thinking that she might refuse what he intended. Except she knew he would not permit her to refuse. And even if she did, Methmeir Irekaì was still there, with his Power that consumed other Immanents and made tools out of dead men. Whatever she thought of Innisth personally, she knew the King of Pohorir would surely make a far worse conqueror. Innisth watched her face and saw her form the conclusion, the necessary conclusion, and waited in silence for the answer she must make.

She made it. She said, quite tonelessly, "I'll write the letter."

"Thank you," said the duke, very softly. He considered her pale, set face and added, still softly, "I will take as many of the provinces beyond Coär as I can. But I will protect them. All the lands that I take will prosper under my rule. I will teach your people no fear of me. With you by my side, they will accept what they must. And the people of Eäneté will bless your name forever, as the key to their freedom from Irekay and from Pohorir entire. In this, you are the foundation of all my hope, and the tomb of all my fear."

She made no answer. He did not insist on one. He rose instead, and realized for the first time that the pain in his leg had become much less. The Immanent of Raëh had also done that, he surmised, or showed Eänetaìsarè the way of it, for healing was not something to which savage Eänetaìsarè easily bent itself. Probably Kehera Raëhema encouraged her Immanent toward such gentleness as easily as breathing. And he would return her kindness with cruelty.

But he had no choice. So he said nothing, but gave only the small bow that granted her leave to retire from his presence. Out of the surprising impulse to mercy that inhabited him in her presence, he chose to deliver the final blow as well, so that she should not have to wait for it. He told her, "Whatever response your father sends, the wedding will take place in eight days' time, on the sixteenth day of the Iron Hinge Month. That will give my people time to make ready, so that immediately afterward we may ride into the pass." For a moment he hoped he might find something else to say as well, to soften the blow; as though he might find in himself some sufficient apology. But there was nothing, of course, that could be said, and no apology that could be anything but an insult.

15

The shocking events that had forced the Wolf Duke into open rebellion against the King of Pohorir also left Kehera struggling to find a proper response. Should she submit to the duke's plan? Or should she make one last effort to break away, to get back to Harivir, to Raëh, to her father? What could she actually *do*, if she were at home? She had renounced the heir's tie; that was gone.

But she still held a thinner tie to Raëhemaiëth. And Raëhemaiëth had clearly allied somehow with the Eänetén Power, foreign though the two Immanences must be to each other. Perhaps the Eänetén duke was right to want her here.

The tomb of all my fear. She wondered whether he believed that. Whether he truly believed that her Raëhema blood and her tie to Raëhemaiëth would be enough to let him resist the Pohorin king and the terrible Power of Irekay. Whether he truly thought that Raëhemaiëth would support him in that effort, even if that involved breaking the bond between Coär and Raëh and establishing a new bond to Eäneté in its place.

She thought perhaps he was right about that. If he was, it might be her fault. Or to her credit. One or the other. *She* had carried

Raëhemaiëth into Emmer. Through her, it had seen exactly what had happened in Suriytè . . . seen it as Immanent Powers saw, which was not as human people saw, but even what she had seen had been so frightening. Now she thought Raëhemaiëth had been even more frightened than she. Not that *fear* was exactly what it had felt, probably.

Powers did not feel or think as human people did. If Immanent Powers formed intentions or took actions, it wasn't the way human people did such things. But that Raëhemaiëth preferred the Immanent of Eäneté to the Great Immanent of Irekay . . . that much, she couldn't doubt. She agreed, vehemently. Maybe Raëhemaiëth had decided that allying itself with Eänetaìsarè was the key to protecting itself and its land and all its creatures from the Pohorin king. She could almost believe Raëhemaiëth had meant all along for her to be here. It seemed incredible. But it did not seem *impossible*.

The Wolf Duke believed he might be able to carve out a new kingdom, make himself a king. He thought he was that strong. Or he thought he could make himself that strong if he could take part of Harivir, break it away from Raëh and bind it to Eäneté.

She wished she might tell Tiro everything that had happened. Here she was, with her thin tie to Raëhemaiëth not quite so thin as it was supposed to be, and she was becoming more and more certain her presence in Eäneté reflected Raëhemaiëth's maneuvering. Maybe—it seemed likely now—the maneuvering of the Fortunate Gods as well. As the Unfortunate Gods presumably influenced the decisions and actions of the Pohorin king. The idea that events in the world had become so important that the Gods were moved to touch the world . . . that frightened her.

Did her father know that Methmeir Irekaì was the architect of all these disasters, in Emmer and Harivir and now Kosir? Did he understand what kind of threat he faced, in the Pohorin king and the Irekaïn Power?

What would her father do, what would Riheir Coärin do, if the Wolf Duke demanded Coär as the price of an alliance? If he demanded as well the provinces that were Coär's neighbors?

There were too many questions, and she held none of the answers.

She had known Riheir fairly well, once. When she had been a girl, he'd visited the court in Raëh nearly every year; less often after he took the deep tie. It had come to him young. He'd been, what? That must have been seven or eight years ago, so he'd been twenty-three, twenty-four. Only a little older than she was now. She'd been sorry for it when she heard. She knew what it was, to lose your mother. And taking the deep tie cost a man, cost him years of his life, unless he used the tie the other way, which Riheir certainly would not.

She had always liked Riheir Coärin, even before he'd sent her a poem this spring. She remembered the kites fondly. She'd been sixteen that year, and she'd thought she was too old for such toys, but he must have seen how much she loved the beauty of the kites darting like living things in the sky. So he'd made her one, from paper colored orange and red and gold. She hadn't wanted to fly it for fear it would be damaged, but he'd told her kites were for flying and fire was meant to burn against the sky. She'd flown it a dozen times, and given it to a real fire when it was finally too badly battered to fly again.

Now the Wolf Duke of Eäneté was going to ride through Roh Pass and take Coär, and he was going to use *her* to make Riheir Coärin accept whatever he did. Because he was going to marry her. He would make her marry him. She didn't doubt he could do it. He couldn't make her say the words. But he could tie the cords and light the candles, and even if she didn't tie any of the cords herself, the marriage would still stand.

He would send someone to tell Riheir and her father what he intended, but he wasn't asking permission and he wouldn't change his mind, no matter what they said or did. Or what she said or did. She knew that. And she didn't even know whether she should fight him or accede. She just didn't know.

How long would it take an army from Irekay to march west to punish a disobedient provincial duke? With, presumably, Gheroïn

Nomoris, who had no doubt stepped from this house right back to Irekay, she didn't doubt that the King of Pohorir now knew everything—well, not that the Eänetén duke meant to make himself a new kingdom; probably not that. But that she was here with Innisth Eänetaì and that they were both set against him. Certainly Methmeir Irekaì knew that.

Raëhemaiëth *would* be able to support Eänetaìsarè more effectively if she married the duke. She knew that. Faced with a choice between the Wolf Duke of Eäneté who wanted to marry her and ally himself with her father and her country, and the hollow King of Pohorir who wanted to tear Raëhemaiëth out of her by the roots and destroy first it and then her whole country . . . It wasn't even a choice.

The duke left her alone while they waited for his man to return from Coär. Kehera thought she was glad about that, but she wasn't sure. She had too much time to think, and found herself unable to think at all. Though she didn't believe in divination, she cast her tiahel rods nine times. The King's Rod came to rest with the double-headed Winter Dragon faceup every time. She wished she thought that meant nothing. She was afraid it meant everything.

Luad turned out to be deadly with ordinary play, though. When Kehera found herself afraid to try further divination, he borrowed her set and won first all the slices of crystallized ginger from Tageiny and then quite a lot of copper coins from the Eänetén guards set outside her suite. If Tiro hadn't made the tiahel set for her, Kehera would have just given it to him.

She wished fervently that everything was back the way it should be: her father safe in Raëh and Methmeir Irekaì keeping to himself in Pohorir. . . . Well, maybe they could do without Hallieth Theraön Suriytaiän in Emmer. She supposed now that the Emmeran king's madness might have been the first sign that everything was crashing down. He had been mad for years. Now she wondered if the Pohorin king had been behind even that, somehow.

❄ ❄ ❄

On the tenth day of the Iron Hinge Month, a tap on her door broke into her thoughts, and she looked up.

"Your Highness," Gereth Murrel murmured, stepping into her view, his look grave. "The duke's man has returned from Coär. His Grace asks you attend him."

This was rather before anyone had expected, so she knew the man must have turned right around and come straight back, riding hard. Kehera stood up slowly, trepidation running through her.

The duke had sent his young captain, Verè Deconniy, the one who, it turned out, was engaged to marry timid little Eöté. They were both from Tisain, which was perhaps a bond of sorts; Kehera wasn't sure. But she was ready to like him. He had seemed kind when she'd first met him, and she suspected it had taken a special man to win Eöté's trust. Now, as she came into the duke's study, she looked at the captain with wistful hope, because he brought her news from Coär.

But Captain Deconniy looked back at her with something like pity underlying his professional reserve, and the Wolf Duke had a particularly chilly and impenetrable look in his eyes. An intimation of disaster prickled across her skin and down her spine. She found she had taken several steps forward without noticing and made herself stand still. "What?" she asked the young captain. "Tell me."

The Wolf Duke inclined his head in silent permission, and Deconniy told her, "Duke Riheir Coärin has not precisely agreed to surrender Coär to Eäneté." Every word was clipped and flat. "But he will. Because Leiör's Immanent has been lost, and the Irekaïn Power—'some cold Power carried by the hollow dead' is what Coärin told me—it's pressing Raëh hard. You know how a Power will take up its folk when they die. This one is stealing anyone's dead, using the revenants as its hands and eyes." His steady recital faltered on this horrifying detail. Then he went on. "It tried to break Raëh. It failed; they'd anchored the Power of Raëh right into southern Emmer, so their enemies had to break those Immanences first, and that cost it and kept it away from Raëh. Even so, Torrolay Raëhema was unconscious for two days and—" He hesitated, then finished quietly. "That was on the first day of Iron Hinge Month, and your brother, Tirovay Raëhema, still had not woken, so far as the Duke of Coär knew. His Grace could hardly bear to tell me that. Because he knew I would tell you, Your Highness."

Kehera was only tangentially aware of the captain's obvious sympathy. She was too horrified. "I didn't feel anything," she whispered. This seemed almost too much to bear: that her father and her little brother had been stricken and she had not even known. She didn't understand how such a disaster could have struck and yet she feel nothing through Raëhemaiëth. Had Raëhemaiëth deliberately kept it from her, protected her from it? Or, no—the Eänetén Power. Perhaps its presence had protected her.

But it didn't matter.

She turned to the duke. "I have to go home. Tiro—my father— they need me. Tiro wasn't supposed to be heir; that must be why he hasn't woken. He wasn't supposed to have the heir's tie. It's my fault, making Raëhemaiëth sink the deep tie into Tiro when it should have been in me." It *was* her fault. She hadn't been there to support her father, and Raëhemaiëth hadn't been able to protect Tiro. She said, still more urgently, speaking straight to the duke, "You *must* see, I have to go home."

But she could already see he was going to refuse. He started to say something, some kind of explanation or excuse. But she didn't care what he would say, and didn't stay to listen.

A doubled guard appeared outside her suite almost before she slammed the door. Heris Tageiny told her that, and told her that guards were watching all her windows too, even though her rooms were three stories up. "Not that it matters," he told her gently. "You know he'll have the pass trebly guarded now too."

Kehera nodded. She didn't care about the guards. She knew she had to get home. Back to the precincts of familiar Powers, to lands that were hers in a way that Eäneté could never be. She would reclaim her tie, the heir's tie, and free Tiro from it. Then her brother would wake.

Then she would stand with her father, and together they would show the Wolf Duke that he wasn't the only one with a strong Power, nor the only one who could resist Methmeir Irekaì. Then, if he wanted to ally with Harivir, let him bargain for that alliance, not issue an ultimatum. Let him ask for what he needed instead of demand whatever he wished, and if she was going to be a counter on the game board, she would play as the Harivin princess and not as anybody's pawn.

But to do that, she had to get through the pass.

And there was exactly one person who could help her in her escape from the Wolf Duke: Gereth Murrel, seneschal to this house and this duke, was the man who had the authority to get her through the pass to Harivir. If he could be brought to betray his lord. And Kehera was almost certain she knew exactly how to persuade him to do it.

Luad brought the duke's seneschal to her. No doubt the man had been twice as busy as usual, given all these cascading crises. But whatever urgency Luad had conveyed to him, it had sufficed to bring him quickly to her side.

Dry-eyed and quiet-voiced, Kehera explained. She must leave the duke's house. She must not stay in Eäneté. She must go back to her father, to her brother, to her own country. She must add her strength to theirs. Then Raëh would not fall, and Harivir would stand, and Eäneté could bargain for alliance. Which Harivir would agree to, of course! But if Harivir fell, how long did he think it would be before Eäneté followed? Or did he think the king in Irekay would forgive Innisth Eänetaì's defiance?

And when the seneschal began, despite all her arguments, to demur, she pitilessly invoked the other weapons he had handed. "Please. Please, listen. You know I'm right. Raëh must hold. Harivir must hold. I have to go home. I have to go now, before it's too late. Your duke will change his mind, he'll see he must let me support Raëh, but it will be *too late*. You're my only chance. But not only that. Not only that. Gereth, how many girls are you willing to see wed unwilling to the dukes in this house? Wasn't Jeneil inè Suon already one too many?"

The man flinched at that, losing color. He tried to interrupt.

Kehera did not permit it. Nor did she herself flinch. She leaned forward intensely. "When is the cost of loyalty too high, Gereth? When love requires terrible things, hateful things, is it still love, or just cowardice? If you let him do this to me, and my brother dies, and my father is cast down, and your terrible Irekaïn Power rules in Raëh, then I tell you, even if your duke somehow succeeds in every part of his plan, you will see another child born of despair and rage in this house. And what will you tell that child when it asks you why?"

"*All right*!" The seneschal stood up, the sharp movement of a man who *must* move. "All right," he repeated more quietly. "I'll help you, Your Highness. You had better be right, you had better be right about everything, because I'll do it. I'll help you get through the pass, and may the Fortunate Gods have mercy on us both: on me for the trust I will break and on you for forcing me to break it."

Kehera nodded. It would demean them both if she apologized, so she said instead, "The most straightforward method is best, I think. I know no one questions anything you do. I've sent Tageiny into the city. He's creating a false trail. Luad will join him. I don't know the details." Tageiny had said mildly that it was better that she didn't, and a second's thought had showed her he was absolutely right. She said, "I doubt it will fool the duke long, but maybe long enough—and it will let Tageiny and Luad get away." She wished they were with her now, but her part should be more dangerous than theirs. Tageiny insisted he could manage. She trusted it was true. She had also given him her last pearl and all her money, and promised to cover his feet and Luad's with silver if they made it to Raëh. She hoped they would come. She hoped above almost everything that they would be safe.

But that part was out of her hands now. So she said only, "You do have the authority to get past the guards on my door? And at the pass?"

"Of course," Gereth said bitterly. "I speak with the duke's own voice. Am I not the most trusted of all his servants? Get dressed and we'll go straight down to the stables." He closed the door of her private bedchamber behind him with a gentleness so calculated it made plain the strength of his desire to slam it.

Kehera changed quickly, dressing herself in the simplest, warmest clothing she had. She packed almost nothing but her tiahel set.

The Eänetén guards questioned nothing. Nor did the stablemen. Gereth chose plain, sturdy animals that would not tire in the hard conditions of the pass. Kehera didn't let herself look around anxiously to see who might be watching. She was glad the stables were on the windowless, windward side of the house—far less likely the wrong person might glance out and happen to see her here where she had, saving Gereth's presence, no right to be.

She mounted the gelding Gereth held for her without a word and they rode silently, side by side, across the courtyard and through the gates. The guards there saluted Gereth with grave respect, a salute he returned tensely—he was not a man given to subterfuge. But no one showed the slightest suspicion.

"Surely someone will send a messenger to the duke?" Kehera asked nervously.

"Maybe," Gereth answered shortly. But a moment later he said more gently, "Probably not right away. They're not accustomed to questioning me."

Kehera nodded.

"It's about five miles to the mouth of the pass. There's a guard post there, of course. We'll get a change of horses there, and then there'll be only the winter itself to fight through. If we ride fast and don't stop for anything . . ." He didn't finish the sentence. She knew it was two days to the other end of the pass, for people in a desperate hurry.

Kehera nodded again. The duke would pursue them, of course. Everything depended on the head start they could gain now, at the beginning. She followed Gereth as he urged his horse to a canter.

Under other conditions, she might have loved that ride: the flying speed across the packed snow of the road, past the deep green and black of the winter forest, through the slow, heavy flakes of snow falling from an iron-gray sky. Over all, the mountains, taking up all the sky before them, with the road curving up along their flanks. The forest whispered to her, the mountains did, their beauty caught at her; but the voice was the voice of Eäneté, and she tried not to listen to it, lest it notice her and her foreign tie and whisper to the duke.

The guard post was set in a beautifully defensive position; Kehera could see that, even in the short glance she had at it. She could never have got past the men there on her own, but they accepted Gereth's orders without question. They handed up packets of journey rations and bags of watered wine, brought up fresh horses, and swung open the heavy gate for the travelers to pass through.

They went on, but more slowly. An exhausted animal in the winter pass was an invitation to disaster, and the road ran all uphill now. So it was trot and walk and brief, swift canter. Snow was not a problem; the duke's power kept the pass free of any deep accumulation even through the months of deep cold. The mountains loomed to either side: sometimes powerful gray walls towering to the sky, sometimes gentler, thickly forested slopes, but always impassable. They simplified life, removed options: ahead or back were the only possible directions.

Dusk came early and fast in the pass. Gereth lit lanterns, and they rode on. The horses were no longer eager, but they were in good condition and went on steadily. Kehera passed from pleasantly weary to frankly tired, and her legs and back and rear began to ache. They went on. The moon rose, and the snow and stone picked up the moonlight and threw it back. They blew out the lanterns, no longer needing them to keep to the road.

By now, Kehera thought, the duke would most likely have missed her. Perhaps at this moment he was following Tageiny's false trail. Or perhaps he had already discovered the ruse. Very soon, he might be racing up the pass after them. Perhaps he was already coming.

She did not speak of these fears to Gereth. Whatever personal fears he had, he likewise kept them to himself.

The seneschal's voice came out of the dark to her. "How are you doing? Can you go on?"

"I can manage." Perhaps better than he could, she thought. A night of sleepless travel through the winter had to be harder for a man in his fifties than for a woman of twenty. A night and a day and another night might see them to the other side. Somewhere in the middle, she knew she would step from Pohorir to Harivir. She longed for that.

She said aloud, "I think I have forgotten how it feels to be safe." Then a thought occurred to her, and she added, "You'll be safe, too, Gereth. My father will be very grateful to you for helping me come back to him."

There was a short silence. Gereth answered finally, "I don't doubt he has your generosity. Harivir is fortunate in its royal house. But I won't be going with you past the Coär guard post."

Kehera could not, after the first second, understand why she was surprised. Of course Gereth would return to face his duke. She said after a moment, "I understand why you feel you must go back. But I would change your mind if I could."

"You can't."

"I know." After a moment, she asked awkwardly, "What do you think he'll do to you, for helping me?"

"I have no idea." He added, tone just a little stiff, "Do you mind if we talk about something else?"

Kehera began to tell him about Raëh, about her father's house, about anything she could think of in that moment. But what she was thinking was, if she got the chance, she might have Gereth held by the Coär guards rather than allow him to return to the duke he had betrayed. She could not decide whether this would be the right thing to do.

She was still occupied with this question half an hour later, when the first of the wolves appeared.

It was one of the great silver-pale winter wolves that haunted the mountains, almost as white as the fresh-fallen snow. For a moment she even thought it might be nothing but a trick of memory and light. But the wolf was real. The moonlight caught in its golden eyes and glinted off its white, white teeth.

The horses halted of themselves, heads thrown back and ears flat. Kehera grabbed for a better hold of her reins, thanking the Fortunate Gods that the horses were well trained and did not bolt. She had no weapon but her little knife. Gereth, swearing under his breath, dragged at the crossbow tied behind his saddle. He got it free just as a second wolf, and a third, followed the first out of the forest. There were a dozen by the time he had a bolt in place. The wolves completely blocked the road ahead. More were still arriving, white and pale ash-gray and an occasional charcoal-colored animal, all with the same wild golden eyes as the Eänetén duke.

Gereth held the bow indecisively, glancing from one wolf to the next. The horses sweated and sidled uneasily, trying to back up.

Kehera held hers on a short rein and said tightly to Gereth, "Why don't they attack?"

The seneschal answered quietly, "They're *his*. I'm sorry. I should have known he could call the wolves."

Kehera shot him an amazed glance and then stared back at the wolves. An enormous gray male yawned elaborately at her, tongue curling, and closed its mouth again with a sharp click of fangs. "We can't stay *here*," she protested. "We can't just wait for him to come upon us." In any tale, she or Gereth would think of something brilliant and subtle and clever and get past the wolves.

"What do you suggest?" Gereth asked her. "I have only a few bolts, and I'm not that good a shot."

"If they're his, they won't kill us," Kehera said, with a perfect certainty she could not have justified logically. "The horses are a problem, I grant you, but can we just—walk past them, perhaps?"

"I very much doubt it." The seneschal saw her expression and added, "I'll try it. Just wait here." Dismounting, he gave her his rein and walked straight up the road, directly toward the wolves. They closed in. Gereth braced himself, took a swift breath, and stepped deliberately forward.

A slim white female slashed at him, cutting the tough cloth of his cloak as though it had been cobweb. Gereth daringly lifted his crossbow to strike her out of his way. Another wolf lunged like a playful dog, snatching the bow out of his hands. The great gray male knocked him down; Gereth threw back his head and disappeared without a sound below the powerful, shaggy backs of the wolves.

Kehera, shouting wordlessly, ran forward. The wolves drew back, leaving Gereth to crawl to his feet. Trembling with relief, she gave the seneschal her hand to help him stand, and he got slowly to his feet. He was unhurt, though sweating and wide-eyed.

"They didn't hurt you," she said, vastly thankful. And then, realizing this, "They gave way for me." Then she shook her head. "Oh, but I can't possibly . . ." She stopped.

Gereth rubbed his hands across his face. But he had already understood, just as she had. After a moment he said, "You're right. You can walk past them. *You* can. They did give way for you. They're *his* . . . and they know I'm his as well. And that you belong to Raëhemaiëth."

Kehera shook her head again, more vehemently. "I can't leave you here."

"I told you. I would have gone back anyway. You can't walk all that way, but if you lead your horse . . . If it were blindfolded, you could lead it past the wolves. I'll be all right. I'll wait here. I don't imagine it will take him so very long to find me."

He was right. That would work. Kehera knew as well as he did that it would work. When she stepped experimentally toward the largest of the wolves, it looked ostentatiously away, yawning. She knew it wouldn't stop her. She belonged to Raëh, not to Eäneté.

She would only have to walk away through the pass and leave the seneschal to face his duke alone. As he had already said he meant to do anyway. She could lead her horse past the wolves and then mount and ride on. Somewhere in the night she would ride out of Eäneté and into Coär, ride out of Pohorir and into Harivir. Raëhemaiëth would rise for her. She was nearly certain Raëhemaiëth would rise. And then it wouldn't matter what the Eänetén duke wanted or planned or needed; he could not set his Immanent against Raëhemaiëth. He needed Raëhemaiëth's support too much.

He needed her support.

Kehera stared into the golden eyes of the big gray wolf and told herself that she should blindfold her horse, that there was no time to dither, that her father needed her, that *Tiro* needed her. She knew it was true. And yet the wolf held her, though it offered no threat. Its yellow eyes, so much like the Eänetén duke's, looked into hers.

"You have to go," the seneschal said quietly. "Nothing has changed. Think of your brother."

Kehera took a breath and let it out. "I know." She turned, met his eyes.

But before she could say anything further, a sharp half-familiar cry cut through the night, and almost at once a falcon flew straight past them, low, winging fast. A white mountain falcon, a bird of daylight, flying now through the dark like an owl. It turned on a wingtip, circled sharply around, and landed on an outcropping of stone hardly ten feet away.

The falcon's head and breast were pure white, its eyes black, the white feathers of its mantling wings tipped with black. It looked for all the world as though it had just that moment been birthed from moonlight and snow and the dark.

"A falcon," the seneschal said out loud, his voice blank.

"Raëh's falcon is red," Kehera said, but she knew it didn't matter. This white mountain falcon was certainly Raëhemaiëth's. The wolves knew it too. They had turned their heads away, pretending not to see the falcon. Except the great gray male, who rose and paced to stand beneath the falcon's perch, then turned and looked deliberately into Kehera's face.

The falcon shifted its talons, dropped its head, and cried once more, the sharp wild cry of the hunt. Then sprang into the moonlit night, climbed in a tight circle, and flashed away. Not back toward Coär and Harivir, but the other way, cutting through the pass toward Eäneté.

"I—" Kehera said. She felt stunned and blank and witless. "Raëhemaiëth—"

"It might have made itself more plain earlier," Gereth said wearily. "Do you trust your Raëhemaiëth?"

"That's the question, isn't it?" Kehera answered, still rather blankly. "I swore I'd never again let myself be used as a pawn in another man's game. I should have included Immanent Powers and all Gods Fortunate and Unfortunate." She paused. Then she said, "I'm a fool. I'm sorry. If I—if we—" She didn't know how to finish that sentence and sat down on a rock. After a moment, the seneschal sat beside her and put an arm around her shoulders, both of them watching the wolves, which showed no inclination to follow the falcon.

Kehera did not know whether it was worse to be trapped though she made every effort to escape, or to make an actual decision not to escape. She felt too weary even to weep. This was the difference between tales and the real world: In the real world, sometimes every choice meant betraying *someone*.

The Wolf Duke arrived with the dawn, as though the light had trailed at his heel like a dog all the way up the pass. The sky had clouded over again as the night had worn on, so the rising sun backlit a sky the color of lead. Snow whispered down, melting on Kehera's hood and skirt, catching on the duke's black hair and in the mane of his black mare. There were men at his back, the guards from the gate. They stopped well back, waiting as the duke rode ahead of them.

Kehera stood as the duke rode up to them. Gereth stood as well, then went to one knee, bowing his head. Kehera did not look at him, hoping to keep the duke's attention focused on her through the first blaze of his anger. She wanted to say something about Raëhemaiëth and choices and the way things were sometimes hard to figure out and not what they seemed, but she knew that in this, none of that mattered.

The duke's glance passed over her with complete, cold disinterest, caught for an instant on the still figure of his seneschal, and passed on to the wolves. His eyes were exactly the shade of the gray male's eyes.

He swung down from his mare, dropped the reins to drag on the snow, and stepped forward. His lameness had almost entirely passed, Kehera realized, though whether that was natural healing or pure pride was not entirely clear to her.

"Thank you," he said softly to the wolves. "Well done. You may go."

The gray male stood up. He yawned and stretched, cast a glance over his pack, and sprang lightly away through the snow. The other wolves followed, shadows of the winter, going back into the winter that had birthed them. They disappeared into the trees without a backward glance.

The duke turned back to the waiting fugitives only when the wolves had entirely vanished into their world of leafless forest and ice and stone. His attention now was only for his seneschal. Kehera found she did not dare move. She stood very still, all but holding her breath.

Gereth did not rise, but he put back his hood. Snowflakes caught in his gray hair and melted like tears on his face. He did not speak.

The duke took a small step toward him. The seneschal waited quietly. Kehera thought he would kneel without moving even if the duke drew a sword to cut him down. . . . It was an appallingly easy scene to imagine. But the duke stopped several paces away from Gereth. And he was not wearing a sword.

"Gereth," said the duke, and through the discipline he had set on his voice, Kehera could hear an echo of the cost of that control: of a pain beyond words, very near despair. "How could you do to me what you have done?"

Kehera closed her eyes in pain. She had known when she had demanded that Gereth help her escape that betrayal could be the worst of all possible sins . . . and she had still done it. It had been his choice at the end, but first it had been hers, to force him to that choice.

The older man started to speak, stopped. He managed at last in an uneven voice, "I have already watched one woman die of despair in that house, Innisth. I could not bear to watch that happen again. Not even for you. I'm so sorry. Not even for you—" His voice cracked. He swallowed, and fell silent.

For a long moment the duke did not move. Nothing moved in the world save for the snow, slipping endlessly down from the leaden sky, accent rather than exception to the terrible stillness. The duke's face was tight-drawn, his eyes fixed on Gereth's face. Kehera blinked back tears.

The duke said raggedly, as if he and Gereth were alone in the world, "*I am not my father.*"

"I know it. Oh, Innisth, I know it. But you are willing to do to this girl what your father did to Jeneil—"

"*Enough,*" said the duke, voice taut.

Gereth bowed his head.

The duke drew in a deep breath and let it out slowly. He said at last, quite evenly, "I no longer require your service."

Gereth did not seem surprised. He flinched, but he did not look up or speak.

"There is your horse," said the duke. "Take it and go. Take it and go, and never return to Eäneté. In memory—" His voice checked for an instant, resumed under tight control. "In memory of what you have been to me, Roh Pass will be open for you. One way only."

The older man stirred. He glanced around, at the snow, tracked with wolf prints. He got to his feet slowly and took a step backward, toward his horse, eyes on the duke's set face. Then his head bowed again. He walked toward his horse, mounted, and turned it toward the west.

Kehera moved quickly forward and laid her hand on the seneschal's rein. She said, not looking at the duke, "Go to my father. He will welcome you for my sake."

Gereth met her eyes for a second. He nodded. Kehera stepped back.

"Wait," said the duke, and they both turned. Kehera had no idea what her face showed, and could not read Gereth's expression. Nor the duke's.

The duke stooped and picked up a jagged fragment of stone from the side of the road: ordinary granite streaked with smoky quartz. He frowned at this for an instant, then closed his eyes briefly. At last he brought it to his lips and breathed on it, his breath clouding in the cold. Then he opened his eyes, walked forward, and held it out to Gereth.

Kehera could see the warmth that clung to it, the glitter that trailed through the air after it, and blinked. An involution—a thin tie; he had bound a thread of Eänetaìsarè to that fragment of Eänetén stone. She knew it. She could see it. She drew a breath, but looked at the duke's closed expression and said nothing.

The duke said to Gereth, with no inflection in his voice, "Take it with you to the house of the King of Harivir. A memory of Eäneté; a tie to Eänetaìsarè. You may find it useful."

Gereth nodded slowly. He took the pebble and tucked it away, and then turned his horse toward the west once more and rode away. He did not look back, and the falling snow filled in the prints his horse left behind.

Kehera watched him go, the tiny thread of the tie scrolling out behind him. Only when the older man was out of sight did she turn to face the duke. She could not read anything in his set face. It seemed cowardly to say that in the end she had chosen not to go on toward Coär. She only said at last, "He meant to come back, you know. To face you."

The duke flinched, a tightening of his shoulders more than an actual movement. He said curtly, "Get your horse and mount."

Kehera obeyed wordlessly. The soldiers fell back as the duke reined past them and closed in again behind Kehera, an escort no less grim than the wolves.

The ride back to the guard post seemed to take forever. Kehera, dizzy with weariness, braced her hands on her horse's neck and stared straight ahead.

The guards at the mouth of the pass slid carefully blank glances past Kehera's face. None of them asked after the seneschal. Once past the guard post, they went more quickly. It seemed no time at all before the walls of the duke's house came into sight. Coming in from the west, the city was not very much in evidence: the great house seemed set alone into the stark winter world of forest and mountains, isolated from all other works of men.

The guards at the gates kept their eyes prudently on the ground as the duke rode by them. He ignored them all, riding in silence across the courtyard to dismount by the great door of the house. Kehera unclamped her hands from their grip on her reins only with difficulty, her fingers stiff with cold and fatigue. It took a similar effort to swing her leg over the horse's back and slide to the ground. She leaned for a second against the horse's shoulder, gripping its mane.

The duke did not move to assist her. He said curtly, "We shall not wait upon the appointed hour. At dawn tomorrow, we shall ride. I have commanded my officers to be sure all is in readiness. We shall wed in Coär, before the eyes of your people as well as mine."

Kehera couldn't answer him. She couldn't tell whether he meant this as punishment. It felt like punishment. He would force her to this marriage and none of them could prevent him. She wasn't sure he meant to demonstrate that. But she felt as though he did.

Unable to think of anything else to do, she went slowly up the stairs to her suite. There were guards on the outer door. They looked at her warily. She stared back. She had been gone. Why should her suite be guarded? Heart in her mouth, she stepped past them and flung open the door.

Eöté leaped to her feet with a gasp. That was all right, but Luad was also there, Luad, who should have been safely out of the duke's house and out of his hand. But Luad was here, and Tageiny was not.

"Where's Tag?" Kehera asked sharply.

Eöté stammered, "Downstairs—"

Luad added urgently, "The duke took us—he—his tie did it, I guess, we didn't even get out of the city, he took Tag hours ago, last night—"

"Eöté, show me," Kehera commanded. She followed the girl's lead, not even noticing until she was halfway down the hall that they had picked up an escort in the form of one of the guards that had been put on her door. She ignored the man, and he did not try to stop her.

The heavy door that Eöté pointed to was not, thank the Gods, locked. Kehera pulled it open with enough force to send it slamming back against the wall with a reverberating crash. There were no lamps lit along the stairs and no light rising from below. Cold air rolled up to meet her, like the darkness itself given body and weight.

"Down there?" Kehera asked Eöté, appalled. And when the girl wrung her hands, nodding, ordered the soldier, "A torch, immediately!"

The man hesitated.

"I'll go down in the dark if I must," she said savagely, "and *you* can explain to His Grace if I fall and break my neck."

The soldier ducked back down the hall and grabbed a torch from the wall. He lit it with a candlelighter and gave it to Kehera, who took it, said, "Wait here," to Eöté, and went down the steps. The soldier followed at her heels. The cold increased with every step down the stair, until she could see her breath smoke in the light of the torch. The light it cast slid along the dark wood of a heavy wooden table and glinted off some of the . . . implements ranked in neat order, but left the far part of the room shrouded in dimness.

Kehera would have been happier if the shadows had hidden all the . . . things. She had not guessed a place like this existed in the duke's house, and looked around in cold horror. She was afraid to make a sound, which was ridiculous. She was afraid the door above might slam shut. She said, "Tag? Tageiny?" Her voice, shaky, not sounding like hers at all, seemed to fall into the dimness and dissipate like the smoke from her torch.

There was the sound of a small movement a little way in front of her, and a stifled gasp that made her jump. Then Tageiny's voice said, not quite evenly, out of the darkness, ". . . Lady." A shape moved in the dimness at the far end of the table. She did not know, at first, what she saw.

Then she did: Tageiny was there, half lying awkwardly across the table, unable to straighten, arms spread wide, his wrists held in manacles set into the edges of the table. Kehera hurried forward. "You're hurt—"

"No," the bodyguard said, his voice hoarse and strained. "C-cold."

He had been stripped to the waist. In this brutal cold. Anger leaped through her in a hot clean blaze. "Unlock those—those—" She gestured furiously to the cuffs that held him.

The wolf soldier answered stiffly, "This man is the duke's prisoner."

"If His Grace wants him back, I'm sure he'll manage to take him," Kehera snapped. "What do you think I'm going to do with him, hide him in my pocket? Right now, I'm telling you, *let him loose!*"

The soldier dropped his eyes and bent reluctantly over Tageiny, hands fumbling over the mechanism. It did not require a key, and Kehera saw the trick of it as the soldier undid the first cuff. She dealt with the other herself.

Tageiny, failing in his grip on the table, slid slowly back to kneel on the stone floor, shaking uncontrollably.

"Help him walk," Kehera ordered the soldier. "Carry him if you must." She led the way out of the grim prison. They went slowly, because Tageiny was a big enough man to make an awkward burden. Kehera was profoundly relieved to emerge again into the light—it was like coming into the air from a lake, when one had no breath left. She turned to swing the heavy door shut behind them.

The light in the hall showed what the torch had not: a film of blood that had dried on Tageiny's face and shoulders and back, cut across with narrow lines of brighter red.

"L-looks worse than it is—" Tageiny said, speaking with difficulty.

"It had better," said Kehera through her teeth. "Can you make it to my rooms?"

"Yes," Tageiny said grimly, and took a stumbling step that forced the Eänetén soldier to jump forward to catch him. Kehera walked anxiously beside them, ready to lend her strength if necessary, but Tageiny made it to her door still more or less upright, Eöté running ahead to open it, Luad coming white-faced to meet them.

Once safe in her rooms, Kehera helped Tageiny lie down on a couch. He looked horribly white. "I'm all right," he said, teeth chattering. "I'm all r-right."

"You're a fool, is what," Luad retorted. "Shut up and lie still and let me fix this."

Kehera asked shakily, "What kind of whip did this? Not a riding whip—"

"Wire," Luad said briefly. "It ain't so bad, for wire. I'll need clean water. And get one of them wolf soldiers to make himself useful and fetch some salve. They'll know what kind."

It was clear the young man knew what he was doing. Kehera was very happy to let him take over the practical treatment. She had no trouble making the soldiers bring salve and—considering how cold Tag was—mulled wine and hot soup. She patiently handed rags and held basins of water for Luad as he cleaned off the dried blood. Kehera leaned her head against the couch and blinked hard to stay awake as the young man finished his work and smoothed the salve over the worst of the whip-cuts. Tageiny endured the treatment in silence, face hidden against the couch.

"Done," Luad said shortly. "Sit up now, and let's see your face."

It took a moment for Tageiny to struggle upright. Kehera handed him a goblet of the hot spiced wine and steadied his hand while he drank. He wouldn't look at her, which Kehera thought probably meant that he was ashamed to have her see him in such a condition. There was nothing she could do about that but get him back on his feet.

Luad dipped a soft rag in the water and cleaned the blood off Tageiny's face, grasping his chin to hold him still when the older man would have flinched away. "Cut it out," he snapped. "Want this to get the fever? Want another scar to make you uglier yet? Hold still."

"Is it bad?" Kehera asked anxiously.

"Nah, not too bad," Luad told her. "Could be lots worse. The duke used a light hand, the fu—the bastard. This should heal clean." The gentleness with which he applied the salve belied his curt tone.

Kehera had to admit that Tageiny already looked much better. The hot wine and the warmth had brought color back into his face, easing the lines of pain and exhaustion that had marked him as much as the whip-cuts.

"You need to rest," Kehera said. She thought longingly of her own bed, and it took a moment to drag her mind back to the urgencies of the moment. "I need to talk to you first, if you can. Wolves stopped us. And Raëhemaiëth. What happened to you?"

"Yeah," Tageiny said. He rubbed his eyes, wincing, forcing himself to focus. "Yes. Well. Not wolves. Wolf soldiers. He'd sent 'em. They couldn't of known where to find us, but they did anyway. Pretty quick about it, too. Just about dusk, it was. I'm thinking he can make the Eänetén Power stand up and dance. Which I figured. But I didn't figure on him being so quick and sure. He stepped right over my decoy trail and got ahead of us." He sounded disgusted.

"I'm sorry."

Tageiny shook his head. "I didn't figure it. How should you?"

"I told you to tell him the truth, if it came to it. He did this anyway?"

"Well, I figured maybe I could buy you a few hours. I said Gereth took you into the city, that you needed a break from sitting and fretting. I asked if he didn't trust his own seneschal."

Kehera winced. "That wasn't very wise."

"Yeah, I found that out. That's when he hit me and took me . . . downstairs. He must have already guessed at that point Gereth was helping you."

"I'm sorry," Kehera said again. "Surely you told him the truth then?"

"Well, not exactly. I said you'd snuck out and Gereth had gone after you, to try to bring you back before His Grace found out."

"I told you to tell him the *truth*, Tag!"

The big man began to shrug, winced, and desisted. "Well, I thought it was plausible enough it might work. It hadn't been too bad, till then. I was pretty sure I could handle it. When—if he really got started, I was going to remind him he told me himself not to betray you. But then the room got kind of tight, and he said in this real strange voice, 'I know where they are gone. They are gone into the pass.'

"Well, I didn't say anything to that. Let me tell you, it fair made my skin crawl. Anyway, he left then, just dropped the whip on the floor and walked out. And that's it, until you came and got me out."

He hesitated for a moment and then added, "For which I thank you. But it was stupid. The duke, he's in a right taking, and that's not likely to help."

"You're mine, not his," Kehera said, more confidently than she felt. "He said so himself. He had no right to do this to you. I'm sorry I let this happen. I won't let him touch you again."

"He—"

"I can handle him." She hoped this was true. If she hadn't cost him his seneschal and friend, she would have felt more confident. But she said with all the authority she could muster, "Now go to sleep." She meant to follow that advice herself. She was so tired. Bath first; she still caught herself trembling a little from time to time. It must be cold and exhaustion because she refused to believe it could be fear. A very hot bath and something to eat, and then nothing would be able to keep her awake.

Then a sharp tap on the door sent her heart racing and drove all thoughts of bath and bed from her head. Eöté flinched and dropped the cloth she'd been holding, and everyone else stared, motionless, at the door. No one moved to answer it, until Luad stood up uncertainly.

"No," Kehera said hastily. "It had better be me." She stood up, waving Tageiny back sternly when he would have tried to get up.

But it was Caèr Reiöft. Kehera let out her breath in relief and then hoped her nervousness wasn't visible to anyone else.

Reiöft bowed his head politely, murmuring some quiet politeness as he set one hand on the door, gently pushed it wide, and stepped into the room. His sharp glance fell on Tageiny, braced on one elbow, the marks of the whip vivid across his skin. He took in Luad's stiff hostility and Eöté's nervousness, and finally settled on Kehera. His quiet self-possession was intact, but even Kehera, who barely knew him, could see that his normal good humor was completely absent. He looked . . . He looked, she thought, like the rest of them felt: stiff and tired and worried. He said to her, "Might I speak to you for a moment, my lady? Privately?"

"*Absolutely* not," growled Tageiny, shoving himself to his feet, almost completely concealing what the movement cost him. Luad put one hand on Tageiny's arm and the other on the hilt of one of his knives, and for the first time it occurred to Kehera that the young man was still armed, that no one had taken his weapons. That had to mean something. Just what, she wasn't sure.

Reiöft cast his gaze upward. "Oh, come now."

"You, least of all. Do you want me to spell it out?" said Tageiny.

Kehera was almost sure *she* didn't. She said hastily, gesturing toward the other end of the room, "Perhaps just over here."

"Hold up, there," Tageiny snapped, and ordered Luad, "Make sure he's got nothing." Tageiny himself leaned against the back of a heavy chair, which Kehera took to mean he was having trouble just staying on his feet.

Luad made quick work of checking Reiöft for weapons—the duke's servant cooperated with no further protest—and then she guided Reiöft to the minimal privacy of the other end of the sitting room. It was a big room, at least.

The moment Kehera settled in a chair and looked at him inquiringly, Reiöft said, his tone low but intense, "I've seen him in a temper, and I've seen him upset, and I've seen him worried, and before his father died, I saw one or two things that would freeze your blood. And he handled all of that. But I've never seen him like he was today. Tell me what happened. Tell me everything."

Kehera studied the man for a long moment. Then she told him everything.

"He let him go through the pass," Reiöft said when she got to that part. "Good. That's good. And you told him to go to your father, and he didn't say anything about that. Good. And he gave him a pebble from the road. A memory of Eäneté. A thin tie to Eänetaìsarè."

Kehera had no trouble following this despite the abundance of pronouns. She nodded. "I think he meant it to protect Gereth. But I—I'm not sure what else he might have meant it to do. He gave it to Gereth after I told him to go to my father."

"He would hardly have given him anything that would make him the focus of a king's anger. No. Protection on the road. I think you're right. Whatever else, I'm sure you're right at least that far. Good," said Reiöft. He ran a hand through his hair and drew a long breath. "That's better than I feared it might be." Some of the stiffness had eased out of his face, but he gave her a long, serious look. "He's under a great deal of strain. I'm sure he's worried about whatever's going on in Irekay. And he hasn't wanted to hurt you. And now there's . . . this." He hesitated. "I know it's hard for you. I know none of this is your choice. But I came . . . I came to tell you that it's hard for him, too, and to ask you to be . . ."

"Brave?" suggested Kehera, when he paused. "Cooperative?"

"Kind," corrected Reiöft. When she stared at him in astonishment, he went on in a low, urgent tone. "He's been hurt. I don't wish to dismiss what you have suffered, or will suffer. But try not to . . . I know you have reason to be angry. But try to be kind to him. Please."

Kehera made herself stop staring. She said, hearing the constraint in her own tone, "Aren't you—I mean, you're—" She tried to think how to frame a question there was no polite way to ask. "You aren't . . . jealous?"

Caèr Reiöft gave her a long, serious look. "I'm trying not to be. No offense, Your Highness, but, all else aside, I'm glad it's you and not someone else."

"Because I'm a . . . woman?" Kehera hazarded.

To her surprise, Reiöft smiled with something of his customary warmth. "You think he doesn't like women? That's not quite right. He thinks women are fragile. Because of his mother, I've always thought, and then later he . . . Never mind. What I mean is, he's afraid he'll hurt a woman. Even if he doesn't wish to, or intend to. So you see, you needn't . . . He's not always gentle with me. But he will be careful with you."

Kehera thought about this. "That's why you don't mind," she said at last. "Because you'll still be the one he doesn't need to be careful with."

This got her a raised eyebrow and a half smile. "That . . . I won't say that doesn't matter to me. But that would be true for any woman. No, it's because you're foreign. There will always be a part of him you can't touch." He met her eyes. He was smiling, but he was serious, too. "Perhaps you should be jealous of me."

"I don't want this, remember?" But Kehera found that she *was* a little jealous of Caèr Reiöft after all. Not for the reason he was suggesting. Perhaps because he cared enough about the Wolf Duke to come to her and ask her to be kind. She wished she'd had, once in her life, a chance to care about someone that selflessly. She said, "He makes me so angry. He's so sure he should make all these decisions for us, both of us, for both our Powers, both our countries. Raëhemaiëth may be determined to ally with your Eänetén Immanent, but I'm angry." She didn't admit to fear, but only went on slowly, "But I know you're right. I know he's been hurt, and I'm sorry for it. I'll remember that, too, despite all the rest."

Reiöft bowed his head briefly in gratitude. Then he met her eyes again. "While we have this little moment. No one else will tell you this, so I will. His tie will strengthen when he's . . . with you. I tell you so that you'll expect it. Don't be afraid. He'll ride it. Let it sweep you up. You'll be . . ." He paused, then shrugged, smiling slightly. "Let's just say your wedding night will probably be memorable."

He didn't pause for her answer, which was just as well because Kehera had no idea how to respond to this. He gave her a smooth bow instead and strode away toward the outer door, leaving her staring after him.

After he was gone, Kehera looked wordlessly around the room—at frightened Eöté and battered Tageiny and worried Luad. And sighed, and shook her head, and said firmly, "Tomorrow's dawn isn't so very far away. All of you: Go to bed." She caught Tageiny's raised eyebrow and added, "I promise you, that's just what I mean to do, and nothing, not even His Grace shouting and throwing things, will keep me awake."

Nor, in the unlikely event that the Wolf Duke actually shouted or threw things, did it trouble her rest. Not even the thought of having to face him at dawn could keep her awake. Kehera was asleep almost before her head touched the pillow. She slept dreamlessly through the afternoon and evening and most of the night, though a few hours before dawn her rest was disturbed by a dream of wolves. They stayed just out of sight among the forest shadows, only their eyes gleaming with reflected moonlight, and she knew they were laughing their knowing, mocking wolf laughter at her.

She woke in the gray dawn, hearing in her ears the echo of wolves singing to the night.

16

Tirovay Elin Raëhema dreamed of white whirling snow and black knife-edged winds, of many-headed dragons whose wings encompassed the sky and whose breath froze air and light and life. He dreamed of the Wall, the great Wall of Storms, where the obsidian winds endlessly slashed through their continual circular path, dividing the world in two: the northern lands where the Fortunate Gods ruled and men yet lived and the southern where the Unfortunate Gods had destroyed everything living except, maybe, dragons. If dragons could be said to live. Scholars argued one way and then the other, but no one knew. As no one knew whether the dragons deliberately brought down the storms, or whether they only rode upon them, indifferent to the devastation they caused to the lands below.

Tiro dreamed of the Iron Hinge days, of midwinter storms spinning away from the Wall of Storms, one mad gyre of deadly winds and then another and another, each bearing one or two or three dragons into the lands of men. He saw how the dragons blurred into one another, not like mortal creatures but like storms themselves, dividing and recombining, the storm winds filling them up until the tangle of dragons became just one dragon and that one rode the winds on translucent obsidian wings as broad as the sky.

The winter dragons rode the knife-edged winds, and far below mortal creatures fled for shelter. . . . Tiro saw it, memory or anticipation. No scholar's description could capture the terror or wonder of the dark turn of the year. Of course none of the folk who lived near the mountains or anywhere near the Wall of Winds set either window or door into the windward side of their homes; of course they all turned their stables and byres to block the midwinter storms, without concern for ordinary summer storms that came from other directions. Wild creatures too must make their dens so that they could hide from the black winds and the shadows of the winter dragons. Deer must shelter in the lee of cliffs and thickets, birds creep under the cover of thick firs, the whole world take shelter until the Iron Hinge should turn and the world rise back toward gentler days.

He was dimly aware of the memory of summer. Slow sunlit days and quiet moonlit nights . . . Raëhemaiëth tried to show him summer, tried to carry him out of the winter, but the shadow of a double-headed dragon cut between them, obsidian winds glittering, bitter and knife-edged, dividing Tiro from Raëhemaiëth, driving them apart.

Raëhemaiëth spoke to him, not as a person spoke, but in the way of an Immanent, wordless and certain. He heard it, and then lost its voice beneath the ceaseless voices of the winds, which were also the voices of the dragons, layering one upon another like the endless reverberations of shattering ice.

A storm like this had come upon Leiör. Tiro remembered that, or something like that. It was confusing, because surely it was not yet midwinter. Surely the black storms had not yet come. And Leiör was neither far enough south nor near enough the mountains to experience the full peril of the midwinter winds. He had been in Leiör, though. . . . He *had* been in Leiör. He was certain of that. He remembered Taraä inan Seine Leiörian, with her willow tree and her ax. Only he had sent the ax away . . . across the river, he had sent it to Emmer, though he couldn't quite remember why. She must have agreed. Surely he wouldn't have sent Taraä's ax to Emmer without asking her first. Though that was a little confusing, too, because he knew the ax was actually his . . . not exactly his, but it had belonged to his great-great-great-grandfather. He remembered that story. . . . He remembered all the stories, but now he seemed to have forgotten. Raëhemaiëth was trying to tell all the stories to him again, but he couldn't hear them properly because the dragons were crying too loudly. . . . He'd sent the ax away and something terrible had happened. . . . The great willow tree had gone down in a storm, or maybe he had dreamed that. Poor Taraä, that would have been terrible for her, losing her ax and her tree and her city. . . . She had lost her city, Leiör had been lost, the willow had split from the crown right down to the roots, and Leiöriansé had been eaten by the winter dragons, and all of it was Tiro's fault. He didn't remember what had happened, but he knew it had been his fault, for taking the ax and for failing Raëhemaiëth.

Someone was calling him. Someone was calling his name. But Tiro couldn't quite hear through the shattering of the winds. It might have been his father's voice. But he thought it was someone else, a man he knew, someone he'd been arguing with recently. Someone as confident and assured as his father . . . He couldn't quite capture the name, but Raëhemaiëth gave it to him, beyond sound and sense: *Enmon Corvallis.*

That was it. Enmon Corvallis. General Corvallis. The Emmeran general who'd served the Mad King. The Mad King had taken Kehera away and she hadn't come back, and now Tiro had to be heir, only he'd failed Raëhemaiëth, failed his father and Raëh and Harivir. He'd lost Leiör; he'd let Hallieth Theraön Suriytaiän ruin Leiör, eat its Immanent, leave the city and the province hollow and empty. . . . But that wasn't right. It hadn't been Hallieth Suriytaiän. The Suriytè Power was gone, too, and Hallieth Theraön was no longer the Emmeran king. Hallieth Theraön was dead, or . . . not dead, but lost in the whirling black midwinter, as Tiro was lost.

Either way, Emmer had no true king, not anymore. That was what Enmon Corvallis wanted: to be King of Emmer, and Tiro had thought that would be fine, but he would make Corvallis give him something in return. Leiör. Or, no, Leiör was gone. And anyway, it hadn't ever been Corvallis's to give away. Sariy. That was it. Tiro had demanded Sariy, on the other side of the Imhar, there at the confluence where the river was so wide. He'd carried Raëhemaiëth across the river and rooted it into Sariy, in order to set a border and a bulwark between the storm coming down from the north and Leiör. He had almost saved Leiör. But not quite. Leiöriansé had been too much at odds with . . . Sariänesciör. Yes. Sariänesciör. That was the name of Sariy's Immanent.

Tiro had anchored Raëhemaiëth into Sariy, he'd invited a bond between Sariänesciör and Raëhemaiëth, and at first the lesser Immanent of Sariy hadn't wanted the bond, but then the obsidian winds had come down upon them all. Sariänesciör had felt the dragon's shadow fall across its lands, and so at the last moment it had taken the bond after all and sheltered from the midwinter storm behind Raëhemaiëth's deep-rooted strength. And the winter dragon had passed over Sariy and lain its shadow across Leiör, and Tiro hadn't been there; he'd been across the river. So Leiör had fallen silent, but Sariy's Immanent was still present in its land.

It wasn't fair. It was utterly unfair. He'd done everything wrong. His father had trusted him to protect Leiör, Taraä had trusted him, but he'd failed them both, and now Leiör was empty. Hollow. And it was all Tiro's fault.

Somewhere, his father was calling him. Or Enmon Corvallis. Or someone. He heard Kehera's voice, and then thought no, it wasn't his sister, it was Taraä. Then he thought, no, it was Raëhemaiëth. It was the still, soundless voice of the Immanent Power.

But the bitter winds cut between them, between him and every voice and every memory of other sound, until he could hear only the many-headed winter dragon crying with all the voices of the winds.

17

Kehera rode, on a white horse and cloaked in white, at the left hand of the Eäneté duke. They rode at the head of his column of troops, through the icy fastness of Roh Pass, through the gray dusk of the fourteenth day of the Iron Hinge Month, as the year slid inexorably toward the dark turn of winter. Above them flew their standards: the yellow-eyed Wolf of Eäneté, and beside it, the Falcon of Raëh. Only it wasn't the powerful red and black Falcon like the one Kehera's father carried; this was a white Falcon, a delicate kestrel, with sapphire eyes and all its feathers outlined in blue. All her people wore the White Falcon badge now, setting them apart from the Eänetén wolves.

Kehera was a bright mirror image of the duke, and although she knew perfectly well that her bright appearance had been carefully designed, she also had to admit that it was effective. Anyone seeing her White Falcon flying above the Wolf could not help but look to her for hope of mercy. It was exactly the effect the duke intended. Knowing this made Kehera feel . . . she wasn't even sure. Angry at the Wolf Duke's presumption. Hopeful because he thought of such details and never let anything slip.

And she was, in a sense, letting herself be used that way. It was too late now for her to slip the duke's hold and ride to Harivir before him, go to Tiro and . . . make things right, somehow; make Methmeir Irekaì's horrible Immanent Power let him alone. She couldn't do that. But she thought of Gereth Murrel and the pebble the Eänetén duke had infused with a little tie to Eänetaìsarè, and hoped that the duke's seneschal would somehow do what she could not. Raëhemaiëth had helped Eänetaìsarè; surely the Eänetén Power was willing to return the favor. If it could.

If Gereth carried a tie to Eänetaìsarè into Raëh and so let Eänetaìsarè anchor itself even so far away from Eäneté—if Raëhemaiëth let the Eänetén Power anchor itself into Raëh through that thin tie—if the two Immanent Powers together could indeed help Tiro break free of the Irekaïn Power, then maybe she could take that as proof that this alliance was after all the best decision any of them could make.

And if they had to make this alliance work, then she had to admit, it probably was better to perform the wedding ceremony in Harivir, among her own people as well as the Eänetén duke's, so that everyone could see her tie the cords herself and no one could doubt the validity of the marriage.

Presuming she did tie the cords herself. But if she refused publicly, Riheir Coärin would probably start a war right there, and that wouldn't do at all.

Soon she would have to decide what to do. They had pressed the pace, up and up into the teeth of the mountains, until Kehera's thighs and back ached with the strain of leaning forward in the saddle. They had crested the pass just before dusk. There, where Roh Pass wound between the sharp peaks, she had glimpsed for one terrifying moment a winter dragon. Wonder and horror held her transfixed. Just as stories held, the winter dragon was triple-headed, its long sinuous necks and long snakelike body rippling in the violent winds that cut around the sharp-edged stone of the farthest heights. Those winds were streaked with translucent black, but the dragon that rode upon those obsidian winds, though monstrous, did not come down. She knew it must be waiting for the Iron Hinge days. It did not cry, with the voices of the winds or of doomed souls or any voice she heard, and after that one glimpse it disappeared behind the black winds and the naked stone. But even after it had gone and she was once again able to focus on the ordinary world, Kehera was glad to leave the high crest of the pass behind and begin the slow ride down.

Now they rode down and down, straight into the lowering sun. Shadows filled the pass behind them, but daylight lingered above and ahead, the granite glowing rose and carmine in the late sun. Soon the sun would slide down below the edge of the world and they would ride through the dusk a second time and into night. But the Wolf Duke had not yet signaled the halt.

It was snowing. It had been snowing all during this ride: tiny grains of ice or fat lazy flakes, but always snow. But Eänetaìsarè swept the pass clear of any accumulation. It was not at all like Gheroïn Nomoris in Anha Pass: This was no local, temporary blaze of power. The snow here simply blew aside before it could touch the road, sweeping off to fall on the mountains beyond. Kehera found it endlessly fascinating to watch snowflakes almost land on the duke, only to slide aside at the last moment and spin away. They landed on her easily enough, frosting the fur of her gloves and hood and the mane of her horse with a glittering white-on-white veil.

The column of soldiers that rode behind her was also snow-dusted. The column stretched, she knew, for many miles back toward the eastern mouth of the pass: thousands of men in the gray and silver of Eäneté with the Wolf leaping at every shoulder.

It had shocked her that any provincial duke, no matter how powerful, should have been able to raise so great a force, not to mention the ancillary staff necessary to support it in the field. It had shocked her more that he was willing to strip his own lands to do so. He had only said that if he needed more than a handful of soldiers to guard Eäneté proper, he had already lost. Kehera had not asked him why he had so many soldiers if he did not need them. She knew—it was obvious now—that he must have already meant to break with Irekay. He must have been working toward this for years.

He knew his own power, that was certain. So did she, much better now. Because he could handle more than the delicacy of falling snow. When they had come only a short way into the pass, an avalanche—set off, perhaps, by no more than the sound of ten thousand men breathing—had rumbled with slow, breathtaking power down the slopes before them. Kehera had checked her mare, gasping, and behind her the voices of officers had lifted to command stillness and order of the men. The duke had said nothing, but gazed at the tumbling snow with abstracted calm. Kehera had judged the avalanche would pass safely in front of them, but how they were to get past the barrier it would form was a question.

No sooner had she wondered about this than the question was answered for her. The descending wall of snow had passed over the road in front of them entirely and roared its implacable way *up* the slopes on the other side of the pass and down the other side of those peaks, out of sight. She had listened to its diminishing thunder as they rode past the spot it should have filled, knowing that the sight of the hurtling snow and the sound of its thunder would be a vivid memory for a very long time.

Even while turning the avalanche, the duke had looked exactly as he did now: faintly distracted but unconcerned. His lean, spare face was remote as the sky, and whatever occupied his thoughts, he clearly did not intend to share them with her. Or with anyone, probably, since Gereth Murrel was riding somewhere before them. He was probably already out of the pass, maybe already riding north toward Raëh. She was sorry for that—for the duke's solitude. Especially since it had gained her nothing.

Working out what she felt about Innisth terè Maèr Eänetaì was hardest of all. Certainly she would never have claimed to *like* him. She resented his arrogance and high-handedness and willingness to dispose of everyone else's life just as he pleased, and yet at the same time she couldn't help but admire him. She couldn't help but believe he might offer Harivir its best chance of throwing back the aggression of Methmeir Irekaì.

It was all very exasperating and hard to sort out. It was easier to just watch the snowflakes fall around the duke without ever quite touching his horse or his cloak or his still, remote face. He was not ill-favored. Far from it. But she wondered if he had any passion in him at all. Then she thought of his voice cracking as he faced his seneschal in the pass and knew his coldness was like ice masking the violence of the storm.

He frightened her. But she knew Caèr Reiöft was right, too, and that he could be hurt. And though she couldn't quite sort out what she felt for him, she was beginning to be certain she didn't want to hurt him.

Soon, even though they chased the sun down this side of the pass, it would be too dark to see the falling snow. Very soon after that, it would be too dark to see even the man who rode beside her. Especially with his black cloak and black gloves and black mare. He would be able to see her much longer, which did not seem quite fair. Kehera turned to Tageiny, riding on her other side, and started to say something—she hardly knew what—and then her vision blurred with more than the gathering dusk.

Warmth rose around her, dizzying, so that she blinked hard against the sudden vertigo. She glimpsed whirling snow and sky, and . . . the mountains reached up and caught her. She blinked dazedly up from where she lay, confused. Behind and above and around and within her, the tie hummed, deep and warm, like a voice made of harp notes and summer. Raëhemaiëth was very pleased. There was trouble, yes. A ragged darkness to the north and the east that grasped and froze and broke and rose again, a cold, clutching darkness that sometimes ebbed, but never far enough. But despite that, Raëhemaiëth was very pleased. She was back in precincts it knew, lands to which it was allied, and it knew her and was pleased.

Kehera smiled involuntarily. She knew she had come home.

Except she wasn't home at all. For a long moment, she had no idea at all where she was. *Her* home stretched out across farmlands and into the gentle slopes of foothills. The stone beneath her should have been sandstone rather than this polished granite. . . . The earth should have been deeper. The fire here was close to the surface. . . . She did not know where she was. . . . Cold stone hiding fire, and long shadows, and the nearby bulk of horses. . . . She was lying on the ground. Yes. But braced against a warm, solid bulk. Someone's knee. Someone was touching her. A firm hand on her cheek, reminding her that she was herself, human and mortal. Helping her sort herself out from the Immanent Power of Raëh.

The Wolf Duke. He held her. He knelt on the cold stone of the road. Her head was on his knee. It was his hand on her face. She blinked, and shifted, and he drew back a little.

Tageiny knelt on her other side. He was touching her, too, one hand gripping her wrist, but she had not been aware of his hand until now. He wasn't looking at her. He was staring at the duke, fury in his eyes. The duke was pretending not to notice, but his mouth was tight.

Frightened for Tageiny, Kehera sat up quickly and caught his hand in both of hers. "It's all right," she said breathlessly, "I'm all right, Tag."

The duke said quietly, letting his hand fall away from her shoulder now that she was sitting up on her own, "It was the Raëh Power, of course. You are in Harivir again, and the tie has risen in you. Is it close? Is it strong?"

"Yes," she said, thinking, *Of course the Eänetén duke understands.* "It's not like it was. It's not like the heir's tie. And I can't—I can't find Tiro in it." She hesitated, then shook her head. "No. But I think Raëhemaiëth still holds him. I think so. He's not quite lost. I don't think he is." She closed her eyes, shuddering. If that was so, if Tiro was not lost, if he could yet be saved without her efforts—by Gereth, maybe—then perhaps she had been right to trust Raëhemaiëth and turn back and stay in Eäneté. She could hope she had been right. She said, "I should have expected the tie to come up fast and—and violently. I'm sorry." Then she blinked and said, "You *did* expect it. That's why you were ready to catch me." And then, as she realized this must be true, she added in surprise, "*That's* why you didn't want to stop earlier. You were waiting for this."

"Yes," said the duke. He glanced up the slope of the pass the way they had come, back toward Eäneté. Then he looked at her, and his eyes narrowed in satisfaction. "This is earlier than I'd hoped. Good."

"You might have"—*warned me*, but Kehera cut that off. She shouldn't have needed a reminder. But she had grown so used to lacking the close tie. . . . She looked into the humming awareness that had opened behind her mind and knew that whatever else might have happened, however many miles still lay between herself and Raëh, Raëhemaiëth was right *here*. Raëhemaiëth was with her. The knowledge was immeasurably comforting. She drew a deep breath— it felt like the first deep breath she'd taken in months—and accepted Tageiny's help to get to her feet.

"Very good," said the duke, watching her. "We will camp here."

Kehera nodded, unsurprised by his consideration. And then surprised, a little, to realize she had expected it. It was not kindness, exactly. But he was always so deliberately considerate. And she had known he would be.

She thought she might need the rest of the night to think about that. And to recover her balance amid the warm awareness that was her tie to Raëhemaiëth. But she was no longer tired at all. She wished for dawn, for light enough to ride, for the moment when they would come around the last curve of the pass and find Harivir opening out before them.

But the next day, riding into the lowering sun that gilded the stone before the hooves of their horses, she found that actually arriving at the Harivin end of the pass felt . . . very strange.

This homecoming had been Kehera's hope for months. Now she

was home, by any reasonable measure. A glimmering net of *presence* stretched out before and around her, centered far to the north—Raëhemaiëth, of course, allied to the Immanent Power of Coär. Her restored sense of Raëhemaiëth was like sight after she had been all but blind; it was like coming into free air when she had been hardly able to breathe. It should have made her feel more at home. But she did not feel like she was coming home at all.

This might have been because she was surrounded by people whom she had known only in Eäneté. Tag, Luad, Eöté . . . those were the people for whom she had spent thought and worry in these past days. Though in a way the Wolf Duke himself more than any of them. She was almost sure this wasn't anything he had done to her on purpose. It was only that he seemed so much more real, so much more present, than other people—in his profound confidence, in his pride, in his certainty that what he did *mattered*.

Or it might have been because the moment she entered Coär proper, the first thing she would be called upon to do was look Riheir Coärin in the eye and tell him . . . She still wasn't sure what she was going to tell him. That he must surrender Coär, all his people and lands, to a Pohorin lord, and that somehow this was all right? That she was going to marry the Wolf Duke of Eäneté and *that* was all right? This spring, he'd sent her a courting poem to let her know he meant to speak to her father. What was Riheir going to think of her now?

Beside her, the Eänetén duke murmured, "There are men waiting there at the mouth of the pass. You see, just there. Remember that you are their princess and that you bring them an alliance they must have. Trust that you have done well and that you will do well."

"Yes," she said. Just "yes." But his face, turning for a brief moment to hers, held that subtle lightening of expression that was closer to warmth than he had come since sending Gereth away.

Riheir Coärin was himself in the forefront of his people. The proud White Stag banner of Coär, gripped in the hand of a boy at his side, rippled in the wind that blew through the pass, its silver antlers gleaming dully in the pale winter light. It had always been one of Kehera's favorite Harivin standards, and she did not look forward to seeing it humbled. She could only imagine what Riheir must be feeling.

It was immediately clear that Coär did not intend to resist the Eänetén duke; very few of the people with him were soldiers, and those were old men. Kehera guessed he must have sent his soldiers to her father to help defend the north, relying on the Wolf Duke to defend Coär. That was . . . that was quite a statement. It drove home the desperate circumstances Harivir must be facing. So she knew the Wolf Duke had been right. At least so far.

As they drew nearer, it became possible to pick out Riheir's expression, which was set and grim: the expression of a man determined to maintain his pride in the face of surrender. It made Kehera feel slightly ill.

The duke lifted his hand. Behind them, Kehera felt and heard the army come to a crashing halt. It wouldn't have been proper to look over her shoulder at them, so she didn't. She didn't have to look. She knew from previous glances just how grim and impressive the long ranks of gray-clad Eäneté soldiers looked with the Wolf of Eäneté running over their heads.

For a moment no one moved. The duke's lean face was unreadable. Before her, Riheir Coärin's face was no less blank, though his gaze touched hers briefly before going to the Eäneté duke. Riheir looked older than when she had last seen him, just this spring. He was, she knew, only just thirty. He looked older. Thinner. Worn, as though the past few weeks had been years. She had no idea what her own face showed.

Just as she began to believe that no one else was going to break the intolerable silence and she would have to do it herself, Riheir moved. He reached out, not looking away from Eäneté, and took the Coär standard from the hand of the boy who had been carrying it. Holding it high, he swung one leg over his horse's back and slid to the ground.

One of his men leaned over and took the gray's rein as Riheir came forward on foot to meet the Wolf Duke.

It seemed like a long time that the Duke of Coär stood in the snow in front of the Duke of Eäneté, holding the White Stag banner in both his hands and looking steadily into the face of the man with whom he had shared a border all his adult life but never met. The Wolf Duke, not moving, returned the gaze with a look that gave away nothing.

Riheir said to him, "Will you protect my people? Will you set your strength between Coär and every peril, and guard my people from all dark Powers that would enslave them, and stand for them before Fortunate and Unfortunate Gods?"

The Wolf Duke lifted one eyebrow. "All this I will do, for *my* people."

Riheir looked past him, to Kehera. "Kehy," he said quietly. "Can he be trusted?"

Kehera's throat ached. She said, "To protect everything and everyone he holds in his hand? Yes." Just "yes," very simply.

Riheir took a long breath and let it out. It seemed he stared up at the Wolf Duke for a long time, but probably it was no more than the time it might take for an arrow-shot stag to fall, or for a heart to break.

Then Riheir Coärin knelt in the snow and with his own hands laid down the White Stag of Coär before the fierce yellow eyes of the Eänetén Wolf. For a long, stretched instant, no one moved. Kehera's eyes filled with tears that she refused to let fall.

The Wolf Duke lifted his hand. One of his men rode forward, swung down from his horse, gathered up the fallen standard, and carried it to Eäneté's own standard-bearer. This man shook it clean of snow, swept it upright, and let the wind open it again to the sight of the world. He thumped the haft of the banner home in his stirrup, specially made to support such things, and held both standards in one hand, the Coär White Stag behind the Eäneté Wolf and Kehera's own Falcon.

Regarding the bowed head of Riheir Coärin with dispassionate calm, the Wolf Duke asked in a soft, carrying voice, "What is it, Riheir Coärin, that you offer me?"

Riheir lifted his head to meet the Eänetén duke's yellow wolf's eyes. "My lands. My people, if you will protect them." Riheir paused and then added, with a hard, bitter edge to his voice that Kehera had not even heard from him the year his wife had died, "My obedience to your will, so long as you keep faith."

"All this, I accept," said the duke. "And one thing more." He tossed his reins to a waiting soldier and dismounted, striding forward. Riheir got quickly to his feet, and the two men faced each other for a moment in silence.

Much of an age, both had come to power young. Occupying opposite ends of Roh Pass, they must have come to be familiar with each other at a distance. Now each met the other's eyes. The Wolf Duke's manner was cool and deliberate. He was somewhat the taller, and to Kehera's eyes, he seemed both more dangerous and more powerful. Coär was a little stockier in build and normally, at least, had a comfortable warmth to him. That warmth was not in evidence now.

The duke beckoned to one of his soldiers without looking, and the man dismounted and moved to stand behind Riheir, who did not deign to glance back at him.

Deliberately, the duke extended his hand to Riheir, who stared at him but did not move. "If you please," said the duke, with excruciating politeness.

There was a pause. Riheir said, "Coär has always been allied to Harivir and to Raëh. You can't know the outcome for certain," and Kehera blinked and drew a breath, understanding suddenly what this was.

"I can. I do. Raëhemaiëth will yield its bond. And where I stand, *is* Eäneté."

Riheir hesitated a moment longer. Then he slowly answered the other man's gesture. They gripped one another's wrists for all the world, Kehera thought, like a greeting between old friends.

The duke said in his most distant tone, "Eänetaìsarè."

Raëhemaiëth surged upward. The sense of its waiting presence was overwhelming. Kehera shuddered, for a moment blinded by its sharp, glittering awareness. But it ebbed almost at once, and she blinked, and blinked again, leaning on her horse's neck, shaking her head, trying urgently to see the ordinary world of men through its lingering haze.

Riheir Coärin had collapsed. She saw that first. He sagged in the soldier's grip. The effect on the duke had not been not as extreme. He had lifted one hand to cover his eyes. Lines of tension and pain had sprung into existence around his mouth and between his eyebrows as though he had suddenly been stricken with a severe headache, but he did not fall.

Before Kehera could think what to do, Riheir moved to get his feet back under himself. The soldier braced him with professional, impersonal care until he seemed steady, and then let him go and stepped back. All of Riheir's attention was on the duke. He took a step forward and opened his mouth, but closed it again without speaking.

The duke rubbed his forehead with the tips of his fingers, looking slightly fatigued. Meeting Riheir's eyes, he lifted one shoulder in a tiny shrug. "Eänetaìsarè is a jealous Power. But your . . . Coäiriliöa . . . was not harmed by what I did. You know that is true. That is why Raëhemaiëth did not fight us. Me. Eänetaìsarè."

"Yes . . ." Riheir didn't sound quite sure. He gave Kehera a quick look, mouth tight. "You've still got a tie to Raëhemaiëth, have you?"

Kehera said quietly, "Immanent Powers are . . . You know it's hard to understand what they do sometimes. But Raëhemaiëth . . . it's seen the Irekaïn Power. It's frightened of it, I believe. I know it allied willingly with Eänetaìsarè the moment it got the chance."

"Did it? Willingly? Do you think your father will be happy about what you've done, bringing the Wolf into Harivir?"

The Wolf Duke said sharply, "Her Highness has done nothing of which she need be ashamed. She has acted with courage and resolution throughout. Speak to her with respect, Coärin."

Both Kehera and Riheir Coärin stared at him. Kehera did not know which of them was more surprised. She rubbed her hand across her mouth and looked away.

"Get your horse and ride with me," the duke ordered. "Is the city open?"

Riheir beckoned for his horse to be brought up. "Yes," he said. "But—" He glanced away from the duke, along the endless column of gray-clad wolf soldiers.

The duke raised an eyebrow.

"We are expecting attack," Riheir said grimly. "Coäirilïoa is expecting attack. It feels a cold Power gathering strength. It expects attack. At any time. My king tells me he perceives the same from Raëhemaiëth."

"Torrolay Elin Raëhema is no longer your king," the duke reminded him. "But tell me of this attack you anticipate."

Riheir took a breath. "We believe the threat comes from the north and the east. I thought at first my Immanent was warning me of you. But it was never your . . . Eänetaìsarè. That's clear now, beyond any possible doubt. The threat Coäirilïoa showed me was always a different Power. Darker and colder and greater than yours."

"I see." The duke considered him. "I do see. Thus you were brought so easily to yield."

"Yes," Riheir said, rather through his teeth.

"'My lord,'" the Eänetén duke prompted him, with terrible precision.

For a second Kehera thought Riheir Coärin would defy him, and held her breath. Then Riheir bent his head stiffly. "My lord."

"Meilin Gap," Kehera said quickly, before the tension could wind any tighter. She knew it must be true. She thought she could feel the dark pressure herself now that she knew to look for it. Raëhemaiëth showed it to her. North and east, not so very far. She tried to visualize that country. Meilin Gap wound its narrow way through the mountains just north of Coär, between the smaller province of Viär and some part of Pohorir north of Eäneté. Kimsè, probably.

Meilin Gap should have been closed; winter always closed such little passes well before the Iron Hinge days. But she thought of how the Eänetén duke had sent the avalanche aside in Roh Pass and knew that this year, cold and snow and winter storms offered no protection.

"Your soldiers, Coärin?" the Eänetén duke inquired. "I presumed you had chosen to hold them at Coär, or that you had sent them to Raëh."

"I sent most to Raëh. But some to Viär, to guard Meilin Gap." Riheir met the Eänetén duke's yellow eyes without flinching.

"Indeed. Well. We will not delay at Coär, I think. We will proceed north immediately."

Riheir let out a breath, nodded, and swung up onto his waiting horse. Back rigid, he moved his gelding to a place at the Wolf Duke's shoulder, on the other side from Kehera. She thought he was deliberately avoiding her eyes, but she could not think of anything she could do about it.

The duke kept his mare to a steady walk as they exited the pass and came out onto the shoulder of the mountain above the city of Coär. Whatever waited for them at Meilin Gap, he plainly meant to meet it in good order and with men able to fight, not worn out from a forced march. "How many soldiers of yours shall we find at Meilin Gap?" he asked. His voice, though cool, was neither hostile nor gloating. He spoke as he would to an ally, or to a servant.

Riheir Coärin's tone when he answered was just barely civil. "Not enough to hold if Methmeir Irekaì opens the way for a real army. Not nearly as many as you've brought with you, I think." He glanced illustratively over his shoulder at the long, long column of gray-clad wolf soldiers. "You're right to surmise I sent the better part of Coär's men north to support my king."

"Torrolay Raëhema is no longer your king," the Wolf Duke reminded him.

"My lord," Riheir said grimly, acknowledging this. "I left nothing in Coär. I swore to my people that you wouldn't let any enemy through Roh Pass, that you wouldn't come as an enemy yourself, that you'd protect our lands and families as though they were your own." He said this last in a hard, calm voice, but his eyes went involuntarily to the Wolf Duke's face, gauging his response. Kehera watched Riheir's uneasy resentment with the sympathy of one who had been there herself.

"They are my own," said the Wolf Duke without emphasis. Merely a flat statement. "Everything shall be done as I have said it would be done. You have prepared the people to accept my rule?"

"My lord, nothing could have done that. I've done what I could. It helps—" He stopped.

"That I am accompanied by Kehera Elin Raëhema. Yes," said the duke. "That was the intention. I had intended to wed her in Coär."

If he had wanted to get a rise out of Riheir Coärin, he could not have done better. Riheir turned sharply in the saddle and bit out, "Everyone in Harivir will hate you for taking her, *my lord*!"

His vehemence did not surprise Kehera. She doubted Riheir had ever been in love with her, courting poem or no courting poem; but he liked her and he'd decided he wanted her and he had certainly not wanted a foreign duke to marry her. He was glaring at the Wolf Duke with such fury that she was afraid for him. But the duke only answered, his tone suspiciously mild, "I know. They will fear me for my country of origin and resent me for my strength against their king, but they will hate me for taking their princess by force. Your Highness?"

No one had ever said Kehera couldn't recognize a cue when she was handed one on a gilded platter. Collecting herself, she said to Riheir, "You know, the idea of cementing a political alliance by marriage is hardly new. Neither are land concessions to an ally, when the circumstances are desperate enough. Harivir needs Eäneté, which you know, or you would hardly have laid down your banner. Which was very brave," she added. "But I always knew you were brave."

Riheir stared at her, angry and astonished and probably wounded in his pride—she hoped not his heart. She hoped she wasn't wrong about his feelings, or her own.

"I've seen Enchar, Kimsè, and Eäneté," Kehera told him, feeling her way through an unexpected emotional tangle of thorns. "At least in passing. And I've spoken to people from Tisain, and believe me, there's no comparison. His Grace will do very well by our people. If I wasn't convinced of that, I'd cut my own throat before doing anything to help him, and you ought to know it, too, Riheir," she added reproachfully.

Riheir Coärin opened his mouth and shut it again without speaking.

The Wolf Duke said mildly, "And if you think I could have gotten a speech like that out of her by force, Coärin, you don't know her as well as you ought."

There wasn't much that Riheir could say to that without offending him or insulting her. After a moment, when Riheir did not answer, the duke went on. "Very little in Coär shall change. I think you will find that a bond to Eäneté does not lie bitter on this land."

There was a short silence. Then Riheir said, not quite as grimly, "I understand, my lord. May I ask a question, my lord?"

The duke barely glanced at him. "Ask."

"How do you expect to stop yourself losing Eäneté proper to Irekay, now that so many of your men are here? Are not your own Immanence's precincts vulnerable, now that you have come through the pass and entered foreign lands?"

The Wolf Duke gave him a flat, hard look. "No one will take Eäneté from me. I have sealed its borders entirely. I have raised up Eänetaìsarè in all its strength, and forced bonds to lesser powers in the region. Raëhemaiëth supports me, as you have seen. Now your own Coäriliöa supports me as well. Nothing of Irekay will come through Roh Pass."

His voice carried that absolute certainty that compels belief despite any rational doubts. Kehera believed him. She watched Riheir Coärin try not to believe him, and was fairly certain that he failed.

The duke said, "It is early yet. We will not halt until the light fails. How far is Meilin Gap? Seventy miles, perhaps, is that so? We shall let the wagons trail, I think, and allow the mounted companies to press the pace. Of all things, it will not do to come there too late and find that Irekaì has already established a strategic position on this side of the mountains."

On that point, Kehera was sure, they one and all agreed. It might not be enough to make them friends. But she thought it might serve to at least brace up this reluctant alliance.

18

Gereth Murrel arrived in Raëh late in the afternoon of the nineteenth day of the Iron Hinge Month in the company of a large number of refugees. *Other* refugees, for he was a refugee no less than they, for all he did not share their particular fears.

At first Gereth had ridden swiftly, trying to outdistance the memory of Roh Pass. But dread of his arrival at Raëh gradually overpowered grief, and so by the time he came within sight of the city, he was moving much more slowly. Most of the refugees did not have horses; few enough even oxcarts on the road. All of this day and the previous day, Gereth had carried one child or another before him in the saddle. The current child was a dark-haired wisp of a girl, perhaps four years old. She belonged to a woman who walked beside the horse. The woman was also burdened with an infant, and had a boy of ten years who stayed solemnly by her side. The woman had been grateful for Gereth's offer of assistance.

Gereth had been glad to offer. He admired her courage, for taking to the road with such a family—the courage of the desperate, yes, but real courage nonetheless. He wanted to tell her that the Wolf Duke would not have harmed her, would not have permitted his soldiers to harm her, except he dared not explain his confidence. But the company of this small family was useful to him. Anyone who saw him with this family assumed he was the child's grandfather. That was a great advantage for a man who wished to pass without comment. Now, as he passed into Raëh through open gates and between harried watchmen, no one gave him a second glance. Gereth let his horse shoulder a way gently through the crowd to a quiet spot by the lee of the gate, and nodded gravely to the woman. "Is there anywhere I can help you get to?"

The woman smiled back gratefully. "No, thank you, sir. I'll do well enough now." She reached up an arm to swing the child down from Gereth's saddle and added, "My cousin's not far, I think. I'm sure we'll find the way." Over the past day, she had told Gereth more than a little of her cousin, a metalsmith in the city, with whom she hoped to find safety until the trouble passed. She added now, with tentative but genuine hospitality, "My cousin might find room for you, too, sir, for the night, if you've nowhere else to go."

"Thank you," Gereth said, touched. He had not spoken of his own family to this woman, and evidently she was concerned that he might have none, and so no welcome in this city. She was right, of course, but he said courteously, "I've a destination of my own, but I do thank you."

The woman smiled at him one more time and threaded her way determinedly into the crowds. Gereth guided his horse back into the street, heading deeper into the city, where he knew the king's palace would be located.

Raëh was a sprawling city, built largely of a handsome, understated pale-gold stone that must have been quarried from the low foothills that rose as a sweeping half-circle backdrop to the east. It gave the city a wholly different appearance than Eäneté, which was built more of dark wood and of a different kind of stone. Raëh was walled, of course, but Gereth had seen how the city spilled over those boundaries and ran into the countryside. The city seemed almost an outgrowth of the hills, as deeply rooted and ageless as they. But it was crowded with far more people now than it had been built to contain.

The Harivin king's palace, when Gereth found it, was no larger than the Eäneté duke's house, and considerably less imposing in height and form. It had been built along low, graceful lines, of the same pale stone as the rest of the city. It was set apart from the city proper by a fairly low wall that presented little barrier, not at all like the Pohorin king's palace in Irekay. The gates of this wall stood open. Men and women came and went quite freely between the city and the outer courtyard of the palace. Having no better idea, Gereth dismounted at one of the posts that stood around the periphery of the courtyard, threw the reins of his horse over the bar, loosened the girth and slipped the bit, and turned toward the busy doors that led into the palace. And stopped. He stood for a long moment next to his horse, resting his hand on its neck, thinking how easy it would be to get back in the saddle and ride away again.

It had been a long time since Gereth had experienced an attack of true panic. Not since the old duke's death, more than seven years ago. It was not the same as merely being afraid; this panic froze body and brain alike in a stiff, paralyzing terror. Abruptly, it seemed a very bad idea to walk into the house of the Harivin king. No matter what messages or gifts he carried, or might carry—and he wasn't even sure what it was he brought with him. All the carefully reasoned arguments that had brought him this far dissolved and left him standing, locked in fear and indecision, in the courtyard.

No one seemed to notice. Men and women came and went past Gereth in quick flurries of activity with no attention to spare for an ordinary man with a plain horse, even if he was momentarily in their way. Finally one man in the uniform of a Harivin lieutenant rode up close beside him, dismounted, tossed the reins of his horse over the bar, swung down, and eyed Gereth with sudden attention.

"Here, sir," he said, his tone mingling impatience with concern, "are you all right?"

"Yes," said Gereth huskily, and then cleared his throat and said with more assurance, "Yes, thank you, young man. Excuse me. I hadn't realized I was in your way."

"No difficulty at all, I assure you, sir," said the lieutenant politely. "May I help you find your direction somewhere, then?"

Gereth reflexively began to demur. But then, recovering his nerve and his brains from whatever hiding place they had crawled into, said, "Actually, yes. Please. My name is Gereth Murrel. I . . . have a message. From Eäneté. For your king."

The Harivin lieutenant did not move for a moment. Then, taking a step back, he gestured Gereth to come from between the horses into a clear space. "Who did you say you were again?"

"Gereth Murrel," Gereth repeated patiently. "From Eäneté. I need to speak to His Majesty," he added patiently as the captain continued to look at him without speaking. He expected . . . he did not know. Pohorin-bred reflexes told him he should fear any soldier in the service of a king. But this was not Pohorir. And, attacks of sudden panic aside, he knew it was not. He found himself much calmer now that the rods had been cast out to fall as they would.

The lieutenant took Gereth inside the palace, to a quiet little room without windows where soldiers stood guard at the door. But he was polite about it. He offered no violence. And there was a comfortable couch in the room, where Gereth could sit. Being tired, he was grateful for that mercy.

Other men came, some soldiers and some not. But no one threatened him. None of them even raised their voices. They showed no impatience with a man who refused to expand on his odd story or amend his outrageous request. After a while, the first men went away, and others came in their places, to hear exactly the same words as their predecessors.

After a long time, the original Harivin lieutenant brought him watered wine. Gereth thought it might be drugged. Sweet cone bark would make him sleepy and less guarded in speech; the dried leaves of maiden's blush would have something of the same effect and would be nearly tasteless in any sweet wine. He drank the wine anyway, being thirsty and having no recourse if they chose to drug him. It proved to be simply watered wine.

The Harivin men were patient, but they were also persistent. Gereth, just as patient, refused to expand on his original explanation or request, fearing to give too much away. What if the court lord to whom they reported, disbelieving what he told them, chose to order him dismissed, or even killed, without ever allowing him to speak to the king directly? As long as they did not know what information he carried, they could not make such a judgment.

"I'm Gereth Murrel," Gereth patiently repeated one more time, to a graying Harivin captain with a stern expression and a quiet manner. "I'm from Eäneté," he repeated wearily. He rested his head in his hands for a moment, fingers over his eyes. How long had it been? He did not know. There were no windows in this room to mark the passing of time. He said, as he had before, "I would like to speak to His Majesty, if he has a moment."

Another man came in just then. This man was in good-quality clothing, not the uniform of a soldier, but the sort of clothing that a minor lord might wear. He had the very light hair one seldom saw in the south, and gray eyes, and a quiet manner. From the captain's mildly deferential manner, he seemed most likely to be of high, but not exalted, rank.

"He has not said anything more," the captain told the lord.

The lord nodded and asked Gereth, quiet and polite, "You are from Pohorir. From Eäneté."

"Yes, my lord. As I have said."

"You must be weary. Would you like wine or tea? Perhaps something to eat?"

"No, thank you," said Gereth, feeling his stomach clench at the thought. It was all very well to judge Torrolay Elin Raëhema by his daughter. But he fully expected to be brought, before too much more time had passed, if he maintained his stubborn silence, before the king.

He was Pohorin enough to be frightened at that thought. The idea of food revolted him. He very much did not want to throw up in terror at the feet of the Harivin king.

The man made a polite, dismissive movement with one hand. "It is not our intention to question you until you collapse from hunger or weariness. If you change your mind, you have only to ask." At Gereth's repeated disclaimer, he went on, in his quiet voice, "Now, if I may ask, how did you get past the Coär end of the pass, coming as you were from Eäneté?"

No one had asked that particular question before. Gereth hesitated. Then, deciding, he spread his hands. "I had a token from the Eänetén duke. For service I had done him, the duke gave me leave through the pass. They did not see me in Coär. I think it was the Eänetén Power, hiding me within a thread of its awareness." That pebble hadn't implied forgiveness. He knew that. But . . . a chance to redeem something good from the terrible mess he'd made of everything. A chance beyond price.

"For service you had done him," repeated the quiet lord, perhaps hearing something of this in Gereth's voice. "For service you had done the Eänetén duke, he gave you leave through the pass and a thread of his tie. Who are you?"

Gereth hesitated. There was something about this man. Something he almost seemed to recognize. He said slowly, "He dismissed me from his service. But Kehera Elin Raëhema asked me to go to her father, and His Grace gave me his token and leave through the pass."

The Harivin captain jerked his head up at that. But the lord sprang to his feet, nearly knocking over his chair. Then collecting himself, he sat down again. But he did not manage to conceal the eagerness when he said, "Kehera Raëhema herself sent you to us—our lost princess. She, herself, and not the Eänetén duke? But why would she send you to her father?"

"I think, mostly, so that I should have a place to go. She is a kind child."

"Yes," breathed the man, and lowered pale lashes over his gray eyes, bringing his folded hands up to press against his mouth.

And Gereth putting two and two together and coming up, very abruptly, with four—stood up suddenly with a stifled exclamation of his own.

The man looked up swiftly, and the Harivin captain took a step forward.

Gereth immediately dropped to his knees and bowed his head. He had been, he knew, a fool; oh, he had done it up in ribbons. But he had not expected—how could he have expected?—the *King of Harivir* to keep other than formal state. He had not expected Torrolay Raëhema to come, himself, without attendants, to question a man who had shown up at his door with odd claims and odder requests. He had been very stupid. Because it had taken that moment, in which this man had suddenly looked so much like Kehera herself, to show him what he should have guessed from the moment the man had stepped into this room.

He expected—he did not know what he expected from Torrolay Elin Raëhema. A Pohorin lord would not have been forgiving of any show of disrespect from a prisoner, even in the midst of such a deception. In a moment like this, a Pohorin lord would expect a prisoner to go down on his face in terror. Even the Eänetén duke would expect that. Would demand it.

But this was not a Pohorin lord. The Harivin captain retired quietly to his post by the door. And after a moment the king's voice, no colder or more forbidding than before, said above him, "Please, get up. You have not offended me. Get up, please."

Gereth straightened his back cautiously, glancing up and then immediately lowering his eyes again. Now that he knew to look for it, the resemblance was obvious. This man had the same broad forehead, the same oval face as his daughter, though in a masculine form. Gereth said, keeping his gaze on the floor, striving for calmness in his tone and manner, "I meant no disrespect in failing to address Your Majesty properly. I beg Your Majesty will forgive my most appalling failures of intelligence and manners."

"You have not in any way offended me," repeated the Harivin king. "Please get up. Sit down again, if you like." He gestured for Gereth to resume his seat.

Gereth rose, and then stood for a moment waiting for the lightning strike of this king's hidden anger to fall upon him. It did not come. He reminded himself, *This is* Kehera's *father,* and sat down again on the low couch, letting his breath out slowly. His hands were trembling, and he clasped them together in his lap.

Torrolay Raëhema did not appear to notice. He said gently, "Tell me about my daughter. How is it she came to send you to me?" When Gereth did not at once respond, he went on, patiently, "You were the duke's man, but he dismissed you? How did that happen?"

"Your Majesty, it's all part of the same thing," Gereth said, and paused. And then went on, very carefully, because there were things Kehera's *father* would certainly not want to hear. "He intended to wed her. You are . . . Of course you are aware. Perhaps he has done so already. He intended so. She would have accepted the marriage. My duke is a . . . hard man in many ways. But he was gentle with her, Majesty. I swear that is true. And she saw the sense of it when he laid it out for her."

"But?" Torrolay Raëhema was sitting very still.

"She heard about Leiör. And about your son. That's when she asked me to help her get through the pass. Until very lately, I was the duke's seneschal."

"Ah," the king breathed. "Go on."

"I . . . agreed. For reasons of my own. She—Her Highness could have gotten through the pass. But Raëhemaiëth . . . There was a falcon. I don't know whether you . . ."

"I know very little with certainty. But I have been aware that Raëhemaiëth favors the Immanent of Eäneté—it proved willing for Coär to go into Eäneté's keeping—or I should hardly have agreed to any of your duke's demands, whatever other exigencies I or Harivir might face."

"My duke has set his own stamp on Eäneté. He'll do no harm to Coär, not to any Harivin province—"

The king made an impatient gesture. "I'm pleased to hear so, though far less pleased to put such an issue to the test. Personally, I find it appalling to think that any Harivin province should be influenced to any degree by any Pohorin Immanent. But as I say, Raëhemaiëth did not protest. And I had no choice. Go on."

Gereth nodded, fumbling for coherent thought. "Your Majesty, because I had helped her, my duke dismissed me from his service. Her Highness he took back to Eäneté. I swear to you, Your Majesty, he will have resumed his gentle manner toward her. His anger was with me, not with her. And with himself. But not in any part with her. I will swear that is true, Your Majesty."

"Why angry with himself?" The king's tone was reserved.

"For allowing her to break away from him. Innisth terè Maèr Eänetaì is not accustomed to lose track of anything. But Her Highness has a . . . a strength that is quiet. Contained. He knows it, but I think it still took him by surprise. He doesn't like being surprised. But I swear to you, he will show her no shadow of cruelty."

"And yet you betrayed him in favor of my daughter. Why, if what you say is true, would you ever have done such a thing?"

Gereth winced at this. But he lifted his eyes at once to meet the king's and answered earnestly, "The princess appealed to me in the name of . . . another young lady, who was married against her will to the old duke, and died of it. It was not the same. But I . . . It is hard to deny her what she asks."

Torrolay Raëhema drew a breath and closed his eyes briefly. Then he said, looking up again, "Why should the duke care for her feelings if he can compel her obedience?"

It was a better question, perhaps, than the Harivir king knew, and spoken with all the bitterness of a father who could not protect his daughter. But Gereth answered immediately and without, he hoped, a sign of doubt. "He wants her as a willing ally, Your Majesty. He values her for herself, not only for her tie to your Raëhemaiëth, though he believes he can use her tie to free himself from Irekay and break away from Pohorir."

"He is ambitious. But Raëhemaiëth supports him." The king considered this for a moment. Eventually he went on. "Your duke must have been very nearly on your heels through the pass. Raëhemaiëth has lost its bond to the Immanent Power of Coär. The Power of Eäneté has taken that."

Gereth bowed his head. Of course he had not outrun that news. He said, "Even so, I hope Your Majesty will think kindly of the Eänetén duke. He will protect all he holds against Pohorir. Your Majesty may trust that he will. He sent me with a token, as I said. But he gave it to me only after Her Highness told me to come to you. I think it . . . may also be a gift, Your Majesty."

"A gift."

Gereth took it out, the little fragment of stone, plain granite with a little quartz inclusion. To him it seemed an ordinary pebble, save that if he paid careful attention, he could half perceive . . . something. Very faint. By Torrolay Elin's sudden indrawn breath, he knew that the Harivin king must see more than he.

"A thread of a tie," said the king. "Set into the native stone of Eäneté. And you brought this here?" He sounded as though he was trying to decide whether to be outraged or merely surprised.

Gereth ducked his head apologetically. "I hope I was right to do so, Majesty. I think . . . your son. We had word that when Leiör fell, the young prince suffered some injury. That the Power of Irekay struck at his tie somehow." He held the pebble out toward the Harivin king. "The king of Irekay is your enemy. He is everyone's enemy. The Immanent Power of Irekay is very strong and very aggressive. But His Grace means to defy him, and to ally with Your Majesty to defy him. And he gave me this."

"I . . . see."

The Harivin king did not seem altogether to trust this assurance, for which Gereth could hardly blame him. He said carefully, "His Grace gave me this. But as I say, only after Her Highness told me to come to you."

Torrolay Raëhema reached out with one hand, but then did not touch the pebble after all. Instead he drew back once more and folded both his hands on his knee. He was silent for some time, considering. Then he murmured, "So this gift comes from the hand of . . . a man who would prefer, perhaps, not to be my enemy? Or would he prefer to clear Harivir of rivals? Perhaps your duke is working for Methmeir Irekaì after all." He gave Gereth a sharp look and smiled suddenly. "You needn't look so horrified. I think that unlikely. Still . . ."

The Harivin captain said quietly, "Your Majesty, as your daughter was present when the Eänetén duke gave this stone to this man . . ."

"Yes," said Gereth at once. "She was there."

"True. True. She would have seen that thread," acknowledged the king.

"His Grace isn't such a fool that he wishes to face the Irekaïn Power alone."

"I understand." There was another slight pause. Then Torrolay Raëhema rose, and gestured Gereth to his feet as well. "This way. Bring that."

It was a surprisingly short way: up a flight of stairs and down a curving hallway, and then a suite, and a small, neat bedchamber, with a wide window that looked out over the gardens, open to the air. A woman servant rose from a chair drawn up close to the narrow bed. She nodded to the king, murmured, "No change," and stepped aside.

Torrolay Raëhema stepped forward to his son's bedside.

The boy was seventeen, Gereth knew. Or perhaps eighteen. He looked younger, tucked in that bed. He looked young and thin and pale and vulnerable. He lay quietly beneath the blankets, but there was a strange tension in his face and his neck and shoulders and hands, very unlike the relaxation of ordinary sleep.

"You see," the king said over his shoulder. "Since Leiör. It is many days now. He does not decline. Raëhemaiëth sustains him, though he takes little water and less nourishment. But he does not wake."

"Yes," said Gereth, understanding.

"Your duke's . . . gift. What would you do with it?"

"I will put it in his hand, Your Majesty, so that the Immanent Power of Eäneté can find your son. And if it does not help, I will pray it does no harm."

"You *should* pray for that," said Torrolay Elin, an edge to his voice. But then he rubbed his eyes, sighed, and glanced at Gereth. "No. Forgive me. I do believe, at least, that you offer this in all good faith. If you are mistaken . . . If we are both mistaken, I will try not to blame you for it." He gazed down at his son for another long moment. "Very well," he said at last. "Set it in my son's hand."

Gereth didn't let himself hesitate. He stepped forward, took the young prince's hand, turned it palm-up, tucked the pebble into it, and folded the boy's fingers around it. He stayed by the bed afterward, holding the prince's hand in both of his, his gaze on the young face.

At first nothing seemed to happen. Then the king made a slight movement of surprise, stiffening, and a second later, Gereth felt the reverberating presence of a rising Power. A deep hum pervaded the room, intangible, invisible, but as though the very air had become heavier all around them.

Here in this place of its strength, Raëhemaiëth shook the world as it rose. It was not like the Eänetén Power when Innisth called it up. The Power of Raëh rumbled through the world as though the earth itself purred like a great cat. It seemed indeed very much a thing of earth, warm and deep, immensely strong but far less frightening than the Eänetén Power. Below Raëhemaiëth, Gereth could perceive Eänetaìsarè as well, vivid and violent, like shattering rock and savage fire.

But there was something else, something beyond and underneath both Raëhemaiëth and Eänetaìsarè. Gereth realized this only after the king, who swore under his breath and then snapped, "*Raëhemaiëth!*"

The Raëh Power surged upward and outward. The room trembled with it—the very light took on a heavier, richer appearance—cold bit Gereth's fingers sharply and he opened his hands, gasping. Frost spread suddenly across Tirovay Elin's hand and continued in a glittering web up toward his elbow; frost grew across his eyes and his hair. The boy drew a shuddering, painful breath.

"Fortunate Gods!" said Torrolay Elin, a prayer, and again, *"Raëhemaiëth!"*

"Eänetaìsarè," Gereth added. "Eänetaìsarè!"—though he did not know whether the Eänetén Power could hear him. But the Raëh Power surged strongly through the room, all warm earth and burgeoning summer, and the frost melted, running down the young prince's face like tears. Tirovay Elin Raëhema drew in a sharp breath, and then another.

Then he sat up, so suddenly that Gereth flinched.

The prince closed his hand hard around the stone he held and brought it to his mouth. He touched it to his lips—perhaps he breathed on it. Then he clenched it in both hands. He said to Gereth, in a tone of surprise, "But *you* don't hold a deep tie."

"No," said Gereth.

"But you brought it," said the young prince. He sounded perfectly coherent and aware. "It broke the other Power. Raëhemaiëth held it back, but Raëhemaiëth couldn't break it until your Power gave its strength to the effort."

"Yes," said Gereth. "I think that was the intention. Or at least the hope."

The boy nodded. Then he looked at his father and said in a smaller voice, "I failed Leiör. I'm sorry. I'm really sorry. If you'd been there . . . or Kehy . . ."

"Raëhemaiëth failed Leiör," Torrolay Raëhema told his son, quietly firm. "We faced too great an incursion, all along the river. We faced both the mortal armies of Emmer and an incursion of midwinter cold from Pohorir. You did well."

Prince Tirovay stared at him, seeming to have trouble taking this in.

"Had I been at Leiör, I probably would not have made common cause with Enmon Corvallis," said his father. "Then we would be facing worse trouble along our border with Emmer. *You* supported Sariy, and

Corvallis blocked the Mad King's mortal army while Raëhemaiëth blocked the Irekaïn Power."

"But Leiör—"

"Even though Leiör is now a hollow province, at least Methmeir Irekaì found no way to anchor his cold Immanent into that land. Meanwhile, the north bank of the Imhar stands now as a buffer between Hallieth Theraön and Harivir, exactly as you intended, my son. If we hadn't bound Raëhemaiëth into Sariy, then once Leiör fell, we would most likely have lost everything north of Raëh. Because of you and because of Enmon Corvallis, we lost not an inch of land, but rather gained a new foothold on the northern bank of the river. Though Leiör is hollow, the land is not actually lost, nor has the Immanent of Irekay found foothold there. I assure you, it makes a great difference to the folk there that the province still lies in Harivir and has not fallen to Emmer."

His son stared at him.

The king laid one hand on his son's shoulder. He was not smiling, but there was an intensity in his gray eyes that went well beyond a smile. He said, "You did well, Tiro. And you *will* do well, now that you are come back to us. Are you hungry? Can you eat?" Without waiting for an answer, he added to the woman, "Have someone bring my son broth and bread."

Then he turned to Gereth. "Thank you," he said simply. "Thank you for what you have done. Will you ask me again to think kindly of your duke?"

After a second, Gereth found his voice. "Your Majesty, I do ask that."

"Then I will," said the king. He nodded to the Harivin captain. "The blue suite. This man is my honored prisoner. I want him under close but extremely courteous guard." He did smile, then. "Challenging as such an order may be to carry out."

As the captain bowed acknowledgment, the king said to Gereth, "I will speak to you again. Soon. I am favorably disposed to hear anything you have to say. But I will ask you to be patient."

"Your Majesty," Gereth answered, bowing. "Of course." He was surprised to find himself smiling—he had found little to smile about during the past days. He nodded to the young prince. "Your Highness."

Tirovay Raëhema returned his nod, looking faintly puzzled. "Should I know you?"

"You don't know me at all," Gereth assured him. "But I am very glad to see you recovered, Your Highness." He was. The young prince's recovery was one good thing, one excellent thing, to save out of the difficult, painful disaster of the previous days. He wished he could tell Kehera Raëhema that her brother had been freed of the Irekaïn Power and had recovered.

Perhaps Torrolay Raëhema would allow him to write a letter. Even if he could not bring himself to write to Innisth, he could write to Kehera. Yes. That would be . . . He could do that. He would ask.

Though not just yet. It was clear Torrolay Raëhema had no time for anything but his son just now.

19

Lord Laören Peris felt uneasy. It wasn't clear to him exactly why. He knew there was no danger in this little operation. Certainly not to himself. The six companies of regular soldiers the king had loaned him would see to that—not to mention the king's servant and sorcerer, Gheroïn Nomoris. The king had set a deep tie in Gheroïn, which Laören might have been jealous of, except very soon he would hold a deep tie himself

Besides, forcing the tie and becoming a sorcerer had done very little for Gheroïn's personality or manners, in Laören's opinion. He'd known Gheroïn Nomoris for years, off and on, and he'd always had a sense of humor until late last year when the king had granted him the tie. Shame to ruin a man who'd been a decent companion. Still, it was well worth sacrificing Gheroïn to make a sorcerer, if he could in turn force the Eänetén Power to abandon that stiff Maèr provincial and set its deep tie in a loyal Irekaïn lord instead. Which Laören had no doubt the sorcerer would do.

Yet he was still uneasy. The closer they'd come to Eäneté, the worse his uneasiness grew. And he didn't know why. Provincial in the worst sense of the word, not merely lacking in but contemptuous of sophistication . . . Sullen peasants, all of them, including the Maèr Eänetaì. It would be a pleasure to humble *him*. Oh, Gheroïn might pretend to think the Eänetén Power a somewhat difficult Immanent, but Laören wasn't concerned about *that*. Mastering a recalcitrant Immanent was undoubtedly akin to mastering a disobedient woman, and he was quite accustomed to such pursuits. Besides, when all was said and done, Eäneté was a province of middling age and size. He was quite certain he would enjoy mastering its little Immanent.

The mountain road was clear. There was no problem there. The weather was good, considering it was the twentieth day of the Iron Hinge Month. It might be unpleasantly cold, but there hadn't been snow for days and travel was easy enough. Off to the left rolled pastures, empty stubble as far as the eye could see, snow clinging to the yellowed winter grasses, patches of ice glittering where the land was low and marshy. On the right, the low hills marched up to meet the mountains, black leafless forest giving way in the heights to bare gray stone. Far too much empty land, altogether a dismal scene, but Laören's senior captain had pointed out that nothing could move close to the road among those naked trees without being seen, so that was something.

Laören glanced sidelong at Gheroïn. The man rode with his eyes turned steadfastly forward, as though thoughts of wine and women never entered his mind. Laören found him unsettling. No doubt that accounted for his general unease.

"Eäneté province begins just around the curve of that next hill," Gheroïn said abruptly. His voice and manner expressed neither pleasure nor anticipation.

Indeed, it was a most disconcerting flatness of manner. Laören nodded acknowledgment and thought privately that, truly, it was not an Immanent that would have suited him at all well.

At least the tedious part of this little exercise was nearly past. Once on Eänetén land, Gheroïn would break its rebellious Power, set the tie into Laören, and they would all enjoy a leisurely journey to the central town, where no doubt it would take the rest of the winter to put affairs in proper order. Laören did look forward to seeing the arrogant Eänetén duke on his knees. He would have to make sure his captains understood Innisth terè Maèr Eänetaì must be taken alive and unharmed. Though the man would not be Eänetaì by then, of course.

Then they breasted the hill, and Laören looked down the curve of the ground into Eäneté.

Along the east side of the road, the land rambled off for a long way in harvest stubble and frozen marsh. To the west the forest had been hewed back for only a short distance before the slopes grew rocky and the land too poor to be worth the effort. In the road, and to each side of it, waited men.

They had constructed a barricade of logs cut from the nearby forest and sharpened. It was nothing horses could charge into, certainly, especially with a shallow trench hacked out of the frozen ground before it. But behind this barricade was merely a scattering of soldiers in their Eänetén gray, and with them, a scarcely larger number of townsmen and farmers less well equipped—pitchforks and axes as common among them as swords.

But the Eänetén duke himself was not there. Laören looked for him at once and was both disappointed and relieved not to find that tall cold-eyed lord among the defenders.

"Few horses, not that they've much use for horse in their position," murmured Laören's senior captain, Criof. "And their numbers are certainly paltry."

"Excellent," Laören agreed, wondering why the captain was bothering him with such trivial details instead of just going on and dealing with it. "I'm sure they'll give you no trouble."

The captain said apologetically, "Well, it may take a bit longer than we'd like, my lord. All that land east of the road is too damn wet to take our horses through. The animals would go through the ice more like than not and break their legs. And then that wood on the other side is nice cover for hidden soldiers."

"Well, then?" Laören demanded. "Don't tell me you can't take them, Captain."

"Of course not, my lord. It'll be easy enough. Just slower than it might have been had they chosen worse ground. Unless—" He glanced sidelong at Gheroïn. "Unless His Majesty's sorcerer can break through their line for us, my lord?"

"Not until I set foot on Eänetén soil," Gheroïn said impassively.

Laören shrugged. "It seems we'll have to do it the hard way."

The captain sighed, not quite audibly. "So, then. I'll set one company to guard against that wood, just in case. Then I'll send a company of foot through the marsh. They'll be slow, but the Eänetén commander won't be able to ignore them. That'll draw defenders off the road, and leave four full companies to get through the barricade, not that so many will be necessary. Once we get a few men set on the other side to hold off the Eänetén soldiers, we'll have that barrier out of the way fast enough. Then we'll be able to bring in the heavy horse for one mop-up sweep, and that'll be that."

"Whatever you like. Just make a way for us into Eäneté."

"Yes, my lord," Criof acknowledged. "If you would please retire a little way back along the column, my lord. It wouldn't do for you to take an unlucky arrow."

Laören certainly agreed with that. He reined his horse away. Gheroïn didn't follow, but no doubt he could judge such matters for himself and certainly Laören wasn't going to argue with him.

At first, Criof's plan seemed to be working perfectly, though of course Laören had not paid much attention to the details. The Irekaïn detachment of foot troops picked a careful way into the frozen marsh, swinging wide out of bowshot and preparing for a quick advance. As he clearly had to, the Eänetén commander separated some of his men from the main body of the defenders and sent them a short way into the marsh, which would surely weaken his frontal defense . . . or Laören supposed so; he felt in general such matters were best left to soldiers, who had nothing better to do than consider tactical matters.

A few Irekaïn soldiers fell; the first defenders as well, and suddenly it was impossible to make out anything clearly amid the chaotic struggle on and around the road. He supposed his Irekaïn soldiers would shortly trounce those upstart Eäneténs . . . and then Captain Criof sounded the withdrawal. The staccato beat of the call sang out above the clash of battle below. At first Laören wasn't certain of the meaning of that call, but then the Irekaïn soldiers began an orderly retreat, guarding themselves and taking their wounded out with them.

Laören pressed his horse forward toward Criof. "Captain!" he said. "What is this? Do you not understand the urgent necessity to make a way for the king's sorcerer into Eäneté?"

"Look again, my lord," Criof said in a tight, abrupt tone. Laören was half minded to reprimand the man, but he did look again . . . and then forgot the man's insolence.

Where Irekaïn men had fallen and died, they still lay. But where Eänetén defenders had died on Eäneté soil, they did not stay dead. Or not quite in the usual way, at least. Laören watched one man, mortally wounded, throw his head back and die, coughing blood. And his body blurred, and at once, fast as thought, there was a large ash-colored wolf struggling to its feet where the man had lain. The wolf tilted its muzzle to the sky and voiced the long singing cry of northern winters, and in its wild voice there was nothing left of the man it had been.

Laören found this difficult to believe. The Immanent might have taken up its dead, certainly. But it was only a provincial Power, a lesser Power. It should not have been able to reshape its dead and pour them back into the world. Yet all through the ranks of the defenders there were now wolves, two dozen or more mist-colored animals with savage yellow eyes. They flowed over the low barrier the Eänetén men had constructed, heading directly for the Irekaïn soldiers.

"Just how strong *is* the Eänetén Power?" Laören said to Gheroïn Nomoris. "You didn't tell me it was Great! Can't you stop it doing that?"

"I warned you it was recalcitrant," Gheroïn said coldly. "Of course I can stop it. Once I set foot within its precincts."

Laören glared at him, then turned to Captain Criof. "Do something!"

Captain Criof said to his signaler, sounding perfectly calm, "Instruct all archers to fire on those animals at once," and the young man lifted his horn to his lips with hands that trembled. Arrows sang through the air. Many found their targets. With very little effect. Laören was looking directly at one immense wolf when it was struck by three arrows in quick succession. The wolf was solid enough to stop the arrows' flight. But unlike an ordinary wolf, the arrows did not seem to bother it very much. They certainly did not slow it down. That wolf, and all the others, continued to pursue the retreating Irekaïn soldiers. The soldiers, from an orderly retreat, began to move a great deal faster, and with a great deal less concern for the order of their ranks. Here and there two or more soldiers, working together, managed to hack a wolf to pieces. But there were a lot more men dying out there than there were animals.

But then Gheroïn Nomoris moved at last. The king's sorcerer rode forward, took out a short dagger no longer than his palm, and threw it out toward the wolves. It struck the earth almost directly in front of the lead wolf, which tumbled off its feet as it met some unseen barrier. The wolf scrambled up again, snarling. All the other wolves pressed forward, but none seemed able to pass the knife where it stood in the ground. Nomoris continued forward, and the wolves fell back before him, retreating finally back beyond the barricade. There, they did not fawn on the men as dogs might have, but formed instead a separate pack of their own, on the side where the leafless forest made its closest approach to the road.

"Well, that's all right, then," Laören said, trying to sound as though he had never been even momentarily concerned.

"While they are off Eänetén soil, I can break them. Not on Eänetén soil. Not until I too can stand on that land and break that Power entirely."

"Of course, of course. You must clear a way past that barrier, Criof."

"I understand." Criof cleared his throat. "It will be more difficult than I anticipated."

Laören gave him an incredulous look.

Criof cleared his throat again. "Of course we shall succeed, my lord." He regarded the field, considering. Then he said to an aide, in a clear, carrying voice, "Pass orders back that the men are to fight to cripple. Not to kill, as they can avoid it; the men are less dangerous than the wolves. Our men must work in pairs on those cursed wolves. If they keep their heads, they can cut them apart."

The aide saluted and reined away.

The second attempt to break the Eänetén barricade was very different in tone from the first. The Irekaïn soldiers were much grimmer about it. Laören leaned forward, trying to make sense of it. The wolves were a threat, obviously, but as Criof had said, two or three men working together could cut them down. And the Irekaïns had soldiers to spare, for the wolves and the Eänetén men besides. It was inevitable, then, that the barricade would be broken. It was inevitable that Gheroïn Nomoris would ride forward, dismount, step over the invisible line that separated Eäneté proper from all the lands to the east, and raise his sword with a hiss of triumph, ready to plunge it into the dark earth at his feet.

But he never completed this gesture, because suddenly a man in the uniform of a Pohorin soldier ran forward between his fellows, caught Nomoris by the arm, spun him around, slammed a long, slender knife up under his chin, then lifted him entirely off the ground and cast him down onto the earth.

In the space of a single heartbeat, while Laören stared in astonished dismay, a young black sapling taller than the height of a man and as big around as a man's wrist burst from Nomoris's body. It reached upward with slender branches, carrying the sorcerer along with the force of its swift growth. Nomoris hung there, limp, struck through the body by the graceful branches of the young tree, his eyes open and blank, the knife still jammed into his skull. Where drops of his blood fell, red and full, onto the dark ground, the cold earth smoked. Flowers, white as snow or death, sprang from the bare twigs of the new tree with all the power and life of a remembered spring. Though the Irekaïn Power had raised him once, Laören found himself unable to believe it would be able to do so again. No, this time the king's sorcerer was truly dead.

Then Laören cried out, as an immense cold pressure closed around him. He had just time to understand that this was the Great Power of Irekay, cast out of Gheroïn Nomoris and seeking another mortal body in which it might anchor itself, another body with the eyes and mind of a man. He had just time to understand that, and then Irekaìmaiäd crushed his mind and heart and soul and he vanished within the endless white winter.

Verè Deconniy, commander of the one company of Eänetén soldiers left in Eäneté proper and thus by extension of all the townsmen and farmers as well, watched with amazement as one of the Irekaïn soldiers killed the sorcerer, as the black sapling struck upward through the sorcerer's body, as the tree burst into flower, its blooms white as winter. Other saplings rose among the dead, thickening into young trees, black branches shining with a glaze of ice, flowering despite the season. Among the Irekaïns, someone sounded the retreat; the stuttering notes echoed in the appalled pause that had gripped both sides . . . and Lord Laören, safely back from the violence and death, toppled from his horse as though arrow shot.

Verè only wished the man *had* been shot. Probably he had merely fainted. That suspicion was nearly as satisfying, in its way.

He had been appalled to see Laören in command of those troops; sickened at the idea that *Laören,* of all men, had been appointed to take the lordship of this province. He had not been at all certain he could prevent that, with the limited resources His Grace had left for defense. Then the Eänetén Power had risen, and he had become more confident.

And then Gheroïn Nomoris had ridden forward and Verè had known, dismayed, that even the Eänetén Power might not defeat the Irekaïn sorcerer and that if it could not, *he* had no way to prevent anything of the disaster that would come down on Eäneté.

And now this.

His Grace had told him. He should have trusted his orders. His

Grace had said right out plainly, *When our Immanent is roused, the dead of Eäneté are not likely to rest. Even some of the living may be taken up. A man from Tisain may be a better choice for commander, when Eänetaìsarè rouses.* It hadn't been . . . enough of a warning. Not enough for him to honestly be prepared for . . . this. But he suspected that nothing could have been enough. Not for this.

The wolves had gone, at least. Melted away into the winter woods. Verè was glad of that. A man born and bred in Tisain had little fondness for wolves; not like the Eänetén townspeople who sometimes killed calves and left them for the wolves. He understood that custom better now.

Though at least there would be no need to form a burial detail. The bodies of the fallen Irekaïn soldiers could be left where they lay. He imagined the wolves would drift back to this killing ground once the soldiers had gone. Actually, he would have preferred not to imagine it.

The soldiers that remained on their feet were more of a concern. The surviving Irekaïns were definitely retreating, but Verè thought it deeply unwise to allow them to regroup. And he wanted, for both personal and professional reasons, to be sure of Lord Laören. He glanced around, taking in the men he had left. He could wish the wolves had not gone just yet, actually. His men were still outnumbered . . . though with the Irekaïns so thoroughly unnerved that might not matter.

Then, hardly more than a bowshot away, Lord Laören got to his feet and leveled a hard stare across the abandoned field where the lithe black-barked trees grew amid the dead. He looked very different, somehow. He stood straighter or something, and he inspected the scene with a strange kind of indifference that sent cold prickling down Verè's spine.

Then Laören turned and took one step back toward the east, toward Irekay. The light around him grew brilliant with prickling cold, and he vanished. And all the Irekaïn soldiers vanished with him, all the remaining living men and a good handful of the dead that had fallen farthest from the border of Eäneté.

Verè took a hard breath.

Beside him, one of his sergeants said, in a resigned tone, "Well, better to have fed the whole lot to the wolves, but if the Fortunate Gods are kind we won't see them again anyway."

"They may have retreated in order to regroup," Verè pointed out. "We'd better lay plans to face them again, just in case. Though I don't imagine any normal man would be overeager to challenge Eänetaìsarè after that." He hesitated, wanting to ask, *Did you see something strange about Laören? Do you think he is a normal man, still?* But in the end he didn't ask, perhaps because he didn't want to hear his sergeant's answer.

The man who had killed the Irekaïn sorcerer . . . That man was a more immediate concern. He was still alive, and still right here, still on Eänetén ground. He did not seem inclined to fight, but simply knelt, holding out his empty hands to the first Eänetén soldiers who approached him.

The man had been slightly injured in the fighting, a shallow cut that marked his right arm at the elbow, but he did not appear to have suffered any serious wound. He showed no wariness of the new young trees that now crowded what had been a road, and for whatever reason, Eänetaìsarè did not seem to resent his presence.

He looked perfectly ordinary. He had hair that was darker than average, but not so dark as to catch the eye. The cast of his face and the paleness of his skin spoke more of northern ancestry, but many people of Enchar had similar features. On the other hand, he did not seem particularly disturbed by his position, even when one of the soldiers, answering Verè's gesture, pulled him to his feet, bound his hands roughly behind his back, and brought him over.

"Well?" Verè asked him. "Explain yourself."

The bound man bowed his head, appearing unafraid. He said, "I am not Irekaïn, but rather a servant of the Fortunate Gods and an enemy of Irekay."

"Oh?" Verè said with careful neutrality. "A servant of the Fortunate Gods. I see." He had never heard of such a thing, but perhaps it meant this man was something like a sorcerer. Or that fortune and chance bent around him. For the moment, he asked merely, "Where are you from, then, if not Irekay?"

"I am Harivin. Originally."

"Indeed. Harivin." Verè looked the man over with open skepticism. All of his clothing and equipment seemed standard issue for an Irekaïn soldier.

"I suppose he was riding with the Irekaïns for his personal amusement, or for the exercise, perhaps," commented the sergeant, a level-headed man named Tegen.

The man shrugged as well as he could with his arms bound. "It seemed the likeliest way for a man to get into Eäneté with reasonable speed. Also, you will forgive me if I observe that even your impressive defense could not have protected your land from a man such as Gheroïn Nomoris. I needed to be sure I was in a position to intervene."

Verè could not deny this man's intervention had been important. Even decisive. He had clearly seen the look of triumph on the sorcerer's face at that last moment. He'd had one flashing moment to think that he had failed, they had failed, Methmeir Irekaï's sorcerer would force the Immanent Power of Eäneté to submit to Irekay, and the king's men would roll over their defense, and Lord Laören would do as he pleased with the province and its people. He had had one sharp instant to be grateful the Harivin princess had taken his little Eöté with her, because of all the folk of Eäneté, Verè wanted least to see Eöté at Laören's mercy. . . .

And then this man had driven his blade through the Irekaïn sorcerer's skull and handed Eäneté the victory after all.

He said, "It's plain you served Eäneté by your actions. I will admit, a dagger is not the weapon I expect to strike down a sorcerer. I've seen blades rebound from that man before."

"My knife carried the blessing of the Fortunate Gods. Sometimes it does."

Verè considered this. The prisoner merely waited. It did not seem to occur to him he should attempt to argue further in his own defense.

At last Verè asked him, "Did the Irekaïn Power take Lord Laören, there at the end? Will he return and try to do what Nomoris failed to do?"

The prisoner tilted his head, considering. "The tie went somewhere," he said after a moment. "Into Laören? It might be so. Will he return? He may. But I think not here. When it took Gheroïn Nomoris, Eänetaìsarè also took up some of Irekaìmaiäd's strength. Irekaìmaiäd will not wish to risk facing Eänetaìsarè directly upon its own precincts again. It is far more likely to strike against the Eänetén Power elsewhere, upon foreign lands it has claimed, and not here."

"Well, that's something," muttered Sergeant Tegen.

If it were true. But Verè thought it probably was. He glanced around, thinking. The aftermath of the battle surrounded them. There were the wounded to tend. The bodies of the Irekaïn soldiers could be left to the trees and the wolves, but their horses would have to be cared for, or put down if too badly injured. All the tasks that followed battle would take time.

Turning back to his prisoner, Verè ordered, "Put this man on a horse. He'll go back to the duke's house with me right now. Sergeant, you and your squad will ride with me. Lieutenant Tejef, deal with things here."

The prisoner made no comment to any of this, not when a horse was brought for him, not when he was helped to mount, not when a soldier took the lead rope and fell in behind Verè. Verè kept an eye on him, but the prisoner seemed disinclined to cause trouble.

Four days to the city. Three, if they pressed hard and none of the horses went lame and no other disasters got in their way. The prisoner had better be right about Laören not coming against the border here a second time. But the man was surely right that the Irekaïn Power had gotten its arrogance trimmed today. He hoped that such a great magic had not dragged the duke's attention from anything important . . . wherever he was this moment and whatever he might be doing.

❄ ❄ ❄

Three days to the town of Eäneté, nearly, and hard on the horses to hold that pace, but they made the distance in very good time for all that. The wolves paced them the whole way, gray shadows glimpsed now and then when the woods opened up to cleared land. The prisoner gave no trouble, but no helpful answers either. He answered whatever questions were put to him, but elliptically, and Verè could not tell whether every word off his tongue was a lie. It would be different, Verè was determined, when they came to the duke's house.

Once they had finally arrived, he had the man taken at once to the cells downstairs, below the main floors of the house, while he went to his own quarters to hear reports and make his own to Geran Lhiyré, senior among Gereth Murrel's factors and now, since Gereth was gone, standing the seneschal's place. It was a hard place to fill, but Lhiyré was a quiet, thorough man who seemed to know his job. Verè would have very much preferred to have Gereth in charge, but he liked Lhiyré well enough.

The house seemed empty and quiet with so many of the staff gone with His Grace; and Verè missed Eöté's quiet little presence more than he had expected. She effaced herself so thoroughly you could forget she was even there, poor timid little Eöté, yet she was always doing little things to see to a man's comfort. The Raëhema girl was kind, at least. He could trust that the Harivin princess would protect Eöté. He thought he could trust her to do that. Or if not her, then His Grace, who took such strict pains to be . . . not kind. But careful.

Verè took a breath, let it out, and disciplined his thoughts to consider his own duty. In an hour or two, the prisoner, having been led past the racks of torture implements and then left in a cell to think about them, would probably be very uncomfortable. Here in this house where the Eänetén Power seemed to inhabit every stone and linger in the very air . . . this was the place to get answers from a man who thought himself too clever to be caught in a lie. Verè was certain he could get the truth from his prisoner *here*.

And if the truth was that the man truly was a servant of the

Fortunate Gods . . . well. He could already imagine the report he would have to write. He hoped he would not sound too much a fool, writing about servants of the Gods.

So, downstairs. It could have been worse. The cells at the back were dark and cold, but the big room at the bottom of the stairs was well lit, with heavy, ornate brass lanterns set along the walls, three fireplaces set into the near wall, and candles lining the huge oaken table that took up a large part of the room. The lamps and candles were all lit, and there were fires burning in all three fireplaces to take the edge off the chill in the room. The oil the lanterns burned was scented with clove oil, and the wood in the fireplaces was cedar, so that the air was fragrant with their smoke. The other smells, below the smoke, were nothing more sinister than those of hot wax and the sweet lemony scent of the oil used to polish the long table.

But lining the long wall nearest the table were pegs and racks where whips and knives and irons, and other less-identifiable implements, were neatly hung and arranged. There were several sets of metal and leather clamps set into one end of the heavy table. And in the polished stones of the floor, channels had been incised, to make it easy to wash the blood away.

Geran Lhiyré had—rather bravely, in Verè's opinion—accompanied Verè to observe the interrogation. Now Lhiyré looked at those implements and paled slightly. Verè didn't count that against him at all. "I hear it was a great deal worse when the old duke ruled here," he commented.

"Oh, it was," Lhiyré agreed, in a voice pitched slightly too high. "I kept clear of him, fortunately, but I heard tales of this place. And saw a man once, after he'd been released. You can't imagine."

"I prefer not to imagine it, thank you." There was only the one chair, but Lhiyré glanced at it and then gingerly leaned his hip against the table, so Verè took it, not to seem intimidated. It was a very comfortable chair, but he had to admit he was not very comfortable in it.

At a gesture, the two men-at-arms set to guard the prisoner went to bring him out.

He came blinking into the light, by which Verè gathered that no one had troubled to provide him with a lantern of his own. He was shaking all over, slight tremors that racked his body. But he did not actually appear to be afraid. When the soldiers led him toward the table with its nearby fires, he showed no hesitation about accompanying them. His eyes passed over the neatly arranged implements without obvious concern, or even much apparent interest. Verè had to admire his nerve.

The soldiers fastened the set of manacles closest to the end of the table around the prisoner's wrists, leaving the man held uncomfortably half bent over the end of the table, with his arms spread wide to either side.

The prisoner shifted his weight a little, turning his wrists in the manacles, testing the limits of his confinement. Then he went to one knee on the stone floor. It was a more comfortable position for him, allowing him to straighten his back and lift his head.

He still wore the uniform of an Irekaïn soldier. The uniform shirt was thin; threadbare in places. It was no wonder he'd been cold in the unheated cells. He still trembled a little, but less now, with the heat of the fires against his back. For a long moment he met Captain Deconniy's eyes directly, and then, as though it went against his nature, bowed his head. There was no fear in his face or manner.

"Your name?" Verè asked him quietly.

The man lifted his head again. "Quòn," he said.

Lhiyré said sharply, "Indeed?"

The man shrugged and turned his hands palm-up where they rested on the table. "It's the only name I have. If it does not content you, I would be glad to invent a better name for your pleasure. You would then be pleased by a lie, but that is your affair."

Lhiyré was clearly taken aback by this answer, and Verè leaned forward. "I would suggest a more careful courtesy would be wise for a man in your position."

The man bowed his head at once. "I ask your pardon, if I have been impolite," he said, without emphasis or expression. "I meant no offense."

"Quòn." Verè tasted the word on his tongue, glancing at Lhiyré.

"Burned," said Lhiyré, who was, naturally, an educated man. "Charred black. Burned to ash and char."

"Hmm." Verè raised his eyebrows at the man.

"I have gone by other names as well, but that one is as true as any."

Verè rested his arms on the oaken table and looked steadily at him for a long moment. Then he said, "Quòn, then. Quòn of Harivir. Who are you, exactly? How did you kill the sorcerer, if you are not a sorcerer yourself? *Why* did you? I've no interest in pulling your story from you piece by tiny piece. This is your chance—your last chance—to simply tell me. If I don't believe you, we can go on from there."

"An admirable strategy," the man agreed, so completely without expression that it seemed like deliberate mockery. Verè found his hands closing into fists, and opened them, taking a breath. Quòn, looking consideringly at him, added, "I beg your pardon, if I have been impolite."

"Just go on," Verè told him.

The man said in his cool unconcerned tone, "I intended to find and protect Kehera Raëhema from any enemy. The King of Harivir gave me this trust, as he believed that I was his man."

"Fooled him, did you?"

"For that time, I served the Fortunate Gods by serving Torrolay Elin Raëhema. Now I serve the Gods in seeking Kehera Elin Raëhema. I lost her in Suriytè, but I caught up to her on the road and assisted her to break free of her captors outside of Enchar. I was unable to follow her at that time, however, as Nomoris proved an . . . unusually capable enemy. I killed him, but unfortunately the Irekaïn Power raised him up again. Most disconcerting. Perhaps you were aware he was already dead? That the Irekaïn Power moved him and spoke with his voice?"

"He didn't seem dead there at the border. Until you killed him."

"He is certainly more dead, now," Quòn agreed with cool satisfaction.

"Entirely dead. Unfortunately, this is unlikely to prove more than a minor inconvenience to the Power of Irekay. Irekaìmaiäd has become far too strong, far too capable of investing itself in persons it should not be able to touch."

Verè said, sticking to the main point, "So you have killed Gheroïn Nomoris twice, and now he is truly dead."

"Indeed. But the first time, he took me by surprise." Quòn did not seem particularly embarrassed or ashamed to admit this. He simply said it, as though it were one unimportant fact among many. "He took me prisoner. Or Methmeir Irekaì did. Or Irekaìmaiäd, to speak more precisely, for the Power itself has become master of the tie and the man."

Lhiyré leaned forward. "Wait. The Power of Irekay has mastered the *king*? Is that what you'd have us believe?"

Quòn lifted an eyebrow. "I believe that is what I said, yes."

Verè looked at Lhiyré, who explained rapidly, "When a Great Power masters its tie and its line and the man who ought to hold it . . . It's dangerous when any Immanent Power breaks the bonds that hold it to its land and its people; sometimes it goes on to apotheosis. That's always dangerous, but a Great Power . . . something just like that is said to have led to the destruction of the southlands and the creation of the Wall of Winds."

"That is not quite correct," Quòn said calmly. "The Great Power became a God, it's true. A number of Immanences followed suit. Unfortunate Gods, of course, or they would not have done quite so much damage. The southlands were indeed destroyed by the ensuing . . . tumult. The Wall of Eternal Storms was then raised up by the Fortunate Gods to prevent the destruction from consuming all the north as well."

"Oh, this sounds splendid," Verè muttered, not quite under his breath. He didn't believe it. He didn't want to believe it. Except what this bastard said made sense of so much. The trouble in the north, in Emmer and Harivir . . . the sudden swift fall of Kosiran Immaör, perhaps all of Kosir . . . Gheroïn Nomoris, whom His Grace had struck down though Her Highness had said he was already dead; certainly Her Highness had declared Nomoris dead and hollow after that. He might not trust this prisoner, but surely Her Highness would not have been misled herself, nor misled His Grace.

The prisoner had paused for a moment inquiringly, but when no one asked him another question, merely went on matter-of-factly. "It took me some time to free myself, and by then the borders of Eäneté had been closed. It seemed appropriate to allow Nomoris himself to clear the way for me into Eäneté, as he had put me to such considerable trouble. That this gave me the opportunity to permanently disembody Nomoris was certainly an added benefit."

"He gave you trouble, did he? But not so very much, we gather, as you killed him. Or disembodied him. Because you are a servant of the Fortunate Gods and an enemy of Irekay."

Quòn inclined his head just a fraction. "Just so."

"Yet you are a friend to Her Highness."

"I surmised, from the opportunities that fell my way, that in serving Her Highness as she might require, I would also strike a blow against the Power of Irekay. I believe that is still true."

Verè shook his head. "Well, it's an entertaining tale, and certainly one that shows *you* in an unexpectedly heroic light." He didn't believe a word of it, though at the same time he wouldn't have laid a single base coin on a bet that it was false.

"I've told you the truth, Captain Deconniy. If it does not please you, tell me what tale would, and I will be glad—"

"To tell me what I wish to hear," Verè interrupted him. "I'm sure."

Quòn shrugged.

He was certainly very difficult to read. Verè ordered, "Look at the wall to your right. Look at it!"

The prisoner turned his head, examining the tools that lined that wall without expression.

"You're telling tales to frighten children. Is any of that the truth? I have severe doubts about that, I truly do. And I've the tools to be sure. Do you think you have the strength to withstand the kind of questioning I can bring to bear?"

Quòn turned his dark eyes back again to rest on the captain's face. "I sincerely doubt it," he answered without emphasis. "I've no intention of trying. I have told you the truth. If you wish greater detail on any part of it, simply say so. I'll be glad to go into as much detail as you require."

"I wouldn't believe that, either," Verè said, letting his voice lift with open scorn. He leaned forward aggressively, trying to frighten the man, wanting to see whether his tale might falter. "You're a servant of the Fortunate Gods? Of course you are! That's why Nomoris took you in the first place! Yet you got away from him, so you say. You attached yourself to his own command and he didn't *notice*? A sorcerer like that?"

Quòn shrugged as well as he could—not very well, bound as he was. "I'm a resourceful person. And the bond I bear to the Fortunate Gods, though deep, is quiet. It is truly unlike the tie to a Power."

"I'm not so sure you bear any tie at all. Shall we see whether the Fortunate Gods protect you?" Verè gestured to the soldiers. Stepping forward, they drew their knives and cut the prisoner's shirt off his body. The shreds of it settled to the table and the floor in several pieces.

The skin of Quòn's back shivered and tightened at the delicate touches of the knives, though the soldiers did not nick his skin. But his tone when he spoke was merely exasperated. "What would you believe? That your own Eänetén Power destroyed the Irekaïn soldiers but missed me by mere chance? I wished to disembody the aspect of the Power possessing Gheroïn Nomoris. I did so. Now I wish to find the Raëhema heir, who I believe will prove important in what is to come. I have no personal interest in who rules in Eäneté, nor by what means."

Verè stood up, walked forward, and leaned his hip against the table a few feet from the prisoner. He held out his hand, and one of the soldiers took an implement from the wall and handed it to him. It was one of the little whips, the one with tiny metal hooks set into its braided thongs, which were now coiled loosely to fit into the hand. It wouldn't have been his first choice, but he did not say so. He brought it forward to touch the prisoner's shoulder, gently, letting him feel the sharp bite of the hooks. "Does this frighten you?" he asked. "It should. There are heavier whips, but this is one of the cruelest. The scars it leaves will last all your life. Even if that should unexpectedly be long."

To the side, Lhiyré put a hand over his mouth and turned his face away. Neither Verè nor Quòn glanced at him.

"Of course it frightens me," the prisoner said calmly. "Whatever you want to hear from me, I will tell you. But in the end, if you will not accept the truth, you will find that you have been satisfied with a lie, and what benefit will that be to you, or to your duke?"

Verè shook the little whip out across the table. Its spines scraped across the polished table with a small, deadly sound. That would be work for some unfortunate servant, later, who would have to come down to this room and polish those scratches out of the wood.

"Have you leave from your duke to do this?" Quòn inquired, in a tone of academic curiosity, dark eyes fixed on the captain's face. "Should you not carry my tale to His Grace and permit him to decide whether he believes any part of it? I ask you to do so. I think you will find the Power of Eäneté recognizes my bond even if you do not."

"His Grace is not here," Verè told him. "If he were, this would be his duty, and his pleasure. But in his absence, I have all authority."

Quòn's eyes widened slightly. "If he is not here, where is he?" And, immediately answering his own question, "He has already gone through the pass into Harivir." And then, "No wonder Gheroïn Nomoris came so near destroying the Eänetén Power, if His Grace is not even here in Eäneté to support it. How very fortunate I was at hand to balk Irekaìmaiäd at the last. And Her Highness? Of course His Grace took her with him?"

Verè cursed inwardly. He had not meant to give so much away. He was thoroughly annoyed with himself. He snapped, "That the King of Harivir sent you, I certainly believe! You are an assassin, sent to murder His Grace and recover your princess."

"I came to give Her Highness what assistance I am able. I am not interested in your duke at all."

"Why you?"

Quòn shrugged. "I'm a helpful sort of person."

"Because you're a servant of the Fortunate Gods."

"Yes."

Verè and the prisoner looked at each other. Lhiyré watched them both in tense silence.

Not breaking his gaze, Verè flicked the little whip back and then sent it curling forward. It wrapped in a deadly line around Quòn's shoulder and across his back. He hardly knew how to handle any whip, much less this spined lash, and so flicked it back with a little more strength than he intended; the metal hooks tore savagely through the prisoner's skin and flesh, leaving deep and bloody tracks.

Quòn did not try to pretend that it did not hurt. He threw his head back, body recoiling as far as the manacles would allow, and cried out without inhibition. His short, hoarse scream echoed in the confines of the stone room. Lhiyré flinched, and even one of the soldiers hissed between his teeth.

Verè, coiling the whip back into his hand, laid the gathered bloody loops of it gently against Quòn's face to turn it back to his. "You're an assassin," he said levelly, "and you came to Eäneté to murder the duke."

Face white with pain, Quòn answered raggedly, "Yes. Of course. As you say."

"You can't believe that!" Lhiyré cried, almost as pale as the prisoner.

Verè tossed the whip down on the table. "If necessary, one can bring a man through all hope of deception, past all the lies, back to the truth. Is that not so?" he added sharply, speaking now to the prisoner.

Quòn, his breath still coming a little unevenly, said, "Yes."

"Yes. Of course, it helps if one is able to recognize the truth when one hears it, at the end."

The prisoner knelt, arms spread wide across the surface of the table, blood trickling down his back from the cuts of the whip. He said, "Why go to the trouble? You've already had the truth from me."

"Indeed." Verè paused.

RACHEL NEUMEIER | 369

"Send him to the duke," suggested Lhiyré.

Verè lifted an eyebrow at the prisoner.

Quòn bowed his head. "I would be glad to explain myself to your duke."

"What, shall I send His Grace a possible assassin? I've heard better notions." Verè turned to the soldiers. "Put him back in his cell. Give him a blanket and coal. And I want one of you where you can watch him at all times."

"Sir," said one of the soldiers, and bent over the manacles.

Quòn slumped back on his heels as his wrists were freed, and then stood up carefully, letting the soldiers take his arms without protest.

When he was gone, Verè said to Lhiyré, "I don't like him, or his story."

"But do you believe him?"

"I don't know. Maybe. I don't know." Frustrated, he ran a hand through his hair and shook his head. "I don't want to. Gods and Powers, disasters and miracles! I need to send a message to His Grace, but what to put in it, I confess I don't know." He drew a breath and let it out. "Is that true, what he said about the Gods and the Wall of Winds?"

"I don't . . . I was never a scholarly man, Captain Deconniy. Something of the kind happened, I believe."

"Something of the kind." Verè glanced toward the cells. "I promise you, I'll have the truth out of him eventually. And he knows it. Let him think about that for a while. I'll question him again in the morning and see whether he tells the same tale then." He walked toward the stairs.

The new seneschal, following him, winced slightly.

"You don't have to watch."

"I don't know that I have the nerve," Lhiyré admitted. He set his foot on the bottommost stair, cast a misgiving look over his shoulder back toward the table, and shuddered. "Poor man. I wouldn't be in his place tomorrow morning for any possible reward." He followed Verè up the stairs, closing the door behind them with open relief.

But in the morning, the cell was empty and the prisoner was gone. The guard set to watch the prisoner lay dead on the stones of the floor, stripped of clothing and weapons.

Very soon after that, Verè found out about the dead men at the mouth of the pass, and the heavy gates standing open.

It was the worst possible failure of duty he could imagine.

"I'd meant to send a man," he told Geran Lhiyré, trying to keep the grim fury and worse, the edge of terror, out of his tone. "But I don't see that I can send anyone else to carry *this* word to His Grace. I'm the one who saw Gheroïn Nomoris die the second time; I'm the one who spoke to the prisoner, and lost him, and let him through the pass. I'll have to go myself. I'll ride light, with two spare horses."

The new seneschal only nodded, but Verè's senior lieutenant objected. "His Grace left you in charge of the men here, sir."

Verè was acutely aware of this. Disobedience if he went, dereliction of duty if he stayed; the choice was plain enough. He said, "And I'm leaving you in charge, Lieutenant Tejef, under Lhiyré's authority. You'll get a promotion out of it, I expect, since I've no doubt you'll do a fine job. Two spare horses. See to it."

"He's not wrong, though," murmured Lhiyré once the lieutenant was out of earshot.

"I know," said Verè, rather through his teeth.

"His Grace won't like this tale—"

"*I know*," Verè said again. He hardly needed anyone to point this out to him. "I'll count on you to advise Tejef if anything comes up. You're both sensible men. You'll do fine."

"I wish Gereth were here," Lhiyré muttered.

Verè didn't answer. But he wished that too. Very much. Or better, that the seneschal was with His Grace, so that a man might count on his calming influence when he had an uncomfortable report to make.

But there was nothing to do but wait the few minutes necessary for the animals to be readied while he tried to find a way to change his mind about what he had to do. He already knew there was no way. He could hardly send Lhiyré. He was aware, to his shame, that he would have sent another man in his stead if it had been possible. But it was impossible. When the horses were brought up with their light-loaded saddlebags, he swung up onto the foremost gelding without a word and rode out of the yard without looking back.

20

*The weather was bad, mudslides and freezing rain had made an appall-*ing mess of the road, and the uncertainty of this whole winter was worse than either weather or road. All this exacerbated the tension between Riheir Coärin and the Wolf Duke.

Everything was hard for poor Riheir. Kehera knew it, and she did sympathize, she truly did, but she found herself impatient as well. Surely he understood that this was hard for her, too. It was hard for *everyone*.

She knew perfectly well that part of her impatience was just embar-rassment. Only this past spring she had accepted a courting poem from poor Riheir. And now the Eänetén duke had declared he would marry her and she . . . well, she had not refused. She had even more or less agreed. All right, to be fair, in the end she *had* agreed. Only events had flown ahead of them so that the actual wedding had been delayed once and then again. And yet they were all still acting as though they were allied. It seemed to Kehera that they might all perfectly well go on just as they were: as allies, with no need for the bonds forged by marriage. If they chose.

Though she couldn't help but be acutely aware of the tension between Riheir and Innisth. If she were married to either one of them, that situation, at least, would surely become easier. Only she didn't want to wed the Wolf Duke of Eäneté . . . or she thought she didn't want to, or at least she thought she *shouldn't* want to.

It was difficult to sort out her own knowledge and feelings from Raëhemaiëth's. Now that a deep tie had once again awoken in her, she had rediscovered how very challenging it could be to sort out what was hers from what was the Power's. And Raëhemaiëth wanted this alliance. Or the proposed marriage. Or something.

Kehera also had to admit that somehow, Raëhemaiëth aside, she kept finding her gaze wandering to the Wolf Duke. She liked to look at him; she couldn't deny it. She almost fancied she could see his Immanent Power surrounding him, like a shimmer of sunlight even in this dreadful weather. But even without the tie, she suspected he would make a compelling figure. Those yellow eyes. That spare, ascetic face. The cold manner beneath which hid such depths of heat and anger . . . He *was* compelling.

He could be cruel. She'd seen that herself. Yet she thought she understood now why he drew such devotion from his people. Because he gave that devotion back. You could see it once you learned how to look.

She found herself gazing at him again, at the lines of his shoulders and back where he rode ahead of her. When he rode ahead of her like this, she couldn't help but take the free chance to look at him as a gift.

She was at least sure now that she could never imagine marrying Riheir Coärin. She was fairly sure poor Riheir had guessed as much. This made her feel uneasy about everything he said and did, and that made her feel impatient. She knew it wasn't fair. But she couldn't help it.

And besides that, they were all tired. She and the Wolf Duke and the Eänetén force had entered Coär's precincts on the sixteenth day of the Iron Hinge Month and it was now the twentieth day, and Kehera felt none of them had yet had a chance to take a single free breath.

They should have come by now to the town of Viär, in whose precincts Meilin Gap lay, but first they had delayed so that Riheir could arrange for wagons and support from Coär and then the weather had turned cruel, icy rain spitting from a heavy sky. Harivin roads were generally good, but where the road lay through a low place, the stone sank into the mud. These low areas were a torment for horses, worse for men afoot, and especially brutal for narrow-wheeled wagons. This part of the road, outside both Coär's precincts and Viär's, was worse than any. When it was no one's duty to carry the stone necessary to maintain the road, the task tended to be neglected, and of course the problem was worse this year because nearly all the men had been called up by their lords to defend Harivir's northern border. The Wolf Duke had been freezingly polite to Riheir about the bad sections of the road, and of course Riheir had taken that poorly, especially since he knew very well he should have made sure someone saw to the road before winter set in.

This was the third time they'd had to halt the column and task the men with tearing down the nearest farmers' walls and hauling rock for the road. The walls were not that close to the road and the rain made the labor still more unpleasant, and if Kehera was any judge, the Wolf Duke was just about to stop being freezingly polite and become cuttingly acerbic instead. She was fairly certain that would not be helpful. Nudging her horse forward, she said soothingly, "Once we're past this low part, I think it's uphill all the rest of the way to Viär, so this shouldn't happen again."

"It shouldn't have happened at all," snapped the Wolf Duke.

"I know," Kehera said even more soothingly, before Riheir could retort with unwise heat. "But of course no one could guess your king would be so insanely ambitious as to make sorcerers and then find a way to feed other Immanences to the Power of Irekay and then start attacking everybody in the world. If you had realized, Your Grace, I'm sure you would have sent warning and so we would all have been better prepared."

She was quite certain it would never have occurred to him to warn Riheir or anyone else, even if he'd known all about his king's plans from the beginning. Since it was obviously true that they'd all be a little more secure now if he had realized sooner what the King of Pohorir was about and passed warning across the mountains, her comment held enough justice to bring what might have been an incipient tirade to a dead halt.

Kehera added, turning to Riheir, "Of course, obviously once the trouble with Emmer began—"

The Wolf Duke gave a sudden hard gasp, and Kehera forgot what she'd been about to say. She reined her horse a step closer to his, reaching to touch his hand. "Your Grace!" she said sharply. "Are you well?"

He plainly wasn't. A couple of his soldiers were near at hand, but they obviously had no idea what to do. But Tageiny jerked his horse's head around, came up on the duke's other side, and seized his arm, keeping him upright in the saddle. As far as she could tell, the duke did not notice either of them.

"Eänetaìsarè has risen," she told Riheir. She couldn't exactly feel it, not in her own heart and body, but she could feel Raëhemaiëth's response to the other Power's rising. Probably she didn't need to tell Riheir; probably he felt it, too. She said, striving to be sensible and calm, "The Pohorin king has moved against Eäneté. I'm sure that's what's happened. We expected this." She didn't allow herself to worry. Of course Eänetaìsarè would throw back any attack, even from the Great Power of Irekay. Of course it would. Shaking off all possible doubts, she said firmly, "Get canvas up. Don't *argue,* Riheir. Canvas, fire, hot spiced wine, in that order. How long is it till dark? A few hours?"

In ten days they would reach the dark turn of winter. Kehera, like everyone else, hated the uncounted days of the Iron Hinge. Sensible folk avoided setting hand to any new endeavor during the Iron Hinge, for good rarely seemed to come of any such effort. This winter . . . this winter, the potential for misfortune seemed much greater than during a normal year.

But given that dusk would come terribly early, it seemed foolish beyond reason, now that the duke would be incapacitated for some unknown length of time, to press forward through this terrible stretch of road. She said firmly, "We will make camp now. Send for Caèr Reiöft. I'm sure he's back with the first wagons." Which carried the duke's personal belongings and tent, and was therefore Reiöft's proper charge. She paused and then added sharply, "Well?"

The nearby Eänetén soldiers looked from her to their duke and moved to obey. They moved tentatively at first, but no one could dislike the idea of canvas and fire. Riheir glowered at her, but he nodded abruptly, and his men, too, moved with fair alacrity to carry out these orders.

"I'll help you with him," he said to Kehera, moving to dismount.

"I have him," Kehera said, more tersely than she had intended. "If you would see to everything else, Riheir, please?"

Riheir's glower deepened, but he gave her a curt nod and turned away.

"That Harivin duke wouldn't have—" Luad, at Kehera's side, gave a tiny, illustrative twitch of his hand.

"He couldn't be such a fool," Kehera told him. "We all depend on Eänetaìsarè." But she added, "Even so, please go find Captain Etar and explain what's happened." And if the senior Eänetén captain happened to want to assign a guard to his duke, here by this Harivin road where the land didn't quite belong to any specific Immanent, she wouldn't call him unwise.

A couple of hours later, Kehera sat, wrapped in furs and much more comfortable, just within the door of her own private tent, watching the rain slant down across the quiet camp.

Men were still working on the road, but the job wasn't so brutal now that they could take their time with it. They worked in teams, with hot soup and spiced wine waiting for anyone who came in out of the cold.

Kehera's tent was set at the western edge of the camp, on a small hill where the ground was not quite as wet, near the duke's own tent. Her White Falcon standard stood before her tent; the duke's people were punctilious about such matters even in this spitting drizzle that made all standards hang equally limp and unreadable. Her women were with her: timid Eöté and an older Harivin woman named Morain Lochan, whom Riheir had found for her, a placid woman who never seemed disturbed by anything and who was already proving a great comfort.

In a way, Kehera would have liked to sit with the Eänetén duke and just . . . make sure he was all right. She had been at his side for a while. As far as she could tell, Raëhemaiëth had never risen, which she assumed meant that Eänetaìsarè had not needed help defending its precincts. But she had wanted to stay close by the Eänetén duke, in case either of the Immanent Powers changed its mind. But the attack—if that was what it had been—hadn't lasted so terribly long. When the Wolf Duke had drawn a shuddering breath and blinked, human awareness coming back into his yellow eyes, she had nodded to Caèr Reiöft and withdrawn, for decency's sake, because she and Innisth terè Maèr Eänetaì were not, after all, married.

It seemed a trivial consideration, under the circumstances. But she was fairly certain no one of Harivir would agree.

Tageiny, leaning against one of the heavy poles that framed her tent, commented idly, "You know, this would be a pretty good time to get you away. If you wanted. Nobody's watching. They're all too busy cursing the mud or hiding from the rain or staring at His Grace's tent, and the horse lines are right over there. Luad and I could get you straight north to your father's door, if you wanted to give that order."

Kehera gave him a look. "And let Methmeir Irekaì break through Meilin Gap?"

"Ah, well," muttered Tageiny. "Yeah, that's a point."

"I appreciate the suggestion. But it hardly seems practical."

"*Hst!*" Luad murmured warningly. "Here comes himself."

Kehera frowned, not at all sure that the duke ought to be out in this weather.

But in a moment, he stepped under the portico of her tent and paused, ignoring Tageiny and Luad but studying her with close attention. He seemed untroubled by the cold, for his hood was back, and he wore no cloak. His austere manner showed her nothing besides a mild exasperation. Kehera suspected he was actually worried or tired. She studied him, but he *seemed* well enough. Probably.

But he surely shouldn't be out in the cold. She said firmly, not really a question, "Your Grace, I'm sure you would like to come in out of the weather."

The duke inclined his head in courtesy, and a little more to avoid bashing his head on the frame of her tent. "Your Highness." He stamped mud off his boots and came in, folding his legs to settle among the cushions Kehera indicated. He said without preamble, "So the Winter Dragon has tried Eäneté. As we expected. And broken its teeth for its trouble. Did you feel Eänetaìsarè rise?"

"Not really. Not exactly. I knew it had. Raëhemaiëth didn't help you. I would have felt that. It seemed more to . . . draw inward."

"It is hiding from the Irekaïn Power—but it is hiding in ambush, not in fear."

"Yes," agreed Kehera, surprised, but feeling as soon as he'd said it that this was true. "Yes, I think you're right."

"Your Raëhemaiëth is more aware of itself and its purposes than most Immanences, I believe. That's something else you've given it, I presume—you and your father and all those of the Elin line. An awareness of itself, and subtlety, and a sensible caution."

He sounded coolly approving, but Kehera didn't know quite how to answer this. She thought his Immanent gave Raëh something, too, something it otherwise lacked. Ferocity, perhaps. She said tentatively, "So your borders held secure and Eäneté is safe."

"Eänetaìsarè has held," murmured the duke. He met her eyes. His own seemed filled with fire. Kehera could feel it in him, burning beneath his skin. She could not look away. He said softly, "Eäneté is safe. But Methmeir Irekaì will strike soon at Meilin Gap. And we are here, even yet a day's march or more distant. Too far."

"Don't blame Riheir for halting here. That was my decision."

"Your decision was correct," the duke conceded. "However, the halt would have been unnecessary had the road been kept in proper repair."

Kehera sighed ostentatiously. "Please don't start that again. The truth is, I would have ordered camp made even if the road were dry, smooth, clean, and shining under a clear sky. Don't tell me you could have been carried in a litter. What if a litter-bearer had tripped and dropped you and poor Eänetaìsarè had been distracted?"

"In that event, I am certain your Raëhemaiëth would have put forth its strength. But as well it was able to remain hidden and subtle." The duke hesitated. "And you . . ."

Kehera tilted her head, puzzled. "Your Grace?"

"I merely wished to assure myself that you remain well, Your Highness, and that Raëhemaiëth remains clear in your awareness."

"Of course, Your Grace." Kehera thought that was a remarkably silly reason to leave the shelter of his perfectly good tent and venture through the rain to hers, but she said only, "As you see, we are all quite well here. Now that we have been reassured as to your own continuing good health and the security of Eäneté."

"Indeed." The Wolf Duke rose, just a little stiffly. He hesitated a moment longer, then gave her a slight nod and withdrew.

"Well," Kehera said after a moment, a little blankly. "What was that about?"

"I can't imagine," Tageiny drawled, shifting so that he could keep an eye on the quiet camp.

Kehera stared at him.

"He likes you and wants to be sure you're safe and values your good opinion," said Morain Lochan, nudging her way past Eöté and glancing out at the rain without favor. "I expect they've more soup ready, and biscuit if we're lucky, and maybe some of that spiced wine. Here, you, boy, you can help me carry the trays so's I don't have to make more than one trip."

At Tageiny's stern look, Luad smothered what was plainly going to be an outraged refusal. "Right," he said meekly, and followed the woman out into the rain without further complaint.

"He likes me?" Kehera said blankly.

"You're not afraid of him," Tageiny said kindly. "I doubt he's met all that many girls who aren't scared of him." He met her mute stare and shrugged. "Or that's how I figure it. You should talk to that man of his—Reiöft."

"Maybe I will," Kehera said, still feeling rather startled, and stupid with it. He liked her? She admired him. . . . Would she go so far as to say she *liked* him? Surely not. Only now she was not quite so certain. She looked after the duke, as though the sight of him would help clarify her feelings, but he was already gone from view.

An hour after full dark, Caèr Reiöft came to her tent door, with an ironic tilt to his head that almost disguised his genuine worry. "I do regret waking you," he told Kehera, after Morain Lochan had wrapped her in a robe. Reiöft's tone was ironic too: light and amused. But she heard real concern behind the amusement. He went on in that same light tone. "I'm afraid your friend Coärin may have gotten himself into a bit of trouble, arguing about mud and roads and the hour of departure in the morning and the order of the march and who knows what else. His Grace's temper is pushing him hard just now, you know, and I don't believe Coärin quite realizes what kind of trouble he's likely to get into."

Kehera was not surprised that the two men had finally reached a crisis. She knew exactly who would win any contest too—and she wasn't sure Riheir could stand to lose. She did not even like to take time to dress, and was grateful for Eöté's swift assistance.

Before she left her tent, acting on a half-thought impulse, she caught up her box of tiahel rods and took it with her.

"You think those Coäran soldiers will let you by?" Tageiny asked, falling into stride beside her as she hurried out into the cold. "Or those Eänetén soldiers are more of a concern, I suppose."

"They'll all let me by," Kehera assured him.

"Especially if you threaten to stand outside His Grace's tent and scream," murmured Caèr Reiöft

"Exactly."

Tageiny's eyes crinkled with amusement. "Ah, well, yes, that should do it."

"I'll go in alone," Kehera told both men. "You can wait, though. In case I call you. All right?"

"If you call anyone, I trust it will be me," Reiöft said firmly. "He ordered me not to come until he called for me, but if *you* call for me, I expect that will do."

Kehera gave the man a sideways look. She liked Caèr Reiöft. She trusted him, and she was glad he was with them, and she was grateful he knew Innisth terè Maèr Eänetaì so much better than she did, and she was not the *least bit* jealous of him. Or she thought not. Except that every now and then she was not quite sure.

None of the various guards tried to stop her from entering the duke's tent. And the moment she did, Kehera knew Reiöft had also been right to ask her to intervene and that she had been right to hurry.

The duke reclined on one long bolster, surrounded by luxurious draperies and cushions and lanterns swaying from ornate wrought-iron stands. He looked entirely relaxed. Riheir Coärin, in contrast, down on one knee a few steps away from him, looked anything but *relaxed*. She could see the taut fury in the line of Riheir's back from the doorway. And something else that she suspected was not exactly fury.

The Wolf Duke looked at Kehera without expression. Riheir looked at her with humiliated anger and something else, a kind of bewildered confusion that Kehera thought she understood all too well. She could feel Eänetaìsarè in the air, an inaudible deep hum that prickled across her skin, not unpleasantly.

Kehera flicked the catch on the tiahel case and scattered the rods and dice across the floor of the tent between herself and the duke.

"Those," she said distinctly, "are game pieces. This, on the other hand, is a man."

The duke lifted his gaze from the scattered tiahel rods to her face. His yellow wolf eyes held very little she recognized. "Perhaps, to me, there is no difference."

His tone was faintly mocking and faintly amused. But behind the mildness was a deeper, more dangerous emotion. She was sure it wasn't entirely his. So she said, trying to sound impatient rather than frightened, "Nonsense. You? As though I would believe that. I know: Eänetaìsarè is very strong now, and you're very tired. But you can rule it." She walked forward and sat down, uninvited, on a large cushion facing the duke. "Riheir, go away."

Riheir Coärin looked at the duke, clearly both longing to get away and not daring to move.

The duke said gently, "Stay. Her Highness will retire."

"*No*," Kehera said with absolute finality. Of course, she didn't have the authority or the power to insist. What she meant was, *You had better think about whether this is really something you want to do.*

The duke lowered heavy lids over his eyes, masking his thoughts.

"This is your man now, as he agreed and you accepted," Kehera told him. She waited a moment for that reminder to sink in. Then she said, "He argued with you, I know. But he is allowed to argue with you. He didn't defy you." She hoped this was true, but wouldn't add weakly, *Did he?* She said instead, "What you command, he will do. Isn't that right, Riheir?"

Riheir Coärin gave her a furious look. But whatever he felt of Eänetaìsarè and the Eänetén duke's strength, it must have impressed him, because he also muttered through his teeth, "Yes. My lord." He bowed his head. Stiffly, but he bowed it.

"You see," said Kehera. "He has yielded everything. He's not happy about it, but who can blame him for that? You can afford to be generous. Are you going to try to tell me you don't rule Eänetaìsarè?"

Profound anger glinted for a brief moment in the wolf eyes. Then, as the duke mastered it, the anger was replaced by reluctant appreciation. One corner of his mouth quirked upward in faint, self-mocking humor. Kehera couldn't help but smile back. She thought she might truly like him when he was like this. At least a little.

He said after a moment, "You may go, Coärin. At dawn, we will continue north. I wish to reach Meilin Gap before noon. See to it."

Riheir Coärin got to his feet. Jaw set, he jerked a short nod, not quite a bow, to the duke and then to Kehera, turned on his heel, and stalked out.

There was a pause. Then the duke said to Kehera, "He is recalcitrant."

Kehera gave him a look. "Riheir has been my friend since I was a girl."

"When you were a girl, I'm certain he was your friend," the Eänetén duke agreed, a thread of humor coming into his voice.

Kehera sighed, shook her head, and moved to sit next to him—then hesitated and perched instead a little farther away than she had planned. "I imagine poor Riheir is very confused right now. Eänetaìsarè is not very . . . subtle." *She* was not confused, or she thought not. But that suddenly made her more uncomfortable, not less. She was intensely aware of the cold outside, and the warmth of the tent, and particularly the warmth that seemed to radiate from the duke. She felt that she might have flushed. But she did not allow herself to look away.

For one moment the duke actually looked embarrassed. "Yes," he said, a little stiffly, glancing away from her. "It is possible that I may owe you a debt of gratitude, in fact, for this particular interruption. Very well. I thank you. However, you may go back to bed. I will send for Caèr."

Kehera wasn't certain whether she was relieved or offended. But she said, following an impulse she only half understood, "I couldn't possible sleep now. I'm far too wide-awake. Would you mind keeping me company for a while?"

His gaze, curious and ironic but no longer angry, rested on her face. "If you like." He glanced at the scattered rods and dice. "Perhaps a game of tiahel?"

"I think I'd like that." That would be better. A game of tiahel, such as she had played with her brother. She could do that. She moved to gather up the game pieces, but the duke forestalled her with a lift of his hand.

"There is no need for you to trouble yourself," he said, expression unreadable. "Please stay there." He knelt himself, down on the floor of the tent, head bent as he searched through the rugs for the dispersed tiahel pieces.

There were thirteen rods in a tiahel set. Thirteen rods and four dice. In Kehera's set, two of the dice were agate and two jasper; and six of the rods were blackwood and six blond maple. The King Rod was polished oak, the signs of the Four Kingdoms carved in careful relief on its faces and then painted. It had fallen with Harivir's Red Falcon uppermost. Kehera picked it up herself and turned it slowly over in her hand, thinking about signs and symbols, about divination and the unknowable future, about winter dragons and winter storms. She turned the rod over and traced Pohorir's double-headed Dragon with the tip of her finger. "I suppose we'll need five-sided King Rods for tiahel, after this," she said, not looking up. "If you succeed in your aim, I suppose there will be a fifth kingdom between Harivir and Pohorir, with the Gray Wolf as its sign and seal."

"Or the White Falcon, perhaps."

Kehera looked up quickly. The Eänetén duke met her eyes, his hands filled with tiahel pieces. There was an edge of mockery in his tone. But there was something else in his voice as well. Something harder to read and more disturbing. This time she was certain she blushed.

The duke did not seem to notice. Rising, he resumed his seat, laying out the rods in neat order, setting the dice in their shorter row above the rods. The air of predatory relaxation had passed off, but she could not read his expression. Or his mood. She said after a moment, "You had that banner made for me. That was your idea, not mine."

"Banners are like game pieces. Save that they are carried by living men onto bloody fields. Kings and dukes cast them out and gather them up again. As I have done, and shall do; yours among the rest." He met her gaze again, his golden eyes filled with fire in the lantern light. He said, with a dangerous curl of his lip, "But I shall see to it that yours does not fall." Then he smiled and added smoothly, "Nor mine, to be sure."

Kehera was silent. She was very aware of the Wolf Duke; of his physical presence and of the leashed passion he held back. Part of that was his Immanent, but she knew part of it was his own. The chain with which he bound back Eänetaìsarè . . . that was all him: a hard-held discipline she had to respect. Despite moments like this one tonight. It troubled her, though she knew, or thought she knew, where that crack in his discipline had come from, and why. Methmeir Irekaì was hardly likely to leave off his efforts to conquer all the northlands. If the duke found himself hard-pressed now, how much worse would that get?

The duke's fingers as he arranged the tiahel pieces were long and elegant. Indeed, he was long and elegant throughout. She stole a glance at him. He did not have the open, friendly good looks Kehera had always appreciated. His features were severe, his manner restrained, his temper biting. But she had to acknowledge that he was growing on her. Especially as now, when she glimpsed the vulnerability underlying his . . . not quite limitless strength.

He was twenty-seven, she knew. Not so much older than she was. He seemed far older. Of course, he had held the ruling tie to the Eänetén Power for seven years. After killing his own father to take it. And then holding Eäneté safe against his own king. Little of that was easy for a Harivin to imagine.

He liked her. He valued her good opinion. Morain Lochan had said so, and Tageiny had agreed. She was still uncertain that she could say she *liked* him. But she thought it was at least possible she would learn to.

He had let her send Riheir Coärin away. And now he was sitting there patiently, the blackwood tiahel rods on his side of the table, waiting for her to pick up the six made of maple and roll the smoky agate dice.

❋ ❋ ❋

Kehera did not go back to her own tent until almost the hinge of the night, when she judged the Eänetén Power finally settled enough that they both might rest. She felt, when she stepped out into the cold and caught the eye of Caèr Reiöft, rather like one soldier handing an important duty over to another, and while she was sorry that Caèr—and Tageiny, whom she had all but forgotten—had had to wait so long in the weather, she also felt that she had done well.

They reached Meilin Gap an hour after noon on the twenty-first day of the Iron Hinge Month.

To the right of the road, the mountains marched away to north and south, towering peaks of stone and snow and tangled frozen forest as far as any eye could see. Meilin Gap should not have been readily apparent in this season. But snow and ice had plainly exploded outward from the gap, the debris spreading out like the devastation that followed an avalanche, a wide fan of destruction across the field below the mountains, where even now men and Powers strove.

Kehera knew very little of battle, and what little she knew seemed to translate poorly to an actual field where real soldiers and lords and Immanences fought for dominance. She saw Riheir Coärin's White Stag banner on the field below—yes, of course he'd said he had sent men, and obviously that had been a very good idea. And there was the graceful Black Swan of Viär—that was good; all this land lay within the precincts of Viär. This was a small province, much smaller than Coär, its Immanent having emerged from its rough mountains only four generations ago. The land here, subject to nearly the worst fury of the obsidian storms of midwinter, could not be settled until it possessed an Immanent Power that could provide protection. Yet the lord of Viär had done well since his great-great-grandmother had taken the tie of the young Immanent Power. Kehera didn't know the current lord, Toren Viärin, very well. But she knew her father had always liked him and approved of the stamp his line was gradually putting on Viär's small Immanent. She had felt Raëhemaiëth moving subtly all day; it was supporting Viär, she guessed now, though quietly.

But a lot more of the men down on that field seemed to be following a different banner. The long snaky form of the Irekaïn Winter Dragon whipped in the wind, double-headed and monstrous, and from what she could see, it had all but won the field. She said in a low voice, "There are so many."

Tageiny, setting a reassuring hand on her arm, said calmly, "Not so many more than we have, really, and they're not set up to meet a force coming against their flank."

Kehera glanced at him, then looked distractedly at the Eänetén soldiers, who were leaving the road and raising up the Wolf banners and the White Stag of Coär to show they came as Harivin allies. They looked orderly and tough and there were certainly a lot of them, but it all seemed so agonizingly *slow*. The duke himself had drawn off a little way, with Riheir Coärin and a handful of officers and soldiers, toward a slope that offered a good view of the struggle below. She couldn't see anything like fear in his posture. Nor in Riheir's. But then, she wouldn't. It was their duty to look fearless and commanding. That was her duty, too, of course, so she tried not to sound nervous as she asked, "Won't the Pohorins have plenty of time to get themselves set any way they want?"

"Well, yeah," Tageiny allowed. "Only if they try to form up to meet His Grace's wolf soldiers properly, those Black Swan soldiers down there will take 'em in the rear. No, they've got to face both ways at once and that'll mean they've got to pull back toward the mountains, and pretty quick, too, or risk being overwhelmed. We've a good chance of taking that field, I should say, and a stroke of good fortune we weren't an hour later."

"Oh," said Kehera in a small voice, wishing she'd studied tactics rather than embroidery while she'd had the chance. She wondered whether Tageiny was just trying to reassure her, or if he honestly knew.

"Of course, the Irekaïn Power did blow up half the face of that mountain over yonder," the big man added, not quite so confidently.

"So I won't say His Grace necessarily has it all his way just now, either."

This time it was Kehera's turn to reassure him. "We have our ties, too. Remember that just yesterday, in Eäneté, His Grace's Immanent defeated Methmeir Irekaï's."

"Well, that's so," Tageiny began, and then leaned forward sharply. "Now, what's this?"

"Oh!" Kehera was surprised, though perhaps she shouldn't have been. "That's Toren Viärin, but I wouldn't have thought he'd come himself. Of course he can't actually join the battle, so perhaps it makes sense." Toren Viärin's heir was just a little boy, so it would be a disaster if Toren fell. A child was not likely to hold Viärinéseir, especially not with the Irekaïn Power ready, she was sure, to interfere. So she could see why Lord Toren would leave his vantage point above the field and ride to confer with Riheir Coärin and the Eänetén duke. She kneed her horse in that direction, ready to play her role as peacemaker and cornerstone of the alliance.

Toren Viärin didn't even glance at Riheir, and he rode right past the wolf soldiers, who fell back at the duke's gesture. He did spare a glance and a curt nod for Kehera as she arrived, obviously recognizing her. But he swung down off his horse and strode toward the duke without a word to any of them, moving with long, angry strides and a total disregard for propriety. He was an older man, older than Kehera remembered from his occasional visits to Raëh; his bony face was grimly humorless and not at all handsome. But she knew he must be passionately devoted to his land and his people, because all the Viärin line was like that; that would have aged him too.

Now Toren Viärin stripped off his gloves without breaking stride and flung his mud-spattered cloak to the nearest soldier, who caught it, looking startled and impressed.

Innisth dismounted unhurriedly to face Lord Toren, saying absolutely nothing, neither of welcome for the other man nor censure for the manner of his arrival.

Lord Toren said fiercely, with no preliminary greeting or

acknowledgment, "Viärinéseir can't hold that bastard king of yours. It can't hold. Fortunate Gods! That bastard Irekaì blew through Meilin Gap like a stroll on a summer day, and where were *you*? Yesterday would have been more timely, or better yet the day before!"

"I know," said the duke. "I am here now."

"And for all any of us know, too late!" Despite his obvious fury, Lord Toren took two steps forward and dropped to one knee, holding out his hands to the Wolf Duke. "Force the bond, then," he snapped. "Viärinéseir *will* yield, and your Power had best be strong enough to hold for both of us." He sounded not merely determined, but fiercely impatient.

Kehera stared in amazement—everyone was staring, except the Eänetén duke, who simply took the other man's hands in a firm grip, met his eyes, and called up his Power.

And the Eänetén Power rolled forward. Kehera almost saw Eänetaìsarè rise around the Power of Viär and snap its jaws closed like a wolf on a swan.

Lord Toren gasped, a small, pained breath, and the Power of Viär rose in turn, but immediately yielded. Kehera perceived it through Raëhemaiëth. She saw the Immanent of Viär as a bright sweeping Power, like a cool mountain spring and feathers ruffling in the wind and sunlight on a breeze-blown lake, but harder underneath, as the stone of the mountains lies below woodlands and fields. It was strong, for a lesser Power, but it yielded and allowed Eänetaìsarè to force a bond upon it.

Then Raëhemaiëth, that had held a bond to Viärinéseir since almost the founding of Viär, gave it up. It hurt, an odd sharp pain that Kehera didn't really feel. She gasped and flinched, but for her it was over almost at once; Raëhemaiëth had not fought Eänetaìsarè at all. And the bond the Eänetén Power took was a strange one, not anything Kehera had ever seen or quite imagined. It was as though the bond forced upon Viärinéseir was more or less folded through Eänetaìsarè, so that the Wolf Duke himself could hold both ties at once. It was like the ruling tie a king might hold to a lesser Power, but . . . different. Kehera wished again, as she kept doing, that Tiro were here. Her brother knew about Immanences and their bonds. More than she did, at least.

Toren Viärin still knelt on one knee, now with his head bowed against his fist. Whether he had chosen this or not, the change in the ruling tie had plainly not been easy for him. Innisth stood gripping the other man's shoulder, one of the few sympathetic gestures she had ever seen him offer to anyone. He said, "I cannot grant you surcease. This battle must still be won." There was no gentleness in his tone, but when he offered a hand to help the Lord Toren rise, Toren took it.

"So long as we *win*, it will have been worth everything," Lord Toren said, and added grimly, "My lord." He was not quite swaying where he stood, but Kehera thought that was an effort of will. He started to turn back to his horse, and *did* sway, but the duke caught his arm and steadied him. Lord Toren gave him a curt nod, closed a hand on his horse's bridle and stopped. "Kehera Elin," he said to her. "I'd word of you and what you'd done, letting the Wolf into Harivir. Your father sent word to everyone."

Kehera hardly knew how to answer this. She said after a second, "Lord Toren, you've done well and generously, and if we carry the day here, you will be due all our gratitude."

Lord Toren snorted. "I was desperate, and Gods grant I won't regret it!" He looked her over quickly, then nodded, though Kehera wasn't sure what he thought, or about what, exactly. But he said, kindly enough for all his impatience, "Hope of spring in the dark of the winter, that's what you've brought to Viär. Two days ago I wouldn't have said so. But I say so now."

"Thank you," said Kehera, which was all she could manage.

Lord Toren swung up onto his horse, kneed it around, and looked over his shoulder at the Wolf Duke. "I'll see to my people," he said sharply. "Only you see to yours, my lord!" He reined away, back down the slope toward the battle and his waiting officers.

"A good man," the Eänetén duke said calmly. "In later days, I think we will be most comfortable with a hundred miles or more between us." He glanced down toward the battle. "Let us see," he murmured to Riheir, "if together we may drive the Winter Dragon back through Meilin Gap." He spared Kehera a brief nod and took the rein of his tall black mare from the man who held her.

Tageiny and Luad set up Kehera's tent on the high slopes above the field of battle, so that she might be out of the wind and yet witness all that passed. It felt very strange to be at once so separate from the battle and yet feel so intimately connected to events below.

The duke was distant now, but easy enough to pick out, black cloaked on his black mare, always keeping back out of the battle, on the higher slopes that gave him a view of the field below. Kehera thought she could see the fire that lay underneath all that darkness, like the fire that lay buried beneath the mountains of Eäneté.

Raëhemaiëth was with her; she felt it. But she felt also that most of its attention was elsewhere. With her father, she knew. She felt that some other battle was taking place to the north. But here, the Immanences of Viär and Coär and Eäneté were slowly pushing Methmeir Irekaï's soldiers and his Power back through Meilin Gap.

"Getting a little close, here," Tageiny commented, keeping a wary eye on the shifting battle. "They keep coming this way and pretty soon we'll be in bowshot."

"Surely they won't come all the way up here," Kehera protested.

"Well, maybe not quite," the big man allowed. "No, that little knot of wolf soldiers is probably going to get—yeah, there, that's better. But if I tell you to get back, listen; there may not be time to dally."

"Of course, Tag," Kehera said in mock surprise. "You know perfectly well I always do exactly what you say."

Luad laughed outright.

Kehera was glad that to them the battle below seemed to make sense. To her, nothing about it made any sense at all. But Tageiny said, "It's going well. Look, do you see? That Swan officer is taking his company around their flank and he's going to get all the way around it, too, if the Irekaïn soldiers don't move their tails. Right, there they go. See that, boy?"

Luad, peering interestedly down the slope, said, "Yeah, Tag. We've got them cut off around to the north. Right? They can't get away into Harivir, no matter which way they break. Only way they can go is back through the gap." He added after a moment, "Not that it looks to me like they're trying too hard to get away."

"But they should be," Tageiny said. "Fortunate Gods, what are they thinking? It's like they don't think they can die. Yet their Power can't possibly take up their dead, not here. I mean not even the local Immanent's taking up its own dead from that field. Look, you can see the dead are staying where they fall."

Once he had pointed this out, Kehera saw it was true. It did seem odd. And a little disturbing.

The Wolf Duke had now taken a place on a slope quite near the field of battle. As Kehera watched, he brought his mare around and spoke to the men who surrounded him, and riders went out from his position to carry his commands through the battle.

"Fortunate Gods!" muttered Tageiny, "Does he think he's invisible? We're not the only ones as have a good view of him up there, and he's not even carrying a shield."

Kehera started to ask what he was worried about, and then saw for herself as a sudden flight of long black arrows rose out of the Pohorin army. She caught her breath.

Below her, the duke reined his mare about again, but not to flee the descending arrows, which he did not appear to notice. As they arced down out of the air, they scattered, their smooth paths broken, and not one even struck the hill that he occupied.

"What the fuck?" Luad exclaimed, and then quickly apologized, as Tageiny glared at him, "Sorry, sorry, m'lady."

"Eänetaìsarè looks after him," Kehera said, relieved, trying to sound like she had expected that.

"*Now* they're trying to retreat," Tageiny said, with great satisfaction. "Figured out they can't break his Immanent, I guess."

"Yeah," said Luad, pointing. "But what about them there? They don't look like they've given up."

He was indicating a small group of archers, a group that stood high up on the slope of the mountain, just below the gap, and sent flight after flight of black arrows raining down on the hill where the duke overlooked the battle. He never even lifted his head to track their course, and they always skidded aside on the air and fell harmlessly to the ground, but Kehera leaned forward anxiously. "He has a tie," she said. "One of those men. Look. That one who doesn't have a bow. He carries a tie. Can you see it?"

Tageiny jerked his head *No*. But he said disgustedly, "Yeah, of course he does."

"Eänetaìsarè is blocking him. But he's strong. He's—where he stands, that *is* Irekay, I think. He's anchoring his Power into this land that should belong to Viär and Harivir." She looked anxiously back up at the hilltop where the duke sat his black mare and surveyed the battle.

And so she was watching when the winter dragon came floating down from the eastern mountains, riding the winds down from the teeth of the high peaks. It looked like nothing real, like nothing that had ever been real. Its long body divided into five coiling necks and five slender heads; its breath was killing frost and its many-tongued voice held all the bitter violence of winter storms.

They came down from the heights during the hinge of winter, these dragons, and men penned up their cattle and kept their children indoors. In the woodlands natural creatures sheltered in dens and beneath thick stands of firs, and the world waited for the dark days to pass. But dragons did not come ten days early, and they did not come into the precincts of Immanent Powers. And yet this one was here.

The dragon glittered like glass or ice or winter itself. It was the color of the terrible winds from which it had been born, translucent black streaked with white and silver and carnelian. One could see right through its wings, but the sky on the other side was dark and the light that struck though those wings turned a strange nacreous silver. Where its shadow fell, the very air tasted of darkness and storms and despair.

Kehera could not keep from looking to the Eänetén duke as though he could stop even this, though she knew it must be impossible.

But the Eänetén duke dropped his reins and lifted his hands, and Eänetaìsarè rose through him. Fire bloomed. . . . For that first instant, Kehera thought it was real fire. Then she knew it was Eänetaìsarè, rising like fire. Like a storm of fire that might crack the very stone beneath his feet and pour from the earth.

The dragon of wind turned in a slow drifting arc and soared away, back over the high mountains. The shadow from its wings shredded into cold gusts of wind and a spatter of freezing rain, and the light fell naturally across the woods and the fields and across the men who had paused in their struggle to stare upward in amazement and terror.

Then, while Innisth terè Maèr Eänetaì still gazed upward after the dragon, a single narrow black arrow sang down out of the air toward him. This one was not deflected by any invisible force. It dropped straight and clean, and struck him in the chest, with an impact that Kehera almost thought she could hear, almost thought she could feel in her own body. Maybe she could. Maybe Raëhemaiëth felt it for her.

Innisth crumpled slowly from his horse. The officers and aides about him simply stared, shocked, as he fell. Not one made a move to catch him, and he hit the ground, it seemed to Kehera, watching in horror, with terrible force.

She found herself on her own horse with no memory of how she had gotten up on it. But it seemed to her that her body, acting independently of her mind, had had an excellent idea. The horse had been left saddled and ready, and she tore its tether free and turned its head up the hill.

Tageiny threw himself in front of her, grabbing for her reins, and she leaned forward and struck him across the face with all her strength. He fell back, undoubtedly more shocked than hurt, and she kicked her horse forward. Behind her, she was narrowly aware of the big man cursing roundly and hurling himself onto one of the other horses, and Luad scrambling after him for the third.

She did not wait. She whipped the reins across the neck of the horse and sent it racing across the slope at a pace that was just barely controlled. It seemed to her that it took a very long time to cover the distance to the duke's hill. She skirted the edge of the battle, with Tageiny, still cursing, coming up hard to her side to ward off any chance attack. Luad, not such an accomplished rider as either of the others, trailed them by a few lengths.

Then she was on the hill, pulling her horse to a skidding halt on the frozen earth, swinging down from its back. The men there were arguing ferociously, but they fell back in astonishment at her precipitous arrival. One of them, she noted, was Riheir Coärin, and in passing she grabbed his arm and pulled him around to face her. His shocked eyes met hers, but she cut off whatever he had opened his mouth to say.

"Don't you dare let us lose now," she said furiously. "Don't you *dare*, Riheir. You take these men and do something useful with them! And you!" She rounded on the nearest Eänetén officer, who had his mouth open in what might have been protest. "You make sure your people cooperate with his! There are only two armies on this mountain and one of them is Pohorin! All the rest of us are *on the same side*."

"*Yes*, my lady," the man said with great earnestness. "But—"

"I don't care!" snapped Kehera. "*Deal* with it until we get Eänetaìsarè anchored here again!" She flung herself down beside the duke. She was aware, dimly, that the icy moisture of the ground was rapidly soaking through her skirts, and that this was uncomfortable. She was also aware, in much the same way, that Tageiny and Luad had found canvas somewhere and were putting up a barrier of some kind that would stand between her and any more of those little black arrows that should come their way. She noticed this mainly because the canvas got in the way of the light.

The duke was still alive. She knew that almost at once. Someone had found time, before she had arrived, to stretch him out on a cloak and cut through his shirt to show the arrow, where it stood in his chest. It rose and fell with his breathing. His head had been turned to the side, and she saw that blood bubbled out of his mouth with every exhalation. Reaching out, she touched the shaft of the arrow very gently, with the tips of two fingers.

"It's in the lung, Your Highness," a diffident voice said beside her, and she turned to look into the tense face of a man wearing the poppy-and-thorn badge of the physicker as well as the leaping Eänetén wolf. "There's nothing either of us can do for him now but ease his passing. Taking the arrow out would only speed his death—"

"Not acceptable," Kehera snapped. "If he dies, we'll lose; if not today, then soon. So he won't die."

The man made to protest. But Luad, stopping behind him, gripped his arm and growled in his most forbidding tone, "We both heard the lady, man. Shut your mouth."

Then Caèr Reiöft arrived, white and stricken, and with unarguable authority told the physicker, "Shut up, get out of the way, and wait till you can do something useful." Then he turned to Kehera.

Kehera barely noticed him. She put her left hand on the duke's chest, close by the arrow, and curled the fingers of her right about the shaft of the arrow.

Tageiny, dropping to one knee on the muddy ground on the duke's other side, said, his tone rough with distress, "You don't want to hear it, but the physicker is right, you know. If that arrow comes out, his life will go out with it. I've seen it before."

Kehera looked up at him. "If Eänetaìsarè can't hold him, Raëhemaiëth will have to. He's dying anyway, after all." And, taking hold of the arrow, she pulled.

The duke made a horrible wordless sound, body contorting. His eyes opened, but without awareness. Bright red blood ran out of his mouth. The arrow moved sickeningly, but it did not come out.

Someone made a low whimpering noise, and after a moment

Kehera realized it was her own voice. It didn't seem to matter.

Tageiny reached over the wracked body between them and took the arrow in his own hand, close to where it entered the flesh, and twisted sharply as he pulled. It came out. A flood of bright blood followed it.

And Kehera drew in her breath hard, laid her hand over the hole, closed her eyes, and said sharply into the stinging silence she found in the back of her mind, "Raëhemaiëth! *Raëhemaiëth!*"

A hot, heavy presence flooded over the world. It was like being smothered by summer, like being buried in the earth. It was not like either of those things. Though it did not hurt, Kehera cried out. And the duke cried out as well, in a deeper voice, and opened his eyes.

Then a more savage Immanent rose, brutal, and Raëhemaiëth's warm presence swooped and swelled and receded, and . . . broke. . . . It burst and fell away from her, not toward her father, but toward Tiro. And Kehera, half aware of crushing disaster not here but elsewhere, followed a terrible sense of loss and grief and guilt down into the darkness.

She woke in her own tent, in a nest of blankets, in the dark. A single lamp, hanging from the roof of her tent, cast its warm yellow light over the pillows and the canvas walls of the tent, and a brazier glowed near at hand. Despite the blankets and the brazier, she felt very cold. Too cold to shiver. So cold she wondered if she might be already dead after all, and this seeming to wake just a dream.

The tent looked strange to her. Although she knew at once where she was, for some reason she had expected to wake in Raëh, in her own room. Without knowing why she should, she felt wretched. Tears threatened, and her throat felt tight and constricted. And she had a pounding headache. Grimacing, she turned her head.

Sitting in a chair beside her makeshift bed was the Eänetén duke. His long legs were stretched out in front of him, his elbows supported by the arms of the chair. His forehead rested on his interlaced fingers, and she could see that his eyes were closed. He might have been asleep, but she knew he was not. Although his attitude spoke of weariness, even of grief, he was immaculate. There was no sign that he had lately been injured; no sign at all that he had lain bleeding and dying on a muddy hillside with blood coming out of his mouth.

She sat up.

Hearing the rustle of the blankets, the duke opened his eyes and lifted his head. For a long moment he only looked at her. The lambent light caught in his eyes, turning them to a bright flame-gold. He lowered his hands to grip the arms of his chair, but he made no other movement. He did not speak.

Kehera said, and was surprised at the high shakiness of her voice, "Are you all right?"

He moved slightly, as though he might get up, but then he was still again. "Yes," he answered. His voice was very quiet. "And you?"

"Me?" Kehera said uncertainly.

His long fingers tightened over the arms of his chair, though no shadow of impatience touched his face or his voice. "Are you well?"

"Oh," said Kehera, and her voice rose sharply and broke. "No. My father is dead." As she said it, she knew it was true. She had called Raëhemaiëth, and it had come; her father had let it come to her and . . . something had happened.

She had thought their own battle was enough. She should have remembered there were other battles, too, and that her own need for Raëhemaiëth was not the only need.

The tears that had threatened did come, then, and she sobbed once out loud and covered her face with her hands.

The duke left his chair to kneel beside her, reaching one tentative hand out to touch her shoulder. Lost in grief, she caught his hand in both of hers without thought and clung hard, pressing her face against his chest. The fine linen of his shirt was smooth against her cheek.

For a long moment he did not respond at all, but only held very still. Then, carefully, he shifted to a more comfortable position at her side and laid his other hand over her shoulder. He said nothing.

Through tears, Kehera cried, "Why did you let yourself get hit?"

She could not weep prettily, as some girls could; her nose ran, and she pulled away from him to hunt, without success, for a cloth. Her voice, thick with misery, was hardly understandable.

But the duke understood her. He handed her one of his extremely elegant black silk handkerchiefs and said, in a strict tone more expressionless than any she had ever heard from him, "I did not intend to allow that to happen. The calling of the dragon was something I did not anticipate. I am . . . sorry."

Kehera blew her nose and wiped her eyes. And said savagely, wanting to hurt him as she was hurt, "Why were you up on that hill anyway? You were showing off. You could have carried a shield like a normal man! It was nothing but vanity to make yourself a target."

He did not respond, but only looked at her with a perfectly still face, which she saw for the first time was pale and drawn with weariness. There were dark circles under his yellow wolf's eyes.

Seeing this, and knowing she had hurt him, made Kehera feel guilty, even in the midst of her own distress. Gripped by a furious feeling, she cried, "My father was distracted, too. By the tie. Because I called Raëhemaiëth. I killed him, saving you! He died in your place! It's your fault he's dead!"

She knew as soon as the words were out of her mouth that not only was this unforgivable, but it was also not true. It had been her choice to call on the tie, not the duke's. It was not his fault. It was hers. She pressed her hands over her mouth and sat frozen, tangled in the blankets, staring at him with wide eyes.

Whatever he saw in her face sent the duke to his feet in one sharp motion. He strode for the door, brushed the hanging door out of the way with a violent gesture of one hand, and disappeared into the darkness.

Kehera, watching him go, was consumed by an absolute desolation.

But the next moment he had returned. He carried a round pot in both hands, with a single small cup hanging from his finger. Coming back to where she lay, he knelt at her side and poured from the pot.

The rich, sweet smell of the spices filled the tent like incense. He held the steaming cup out to her and said, "Drink." There was no anger in his voice, and no impatience, though the set of his jaw and the corded tension in his arms betrayed both emotions, or perhaps others that she could not recognize.

She took the cup and drank. It was hot wine, liberally laced with spices and herbs. Even in her distress it warmed her.

He said, "I grieve for your loss. It was certainly not your fault, however." His voice was cold, but so definite that she felt obscurely comforted. He took the cup away from her with delicate care, his fingers barely touching her hands, filled it again, and gave it back to her. And commanded curtly, when she only stared at him through the steam that rose from it, "Drink."

She drained the cup obediently, and he filled it a third time and lifted a strict eyebrow at her when she would have refused it. She lifted it to her lips and sipped.

"In preserving my life, you saved not only me, but also the shield I hold between Pohorir and your father's country," he told her, with the same cold assurance. "Drink that. Drink it."

It would have taken too much energy to resist, and so she obeyed, and he poured again. She blinked at him dizzily through the fragrant steam, and her hand, holding the little cup, wavered. The hot wine sloshed and nearly spilled.

The duke took the cup out of her hand with a deft impersonal touch and held it to her mouth with his own fingers. He said curtly, "I don't expect that knowledge to comfort you now, but perhaps you will find it of comfort later."

It seemed ungrateful not to drink, and besides, he seemed to expect it, so she did. It took her a moment to put what he had just said in context, but she said, once she had succeeded in doing so, "But it's my fault he died." Her voice sounded unhappy to her ears, but no longer hateful.

"It was the fault of war that your father died," he answered shortly. "In war, such things happen. Was it your hand on the sword or bow that took his life? No. It was a Pohorin hand. You may be right to blame me. I was on that hill to be seen, and I was, and you are right that that is why I was struck. But it is nothing but child's foolishness to blame yourself. Drink this."

"I don't want it," Kehera protested querulously, trying not to be comforted by his words. She closed her hands into fists, refusing the cup, and added out of the odd certainty she felt, "It was an arrow, like it was for you. Raëhemaiëth couldn't save him. Too much of it was with me. It couldn't return to him in time." The knowledge was almost like a memory of the arrow slicing into her own throat, as she knew, beyond doubt, it had struck her father's. She remembered the sharp blow of it, and the coldness that had spread out from the arrowhead. Shuddering, she subsided slowly back into her blankets, barely seeing the wavering light of the hanging lantern that seemed to sway gently back and forth above her.

The duke regarded her narrowly. Then he tossed the cupful of wine down his own throat and put both cup and pot aside. "Go to sleep," he said. His hands on the blankets were as impersonal as his tone, but his touch as he tucked her in was gentle.

She was tangentially aware that he had risen. But she said, drowsily, "Don't leave. Please don't leave me alone."

Above her, the light of the lantern flickering across his face, the duke paused. Then he sank down again at her side, drawing his knees up and lacing his fingers around them. He did not speak. But he was clearly settling down for a long stay.

As she let herself drift off again into unconsciousness, she was aware of the lantern light sliding across his still face and glowing in his golden eyes.

21

Tirovay Raëhema remembered cold. He remembered being lost, blinded by whirling snow, hunted by a terrible winter that knew his name and wanted him to die. A winter dragon, many-headed, white-eyed, obsidian-winged, had hunted him through the storm, crying with all the voices of the winter winds. Though he had fled from it, he had been unable to find his way out of that deadly wind-struck winter until at last a thread of warmth had spun through it and past it. Then at last Raëhemaiëth's strong solidity and warmth had followed that thread and found him and lifted him out of the cold.

Tiro remembered every minute of the terrible confusion that had held him, though. So, when Riheir Coärin sent word that he expected the King of Pohorir to try to break through Meilin Gap and Tiro's father decided, on the strength of that likelihood, that the Pohorin king might very well try the Anha Narrows at Eilin as well, Tiro knew exactly why he had to accompany his father to Eilin.

Enmon Corvallis would hold the northern border. Tiro trusted that he would. His father trusted that too. They had to trust Corvallis would hold because it had to be true. That border lay now through what had been the south of Emmer, well north of the Imhar; an uncertain border held mainly by strength of arms and only very tenuously by recourse to Raëhemaiëth or lesser Immanences. Tiro had made that much possible when he had forced a tie to Raëhemaiëth on Sariy. Now his father had done the same to a handful of other of the smaller southernmost Emmeran provinces, those along the border between Emmer and Harivir. Most importantly Niaft and Daè. So it might be possible, they all prayed it would be possible, for Corvallis to keep that border secure against the Mad King and prevent further attacks from the north. For a while, at least.

That freed Torrolay Raëhema and Tiro to hold the east against Methmeir Irekaì if the Pohorin king struck through the mountains at Eilin.

So Torrolay took three companies of men marching under the Red Falcon of Raëh, and his own deep tie to Raëhemaiëth, to Eilin. And Tiro rode with him because he needed to be there, watching from a very safe place high on the walls, just in case anything happened to his father. His own presence, in fact, freed his father to take the field—because if the worst did happen, Tiro would be right there to take the tie.

Nevertheless, that *just in case* scared Tiro badly, not just because he didn't want anything to happen to his father, but because he was afraid of the tie. If the ruling tie came to him, he feared he would prove unable to help Raëhemaiëth against the cold, dragon-haunted Power of Irekay. He had failed Raëhemaiëth once before, at Leiör. He was terrified that if everything depended on him, he would fail again and this time lose everything. Worse, *he* had no heir. If *he* lost the tie to Raëhemaiëth, none of them knew where the tie might go or, in an uncertain, violent succession, what damage might be done to the bonds that held all the Harivin provinces together.

And if the Fortunate bonds between the Harivin provinces broke, Tiro was certain the Mad King or Methmeir Irekaì of Pohorir—or both of them—would move quickly to seize everything they could. The very character of every Harivin province would change beyond recognition if the Pohorin king seized them and forced a ruling tie on them. None of them would have the age and depth and strength to resist the white Immanent of Irekay. Tiro had seen it firsthand, and he knew.

Tiro didn't want to think of what would happen to Raëh and all Harivir if Raëhemaiëth were destroyed or, maybe worse, forced into a subordinate tie to a vicious Immanent like the one in Irekay.

So he asked his father to make sure Gereth Murrel of Eäneté came with them. Because if the worst *did* happen—which it *wouldn't*, of course it wouldn't, but if it *did*—he still had the little fragment of granite the Eänetén man had brought. He kept it with him all the time. But he knew he wanted Gereth with him too. Just in case. If the Immanent Power of Eäneté would help Raëhemaiëth . . . if the ruling tie came to Tiro, he was going to need whatever help he could get.

So now on the twenty-second day of the Iron Hinge Month, only eight days before the uncounted days of the Iron Hinge, Tiro stood high up on top of a guard tower on one of Eilin's walls, along with Gereth Murrel and Viy Laseïn, Lady of Eilin, and half a dozen soldiers for a personal guard. They all stood up on their toes to see over the balustrade and watched Torrolay Raëhema arrange his forces between Eilin and the mountains.

"This does seem a good, defensible position," Gereth commented to no one in particular.

Lady Viy nodded. "We are small, but we have the mountains." She was about Gereth's own age, with considerable presence and a decided, forceful way about her. She went on. "And you see how well these hills lend themselves to a crossfire from archers, should any enemy come through the Anha Narrows. Which, in this season, should not be possible. But if they do." She nodded again, as though to reassure herself. "We have many fine archers here in Eilin."

"I believe—" Gereth began, but just at that moment a brutal white strength blew a pathway through the mountains and came flooding out across the beaten snow of Eilin's pastures, followed by a second, narrower flood of Pohorin soldiers, the bloody-jawed Winter Dragon of Irekay flying on a banner at the forefront, one head snapping forward and the other turned back over its shoulder as though the monster were driven by contrary winds.

Tiro had closed his eyes involuntarily against the brutal intrusion of the Irekaïn Power, but Raëhemaiëth rose within and around him and he found himself able to open his eyes again, blink away the shattering brilliance, and lean forward to search the field for his father.

He located his father almost at once and then couldn't look away. Torrolay Raëhema rode out to meet Harivir's enemies, slowly, alone, keeping his bright chestnut horse to a high-stepping walk. The Pohorin force he rode toward looked . . . unstoppable. Ribbons the color of clotted blood fluttered from the wrists and helms and boots of the advancing Pohorin soldiers and streamed from the ends of their long bows and the hilts of their swords. Ribbons white as death had been braided into the horses' manes and tails, and the standard-bearer who carried the double-headed Winter Dragon rode a white horse whose mane and tail had been braided with ribbons of white and dark red.

"That's not your king? That's not Methmeir Irekaì himself?" Tiro asked Gereth, appalled.

"Not *my* king," the Eänetén man corrected quietly. "Not any longer. I can't tell from here whether it's Irekaì himself. It might be a cousin, perhaps. It's someone carrying a deep tie, obviously; someone who can serve to anchor the Irekaïn Power here in Eilin. I'd have thought Irekaì would reserve his main strength for battle farther south. But perhaps he counts your father as his greatest opponent—probably your father *is* his greatest opponent, even counting my duke." He paused and then added, "That's a small army he's brought with him. But perhaps he's got more than he's yet shown. And, of course, where kings take the field, strength of arms isn't likely to be decisive. Your Raëhemaiëth is very strong."

Torrolay Raëhema rode forward slowly and steadily to meet the Pohorin force. He looked every bit a king, and Tiro was proud of him, proud of all the men of Raëh and Eilin and all Harivir who rode with him.

Tiro's father had not yet drawn a weapon, but he carried his own banner, so that the Falcon of Raëh flew over his head, a bright, brave scarlet like holly berries. His cloak was violet, and someone had found the time to braid his chestnut horse's flaxen mane and tail with ribbons of violet and gold. Raëhemaiëth was so strongly gathered around his father that Tiro saw all this only in dazzled glimpses, and for a long moment he thought that his father might simply break the Irekaïn Power and hurl it out of Eilin by main force.

Then the blank white winter rose and struck through Raëhemaiëth's rich warmth, and Tiro knew it would not be so easy, that nothing would be easy.

His father knew it too, and reined his chestnut in. It reared, striking out with its front hooves, and Torrolay Raëhema dipped the Falcon and swung the banner forward, and his Harivin companies surged into motion.

Even then, Tiro thought the battle might not be so difficult. Raëhemaiëth might not be able to throw the Irekaïn Power out of Harivir, but it could hold it away from Eilin and stop it from forcing a bond to the minor Immanent that had grown up from this land. And the Pohorin force was not so very large—perhaps a third the size of the force Torrolay Raëhema had brought with him.

It was Lady Viy who realized first that the advantage was actually all on the other side.

"The dragon," she said, and Tiro thought she meant the banner, but she said it again, "The dragon. A dragon is coming through the Narrows." The lady stood on her toes and leaned forward. Already pale, she looked suddenly deathly, and Tiro gripped the balustrade hard with both hands as knife-edged winds streaked with black whirled out of the Anha Narrows. The vast, unearthly form of a three-headed winter dragon rode the bitter, stinging winds down across the field of battle below. The man bearing the Irekaïn tie and the Winter Dragon standard spurred his horse, which leaped forward with a scream so shrill it carried right up to the tower where Tiro stood frozen with cold and horror.

Still, the charge checked when Tiro's father met it. The Red Falcon burned bright even through the whipping snow; it put heart into the defenders, and Torrolay Raëhema would not give way, and the field rapidly dissolved into bloody confusion.

"He'll hold it," murmured Gereth, low and fervent, like a prayer, and Tiro was grateful to the Pohorin for saying so, because it felt like it might be true. He thought it *ought* to be true. Raëhemaiëth was matching the Power of Irekay, he could feel it was, and if the battle came down to force of arms, they had the numbers too. . . .

Then Lady Viy exclaimed, sharp and horrified, "The dead! That horrible cold Immanent is taking up *my* dead!" Because this was her land and her town and her tie, and many of the men who had rode out to meet the small Pohorin army were her own, she knew at once when the Irekaïn Power began to take them away from her.

It took Tiro some moments to understand what she meant, what she had seen. Gereth Murrel understood first—Tiro could tell from his sharp, indrawn breath—but Tiro mostly saw the Dragon banner, and the darkly translucent winter dragon floating above.

Then at last he saw how the cold Irekaïn Power came down over the fallen, and filled them, and took them, and stood up in their bodies, and picked up their weapons, and turned on the living men of Harivir.

"How can it *do* that?" cried Lady Viy. "Those are *our* people."

Tiro shook his head. He knew. He knew, but he didn't want to say it out loud, as though refusing to put it into words would make it not be true.

Which was a child's terror. He made himself tell the lady, "There are stories . . ." He stopped, because he could see from her appalled look that the Lady of Eilin didn't know those old tales. He didn't want to have to tell her what it meant, that the Irekaïn Power could embody not only its own dead but also steal hers.

But she said, "Tirovay?"

So then he had to tell her, "Methmeir Irekaì can't have mastery of the Irekaïn Power. Maybe he did once—I guess he must have, once. But he's lost it now. It's mastered *him* and now it's *using* him. It's become partly human. It has learned all the wrong things about ambition and lust for power, and now it's using the man carrying that deep tie. It has mastered him, and it's using him to anchor itself in foreign lands so it can break its bonds with the land that gave it birth. Oh. Oh, it makes sense now. Now everything makes sense. . . . No wonder I couldn't hold Leiör. It wasn't just that I was in Sariy. It must have had a man in Leiör. . . . No *wonder* it's been devouring other Immanences and yet not taking their lands for itself. . . ."

"Your Highness!" Gereth said sharply. "Will you explain?"

Tiro closed his eyes. But though watching events play out below was bad, not seeing was worse, and he opened them again. He said tensely, "I don't have to tell you. You already know what happens to a Great Power when it masters all its deep ties and breaks its bonds to its people and its land. It's becoming a God."

And he had to watch while the realization of what that meant drained the color from his companions' faces.

"A God," Lady Viy said. And grimly, "An Unfortunate God, of course; how else with such a violent apotheosis? It will rise to Godhead *here in Eilin.*" She drew a deep breath, leaning forward, staring down at the battle. "It won't. It would destroy us all—it would destroy all of Eilin, the whole province, all my people. No. We'll stop it. How can we stop it? Can your father stop it?"

Tiro shook his head because he couldn't imagine how anything could stop it. But he looked for his father, in case he was wrong. "Raëhemaiëth," he muttered, not loudly, to himself, and looked again, and spotted first the depth and warmth of Raëhemaiëth and then his father at last, riding through the battle. Then he guessed that maybe they might hope after all to stop the Irekaïn Power's apotheosis—at least to delay it. Because wherever Torrolay Raëhema rode his golden horse, he cut a wide swath through the Pohorins. When men fell to his sword, they did not rise again, and when he passed near any dead Harivin soldier, that man collapsed and did not rise again.

"He'll do it—he'll beat them," he said out loud. He wanted it to be true. He hoped it was true. "Look, it's just like all the tales—" All the ones he wanted to remember, anyway. One bright tie, one Great Power that supported its king, and all their terrible enemies could be cast back into the dark. . . .

But Gereth did not appear convinced. "The histories only get written if someone survives to write them, Your Highness. No one ever wrote down the story when the northern desert was made in Emmer, and to this day we have no idea what dreadful things are hidden behind the Wall of Storms. Except, of course, we know winter dragons are born from those terrible winds at midwinter, and we know the sign of Irekay is the Winter Dragon."

"Yes, but look!" said Tiro, leaning forward. "You can see how if the—the dead are killed *enough*, they don't get up, our enemy can't touch them."

"True. That's true," said Lady Viy. She nodded hopefully, peering down toward the battle. "The king is turning back even the winter dragon. Look, you can see it turn when he rides toward it."

"Yes, you see!" Tiro said warmly. "She's right!" He thought she was—he hoped she was. Even now the battle might be all but won, because he could see men and a few women beginning to move among the fallen under the sign of the poppy-and-thorn, sorting dead from wounded and carrying the latter hastily into the city.

The battle itself had moved farther from the city walls, and the Pohorin army was indeed clearly hard-pressed. And the harder Torrolay Raëhema pressed the Pohorins, the fewer dead men seemed able to climb to their feet. Tiro's father moved through the chaotic battle as though a light was fixed upon him; he seemed to blaze with his own radiance, the pale-haired king on his golden horse, and no Pohorin could touch him. The black Pohorin arrows fell around him like rain, and he paid them as little heed.

The Dragon standard wavered in the hand of its bearer, and faltered, and Torrolay Raëhema sent his horse flying that way. Light streamed golden down the length of his sword, and the standard-bearer fell. The double-headed Dragon toppled slowly, like a great tree coming down under the ax, and fell at last into the trampled mud, and high above the great triple-headed winter dragon cried out with a voice like midwinter frost and turned back toward the heights.

Tiro didn't see the banner hit the ground. He knew only that Raëhemaiëth suddenly rushed away south, leaving his father unprotected. He knew only of another arrow that flicked down out of the sky and did not miss, and he knew Raëhemaiëth rushed back, but too late. And then he was aware of nothing but a whirling storm of brilliance and cold and jagged flashes of fire and bitter crystalline wind. Somewhere past the storm, he knew his father was dead. Grief broke over him, and terror, and then the howling winter fell over him like an avalanche.

Tiro was aware, dimly, that he had fallen to his knees, and that Gereth Murrel supported him from one side and Lady Viy from the other. He was not lost so deeply in the white cold this time as he had been before; this time Raëhemaiëth seemed better prepared to counter the Irekaïn Power, and the lesser Power of Eilin was doing what it could to support him, and Gereth was there with his thin tie that led right out of Harivir and rooted itself in distant Eäneté.

Over his head, Tiro heard Lady Viy say huskily, "If Tirovay Raëhema can't hold Raëhemaiëth—"

He didn't hear the rest of it, but he didn't need to. He already knew what would happen if he couldn't hold Raëhemaiëth. His father's death would be only the beginning of this disaster. It would be everything he had feared. If Raëhemaiëth could not cast back the strength of the Irekaïn Power, that would surely be the end of them all; and if the Great Power of Raëh threw back the foreign Power but Tiro couldn't master it, and it lost its hold on its place and its people, that might be almost as bad.

His father was dead. Raëhemaiëth had *let that happen*; it should have protected his father and it *hadn't*. Beyond his terror and grief, Tiro was *furious*. Yet he knew he had to forgive Raëhemaiëth, which surely had not deliberately sacrificed its king. But even if he didn't understand what had happened, Tiro had to forgive Raëhemaiëth and accept the ruling tie.

Eilin was helping them. That seemed impossible: a minor Immanent Power holding against Irekay to buy the Great Power of Raëh time to forge its new tie. But the Immanent of Eilin was determined; it drew on Lady Viy's determination, and it was still holding. There was a lesson in that. Tiro could see how will and purpose fed back and forth between the little Immanent and Lady Viy, different for Power and woman, yet they were drawing one on the other so their strength held and held where it should have failed.

Raëhemaiëth was so much stronger. If they broke, Tiro feared *he* would be the one at fault.

Gereth Murrel wrapped one hand in Tiro's shirt, hauled him as nearly upright as possible, and slapped him across the face, quite hard. That helped. Tiro gasped and blinked, clinging to the shock of the blow, using it to locate himself in the midst of the storm of power that surrounded him. He managed to meet the Pohorin man's eyes. He nodded, and Gereth slapped him again and said sharply, "Tiro! You must master your Power!"

Tiro knew that perfectly well. He was *trying*. But though he could reach after Raëhemaiëth, whirling ice and black winds came between them.

Lady Viy gripped his chin, turned his face toward hers, and said with quiet intensity, "Tirovay Raëhema! Your bones are the bones of the earth. Your body is the earth of the fields and the pastures and the woodlands. Though the year hesitates before the dark turn of the Iron Hinge, Raëh remembers a thousand summers. Eilin remembers. Follow Eilin."

"Follow Eäncté!" Gereth said urgently. He pressed the fragment of Eänetén granite and quartz into Tiro's hand, folding his fingers around it. Tiro clung to the piece of stone. It helped. He could *feel* how the violent bond between the Immanent and the Duke of Eäneté was forced out of grim determination and yet a willingness to give.

Tiro found himself able to straighten his back and take a deep breath and stare through the storm. And reach past it and through it. And down and back, from Eilin to Raëh, until the slow swelling warmth of Raëhemaiëth rose beneath him. This time, Tiro let it come. He made himself welcome it; he stepped sideways in himself to make a place for it, and though the storm screamed around him—around them all—it was no longer deafening.

When Tiro moved to get to his feet, Gereth helped him stand and supported him to go to the balustrade. "You have the full tie, the ruling tie?" Gereth asked the prince, sounding worried. "You're certain?"

Tiro had no way to explain just how impossible it would be to mistake it. "Oh, yes," he said at last. "Yes. I *am* Raëh. The tie is made now, beyond the reach of your terrible Irekaïn Power."

"Not *mine*," Gereth protested.

Tiro spared him a quick glance and a nod. He tried to smile, though he doubted he succeeded very well. "No, I know. The Eänetén Power was here, you know. You brought it to me again. A thin tie. But I think it saved me. Again." He turned toward Lady Viy. "So did your Eilinïen. For which I thank you. But this can't go on. That out there—" He pointed down toward the battle. "You know that can't go on."

For a long moment, they all stared down at the field, where flights of arrows arced down from both sides toward the close ranks of the Pohorin army, which was once again advancing. But far too many of the men struck by those arrows did not fall, or else fell but got up again. An officer on a red horse rode out of the melee of Pohorin soldiers, bent low from the saddle, and rose again. In his hand, the Pohorin standard swept upright, and a cold wind caught the banner and opened it out. The double-headed Winter Dragon with its bloody jaws seemed to laugh, and far above the true dragon turned again and came down once more.

A cry went up from the Harivins, and this time it had the sound of despair.

Lady Viy shuddered, gripping the balustrade hard.

Tiro turned to her. "You saw how the Eänetén Power supported Raëhemaiëth? *Did* you see that?" When she nodded, he went on quickly, "That was a very thin tie. Eilin isn't as strong, and I know, I *know* it's supposed to draw strength from Raëh, not the other way around. I know if Raëh draws from Eilin, that's an Unfortunate bond and—and it can lead to—" He stopped. Then he said, "I won't let Raëhemaiëth consume Eilinìen. It doesn't even want to. Raëhemaiëth doesn't *want* to be a God. But we need Eilinìen's strength. If you'll give me that—if you'll let me take a deep tie to Eilinìen, anchor Raëhemaiëth here into your land, we can make a tie that'll stand against even that white Power out there. But you can't let Eilinìen fight me—no, listen. I *know* it's a terrible thing to ask, but I swear, I swear to you, Raëhemaiëth will not force Eilinìen out of this land. We know it's the rightful Immanent here. Raëhemaiëth will take the tie *through* Eilinìen—"

Lady Viy held up one hand: *Enough.* She stood for a long moment, her attention turned inward, thinking or somehow asking her Power what it wanted to do; Tiro couldn't tell. Then she blinked, and looked over the parapet once more, and then turned again at last to meet his eyes. "A deep tie," she said. "Just like the Mad King forced on lesser Immanences so that his Power could devour them. Or worse than that: You want Raëhemaiëth to *possess* Eilin. That's what you're asking for."

"They can *share*," Tiro said urgently. "It'll be a Fortunate bond in the end, we'll make it work, Eilinìen helped me with Raëhemaiëth just now, it'll be willing to help again!"

He didn't say, *It had better be.* Lady Viy rubbed her face, looking old and uncertain.

Tiro said, "Listen, before the northern desert was made, there was a town there called Liën. Did you ever hear that story? The Lord of Liën was a friend of the Lord of Tamad. When the Immanent Powers of the sea sent a great wave washing over the coast, Liën gave a tie to Tamad. Together they threw back the weight of the tsunami. Both provinces survived; neither harmed the other. They were allies! They *both* prospered."

"Tirovay . . ." Lady Viy rubbed her face again. "You know the strangest stories."

He did. In a sense, all his life Tiro had been studying to advise his sister. But now he had to be king himself, and he did know all the stories. He said as gently and firmly as he could, the way he imagined Kehera might have said it, "Lady Viy, we have no choice but to try this. But you have to know Raëhemaiëth is exactly the right kind of Immanent to try it with."

"Well. Perhaps." The woman looked down at the battle for another moment, then nodded decisively and turned back to the prince. "Very well. It may work. I'll try to force Eilinìen to yield . . . that kind of tie. I think it will, if the alternative is facing *that* alone. It trusts Raëhemaiëth." She took another breath. "And I trust you, Tirovay Raëhema. Everyone knows those of your line can be trusted. We'd better know that."

Tiro let his breath out and held his hands out to her. Lady Viy took his hands in hers, and they were both silent for a long moment. Then Tiro said, though he knew it wasn't necessary to speak aloud, "Raëhemaiëth!" He blinked, his awareness shifting and turning and widening, and murmured, "Eilinìen."

Lady Viy swayed. Gereth Murrel caught her and beckoned to one of the guardsmen to help him, but Tiro drew one breath and then another, and then a third, and finally nodded and let go of her hands. The lady sat down right on the stones of the wall and put her face in her hands, but Tiro stepped firmly back toward the balustrade, stared down toward the battle, and said, surprised by the steadiness of his own voice, "You see their standard-bearer. He's the one with the tie. The rest don't matter. Let him past. Let him in."

"Let him *in*?" Gereth repeated, startled.

"He wants to break us." Tiro spoke distantly, listening more to Raëhemaiëth and Eilin than to any human voice. "Let him try. Let him in."

And Viy seconded this: "We have this. We hold Eilin. His Highness is right. Let that cursed Irekaïn come in, if that's what he wants so much."

Gereth stared from one of them to the other. Then he turned to the lieutenant of their guard and said, "You heard His Highness. Pass that order down: Get our people out of the way and let the standard-bearer through. Run!"

The lieutenant started to speak, shook his head, turned on his heel, and ran.

A quarter hour later the Harivin defenders began to fall back, leaving the way clear for their enemies, straight across the trampled pastures to the city walls and the gates.

A few minutes after that, the Pohorin standard-bearer jerked his horse back on its haunches, reined it around, and reached out to lay his hand on the gate of Eilin.

Tiro had thought he was prepared for the massive surging blankness that slammed out from the Irekaïn standard-bearer like a wall of solid fog. But it would have been impossible to be prepared for that. He lost track of himself immediately—he fell straight into the burning white cold. Claws of ice tore great ripping wounds in his soul; blinding frost struck deep into the land. Dimly, he was aware that Gereth Murrel supported his body. Far more real was the furious weight of Raëhemaiëth, fully roused and defiant, throwing back the winter that tried to smother it; and wrapped up within and around Raëhemaiëth, the small bright fury of Eilinìen. Eänetaìsarè of Eäneté was far away, barely perceptible, but Eilinìen was bright and clean and vivid, and Eilinìen was *right here*. It was in him; it was part of him; it was folded through Raëhemaiëth, and when he reached out he could take its strength so easily.

Tiro could see—though perhaps not with his eyes—the mist that poured out of the earth around the Pohorin standard-bearer. The double-headed Winter Dragon snapped in a savagely cold wind that raced down from the mountains, but the mist did not disperse. A skim of ice spread across the walls of Eilin, intricate webs of crackling frost.

Tirovay actually had his eyes closed. He knew that suddenly, but he was aware of his own people flinching back from that racing net of frost, and he knew it when the ice twisted its swift deadly way up their legs like a clinging winter vine and spread across their eyes and mouths. These men did not die. They moved, whatever their allegiance had been, to strike out at the remaining Harivin defenders.

Eilin was buried, frozen, under its layers of ice. The ice spread deep into the land. Eilinìen was trapped in it, frozen into its white blinding silence. But the Pohorin winter could not reach to encompass Raëh, not all the way from Eilin. Raëhemaiëth remembered the spring, remembered the swelling grain in the fields, remembered rising sap and new-born lambs, and the singing of tiny birds in the trees of the woods and the eaves of the towns. Raëhemaiëth remembered warm springs and rich summers and the long turning years, and rode those slow nonhuman memories out of the blinding silent winter. And it brought Eilinìen with it, out of the winter, into a memory of summer.

Tiro opened his eyes—he really did this time. He stared down through piercingly brilliant air at the gates of Eilin, and the Pohorin standard-bearer, with the terrible real dragon riding the winds above him in its frozen veil of mist. He could not speak; he had forgotten human language. But he was with Raëhemaiëth when the Raëh Power took the strength of Eilinìen and sent it back again, warm with the memory of summer. It was Eilinìen that screamed, high and wordless, through the voice of the Lady of Eilin. Blood dripped from the woven fangs of the Dragon on the Irekaïn banner. Eilinìen and Raëhemaiëth together took that blood and changed it, and where it fell smoking on the earth, it sent down deep roots, and the briar rose that was the symbol and the sign of Eilin twisted upward. Slender vining tendrils coiled about the wooden staff and pierced the arrogant Pohorin banner with its thorns.

The Irekaïn standard-bearer shouted once, letting the banner fall, and his cry was a human sound. The blank white winter had abandoned him, the winter dragon turned and rose, and the black winds carried it away. The bitter winds fell silent, and the standard-bearer tried to rein his horse back, but briars flung themselves up out of the earth and tangled around the animal's legs. Eilinìen couldn't have done that, but Raëhemaiëth did it, allowing itself to be guided by the lesser Immanent. The horse tried to rear, screaming, but the briars tore it down. Small sharp thorns tore savagely into the man's hands as he tried to rip away the briars, and thorny vines coiled about his shoulders and throat, red-veined green leaves rustling heavily as he moved.

The standard-bearer's blood fell on the earth, watering the briars, and slender vines, heavy with crimson buds, burst out of his eyes and mouth. The buds swelled rapidly and surged open into great brilliant flowers the color of fire or fresh blood, which shed golden pollen into the air. The wind carried the pollen across the land and swirled it high against the wall and through the gates and into the streets of the town. The air turned opaque and golden with it, and a piercingly sweet scent filled the air. Where the pollen touched the spreading frost, the ice melted as though touched by the sun.

Wherever the pollen touched a man's skin, it clung. When the man was Harivin and living, it only coated his skin with gold. But when the man was Pohorin, the pollen turned red and dripped heavily like blood, and where it fell on the earth, briars sprouted swiftly out of the ground and twisted upward, clinging, flowering upon the falling bodies of the men they tore down. And when the man was one of the walking dead, the golden pollen blew over his eyes and face and into his mouth, and he died a second death, from which he did not rise. Briars heavy with foliage burst from the bodies of the Harivin dead as they fell and opened their round crimson blossoms, casting more pollen upon the wind.

"Fortunate Gods," Gereth said quietly. Pollen streaked his face and hands, like sunlight given form and solidity. He did not appear to have noticed. He stood at the edge of the wall, leaning far out over the balustrade, staring downward.

Without Gereth's support, Tiro found himself sinking down to sit cross-legged on the wall. He tilted his head back against the stones of the balustrade, breathing through his mouth. The pollen tasted of roses and summer. When Tiro rubbed his hands over his face, they came away streaked with golden pollen and red blood. He looked at them, puzzled. "Am I bleeding?"

Gereth glanced down at him and shook his head, distracted. "You wept tears of blood. Just before the briars tore down the Dragon standard."

At the moment, this seemed perfectly reasonable. Pollen billowed in the air, a thin golden mist.

"What now?" Gereth asked quietly.

"Now?" Tiro blinked into a sky filled with golden clouds of pollen, trying to gather his thoughts.

Lady Viy accepted a hand from one of the guardsmen, clambering stiffly to her feet. She wasn't quite looking at Tiro. He didn't blame her. He hardly knew how to look at her, either. He could feel his new tie to Eilinìen coiling around his heart and mind, weaving in and out around the constant warm presence of Raëhemaiëth. Raëhemaiëth was very much stronger. He held them both.

But Lady Viy only said, her voice uninflected if a little hoarse, "We may have shut the Anha Narrows for . . . some time. This wasn't . . . Eilinìen isn't a Great Power, I don't quite . . . I think those briars stretch all the way from the walls of Eilin to the mountains. If that's so, anyone trying that road is going to have a problem. Though I imagine these particular briars will always flower at midwinter, which can only improve the Iron Hinge days." She glanced down at Tiro, and away again. "I would lose the Narrows three times over to be rid of Pohorir today."

"We've won," Gereth said, not quite believing it.

"No," said the young king. He rubbed his face hard, blood streaking across his cheeks. He said, "Yes, here, but no. Not in the end. It's too late. Or maybe not quite, but . . . very nearly." He glanced up at their puzzled, worried faces. "You didn't feel it? It's already halfway to becoming a God. Every Immanent it devours pushing it a little bit further. Very soon, all it will need to do is break its ties with its own place, and then no one will be able to stop it. I won't. Raëhemaiëth won't. We don't have the strength." He looked at Lady Viy. "Not even with Eilin's help."

There was a short pause.

Then the lady said, "No. We will stop it. If we have to force every single Power in Harivir into an Unfortunate bond with Raëh, we will. And trust your Raëhemaiëth won't tear out all our Immanences by the roots."

Tiro started to protest that his Immanent would never do that, but Lady Viy held up one hand and went on sternly, "But even if it does, I'd rather see Raëhemaiëth become a God than that Irekaïn Power. At least Raëhemaiëth would become a Fortunate God. Better that than . . ." She gestured wordlessly to indicate the field of blood and briars.

"Oh . . . Gods Fortunate and Unfortunate." Tiro pressed his hands over his face. "They'll hate it," he said. He already knew he was going to have to demand exactly this risk not only of his own people, but of as many Emmeran lords as still held ties to Immanences. "They'll hate it," he said out loud, meaning the lords of Emmer and Harivir both. "They'll hate it, and they won't do it."

Gereth asked, "Will they like it less than they like that?" Echoing the lady's gesture, he pointed over the balustrade at the red and bloody field where flowers bloomed from the corpses of men.

Lady Viy nodded, her expression set and grim.

Gereth added, "And if all your northern Harivin Powers are willing to forge Unfortunate bonds between their lesser Powers and Raëhemaiëth, Your Highness, I wonder whether those in the south . . ."

Though the foreigner didn't complete the thought, it wasn't a question. Tiro nodded. "Whether those in the south might yield the same to your duke, you mean."

"For the protection of us all," Gereth said quickly.

"Yes, I'm sure your duke would be glad to take a third of Harivir into his hand and force all the southern Immanences into Unfortunate bonds with his." Tiro heard the edge in his own voice, though he had to agree that it might be the very best any of them could do, now.

"You can't hold the south, Your Highness. . . ." Gereth hesitated. "Your Majesty. But Innisth terè Maèr Eänetaì might."

Tiro nodded. He understood that. He didn't need Gereth to explain it to him. He said, "I'll write to General Corvallis. And my sister. And you'll write to your duke. Lady Viy." He waited for her to meet his eyes. Then he said, "Perhaps you would write to the lords and dukes of southern Harivir yourself."

The Lady of Eilin looked out on the silent fields, filled now with crimson-flowered briars. At Irekay's banner, buried beneath thorns and flowers. At the air, hazed with golden pollen. She said slowly, "I lost a lot of men out there. But Eilin didn't lose them. Because Eilinìen took them up, in the end. I'll tell them that. You get Taraä Leiörian to write as well, and they'll do this. If it's a choice between losing their Immanent Powers and then their lands and their people to one of the mad kings, or yielding a deep tie and an Unfortunate bond to Eäneté . . . they need to understand that the Eänetén duke is your ally."

Tiro nodded. "I'll say so. It will be true." He looked at Gereth. "It had better be true. Despite what he's forced on my sister. I would kill him for forcing marriage on Kehera. I will, if the chance comes my way." Though that didn't seem very likely. But it didn't matter. Tiro added, "But for all he's done, you've sworn he's not our enemy, not as the Mad King is, not as Methmeir Irekaì is, not as the Irekaïn Power itself is. You've sworn that."

"I do swear it," Gereth said earnestly.

"And I believe you. It has to be true. It had better be true." Tiro pried himself up, accepting a hand from the older man in order to make it. All his joints hurt. His back hurt. His head ached, though that might have been Raëhemaiëth's glitter, which he still saw in his mind's eye. But he said, with all the decision and determination he could muster, "We'll summon them all. And then we'll see what we can wrest out of the jaws of the Winter Dragon. Hopefully more than briar-choked fields and hollow provinces—" He stopped.

"Tiro?" Lady Viy asked.

"Your Majesty?" Gereth said, just a little pointedly.

Tiro hardly heard either of them. He said slowly, "All those empty provinces."

All those hollow lands, where the Irekaïn Power had torn out and devoured the lesser Immanences. But Methmeir Irekaì hadn't made any effort to create new Immanent Powers in those lands, had he? Because even if the King of Pohorir would have thought of it and dared take such a risk, it wasn't him, was it? Not really. It was the Immanent Power of Irekay. And Immanent Powers didn't think the way people did. Creating new Immanences . . . that was something an ambitious king would think of, wanting to take their ties and possess them and rule them and their lands.

Catastrophe. That was how catastrophe had fallen across the southlands: because of the king who held the tie to the lost land of Sierè. He had cast out the proper Immanences of neighboring lands in order to make new Immanences that he could rule. He had succeeded, perhaps. Or failed. It hardly mattered, after all those cast-out lesser Immanences ascended into Godhead and the Great Power of Sierè, unexpectedly tempted to follow them into apotheosis, destroyed all the southlands.

But those empty lands in Emmer and in northern Harivir had no Immanences now. Those Immanences hadn't been cast out. They had been destroyed. Even though the Iron Hinge of the year was fast approaching, it didn't matter. No one now had to worry about those dispossessed Immanent Powers ascending. Irekay had seen to that.

And that *should* mean it would be perfectly safe to create new Immanences in each of those provinces.

"It would be *perfectly safe*," Tiro said out loud.

"What would?" Gereth and Viy asked together, equally wary.

Tiro looked at them and shook his head and laughed, incredulous at the audacity of his idea. "It probably won't work," he said. "And Corvallis might not agree. Or I might be wrong; this might go completely wrong, and that would be even worse than anything the Irekaïn Power is doing. . . . ”

"What?" demanded Lady Viy, sounding perfectly exasperated.

Tiro took her arm, and Gereth's, and turned them both toward the tower door. "I'll tell you. Come in with me, and we'll find paper and ink, and I'll tell you both."

22

Innisth stepped quietly out of Kehera Raëhema's tent and simply stood for a long moment, gathering the strained remnants of his self-control. Then he flicked a glance across the several men worriedly hovering in the immediate vicinity and said shortly, but very softly, "She is sleeping. No one is to wake her."

"I—" began Riheir Coärin.

Innisth impaled the man with a cold stare that had nothing in it of tolerance, and Coärin stopped and swallowed. But he then said stubbornly, if very quietly, "I would only ask, my lord, is she well?"

"She will do." Innisth strode away, requiring them all to follow.

His own tent was larger than Kehera's, and furnished more plainly. Innisth gestured that Coärin should enter. There were no chairs in the tent other than his own. Innisth did not sit, but stood regarding the other man for a long moment, his head just brushing the ceiling of the tent. He said at last, "Coärin."

A muscle in the other man's cheek jumped, but he inclined his head in stiff courtesy. "My lord."

"You did quite well with the last part of our battle. I am grateful for your immediate attention to necessity and your excellent handling of the aftermath of the battle."

"My lord," Coärin repeated, his tone flat.

Innisth went on, making no attempt to soften his words, aware that to draw this out was no kindness. "I regret to inform you that Pohorir engaged in another attack on Harivir simultaneously with its attack here. Torrolay Raëhema met the Pohorin force. However, he did not survive the battle. Kehe—Her Highness felt her father die."

"Fortunate Gods," Coärin breathed, clearly stricken. He made an abortive moment as though he meant to leave the tent, but then he changed his mind and only turned his face away.

Innisth had little sympathy to spare for the other man. He told him, his tone flat, "Tirovay Raëhema mastered the Immanent Power of Raëh, which held. I therefore presume Pohorir has been thrown back in the north as well as here. I shall write to the young king immediately. We must coordinate our efforts in order to consolidate today's achievements."

"Our achievements. Our *achievements*!" Riheir Coärin did not storm out, or turn and hit the side of the tent, but Innisth thought it was a near thing.

"Do not allow your grief to blind you to today's victory," he said coldly. "Pohorir has been thrown back twice in one day. I imagine Methmeir Irekaì is far from pleased. I will, as I say, write to Tirovay Elin. You may advise me. I value your knowledge of the young king and your understanding of Harivin expectations."

"My lord," the Harivin duke said, after a moment of obvious struggle.

"Methmeir Irekaì will surely not forget his ambition and retire meekly to Irekay. Nevertheless, I strongly suspect we will face a quiet few days as he reassesses his tactics. We will have leisure to consider possible strategies. We shall withdraw as far as Viär, where we may consider our next steps in relative comfort."

"What of Kehera?"

Innisth said coldly, "You need not concern yourself for Her Highness, Coärin. I will guard her well-being with the greatest care. You may set your mind at rest on that account."

Riheir Coärin flushed dark red, snapped off a sharp little bow that was almost an insult in itself, turned on his heel, and stalked out.

Innisth stared after him. He was very, very angry. He wanted to call Coärin back. That would not have been a good idea. It would, among other reasons, probably upset Kehera Raëhema.

He had already hurt her. Too late to make a different decision, too late to protect himself more carefully from Pohorin arrows. Too late to warn the girl that if she called on her tie to the Power of Raëh, it might find its attention lethally divided at exactly the wrong moment.

It was quite plain to him that Coärin had hoped for more than friendship from Kehera Elin Raëhema. But it was far too late now for Innisth to step backward through the years and court her properly himself, before she thought of other men. He had every hope of gaining great tactical advantage through marriage to her, but now—too late—he found himself wanting so much more than *tactical* advantage.

Kehera Raëhema possessed nothing like Eöté's delicate beauty. Yet somehow Eöté's fragile loveliness no longer seemed anything a man would want in a woman. Now Innisth found himself appreciating Kehera's quieter, sturdier attractiveness. She would not make a man's head turn when she stepped into a room. But she had an assurance that filled the eye, if a man had the sense to take a second look, or a third. Then it grew difficult to look away.

Kehera Raëhema was more than merely pretty. She possessed the steadiness and resilience and clear sense and calm nerve that Innisth had never known he valued. He was aware of his growing desire to see her happy. Worse, he was aware of his growing desire to *make* her happy. And he knew he had no hope of achieving that.

She was kind. Innisth might have assumed as much, if it had occurred to him to think of it at all. They were reliably kind, all the Elin Raëhema line. He had always appreciated that quality, though distantly, as one he did not possess himself. It had never occurred to him that he might ever discover in himself any desire for kindness. Now he made that uncomfortable discovery. Her Raëhemaiëth seemed by its very nature to soothe and settle the worst inclinations of his own Eänetaìsarè. For seven years he had been so tightly focused on his own lands and his own needs and his own desires. How stupid he had been not to realize what his own needs and desires actually comprised, until he found Kehera Raëhema in his hand. And now he had no hope of winning anything from her but reluctant obedience.

As her father's heir, Kehera Raëhema would never have thought of marrying for other than political reasons. He had proposed the match for such reasons; he had set forth the benefits in those terms. Now he realized that *political* benefit was not enough. But now, through his carelessness, disaster had fallen on her. She would hate him for that, and he would not be able to say she was wrong. Too late, too late, too late, and he could not now allow himself to destroy Riheir Coärin, no matter that the other man had once proposed to marry her himself. No matter how much he longed to.

He paced instead, seven long strides one way and then back again, all that the dimensions of the tent could afford. Seven strides and back again, but he only grew angrier.

A servant put back the canvas door and came a tentative step into the tent. "Caèr asks—" he began.

"No," snapped the duke, bitterly furious. He should say something reassuring. Nothing occurred to him. He ordered instead, "Bring me Her Highness's man. Heris Tageiny." Then he resumed pacing.

Waiting was difficult. He did not want to sit down; he did not think he would be able to get up again. Exhaustion should have smothered his anger, but he had learned long ago it didn't. It couldn't. It never could. He pressed the heels of his hands hard against his eyes. It did not really help.

In not very long, there was a discreet tap at the door of his tent. Tageiny ducked through the flap and came in, to stand at careful attention. Innisth assumed he was afraid, but his manner showed only wary deference. "Your Grace?"

Innisth demanded without preamble, "What was Her Highness doing on the field of battle, with arrows still falling and the day undecided?"

Tageiny immediately dropped to one knee, bowing his head. "I have no excuse to offer, Your Grace."

"I should hope you do not. What excuse could there possibly be? Her Highness's safety is your responsibility."

"Your Grace."

"She has lost her father. Had you heard?"

There was the slightest pause. The man's expression didn't change, but he said even more quietly, "No, Your Grace. I am sorry to hear so."

"Indeed. She is considerably distressed. You can perhaps imagine," said Innisth, who personally could not. "I do not wish to distress her further. That is all that protects you in the face of your failure. This time. Fail again in such a manner, and I will grant the Falcon badge to someone more reliable. In that case, *you* will no longer have need of any badge. Do you understand me?"

"Your Grace is exceedingly clear."

"Then go."

Tageiny got to his feet. But he said without turning, "Your Grace cannot reproach me more severely than I reproach myself. I assure Your Grace, I would never willingly allow Her Highness to endanger herself merely to save Your Grace's life."

There was just a little bite on the last few words. Innisth stared at the man for a moment in astonishment.

Then he laughed because the savage relief of being presented with a target for his anger was so great. The other man blanched, and Innisth laughed again. "Kneel," he ordered, and when Tageiny hesitated, snapped, "At once!"

The big man composed himself with an effort that was hardly visible and went down again, this time to both knees. Innisth stepped forward and lifted his hand.

Tageiny visibly braced himself for a blow. Innisth touched his face, instead, in a deliberate caress. Eänetaìsarè rose, fast and brutal. At the powerful surge, the man's breath hissed out in shock.

"How confident are you of your lady's protection?" Innisth asked him, allowing his voice to become husky. He brought his other hand up to cup the man's face. Not a handsome face by any ordinary measure. But a face with character and strength.

"Will she forgive you this?" Tageiny asked. His voice was steady, but he could not quite conceal his reaction to the intensity of the Eänetén Power's fury and passion.

Innisth laughed again, feeling the seductive pull of the man's continued defiance. He felt Tageiny recoil, a flinch more felt than seen. "Will you tell her? How great is your loyalty to the lady who claimed you out of slavery and freed you, who took you into her own service and trusts you now with her life? What might such loyalty possibly encompass?"

Tageiny drew a breath that shuddered in his chest. "It encompasses anything you're likely to do, Your Grace, since I don't imagine you'll want to leave marks."

"Indeed." Innisth gripped the man's hair and pulled his head back sharply. Tageiny's pulse beat in his taut throat. He half-lifted his hands and then lowered them again, effortfully, to rest open on his thighs in careful, deliberate submission.

"How shall I punish your impudence?" Innisth asked him softly.

Tageiny answered with difficulty, his head still back at that awkward, straining angle, "However you please, Your Grace."

"Just so," breathed Innisth. He was still for a long moment, savoring the possibilities inherent in the situation. Then he twisted his body and threw the larger man forward to the thick rugs, letting him go. Dismissing Eänetaìsarè was not so easily accomplished. The Eänetén Power was difficult to settle. But he rode it and mastered it and did not let it master him.

Tageiny remained as he was, on the floor of the tent, one hand flat on the rugs for balance, head lowered. His unsteady breathing was quite audible.

Innisth himself was breathing little more easily. But he had not come near to losing his control. Or not very near. When he spoke, his voice was almost as cool and expressionless as usual. "As you are Her Highness's man, and as your loyalty to her pleases me, you may go."

The other man looked up warily.

"Unless you would rather stay," Innisth suggested, and smiled at him slowly, without warmth.

Tageiny stood up smoothly and bowed with perfect correctness. But he backed out of the tent, not to turn his back to the duke.

Innisth watched him go. Although it was not visible in the uncertain light of the lanterns, he knew the man was shaking. So was he. Eänetaìsarè's presence still filled the tent—filled it and filled the world, until Innisth seemed to see everything only through a yellow curtain of anger and heat. Eänetaìsarè did not understand why he had let the man go. Innisth himself only barely remembered. He thought of summoning Caèr Reiöft, but he was far too angry.

It occurred to him at last that there might be other, more fitting options.

Kehera's second waking was much better than the first. She felt, drowsily, that she had recently been very unhappy, but she could not immediately remember why and she was not eager to probe the question. Her head felt stuffed with wool, but not unpleasantly so.

She sat up. Her body was stiff, too, as though she had recently run up a mountain trail or fought against some enemy. . . . She thought about that hazily, and stumbled accidentally into memory after all. There had been a battle—an arrow. It came crashing back: the slick line of the descending arrow, the crumpling body of the duke—the *other* arrow, that had come out of the sky to strike her *father*. She made an inarticulate sound and pressed her hand over her mouth.

A hand put back the tent flap at once, and Luad leaned in to look in at her. "Lady," he muttered. And withdrew, letting the tent flap fall closed again. Voices called outside.

Kehera rolled forward onto her knees, gathering the blankets over her lap, and brushed the curtains out of the way, the heavy cloth soft against her fingers. It was dark, and very cold. Cooking fires burned here and there, their light drowning all but the brightest stars. Wisps of clouds blew a narrow moon. The shapes of unfamiliar mountains showed dark against the sky. In the distance, a mountain cat screamed, high and thin. The sound seemed to pierce right through her. She shivered.

Morain Lochan came in, dropping down to kneel near Kehera. "Lady. You all right?"

"Of course," Kehera assured her. *My father is dead*, she did not say. It was true, and she felt that emptiness in her mind. She still had her own tie to Raëhemaiëth; she could tell that, but it was not the deepest tie, the ruling tie, and she was glad. Because that meant Tiro must have it, and that meant her brother must be alive. But she had not regained the heir's tie, even now. If anything happened to Tiro . . . Nothing had better happen to Tiro. He would be careful. Surely he would be careful. Maybe her brother would figure out how to set a clear heir's tie in one or another Elin cousin, someone who might be able to master Raëhemaiëth, if worse came to worst.

But no matter how well Tiro handled things for Raëh and for Harivir, their father was still dead. She didn't say it. She tried not to think it, as though if she pretended it were not true it might cease to be so.

From farther away came the sounds of people moving quietly about normal camp chores, familiar, comforting sounds. She was so tired. She wanted to lie down again and go to sleep. But voices arguing nearby made her rub her face and straighten her back. One of the voices was Riheir's and one was Tageiny. She trusted Tageiny to handle almost anything. She didn't care about the argument. But despite her lack of interest, she found herself trying to hear more clearly.

Outside, the voices grew more vehement, although no louder. So eventually she hauled herself to her feet and nodded for Morain to bring her a plain traveling dress rather than simply lying down on the cot again.

Not a dozen feet from Kehera's tent, a small group of men stood. They were still arguing, but as she watched, one and then others turned in her direction, and the argument died. Several men broke away from that group to come toward her: Riheir Coärin, Tageiny, a captain from Viär, Caèr Reiöft, a few others. For an instant Kehera was seized by an urge to duck back into her tent and let them go back about their own business, whatever it was.

Then Riheir came close, reached out, and took both her hands in his, looking searchingly into her face. "Kehy," he said, so gently it brought tears to her eyes. "I'm so sorry."

"Oh, Riheir—"

"Shh. It'll be all right, Kehy, you'll see."

It would never be *all right*, but this was still nice to hear. It was nice to hear from a friend, someone she'd known all her life, speaking to her so tenderly. Kehera wanted to put her arms around Riheir and let him hold her and tell her everything was all right, that she'd just had a bad dream, that everything was just fine.

Nothing was fine, but she didn't want to care. She wanted to go to sleep and wake up in her own bed in Raëh, with Tiro bouncing on the foot of her bed and telling her she'd better wake up; their father was waiting breakfast for her.

It was all impossible. After a moment, she straightened, took a step away from Riheir, and turned to the others. She looked from Tageiny to Caèr Reiöft. "What's wrong?" She knew something was wrong. Tageiny was scowling thunderously, and Caèr had a worried line between his eyes. She asked him, "Where is His Grace? Is he all right?"

Caèr took a step forward, but before he could speak, Riheir said crisply, "These men and I were just . . . having a discussion. But I've been worried about you, Kehy. You've got to be starving. Let me get you something to eat."

No one contradicted him, but Tageiny frowned and exchanged a glance with Caèr.

"I'm not hungry," Kehera said. "Tag, what?" She felt an unexpected and deep stab of terror. "What has happened?" she said, her voice rising involuntarily. "Caèr, is His Grace all right?" She couldn't imagine what might have happened to him. Had there been another battle, that she had slept through? Had he been wounded again, and this time she had not been there to call on the Raëh Power?

"*He's* fine," Riheir said, his tone savage, but then added, in a much gentler tone, "It's you we're all worried about, Kehy. You should rest. And eat something. Soup or something." He threw a look at a man she didn't know, who left, presumably to find her some soup that she emphatically did not want.

Kehera asked sharply, "What is it that none of you want to tell me? Tag, do I have to ask you twice? *Tell* me!"

"It's nothing you should be asked to deal with," Riheir began, with a deadly look at the bigger man.

Tageiny cut him off. "That's her choice, Your Grace, not yours!"

"She's in no shape to deal with such things right now! And she shouldn't have to at all!"

Kehera stepped back from them both and said through her teeth, "Riheir Coärin, I am not yours to rule! Heris Tageiny, whose orders do you take above mine?"

The big man drew a breath and straightened. "No one's."

"Then tell me," she commanded.

"No!" snapped Riheir.

"His Grace," Tageiny said, in a voice from which all expression had been carefully stripped, "has one of the captured Pohorin officers . . . up in the mountains. With him. My lady."

For a long moment, none of them moved or spoke. High and remote, the mountain cat screamed again. It did not, if one listened closely, sound exactly like a cat after all.

Kehera looked at Caèr Reiöft.

"I can't go to him," the man told her quietly. "I would. But he hasn't allowed me near him since . . . you brought him back. His orders concerning me were unfortunately quite explicit." He paused, touching his fingertips wearily to his eyelids. "He does get these protective impulses. At the worst possible times, generally."

"But he didn't leave any orders for me," Kehera said, knowing this was true.

Caèr dropped his hand and met her gaze. "No, he didn't. He didn't leave any orders commanding you to do, or forbidding you to do . . . anything."

Kehera straightened her shoulders. "Do you know where he is?"

"No," Riheir said, face white and strained.

"Yes," said Tageiny, stepping forward. "But I will warn you, he's in a savage mood."

"I don't care. Take me to him," Kehera ordered. "Get me a horse and take me to him."

Tageiny turned on his heel and strode into the darkness.

Riheir came close and took her hands again, his grip urgent. "Kehy, listen to me. This isn't something for you to interfere with. He's not a safe man. I wish above all things you weren't in his power. There's no telling what he may do if you go up there—"

Kehera let her hands lie still in his, not returning his grip, and answered quietly, "This is not yours to decide. It never was."

"He won't harm Her Highness," Caèr Reiöft said quietly. And to her, "When you brace the wolf, it's never wise to back up."

Tageiny led two horses out of the darkness, a tall roan and a smaller gray, by the reins. The two pale horses loomed out of the night as though caught in their own personal pools of moonlight.

"You must *not*—" began Riheir.

"We had better not quarrel," Tageiny said flatly. "Think of the example it would set for the men." He met Riheir's eyes without flinching, and the Duke of Coär paused.

Kehera threw the reins over the gray's neck. Riheir made as

though to approach her, but Caèr stepped between them, deferential but unyielding.

"You've got to stay here," Kehera said to Riheir over her shoulder, and swung up into the gray's saddle. "You know that, Riheir. There has to be a commander here that both armies are willing to look to, and I don't see Toren Viärin anywhere about. Gone back to Viär, hasn't he? Then you've got to stay here and you've got to work with the Eänetén officers. I shouldn't have to tell you that!"

Riheir stopped.

"I'll take care of him," Kehera promised Caèr, and was absurdly flattered when the man nodded as though he trusted this promise. She booted the gray in the ribs, and it jolted off after Tageiny's roan. Its gaits were brutally rough, and for a moment Kehera thought of how much she would rather be lying on her cot, in her tent, wrapped in blankets rather than a cloak.

No one challenged them as they left the camp, although Kehera saw one sentry, and then another. They recognized her, perhaps, for they lifted their hands in salutes and stood aside. Tageiny reined his tall roan back beside her and told her, speaking clearly to be heard over the sounds of hooves and creaking harness and cold wind, "The trail's narrow—if you can call it a trail at all; it's more a goat path. The horses should stay on the path, but we'll have to go single file, and there's damn all for light, with the moon so thin. That's why I picked light-colored horses. If I get too far ahead of you, give a yell."

Kehera nodded, realized that of course he couldn't see her, and said, "Yes."

Tageiny brought his roan in front of her gray. Its dark tail flicked back and forth between nearly white thighs, easy enough to follow. Kehera let her horse pick its own way, taking care only to keep it headed in the right general direction.

The ground rapidly grew steep and rugged. The hooves of the horses rang against stone, and her gray put its head down almost to touch the ground, picking its way more by feel than by sight.

Above them, another scream cut through the air, much closer than before. It did not, now that they were so close, sound at all like a cat. Neither did it sound human. Kehera closed her hands on her horse's mane until they ached.

The path, if one could dignify it by that name, leveled off and then steepened again, and then gradually leveled once more. The scrubby trees opened out to tough wiry grasses yellow with winter, and bare rock, and patches of snow. A great fire burned before them. No, Kehera saw, there were two fires, some little distance apart, and between them, the dark silhouette of a tall man.

"Tag!" she said urgently, and when he turned his horse back toward hers, added, "I want you to go back to camp—*don't* argue, and don't disobey me. I'm far safer here than you are."

Without a word, the big bodyguard turned his horse in a circle and put it into a slow, careful walk down the slope they had just climbed.

Kehera sent her gray forward, toward the fires.

The Wolf Duke heard her coming, of course. He waited for her between the fires, their light sending his shadow leaping on the cliffs that lay to either side. Although the air had been quite cold, it was not cold near those fires; the steep cliffs flung their violent heat back at them, and it became uncomfortably hot as Kehera approached.

The duke was clearly prepared to be furious with whoever had the temerity to approach him, to interrupt him here, about this . . . activity. He was shirtless, and for the only time she had ever seen him, with the sole exception of when he had been lying on the ground with an arrow in his chest, he was not immaculate. Blood streaked his chest and arms. Ribbons of it curled around his fingers. His face shone with sweat from the heat, but the expression in his eyes was wintry.

Behind him, on the ground, a man lay spread-eagled and naked, wrists and ankles bound to stakes pounded into the rocky ground. Kehera was glad she could not see the details clearly. She could hear the man breathing, deep raw breaths that were half groans.

She drew her horse to a halt and put her hood back. Her hands were shaking. She kept her eyes firmly on the duke's face.

And so she was watching when the leashed rage in his yellow eyes changed gradually to appalled shock. There was little enough sign of it; another person, watching less closely, or less familiar with his minimal expressions, might have missed it entirely. He did not speak.

Kehera said, hardly recognizing her own shaking voice, "Innisth, how can you *do* this?" It was the first time she had ever addressed him by his name, and she saw it have an impact. The duke drew a slow, shuddering breath, dropping his gaze to the ground. But he did not answer.

Kehera slid down from her horse and started to walk forward, past the duke and between the fires. He put out a bloody hand to bar her way. "You do not want to see that." His voice was flat, empty of expression.

"What I want," Kehera answered tautly, "is for that not to exist."

The duke turned on his heel, walked back to stand beside his victim, plucked a knife off the ground, and hurled it downward with a neat economical movement. The man lying there shuddered in one great spasm, and went limp.

Kehera put one hand over her mouth and turned away. The heat of the fires leaned like a physical weight against her back.

The duke said distantly, from quite near behind her, "I shall take you back to your tent."

"No," Kehera said. Behind her, he took a breath, more felt than heard, and she added, shocked by the steadiness of her own voice, "I want to know why you did this."

"There are times I must do it."

"No. I don't believe that. What I believe"—her voice shook now, uncontrollably—"is that you want to do it." She turned once more to face him, having to tip her head back to meet his eyes. The fires behind him cast moving shadows across his expression. She could not make out any details of his face. But she felt his fury, blazing out of him like the heat of those great fires, ready, if it slipped the leash of his control, to burn out over this whole mountain.

He said coldly, "If I cannot draw on Raëhemaiëth's calm, I must assuage Eänetaìsarè another way. Should I use one of my own men? Or yours?"

Kehera shook her head. "Innisth, I am *willing* to give you Raëhemaiëth's calm." She *was* willing, she found, and in the moment, this understanding somehow did not surprise her. She said, "I am willing to have you draw on Raëhemaiëth through me. You said you would marry me, and told me your reasons. You didn't say that one of those reasons was so that Raëhemaiëth would moderate Eänetaìsarè's demands. But you hardly have to say so. All your reasons stand, including that one. So I will marry you. You will not put this off again. I will be your *wife*, and you will *never do this again.*"

The quality of the silence after that told him she had struck home. She said, following up her advantage with a precision she had not known she could command, "Don't tell me you would hurt me. I know that's not true."

"I cannot marry you," he answered, and for the first time in his voice there was a raw sound of naked emotion. "I intended to. But how can I bring . . . *this* . . . to you? You say your Immanent will moderate Eänetaìsarè. But the reverse is also true."

Kehera looked into his face. The shadows moved over it, and she could see nothing there she recognized. But she could hear his voice clearly, even over the sound the fires made. She said, and this time her voice did not shake, "You will give me something of Eänetaìsarè. And I will accept it. Do you think I am so craven that I fear that? If you think so, you are much mistaken." When he started to interrupt, she added firmly, "And you must go forward with the marriage. What will you do if you have no heir, and another arrow that you cannot send aside comes down out of the sky? What will Eänetaìsarè do then?"

He drew a sharp breath, and she knew she had struck home a second time.

She said before he could find an answer, "And you must, because I will have it so. I will be your wife, Innisth, and I swear, Fortunate Gods witness, that you will never again lay your hand on any man, or woman, as you have done here tonight. If you do, I lay on you a cold bed that will never grow warm. I call on all Fortunate Gods to hear me: If you do, I lay on you that you will never get a child by me nor by any other woman. A cold bed and a cold wife you will have, all the days of your life, and no child to come after you—"

He took the one step necessary, caught her shoulders, and shook her once, hard. "Kehera! Woman, what are you trying to do to me?"

And that was the first time *he* had ever called *her* by name. She knew by that she had won. But she had known it anyway. She did not try to break free of his grip. But she found now that she could see his face clearly, even in the uncertain light. His yellow wolf's eyes were wide, shocked. Vulnerable. "Kehera," he whispered, this time quietly, with a deep weariness behind every word that frightened her more than anger would have done. "Kehera, I will not be able to protect you from Eänetaìsarè."

She brought her hands up to close around his wrists, where he held her shoulders. His skin was sticky with sweat, or blood. She held him tightly. "I don't require protection. I'm not fragile. Besides, your Immanent will moderate its desires for Raëhemaiëth's sake." She paused and then said more gently, "But you're wrong anyway. You will protect me if you need to. Do you think I don't know you can hold your Immanent in the palm of your hand? You *can* deny its worse desires, if you will have it so."

"Do you think I have never tried?"

She shifted her grip to his hands and held them firmly in hers, not letting him pull away. "I think you've never tried with a Harivin Raëhema standing next to you."

For a long moment there was no sound in the night but the crackling roar of the fires.

"Swear it. Swear you will never again look to another person's pain for your release." She thought for a moment that he would break her hold on his hands and walk away, and she knew that if he did, there would be no way to go after him.

But after that moment, he stood still again, his inhuman golden eyes swimming with fire.

"Swear it," she insisted.

And he sighed and said quietly, "I so swear." He did break her hold then, and turned a little away. But he did not walk away and leave her standing behind him. He stood still, looking into the fires, or perhaps at what lay between them.

She said, speaking as quietly as he had done, "Then I will marry you. You must send me a poem."

He turned his head, clearly taken aback.

"Every woman expects a courting poem from any serious suitor," Kehera told him. "*I* expect one." She hoped composing one on such short notice would help him regain his own accustomed self-possession as well. Though he might have been turning lines over in his mind since his earliest declaration that he would marry her. She would not have been surprised.

He did not object to her demand, but only bowed slightly, though he still stood before her shirtless and streaked with another man's blood. "Your wish is, evidently, my command."

"Good. We will marry tomorrow." She looked up at the star-dusted sky. "Today," she said, because she could feel the approaching dawn. She said it again, "Today." It sounded certain. It sounded right. She had never felt so sure of anything in her life.

"As you wish." He held out his hand. "May I escort you back to your tent?"

"What, like that?"

He glanced down at his naked chest, his bloody arms. "I have a towel. And a cloak. With my horse." He collected both, taking his time about it, and came back to where Kehera waited for him, holding the reins of her own horse. He had cleaned the blood off his hands. Wrapped in his black cloak, he looked severe but no longer savage. He held a bowl of water, which he poured over Kehera's hands to wash off the blood she had gotten on her fingers, touching him.

After that, she allowed him to help her mount. As they turned their horses toward the little trail that would lead back to camp, she hesitated and asked, "What about the fires?"

He spared a glance over his shoulders to them, the flames catching in his eyes. He said, in a tone Kehera could not interpret, "Let them burn. Let them burn to ash and nothing." And turned forward again, and lifted his black mare into a dangerous canter down the sloping trail.

The falcon flies swift on the wing—
Bright her brave flight
Against the pale sky.
Out of the clean dawn,
The wind-swift bird appears—
These walls do not prison the bird
Although I am prisoned here.

To our shattered dreams we cling:
Bright we dreamed them,
Long we cherished them,
High we builded them,
But they break against the beating
Of our deepest hearts and fears,
And we cut our fingers to the bone
On the shards of passing years.

Is it for me the falcon cries?
Brave her song falls
From the open sky!
From the tumbled walls the echoes ring.
In all her dreams she perseveres—
The foundation of all my hope,
And the tomb of all my fears.

23

Tiro knew all the stories. He leaned against the heavy windowsill of this high tower room, gazed out over the windblown homes and towers of Talisè, and let all the scattered details of those old tales fall through his mind.

For example, the one about the Great Power of ancient Sierè in the south. It had forced the apotheosis of many southern Immanences, or so scholars thought. Of course, nothing was left of Sierè now, or any lesser Immanent of the southlands. No one was entirely certain whether the Power of Sierè had *meant* to devastate the south, but if anything besides the chaos of black storms and obsidian-winged dragons now existed in the south, no one knew of it.

Tiro had certainly not driven the Immanent of Eilin from the land that had birthed it. But he had taken not merely a light tie, but a full ruling tie to the lesser Immanent. He had anchored Raëhemaiëth into Eilin, through and past the rightful Power of that land. Through and past the tie rightfully held by the Lady of Eilin. Lady Viy still held Eilin. But now she held town and province and Immanent Power largely at his own sufferance. If he put his will on Eilin, Tiro was fairly certain he could take the tie away from Lady Viy entirely and keep it for his own or bestow it elsewhere as he pleased.

It was a terrible ability. Just how similar it might be to what the King of Sierè had done . . . he really did not know. But it was certainly just the kind of thing an ambitious king might do.

He had *tried* not to disturb the Eilin Immanent. He hoped Raëhemaiëth had not disturbed it. But he knew possibly the disaster in Sierè had begun very much this way.

This was why no one was supposed to experiment with establishing different kinds of bonds between one Immanent and another. Nor with creating new Immanences in empty lands where none had yet formed naturally. Because no one knew exactly when ambition and audacity might lead to calamity. The ordinary bonds between a Great Power and a lesser . . . yes, that kind of bond could become Unfortunate. But everyone knew the limits of that kind of bond, either way.

Tiro did not know where the limits of this new kind of bond between Raëh and Eilin might lie. Far less what would come of this new notion of his, based on what he'd done at Eilin, but . . . different. No one knew.

So he would try this mad stratagem with Raëhemaiëth. It *was* mad. But Tiro was, amazingly enough and in defiance of all good sense, King of Harivir. He hadn't wanted the ruling tie. He didn't want it, but he held it and he was going to do what he had to, anything he had to, to make sure that whoever got the tie after him, it wasn't any mad foreign king. Or, worse, any mad foreign Immanent Power that was right on the edge of tearing itself free of the earth and becoming a God.

That was why Tiro had left Harivir proper, crossed the Imhar, and come to Talisè.

He hadn't wanted to try this with Talisè specifically. But he hadn't been inclined to try anything so risky in a Harivin town, not the first time at least, and Enmon Corvallis had been all in favor of beginning with an Emmeran town. Corvallis had suggested Talisè. It seemed a fitting town for this experiment, this Emmeran town that lay directly across the Imhar from Cemerè, where everything had started.

That wasn't quite true, of course. But for Tiro and Kehera and their father, it had all *seemed* to start in Cemerè. The destruction of Cemerè's Immanent had led to their first clear knowledge that something beyond ordinary mortal ambition threatened Harivir, and to Kehera being forced to leave Harivir, and then from there to . . . everything else.

So, Talisè. For most of the year, the winds here must blow from the north and the west, Tiro knew. The winds would sweep across the wide flat lands of Emmer, through small stands of neatly tended woods and through harvest stubble left in the fields, carrying the fragrance of warm earth and growing things. But as midwinter approached, the winds shifted and came from the south and the east. These were cold, unfriendly winds that hissed now up and over the pale-yellow walls and whipped the banners strung on the towers out to their full lengths and brought tiny whirlwinds of dust and leaf litter to brief life in odd corners. Not the black winds of the Iron Hinge. Not yet. But that was coming too.

He supposed they should all be grateful they still had seven days till the actual Iron Hinge began. It had taken practically forever to coordinate everything, but it was impossible to imagine taking this kind of risk during those dark days between the ending of the old year and the beginning of the new. Though he would have done even that rather than gambling everything on waiting for the new year to dawn. Certainly Corvallis wouldn't have waited; he was perhaps the most ambitious man Tiro had personally ever met.

A step behind him made him turn. It was Gereth Murrel, of course. A man who belonged neither to Harivir nor to Emmer and so had found himself the one person who could speak to anyone equally without ever giving offense. Of course, part of that was the man's natural talent.

Tiro gave him a nod. "Everyone is here?"

"All that I think we'll have, Your Majesty." Gereth never sounded ironic when he called Tiro by that title, which was helping Tiro become accustomed to it. "The Talisaiän heir, Lady Maené. Lord Liyè, of course, has come across the river from Cemerè. Lady Taraä of Leiör, whom I understand has brought you your . . . ax."

Tiro couldn't help but laugh. She had, though she'd added wryly that with the situation so dire, she doubted he'd need to intimidate anyone into cooperation.

Gereth was going on, not needing to consult any sort of notes. "Lady Senen of Daè and Duke Miya of Nuò have come from Emmer. I'm sure they're both impatient to see what will happen here. If you do manage to restore an Immanent to Talisè, even one to which you hold a new kind of ruling tie that can compel its submission to Raëhemaiëth, then I'm sure you can expect an instant uproar as every ruler of an empty land will wish theirs to be next."

Tiro sighed. In all known history, relatively few lands had ever been hollowed out once they developed an Immanent Power. But those tales did tend to stick in the memory, as vivid warnings against the venality of men or the enmity of the Unfortunate Gods. Empty lands suffered terribly during the midwinter storms, generally serving as object lessons for generations before—hopefully—eventually giving rise to young new Immanents and recovering. He was certain anyone who loved a land would agree to almost anything in order to recover the protection and resilience an Immanent Power provided.

He said, "Corvallis will undoubtedly try to insist that Suriytè come next. I don't know whether he expects he'll find a way to hold any Immanent of Suriytè on his own and not through me or Raëhemaiëth, or whether he'll plan to break with us after . . . afterward, through sheer force of will."

"Ah. Yes, the latter, I expect."

There was a dry note to Gereth's voice that made Tiro look at him sharply. "You're thinking I won't permit him any such thing? You're right. I'll do my best to prevent any Immanent of Suriytè from gaining independence from Raëh. If this works, Cemerè will be next, and then Leiör. Then Daè and Nuò. Suriytè at the very end, when my position is as strong as possible."

"But you will permit Enmon Corvallis to take Suriytè, if he can."

"I have to. I need him. But I don't plan to let him take much more than that one province, if I can stop him. And I'll be sure the new Immanent of Suriytè remains subordinate to Raëh, if I can. I think we'll all be more comfortable with Corvallis as King of Emmer if Emmer's influence is substantially reduced." He hesitated. "Anyway, we—I can't be sure any of this will work. It could still just go horribly wrong."

"It will work. It won't go wrong."

Gereth couldn't know that. But he offered this reassurance with cheering certainty and without a trace of condescension, so that Tiro immediately felt more confident. Gereth did have a gift. He must have been a very good seneschal.

Tiro took a breath, let it out, and nodded to the older man to lead the way.

The others, those Emmeran and Harivin lords who had lost their Immanences and had come here in the hope that Tirovay Elin Raëhema had found a way to give them back what they had lost, were gathered in the courtyard of the lord's four-cornered house, where the high walls blocked the cold wind yet they could stand upon earth that belonged to Talisè. Lords and ladies of Harivir and Emmer, Enmon Corvallis and a couple of his men, Tiro and a couple of *his* men, and Gereth Murrel of Eäneté. It was a most peculiar gathering under any circumstances, possibly the strangest this house had ever hosted. Corvallis was at the center; the man possessed such natural authority that this was probably inevitable. He was the oldest, too, except for Duke Miya; and Miya Nuòseir was not nearly so . . . forceful.

The rest stood in a loose, uneven circle, with a good deal of space left between the three from Emmer and the two from Harivir. Everyone turned toward Tiro when he came in, variously anticipatory and nervous and skeptical. He took care to nod to them all equally, not favoring his own folk. But it was Lady Taraä who stepped aside to make room for him beside her. She was fairly forceful, too, even if she were a woman and not much older than Tiro. She had brought her ax. His ax. The ax that figured in stories of both their families. She had planted the ax-head against the earth and was leaning comfortably on the haft. She was a big enough woman that it was quite possible to imagine her doing more with that ax than just leaning on it. Everyone else in the circle was leaving her plenty of room. When she caught Tiro's eye, her lips twitched, and even under the circumstances, he was hard put not to grin back.

Tiro stepped into the circle beside Taraä and paused, studying Enmon Corvallis. Everyone else followed his gaze, which did not seem to make Corvallis at all uncomfortable. The man looked like nothing had ever made him uncomfortable in his life. Tiro knew he must be at least a little nervous, no matter how calm he seemed. Probably serving the Mad King had taught him that impenetrable composure.

Lady Maené was much easier to read. Of them all, she had reason to be the most anxious—after Tiro, perhaps—because she was the heir of Talisè. Her uncle the Lord of Talisè had killed himself when he'd lost his Immanent. Tiro had been quietly appalled when he'd learned that. He was not entirely happy about binding a new Immanent to the heir of a line capable of such a failure of nerve, such an abdication of responsibility. But she was the heir, and that might matter. It might make all the difference.

She might regain . . . not exactly what she had lost, but *something*. If this worked. So might they all. *If* this worked, she would hold Talisè. Truly hold it, with no need to wait for years or generations for the slow, natural emergence of a new Immanent; the lady would leap all at once from holding no tie at all to taking a ruling tie to a strong Immanent.

If this didn't work . . . Tiro had no idea. He supposed no matter what happened, they would all do their best to withstand Hallieth Theraön and Methmeir Heriduïn, or the terrible Power that had mastered both kings.

"You have the Eänetén stone?" he asked Gereth, who had come quietly, as he was always quiet, to stand near at hand but outside the circle. "May I hold it?" Then he looked around at the small gathering. They all knew what Tiro meant to do. And they had all seen the fragment of stone before, with its tiny involution containing an infinitesimal thread of the Eänetén Power.

"All right," Tiro said, trying not to sound nervous. "In none of the old tales does anyone succeed at this, exactly. Or not without dire consequences. But I trust Raëhemaiëth—and if we do nothing, we'll almost certainly face dire consequences anyway. Even so, I can't deny that trying new things with a Great Power carries a certain hazard."

"Of course we all understand that," snapped Duke Miya.

"We just have to hope it will go well," added Lady Maené, gripping her hands together.

Lady Taraä said firmly, "It's not a matter of luck or hoping. You'll make it work, Your Majesty." She swung the ax lightly in her hand and set it back against the earth. "Your great-great-great-grandfather would have made it work, and so will you."

Tiro didn't think it would be right to smile openly, but he nodded to her.

Enmon Corvallis said in a calm, level voice, "I honestly believe that even if this doesn't work, it won't go all the way wrong."

Tiro nodded again. That was the important point; trust Corvallis to go straight to the heart of the risk they were taking. The Emmeran general didn't have to say anything else. Everyone here knew what *all the way wrong* entailed. Everyone knew about Immanent Powers and Gods and the risk of apotheosis. They all knew what Tiro was going to try to do. He should stop explaining and just go on. Nervousness always made Tiro want to *explain* things. He knew it was time to just move forward.

So he met Enmon Corvallis's eyes one more time and then turned to Lady Maené. And when the lady nodded, Tiro knelt on the cold ground and laid his hand on the earth of Talisè, the empty earth which the Immanent Power that had risen out of this land should have filled.

And he called up Raëhemaiëth.

The Immanent of Raëh came immediately, as though it had been waiting for his call. It swelled up within Tiro and around him, warm and heavy as summer despite the bite in the air above and the frozen earth below. Raëhemaiëth came, and Tiro anchored it into the land of

Talisè, as an ambitious king would do to dominate a smaller land and expand his kingdom. . . . It wasn't quite as simple as Tiro had imagined. There was no lesser Power here, and now he saw that a lesser Immanent would have given Raëhemaiëth a . . . pattern, a line, a web . . . none of those were right . . . a living soul and presence already shaped to Talisè, to the land and the people, the beasts and the dormant growing things. Without that, Raëhemaiëth had nothing to follow, nothing to guide it as it tried to settle into the earth and the creatures of Talisè. It settled itself into and around Tiro instead, recognizing him, and spread out into the land only very slowly.

For the first time, Tiro thought he might understand why the ruthlessly ambitious Irekaïn Power had not set itself into all the provinces it had hollowed out, why it needed a man to carry its tie into a foreign land before it could act. He wanted to think about that. It felt important. It felt like a revelation he should try to remember, but Raëhemaiëth was so . . . enormous . . . it swelled and swelled and flowed through Tiro into the land, until he lost awareness of everything else. He couldn't tell whether it understood what he meant to do. Immanences weren't like people. They didn't exactly *understand* things. He didn't know how to explain what he meant to do. Or try to do. He didn't know how to ask if it would approve.

If it didn't . . . if it fought him . . . Tiro could guess what might happen. He had mastered Raëhemaiëth once, when his father had died. But then Raëhemaiëth had *wanted* him to master it. If it fought him now . . . he might do worse than fail. He might lose the tie.

Which might go to Kehera, held in the south by the ambition of the Wolf Duke. That would be all right. Tiro wouldn't mind that, or he thought he wouldn't mind it. Or not much. Or he would hate it; if he lost Raëhemaiëth now, he would *hate* that. But if Taraä and Liyè and everyone could stand losing their ties, he could, if he had to.

If Raëhemaiëth rejected the Elin line entirely, that would be worse. He would be very sorry for it, but it could set its deep tie elsewhere and, again, Raëh would be all right. Harivir would be all right. He trusted Raëh not to choose anyone unsuitable.

But it might tear itself free from Tiro *and* from all its other bonds. He didn't *think* that would happen. But it *might*. And then Raëhemaiëth would become a God, and that would be far worse than just Tiro losing its tie. Worse for Harivir, and far worse for Raëh, and probably pretty bad for Talisè, too. They had all talked about that possibility and decided to take the risk. Because if the worst happened, everyone trusted Raëhemaiëth to become a Fortunate God, and then, if it remembered its people at all, if it were sorry at all for destroying Raëh and probably Talisè, at least in the violence of its apotheosis, it might do something about the Irekaïn Power. Then at least the rest of the Four Kingdoms would be safe.

It seemed to take a long, long time for Raëhemaiëth to anchor itself firmly into Talisè, to shape itself to the pale-yellow sandstone and the ceaseless winds, the folk of the city and the surrounding lands, the creatures of the broad fields and narrow strips of woods, the earth and the air and the nearby Imhar River. But once it had made itself part of Talisè, Tiro closed that part of Raëhemaiëth away from the part that was still solidly grounded in Raëh. He made all of Talisè a single great involution containing that part of Raëhemaiëth and . . . gave it up, closed it off, shut it away. He didn't know what he did, exactly.

It hurt. It didn't exactly *hurt*, but . . . it hurt. It was like pouring the strength of Raëh into a lesser Immanent, except . . . different. Raëhemaiëth did not exactly fight it, but . . . it fought. Cutting the involution free would weaken Raëhemaiëth, and it didn't understand things the way a person did, but it understood weakness and strength, and it fought what Tiro was trying to do to it, what he was trying to make it do to itself.

In another way, it didn't actually fight at all. If Raëhemaiëth had truly refused, he could never have made it do anything. Certainly not pour a part of itself into Talisè, create an involution, and cut that part free to shape itself to a land that was not Raëh, that had never been part of Raëh.

Raëhemaiëth did not quite refuse, and the new Immanent that had been poured into Talisè and shaped itself to the new land, to sandstone and wind, plains and river, border and border people . . . that part accepted the separate involution Tiro offered.

Losing it weakened Raëhemaiëth. But the new Immanent was bound to Raëhemaiëth, and its strength poured through the bond . . . strength poured both ways, through a bond that was neither Fortunate nor Unfortunate. Or in a way it was both at once. Tiro had hoped for that . . . or for something like that, he couldn't remember any longer what he had hoped for; he was too lost in what was actually happening to remember what he had guessed might happen.

The new Immanent was anchored to the earth; it was anchored to Talisè. It spun itself into all the people of Talisè, all the creatures; it settled into them, became a part of them. Raëhemaiëth knew how to do that. It couldn't have done that itself. But it knew how, and the part of itself that was now part of Talisè bound itself to the land and the people alike.

But it was not held by a deep tie. It was not held by any single person. It had not been mastered. If no one held a deep tie to the new Immanent, it could cradle Talisè and protect it against storms and ill luck and dragons, but it could not work with people. Not properly. Not as it would need to when the terrible cold Immanent of Irekay came down against it. It knew that. It knew it because Raëhemaiëth knew it. It *wanted* to be bound, as Raëhemaiëth wanted to be bound. It couldn't take an ordinary deep tie to Tiro, though in a way it was already bound to him; that would have made it back into merely a part of Raëhemaiëth.

So it set its tie elsewhere. Tiro wasn't sure at first where the tie went. Into someone with the strength and determination to master the new Immanent and be sure it saw the world partly through mortal eyes rather than only through its own strange perception . . . Tiro opened his own eyes. He hadn't realized he'd closed them, but he opened them now to the ordinary, solid world of men, and found himself meeting Enmon Corvallis's eyes and looking through him into the heavy presence of . . .

not Raëhemaiëth. The new Immanent, bound to Talisè.

Tiro couldn't speak. He had forgotten how to speak, but even when human language slowly opened up within him once more, he didn't know what to say. All his efforts and Raëhemaiëth's sacrifice had worked so well, and so unexpectedly.

Corvallis was going to be furious. He *was* furious; that was obvious. It didn't really show in his face or manner, but the older man's anger was as vividly plain to Tiro as though he had shouted. Talisè was not the city or the province General Corvallis had wanted. He would have rejected both and taken Suriytè if he could. But the tie had come to him anyway, the new Immanent setting its tie where it found the clearest echo. Enmon Corvallis held it now, and Tiro knew without a word having to be spoken that the man would not be able to give it up. Not now that he held it.

Not even though the new Immanent was still bound to Raëhemaiëth. The new one had been folded somehow *through* Raëhemaiëth, so that Tiro held a deep tie to both Powers at once, to the new one through his own. . . . It was indeed a different kind of ruling tie, one that gave Tiro a firm hold on Talisè as well as Raëh. It had worked almost exactly the way Tiro had hoped. He could see that he might indeed strip the tie out of Corvallis and set it elsewhere; that he could strip vigor and strength from Talisè, from the new Immanent and the land itself. That Talisè was not and would not ever be truly sovereign, but would always be subordinate to Raëh.

Corvallis had realized that too. He would never be King of Emmer now. He held Talisè, but his was not a ruling tie. If Tiro created many new Immanences of this kind and bound them all to Raëhemaiëth in this way, then if anyone became King of Emmer, it would be *him*. Corvallis had already understood that. No wonder he was so furious.

"Raëhemaiëth never meant to lessen itself in order to shape . . . Talisamaiëth," Tiro said to him. It was as though the two of them were alone in this courtyard, in the heart of Talisè. He went on honestly, "It always meant to make . . . this kind of bond. I'm not—I can't be sorry for it, though I meant the tie to go to Lady Maené." He spared the lady a slight nod of regret, but made sure not to imply apology. She might have been easier to work with in some ways, but he couldn't regret what the new Immanent had done.

"Talisamaiëth chose where it would go," he said, still speaking directly to Corvallis. "But it had to be this kind of bond. It would have been disastrous to weaken Raëhemaiëth. You know that. This doesn't weaken Raëh. You know this was the only way to do it."

"I know," Corvallis said, rather through his teeth.

Lady Taraä swung the ax from one hand up to rest over her shoulder. She was tall enough and strong enough to handle the massive weapon easily. It wasn't exactly a gesture of intimidation. But the ax was big enough and impressive enough to make everyone, even Enmon Corvallis, look at her. Then she said in her calm way, to Corvallis but really to all of them, "It would have been the same in Suriytè. Unless you had let the Immanent there rise naturally from the land, and there wouldn't have been time. I know this wasn't what you wanted. But we can't be cutting at each other. We can't be at odds. Not now."

"*I know.*" Corvallis glowered at Taraä and then at Tiro. Then he finally took a deep, deep breath and let it out, locking down his fury. "Your Majesty," he said to Tiro. Grimly. But he said it.

Tiro set himself and nodded back, not letting himself glance at Taraä, though he knew her support might have made the difference. She was right. They all knew she was right. Even Corvallis. Now he had to trust that the man—Enmon Corvallis Talisaiän, now—wouldn't change his mind. At least not yet. Not until they were through the dark turn of the year and one way or another this grim business with the Irekaïn Power was settled. He didn't think the man would be able to break the ruling tie between Talisè and Raëh later, either. But if he chose to try, later was definitely better.

Then Tiro looked around, wondering belatedly whether the other rulers of the hollow provinces would be willing to go on with this now that they all understood that even in the best case they would be tied to Immanences that would be unavoidably ruled by Raëhemaiëth and by Tirovay Elin Raëhema, before even their own will or desires. That was very different from an ordinary ruling tie. Tiro wasn't sure what to call it: not just a ruling tie or a king's tie. An overlord's tie, perhaps. A high king's tie.

"Can we do Leiör next?" Lady Taraä asked in a decisive tone that made it clear *she* wasn't worried about any of that. "Or, I *suppose* Cemerè, since it's right across the river. But then Leiör next after that. And then Nuò, I suppose, to set the border against anything coming down from Suriytè." She raised her eyebrows at Duke Miya Nuòseir, who of them all seemed the most skeptical. "Surely no one thinks it's better to leave their province echoing and empty?"

"The lady's grasp of strategy is adequate," growled Corvallis. Lord Enmon. Or he might be a duke. His Immanent might be powerful enough for that; if not yet, then soon. Talisè was a fairly large province, and Corvallis a great deal stronger-willed than the former line that had held Talisè. Now he gave Tiro a grim little nod and went on. "Cemerè is not actually essential, however. Nor is Nuò; I hate to give it up, but if we have to, Talisè can serve as our northern border." Duke Miya, obviously dismayed, began to protest, but Enmon ignored him. "We must have Leiör to cover anything coming against us from the northeast. And that ruthless wolf's whelp in Eäneté had better keep his promise to cover us from the southeast and south."

"I'll write to the Duke of Eäneté." No. Tiro would write to Kehera, and trust her to make sure the ruthless wolf's whelp who had forced himself on her would keep his part of the bargain. Surely his sister would be able to do it. She might even persuade Innisth terè Maèr Eänetaì to join the rest of them, actually tie his obviously very strong Immanent Power to Raëhemaiëth. . . . Well, no, probably not. The Eänetén duke was ambitious enough to annex southern Harivir into what he plainly meant to make into a new kingdom—and callous enough to force Kehera to help him do it. A man like that was not likely to surrender anything he held or owned to Raëhemaiëth.

If they all survived, if they all survived intact, or intact *enough* . . . he swore to himself that he would find a way to punish the Eänetén duke for what he'd done to Kehera and to Harivir. It almost physically hurt to know that if Innisth terè Maèr Eänetaì held the south and southeast and protected all those lands from the Irekaïn Power, he would actually *owe* the man.

He didn't say any of that. It was none of Enmon Corvallis Talisaiän's business.

"I don't—" began Duke Miya, finding his voice at last.

"We'll do what we have to," Enmon said grimly. "All of us. We've no choice now."

"I know," said Tiro. And what they could do would have to be enough. Seven days until the Iron Hinge of the year; only seven days. He was almost certain the Irekaïn Power meant to achieve its apotheosis during the Iron Hinge days. No later than midwinter itself. Nine days. At most.

He was not at all sure it would be enough.

24

Kehera had attended many weddings, of course. The people of Raëh had all her life taken her presence at their weddings as a sort of charm. Dyed wheat, apple blossoms, blown robins' eggs of the most delicate blue, and the cheerful presence of the Elin Raëhema heir: all good signs for a long and happy marriage. Kehera had always wondered, watching ardent or glad or resigned women and men tie the cords and exchange their vows, what it would be like to take the bride's part of such a ceremony. This . . . was not quite what she had ever envisioned for herself.

Weddings normally took place during Apple Blossom Month, of course. Or sometimes, daringly, during the Golden Hinge Month, as spring turned to summer. The Golden Hinge was a chancy time, for the bright turn of the year meant not only burgeoning warmth but also change and transformation, not always in predictable directions. But Kehera's women had liked to tell romantic tales about poor but audacious couples who married during the Golden Hinge days, thus changing their fortunes and carrying their families to brighter days.

Apple Blossom Month or the Golden Hinge Month, those were the most auspicious times for weddings. Couples seldom wed at other times of year. Certainly never during the Iron Hinge Month. The whole dark month carried ill fortune. Yet Kehera made ready for her marriage to the Wolf Duke of Eäneté on this winter afternoon with the hinge looming before them like a dark storm, only four days removed.

They had at least withdrawn to Viär rather than holding the marriage ceremony in a tent at the edge of the trampled and bloody mud below Meilin Gap. Viär was nearly in sight of the gap, so it was simple to repair to the town for a night and a day to recover from . . . everything, and hold something like a proper wedding ceremony. Though it was not a large town, Kehera could see it had remained prosperous despite the recent long years of drought. No wonder Lord Toren seemed so much older than she remembered from only a few years ago; he had poured his own strength into his land so that it should not suffer.

The homes of Viär were mostly large, as was the custom in towns and villages near the mountains. They were meant to house extended families over generations, these homes; built solidly of local stone and timber, with wide windows to the west and the south to catch the sun that spilled across the barley fields in summer. They had no windows at all facing the mountains from which came the black winds of midwinter.

Lord Toren's house was of that same sprawling construction, easily large enough to house the lord and his young wife, her children and his son by his first wife, his brothers and their wives and children, and innumerable cousins of various degree. All of these folk appeared determined to attend Kehera's wedding.

She missed Tiro, though she didn't want to think of what he might say about this wedding of hers, which would bind her to Eäneté and bind Raëhemaiëth to Eänetaìsarè. She thought all this was as much Raëhemaiëth's doing as hers, or even the Wolf Duke's. But she couldn't decide whether Tiro would agree with her about that, or whether he would be horrified by the very suggestion.

She missed her father so much. Not only because she longed to ask his advice and counsel, not only because she could imagine how frightened he must have been for her, but simply because his absence was a stone weighing down her heart. When she had been a girl, it had never occurred to her that she might marry among strangers, with none of her own people around her.

On the other hand, she had been prepared to marry the Mad King of Emmer if he had forced her to it. Compared to that, she was *entirely* content to marry the Wolf Duke, in Viär or a muddy camp or anywhere else.

Of course, she had never intended to *stay* in Emmer. She'd always meant to escape, or at least *try* to escape. Though after that horrifying visit to Hallieth Suriytaiän's tower, she'd never believed she would get away unscathed.

And of course she hadn't. Not unscathed. She'd lost so much. She missed Eilisè even more than her father, which in a way made her feel guilty. But Eilisè had been her own age, and a woman, and her friend. Kehera would have felt so much less alone if Eilisè had been with her here.

These days were so perilous, anything might happen. They might yet all be crushed beneath Irekay's cold Immanent. But Eilisè should have had her chance to fight through these days in her own quiet woman's fashion, and live, and make a life for herself, and someday marry for love the way a princess could not. Kehera should have looked forward to going to her friend's wedding, to throwing handfuls of dyed wheat over her and giving Eilisè her own wreath of apple blossoms. It seemed so bitter that none of that could ever happen.

They stood in the great hall of the house, surrounded by Lord Toren's household. Kehera, of course, had only Eöté and the thankfully calmer Morain Lochan to attend her. But the Wolf Duke, having left his soldiers encamped at Meilin Gap, was even more sparsely attended than she. Kehera was sorry for that, too; sorry that Gereth Murrel could not be here, sorry that the duke had no brothers or cousins or, so far as she knew, friends, to stand with him. Even Caèr Reiöft had absented himself, showing a delicacy that did not actually surprise her at all.

Kehera glanced covertly sideways at the closed expression and unrevealing eyes of the Eänetén duke. Innisth terè Maèr Eänetaì. She wondered what he was thinking. All these days in his company, even some sort of understanding between their two Immanences, and she still couldn't tell. Except that when she had demanded this marriage go forward, he had acceded. Princesses did not marry for love; nor did dukes. But as she had asked, he had sent her a courting poem written with his own hand. Perhaps he cared for her . . . a little, at least. She had to admit, if only to herself, that she might have learned to care for him. At least a little.

He was not a comfortable man. But she admired his strength of will, his dedication to Eäneté and to his people, even his ambition. He was not exactly kind. She would not have said *kind*. But he was often generous, though he seemed not to realize that himself.

And he had certainly taken some pains for the ceremony. Kehera looked at him sidelong. The Eänetén duke was not smiling, but his austere features did not seem well suited to smiling. He was perhaps a little pale, though that might have been the chilly light of the season. Eilisè would have pointed out that his height and the breadth of his shoulders showed off his elaborate wedding coat to very nice effect. Kehera couldn't help but wonder whether Caèr Reiöft might have packed that coat with his own hands, or whether that was a garment borrowed, like the house, from Lord Toren.

The duke's coat was stiff with embroidery. Blue for marriage, of course, and gold for strength, both against Eänetén gray. Kehera had borrowed a dress from one of Lord Toren's cousins, an azure and violet gown with abundant skirts and gold embroidery on the bodice. She and Eöté and the cousin and the cousin's two daughters had taken up the hem and fitted the bodice and added dozens and dozens of tiny pearls to the panels of embroidery, because the cousin was determined to have the dress fit for the Raëhema heir. Kehera had thought the pearls unnecessary, but she had to admit the gown was beautiful.

It had taken Kehera almost half an hour to get into the dress even with the girls to help, and then the cousin had insisted on arranging her hair with strands of lapis beads and more pearls. Then she added the weightless strand of hollow robins' eggs, which was like being crowned with a strand of hope and belief in the possibilities of future days.

After all that, Kehera had actually felt quite shy when the duke had called at the door of her borrowed chamber to escort her down to the central hall of Lord Toren's vast house.

She hadn't been able to help noticing the slight widening of the duke's eyes when he saw her, the minimal change to the stern line of his mouth. Kehera had laid her hand gravely on his arm and wondered if there was the slightest chance that he was glad to have it there, not because she bore a deep tie to Raëhemaiëth or he would find her useful in the struggle with Irekay, but just because it was her hand.

Now their hands were clasped together, her fingers interlaced with his, with the twice-braided cord of black horsehair and bleached flax looped around their hands and wrists in token of a binding that was supposed to last all the rest of their lives. The knot was complicated. The cord was not supposed to be untied.

The vows were very simple: his to protect and cherish, hers to be faithful. But when it came to the moment for the vows, the Eänetén duke swore to protect and cherish not only her and her children, but her people as well. She was not surprised at all. Generous, yes—if not kind. She met his eyes and nodded to show she trusted his vow. His yellow gaze was inscrutable as the gaze of a wolf. But he nodded back gravely.

When it was her turn, she swore to remain faithful and cleave only to him for the term of his life and hers. It occurred to her that she could rather easily imagine that, despite everything, despite Methmeir Irekaì and his horrible Immanent Power, their lives might prove to be long. But what surprised her was that she thought she might not mind living a long life with the Eänetén duke, however unlike her imagined life that might prove to be. She still did not know whether she *liked* him. But she thought she trusted him, in a way that she could not define even to herself.

Then it was done. They held their bound hands over the candle, and the cords went up in a brief, dazzling burst of flame that was over so quickly the fire did not have time to burn their skin. Kehera rubbed the faint red mark that was the only sign of the burning and then slowly dropped her hand back to her side. She tried to decide whether she felt any different, but she could not tell. She looked at him—at her husband. He gazed back, his expression remote. He honestly did look very forbidding. Kehera thought, with a faint sense of surprise, *He is almost as nervous as I am*, but then she was not sure whether this was true.

The duke touched her arm, and they turned together to face the assembled folk. There was a little cheering, not loud and joyful as Kehera had heard—and participated in—at other wedding ceremonies, but subdued. The household had lost loved ones at Meilin Gap, and feared what next might come from the east, and were not certain they should wish her happy in her marriage to this foreign duke. But the children threw handfuls of dyed wheat nevertheless. Kehera made herself smile at the gathering with all the reassurance she could muster, and was rewarded by a slight relaxation of the tension in the room. But she was glad enough to escape to the privacy of the hall when the duke conducted her out of the great hall.

"I will escort you to your rooms, if you will permit me," said the duke expressionlessly. Her rooms were on the second level of the sprawling house, above the bakery ovens, where it was warm and comfortable even in midwinter. She had not asked what rooms the Wolf Duke had been offered. Lord Toren's own, probably. He did not touch her now; he did not so much as offer his arm.

Kehera nodded and walked obediently at the duke's side through the halls. They met no one. No doubt Lord Toren's staff had made sure to clear the way, in case either she or the duke did not wish to be observed in this first interval of their married life. She appreciated their discretion.

At the door to her outer room, they paused. For a moment the duke examined the wood in front of him. Then he turned his head to look at her. "I will come to you in half a glass," he said, surprising her with the constraint in his tone. "I hope . . . That is, you do not need to be afraid. Whatever you may have heard of me, or guessed . . . or seen . . . you will have no cause to fear me."

She had already known that. Even without Caèr Reiöft's reassurance—that seemed so long ago now!—she would have known that. But she still could not find her voice to answer. If he had stayed, perhaps she would have found some words, but he turned away toward his own rooms. She went into hers, to face her own private audience, with her head high and her expression carefully composed.

Her women had arrived back in her suite before her. They had been able to hurry, of course, while she had been constrained by the duke's slow, formal pace. Eöté jumped to her feet, gripping her hands together, but Morain Lochan, calm as ever, only heaved herself up and nodded placidly.

Tageiny had been leaning against the opposite wall, fretting, no doubt, because she had not been able to permit her personal guardsmen to attend her during the ceremony. He pushed away from the wall and gave her first a straight look and then a little nod as though he were satisfied with what he saw. Luad, who had a clear sense of priorities, hastily stepped away from a platter of cakes he must have stolen from the kitchens while everyone else had been distracted. But he looked worried, despite the sticky fragment of cake he still had in his hand and now attempted belatedly to hide behind his back.

"It was fine," she promised them all. "The cords went fast and neither of us was burned." And because they would be wondering, she added, "He's coming here. In half an hour." She moved across the room to reverse an hourglass, not wanting to lose track of the passing moments, then turned back toward the others.

Eöté had gone noticeably pale. Luad flushed and looked anywhere but at her. Kehera concentrated on keeping her own expression serene. Tageiny, thankfully, seemed completely undisturbed.

She said, "Eöté, please help me with this dress, and then you can go for the night. Be sure you take some of those cakes; not even Luad can eat that many by himself. Tag, I don't expect bodyguards are quite necessary just at the moment. Why don't you and Luad take the rest of the cakes and go . . . somewhere."

Eöté and Morain had been given a little room of their own adjoining Kehera's, with a connecting door that could be left open or shut, as was suitable for her personal women. Kehera didn't know what arrangements had been made for the men, but was sure Tageiny could cope with anything from a nearby chamber to a servant's attic to a loft in the stables. Now Tageiny set aside half the cakes for the women, quashed the younger man's protests with a glance, and waved him out the door. The look he gave her himself was unreadable. "You'll be fine," he told her. He tapped a hand to his heart in the gesture that wished her good fortune, and swung easily out the door and away.

Kehera preceded Eöté into the bedchamber, standing patiently for the girl to undo the complicated stays of the blue wedding dress. She breathed a deep sigh of relief as the constriction was relaxed. The dress did not, thankfully, take as long to remove as it had to put on.

"Shall I draw you a bath, my lady?" asked Eöté. She laid the dress aside and picked up a light robe.

"Yes," Kehera decided. "Yes, thank you. Then you should go. His Grace—" She stopped until she could finish steadily, "His Grace will be here soon."

"Yes," Eöté whispered. But then she said. "My lady, you should know, I've never . . . He never . . ."

Surprised, Kehera turned her head. "Really?"

"Everyone was supposed to think so. Because Lord Laören wanted me, so His Grace . . . he made it seem . . . but he never. I'm not supposed to say. . . ."

"Oh."

"Only with Verè," Eöté blurted, barely audible, and fled to draw the bath, leaving Kehera with at least one unanswered question she was too embarrassed to ask.

The duke came down the hall exactly on time. Kehera was surprised at how easy it was to recognize his step—the lightness and length of it, with just the faintest unevenness in the stride, the only reminder now of the leg injury that had so nearly killed him.

He stopped, of course, just outside her door.

Kehera opened it. The duke stood quite still in the hall. He, too, had bathed since the ceremony, and changed into lighter, less formal dress. His plain shirt was dark blue. It actually suited him just as well as the black and gray he ordinarily wore. His expression was unreadable, his dress and manner impeccable as always, but she could feel the Eänetén Power lying beneath his skin, like heat haze in the summer. She could not perceive any answering pressure from Raëhemaiëth. But she suspected she would, soon enough.

"My wife. May I enter?"

Kehera fought down a brief, cowardly impulse to refuse permission. "Yes," she said through a tight throat. "Of course. My lord."

The duke stepped through the doorway. But then he stood still again, not moving closer. Kehera took a deep breath. "Well," she said. "I suppose we should get this over with."

The duke made a small movement, instantly controlled. He said after a second, with unaccustomed tentativeness, "I beg your pardon, but . . . I think you have never been with a man?"

"Of course not!" said Kehera, shocked. "What do you think I am?"

"I beg your pardon," the duke repeated. Kehera saw with amazement that he had flushed slightly. He said, still almost hesitantly, "It need not be a . . . terrible thing. If you do not find me actually revolting."

"Does it matter?"

"Yes. It matters to me. I have no wish to hurt you, Kehera. Eänetaìsarè . . . you understand, Eänetaìsarè is not a gentle Power. But it does not want you to be afraid, or hurt. Nor do I."

"Well, good." She knew very well now just how hard the Eänetén Power pressed the duke toward savagery. She had never been more glad of the nature of her own tie.

And that marked perhaps the first time he had ever used her given name. Or . . . no. The first time except on the mountainside above Meilin Gap, when she had driven him to it. She found, somewhat to her surprise, that she did not mind the familiarity . . . which was just as well, since she no longer had the right to object.

And it was surprisingly easy to believe him. Kehera found that she did not want to hurt him, either. She said after a moment, "I believe you. And no. I mean . . . you are not revolting to me." She studied his spare face, his wolf-pale eyes, his narrow-lipped mouth that never smiled. There appeared to be nothing soft or gentle about him. But softness or gentleness would not have suited him. She did not quite know how to explain how far from revolting he had become to her.

A flicker of expression crossed his face and was repressed. Even a few days ago, Kehera would probably have missed it, though it seemed clear enough to her now. Not that she could easily guess what emotion it had been, but at least she had known that in some way she had affected him.

He said, "We need not use your bed. If you would prefer to maintain that privacy."

"What privacy?" Kehera asked, but his careful thoughtfulness did not surprise her. She said more gently, "No, it doesn't matter. I don't mind." She backed away, into her bedchamber.

After a moment the duke stepped through the door after her.

Standing by the bed, Kehera looked at the Wolf Duke—at her husband—and waited for him to tell her what to do.

The duke removed his shirt, laid it neatly over the back of a chair. His face, as always, was unreadable. His skin was very pale, more even than one expected at midwinter, as though he had never in his life gone without a shirt in the summers. He turned away, still very slowly, to stand with his back to her.

It took a moment for Kehera to realize what had caused the tracery of fine white lines across the skin of his back. She caught her breath.

The duke turned back to face her. "I did not want to take you by surprise."

"Fortunate Gods—your father did that?" She knew it had been his father. She still could hardly believe it. "To his own son?"

He said softly, "It was over a long time ago."

"I wonder," Kehera said gently, "whether something like that can ever be truly over." She was afraid, as soon as the words were out, that he would be offended or annoyed at her unasked sympathy; she didn't have to think about it to know that he would answer any offer of pity with the most extreme distaste.

But the duke said only, "It can. It is." He spoke with perfect finality. When she didn't answer, he went on, a little more slowly, as though he were choosing his words with care. "It has to be over, you see, Kehera. One has to choose in the end whether to let it be a thing of the past." He paused, and then added, "Anyway, I won, in the end."

Because he had killed his father. Kehera did not know what to say. She thought she could quite easily hate the Eänetén Power. Except it was part of him. And at the moment, she did not want to hate any part of him.

"Do I repulse you? I hope not; I cannot leave you now, you know."

Kehera looked at him with real astonishment. "You can't mean because of the scars? What possible difference could that make?"

The duke almost smiled. Then, as he looked at her, his expression closed again. Perhaps it was merely habit that made him close up like that. Perhaps he thought it made him less intimidating. She wished she knew how to tell him it didn't work like that.

He down on the edge of her bed. He reclined against a bed-post, hands laced easily around a drawn-up knee, a deliberately easy, unthreatening pose, for all she could still sense the heat in him, locked beneath that control like fire beneath stone. He touched the place next to him. "Come sit here," he said. Not commandingly at all. As matter-of-factly as though nothing at all were out of the ordinary.

Perhaps to him nothing was. Maybe he had had many lovers before her. Kehera still did not know. She only knew that Eöté had not been one of them. And that, however many there had been, Caèr

Reiöft had somehow managed not to be jealous of them.

She shouldn't ask. She knew she shouldn't ask.

She couldn't help it. She asked, "Have you—have there been many women for you? Or . . . men?" She knew she was blushing.

The duke did not seem either embarrassed or offended. "No, in fact, not in the way you mean it. You have heard—what exactly is it that you have heard about me?"

Well, she'd started it, hadn't she? Kehera pulled her robe around herself and sat down, not on the bed next to him as he had indicated, but on a chair a little way removed. She said carefully, "One can't help hearing things sometimes. But Eöté said . . . I think sometimes what people think isn't necessarily so. But then, it's clear to me that your, um, your relationship with Caèr Reiöft is not, um, not . . . quite . . ." She didn't know any nice way to put it.

"Not quite . . ." the duke agreed dispassionately. "That is perfectly true, Kehera. Eöté told you I did not touch her? That is true. She was not supposed to deny it, however."

"You won't punish her." Kehera had no doubt of this.

"No. She is yours now, more than mine, so of course she told you. I would have given her permission to tell you the truth. I didn't think of it, which is my fault. Did she tell you I also did not touch Verè Deconniy?"

Kehera felt her blush deepen. "From what she said, I wasn't quite certain," she admitted.

"I did not. That was a ruse as well, though one widely believed within my household, I imagine. They wed because Captain Deconniy wished it, and Eöté acceded to it."

"Yes, that . . . surprised me a little, actually."

The duke inclined his head. "He is enamored of her, I believe. I suspect more so than she of him. I suspect Eöté wished a protector, and found it more nearly possible to trust a man who had also . . . endured Laören's attentions."

Kehera was not at all inclined to ask for any more detailed clarification about the implication of that observation.

"The match offered her protection and standing in my household. And of course it is important for any woman of your household to be respectable." The duke paused. "Of course, the ruse was only believable because there have been others. So you were right to be . . . not quite certain." He paused, and then went on. "The Eänetén Power is very strong. I know you, of all women, understand what it is to hold a deep tie. But the Raëhema family is kind, and your Power is kind. The Eänetén Power is . . . not. It was tied to my father, and before him, to my grandfather and all those of my line, and few enough, I think, gave it anything that would gentle it. It is strong, but it is cruel; it delights in pain and fear, and so do we who hold the tie. For us, the urges of the body are bound up with that cruelty. Continence is not something we can easily practice, and fear or pain in those we take to our beds pleases us. This is how I am. I tell you so you will know." He paused again, eyes on her face.

Kehera nodded again. She felt faint with horror and pity, but she felt no surprise or disbelief. She could imagine exactly what he meant.

The duke was continuing, in his quiet, most matter-of-fact voice. "Women are fragile. It is easy to harm a woman. Beyond that, I must not get an heir carelessly. So I have seldom taken a woman."

"I see," Kehera said soberly, reflecting that she'd gotten rather more frankness than she might have wanted. "It must be a little hard on your men."

"I am careful of my people," he said, perfectly calmly, just as though he allowed her a right to question his habits. He added reluctantly, as a man compelled by a sense of justice to a perhaps unwelcome precision, ". . . as careful as I am able to be, which is sufficient, most of the time. Caèr Reiöft is far from fragile." A faint warning came into his tone. "You understand, I do not mean to put Caèr aside."

Kehera nodded. It had not occurred to her that he might.

"With you . . . It is easier for me with you, because you are not afraid of me, and because your Raëhemaiëth quiets Eänetaìsarè. I do not *wish* you to fear me."

Kehera believed him. Although he was wrong about one thing, at least, if he thought she wasn't afraid of him. They sat in silence for a few minutes, she robed and in the chair; he shirtless and resting in apparent comfort on the edge of her bed.

"Is there anything else you would like to ask me?" he said at last.

There was no trace of impatience in his voice or face. But she couldn't think of a single thing, although she wondered whether later she would regret the lost chance. Mutely, she shook her head.

The duke didn't touch her. He held out his hand instead, palm-up, invitingly. "I swore a vow today," he said soberly, "to cherish you, Kehera. I mean to hold to that vow. I hope you will trust me to be your own right decision. Will you take my hand?"

Kehera, meeting his eyes, laid her hand in his.

25

On the morning of the twenty-eighth day of the Iron Hinge Month, two days before the beginning of the uncounted days of the Iron Hinge itself, three days before the actual midwinter dawn, Innisth terè Maèr Eänetaì lounged like a lazy wolf before the fire in his borrowed apartment in Viär. He found himself quite well pleased with the solidity of his position in this province and this town and this house. In these new-claimed lands, which had recently been part of Harivir and now belonged to Eäneté. He was aware of the quiet murmur of Viärinéseir: a presence like the sound of the wind through the cedar branches, or through the feathers of great outspread wings. He felt this presence through and past his constant awareness of his own more savage and stronger Power . . . yet even Eänetaìsarè seemed more contented and less violent now. Since the wedding.

Innisth felt his affairs could hardly have been better arranged had the year been approaching the Golden Hinge rather than the Iron. Yet he did not wish to offend his new people . . . his wife's people . . . by open disregard of the ill luck of the month. Quiet and good order and attention to homely comforts, that was what he wished for his people . . . for his wife . . . during the approaching days of the Iron Hinge. And when the obsidian winds came down from the heights, let all men and beasts shelter within the strength of Eänetaìsarè. His Great Power would turn aside any winter dragon and any storm that tried to come down upon the lands that it encompassed. Thus all these new lands of his would understand that to belong to Eäneté was no ill thing.

So let Meilin Gap be sealed by avalanche; let the high Takel Mountains shrug off their clinging burdens of snow and close the narrow pass, let Eänetaìsarè lay its strength all through these lands and see that no other Immanent Power, no obsidian-winged dragon, no bitter king who had failed his own people dared intrude into the lands it had made its own.

Innisth could not, of course, guarantee that Methmeir Irekaì might not even yet confound his ambition and endanger the integrity of the new kingdom he was making. But now that he held Viär, now that he was in position to anchor it to the western slopes of these mountains where its awareness had never before reached . . . now he could offer Eänetaìsarè considerable support. He *would* support his Power. He was fixed on that purpose. He would hold the land on *both* sides of the mountains, *they* would hold all these lands, and they would never let them go.

Innisth had sent for the lord of nearby Loftè, a town that lay to the west of Viär. It was not a great town, hardly larger than Viär, but he meant to take it into his hand. He had sent for other Harivin lords; some would probably answer his summons and others defy him. He might tolerate defiance, for a while.

The province he was determined to have was Risaèn, south and west of Viär. He had sent for the Duke of Risaèn: Gheres enin Moran Risaniòn. He expected defiance from His Grace of Risaèn, but he was determined he would take that city for his own. In all southern Harivir, Risaèn was second only to Coär. It was central and important and he *would* have it yield to Eäneté. Gheres Risaniòn would come, and Innisth would bind Risaèn as he had bound Viär. He hoped to do it without setting foot himself in Risaèn, though he would travel there if he must. It would be a journey of some days, and he did not wish to leave the mountains that divided his new greater Eäneté unguarded if he could avoid it; certainly not during the Iron Hinge of winter when the high country was most imperiled by winter dragons.

He had sent a message to Gheres enin Moran Risaniòn that should make it clear that the man must come. With a warning that should suffice: an involution containing enough of Eänetaìsarè that a wise man would understand he must yield. If Innisth must go to Risaèn himself to answer the duke's defiance, he would be angry. Risaèn's tie need not belong to the Moran line. That, too, he had made clear. If Duke Gheres defied him, Innisth would master Risaèn's Immanent, tear its tie from Duke Gheres, and set it in someone more compliant. Let Duke Gheres understand this and choose to obey. That would suit them both better, in the end.

Just as Harivir yielding these southern provinces, passing them from Raëh's care to Eäneté's, would in the end best suit both himself and young Tirovay Elin Raëhema. Every province that yielded to Innisth's hand and came within Eäneté's protection was one more province that the young Harivin king need not defend himself. Hard-pressed as Kehera's brother must be from the north, he *must* give up the south . . . and giving up Harivir's southern provinces to his sister's lord could not horrify the young Raëhema king a tenth as much as risking their fall to Methmeir Irekaì and Pohorir.

Thus all seemed well, and Innisth had every hope and expectation that he and all his lands, new and old, would weather the Iron Hinge and come into the new year well set to withstand any continuing threat from Methmeir Irekaì.

In the meantime, Innisth was content to linger in Viär until the days of the Iron Hinge had passed. This was an agreeable town. Small, yet larger than it at first appeared, with wide-scattered villages and hamlets and homesteads sheltered within the precincts of its Immanent. The town and all this small province showed every sign of good management. It was prosperous. Comfortable. Lord Toren Viärin's house offered a pleasing abode, if one wished to spend the few remaining days before the midwinter hinge in quiet amity with one's wife while preparing to expand and solidify one's new borders. The midwinter would undoubtedly be difficult. Let them have these few days of rest.

Lord Toren had shown himself to be a practical man, with the sense not merely to yield his small province and his house and his personal apartment to Innisth, but then also to keep out of his new overlord's way. This was a not-inconsiderable respite, after Riheir Coärin's moods and tempers. Innisth was perfectly well aware Coärin had wished to marry Kehera Raëhema. He was quite certain that Coärin would never have suited her. The man was neither sensible enough nor intelligent enough. Nor was the Immanent Power of Coär strong enough to match Raëhemaiëth.

Though Innisth would have liked to be perhaps a little more confident that his wife agreed on all these points. Still, *she* was the one who had finally insisted on the marriage. Under difficult circumstances, perhaps, but still, she *had* insisted. That had been . . . disconcerting. But peculiarly satisfying. Though he could not pretend to himself that she cared for him personally. He would have wished . . . Well, perhaps it was unwise to dwell on what he might have wished. The world was as it was, political exigencies as they were. Personal desires were nothing. Could be nothing. For either of them. He had no intention of asking his wife what she thought or felt or hoped. If he asked, she would certainly tell him, since she feared him not at all. And he did not want to know.

But she had been correct. He had not quite believed that she *could* be correct; and yet since their marriage, he had been aware that her Raëhemaiëth had become firmly bound to Eänetaìsarè, and that, unquestionably as a result of the Harivin Power's influence, Eänetaìsarè no longer pressed him so hard or in quite the same manner as it had.

His wife, too, must have traded some of her Immanent's calm and gentleness and warmth for some of Eänetaìsarè's violence and heat. He was sorry for that. He did not intend to ask her whether she considered the price she had paid to be worth what he had gained.

Nevertheless, for this one moment, Innisth was fairly well pleased with what had been thus far accomplished. Eäneté was secure; and because the King of Pohorir could not come at Coär save through Roh Pass, so was Coär. Now Viär. The new kingdom he had envisioned was well on its way to becoming a reality. All other concerns were trivial before that one accomplishment.

Then, two hours before noon, Caèr Reiöft came in, quietly, with that particular manner of his that told Innisth he brought news he expected would displease the duke.

Innisth had not quite settled in his own mind what Caèr's position in his household must now be. He had informed his wife, though with some slight trepidation, that he had no intention of setting Caèr aside. He had feared she would be affronted, but she had only seemed surprised he had thought she might protest. He had realized only then that his wife and his servant had somehow contrived to become friends. He had not considered the possibility, and only after he realized it was so had he understood how fortunate a thing it was.

But neither did he quite know how matters lay between himself and Caèr since his marriage. He would have to find out, of course; he would have to determine with more certainty what Caèr wanted, and expected; and what he himself could give. He did not know how to approach any of these questions. It was a kind of uncertainty he had never previously suffered, and he was already impatient with it.

Observing Caèr's manner, he said merely, "You had better tell me." He allowed a little dryness to enter his tone, a trace of humor, so that Caèr would know he was prepared to hear whatever it was without giving way to anger. Then, another thought occurring to him, he asked with real concern, "Nothing has happened regarding my wife?" But even before Caèr could answer, he realized it could not be so. If his *wife* wished to inform him of any event that might displease him, she would do it herself, not ask his servant to act as a go-between. She was so fearless. He smiled slightly, involuntarily, thinking of her. Then he became aware of a particular look in Caèr's eyes and carefully straightened the line of his own mouth.

Caèr did not laugh. He only said, "No, Your Grace; Her Highness does very well, I'm sure. This is another matter, possibly urgent, if I may have leave to bring it to your attention."

And if Innisth refused to give him leave, Caèr would continue anyway, if the matter was urgent. That was one reason the duke valued him. Doubly, since losing Gereth—Innisth still flinched from the emptiness where Gereth should have stood.

His mood was darkening. But that was not Caèr's fault. He said, "Tell me."

Caèr met his eyes, bowed his head slightly, and answered calmly, "Verè Deconniy has arrived, on a horse he's ridden half to death and not looking much better than the beast. He insists he bears urgent news for Your Grace and begs leave to come before you, though if Your Grace will permit me to say so, you might do better to go to him, because I'm not sure he'll make it up the stairs."

Innisth had charged Deconniy to protect the heart of Eäneté. Evidently the man had defied that command and deserted his post and come here. Anger rose. So did Eänetaìsarè, answering that surge of temper. Innisth did not allow his expression to change, but gripped the arms of his chair with careful force and got to his feet without a word.

Captain Deconniy was indeed below, in the entry hall of Lord Toren's house, dripping muddy water on the floor and arguing with one of Toren's servants, who was trying to make him sit down on a bench. But the argument ceased the moment Innisth appeared. Deconniy shoved away from the servant, staggered, caught his balance with an obvious effort, managed one more step, and dropped heavily to his knees, saluting the duke carefully.

Unquestionably, Deconniy had abandoned his post to come here. On the other hand, he had clearly used himself hard to do it. If the horse was in worse shape, Innisth was surprised the animal had survived to reach Viär.

He was aware of the scrambling arrival of others: people of Toren Viärin's household; one of his own officers who had come into town to make his routine report and now found something considerably more interesting to delay him; his wife's man Tageiny. Caèr Reiöft had drawn quietly to one side, ready for any errand his duke might have for him . . . reliable Caèr, who plainly believed leniency was in order.

So when Innisth spoke, it was more gently than he otherwise might, and with no charge—yet—for failure of duty. "Well? Eänetaìsarè does not inform me of any great ill that has befallen my lands or my house or my folk. What, then, is this?"

"Your Grace." Deconniy's voice was hoarse with exhaustion. "Your Grace, Gheroïn Nomoris came himself with Irekaïn troops, but we met them and set them back, as you'll be aware. Eäneté took up many wolves from among our dead; you'll have known it."

"Indeed," agreed Innisth, slightly impatient. "This was days ago. You broke the Irekaïn attack. I was most pleased."

"Yes, Your Grace, only it wasn't us. Not really us. Nomoris, he was going to break our defenses—I think he was—only someone killed him first. But the man who killed him wasn't one of ours, nor one of theirs. He was Harivin, Your Grace, come to Eäneté seeking Her Highness, he said, or that's what he said first off. He killed Nomoris, and if he hadn't . . . if he hadn't, I think . . . I think we might have lost right then, Your Grace, lost everything, maybe. He might have been on our side—he wasn't working for Irekay. I don't see how he could've been. He killed Nomoris—" The young captain caught himself as he began to lose control of his report. He took a breath and went on more collectedly. "He said he was seeking Her Highness, and I would have questioned him further, but he . . . he escaped, Your Grace, he escaped from your cells below the house, and he was ahead of me through the pass, he got past the men at the gate of the pass. . . . I rode as hard as I could, to get here before him, if this is where he was coming."

This was certainly no tale Innisth had expected. He had no idea what he *had* expected, but assuredly not this. "This man escaped," he repeated. "From my cells, downstairs?"

"My fault," Deconniy said faintly. "I should have left more than one man on guard. Should have questioned him properly that first evening. He said he was seeking Her Highness, then he said he was a servant of the Fortunate Gods, but I didn't keep at him, don't know what else he might have said. . . ."

"A servant of the Fortunate Gods," repeated Innisth thoughtfully when the young captain faltered. "Is that what he claimed? How very unusual. A servant of the Fortunate Gods, and seeking my wife."

Deconniy blinked and nodded. "He wasn't Irekaïn. I don't think he was Irekaïn. I don't see how he could have been. He was Harivin, he said, but I don't know. He said he was seeking Her Highness, but I thought . . . I thought maybe he was seeking *you*. The man's an assassin, whatever else he might be, he killed Gheroïn Nomoris, killed the man on his cell, killed a man at the gate to the pass, who else I don't know—"

"No ordinary assassin, to kill a man bound to a Great Power and made into a sorcerer."

Deconniy nodded, swayed, caught himself, and determinedly straightened his shoulders. "He said Irekaìmaiäd had mastered Methmeir Irekaì. He said it had filled up the king, embodied itself in him and in Nomoris, maybe others. I don't know. I don't know about such things. I don't know what could be true or what can't or what it means. But I came . . . I was there when this man killed Nomoris and I questioned him myself, and made a bad job of it, Your Grace, I know that. And—and I'm the one who let him escape. I thought I had better report to Your Grace myself." He squinted as though this decision now seemed questionable to him, then added, "I beg Your Grace's pardon for leaving my post."

"As well you might. However, it does seem I must grant it. Whom did you leave in command?"

"Lieutenant Tejef over the soldiers, Your Grace, and of course, Geran Lhiyré over the staff."

"Well, that was well done, given that you intended to ride out yourself." Innisth studied the young captain narrowly. The tale was difficult to credit. Yet he could hardly believe Verè Deconniy would have created such a story out of whole cloth. He tried to imagine the circumstances that might have led the young man to ride here like this bearing a tale of sorcerers and Gods, rising Powers and dark murder, a tale that was a pack of lies . . . no. No, it was impossible to sustain the effort of imagination that supposition required.

He said, "My captain, if this man indeed intended to come here, you have come before him. You have delivered your warning, and I have heard it. I commend your effort. I shall want your report in a great deal more detail when you are able to deliver it coherently. For this moment, I think you had better rest. Caèr."

With a sober little nod, Caèr Reiöft moved quietly away from the wall and went to set a hand under Deconniy's elbow and help him rise, so Innisth knew his young captain would receive all due care and he might turn his attention to other matters of sudden urgency. He said to the officer, "Send for Senior Captain Etar." Then he ordered one of Lord Toren's servants, "Inform His Grace that I wish him to attend me immediately." Finally, turning to Tageiny, he said with studied formality, "Please inform my lady wife that I request her presence in my apartment, if she has a moment." He was a little surprised, now that he came to think of it, that she was not yet here herself. But then, none of them could have expected so abrupt an arrival as Deconniy's, nor so peculiar a tale.

Kehera Raëhema was the last of the three to arrive, though she had surely been the closest to hand. Lord Toren had answered Innisth's summons with the strict promptness with which he always received the duke's commands. No doubt he hated the Eänetén duke. . . . Innisth could in fact perceive the edge of the other man's detestation through his tie. But since that served neither of them, Lord Toren pretended to a complete absence of feeling in this change of allegiance from Raëh to

Eänété, and Innisth pretended to believe his neutrality. Both of them preferred to keep the width of the house, or better, the width of Viär, between them; and no doubt Lord Toren would be still better pleased when the Eänetén duke and all his men withdrew from Viär's precincts. But Innisth could work with the man. He was grateful for that.

Captain Etar had been, fortunately, not all the way down at the camp by Meilin Gap, fifteen miles and more from the town walls. Since the gap had been closed most thoroughly by avalanche and rockfall, and now that the days of the Iron Hinge were nearly upon them, most of the men had been pulled back to bivouac more comfortably within Viär's walls until the black midwinter storms should pass. Thus Etar, too, had answered the duke's summons promptly.

Naturally, Kehera Raëhema attended her own schedule and not his. He didn't know why he should be surprised. He did not wait for her, but laid out briefly for the other two men the tale Deconniy had brought, briskly acknowledging that he did not know what of it might be true but that he intended to proceed as though it was all true beyond question. Then he permitted Captain Etar to depart upon the urgent business of warning and strengthening the guard set on Viär and on the road and most of all on this house.

Lord Toren was plainly skeptical, and plainly very near saying so, probably in terms Innisth would have to answer with regrettable force. Fortunately, Kehera Raëhema came into the room before matters had become quite that dire. Innisth rose at once, gesturing dismissal to Lord Toren. For a moment he thought the man would refuse, but after a slight hesitation, Lord Toren bowed sharply and said, "I'll inform my people, then, and set a proper guard, and instruct them to work with your people, just as you command. But I assure Your Grace that no one such as you describe will slip Viärinéseir's notice."

"See that no one does," Innisth said flatly, and turned to greet his wife. Her man Tageiny was at her back, but him Innisth ignored. It had not been the custom for her men to stand such close guard in his house, but now the precaution seemed only wise.

His wife had become, he thought, a little graver and a little quieter since the marriage. A little more constrained in her manner. He strongly suspected she was seeking her own way to manage her new close awareness of Eänetaìsarè. He had not asked her whether she regretted pressing him to finally act on his intention to wed her. He had not wished to press her on such a private matter, and . . . perhaps it was also somewhat a failure of nerve, little though he liked to admit it. He had tried to be kind to her; he had tried very hard to moderate Eänetaìsarè's violence while he was with his wife, but even so, he knew she could hardly help but perceive the edge of that ferocity. If that were so, if she must steel herself to endure his touch . . . he knew he should ask. But he truly did not want to know.

He took a moment to consider her, as he had recently found himself snatching one moment or another merely to look at her whenever he was provided with some excuse. He had thought her pretty enough, in an ordinary way, when he had first seen her in the front hall of his own house, in that ridiculous pretense of servitude. But it had taken him a long time to recognize how her quiet composure contributed to a kind of beauty he had never before been wise enough to recognize.

He doubted very much that she returned his increasing regard. If she did not . . . that, too, he did not want to know.

But if an assassin who was also some manner of sorcerer sought to do harm to her, or dared seek to use her in some ruthless stratagem of the Gods, he would take that man and destroy him utterly. He was perfectly determined about that.

He said without preamble, "I presume, given your delay, that you have already heard my captain's report from his own mouth."

"Yes. I'm sorry for making you wait for me, but Tageiny told me what news he'd brought and I thought I'd better talk to Verè myself right away. Poor Verè. He'll be all right, I think, but he's worn to bone and nerve. I told Eöté she could look after him until he's recovered."

Her manner was faintly apologetic, but not in the least defiant. She *was* sorry to make him wait, but it had not occurred to her that he might be angry. Innisth's temper settled in response. "Sensible," he agreed. "And your thoughts on this matter, my wife?"

"It's all very mysterious and disturbing. I know this man Verè speaks of. Quòn—I don't know the rest of his name. He was my father's man. Or my father thought he was. He'd been in Emmer. He brought word . . ." Kehera hesitated, her eyebrows drawing together over her clear gray eyes. She said in her quiet way, "It was this man who brought word when Hallieth Theraön Suriytaiän took the Immanences of Talisè and Cemerè. He seemed a man out of the common way, but then . . ."

"Such men are, who spy for kings," agreed Innisth, rather dry.

"Yes, exactly. I thought that was all it was. My father said he would send him after me. When I . . . when I went to Suriytè. I didn't see him, I never saw him, not through anything that happened there, not when Gheroïn Nomoris took me . . ." Her voice faltered as memory rose up, but she shook her head when Innisth poured a goblet of spiced wine from the pot over the fire and offered it to her. "Thank you," she murmured. "I'm well. I'm quite well. Quòn met us when we came through Anha Pass. He was there before us. I didn't understand how he came there first. Then he said he was a servant of the Fortunate Gods. He told me so then, but I didn't . . . it didn't seem something . . ."

"That you need pass on to me? I imagine not. But perhaps you will tell me now."

Kehera nodded. "He killed Nomoris and freed me. I rode ahead. He was to follow, but he never came. I wonder—I'm sure now that's when Irekaìmaiäd took Nomoris. Quòn killed him and the Irekaïn Power took him; doesn't that make sense?" She looked gravely at Innisth. "We know the Power of Irekay had already taken Nomoris up when he came to you in Eäneté, and you killed him there. Killed him again, and again he didn't die, not all the way. We knew that, but we thought . . . we thought Methmeir Heriduïn Irekaì was still master of the Power. Only now it seems Quòn told Verè that's not true, that Irekaìmaiäd isn't only taking up the dead, but has mastered and taken up the king." She met his eyes. "That's how Great Powers become Gods." Kehera knew this because any king or duke's heir had to know such things. Her father had explained it to her years ago, before she had ever guessed it might matter. She saw that Innisth knew it as well. So that was one duty his father must have kept: teaching his heir the importance of mastery and strength when dealing with his Immanent.

"And are we astonished that Methmeir Heriduïn Irekaì should be foolish and weak as well as ambitious?" Innisth murmured. "So we must be doubly glad that we have established very strong borders around Eäneté. We will certainly claim as much land as possible and protect it all as strongly as possible, in case the worst should come to pass."

"It won't be enough," Kehera said in a low voice. "Not if Irekaìmaiäd achieves apotheosis and rises up as an Unfortunate God. We must defeat it, drive it back, weaken it until it *can't* rise. Destroy it, if we can, and let a kinder Power rise in Irekay."

"Indeed," Innisth said politely, allowing her to hear his skepticism.

"No, listen." Kehera took a folded paper from her skirt and held it out to him. "From Tiro—Tirovay," she explained. "That's the other reason I was delayed. The messenger brought it with the letters for Lord Toren's household, and I was reading it when poor Verè arrived. This is the page that matters."

She was blushing faintly, from which Innisth gathered that the letter had included other pages she did not intend to show him. He did not actually want to know what Tirovay Elin Raëhema might have said about *him*. He merely took the page his wife held out and glanced down the lines of scribe-neat script.

"He, too, is aware that the Irekaïn Power has mastered the king," he murmured. "A most timely warning if we had not heard the other."

"It's his suggestion to try to bind all our Immanences together," Kehera pointed out, which he had already seen. "He—my brother—it sounds like Tiro's creating new Immanences in the lands your king's left empty. I know, not your king—the Power of Irekay. But Tiro is making some new kind of ruling tie, not only to those new Immanences, but to the Harivin Powers already bound to Raëhemaiëth. He's creating Unfortunate bonds, but he's not using them to feed lesser Immanences to Raëhemaiëth. He's not using them to force lesser Immanences out of their lands, but he's binding Raëhemaiëth into their lands *through* them, or something. I don't know if I understand exactly what he's doing. But if Tiro thinks this will work, it probably has a good chance. He knows about things like that." She held out the letter.

Innisth took it without comment. He read to the bottom of the page, then read the final lines a second time. The he folded the page with careful, precise motions and handed it back. He said, hearing the thread of violence in his own voice and making an effort to moderate it, "We need another term to describe what your brother has done, it seems. These bonds of which he speaks don't appear to be precisely Unfortunate, whatever ill fate similar bonds have wreaked on lesser provinces in the past." He paused and then added coldly, "Plainly one effect of what your brother is doing will be to permanently subordinate lesser Immanences to Raëhemaiëth. That is certainly new and daring. It is, of course, out of the question to permit your brother to involve Eänetaìsarè in such a bond."

His wife didn't argue. She asked instead, "Did you read the part about what Tirovay thinks has happened in northern Emmer and in Kosir? If Irekaìmaiäd has taken all those lands and devoured all those Immanences and set its own hollow sorcerers in all those towns, like Gheroïn Nomoris twenty times over . . . If Irekaìmaiäd has set its ties in so many different people, anchored itself in so many different places, then you must see, if we all work separately, we have no chance of defeating it. We have to find a way to do more than just *hold*. If we have a single ruling tie over all our Immanent Powers, that might do. If we don't try something more dramatic, then in the end Irekaìmaiäd will win. And then it will rise up as an Unfortunate God and destroy everything."

"Not everything," Innisth corrected her. "Eäneté will hold regardless." He was utterly resolved that Eäneté would hold. He would entertain no doubts on that point. Doubt was weakness. No one who would hold Eänetaìsarè dared entertain doubts of its strength.

His wife paused, perhaps to master her own temper. He knew she was capable of temper, and passion. Probably more so now, under the influence of Eänetaìsarè. But she would never have yielded when she believed she was right. Nor did she now. She said with quiet determination, "It took the Fortunate Gods to raise up the Wall of Storms. But say you're right. Suppose the Gods set some other barrier to preserve Eäneté. What about everything outside Eäneté? The rest of Harivir, all of Emmer, all of Kosir? That's too much to give up—far too much. Unless Eänetaìsarè is strong enough to protect all the world as well as its own lands?"

Innisth snapped, "I will not subordinate myself to Tirovay Raëhema, nor Eänetaìsarè to Raëhemaiëth. Nor do you wish any such thing. Your brother is no doubt a worthy young man. I have no doubt of it. But you do not want him tied to Eänetaìsarè. He could not hold it. He could not master it."

"You were hardly older when *you* took it—"

"I was bred to hold it. But even were your brother a man grown, you cannot believe I would willingly trade one king for another."

"I know!" Kehera agreed. "But Tirovay isn't Methmeir Heriduïn Irekaì and never will be! Besides, even if my brother established a ruling tie to Eänetaìsarè, it wouldn't *exactly* mean you lost your own mastery—"

Innisth made a sharp, impatient movement. "No. Enough. I will not subordinate Eänetaìsarè to any other Immanent. I will not subordinate myself to anyone, nor return one inch of land I have taken, nor surrender any of the lesser Powers I have brought under Eänetaìsarè's dominion."

Kehera pressed her hands against her lips, bowing her head as she drew a deep breath. No doubt she feared she was handling this argument poorly. No doubt she thought there were better arguments she might make. Of course no argument would persuade him. She must know that. He was sure she knew Innisth had killed his own father to take the deep tie. It must be obvious to her that Innisth knew that all safety, all well-being, and everything good came from seizing power and keeping it tight in his hand. No doubt an Elin Raëhema of Harivir found it difficult to believe that any yielding, any surrender, must bring death and cascading disaster. But she must know she wasn't going to be able to persuade him otherwise.

Nevertheless, she lifted her eyes again to meet his. "Kosir has already been defeated, and most of Emmer has fallen. Tirovay is holding what he can, but if he falls too, what then? Raëhemaiëth is Immanent in *Raëh*! If Raëh falls, I'll be a weakness for you, not a strength! What will happen to Eäneté then?"

Innisth said softly, "You will never be a weakness for me. Though it may be stripped out of Raëh, Raëhemaiëth will anchor itself into our new land through you. Eänetaìsarè will make room for it. You brother should be grateful for that, if he cares for you."

"Yes, I'm fairly certain he *won't* be grateful that you refuse to help him!"

Innisth held up a hand sharply, and his wife bit her lip and was silent. She was very pale, but she knew how to argue without losing her temper and how to stop before pressing him beyond his. Because her steadfast courage deserved full answer, he tried to answer her quietly. "And if I did as you suggest and forced Eänetaìsarè to yield a deep tie to your brother, and he were still defeated? I commend his ingenuity and his resolve. But if he fails, if Irekaìmaiäd becomes a God, then we *must* take our chance to prepare ourselves to hold a smaller land clear of the disaster of its rise. Would it make your brother's defeat less if we joined him in it?"

Kehera whispered, "It might."

He lifted an eyebrow. But she went on with conviction. "Innisth, sometimes it's wrong to take the road that seems safest. Sometimes you have to take the road that's *right* instead, even if it leads into the dark. Don't you know that? Don't you? Innisth, sometimes you have to pick up a sword and join the fight, even when you know you can't win. Sometimes you just have to."

His temper had been pressing him. Now it ebbed. He said, very softly, "I would give you whatever I am able to give. But I cannot give you this."

Kehera was silent for a long moment. She said at last, "Gereth also wrote. But not to me."

Innisth flinched, and controlled himself. He said distantly, "I shall not read his letter. You may, if you wish. But you should not imagine that anything he writes might change my mind."

For a moment he thought she might protest. But in the end, she said nothing.

26

Kehera lay alone in her bed, gazing at the whitewashed ceiling without quite seeing it. Until three nights ago, she had slept alone nearly every night of her life. Strange how cold her bed seemed now, without Innisth to share it. She wished he would come to her. At the same time, she was glad he had not, because she wanted to think and it was hard to think when he was with her.

It was far into the twenty-eighth night of the least fortunate month of the year. In just two days the world would enter the unnumbered Iron Hinge days and the year would begin its dark pivot around midwinter. And she lay alone in her cold bed and wished . . . She didn't know what she wished. Not to have everything back the way it had been. It was too late for that, too late even to *wish* for that. Too much had changed. She wished . . . to be safely through the dark turn of the year. She thought she might wish at least for that.

She wished she believed Raëhemaiëth and Eänetaìsarè together, along with all the lesser Immanenccs they had bound, would be able to defeat the Immanent Power of Irekay. That she believed that they could prevent Irekaìmaiäd from becoming a God. That she believed these Iron Hinge days would not bring disaster down upon all the northern kingdoms. She wished she believed all those things. Her husband did believe them, or he told himself he did. But she could not.

It was hard for her to imagine her little brother with the great tie to Raëhemaiëth and the responsibility for protecting northern Harivir in the face of this great threat; hard to believe their father was not still alive. When she was doing other things, she would forget. And then remember, in quiet moments like this, with a brittle stab of grief and anger and fear that never seemed to get less sharp. She had never realized before how impossible it could be, to tell grief from anger and anger from grief; the two emotions bled together and could not be pulled apart.

Around her, the quiet sounds of the night came to her, demanding no attention. She couldn't sleep. She hadn't expected to sleep. Not on this night, so near the Iron Hinge of the year. She wanted to think about what else she might say to Innisth, what other arguments she might make, but there *was* nothing else and she could not find any way to move him.

A gentle stir of movement in the antechamber disturbed her. For a moment, she thought Innisth had unexpectedly come to her and her heart jumped, but of course he would have announced himself to her women first, and asked her permission to enter her rooms.

Any proper visitor would have done that, in fact.

Kehera gathered herself warily to her feet, reaching for a robe, wondering, if she shouted, how quickly Tageiny and Luad could come. Should she call out? If this was Quòn . . . Could it be? Slipping by the attention of both Eänetaìsarè and Viärinéseir? If it were, did she trust him? He killed easily, from what Verè had told them, and if this was Quòn, he had certainly come like an assassin in the night.

Maybe the sound had been just her imagination.

A dim shape moved, sliding cautiously through the door of her bedchamber; came a step closer, then straightened and became a man, slight and dark and familiar. It *was* Quòn, as she had seen him at the end of Anha Pass, quiet and confident and mysterious. He glanced around, tilted his head back, and said, "Kehera Elin Raëhema," in a voice low and plain and somehow dark as the night. "I—"

And Luad hurled himself silently from the dimness of her women's room, a knife flashing in his hand.

Quòn twisted like a cat to meet him, and they grappled, staggering back against the wall, falling together with a thud that seemed loud. Luad gave a muffled grunt, and Kehera pressed her hand to her mouth, unable to decide whether she should try to stop them, with no idea how she might.

Then Tageiny was there, big and brutal and determined, and there was a sudden flurry of movement that Kehera could make nothing of, and then Quòn was pinned on the floor, facedown, with Tageiny's knee on his back. Her heart began to beat again, and she sat down suddenly on her bed as she found her legs unsteady.

Tag had one hand locked on the man's wrist, pulling his arm up hard behind his back, and a knife at his throat. Luad got to his feet, wincing. Eöté hovered in the door of the women's room, eyes wide.

"If I may—" Quòn began, his voice muffled against the floor. Tageiny jerked his arm sharply, and he grunted and was still.

"You had better let him up," Kehera said, though she couldn't help wondering if that was a good idea.

"Not likely! I'd rather cut his throat," Tageiny snapped. "Fortunate Gods, do you know how quietly this bastard got in here? He's an assassin for sure. It's just luck Eöté's got good ears, and how she heard him I'm sure I don't know. Boy, you all right?"

"Yeah, I'm fine, honest, Tag." Luad stooped over their captive, searching him gingerly. "I don't find shi—anything, Tag. He's clean."

"Yeah?" Tageiny said. "I don't believe it." He leaned a little on the knife he held, until Kehera could see a dark trickle of blood start where the blade bit into the prisoner's neck. "Listen, you. I'm going to go over you myself, and if I find anything unexpected, I'm going to take you apart, you got that? What're you carrying?"

Quòn answered, muffled, "A knife in my boot, that's all." His tone was surprisingly unconcerned. "I didn't come to murder the lady in her bed."

"Yeah, sure, that's good to hear." Tageiny swung his weight off his prisoner and hauled him up, not gently, slamming him face-about against the wall. "Don't move, you. Luad!"

"Yeah, Tag." Luad smoothly took over, pinning the man in place while Tageiny searched him again, much more carefully.

Kehera's heartbeat had nearly returned to normal. Eöté took a step forward, and Kehera glanced at her, surprised to find that for all her nervousness, the girl now stood only a pace away, her back straight and her head tilted in apparently unselfconscious fascination. Her wide-eyed gaze was fixed on the stranger, her lips slightly parted, her breathing quick. But she seemed more interested than frightened.

"He's not armed," Tageiny said, recalling Kehera's attention. His tone was grim, as though he still didn't believe this. "I didn't find anything on him, except the knife he admitted to. He's got one bastard of a whip mark across his back, though, not much more than a couple days old, I make it. I guess that was Verè." He spun the man roughly around and shoved him to his knees, facing Kehera.

The captive lifted one wry eyebrow at her.

"Who marked you?" Kehera asked him. "Was it Verè Deconniy? What cause did you give him? Did you kill anyone there to get away?"

"Captain Deconniy, yes. Little enough cause, in fact. He didn't trust me." There was neither resentment nor even much interest in the man's voice.

"I can't imagine why not." Kehera hesitated. "You didn't find me, you didn't come after me in Enchar, and I thought—but we understand you killed Nomoris at the border of Eäneté? For the third time. And now you've found me after all, but I don't understand why."

Quòn smiled crookedly. "They do say the third time pays for all." She could see, above the open collar of his shirt, the end of the mark Tageiny had mentioned; it was red and vivid against his pale skin. It had been, indeed, one bastard of a whip cut that had made that savage mark.

She wouldn't have thought it of Verè Deconniy. But this man made her uneasy now, in a way he hadn't before, and she could imagine how he might have spooked Verè.

Quòn's gaze traveled from her to Eöté to Luad, seeming to assess every person and piece of furniture in the room. Then he nodded to Kehera and said smoothly, "Forgive my tardiness, Your Highness. I made a slight error of judgment with Nomoris that occasioned a regrettable delay." He spoke calmly, not seeming disturbed to be held on his knees with a knife at his throat. "By the time I dealt with that matter, you were well ahead of me. Then you proved difficult to approach. Did you know that the Eänetén duke and Lord Toren of Viär have each established independent guard over you? But I gather these are your own men." He glanced at Eöté and added, "Your own people." He paused for just a heartbeat, studying the girl curiously, which seemed odd, as he hardly seemed the sort to be distracted by a woman, even one as delicately beautiful as Eöté. But he turned back to Kehera before she could frame an answer, continuing. "Your Highness, can you trust all these people? I have created a hole in this house's defenses, but it will not last."

"Oh, you haven't killed anyone. . . ."

"Not here," Quòn said impatiently. "Not yet. I will try to avoid doing so if you prefer, though all men die in the normal course of the world. The Fortunate Gods are not concerned with natural death, but with the appropriation of mortal souls by the Unfortunate. Or by their servants." He paused, shrugged, and added, "But that is beside the point. I meant to say: if your people will be quiet for the night, I could take you out of this town by morning and have you in Raëh in a week." He glanced once more at Eöté and added, "You and your woman, if you wish. Less than a week. Much less, if the Fortunate Gods are kind, as I think they would be. You would find it easier to support Raëhemaiëth from the heart of its land, and it would find it much easier to support you." His tone was completely matter-of-fact. He sounded perfectly certain of himself.

Tageiny had gone quite blank. Luad glanced warily from one of them to the next, his face trying to settle on one expression and failing. Morain Lochan looked placidly unmoved by the proposal. Eöté took a small step forward, toward Quòn; then she hesitated, glancing at Kehera, and said in a small voice, "I would go, my lady. I would go with you."

Surprised at the girl's uncharacteristic bravery, Kehera said, "Thank you, Eöté, but I can't possibly leave this house."

Tageiny and Luad visibly relaxed, but Quòn said briskly, "Of course you can. If the Fortunate Gods wish you to be secure in Raëh, I assure you, I can conduct you there. I'm a very competent person." He flicked a glance around the room and added, "Present appearances notwithstanding."

"You didn't get to your knife very fast," Tageiny commented in a neutral tone.

"I wasn't fighting. I was preventing you from killing me."

"Maybe," the big man admitted. He moved his shoulders uncomfortably. "All right. That could be true."

"It is true." Quòn turned back to Kehera. "If Your Highness will trust me, I assure you, it is entirely possible for you to leave this house."

Kehera nodded. "I'm afraid I expressed myself badly. It may be possible for me to leave the Eänetén duke, but it's unthinkable. He needs me too much. He needs my tie to Raëhemaiëth. Without me . . ." She wasn't sure how to finish that sentence, and said instead, "I can't leave."

"But—" began Eöté, then stopped, blushing.

Kehera glanced at her curiously, and Quòn raised an eyebrow. But Quòn only said to Kehera, "You believe your Immanent supports the Immanent of Eäneté? Interesting. Perhaps it does. One might imagine that Raëh's influence could be useful in several exigencies. Eänetaìsarè is precisely the sort of Immanent Power that might rise in either direction." He considered for another moment and then concluded, "If you are quite certain you wish to stay in the keeping of your . . . husband, then that might indeed serve the needs of the Fortunate Gods."

Kehera studied Quòn for a long moment. She couldn't read him at all. She said carefully, "So . . . . may I trust that the Fortunate Gods don't *demand* I go to Raëh immediately?"

"I don't believe so. No. Yet I am somewhat surprised that I should have come here for no purpose." The man flicked a glance at Eöté, who blushed again and then paled. But the girl said nothing, and Quòn asked merely, "As I am here, perhaps I might do some other service for Your Highness?"

Kehera didn't understand the interaction between Quòn and Eöté at all. But she said, "I do have something else you might do for me, if you would. You see, I want His Grace to—to get the Eänetén Power to share a deep tie with my brother. To let Tiro take a ruling tie to Eänetaìsarè, through Raëhemaiëth. Only if he did that, my brother would hold Eänetaìsarè himself, in a way that even His Grace couldn't break, so you see why His Grace is . . . reluctant." She hesitated at this extreme understatement. But then she said firmly, "I think it's very important that Innisth should do this. I think it may be the only chance we have to truly defeat the Power of Irekay."

Quòn tilted his head to one side. "A most interesting suggestion. And a goal devoutly to be wished. Yes. I see. I do see. One rather suspects the Fortunate Gods also find this notion compelling. Yet His Grace has proven recalcitrant?"

She nodded. "I couldn't persuade him. But there is one man who might."

"Indeed. Who?"

"He's in Raëh now, I hope. An old man, in his fifties, I think. Gereth Murrel. I think he's with my brother. I hope he is. You wouldn't have any trouble finding him, if he's with Tiro."

Quòn said calmly, "If this is to the purpose of the Fortunate Gods, I won't have any trouble finding him wherever he may be."

Kehera nodded, though uneasily. She said nevertheless, keeping to the important point, "If he were here. If he could explain to Innisth.

He—if anyone can make Innisth understand, Gereth can." She opened her hands. "I can't. I . . . can't."

Quòn bent his head politely and said, "Very well. I will do it, provided the Fortunate Gods do not set a different task in my way. Have you a token for me? To show this man he should come with me?"

Kehera hesitated. Then she quickly found her tiahel set, the set Tiro had made for her. She paused over the pieces before selecting the King Rod and offering it to Quòn. "I don't think Gereth will recognize this. But show it to my brother, and he'll know you came from me."

Quòn inclined his head, took the rod, and rose to his feet, neat as a cat. He said to Tageiny, "May I have my knife back?"

At Kehera's nod, Tageiny shrugged and handed it over, and Quòn nodded, glanced once more at Eöté, and went out. There was no sound of footsteps, or of the door to her suite opening or closing. There was certainly no outcry from a sentry.

"That," said Tageiny after a moment, "was very strange." He shrugged, let his breath out, shook his head, and added, "Granted, it's the strange ones you sometimes need." He looked at Kehera. "His Grace may not . . . be very happy to see the seneschal here."

"No," Kehera answered slowly. "No. I think . . . he will be very happy to see Gereth again."

"Well, then," Tageiny said. Now that the alarm was past, his discomfort at her dishabille was visible. He kept his eyes strictly on her face.

Luad, watching him, grinned, much less concerned with propriety.

"Go back to bed, both of you," Kehera said, rescuing Tageiny. "I sincerely hope the rest of the night will be less eventful." She added, "Thank you. Both of you. You were both very impressive tonight."

Her praise embarrassed Luad as her robe had not. He bowed quickly and backed out of the room, muttering inaudibly.

Tageiny bowed more properly and also left her.

"Eöté . . ." Kehera began, but then did not know what to say. The girl was staring at her in mute appeal, but she looked frightened again, and

Kehera couldn't tell what frightened her. She said gently, "You know, if you are unhappy in my service, or unhappy with Verè Deconniy . . . I couldn't help but notice you didn't ask me for leave to go to him tonight. If you are unhappy at all, I hope you would tell me, and I will try to—"

"No!" Eöté said quickly. "No, my lady." Her eyes had gone wide in what seemed genuine astonishment.

"So Captain Deconniy—"

"No! No, Verè is always good to me." But her tone lacked conviction, and she glanced away in the direction Quòn had gone.

It wasn't exactly a question, which was good, because Kehera certainly had no idea what to answer. She said, "Verè *is* good to you?"

"Of course," Eöté said. She now sounded faintly dismissive, but at least not nervous. Or not nervous of her husband. "I'll fetch you mulled wine, my lady." She ducked away, into the women's room, presumably to light the brazier and warm wine.

Alone, Kehera slowly tucked herself back into the bed, hugging a pillow and staring at the ceiling, not quite ready to blow out the remaining lanterns. She felt rather as though something else might leap out of the darkness at her. It had, indeed, been an eventful evening.

27

Tiro had believed he'd been afraid when he'd been forced to take the heir's tie and watch Kehera ride away to marry the Mad King of Emmer. Then he'd thought he'd been afraid when they'd first understood that their actual enemy was Methmeir Irekaì of Pohorir and that he had found a way to let his Immanent Power of Irekay consume other Powers. Then, worst of all, he'd understood the Irekaïn Power had mastered its fool of a king and acted now on its own behalf. Then he'd been terrified of what might happen when he tried to answer this threat by creating a new Immanent in Talisè, and by binding all the Immanences he could reach into Raëhemaiëth.

But after they'd all survived that, he'd actually believed that at last they had a chance to stop the Immanent of Irekay from its insane ambition to become a God. He'd believed they might pivot around the dangerous days and come to a safer time of year. They didn't even have to win, exactly, just hold back the Irekaïn Immanence from its ambition until the Iron Hinge had passed. If it missed its chance at midwinter, they'd have a whole year to figure out what to do before it had a chance to try again for apotheosis. Only during the days of the Iron Hinge were the boundaries thin enough between the mortal realm of Immanents and the realm of black storm-ridden chaos where dragons tore at the edges of the earth and the Fortunate Gods strove eternally against the Unfortunate.

Or at least that was one scholarly notion. There were others. But Tiro at least believed, or was fairly certain he believed, that the Irekaïn Power would achieve its apotheosis during the Iron Hinge days or miss its chance for the winter and the year. Certainly every child knew the Unfortunate Gods were always strongest during the Iron Hinge days.

So he'd written to Kehera to explain everything he'd done and everything he'd figured out about Immanences and about the Irekaïn Immanence in particular, and he'd really believed she might get the Eänetén duke to ally with the rest of them. Or he'd told himself he believed that. He wanted to smile now at his belief that they might have gotten past the worst. Except it was nothing to smile at.

Now Tiro held ties not only to Raëh but to all the lesser Powers of northern Harivir and some of those Immanent of southern Emmer. He'd created new Powers in as many hollow provinces as he could, and if Raëhemaiëth wound up destroying all of them and becoming a God itself, it would be his fault. Even if he meant to balance the bonds between all the different Immanent Powers, even if he had every intention of making sure all those bonds remained Fortunate . . . that only gave him a chance to fail more spectacularly. If the terrible Irekaïn Power poured its winter over Raëh and became a God and consumed the whole world, that would be his fault too.

And he'd never even wanted to be *heir*.

It wasn't fair. If he'd had time for it, he would have dwelt at great length on how entirely unfair it was. He'd never even had a moment for *that*. That *really* wasn't fair.

But Raëhemaiëth was holding; and so they held all of Harivir and bits of Emmer and even a little bit of Kosir. For the moment.

It was close to midnight on the twenty-ninth day of the least fortunate month of the year. If this had been a normal month, the sun would rise tomorrow on the thirtieth day. Instead, they would enter the days of the Iron Hinge. Tiro stood in the dark and the wind, at the top of the highest tower of the king's palace in Raëh, and listened to his kingdom. He was so very tired. But he couldn't rest. He needed to stand in the open air and *feel* that everything he had held at dusk was still safe as they came to the turn of night that led into the dark hinge of the year.

The coming dawn would be late and reluctant, and the obsidian winds would descend toward the earth. Many-headed winter dragons would ride those winds, carrying storms in the shadow of their wings and misfortune on their breath, and the world would pass into the Iron Hinge of winter. Four uncounted days after that, it would come out the other side and the new year would dawn. Tiro just hoped they would all *see* that dawn. Midnight was a hard time for optimism. Especially as midwinter approached, when one could already see the black winds streaking the face of the moon.

It was cold. That was why Tiro shuddered and pulled his coat close around himself.

"You're cold," Gereth Murrel said behind him. "Your servants are worried about you. You should come in where it's warm, have some spiced wine or cider . . . deal with Rosaën Tinìenas, who rode through half the night to get here and, it seems, is very upset at having my duke on his border."

Tiro rolled his eyes, though actually he felt the distraction of Lord Rosaën's upset would be welcome.

He hadn't heard Gereth come up the tower steps nor out onto the balcony, but he didn't mind. The Eänetén was an accustomed presence these days, and a reassuring one. A link to Tiro's sister, maybe. Or maybe Tiro felt he was welcome because Raëhemaiëth approved of him. *That* was reassuring, in a number of ways. And, though Tiro already had a seneschal taking care of things in Raëh, Gereth seemed to slip naturally into that kind of supportive role.

He knew that Gereth was doing a great deal of the work involved in handling the various lords of other provinces, many of whom Tiro had summoned to Raëh in the hope that their presence here would help broaden the bonds between Raëhemaiëth and their own Immanences and in the end better protect all their lands. He wasn't sure his reasoning was sound in that, but he also thought he might actually not be acting on his own, but according to Raëhemaiëth's urging. It was important to trust Raëhemaiëth. His father had said that. So had Kehera. But he would have known that was true anyway.

"I'm not really cold," Tiro said. "I'm mostly scared." He was glad of Gereth's presence partly because there was no one else he could admit that to. Gereth wasn't *his*. The man was still Eänetén to the bone. So it was all right for Tiro to say to him, *I'm scared*. He said now, "There are more black winds in the heights than last year, I think."

Glancing upward, Gereth said judiciously, "That looks about the same as always to me. Of course, Eäneté is a good deal farther south and hard against the mountains."

"Raëhemaiëth will protect us."

"Irekaìmaiäd brought a dragon with it through the Anha Narrows eight days ago, well before the black winds were supposed to spin off the Wall of Eternal Storms."

Tiro gave Gereth a *look*. "Aren't you supposed to reassure me?"

The Eänetén came over and leaned on the tower wall beside him. The moonlight bleached the color out of the older man's graying hair and turned the bricks of the parapet to a color darker than blood. "Better to expect the worst. Then any surprises will be good ones."

"Ha," Tiro said skeptically. "You think it's possible to expect the *worst*, do you? Whatever *I* think of, I'm sure the Power of Irekay will come up with something *even worse than that*." He knew Gereth was right, though: He should go in out of the wind. But he somehow felt that something terrible would happen the moment he turned his back.

That was foolish, of course. He could hardly stay awake right through the Iron Hinge, and if he tried, he'd be too exhausted to deal with . . . whatever terrible thing eventually did happen. He was certain that something terrible *would* happen.

The city was still well enough tonight, though. Raëhemaiëth was deeply rooted in Raëh; in the city and the dark, rich earth beyond the city walls, the broad fields, the wooded copses, the many streams that wandered out of the hills and the lakes that were fragrant with water-lilies in spring. It was rooted in the souls of the folk who made their homes within its precincts, the brick-paved streets and orderly homes and the pots of brilliant flowers that lined the edges of its roofs in the summer and graced the indoor rooms during the long winter months.

Behind all this, Raëhemaiëth was now also solidly rooted well to the east, in the bustling river towns of Leiör and Sariy and Las, the rose-pink and ivory stone of West Daman and East Daman, which had never been Harivin before, and the mountains of Eilin, which had belonged to Harivir for a hundred years and more. And in the west, Raëhemaiëth was bound to the fine-boned people and the ancient trees of Ghiariy and to the bright-sailed fishing boats and busy markets of Timir, where the winds spoke always of the sea. Emmeran and Kosiran and Harivin provinces alike were now contained within Raëhemaiëth's precincts; whatever they'd had time to claim and bind to Raëh.

To the south, of course, Raëhemaiëth now reached only to the rolling hills and farms of Tinìen. Everything past that belonged now to the Eänetén Power. That was bitter, and Tiro couldn't blame the Lord of Tinìen for being upset, but he was fairly certain he wouldn't have had a chance to withstand the Irekaïn Power if he'd tried to hold much more territory than was now bound to Raëh.

Right now, standing in the heart of his strength, in Raëh, a city built out of the bones of the mountains and the bones of the folk who had lived and died here, he wasn't sure he could even hold what he still possessed.

"Everyone will support you," Gereth said, watching him. "You were wise to call them all in, I think."

Tiro nodded, though he wasn't sure. The other Immanent Powers would support Raëhemaiëth with all their strength. They had no choice now. They spread like a shining web across the face of the land, from point to point, wherever the Power of Irekay had not broken and destroyed them; wherever Raëhemaiëth had restored them; wherever enough men had lived for a long enough time to pour their fears and their hopes and their brief brilliant lives into the realm that lay behind and beyond the world of men. Raëhemaiëth drew life and vigor from all these lesser Powers; it sank roots into the land all across the kingdom, wherever Tiro held a tie, and so all that he held, held firm. But whether he'd been right to summon all the lords and ladies who held those other provinces to Raëh . . . He *thought* they would be able to do more to support Raëhemaiëth here than from their own provinces.

His father would have known what to do. *Kehera* would have known what to do. It was appalling that *Tiro* was the one at the center of all this effort.

"You're the one who figured out how to create new Immanents without losing Raëhemaiëth," Gereth pointed out. "You guessed it might be possible to bind lesser Immanences to Raëhemaiëth with bonds that are that strange mixture of Fortunate and Unfortunate."

Tiro had to laugh. "How do you guess what I'm thinking?"

The Eänetén smiled. "Long practice. Innisth took Eäneté when he was hardly older than you are now. Though he intended to, of course, and prepared himself for it, so it wasn't as hard for him." The smile faded. He added in a low voice, "Nothing was as hard after the old duke was dead. I'd hoped Innisth would never face anything worse than that."

When it came to taking a ruling tie, "intended to" and "prepared himself" were phrases that had some fraught implications. Tiro didn't make a single comment about overweening ambition—certainly not about murder. He knew the old Duke of Eäneté was supposed to have been terrible. Besides, he was aware—Raëhemaiëth was aware—they were always aware of the looming pressure of the Irekaïn Power just outside their borders. Tiro had no choice but to depend on the Eänetén duke to defend the south and most of the east. And he told himself that a man who had made Gereth Murrel his seneschal and had won his apparently unshakable loyalty couldn't be *entirely* wicked.

"I think—" he began.

And at that moment, as the black winds swept across the moon and the silvery light dimmed, someone unfamiliar stepped soundlessly out of the deep shadows and walked toward them along the tower's balcony. He held his hands at his sides, palms turned forward to show he carried no weapons. Other than that, Tiro could see very little of him.

Tiro had an impression of *dark* and *quiet* and *dangerous*, and a fainter impression of familiarity, as though he might have met this man somewhere once or twice before. He couldn't remember where that might have been and drew breath to call out. Gereth began to step forward, but Tiro caught his arm and pulled him back, because if this were some strange attack by an agent of the Irekaïn Power, he trusted Raëhemaiëth would protect *him*.

But the man stopped. He said in a calm, uninflected voice, "Tirovay Elin Raëhema. I wasn't seeking you, but it's a fortunate meeting. Perhaps the Gods set us both here at this moment. Do you know me?"

Tiro tried to pick the man's face out of the shadows, but it was too dark. There were no lanterns on the tower balcony, because men on duty here at night were supposed to be careful of their night vision. He said, "Tell me your name," and was pleased at the firm, fearless tone in which that came out.

"I am called Quòn," the man told him.

After a moment Tiro remembered that name. "Quòn. Yes, I remember you. My father sent you to take care of Kehera." His voice tightened. "A job you don't seem to have managed very well."

The man shrugged. He said without a trace of either offense or apology in his voice, "Kehera Elin Raëhema is in the hands of the Gods and does very well there. She sent me here."

"*Kehera* sent you to me?" Tiro realized he'd taken a step forward, and made himself stand still.

"Not to you, but to Gereth Murrel," Quòn corrected, his tone perfectly unconcerned. "But she gave me a token for you, young king." He held it out: a finger-length tiahel rod, carved with the symbols of the Four Kingdoms.

Tiro drew a slow breath. He had to force himself not to snatch the rod out of the man's hand. He took it gently, turned it over in his fingers, and said, with no doubt at all, "Kehera gave this to you." And then, "But she didn't send you to me?"

"You do well enough as you are, young king. As she does well enough where she is. It is Gereth Murrel who is out of his place. It was impossible to come earlier, but fortunately it was also impossible to come later. At the hinge of the night, with the favor of the Gods, one may sometimes step across the miles."

He turned to Gereth, who now stood very still at Tiro's right hand. "I think you would do well to come. Innisth terè Maèr Eänetaì has need of you."

"*Innisth* sent you for me?" Gereth said disbelievingly.

"Not he," Quòn said patiently. "Kehera Elin Raëhema, for Eäneté's sake and for the sake of the world. I think it's very possible chance and fortune will pivot around Eäneté this midwinter. You *will* come."

This last did not sound at all like a suggestion. Tiro said sharply, "If you were my father's man then you're mine now—"

"I was never any man's servant, though it suited me to serve Torrolay Elin Raëhema for a time," Quòn said. "I am a servant of the Fortunate Gods. You must not balk me. I warn you, there's little time. The hinge of the night does not stay for the hopes of men."

Tiro called on Raëhemaiëth. His Immanent stirred, but it did not rise, evidently finding no threat here. Tiro let out a breath, nodded, and laid a hand on Gereth Murrel's arm. "I don't know this man. But Kehera wouldn't mislead us. And besides . . . if Eäneté doesn't hold . . ."

"Yes," said Gereth, but his tone was distracted, and Tiro was fairly certain he hadn't heard anything after this strange servant of the Gods had said that the Eänetén duke hadn't been the one to send for him. His expression was hard to read in the dark-streaked moonlight. But he said in a low voice, "I'll come, of course." And he held out his hand, stepped forward, and allowed Quòn to take his hand and grip his arm and draw him forward into the shadows.

"Good fortune go with you!" Tiro called in a low voice.

"It will," Quòn answered. "If the Gods of the living earth win out over the Gods that summon the deathly winds. Or else we will all of us fail and fall. Trust Raëhemaiëth. Your line has taught it to be trustworthy, and it has long cared for its little ephemeral creatures. When the moment comes, trust Raëhemaiëth."

"What moment?" Tiro asked, baffled. "Trust it to do what?"

But both of the other men were gone before Quòn could answer, if he meant to.

Then the night turned, and though it would not be dawn for hours yet, the world entered the last day of the year.

Tiro took a breath and let it out. He ran his thumb along the symbols carved into the tiahel rod and then cast it down on the floor of the balcony. It tumbled with a quiet clatter, teetered for an instant with the Red Falcon of Harivir facing upward . . . and then tipped over and came to rest with the Winter Dragon of Pohorir above the rest.

Tiro had never truly believed in tiahel divination. Nevertheless, a chill went down his spine. It was cold on the tower balcony, of course. Even so, he turned the King Rod so the Falcon was faceup before he tucked it away in his pocket.

Then he went inside, back into the warmth, leaving the moonlit night.

28

Hours after sundown on the twenty-ninth night of the Iron Hinge
Month, the grim night before the uncounted days of the Iron Hinge
began, Kehera admitted to herself that she was not going to be able to
sleep and got out of her bed. She wanted to take out her tiahel set but
couldn't quite stand to see the King Rod missing. She wondered where
it was now, how far along the road between Viär and Raëh.

Wrapped in a warm robe and surrounded by relit candles, she
found thread and needles. There was no spare cloth lying about, however. She thoughtfully embroidered a tiny yellow butterfly on the hem
of her robe.

Kehera had not set a single stitch in cloth since helping get her
wedding dress in order. She had been so grieved, and then so busy,
and always afraid. She was surprised now to find how much she had
missed the quiet activity. Sweeping up all the thread, she resettled herself among the blankets and leaned back against the pillows, frowning
at her robe. It was dark blue, lined with soft thick wool and then with
smooth creamy linen.

The work soothed her, even though the thoughts that wandered
through her mind were not particularly soothing. A scattering of other

butterflies joined the first, fluttering over delicate sprays of flowers along the hem of her robe.

The movement of air through the room made the candle flames flicker. She noticed that a good long moment before its import dawned on her, and she looked up.

Tageiny leaned in the doorway. "I heard you moving around and saw the light under your door," he said softly. "But I don't want to disturb you."

"Go on back to bed," she said, smiling at him. "I couldn't sleep, but that's no reason you shouldn't."

"I'm on watch. You never know."

"Words to live by," commented a dry voice, much too near.

Tageiny, who had been stepping back, came all the way through the door instead, his sword whispering into his hand. Kehera had not even realized he was armed. But he had hardly drawn his weapon before he was lowering it again, looking disgusted. "How do you get in here?" he demanded.

Quòn, edging out of the shadows, half-smiled: a quick expression gone almost as soon as it appeared. "Natural talent. And the favor of the Fortunate Gods."

Kehera found herself bitterly disappointed. She had prayed he would be nearly to Raëh by this time. And here he was, back here instead. A whole day wasted. "You couldn't even get out of Viär?" she demanded. "You need something from me—a letter to the men at the gate, a word from His Grace?"

Luad, hearing unfamiliar voices, appeared at Tageiny's back, but his senior waved him down. "It's all right, I think, boy."

"It's more than all right," Quòn said, an edge of irony in his voice. "I assure Your Highness, I seldom require anyone's assistance to come and go. The Fortunate Gods open all paths for their servant." He stepped aside to make way for another, far more familiar, man.

"Gereth!" Kehera exclaimed, and flung back the blankets, going to take the old man's hands with real enthusiasm. "How are you? How is Tiro? How is Raëh?"

Gereth looked tired, and older. When she had first met him, he had seemed strong and very confident, certain of his place in the world. What she saw now in his face was an echo of the uncertainty he had suffered since the duke had dismissed him in Roh Pass.

But he gripped her hands firmly and smiled. "I've been very well. Very well, indeed. Your brother is growing into a true king. He has become quite creative with Raëhemaiëth and allied Immanences. I believe he's written you about it."

"Yes, he has. I'm so glad! I mean, for Tiro, but I'm so glad to see you, too! I got his letter, but I'm not sure I understood everything. Trust Tiro to come up with something no one's ever done before, or would dare do now! I want to hear all about it. But look, you're wet. You must be half-frozen." She pulled a chair around for him and took his cloak, looking around for a place to put it. Tageiny took it away from her and tossed it over the back of another chair, waving to Luad to start a fire in the hearth. "I'd offer wine, or soup, but I'd rather not wake the whole household. They aren't awake now, are they?"

"No," Quòn said. He was leaning, arms folded, against the wall, watching her with an expression of mild curiosity. "Although I suggest quiet, if you'd rather they stayed abed."

"Quieter than you've been," Morain Lochan said, coming in and gently closing the door that connected the women's room from Kehera's. "Or you'll wake Eöté. Shall I stay, my lady?"

By which she meant to imply how unsuitable it would be for a lady to be left unchaperoned with all these men. Though Kehera doubted the woman would be shocked at anything a lady might choose to do.

"Yes, that's fine," Kehera said. "In fact, if you could lay out a dress for me, I think I'll be wanting it."

"Fine and showy? Strict and formal? Practical, for climbing out windows?"

"Plain," Kehera decided, "but nice. Nothing to catch the eye or draw attention."

The older woman inclined her head and tapped Tageiny on the

shoulder, moving him out of the way so she could get into the wardrobe.

"Quòn," Kehera said, "Thank you. I don't understand how you could have gone to Raëh and back so quickly—you must mean the Fortunate Gods literally opened a path for you?" She remembered how Nomoris had stepped through the air, stepped across miles; the Irekaïn Power had done that, opened a way for its servant. For the first time it seemed not just possible, but certain that Quòn really *meant* that he served the Fortunate Gods. This made her uneasy. But it also, under the circumstances, seemed like a very good thing.

Despite their low voices, Eöté opened the door to the women's room and stood blinking in the light. The girl was wearing only a sleeping shift and a light robe, but she didn't seem aware of that. Her eyes, wide and unblinking, had gone straight to Quòn.

Kehera looked from one of them to the other. She said hesitantly, "You must be cold, too, Quòn. I'm sure Eöté would bring you a robe or hot tea."

Quòn shook his head, although beads of moisture gleamed in his dark hair. "I need nothing. Or nothing a robe or tea could provide."

"As stoic and mysterious as he is insistent," Gereth commented.

Forgetting Eöté, Kehera had to smile at his tone. "Don't tell me he dragged you out of Raëh without even letting you grab a cloak."

"Very nearly. But the journey was, as you've gathered, one of quite astonishing brevity." Gereth hesitated, and then went on more soberly, "Allow me to offer my most sincere condolences for your loss. I hardly knew your father, but he was kind to me. All the world knows he was a good man and a fine king. I will always be grateful for the hospitality I met in your father's house."

Kehera nodded, unable, at that moment, to answer.

Perhaps seeing this, Gereth went on much more briskly. "Quòn told me you sent for me most urgently, but not why. Has Innisth . . . ?"

Kehera saw his anxiety and said quickly, "No, he's well—mostly well. But he uses his strength prodigiously shoring up our borders, until I fear it will be used up. He still thinks he must resist Irekay all by himself—or he did. What Tiro's done, he's done that too, or something like it, with Coär first and then Viär and now Loftè and Risaèn as well."

"Good!" Gereth said. "Very good. Has Innisth thought—I don't suppose he has considered—of course he probably will not consider yielding a tie of this new kind to your brother?" This, from his resigned tone, was not actually a question.

Kehera lifted her hands in a helpless gesture. "I haven't been able to persuade him. Caèr won't take my side, though I think he thinks I'm right. But you—"

"You think I might persuade him? I'm not confident. Although Innisth must surely be having qualms about his hope to break free of Irekay by now. No matter how strong his position seems here. Nor am I confident that . . . he will tolerate my presence here at all." Gereth bowed his head slightly, looking at his hands, where they lay in his lap.

Other than herself, Gereth was the only person Kehera knew who ever used the Wolf Duke's first name. He'd been doing so, no doubt, for more years than Kehera had been alive. She said, more certain than ever, "*I* have no such doubts. Not about that. He may not take your advice, Gereth. But he'll be glad you've come, and he'll listen to you."

He opened his hands, uncertain but hopeful.

Morain Lochan laid out a dark green dress with silver trim.

"All of you go away," Kehera said to the roomful of men. "Be discreet. Quòn . . ." She was fairly certain now that she didn't have the authority or the nerve to try to give *him* orders.

The dark man tilted his head consideringly to the side. "As always, if I see a task that seems good to do, I will set my hand to it. If I see a useful chance, I will take it. But as I am here now, I imagine this is the place I am meant to be. If you need me, I will probably be here."

"Good!" Kehera said gratefully, though this was not a very reassuring . . . reassurance. Nor was there time to think about it just at the moment. She said, "Gereth, take a moment to rest, but after I'm dressed I want to talk to you about what I have in mind. Stage management, so to speak."

"I look forward to hearing it." He nodded to her and followed the other men from the room. Except for Quòn, who seemed to have decided he might like tea after all, because Eöté had moved the pot over the brazier and he had gone to join her.

Kehera refused to worry about either of them right at this moment. She felt she had more than enough to worry about already.

Captain Deconniy stood outside the duke's apartment, speaking to the sentry. No one, Kehera gathered, was getting much sleep tonight. So far as she could see, only determination was keeping Deconniy on his feet. He ought to be granted a lot more than one day to recover, in Kehera's opinion, but Innisth and Senior Captain Etar seemed to think he'd do better back on duty. Maybe they were right. Certainly he hadn't seemed exactly happy while he'd been abed. Fretting over having left his post, she'd thought at first, though Innisth had pardoned him for that and Senior Captain Etar had agreed it had been the right thing to do. Fretting over Eöté, it had occurred to her later; Kehera had come to suspect theirs was a more complicated match than she'd initially guessed. And now the girl's strange response to Quòn—she didn't understand that at all.

But she didn't have time to worry about any of that just at this moment. She only nodded to Deconniy and the sentry.

The sentry bowed, and Deconniy inclined his head. "My lady? It's very late."

"Or very early," agreed Kehera. "Is my lord awake within, do you know?" She was certain no one was getting much sleep this night, not with the Iron Hinge dawning tomorrow—they had actually entered the hinge already, since it was past midnight.

"Well, yes," Deconniy admitted. "His Grace sent for hot tea half an hour since. Shall I announce you, my lady? And you, sir?" He peered at Gereth, standing cloaked and hooded beside her.

"You may announce me," Kehera said. "But not, I think, my companion, just yet. He can wait in my lord's antechamber until I send for him to come in."

"My lady—"

"I do insist, Verè. This is to be a . . . surprise for my lord."

Deconniy hesitated. The sentry said in a low voice, "His Grace don't always appreciate surprises much, my lady."

At her side, Gereth put back his hood and smiled at the men. "Verè. Hello, Ceriy."

"Sir!" exclaimed the sentry, and saluted with enthusiasm. "Of course you can do whatever you wish, sir. And welcome back, sir, and all good luck to you, if I may be so bold!"

"You're not bold, and thank you very much, Ceriy. It's . . . good to be back." Gereth looked at Captain Deconniy, waiting for his decision.

"A surprise," muttered the captain. He rubbed his forehead. "I— that is, it's good to see you well, sir. My lady . . . if you're *certain* about this."

"If he's given warning, he might refuse to see Gereth," Kehera explained. "But if he sees him first, do you honestly think he'll send him away? Because I don't think so at all. And if you do anything to interfere and he does send him away, Captain Deconniy, the duke will be very, very unhappy with you. Not that he'll admit it. But you know it's true."

"I think . . ." Deconniy paused. The sentry looked at him anxiously. "I think you're right in every respect," the captain said finally. He nodded to the sentry to open the door.

"*Yes*, sir," the sentry said earnestly, and added to Gereth, "It's very good to have you back, sir." Opening the door, he lowered his voice conspiratorially. "His Grace is in the study. Just let me announce you, my lady, and only you, as you say."

Indeed, Kehera could see the light flickering under the door. "Thank you, Ceriy."

The sentry nodded and crossed the room to rap softly on the connecting door. At the duke's answer, he eased the door open and leaned his head within. Kehera heard him murmur, and Innisth's voice answering. Then he turned back to them and nodded, holding the door a little wider for Kehera to enter.

He shut it after her. The slight click of the door closing had a sound of finality.

Innisth did not seem to have gone to bed at all. There were papers, maps and lists, spread out on his desk, with a half-empty cup of tea holding one stack in place and a plate cleared of all but crumbs weighing down another. He held a pen in one hand, the tip glistening with ink that was still wet.

He stood up politely to greet Kehera, pen still in his hand, wolf-yellow eyes showing a trace of concern. "Yes, my wife?" he said, his tone courteous and just slightly tense.

"My lord," Kehera said softly, "I've come to beg your pardon."

Innisth set down the pen. His eyes followed the movement of his hand and rested for a moment on the cluttered desk. Then he drew in a careful breath and lifted his head again, as though it was not an easy thing to do, to meet her eyes. "What have you done?"

Without a word, Kehera reached back and rapped the door sharply, once.

Gereth pushed it open and came in. He wore no concealing hood now. For all his nervousness before this moment, his expression now was calm and confident, and he met the duke's blank, astonished stare with deep concern, but with no sign of doubt or fear. "Hello, Innisth," he said very softly.

Innisth said, disbelievingly, "*Gereth.*"

Kehera slipped out the door, and shut it behind her.

She went up to the roof, to sit in the open air and wait for the Wolf Duke to make his decision and join her. Or send Gereth away and then turn his back on her as well. She knew now that if he made that choice, it would hurt her. Somehow she hadn't seen that coming, even when she had insisted he go through with the planned marriage. She'd thought about Raëhemaiëth and how its influence would surely moderate Eänetaìsarè. She'd been a little bit afraid of Eänetaìsarè, afraid that its ferocity might influence her own . . . her own idea of herself. But somehow she hadn't quite thought about whether her actual feelings might have begun to be engaged.

Now she couldn't mistake it. But now there was nothing she could do. She had already done everything she could. Either he would come to find her or he would not. So she curled herself into a nook between two crenellations and stared out into the darkness that shrouded the rooftops of Viär and listened to the wind that came down from the mountains. It seemed to her that the wind spoke with the voices of her own land, the many voices of Raëhemaiëth. That was an illusion, of course. She did not need the wind to listen to the Immanent of Raëh. She heard it all the time now. It was afraid. Or Tiro was afraid. Or Eänetaìsarè was afraid . . . though in its case, she would perhaps have said "wary" instead. It gave her courage, or a thread of anger that was *like* courage.

But she knew that they all had such good reason to be afraid.

A pearly tint touched the sky, hardly perceptible at first: dawn approaching at last from the other side of the mountains. Black streaks across the sky traced the curving path of the obsidian winds. The storms were still high, so far. If a winter dragon rode those black winds, she couldn't see it, yet.

Soon it would be full morning; the first morning of the Iron Hinge. And then . . . whatever would come, would come. She waited for it patiently, as she had learned as a child to wait patiently. As she waited for a step on the rooftop behind her.

The morning gradually brightened. For the first time in weeks, the dawn brought neither snow nor sleet nor freezing drizzle. But the sky was opaque, streaked with glassy black. The dawn colors filtered past the perilous midwinter winds and took on strange grayed-apricot and grayed-rose tints. Even the sun looked grayed and dim. Shadows stretched out from the mountains, darker and grimmer than they ever fell during the ordinary days of winter.

Behind her, there was a step. Kehera turned her head.

Her husband came forward to stand behind her. He put a careful hand on the back of the chair, close by her neck, not touching her. He was alone. The rising sun behind him cast his features into obscurity. He said, "You have been here all night? Your people have neglected you."

"They never neglect me. I told them to leave me alone." Reaching up, Kehera put her hand over his.

He turned his hand over and closed his fingers gently around hers. "Gereth will stay by me now."

"I know. At least—I knew that if you had sent him away again, you would not have come to me afterward. I'm glad. I can't tell you how glad I am that you have him back, Innisth. Not because of anything else. Just for that."

"Yes. I know." He stood quietly behind her chair for a little while, her hand in his, looking out across the city toward the mountains. The bitter wind blew through his dark hair and ruffled his heavy cloak.

Kehera leaned her head against the back of the chair and shut her eyes, listening to the wind. It was a spiteful wind, but she was not afraid of it now.

He said at last, "Gereth made all your arguments again."

Kehera opened her eyes. "I know. You're not angry I sent for him."

"No. I do not seem well able to be angry with either of you." He touched her cheek with just the tips of his fingers.

Kehera leaned her face into his touch, though she kept her tone neutral. "But he did not persuade you."

The duke said, "No." But he hesitated just perceptibly before he spoke.

So Gereth had moved him. Kehera had been right to send for him. She and Gereth together might yet change his mind. If there was still time, now that they had entered the Iron Hinge.

"You are cold. Your hands are icy. Will you come in?"

It was hard to stand up. The cold had made her stiff. Innisth put a hand under her arm, and Kehera let him take her weight. The warmth indoors was like a furnace for the first moments, almost painful, but after that it was very pleasant.

But on the stairs, she suddenly found her balance gone, and only

Innisth's quick response saved her from a fall. He spoke to her, but she could not understand his words. She was lost in a surging maelstrom of thoughts and sounds and inhuman memories. Raëhemaiëth. She thought it must be Raëhemaiëth, but the Raëh Power had never felt this way, nor struck into her awareness with so much violence.

The dizziness faded, and redoubled in strength, and faded again so that she blinked past the flurry of sensations and images and strange awareness that assailed her. She was no longer on the stairs, but the world surged and twisted so that she could not tell where she was. Innisth was beside her; she knew that. She clung to him. But though she knew he spoke, she could not hear him. A tangle of clamoring winds rose again, not exactly winds, but deafening and confusing. It seemed to her that beyond that confusion, there was another kind of clamor, metal crashing against metal, and the shouts and screams of battle. And above that, she heard the resonant cry of a winter dragon, full of the violence and fury of the icy winds, the dark midwinter storms that spun down from the heights. . . .

The confusion passed as suddenly as it had come. Kehera blinked, and the world settled into its proper relationship with space and solidity. She was in Innisth's private room in Toren Viärin's house, half lying on a couch. Her husband was there; she was gripping his hand with both hers. Gereth hovered beyond him, and another man she did not know, who had at his shoulder the poppy-and-thorn physicker's badge.

Behind the quiet in the room, she heard again the deadly scream of the dragon. Sitting up, she reached out to her husband, gripping both his hands hard in hers. "Innisth!" she said. "Innisth! Do you not know where the Dragon is? Irekaìmaiäd is at the gates of Raëh; it has come to the very gates!"

She was hardly aware of Gereth dismissing the physicker with murmured reassurances. All her attention was on her husband, who had straightened sharply as she spoke, his expression closing. "Now is not the time," he said. He tried gently to break her hold, but she held fast, and of course he would not use violence to throw her off.

"But it *must* be now," she told him fiercely. Her own ferocity astonished her, but she did not give way; determination rose up in her, hot and angry, and she cried, "*Now* is the only time we will ever have. Don't you know that, Innisth? This is the only chance we have left! If the Dragon wins in the north now, it will win entirely, and then it will feed all the kingdoms into its endless winds! It will never leave you alone! Never think that is possible!"

"You are mistaken," he responded, answering her anger with uncharacteristic quiet. "If I ally now with your brother, we will all be lost together. Eänetaìsarè will not be able to extend itself so far, and we will save nothing. There is nothing I can do to help your brother without losing everything." He hesitated for just a second and then added, "If your brother saves anything from the day, if he comes to me, I will shelter him and any of his people. I will shelter him if I can, Kehera—"

"This isn't about *my brother*!" Kehera exclaimed. She shoved him violently away, furious at his willful blindness. "Do you think this is about *Tiro*?"

Innisth took one step back, caught his balance, and stood still again, looking at her with surprised attention.

Gereth said quietly, "Nor is this about winning. Sometimes one must fight, even if there is no hope of winning. Had you forgotten that, Innisth? You?"

The duke said nothing. But Kehera thought Gereth had struck a true blow, where all she had said had seemed to slip off without leaving any mark. She closed her hands until her fingernails bit into her palms and was silent, willing Gereth to continue.

"You know what has gathered in Raëh," Gereth said. "Every tie remaining in southern Emmer and northern Harivir. They are all there, all bound to Raëhemaiëth. If you join Eänetaìsarè to that, if you set your strength behind Raëh, how do we know what might be possible? If you bring the strength of Coär and Viär and Risaèn with you, do you think Irekay could break you all?"

But Innisth only turned his face away and said, "Gereth. My old friend. It is too late."

"Even if that's true, we have to try!" Kehera retorted. "You can't truly believe the months or years you will be able to wring out of time will be worth leaving the rest of the Four Kingdoms to suffer the destruction as the Irekaïn Power becomes a God!"

"I cannot save the world. If I set my strength here, around this new kingdom of ours, I will win safety for us all. That is all I can do. *I cannot do more.*"

"Innisth—" Kehera began, leaning forward, unwaveringly certain.

But he said, "*It is not possible.* I tell you, Kehera, I am sorry for it. But there is *nothing I can do.*"

Kehera drew a furious breath, let it out, and recovered her temper enough to look at Gereth for help. The older man lowered his head and sighed. He rubbed his hands slowly together, as though he were cold, but his voice was steady. "I think you're wrong, Innisth. I hope you're wrong. But even if you were right, whatever you may believe you'll gain by standing back and letting the north fall, there is one thing you'll lose irrevocably by that decision, and there will be no turning time back to retrieve that."

Innisth flinched slightly. He turned his wolf-gold eyes to meet Kehera's gray stare, and she wanted to say something decisive and final. But then she could not think of anything to say, and so was mute.

"Kehera," he said very softly, and paused.

"Innisth," she answered quietly, using his name as he had used hers. "What shall I say, when I have said everything?" She added in a low voice, "To our shattered dreams we cling, but they break against the beating of our deepest hearts and fears."

"It is I—" he began, and stopped, and went on more softly still, so that she could barely hear him. "You must know, Kehera, this will be no good. No matter what I would do, it is too late. A week or more to reach Raëh. Longer for an army. It is *too late.*"

But Kehera answered with equal intensity, "Innisth, this may very well be the only good we will ever have. Even if it is too late, *we have to try.*"

Then the door opened, and Quòn stepped into the room. Verè Deconniy was behind him; he seemed to have moved to try to prevent Quòn from coming unannounced into the duke's presence, but somehow the man had slipped past him or around him and come in anyway. Innisth straightened in offense, his expression stark and forbidding, pinning Deconniy with a look of hard reproof that made the young captain flinch and duck his head. But Kehera looked at Quòn with sudden hope and said to them all, "Maybe it *isn't* too late—if the Fortunate Gods will help us now."

Quòn gave Kehera a small nod, not appearing to notice the tension in the room or the duke's chilly anger. He said calmly, as though continuing an academic conversation about some abstruse theory that wasn't of much practical importance, "Irekaìmaiäd has learned to use its ties to hollow men in order to transcend the bonds of place and establish bridges between its own lands and distant lands. That is more properly the act of a God; or one might say, such an action is not properly within the purview of any mortal Power. But it has done this, and as fortune would have it, I was not there to prevent it. However, as I am here, I believe the Raëh Power might itself safely form such a bridge between two mortal people, if both hold its close tie and each is willing to yield to the other. It will require the close attention of a God to prevent the apotheosis of the Power, which must afterward be willing to yield its mastery of the ties and resume the bonds of place."

There was a short pause. Then Kehera said uncertainly, "I think I understood that."

Innisth looked extremely forbidding. But before he could speak, Gereth said to Kehera, "I'd lay any odds that your brother would trust you enough for that to work. I think he can hold his end. He's grown since he took the tie."

Kehera looked at him, looked back at Quòn, took a breath, and nodded. "Of course."

Her husband said in a flat tone, "I forbid it."

They gazed at one another. Then the duke lifted one eyebrow, and Kehera said in polite introduction, "This is Quòn. I don't think you've met. Don't blame Captain Deconniy for failing to keep him imprisoned in Eäneté, nor for preventing him from coming here; I'm not sure anyone can stop him going anywhere he wants. He's a sorcerer, or something like a sorcerer. He bears a tie to a God."

"Indeed," said Innisth, in a tone that did not precisely indicate disbelief, but certainly disapproval.

"The Fortunate Gods may act only through men," Quòn said. "Lest they create a disaster worse than the one they strive to prevent." He was studying the Eänetén duke, his expression bland and interested. He added, "The cooperation of mortal men is thus indispensable."

Innisth's expression did not change.

"He saved me from the Irekaïn Power, you know," Kehera pointed out.

"Yes," Innisth said, a little testily. "I recall your mentioning the incident." He gave the man a look of dislike, but he also raised a finger to indicate Captain Deconniy need not attempt to remove Quòn from the room, and he gave the sorcerer a nod that permitted him to speak.

"Three times," Quòn explained absently, as though not very interested. "I've saved you from Irekay three times thus far. I, or the God."

The very disinterest in his tone compelled belief. So did the scattering of fortunate coincidences that had brought them all to this place. Kehera reached out and laid her hand over her husband's. He looked at her, and the hard line of his mouth eased, just perceptibly. Kehera said to him, "Tiro and I can do this. I know we can. But you have to give us the chance to try."

Innisth said softly, "I do not doubt *you*. But in the end, it will not matter. If you create this bridge and I bind Eäneté into Raëh, then we will simply all be destroyed together when, in destroying Raëh, the Irekaïn Power becomes a God. I see no way any man can prevent this now." He gave Quòn another look, no kinder.

"That is certainly one possible outcome," said the sorcerer.

"Even that would be better than doing nothing," muttered Deconniy, then glanced down in embarrassment when the duke fixed him with a cold stare.

Undeterred, Gereth said quietly into the little pause that resulted, "Verè is right. If we do nothing, Innisth, then we'll be destroyed anyway, and we wouldn't have even *tried* to prevent it. How would that be better?"

"They're right," Kehera declared fervently. "They're right, I'm right, Quòn is right, and you know it, Innisth. So I trust you to make sure we all have a chance to do what we must do."

She met his dangerous wolf's stare without doubt, because she knew he would.

29

"They are being destroyed," Kehera Raëhema *said softly and agoniz-*
ingly. "We will be too late."

It had taken so long to organize everything. Too long. Innisth was
almost entirely certain of it. But Quòn, on the other side of Kehera,
said dispassionately, "Until the very end, there is always a chance for
fortune to turn. Bridge the distance."

Innisth half hoped she would refuse. But he knew she would try.
She was brave. So of course she tried. He felt her reach out to her deep-
seated Raëhemaiëth and take the tie from her brother. He felt it through
Eänetaìsarè, which gave her some measure of its ferocious determination. If Tirovay Elin Raëhema tried to keep the tie, Innisth could not
feel it. But Innisth thought the boy did not fight. That was what he felt:
unspeakable trust and a yielding of the tie.

So Kehera took the tie. She took the great tie, the ruling tie; she took
it away from her brother. Eänetaìsarè supported her, and Raëhemaiëth
allowed her to take the tie, and Kehera opened a way between Viär and
Raëh, through the screaming obsidian winds of the Iron Hinge. A way
to step between the earth of Viär where now Eäneté had rooted itself
and the home of her heart; a single step that spanned the hundred fifty

miles between with glittering magic. Innisth wouldn't have known how to do anything of the kind. Perhaps his wife did not know; perhaps it was Raëhemaiëth or the peculiar sorcerer Quòn or the Fortunate Gods themselves that made it work.

Then his wife gave the tie back to her brother. Innisth felt the boy take it.

Innisth knew that somewhere beyond air and earth, the Fortunate Gods battled the Unfortunate to make the chance his wife and her brother had seized. Mortal men had cast a handful of tiahel rods, and the Fortunate Gods were making them fall into the pattern they desired. Only it was men the Gods picked up and cast, and they were ruthless in the design of their hand.

Kehera was shaking. Innisth could do nothing to help her, except tell her what she wished to hear and then see to it that he had told her the truth. So he said, "We will come late to that field. But too late? Perhaps even the Gods have yet to determine that. We need not *win*. Only hold until the hinge has passed. Then Irekaìmaiäd will have missed its chance, and at very worst we will not find ourselves battling a God."

"Four days!" said Kehera, all the dire impossibility of it in her voice.

"As we must do it, we shall do it," Innisth told her flatly. He reached down and took his wife's hand and swept her up into the saddle before him. Then he turned his neat-footed black mare and called out, "Eänetaìsarè! *Eänetaìsarè!*"

And from very far away, from the black forest and the gray rock where the wolves sang, the Immanent Power of Eäneté rose. He called the others, too, all the lesser Powers immanent in these southern provinces and in the lands of western Pohorir. He called them all, and then he lifted his hand high and brought it down in a sweeping gesture, and his mare leaped forward into the air, crossing all the miles between Viär and Raëh in a single stride.

Behind the mare the world cracked open, blazing with all the terrible brilliance of a lightning strike, and the first ranks of their own armies poured after them, followed them across all the miles of air in one lightning-lit instant, and struck the flank of the Pohorin force, hurling it back as a thrown rock will hurl back water.

Innisth steadied his wife as she perched before him, clinging to the black mare's mane with both her hands. She did not seem afraid, trusting that he would not let her fall. He reined his mare sharply aside along the edge of the battle, her men Tageiny and Luad following, but his army—the men of Eäneté and Coär, of Viär and Risaèn all together—had driven hard forward. The Pohorin force seemed to take an astonishingly long time to realize what had come against them was not some little force, but a combined army very nearly as large as the one they already faced. The field was locked in disorder. Almost at once, Innisth gave up trying to understand the battle with ordinary human sight, listening instead to the brilliant, savage awareness of Eänetaìsarè.

"*Are* we too late?" his wife asked him, sounding overwhelmed.

The way back to Viär was gone now, dissolved back into the light. Innisth was almost glad it was impossible to retreat, because he knew with hard, clean certainty that this was the moment at which they must succeed or die.

"No more than we always were," he told his wife, distantly pleased by his collected tone. He stood up in his stirrups, scanning the line of battle. He saw the dead Pohorin soldiers, blank-eyed, but still terribly, remorselessly, on their feet and advancing. But facing the Pohorin army, not too far away, Innisth glimpsed the Briar Rose of Eilin and the graceful Willow of Leiör, sweeping together to cut off and destroy a small part of the Irekaïn forces and then another small part after that, whittling away at the enemy like a man shaving slivers of oak away from a bit of wood he carved.

Eilin and Leiör were Harivin provinces, but Innisth also saw the fawn-colored Hound of Emmeran Nuò and the great-spreading Oak of Daè, both of which lay in the south of Emmer. So he knew that Tirovay Raëhema had done as he had promised, persuading many of the lords of Emmer to support Raëh and Harivir. And he had persuaded many of the lords themselves to take the field, carrying with them the strange unhuman awareness of their Immanences. Even the ladies had courageously ridden out onto that bloody field, unarmed against the empty-eyed dead men belonging to Irekay—unarmed save for the ties they carried. The woman on the tall bay horse beneath the briar rose banner must be Lady Viy, and there beneath the willow rode a younger woman who must be the Lady of Leiör, Lady Taraä. Where they passed, the hollow soldiers fell, though untouched by any ordinary weapon; their Immanences inhabited them and surrounded them and reached out to fight the Immanent of Irekay.

So much Innisth saw. Then curtains of snow came between the Eänetén force and the field of battle, confusing vision; and the light itself became unchancy under the black winds of the Iron Hinge. But he saw, through the snow and the obsidian winds, the Irekaïn standard-bearer ride slowly across the field on a terrible double-headed mount, a beast like a horse and also like a dragon. Behind him dead men rose and took up arms. It struck Innisth with terrible force that despite everything, he might indeed have come too late. He looked for the Gods' servant, Quòn, but he could not see him.

The Winter Dragon standard swept forward and cut down the Blue Swallow banner of Lanis, and Innisth saw how the whole detachment faltered. He saw how ice spread out from the shadow of the Irekaïn banner, how the dead rose to their feet to follow the standard-bearer. He knew, coldly, that not even all the Fortunate Gods together could shift chance and fortune enough to save them in the face of that terror.

Then he felt a tiny shudder go through his wife and said coldly, "Do not fear. We shall throw them back."

Before them, someone more daring or foolhardy than most rode a heavy horse between the Lanis detachment and the standard-bearer and personally draw the Dragon away. The obsidian winds tore past overhead and when a dragon screamed in balked fury, Innisth could not tell whether it was a man's voice that cried out with the voice of an Immanent Power, or the voice of a true dragon overhead.

"Gods!" Deconniy said, fighting his bay horse to stay close beside them. Deconniy was on one side of Innisth's mare, and Tageiny on the other.

The standard-bearer swung the Dragon banner around and sent his mad abomination of a horse leaping forward, and for an instant it seemed certain his challenger would be struck down, but at the last instant, the man spun his horse aside and sent it racing for shelter against the walls of Raëh. And the standard-bearer turned away.

"Raëh still holds," Kehera said, like a prayer. "We have a chance after all."

"Yes," said Innisth. "The city will not hold another hour without us. Your brother will not hold without my support. But we are here, and I am here, and I shall support him as I must, if not as you desire. Perhaps we may yet prevail." And he swung Kehera from his saddle across to Tageiny's, snapped at Deconniy, "Protect my wife," wheeled his mare around toward the battle, and sent her leaping forward.

If his wife said anything as he left her, or reached out after him, he did not know it. It was too late. He had left her behind and entered the battle.

No one—not Tirovay Elin Raëhema, nor Gereth Murrel, nor the cold and brutal Power that had mastered Methmeir Irekaì—could have truly expected the Wolf Duke of Eäneté to abandon his own lands and people in order to cast his strength into this desperate battle that was already lost. The new young Raëhema king had asked for him to do this, Gereth had asked, but Innisth was certain they had not truly believed he might agree. The Irekaïn Power, selfish and ambitious to the core, certainly could not have conceived of the possibility. Only his wife had actually believed that Innisth might choose to risk Eäneté to this end.

Yet she had been right. He had come straight into the jaws of winter, into this dark day of the Iron Hinge. He would not subordinate himself or Eänetaìsarè to anyone. But short of that, he would give what support he could.

There was no dragon above—not yet, at least, though one could not forbear to steal a glance upward now and again. But no winter dragon rode the black winds that streamed above. Those high winds themselves were terrible: the sun seemed to gleam dimly through an obsidian veil; curtains of snow and fine stinging granules of ice whirled among the embattled men so that visibility came and went. The entire field and Raëh beyond had become confused and uncertain.

At first Innisth had hung back, trying to see the underlying order to the battle. He had meant to find his wife's brother so that they might see which of their Powers was greater and forge a bond between their lands stronger than either. He was confident his Eänetaìsarè could not be overmastered by any Immanent born from gentle Harivir and mastered by a boy still in his teens. He was *nearly* confident of that encounter. He would have mastered Raëhemaiëth, brought all Harivir under his own Power, and cast out the Irekaïn Power and all its works. He would have *tried*. But now he saw no way to even find Tirovay Elin Raëhema, far less come to him across this bitter field.

Nevertheless, he sent his black mare racing forward into the teeth of disaster. Eänetaìsarè rode at his back. If Innisth had turned his head, he thought that the tracks his mare left behind her in the churned mud and crimson-flecked snow would be the tracks of a wolf. But he did not turn. He singled out a Pohorin officer who wore the double-headed dragon badge on his shoulder and three marks of rank on his other shoulder, and struck him down. The man did not even have time to turn his head.

The death of ordinary men would not matter on this field, where the bitter Irekaïn Power filled dead men and brought them back to their feet, cold hands gripping their broken swords . . . but the officer's death was still satisfying. Innisth wrenched his sword free and lifted it. The blood of the man he had killed ran down over his hand. He laughed. Eänetaìsarè lifted him up and threw him forward, a savage presence within and around him.

The White Stag of Coär swung into place at his side, and Riheir Coärin lifted his sword and pointed forward, to where, as the veils of whirling snow parted, he saw that part of the Pohorin army pressed the defenders hard. Innisth gathered his mare and sent her that way, with Eänetén soldiers to either side supporting him and the cries of the embattled sounding in his ears very like the singing of wolves.

The Pohorins gave way before the furious attack of these fresh and angry new attackers, and gave way again before the strength of the southern Powers. Anchored and unified by Eänetaìsarè, all the Immanences were for once in full accord with the stronger Eänetén Power that had mastered them.

The hard-pressed defenders cried out hoarsely in a fury of desperate relief and pressed forward with new heart. Before their determination, the Pohorins gave back.

For a long, trembling moment it seemed that the tide of battle might have turned, at least here, at least for this moment.

Then the white rider on the double-headed dragon-horse rode slowly and deliberately across the leading edge of the southern armies. The monstrous animal strode forward at a high-stepping walk, tossing its two heads and snapping its fanged jaws both to the left and the right, and where its clawed feet touched the ground, webs of frost spread outward across the ground. Where the standard-bearer passed, cold mist billowed outward in slowly descending clouds of vapor, and where the mist touched the earth, the mud froze into sharp glittering ridges.

The standard-bearer passed through the ranks that had come from Loftè, from Risaèn, from Coär as though he hardly noticed they existed; and men flung themselves away from his shadow in terror. His dragon-mount seemed to take pleasure in trampling the bodies of the fallen, and it reached out with both its long heads to slash at men or horses that did not flee quickly enough. Innisth could see that the white rider had bent his path toward the blue-eyed Cat of Nuò, and Irreith Nuòriy spurred bravely forward to meet him.

The Winter Dragon banner dipped and swung, its bladed tip glittering. The icy blade cut across the throat of the Duke of Nuò, who seemed to fall more slowly than he should. But he fell. Innisth felt—not his death, but the death of the Nuòrin Power, as Irreith Nuòriy struck the frozen earth at the feet of the Winter Dragon.

At his side, Riheir Coärin swore softly and fervently. "We should not be on this field, you and I."

"We have no choice. Ordinary men cannot defeat that," Innisth answered flatly. "That will require a true tie and a Great Power. Irreith Nuòriy was right to make the attempt. But the Immanent of Nuò did not have the strength."

Coärin swore again. "You can't think *you* can face that!"

Innisth lifted one shoulder slightly in a minimal shrug. "The Power of Eäneté is far stronger than that of Nuò. And, of course, Eäneté is supported by many lesser Powers, including your Coäriliöa."

"For which chance I thank the Fortunate Gods, though I never thought I'd say so. But—"

"Someone must break the Power of Irekay or the day will turn," Innisth said, which was obvious. "Tirovay Raëhema has gathered a great deal of strength to himself, and of course his strength is greatest within the precincts of Raëh. But I think he has not taken the field. Probably that restraint is wise. He is only a boy. And Eäneté is far better suited for this battle." Innisth paused. Then he added, "I will save him if I can, Coärin. If Raëhemaiëth is broken, my wife will break as well."

Their eyes met. The other man said quietly, "All right." Then he said, "I'll ride with you. To be sure no one comes between you and . . . that."

"Yes," Innisth said distantly, and sent his mare forward.

Across the field, the white rider turned his head, his face invisible behind the mask of his helm, and met Innisth's eyes. He jerked both heads of his monstrous horse around and spurred the beast, which reared and flung itself forward, fanged jaws dripping blood and foam. The standard-bearer laughed. Innisth heard him even above the crash and clamor of battle. His laugh was not the laughter of a man.

In the forested depths of his soul, where Eänetaìsarè dwelt, the duke felt a blaze of—not fear, as a mortal man might feel fear, but a vivid awareness of peril. It was Eänetaìsarè's awareness. A midwinter wind, too cold to be natural, came against him, sharp as shards of glass and ice. He shuddered involuntarily, but he did not turn his mare aside, nor look up to see whether he rode into the shadow of obsidian wings.

Coärin's men closed around him, and from the other side a company of Eänetén soldiers. Etar led that company, and Innisth was sorry for that; he knew distantly how unlikely it was that these men would survive even a few moments longer. He was glad Caèr Reiöft and Gereth were both safe in Viär. Except if he himself fell here, none of them would be safe for long. He wished he believed Eäneté would hold if he fell.

It would hold for a little while. He believed that. If whoever took the tie could master it. Otherwise, probably not.

He could hardly believe he was actually here, doing this. The surge of his mare beneath him, the thud of her hooves, the reins in his hands, the bitter wind in his face, none of that felt real. He seemed to have been riding forever across this battlefield, the double-headed Winter Dragon standard snapping in the bitter wind, its hollow standard-bearer, its mockery of a horse. All seemed a dream, distant and unreal. A nightmare.

Here on this ground, before the pale-gold walls of Raëh, where all of its opponents had gathered, the Irekaïn Power would finally win. Innisth knew he could not defeat it. For all his brave words to his wife, he knew that not even all the Fortunate Gods together could make the chance turn now. He had intended to bind Eäneté to Raëh, and only then face the Great Power of Irekay. Now he found no way to do that. Eänetaìsarè had the will and the affinity for destruction, but it did not have the sheer hammering strength it needed to destroy Irekaìmaiäd. Raëhemaiëth possessed the deep-rooted strength but not the savagery.

The men of Eäneté who fell here did not rise from the earth with the song of wolves in their mouths; they did not rise at all, or if they did, it was with the hollow eyes of the walking dead, to follow the terrible Dragon standard. Raëhemaiëth was still shielding its folk from that obscenity. But Eänetaìsarè could not prevent even that.

Eänetaìsarè could never have invested a true tie in a dozen men or more and mastered them all, could never have embodied hundreds of dead men and forced them to rise. No, the Power of Irekay would win. Innisth knew it. It would use the bitter chaos of midwinter to cut itself free of the bonds of earth and leave in the end nothing but ice lying on this field of battle; frozen earth and frozen men, and an endless winter that would in the end bury even the tallest towers of Raëh. It would become a God. Men, such as survived, might even pray to it. Though probably not for mercy.

The standard-bearer met Innisth's attack with his standard, thrusting with its pole as though with a spear, the flying banner cracking like a whip. Innisth blocked that blow, his sword ringing like a bell, but cold struck up his arm to the shoulder; his mare leaped aside or he would have fallen in that moment. He was conscious mostly of irritation: how embarrassing to go down in the very first moment of battle! It was insupportable. He laid the rein against his mare's neck and she whirled and leaped courageously forward, and he ducked under a second blow from the standard and cut at the monstrosity's legs. But the standard-bearer blocked his blow and the double-headed dragon-horse snaked one long neck down and sideways, snapping with fanged jaws, and bit his mare at the base of her neck.

The mare tried to dodge at the last moment, but she did not have room to get out the way. She screamed as piteously as a child as the monster jerked her off her feet, reaching for her throat with the fanged jaws of its other head. Innisth barely leaped clear as she collapsed and rolled, thrashing her long legs in an agony of effort.

The standard-bearer laughed and swung his banner high, the two-headed Dragon snapping out to its full length on the cold wind. Staggering to his feet, Innisth lifted his sword. Eänetaìsarè's heat and fury surged through him, but the standard-bearer laughed again and strode forward, and behind Innisth the black mare blew out a cloud of bloody foam and died.

Innisth, unexpectedly consumed with grief and rage, flung down his sword, snatched a slim-bladed little dagger into his hand from a wrist sheath, took a single step forward, and flung it into the standard-bearer's face, where the helm left a gap for the man to see through. The standard-bearer did not shriek. He hissed like a cat, jerked the knife free, and reined his double-headed beast around, his standard sweeping up and around. Blood spattered from the white banner and curled around the hand of the white rider. Innisth could not tell whether it was real blood or whether it was the blood that dripped from the painted jaws of the Winter Dragon on the banner. In a moment, he knew that standard would slam down like a club and it would be his blood. He did not even have another knife.

But before the standard-bearer could strike, Riheir Coärin brought his horse leaping over the corpse of the black mare and swung his sword in a great overhand blow as though he meant to cleave through the very earth; he struck the monstrous double-headed horse across the back right behind the saddle. It tried to rear but fell, screaming, its rear legs failing; but its rider twisted clear and landed on his feet. Coärin swung again, not at the rider but again at the dragon-horse, this time cutting one of its heads nearly off. The beast thrashed, tearing at the earth with clawed forefeet, but the white-clad standard-bearer stepped out of the way and lifted his banner in both hands. Coärin's horse reared, shrieking, and bolted. Coärin, cursing as his horse carried him away, flung Innisth his own sword, hilt first. And Innisth put out his hand and, to his own astonishment, caught it.

30

Kehera perched in front of Tageiny on his horse, leaning forward tensely, her hands gripping the animal's mane until her fingers ached. Verè Deconniy and a small company of Eänetén soldiers kept near at hand. She was both glad of their protection and sorry to hold them here when her husband needed them, but she knew if she tried to order them away from her, they wouldn't go.

She was trying to make sense of the battle. She didn't understand anything she saw, and knew she wouldn't have even without the curtains of snow that came and went on uncertain winds. It was daylight, but a strange, dim daylight; the obsidian winds of midwinter rushed high overhead, veiling and unveiling the racing skeins of cloud. Captain Deconniy looked anxious and grim, so whatever order he perceived below, he plainly did not like it.

Kehera might have joined the battle herself—not by lifting any ordinary weapon, of course, but by carrying her tie across the field so that Raëhemaiëth could rise and put its will out into the world through her. She *wanted* to, with a savagery foreign to her and yet familiar, which she knew came from the Eänetén Immanent. But she had never studied tactics; she would not have known where to go or what to do. To her, the battle seemed to consist only of scattered, indistinguishable knots of struggling men and horses. Men shouted and screamed, and metal crashed and rang, and the long singing notes of bronze horns rang out over all, and above that came dimly the roaring of the high midwinter winds.

She could recognize banners here and there, from Harivir and Emmer, and nearer at hand the Wolf of Eäneté. But she could not understand the patterns made by those banners. Except she could see that some of the men out there, especially near the Dragon banners, were fighting even though they were dead. She could see it, or maybe Raëhemaiëth knew it and she could tell through her tie. She knew that dead men rose against their own friends and brothers. It was horrible. It was *obscene*.

Innisth would support Tiro and stop that horror. Maybe. If he could. Now that she saw the immense field of struggling men and the distant walls of Raëh beyond, she could not imagine how Innisth would even find her brother. She looked helplessly for Quòn, but she couldn't see him, either.

She had spun the bridge that had brought Innisth and all his people here. She had insisted they must come here to Raëh. And now everyone *else* was out there in that battle, and Tiro was somewhere out there, or more likely up on the walls of the city, the tie to Raëhemaiëth rising furiously through his mind and heart, and she could do nothing to help any of them. Almost she wished she had held the ruling tie, that she held it now. But her brother was the one who had gathered up bindings to so many lesser Immanent Powers. Tiro had to be the one to hold Raëhemaiëth now.

It was unbearable.

Perhaps *she* might find Tiro *and* Innisth. Perhaps through her tie she might find them *both*. Then the two of them might work together after all. If her brother *knew* Innisth was willing to try to work with him, that might make some kind of difference. Anyway, Kehera could not bear to sit here and watch men struggle and die a stone's short throw away and do nothing. She said to Tageiny, "Can't we get closer to the city?"

"We can try—" he began to answer, and then Verè Deconniy flung out an arm, making a short, inarticulate sound of fury and terror, and Kehera, caught by the note of horror in his voice, leaned forward to peer in that direction and saw, terribly clearly even across the distance that separated them, as Innisth met the standard-bearer and his terrible double-headed dragon-horse.

If Kehera had been on her own mount, she would have sent it in that direction. Perhaps that was why Innisth had carried her across the bridge on his own mare and then set her before Tageiny's saddle: because he had known she might do something like that and wished to forestall her. She could tell at once that Tageiny would not listen to her if she told him to take her into the battle, and anyway, she could tell that even if his horse leaped into a full gallop at this moment, they could not possibly come there in time.

Deconniy's horse half-reared at his heavy hand on its reins, but he jerked it down again, cursing under his breath. She knew he wanted to go almost as badly as she did, but of course Captain Deconniy also knew there was no time for either of them to do anything. He had flung up one arm to stop all his men, who shifted and groaned as though they couldn't bear it. Kehera knew exactly how they felt. She tried to slip down to the ground, but Tageiny grabbed her arms and wouldn't let her go. Kehera wanted to hit him, though she knew it would be stupid and unkind, but in the brief struggle she lost track of what was happening.

Then she heard Deconniy shout and whipped her head up again in time to see Innisth's beautiful black mare torn down by the double-headed white horror and Innisth himself disappear from sight.

Quòn said behind them, his voice as coolly disinterested as ever, "It's odd, isn't it, how chance and fortune shatter across every field of battle?"

They all whipped around.

Quòn was sitting calmly astride a chestnut horse, bareback, with neither bridle nor halter on the animal. To Kehera's astonishment, Eöté was sitting before him. The girl was wearing her plain rose-brown gown and light house slippers. Her hair was bound neatly back with a ribbon, and her expression was perfectly tranquil. She might have been sitting before a peaceful fire with embroidery spilling across her lap, not perched before a sorcerer at the edge of a muddy field of battle that stank of blood and rang with terror and rage.

"Eöté!" exclaimed Verè Deconniy, horrified. He snapped, "Wait there!" to his men, then flung himself down from his horse's saddle and took a long stride toward his wife. But she turned her head and fixed her wide, peaceful gaze on him, and he jerked to a stop. "Eöté?" he whispered.

"Every now and again, I chance across someone with the capacity to take a tie to the Gods," said Quòn, his tone too flat to be called gentle. "It is never wise to ignore such a chance. Eöté wished for nothing more than to renounce the world and herself, thus making room for the voice of the Fortunate Gods. Finding her was a stroke of fortunate chance, if you would say such matters are governed by chance. I suspect we will need her before the end. Or if we do not, then we will likely have come to an unfortunate end."

"I'm perfectly well," Eöté told Deconniy. "I was tired of being afraid all the time. I was so tired of being afraid. Now I'm not. I'm not afraid of anything anymore." Her voice, though still light and pretty, had flattened and taken on a kind of remote indifference. She looked at the young captain as though she did not quite remember who he was—or as though she did remember, but did not recall why she should care.

He stared at her, stricken.

"The battle has not ended," Quòn said calmly, ignoring them both. "It's time to seize the chance. The Fortunate Gods have made this moment, and Raëhemaiëth and Eänetaìsarè have entered it, but without mortal blood and will, the Immanent land cannot forge this chance into the future we must have."

Kehera was terribly afraid she understood what he meant. She hurried to take Tageiny's hand and let him lift her back astride his horse. "We have to go!" she said to Deconniy, sharply determined that he wouldn't stop her, that no one would stop her. She cast only one last uneasy glance over her shoulder at Eöté's calm, pretty face, which already held so little of ordinary life and mortality, and then she waved imperiously, commanding everyone forward.

A tight defensive line of Coäran and Risaèn soldiers hemmed Innisth into a close circle, not meaning to pen him into a personal battle with the standard-bearer, but not allowing him any way to retreat. If retreat had been possible. Innisth rather thought it was not, now.

The standard-bearer laughed, stepped forward, and set the butt of his standard hard against the ground not twenty feet from Innisth. The mud froze, cracking with frost. He said, in a voice Innisth heard in his heart, in the place he should have heard no voice but that of Eänetaìsarè, "*What will you yield to me? All the little Powers of the south? They all ride upon your heart and soul. Have you balked me only to come to me here and yield them all unto me?*" It was not in any way the voice of a man, and it made no effort to disguise the fact.

"Methmeir Irekaì," said Innisth, lifting Coärin's sword. "Is that you? I think not. No, I do think not. Irekaìmaiäd has taken you and wears you like a mask. It has consumed your soul and speaks with your voice. No doubt you deserved your fate, but did you have to let your cursed Power free to ruin every other kingdom as well?" He stepped forward deliberately. He was not good with swords, but he lifted it anyway, calling upon Eänetaìsarè, and the Powers of Coär and Risaèn and Viär, and to the smaller, crueler Powers of Kimsè and Tisain. Heat and strength ran through him and straightened his spine; heat ran down his blade, which seemed suddenly lighter in his hands.

"*Eänetaìsarè,*" whispered the cold voice. "*You are known to me. You are mine. I will imprison your fire forever beneath my winter.*"

You will burn only for me. I will consume you."

Innisth set his teeth and began to step forward again, though he knew he could not win this battle. But then his wife's voice called his name sharply behind him, far too close. He spun about in furious horror and found Kehera herself leaping down from her man's horse. Beyond her, Quòn carried another girl he half recognized before him on a chestnut animal, with Verè Deconniy and his men surrounding them all in a tight protective formation. Innisth could not believe Deconniy had brought Kehera into this battle, and swore a silent oath to destroy him for it—by the man's grim expression, he knew exactly what the duke was thinking—but there was no time now, and Innisth knew rationally that the chance was unlikely to present itself. Blood spattered Kehera's face, but she seemed unharmed. And unafraid, though the hollow shell of the Pohorin king stood right there, so small a distance away. Methmeir Irekaì started to speak, or the Irekaïn Power started to speak through him, but Innisth did not listen. He commanded Kehera fiercely, "Get away from this field!"

His wife ignored this command, as he had known she would. But she said—and this he had not expected—"Use me! Use Raëhemaiëth! Here on this field—here where blood from my people has spilled out on the earth—take the tie from me, use it, here where it is strongest of all!"

Methmeir Irekaì strode forward, the Winter Dragon snapping over his head, the blank white winter in his hands. But Quòn set his woman companion down—the woman was Eöté, Innisth realized at last, with mild astonishment, but he had no attention to spare for her. Quòn had sent his chestnut horse mincing forward, between the hollow king and the rest of them. The animal sidled and took tiny reluctant steps and tried to rear, upset by the cracking banner or by the blood that spattered from the painted jaws, and Quòn swung one leg over its hindquarters and leaped free, letting it go. But he turned as the horse raced away and walked steadily toward the hollow king.

Quòn had a knife in his hand and a cool, intent look on his face, and walked forward to meet what was left of Methmeir Irekaì like a man walking to meet a friend, or a lover. For some reason Innisth did not understand, Irekaìmaiäd hesitated and even drew back a step, but then it laughed and strode forward again. That terrible whisper came again, not from the dead king's throat and tongue, but through him in some other fashion. "*What little God do you carry? I will devour it.*"

"Innisth!" Kehera cried. "He can buy us a chance, but we have to turn fortune our way! Take Raëhemaiëth!"

Innisth's awareness narrowed until he was aware only of his wife and the tie that sang in her and through her, and of the ferocious urging of his own Eänetaìsarè. He drove Coärin's sword into the frozen ground, the heat of the sword carrying the blade deep into the ice-struck earth. Then, reaching out, he took his wife's hands in his. He gripped her hands and looked into her face, into her fearless gray gaze.

Then she took back the tie to Raëhemaiëth, and he took Raëhemaiëth through her. Eänetaìsarè reached through him and through her and mastered Raëhemaiëth as it had mastered lesser Harivin Powers, and Raëhemaiëth, though it was here in this place of its strength, lowered all its defenses and yielded its will. It brought with it a tie to every surviving Power of northern Harivir and southern Emmer—even one Immanent Power from Kosir, and how that one had survived long enough to be bound into Raëh, Innisth had no notion.

Far to the south and east, in the heart of its strength, Eänetaìsarè rose and kept rising. Innisth let go of his wife's hands, turned, and strode directly toward the hollow king and the terrible Immanent Power that had consumed him. But then he paused. Quòn, his face blank and still as though he listened to something no one else could hear, was sinking to his knees. Methmeir Irekaì had struck him through the chest with the spear-tipped standard. The man's blood sprayed across the Dragon banner, but Quòn, though he sagged to the ground, did not seem to be yet aware of his own approaching death.

Though the knife had fallen from his hand, his expression had not changed. Something strange echoed in the air around him: as though the very air were changing to crystal. When he set his palm flat on the ground, it rang as though he had struck a bell. Above, the sky darkened like smoky crystal as the obsidian winds came screaming down. Winter dragons rode those winds, two and three and four . . . five, more dragons than Innisth had ever imagined seeing in one place: many-headed and monstrous, their breath cold as midwinter, their wings sharp as glass, their voices the voices of the winter winds. They brought storms and killing cold and sharp-edged winds before which nothing could stand, and Innisth knew they would destroy everything living, tear down Raëh, and then go on to hammer down all the northern kingdoms until nothing remained but the violent winter and the dragons that rode the winds. It was the Iron Hinge of the year, and he knew the world would never come to the other side of these dark days and rise back toward spring.

The hollow king laughed, a low hissing laugh like the wind raking across snow. He jerked his standard back, tearing the ice-blade free of Quòn's chest, and slammed the butt of the standard against the ground. Quòn swayed but did not yet fall. His eyes were open but blind.

Irekaìmaiäd let go of the standard, and it stood upright, thrusting arrogantly out of the ground, its blade red with blood and the long white banner whipping in the sharp wind; the painted jaws of the Dragon seemed to snap, and blood dripped from the standard and fell in drops to the ground. The blood froze as it fell, each drop ringing like a tiny chime against earth frozen hard as iron.

Innisth strode forward, though he did not carry even so much as a knife. The hollow king put out one hand, and Innisth took it, and for a long, long moment they stood so, wrist to wrist, like friends. One of the king's eyes was black and empty of anything human. The other, where Innisth's flung knife had struck, was a ruin, but frost overlay the ruined eye and the Immanent that had taken the place of the man did not even seem aware he had been half-blinded. It was not human eyes he used now to see. It was the other kind of awareness, the savage inhuman awareness of an Immanent Power.

Innisth knew Irekaìmaiäd, and named it, and flung the soul of Eäneté after it, burning into its blank white silence. Innisth was immediately lost in that great stillness, but something guided him—or not him, but Eänetaìsarè. Something he did not recognize; something so wide it encompassed both silence and sound, both the world and the sky; something beyond time and free of all bonds of place; something so vast it staggered both man and Power. A calm, still voice spoke in all that white silence; it was not a voice, but it was like a voice. It was as though the whole world spoke. What it said was a name. One single name. It said, *"Eänetaìsarè."*

And Eänetaìsarè rose in all its brilliant demanding depths and followed Irekaìmaiäd into the place that had once bound the Great Power of Irekay, the land that had given it birth and, in some slight measure, bound it still. Eänetaìsarè roared up around that name and followed its bonds of place and found a glittering bone-white city high on the cliffs above the eastern sea. Dead, it was; all dead; frozen. Ice sparkled on the towers and flowed in gleaming sheets through the streets and rimed the leafless branches of the dead trees and filled the eyes of the people, frozen where they stood, where an Immanent Power of silence and death and cold strove to become a God. It was still anchored in this place. The province and city of Irekay was no longer the source of the Great Power's strength. But it was still its foundation.

Innisth said softly, forcefully, as though it were a lesser Power and he might put his will upon it: "Irekaìmaiäd."

But the Great Power of Irekay did not tamely yield. It had anchored itself widely in the world and could not be torn loose so easily. *"Eänetaìsarè,"* whispered the cold. *"Yield to me."*

In another moment, Eänetaìsarè would have had to. It did not have the strength to resist. But then the Great Power of Irekay staggered suddenly, as a man might who had been unexpectedly struck or pushed. It was not like a physical blow. It was as though an infinite silence opened around them, unfolding like a spring crocus opening through the snow, except the flower was all of spring and the snow only a moment's chill. The voice spoke a single word. It said again, as it had before, *"Eänetaìsarè."* Only it made the name something else, something greater. It spoke the Eänetén Power in its entirety, and Innisth was staggered by it—by its strength and its beauty and its ferocity.

He shut his human eyes and whispered, "Eänetaìsarè," and his Power rose from its uttermost depths, and his. Innisth yielded to it. He gave way to Eänetaìsarè for the first time in his life. He allowed it to master him, and the Eänetén Power *reached*. It reached far below the frozen city and below the cliffs and below the sea that flung up freezing spray, and there it found the always-burning heart of stone. Far beneath stone and sea and earth, so much farther than beneath the sharp-edged mountains of Eäneté, but the fire was there and Eänetaìsarè found it. It took the steady strength Raëhemaiëth offered it, and it took the strength of Coär and of Viär, and of Eilin and all the rest, and it broke the stone and the earth and let out the fire, shattering the chill silence with a roar so loud it went beyond sound. There on the high cliffs above Teilè Bay, the very stone melted and ran burning through the streets. Burning stone flung a thousand feet into the air, and fell still burning to shatter the frozen city and plunge hissing into the sea, and the very cliffs cracked asunder, and the city of Irekay disappeared into a black and smoking mountain that built itself out of burning stone.

The thunder of Eänetaìsarè rushed down every bond and tie and thread of awareness that the Power of Irekay had ever set into any person or any place, and all those bonds and ties and threads burned too. So the Immanent Power of Irekay died with its city. Eänetaìsarè's fire roared up in a wild conflagration, its ferocity growing, and Innisth knew at that moment that he would never reclaim the mastery of his Power. The Immanent Power of Eäneté had burned through him and destroyed Irekaìmaiäd with fire and stone, but now it would burn on. It was too strong; it had become too Great; it was becoming a God. Not Irekaìmaiäd but Eänetaìsarè had met apotheosis, and Innisth could not stop it. He could do nothing but bend the shape of his Immanent so that it might become a Fortunate God, so that perhaps its apotheosis would not destroy all of Eäneté as it rose. But more than that he could not do.

31

Kehera knew when the Irekaïn Power was destroyed. She knew when Eänetaìsarè roused, and she knew when Raëhemaiëth rose in answer, bringing with it all the lesser Powers to which it was bound. Harivir was a network of light that spread across the land, spinning from town to town along roads and pathways and streams, brightest where many men had lived for a long time but sparkling through all the living lands. And not only in Harivir, for the lacework of light spread out across parts of southern Emmer and perhaps half of Kosir, and western Pohorir all along the mountains glittered with light as well. This she saw with an inner eye, unfolding in the other plane of the world; but she saw as well the shadow of dragon wings fall across all these lands and across the empty lands where there were no Immanences to hold back the darkness. The obsidian winds screamed overhead like the voices of dragons, like the screaming of a dying land, and Kehera was afraid.

With her mortal eyes, she saw Quòn move to face the hollow creature that had once been Methmeir Irekaì, and she saw him die, making only a vague, token effort to evade the blow that killed him. A great echoing stillness that was like a great echoing sound rose through him and spread out around him, silencing the terrible midwinter winds and turning the monstrous dragons away from the earth, and this, too, Kehera saw or heard or felt.

Then, though her attention was mostly with Raëhemaiëth, she saw the Wolf Duke take the hollow king's hand. After that she was mostly aware of the shock of Eänetaìsarè mastering Raëhemaiëth, but when she could see again, she saw Eöté walk forward, picking her way across the frozen mud in her light slippers, carefully avoiding the Dragon banner, circling to stay clear of its spattering blood and its shadow. And she watched, unable to move or speak or think, as the girl stooped close by Quòn's body and picked up the knife he had dropped.

Immediately she had to stop Verè Deconniy from hurling himself between Eöté and Methmeir Irekaì. She did not remember moving; she was hardly aware of her own body, of the men surrounding her or of the wider battle that was slowly coming to a halt around them. There was fighting; the dead soldiers still moved and fought, but somehow despite the clamor that still echoed across this field of battle, it seemed to Kehera that a great silence had spread out from Quòn's body and now encompassed the whole field and all the land beyond. She put her hand up and rested her palm on Captain Deconniy's chest. He stopped then, though she couldn't have *made* him stop.

In that space of quiet, Eöté reached out with one hand and cut the human throat of the man whose body housed Irekaìmaiäd. At once the Great Power of Eäneté swept through the emptiness that had been Irekaìmaiäd and mastered Innisth, and at the same time, Raëhemaiëth rose. Kehera staggered. Raëhemaiëth might have mastered her then, too, only it did not want mastery. It did not want to break the bonds that bound it to its place and its people. And Tiro was with her too, not with her in the mortal world, but with her in the tie, so that when Raëhemaiëth reached again for the bonds that tied it to the world, it had somewhere to go.

Eänetaìsarè had a place to go too. It was bound to the land, to the city and province of Eäneté, to the forest and the wolves and the people, to the granite of the mountains and the fire beneath the stone. It had almost forgotten. It had spread out and come unmoored from the place that had birthed it and nurtured it; it had risen in fury and reached out to anchor itself far to the east, by the white cliffs where the storm waves ran; it had risen there and burned away the deathly Irekaïn winter. But Kehera reminded it of its own land. Or Raëhemaiëth reminded it. They both reminded it: It should be bound. It *wished* to be bound. To its land and its people, and to the man who held its close tie . . . "*Eänetaìsarè! You do not want to be a God,*" Kehera whispered to it. Raëhemaiëth reminded it that beyond fire and stone and forest, there was the gentler warmth of the people to whom it was tied. Kehera reminded it that beyond fury and ambition and passion, there was love.

And the great stillness lay over everything, and Kehera blinked and opened her eyes.

Kehera sat on the cold ground beside her husband's unconscious body. Her brother found her there. He didn't embrace her or try to speak with her, but only touched her hair and then her shoulder and then knelt quietly beside her. He was no longer a boy who would demand comfort, but a young man who tried to give it, and she was grateful.

Riheir Coärin strode up too. He stared down for a moment at the Eänetén duke. "Does he live? Or did that kill him?" He spoke in a low voice, to Tirovay and not to Kehera. She was grateful for that, too. She felt utterly incapable of forming words. She held her husband's hand in both of hers, gazing into his still face.

The fighting was over, or Kehera supposed it was. She was not aware of any clamor of battle. People came and went. She paid very little attention. She was dimly aware that Tageiny stood near her, and was distantly glad because she did not feel equal to guarding herself at all.

She knew Eöté was gone. The girl had walked away among the fallen dead, for all the dead were fallen now. She had walked away from Verè Deconniy, who had not tried to follow her. He had let her go, turning away with terse, hard-edged efficiency to direct the raising of a shelter for his duke against the wind.

The brutal cold had broken with the hollow king's death or with the destruction of the Great Power of Irekay. The dragons had risen away from the earth, back into the heights, and the sky was clear, or nearly clear, with only thin streaks of the obsidian winds rushing high above. The storms had passed over the earth, and though the land still lay within the hinge of the winter, it seemed to Kehera that the year had turned and that the air now carried a hint of spring along with the reek of the battlefield.

"He still lives," Tiro answered Riheir Coärin. "Can't you feel it? But his Power mastered him, there at the end."

"He let it," said Kehera, though she didn't look up. "He couldn't do . . . what had to be done. He had to let Eänetaìsarè do it."

Riheir nodded. After a while he said, "It almost felt to me like he took the mastery again . . . afterward."

"Yes," said Kehera. "He mastered Eänetaìsarè a long time ago. He's held it for years and years. It remembered that, at the end. It wanted to be bound. Someday it might want to be a God. But not today."

"Yes," agreed Tiro, because he had been there too and knew this was true. "And there's this, which we may hope will help bring him back to himself." Bending, he put a little quartz-streaked pebble of granite into the Wolf Duke's hand, folding his fingers around it. Then he straightened, his gaze on the Innisth's face.

Kehera leaned forward, but . . . nothing. Nothing.

"Well," said Tiro. "I also brought this." He held a chip of stone out to show Kehera—not granite this time. This stone was a pale creamy gold, the chip smooth on one side, sharp enough to cut on the other. He said, "I broke it off the wall. If I . . . I've never tried . . . It may hold a tiny involuted tie to Raëhemaiëth. But even if I did it right, I don't know if it will help."

Kehera touched her brother's hand and tried to smile. "It will help," she said in a low voice. "They were always allies, I think. From before I ever brought a thin tie to Raëhemaiëth into Eäneté. Besides . . . it helps *me* just to know you tried to do this. Thank you." She put the little shard of golden stone into her husband's other hand and interlaced her fingers with his, so it was held tight between their palms. "Raëhemaiëth," she said softly. "Raëhemaiëth. I know you don't need Eänetaìsarè any longer. But I still need Innisth terè Maèr Eänetaì."

And this time, her husband drew a breath that might have been in response. He did not wake. But Kehera thought—she *thought* she saw a different kind of stillness in him. Something more restful and less . . . fraught. She let her own breath out. Maybe . . .

"Maybe that's done some good," Tiro said. He touched her shoulder again. "We'll move him inside. We'll take care of him. Maybe he'll wake."

"And if he does?" said Riheir grimly. "He's not your ally, Tiro—not anymore. This man isn't anyone's ally anymore. You saw what he did there at the end. He's either got all of Pohorir now, or he can just reach out and take it. And how much more would he take after that? He's dangerous, Tiro: far too powerful and far, far too ambitious. He's probably as dangerous as Methmeir Irekaì—or he could be."

Kehera began a sharp answer, but her brother held up a hand and said to Riheir, "I know. But we owe him, Riheir. Certainly we owe him gentle treatment until we see whether he wakes. After that . . . After that, we'll see."

"You owe him a lot more than that. You owe him *everything*!" Kehera snapped, though she knew her brother didn't need reminding. That wasn't the question. She knew that, too.

"I know," Tirovay said again, speaking not like an impatient boy, but like a king. "But that doesn't mean he'll be safe to leave loose in the world, Kehy. We'll have to see." He paused in case she wanted to argue, but Kehera couldn't say a word. She had been her father's heir, and she was still a princess of Harivir, and she understood what he meant.

Then her brother turned aside and walked over to the fallen white-armored body that lay atop the crumpled white banner, fought briefly with the stiff laces of its helm, and pulled it free. They all looked down at last at the face of their enemy. Even Kehera got to her feet and took the few necessary steps and looked, though she hadn't thought she was interested.

In death, it was the face of a man. Only a man. She recognized him, and was distantly surprised. This wasn't Methmeir Irekaì. This was the Irekaïn lord she had glimpsed in Innisth's house. Lord Laören. A terrible cut had slashed across one eye, but the other was open, blind, filmed over in death.

"Methmeir Heriduïn died some time ago, I suppose," she said in a low voice. "Perhaps that's when Irekaìmaiäd began to embody itself in the dead . . . and learned to enslave the living." She almost felt sorry for Laören. But not quite.

"*Eöté* cut his throat," Verè Deconniy said quietly; disbelievingly, but not as though he didn't believe it. Kehera understood that. He sounded as though he wasn't quite sure whether this was a comfort to him or not. She understood that, too.

Another man came up to the little group and stood looking down upon the face of the dead man. It was General Corvallis, which did not surprise Kehera at all. Enmon Corvallis was limping, but he didn't look like he'd noticed. He said, "So that's over. About time." Then he looked at Tirovay. "And seeing as it's over, Tiro—Tirovay—Your Majesty— what orders do you have for me? I suggest you command me to go to set our common armies in order and arrange for all our peoples to establish themselves inside Raëh's walls. It *is* still midwinter."

"I think the storms are over for this year," Tiro said. "But yes. Please see to that, Enmon."

Corvallis nodded shortly. "Also, there are the enemy soldiers. The living ones, I mean; the dead ones seem to be truly dead at last, thank the Fortunate Gods. But the living. They have to be allowed to surrender—it creates all the wrong incentives to kill enemy soldiers once they've been defeated. Besides, I think no one has the energy to kill them. If you'll permit me, I'll see they're disarmed them and quartered in reasonable comfort . . . somewhere. But the Eänetén soldiers, they're a question—"

"Yes," began Tiro.

"No," said Kehera, very firmly. "I will see to . . . all that. Everything to do with the Pohorins. The Irekaïns can surrender to me—to Eäneté. That would be better, if—when—I mean, it would be better."

There was a slight pause. Corvallis looked like he wanted to object, but Tiro caught his eye and he was silent. "Yes," Tiro said to Kehera. "All right, Kehy. They *are* your people, after all. In a way."

"Yes," Kehera said. "I'll take care of my people."

32

A cell, no matter how finely appointed, is still a cell.

Innisth terè Maèr Eänetaì stood with his hands clasped gently behind his back, gazing out through an expensively paned window at the rising sun that streaked the winter sky with apricot and primrose. He was contemplating the ironies of life.

His chest ached: an intimation of mortality. His heart had not actually stopped and restarted. He had not actually turned to stone and then returned to life. It had not even felt like either of those things, though both images came to mind when he tried to make sense of those memories. He had not become a wolf, or a mountain, or a river of molten fire smashing out of the deep darkness of the earth into the light. But in a way he remembered all those things.

He still did not know how he had recovered the mastery of Eänetaìsarè. On his windowsill, he had placed two fragments of stone: a pebble of Eänetén granite and a shard of the pale-gold stone of Raëh. Neither held even the thinnest or most tightly involuted tie any longer.

He held his own tie still, or again. He still held ties to Kimsè and Tisain in Pohorir. He even held a tie to . . . not Irekay. Not precisely. But to the land where the fiery mountain now loomed above Teilè Bay, where the white city had once stood. Eänetaìsarè held that mountain. All the lands between Eäneté and the sea were slowly becoming part of Eäneté, and some of the lands north and south along the coast. He could feel a slow unfolding of awareness of those lands at the very back of his mind, or his heart.

But they—he—no longer held any kind of tie to Coär or Viär or Risaèn. Those had been taken from him while he lay helpless. There was a message in that, he knew. Though from Tirovay Elin Raëhema or from Raëhemaiëth itself, he was not quite sure. Now distance and Raëhemaiëth blocked any attempt he made to reach after Eänetaìsarè. He knew if he tried to raise up his Immanent, he would not be able to do so. He had not tried. He was weary of battle . . . and he did not want to battle Raëhemaiëth.

He had been held here seven days now. Seven times he had watched the sunrise from this window. The world without seemed peaceful. Quiet. The winter of the new year was a serene season after the Iron Hinge days. Innisth wished he knew how far the seeming peace extended . . . whether it encompassed the world beyond Raëh. He wished he could ask after his people. He wished very much to ask after his wife. But if she did not come, he would not set aside pride so far as to beg news of the guards who stood at his door. And she did not come.

Perhaps she refused to see him. Perhaps now that she was back in her proper place, in the home of her heart, she wanted only to forget everything that had happened to her in foreign lands. Perhaps she wanted to forget Eäneté. That seemed quite plausible.

Or perhaps her brother refused to permit her to approach him for fear that Innisth and Eäneté might yet divide her from her home. That seemed entirely plausible as well. Innisth might indeed have been tempted to take Kehera Elin from Raëhemaiëth and bind her to Eänetaìsarè, except he doubted it was possible. Raëhemaiëth might no longer be a stronger Immanent . . . but he knew that would not matter. He knew Eänetaìsarè would not rise against it.

Also, of course, if he attempted anything of the sort, Kehera would probably hate him. He did not want that.

He wished she would come. Or that he were able to bring himself to ask for news of her. But all he had left now was pride, and that he would not give up.

Tirovay Raëhema had not summoned him yet, nor come to see him. Not during the uncounted days of the Iron Hinge nor, once the year had turned, during the earliest days of the new year. The winter still lay across the land; the Month of Deep Cold and the hungry Wolf Month lay between the dark turning of the year and the new budding of the spring. But even through the cold, he felt the coming spring in the air, saw it in the quality of the light and the slowly lengthening days.

The outer door of the suite was not locked, but it was close-guarded. Besides the men in the courtyard, four guardsmen stood outside his door at every hour. Innisth might have challenged those men. He did not. He understood the implicit terms of his imprisonment: courteous recognition that it *was* imprisonment in exchange for a pretense of civility.

But he would have liked to go home. He dreamed of the forested mountains, now beginning to rise toward spring. Eäneté was so much larger now than it had been. He wanted to ride from the northern border near Enchar east to Teilè Bay and back again west and south to the shadow of the Takel Mountains. He wanted to learn the way the land lay within his new borders. But he held out very little hope that he would see his home again before he died. All his hope now was that young Tirovay Elin Raëhema would permit him to set Eäneté's tie as he chose, and that Eänetaìsarè would accede. He would give it to Kehera, if he could, if her brother agreed and she accepted it, if Eänetaìsarè would allow it. Or to Gereth, if necessary, though he might be too gentle a man to hold it. Or if that choice failed . . . he did not know.

But striving to choose his own heir was now the measure of his ambition. Beyond that, he could do nothing for Eäneté or for his people. So that would have to be enough.

There was a tap on the door, and he turned from the window and waited expectantly, as he was always expectant, and always, to this moment, disappointed.

The guard tapped again and then opened the door. The man was alone. Innisth gave him a distant nod, nothing to show disappointment or query or even interest. But this time the guard bowed and said, "Your Grace, the king is asking for you."

Innisth inclined his head in frigid courtesy and walked as directed through the long wide corridors of the palace.

The room to which he was conducted was large and warm, flooded with light from the fires burning in several fireplaces, and from many porcelain lamps, and from the wide windows fitted with fine panes of clear glass. A tapestry hung on the far wall: a scene not of battle, but of peaceful fields below tall forested mountains, so like the mountains of Eäneté that the image struck him with a feeling almost like pain. The guardsman bowed Innisth within with a slight flourish and shut the door after him gently as he entered.

The new young King of Harivir was waiting there, seated on a heavy chair with carved legs and velvet cushions. Beside Tirovay Raëhema, on a low table, lay a scattering of tiahel rods and a set of carving tools. There seemed to be two King Rods in the set. One showed the Pohorin double-headed Winter Dragon. That one had been snapped cleanly into two pieces. The other, as yet only half carved, had a blank face that he suspected would never show a dragon.

Behind the table, a massive war ax leaned against the wall, an old weapon with a stained blade and an age-darkened haft. As a symbol of authority, Innisth had to admit that it was fairly effective.

Both tiahel rod and ax were fraught objects, under the circumstances. Innisth wondered whether the new tiahel rod would ever be finished. Or whether the ax's blade would ever be cleaned of its stains.

Kehera was not present. Innisth did not allow himself to feel disappointed. Or certainly not to *show* disappointment. Nor would he stand before Tirovay Raëhema like a penitent come for judgment. There was a wooden chair with a tall back against the wall to one side. He took it, swung it around, and sat down on it with his fingers laced over his knee. Then he regarded the young king coolly without speaking.

Tirovay Raëhema said, his tone neutral, "My sister speaks well of you."

"I am pleased to hear so," Innisth answered coldly. He *was* pleased. But he declined to show anything of his feelings to this boy who had become king.

"As, Your Grace, does Riheir Coärin of Coär speak well of you. And Lord Toren Viärin, and all the folk of southern Harivir."

This was more surprising. Innisth did not respond.

"My sister claimed all the people of Eäneté. All the other Pohorins were given into her keeping as well. She sent nearly all of them back to Pohorir, with your Captain Etar in command, under her White Falcon standard so that they might pass unchallenged. Kehera tells me that you would be interested to know this."

"Yes," admitted the duke. He added with exact courtesy, "Thank you for telling me, Your Majesty."

"As you may know, Kehera is my elder by three years. I offered her the chance to take back her rightful place in Harivir, but she would not. Having once renounced the ruling tie, it may not easily be reclaimed. Still, we shared it, there at the . . . end. We traded it back and forth in a most unprecedented manner. I would have tried to give it back, if that had been her will. But it was not. My sister declares the Red Falcon of Raëh is no longer her standard. The White Falcon was no doubt a device of yours, Your Grace, but she has not and will not set it aside."

"Indeed?" Innisth said, since the boy seemed to expect an answer. He wished he knew what this meant—what it meant to Kehera. What it meant to Tirovay Raëhema. Was it possible the young king meant to try to set Pohorir in his sister's hands? Eänetaìsarè did favor her, or it had seemed to . . . and Innisth had no clear heir. But she carried none of his blood, nor any blood of Pohorir. . . .Still, perhaps the tiahel rod would be carved with a White Falcon.

He was prepared to suggest exactly this, but Tirovay Raëhema spoke first. "What I am interested to know now is, what are your intentions toward my sister?"

Innisth lifted one eyebrow. "I beg your pardon?"

Tirovay Raëhema shook his head impatiently. "You meant to use her to compel half my country to yield to your rule. That opportunity has passed forever. If you were to take back Eäneté, what then would be your intentions toward my sister, as she is no longer useful in that way?"

Innisth regarded him coldly. "I am in no position now to possess intentions toward Her Highness. That is quite clear to me."

"You misunderstand me." Tirovay Raëhema stood up and took a step forward. He lowered his voice to speak both more quietly and more intensely. "I ask not as her king, but as her brother. So let me ask more plainly. Innisth terè Maèr Eänetaì, do you love my sister? Will you cherish and protect her for all your life?"

Innisth said sharply, "Am I going to survive long enough to make the question urgent? As you say, I established my own rule over half your country. When your sister fell into my hand, I forced her to marry me; and it was in part my doing that your father fell in his battle. Ah, she did not tell you that, I see. But it is true. I held myself aloof and allowed you to take the full force of Irekay's malice. And then at the end, *I destroyed Irekay.* Do you think I don't know that I am too dangerous to be suffered to live?"

Tirovay Raëhema was clearly shaken, but he waved all this away and said merely, "None of that bears on my question. That still stands. Innisth terè Maèr Eänetaì, Wolf Duke of Eäneté, answer a brother who must know: Do you love my sister?"

There was no mistaking the young man's sincerity. Nor the fact that he did have a brother's right to ask. Innisth said through his teeth, "Yes, then. Yes. Does that satisfy you?"

Tirovay Elin Raëhema exhaled. "It will do for a start." He paused. Then he resumed his seat. "Everything you say is true, of course. Yet you also came onto the field here on my side, though you must have known you might lose everything when you did it. And you did destroy, not Irekay alone, but almost the entire province. Along with Irekaìmaiäd."

Innisth shrugged. "I don't imagine anyone protested. I hardly expect you to protest it now."

Tirovay Raëhema considered him for a long moment, "I don't protest it. It was a remarkable deed, and produced remarkable consequences. I sent a man to Irekay, you know. I should say, to the place where Irekay used to stand. He has only just returned."

Innisth lifted an eyebrow.

"Probably you will not be surprised to know that a great mountain stands there now, rising from Teilè Bay. The mountain is black. Smoke and grit and ash rise from it. Everything for many miles around is covered with ash. The white cliffs are broken all along that shore. I don't know how long it will be before anything lives there again."

Innisth wished he could see it. He lifted one shoulder in a tiny shrug. "It seemed good to Eänetaìsarè that the white city should be destroyed utterly."

"Eänetaìsarè made that choice. It had mastered you."

"Yes."

"But now it has yielded again to your mastery."

"Yes."

"A unique circumstance, to the best of my knowledge. But a circumstance that offers us unforeseen possibilities. So now what shall we do with you, Innisth terè Maèr Eänetaì? What shall we do with Eänetaìsarè, now that it has become so strong and shown itself to be so ambitious?"

Innisth said flatly, "It is your decision, of course. Because you hold all the other Immanences. You understand what Eänetaìsarè has become. You have the strength to destroy it. No one else. Only you. If you choose to do so."

"Yes," the young king said, very quietly. After a short moment, he added, "I once swore that if you ever came into my hand, I would kill you for forcing my sister into marriage."

"No one would say you do not have the right. Many would say that you have a duty to destroy both me and Eänetaìsarè."

The young king acknowledged the truth of this with a little nod. "I know."

Innisth could see he had been wrong in his first estimation of the young man. It was true that Tirovay Raëhema was hardly more than a boy. But he had exceptional presence. He had fought Irekay, fought a losing battle to preserve the order of the world, with the ties to Immanences of three kingdoms gathered into his hands. That would change someone. It had changed this young man. It had made him into a king. He was, in fact, the only true king in all the lands now.

"Tell me, Duke of Eäneté," said Tirovay arrin Elin Raëhema. "What shall I do with Pohorir, now that Irekay has been destroyed, its lands buried beneath stone and fire and ash? What house and family and Power is strongest in Pohorir?" He paused and picked up the unfinished tiahel rod, weighing it in his hand. "What symbol shall I carve on the unmarked face of this rod, Innisth terè Maèr Eänetaì? A wolf?"

Innisth got slowly to his feet and turned to look into the heart of the burning fire in the nearest fireplace. After some moments, he faced Tirovay Raëhema, who had not moved. The room was very silent. They might have been the only two men in the house, or the city.

He said, "If you are going to offer it to me, then offer it."

The king set down the rod and opened his hands. "Will you take it? Innisth terè Maèr Eänetaì, I ask you: Will you take Pohorir? Can you rule it, and create a bond between Eänetaìsarè and each lesser Immanent of Pohorir, and be certain it rules them all, and never permit any of those bonds to become Unfortunate? Can you hold Eänetaìsarè, and master it, and raise an heir who will do the same, so that it never becomes a God? Irekay all but ruined Pohorir, shaping its land in its own cold and brutal image. Then it nearly destroyed us all. Can you forge Pohorir into a greater and brighter land, so that we never again have reason to fear the Immanences that rise from its lands?"

Innisth exhaled, a long, slow breath. "Yes. If you give it to me."

"If I give it to you, you must take it from my hand. With all that implies. Through you, I will take a ruling tie, as I have done elsewhere, in raising up Immanences in hollow lands but also in lands possessed by lesser Immanences. Eänetaìsarè will be subordinated to Raëhemaïëth. You will lose something of your sovereignty." He paused and then went on. "You are right that you are dangerous. Your Immanent is dangerous. But I might trust Eänetaìsarè—if I take a tie to it. I cannot force it to take such a tie. But that is what I must have. So I ask you: If I give Pohorir into your keeping, Innisth terè Maèr Eänetaì, will you take it from my hand?"

There was a pause, stiff with tension.

Then Kehera swung the door open and came in. "He will," she said.

Both men turned, her brother sharply, Innisth more slowly. He felt he could hardly bear to look at her. He could look at nothing else.

She was as self-possessed as ever. She was smiling, but she was serious, too, and she met Innisth's affronted stare with serene, unyielding determination. "You will. Is your pride so great that you can tolerate no king above you? When you were ruled by Irekay all your life until this year? Tiro will do very well. He'll leave you alone to rule as you see fit."

"Will he? And what will you do?"

"She'll go where she will," Tirovay said quickly.

Kehera turned swiftly and walked across the room to take her brother's hands in hers. "Tiro, this is what I want."

"Kehera, are you sure it's not just what Raëhemaiëth wants?"

"I'm sure."

"She believes that she must stay by me," Innisth snapped. "To bring the kind influence of gentle Raëhemaiëth into Eäneté and into my country. This is not true. I am perfectly capable of ruling Pohorir alone." He met her eyes and told her coldly, "Raëh is your home. Stay, then. I shall do perfectly well, I assure you."

"With Gereth? And Caèr Reiöft? And Verè Deconniy?"

"Just so," said the duke, between his teeth. He was furious.

Kehera smiled deliberately into his face. "You would do well enough, I'm sure. But you're not going to, Innisth. Because the fact is, I am going with you—the foundation of all your hope, Innisth, and the tomb of all your fears. Don't think you will put me aside. I go where I will, and that is by your side. If you will master your pride. You can, I know. If you will."

Innisth drew in a slow breath and let it out. Then he turned to study Tirovay arrin Elin Raëhema. At last he came back to where the younger man stood. Then he knelt. Offering the young king his hands, he said grimly, "Take Eänetaìsarè, then. If you can."

A warm, singing tension filled the room: Raëhemaiëth was rising.

Sharp-edged, ferocious, heavy with power, the Power of Eäneté rose in answer, filling the small room with a presence that seemed far too great for it to hold. And met Raëhemaiëth and all the gathered Immanences behind it.

Innisth flinched, despite all he could do, and for an instant he would have broken the young king's grip if it had been possible. But Tirovay did not let go, and the moment passed. Raëhemaiëth slid around and through Eänetaìsarè, and when the king reached through his Great Immanent and took a ruling tie to Eänetaìsarè, still the Eänetén Power did not fight him. Only a little. A very little. Enough to show it could have fought much harder.

Innisth let out a breath he had not known he held. Then he said, "You have it. You hold it. Very well. May the Fortunate Gods have mercy on you if you do not keep faith, for assuredly I will not forgive it."

"But I shall keep faith," Tirovay answered. "As will you. Innisth terè Maèr Eänetaì, I will cherish your honor as my own and hold your lands in high trust."

Innisth lifted his yellow eyes to meet Tirovay Raëhema's darker, more human gaze. Then, because he would have demanded it in the king's place, and so required it of himself, he bowed his head. He said with strict deliberation, "My lord."

The king released his hands. "You have a great deal to do, Duke of Eäneté and Pohorìr. Put your country in order. Bring the other Immanences under your rule, and all their lands, and turn them back onto the kinder path they should have taken all along."

"My lord," Innisth acknowledged distantly. He stood up.

"There are still pockets of Pohorins, I am told, in the Kosiran mountains and the northern Emmeran desert, and all along the coast. Living men, who did not die with the Irekay Power, but have not dared make their way home again. Or who now have no homes to which they might go."

"I understand. I shall see to them."

"Thank you." Tirovay Raëhema paused for an instant and then added, "Kosir was struck the hardest, and Pohorir by far the least affected, by the war your country forced on us all. There will be star-vation in Kosir before the end of the Wolf Month."

Innisth met his eyes, faint amusement struggling to be born through offended pride. "I shall see to it, then. My lord."

"Good. Thank you."

"Is there anything else that you will have me do?"

The young king's eyes touched for an instant on Kehera's face and just as quickly flicked away. "No. Nothing else. Your people have mostly departed Harivir, but some few have been quartered in the city—Kehera can show you where. I'm sure they'll be glad to see you."

"I think perhaps they will," Innisth Eänetaì answered. He offered his arm to Kehera. She came forward with a grave expression and a light step, set her hand on his arm, gave her brother a brilliant smile, and allowed Innisth to lead her out of the room and into the unfurling future that lay before them both.

Or perhaps it was Kehera who guided him, with the forceful determination she had gained from Eänetaìsarè joined to the quiet surety that had always been hers. On reflection, Innisth thought that more likely.